Praise for the Novels of Karen White

"A book you could get lost in."   —*Delta Magazine*

"Gothic gold."   —*The Atlantan*

"White's dizzying carousel of a plot keeps those pages turning, so much so that the book can—and should—be finished in one afternoon, interrupted only by a glass of sweet iced tea."   —Oprah.com

"Readers will find White's prose an uplifting experience, as she is a truly gifted storyteller."   —*Las Vegas Review-Journal*

"This is storytelling of the highest order: the kind of book that leaves you both deeply satisfied and aching for more."
                —Beatriz Williams, *New York Times* bestselling author of
                                                        Tiny Little Thing

"An intriguing and romantic family drama."   —*Booklist*

"A story as intricate and sturdy as a sweetgrass basket, with the fresh, magnetic voices of its headstrong characters."   —ArtsATL

"White entwines historical fact and research seamlessly through the lives of these strong and intriguing women."   —*Library Journal*

"White's ability to showcase her characters' flaws and strengths is one of the best in the genre."   —*RT Book Reviews*

"A perfect read for the summer."   —*The Florida Times-Union*

"Brilliant and engrossing . . . a rare gem . . . exquisitely told."
                                              —The Book Connection

Spinning the Moon

TWO CLASSIC NOVELS:
In the Shadow of the Moon
AND
Whispers of Goodbye

KAREN WHITE

BERKLEY
New York

BERKLEY

An imprint of Penguin Random House LLC

375 Hudson Street, New York, New York 10014

Library of Congress Cataloging-in-Publication Data

Names: White, Karen (Karen S.), author. | White, Karen (Karen S.) In the
shadow of the moon. | White, Karen (Karen S.) Whispers of goodbye.
Title: Spinning the moon / Karen White.
Other titles: In the shadow of the moon. | Whispers of goodbye.
Description: New York: Berkley Books, [2016] | "Includes two classic romance
novels . . . completely revised and together in one volume for the first time."
Identifiers: LCCN 2016012402 (print) | LCCN 2016019591 (ebook) | ISBN
9781101989517 (softcover) | ISBN 9781101989494 (ebook)
Subjects: | BISAC: FICTION / Romance / Gothic. | FICTION / Romance /
Historical. | FICTION / Historical. | GSAFD: Love stories. | Gothic
fiction. | Fantasy fiction.
Classification: LCC PS3623.H5776 A6 2016 (print) | LCC PS3623.H5776 (ebook) |
DDC 813/.6—dc23
LC record available at https://lccn.loc.gov/2016012402

First Omnibus Edition: September 2016

PUBLISHING HISTORY
In the Shadow of the Moon: Love Spell mass-market edition / August 2000
Whispers of Goodbye: Love Spell mass-market edition / October 2001

Printed in the United States of America
1   3   5   7   9   10   8   6   4   2

Cover art: Photo of Southern manor home at night © Jeremy Woodhouse/Spaces Images/ Corbis
Images; photo of moon © johnnorth/ Thinkstock
Cover design by Sarah Oberrender

*To all of my lovely readers whose requests
to read my first two long-out-of-print books
made this publication possible*

Acknowledgments

Thanks to my editor, Cindy Hwang, who read the first incarnation of *In the Shadow of the Moon* before it was initially published and saw promise in me as a writer; to my publisher, Penguin Random House, and the most amazing and supportive sales, marketing, publicity, and editorial team an author could ever want.

Last, but not least, to Anthony Ramondo and the magicians in the art department for finally giving these books the cover they deserve.

Author's Note

During the summer of the Atlanta Olympics (1996), I was the mother of two small children and suffering from a severe bout of book hangover. I had just finished reading Diana Gabaldon's *Outlander* and was finding it impossible to pick up another book to read because I was still living in eighteenth-century Scotland with the incredible characters and setting the author had created.

Deciding to finally listen to all the teachers I'd had since I was in elementary school who told me I should write, I pulled a chair up to my desk and started to type. If I couldn't pick up another book to read, maybe I could *write* a book instead. So I did. I set no goals at first, just wanting to see whether I could write the kind of book I'd like to read. I wrote when the children napped and when I felt like it (oh, those blissful predeadline days!). I laughed and I cried, and I held my breath during the tense scenes—an experience just like reading a favorite book. I let my neighbor read it as I wrote each chapter and I chose to believe her when she told me it was good.

That gave me the confidence to finish the book and submit it to a writing contest. It won, and the finals judge, a New York City literary agent, offered to represent me, then quickly sold it to a small New York publisher. *In the Shadow of the Moon* was published in 2000, and my second novel, *Whispers of Goodbye*, was published in 2001.

Despite horrendous covers and extremely small print runs, I was very proud of these first two books. I loved the stories and the characters I had created, and was overwhelmed by the positive feedback I received from readers. Although the subject matter is vastly different from my more recent books (*Shadow* is a time-travel romance set in Civil War Georgia and *Whispers* is a gothic romance—à la Victoria Holt and Daphne du Maurier—set in Reconstruction Louisiana), the themes of family, home, and a woman's journey from loss to inner strength will be familiar ones to my current readers.

This is the reason why, a decade and a half since their original publications, my current publisher and I have decided to rerelease my first two novels. We believe my readers will enjoy this glimpse into my earliest works and appreciate the stories and familiar themes, and perhaps identify what it is that makes these "Karen White novels."

If you are among the few who had the chance to read these books in their original editions and enjoyed them, please know that I have taken the opportunity to clean up and edit both books, hopefully upgrading the writing style from that of a novice to that of a seasoned writer. But the stories and characters that you first fell in love with are untouched.

Whether you're a new reader to these books or they are old favorites, I hope you enjoy reading them as much as I enjoyed creating them—both times.

Happy reading!

Karen

In the Shadow of the Moon

*The law of humanity ought to be composed of the past,
the present, and the future, that we bear within us;
whoever possesses but one of these terms, has but a fragment
of the law of the moral world.*
—EDGAR QUINET

PROLOGUE

———◆———

The house stood strong and silent, bidding me to come nearer as if it were an old friend needing companionship. The windows stared at me with familiarity, and the feeling of having been there before hit me with a force so strong I had to stop. I grabbed Michael's hand and pulled him back across the brick sidewalk.

"I want this house."

My husband turned to me as if to say something. He was very well acquainted with my particular brand of stubbornness.

Weeds as high as my pregnant swell grew behind the dilapidated picket fence, and the roof over the porch sagged desperately. Shattered panes looked out of the two dormer windows, and the entire place needed painting. A large fan window crowned the massive front door, while white rocking chairs perched invitingly on the porch. It was a remarkable house, but there was something else about it that caused me to pause before it. Some sort of unexplainable connection. Four stately columns stood sentry at the front, and I could picture in my mind's eye beautiful belles and gallant gentlemen from a time gone by sweeping down the still-graceful steps.

"I hate to disappoint you, Laura, but I don't think it's for sale. I don't see a Realtor's sign."

I was already pushing open the front gate, its rusty hinges squeaking in protest.

"We'll never know unless we ask." I waddled up the front steps to the porch, grasping tightly to the chipped and peeling wood banister.

Due to the imminent expansion of our family, our Atlanta apartment was no longer large enough. We needed a house. Not just brick, mortar, and roof shingles, but a home to love and call our own and raise our family in. An older house with creaky wood floors and impossible-to-heat rooms with high ceilings. This was my house. I was so convinced of this that I didn't pause to think how a different approach might be more civilized. But there was something about this house that told me I shouldn't wait.

In the absence of a doorbell, I grabbed the dull brass knocker and banged a little too loudly. Michael had his back to the door and was surveying the wreckage of the front yard and porch. I didn't need to see his face to know what expression he was wearing.

I stood, waiting, ignoring the urge to tap my foot. I was about to knock again when the sound of a latch being drawn from inside rattled the heavy wood door.

The woman who opened the door was tall like me, but her shoulders were slightly stooped. The intensity of her blue eyes seemed to add height and strength to her willowy figure. A halo of white hair framed an oval-shaped face with smooth, supple skin. She could have been anywhere from sixty to eighty years old. I made a mental note to ask her what she used for skin care.

Her smile revealed a row of white, evenly spaced teeth. "Oh, my! You're finally here."

I looked at her in confusion. "Have we met?"

She opened the door wider, and I caught a whiff of mothballs and furniture polish. I inadvertently wrinkled my nose and stifled a cough. My sense of smell had become acutely sensitive since I became pregnant, and even the slightest odor could overwhelm me. I must have staggered a bit, because the old lady grabbed my forearm in a surprisingly firm grasp and brought me inside through the receiving hall to a sofa in the front parlor, Michael following closely behind us.

"My dear, you must be careful of this heat in your condition." She motioned Michael to take a seat opposite me in a fiddleback chair. Her voice was rich with the warm accent reminiscent of the Deep South.

I should have been embarrassed by the situation. Michael obviously was, as he kept trying to stand and offer apologies to our impromptu hostess, but, strangely, I felt very much at ease in this lady's presence and in her house.

The old woman disregarded Michael's sputtering and excused herself to get us all some iced tea and refreshments. Michael was raised up north in Connecticut, where I figured people didn't just drop in on strangers to have tea with them. I'd never done it before, either, but for some reason, it didn't seem as if the owner thought we were imposing on her. There was something in the way she looked at me, as if she knew me.

Situated against one wall was an upright piano, its polished surface markedly different from the dusty, worn pieces of furniture in the room. The ivory veneer was missing on the G key above middle C, as if something heavy had dropped on it and chipped it off.

"Laura, what are we doing here?" Michael busily eyed the cracked wall plaster and water stain on the ceiling. "You can't possibly be thinking of buying this house."

I walked to stand behind him and put my arms around his waist. Standing on tiptoes to kiss him on his cheek, I followed his gaze toward a mess of wires hanging from the ceiling. "Michael, you've got to look beneath the surface to see the real beauty here. Look at those dentil moldings on the ceiling, and the wood floors. I bet these walls are a foot thick." I moved over to one and tapped it lightly to make my point. I didn't really care. The emotions I was feeling had nothing to do with plumbing and insulation. The sense of home surrounded me, emanating from the walls. The roof could have been falling in and I still would have wanted to buy the house.

I sat down just as our hostess came back bearing a large silver tray and tall iced-tea glasses. A china plate in the center was laden with an assortment of cookies and small cakes.

She smiled as she handed me a plate and a frosted glass. "I hope you don't mind me serving you leftovers from yesterday's ladies' bridge meeting. They are just so delicious and my housekeeper and I could never eat them all before they spoiled."

I realized I was starving, but my manners finally interceded. I struggled to sit up. "We really hate to intrude. We're Laura and Michael Truitt, and we were merely inquiring about the—"

"House," she said, completing my sentence. "I knew you were coming. Someone told me to expect you. I just didn't know when. I've been wanting to sell this house for years now, but knew I needed to wait for you." She smiled serenely and settled back against a once-elegant but now-faded sofa. "When you've got your strength back, I'll be happy to give you the grand tour."

I glanced over at Michael, who had edged himself to the front of his seat, as if preparing to make his escape. I, too, was feeling a bit strange, but not in the least bit wary.

"I don't understand." I shifted in my seat and knocked a cookie off my lap and onto the threadbare needlepoint carpet.

As sprightly as a teenager, the white-haired lady leapt up and retrieved the cookie.

"I bet that sounded odd, didn't it?" she asked. "Perhaps I should introduce myself. I'm Margaret-Ann Cudahy." She paused to let it sink in or to wait for a reaction from us. Neither was forthcoming, as the name meant absolutely nothing to me or, I was sure, to Michael.

"Do you know my mother, Mrs. Cudahy?" I asked, trying to find a common thread. "Her name is Nancy Chrisler."

She shook her head. "No, I don't believe so. The person who told me you were coming was my great-grandmother, and she passed on many years ago. She didn't explain it to me fully, since it didn't really concern me, but she said you would understand it all eventually."

Unease brushed the back of my neck, but I was unwilling to leave. The overwhelming feeling of being home surrounded me, and this woman and her house intrigued me.

"How long has your great-grandmother been dead, Mrs. Cudahy?" I asked, trying to figure out how her relative could have known me.

"Oh, since 1935. I remember it well. It was the middle of the Great Depression, and I was nine years old. She died three days after her hundredth birthday."

"I don't understand. I wasn't born until 1985. She couldn't have known about me." I looked at Michael as he sprang from his chair and walked quickly over to me.

"I think we need to be going, Laura." He grasped both of my hands and tried to haul me off the sofa.

I held tightly to his hands, but gave a quick shake of my head.

"No, Michael. Not yet." His eyes searched my face, and then he let go. He kept his hand resting on my shoulder. I reached for him, my fingers brushing his gold wedding band.

I turned my attention to Mrs. Cudahy. "If you don't mind, could we see the house now?"

"Of course, dear." After Michael helped me off the sofa, she slipped her arm through mine.

The house had four large rooms on the first floor and four on the upper floor. A later addition had added a fifth, smaller bedroom upstairs, making for interesting architecture at the back of the house. The rooms had lofty twelve-foot ceilings and were all interconnected within the house. The one exception was a small preacher's room, with a single entrance from the rear porch. The huge receiving hall ran the entire depth of the house, with large doors in the front and back that could be left open to create a breezeway. A staircase rose from the floor at each end of the hallway, the one in the back less elaborate than the other, and presumably for the use of servants.

"Legend has it that some of General Sherman's troops garrisoned here in Roswell rode their horses right through this front hall, slashing at everything with their sabers." Mrs. Cudahy's arm waved back and forth, slicing the air. "Most of the other houses in the area were heavily looted, but not this one. No one knows for sure how, but somehow the family living here was forewarned and had hidden just about everything of value. Bulloch Hall, down the road, was saved from being torched because both the owner and the Union commander were Masons. However, local historians aren't sure why this house was left intact." Mrs. Cudahy paused to run her hands gently over the fine, peeling wallpaper. "They did destroy most of the outbuildings and crops, and confiscated the remaining livestock and slaves. There's a reason why Sherman's name isn't brought up in polite company even today," she said with a smile.

"I hear Sherman was one for the pretty ladies," she continued, giggling like a schoolgirl. "It wouldn't surprise me at all if many of the great houses in Georgia survived Sherman because of the Southern women who personally convinced him to spare their property." Mrs. Cudahy gave me such a cheeky glance that I giggled, too. I wondered at her story. I had read biographies of Sherman for a paper in my AP history class, and I didn't recall any wartime dalliances. But that was merely the written record. Word-of-mouth stories doubtlessly would have been more subjective.

Michael and I held hands as she led us through the back door onto the porch. It was deceptively cool out there in the shade with a soft, warm wind caressing our faces. "The house was built around 1840. As you can see, it is situated on a high point to take advantage of the Chattahoochee River breezes." She caressed the smooth wood of the balustrade, her hands barely marred by time.

"Before the War of Northern Aggression, the property had almost three hundred acres, all planted with cotton, and thirty slaves to work the fields and tend to the house. But that's all gone now, except for the springhouse and chicken house out back." Mrs. Cudahy looked at me with a wide grin. "Don't suppose you'll be raising chickens, though!" Then, as perfect strangers are wont to do, she patted my swollen belly.

"Looks like y'all have been busy! This house sure misses the sound of babies. It's been a long time since the pitter-patter of little feet went up and down these floors." Her voice trailed away as she led us to the master bedroom. I imagined the sound of children's voices echoing through the rooms. *Yes. This is home.*

She preceded us through the doorway, and I stood, paralyzed, at the threshold. I knew this room, as if I had awakened in it many times. A magnificent mahogany half tester bed with an elaborately carved pediment hung with heavy draperies dominated one side of the room. A marble-topped dressing table with graceful cabriole legs stood between the two floor-to-ceiling windows. Fancy fretwork topped the mirror above the dressing table. A splendid armoire towered toward the ceiling at one end of the room. I must have seen this room before in a magazine. I felt completely at ease and could imagine myself at the dresser, brushing my hair.

"This furniture has been in my family for more than one hundred and fifty years. All of it was made by Mr. Mallard himself in his shop in New Orleans for this very room. It's never been moved. Probably too big and heavy to go anywhere else," Mrs. Cudahy explained as she walked over to the bed and smoothed down the faded yellow bedspread. She looked up at Michael and gave him a wide smile. "Most of my ancestors were conceived on this very bed."

Michael, who, until that moment, was not known to be a prude, turned bright pink. He quickly looked at me, and I buried my face in his shoulder, struggling not to laugh.

Mrs. Cudahy smiled gently at Michael. "I'm sorry if I've shocked you. I used to be a ballet dancer and I've traveled and lived in all sorts of strange places. I suppose it's rubbed off on me a little." She winked at Michael. "Plus, I'm an old lady. I'm supposed to be a bit batty."

Michael cleared his throat. "So, this house has been in your family since it was built?"

"Yes, but I'm the last in the line, I'm afraid. My husband and I never had any children. Though it wasn't for lack of trying." She grinned mischievously at me, and I grinned back.

As she led us through the house back toward the parlor, I noticed the finely carved moldings, the thick mahogany doors with leaded-glass transoms and heavy brass door fittings. It was all beautiful but very worn. I could tell that a massive renovation would be needed to restore the house to its former splendor. The same feelings of familiarity I had had when standing in the front of the house came over me. I could clearly picture in my head what I would see when we turned each corner and opened every door. It was almost disconcerting, since I was sure I had never been in the house before, but it was also comforting in a way, as if this were a reunion between friends.

Once we were back in the parlor, Mrs. Cudahy refilled our glasses and motioned for us to be seated. Michael sat next to me, holding my hand, his thumb rubbing circles over my knuckles. The nagging questions in my mind wouldn't go away. "Mrs. Cudahy, I would appreciate it if you could explain further how you knew I would be coming. I'm pretty sure we're not related, so I can't understand how any relative of yours would have known about me."

Mrs. Cudahy stood. "Perhaps if I gave you something, it would explain it better than I can," she said as she left the room, leaving a scent trail of Tea Rose perfume.

Michael leaned over to me and whispered, "She's probably going to get a gun or something. We could leave now before she gets back."

I elbowed him in the ribs. "Very funny. Don't you feel it, though? That feeling of rightness that this is our home?"

He looked at me with a raised eyebrow, then smiled and reached for my hands.

"Laura, I certainly hope it's not your pregnancy hormones talking right now, because if we buy this house, it's going to be a long-term commitment."

"I'm not blind to the condition of the house, but I'm going with my sixth sense here. I really want this house. Please trust me—have I ever steered you wrong?" I squeezed his hands, my eyes searching his.

He opened his mouth to say something, but closed it again when Mrs. Cudahy returned and handed me an object wrapped in yellowed newspapers. "I hope this explains some of it."

I gingerly unwrapped the layers of paper. Dust motes rose from the wrinkled bundle and danced in a shaft of light from the parlor window. Inside the layers lay an ornate picture frame. I rubbed the surface with my thumb, attempting to wipe off some of the black tarnish. I peered closely at the picture and my breath caught. It was a sepia-toned likeness of a woman wearing nineteenth-century clothing. Around her neck lay an unusual necklace with what appeared to be an old-fashioned key hanging from a chain. The straight dark hair was swept up off her face and coiled around her head. The large light eyes staring back at me were tilted slightly at the corners, and her nose was a little too pert for conventional beauty. The upturned lips were reminiscent of the *Mona Lisa* and anything but demure. I had seen this face many times before. I saw it every time I looked in a mirror.

"Where did this come from?" I croaked, unable to find my voice.

Michael leaned over my shoulder. "It's you, Laura, or someone who looks a hell of a lot like you." He tried to pry it from me to get a closer look, but I couldn't let it go.

Mrs. Cudahy moved closer. "It is a remarkable resemblance, but I'm afraid I don't know her identity. I wish I had something to add, but my great-grandmother told me only that a woman who looked like this would come asking about the house. I didn't question her very closely, and she died shortly after she gave it to me. She asked only that I save this picture to give to you." She bent down to pick up the scattered pieces of old newspapers and crumpled them tightly together in a ball.

I turned the frame over in my shaking hand and gently pried off the back. Perhaps something was written on the reverse side. I removed the delicate picture from its frame to examine it more closely, but there were no identifying marks. I studied the key around the woman's neck, hoping it would offer some clue. I thought it was a strange ornament to be hanging on a necklace, and I wondered about its meaning. But the face of the woman was my own. There were no subtle differences to account for generations of genetic progression. Had I somehow lived before in this house? I had no idea, but the thought did not frighten me. Odder things had been known to happen to people. But still I pressed for some sort of logical answer.

"Mrs. Cudahy, perhaps we're related. If you don't mind, I'd like to borrow this picture and ask my mother about it. She can trace our family back to the American Revolution, and if there's a connection, I'm sure she'll find it." I knew I was overlooking her great-grandmother's prediction regarding me, but I had no idea where to look for any answers to that gnawing question. Finding a familial connection would be sufficient explanation for me.

A strong kick from the baby pushed all these thoughts to the back of my mind. I must have gasped, because Michael turned to me and placed his hand over mine on my abdomen. He never tired of feeling our child inside me, and a boyish grin erupted on his face.

"See?" I said, grinning back. "The baby wants this house, too."

Michael leaned his forehead against mine and let go a deep sigh. "If that child is as stubborn as his or her mother, I know better than to fight you both."

Mrs. Cudahy stood. "You can keep the picture as long as you like, dear. As for the house, I've been waiting a long time to sell it. I can certainly wait a little longer while you two discuss it. You know where to find me."

We thanked her for her hospitality and walked slowly to the front door. Impulsively, I leaned over and kissed her on her soft cheek. "Thank you, Mrs. Cudahy. You'll be hearing from us."

I led Michael out into the front yard and looked up at the house, the shadows of its four columns reaching out like arms to embrace us. I kissed him lightly on the lips. "I love you, Michael Truitt."

He kissed me back, his mouth warm and soft. "I love you, too."

A soft river breeze stirred the wilted garden, summoning the scent from the boxwoods and tickling my brain with a remembrance of something I couldn't quite recall. The child kicked again as the wind jostled the leaves of an old oak tree, sending one spiraling down to me like a distant memory. I clutched it tightly in my palm and then held it up again, watching as the wind carried it away.

CHAPTER ONE
———◆———

When beggars die, there are no comets seen;
the heavens themselves blaze forth the death of princes.
—WILLIAM SHAKESPEARE

O ur daughter, Annie, was born exactly two weeks after moving into the house. Although my strange attraction to our new home never faded and questions remained unanswered, I pushed them aside and threw myself into my new role as mother.

An engaging and guileless little girl, Annie had inherited equal parts from each parent. She had bright green eyes and an odd crescent-shaped birthmark on the inside of her forearm from her mother, and fair hair and perfectly shaped ears from her father. But her little personality was all her own. She was everything I could have wanted in a child.

Annie was a gentle baby, which made it easy for us to resume our adult lives when she was still quite young. She went everywhere with us, her fair head poking up over the carrier strapped to one of our backs. We enjoyed being together, our little family.

Annie was only twenty-three months old when we took her to see her first comet atop Moon Mountain. Sky watching was a hobby of mine, introduced to me as a child by my Cherokee grandmother, and I was eager to share it with my daughter. Genetti's Comet would be sharing the sky with a total lunar eclipse—a rare enough event to warrant mention of it in the *Atlanta Journal-Constitution*. Moon Mountain wasn't really a mountain, but rather a largish hill and the perfect vantage point for celestial happenings. According to my grandmother, who was widely known for her eccentricities, it was a place with strong unknown powers. She called it a sacred place to the Cherokee Indians, who had inhabited this part of the country for centuries.

Michael grumbled only slightly when I roused him that Saturday morning. It was usually his sleeping-in day, but I had made plans for an early start at antique shopping and general family togetherness before the lunar eclipse that night. He leaned over and rubbed his stubbly chin on my bare midriff, where my nightgown had ridden up. Resting his head on my abdomen, he gently traced a circle around my navel with his finger. I ran my hands through the thick mane of his hair and sighed softly. He looked up at me with a raised eyebrow.

"Laura, why don't we just skip the shooting star and stay in bed all day?" He rose to nuzzle into my neck, sending delicious shivers down my back.

I pressed my head into the pillow and tapped him gently on the head with the flat of my palm. "It's not a shooting star—it's a comet and an eclipse. It'll really be spectacular."

"Mmmmm," he mumbled.

I shifted my head, enjoying his attentions to my earlobe. Slowly, he worked the spaghetti straps of my nightgown off my shoulder and moved his mouth lower. I looked down at his dark blond head, and my body flooded with love and desire for this man. I sighed, and our eyes met.

His moist lips formed a slow grin. "I've got powerful methods of persuasion, you know."

I sat up, pulling off my nightgown completely. "Yes, you do. You certainly do."

We made love slowly, in the comfortable way old lovers do, and then we held each other close, listening to the sounds of morning outside our window.

"Mommy!" came the shout from across the hall.

The sound made me grimace. Reluctantly, I threw off the sheets. "It was nice while it lasted," I said as I slipped out of bed and into my robe. I leaned down to give Michael a kiss and then hurried to the nursery, where I was being summoned in a tone approaching hysteria.

Annie clutched the top rail of her crib, huge tears of distress running down her cheeks. I tripped over the object of her anguish and bent to pick up her stuffed giraffe from the floor, the apparent victim of a fall through the crib slats. Her chubby arms stretched up to greet me as I approached. I handed her the giraffe and reached for her.

"Hello, morning glory," I whispered as I picked her up and kissed her baby-fine hair. The mingled scents of baby sweat and shampoo wafted up my nose. "Can Mommy have some good-morning butterflies?"

Annie put her face right up to mine and fluttered her eyelashes, tickling my cheek. She then laid her head on my shoulder, a cue for me to sing and waltz. This had been our morning ritual for as long as we both could remember.

"You are my sunshine, my only sunshine. You make me happy when skies are gray," I sang as I twirled my delighted partner, my bare feet padding gently on the hardwood floors of the nursery. "You'll never know, dear, how much I love you. Please don't take my sunshine away."

As I placed her on the changing table to dress her, Michael came in to give Annie her good-morning kiss. "Maybe we should get your mother to babysit Annie tonight. I mean, she'll probably sleep through the whole thing, anyway."

I finished snapping up the bottom of Annie's one-piece outfit and lifted her. "Oh, Michael—I thought it would be so much fun with the three of us. My dad used to take me when I was her age, and I remember watching the sky with him. It's such a magical thing."

He shrugged. "All right. If it means that much to you." He kissed me quickly on the lips and reached for his daughter.

I was fascinated by comets—those ghostly apparitions from the past traveling along sweeping pathways through space and time. Historically, comets have always been harbingers of doom, having made appearances prior to the assassination of Julius Caesar, the Black Death, the defeat of the Alamo, and the fall of Atlanta to the Yankees in the summer of 1863. Ancient man thought that comets were God's messengers alerting mankind of what was to come. Despite Mr. Haley's scientific explanation on the origins of comets, I, too, thought there was something more ethereal about those dirty snowballs of ice and dust.

I was especially intrigued because of something my grandmother had told me when I was a girl. As I was leaving her house after a day of learning about folklore and her own brand of ancient astronomy, Grandma had held my arm and whispered in my ear, "Be careful of moonless nights and speeding stars. Though the magic is there, there is danger, too, and great heartache."

I had no idea what she was talking about, and she refused to elaborate further on subsequent visits. But her prophetic words would always return to me as I climbed Moon Mountain to witness yet another astronomical event.

Double-checking the diaper bag for Annie's hat and sunscreen, I loaded it into the Explorer. As I bent down to tie my shoelaces, a bead of perspiration dripped on my knee. At ten o'clock in the morning, it was already sweltering—a typical August day in Georgia.

It had rained during the night. Not one of those gentle rainstorms found in northern climes, but a powerful combination of window-shaking thunder and daylight-making lightning common to Georgia and other Southern coastal states. But the sky above was now cloudless, a blue dome over the baking earth.

By the end of the day, we found ourselves at the foot of Moon Mountain. The National Park Service had fashioned an asphalt parking lot at the foot of the hill, and I was happy to see that there were no other cars. Even at nine o'clock at night, the heat rose from the blacktop. Perspiration prickled down my back as I stooped to get our sleeping Annie out of her car seat. I had tried to keep her awake in the car, but her exhaustion had finally overtaken her. I hoped she would wake up in time to see her first comet.

Her head lolled to one side and I carefully cradled it as I lifted her out. I zipped her snugly into the carrier on Michael's back and laid a gentle kiss on her sweaty cheek.

The gravel path cut across the hillside and disappeared around the bend. We hastily checked the car door, then began our ascent, refraining from talking so we wouldn't disturb Annie. Despite the additional twenty pounds on his back, Michael kept a grueling pace. The only sounds besides the crunching of the gravel beneath our feet were the constant whirring of the cicadas and the distant hum of traffic from Highway 9. My shirt began to stick to my back and quickly became drenched under the arms. With a quick glance behind me to ensure that we were alone, I slid off my backpack for a moment to remove my shirt and continue the climb in my bra. Michael raised an eyebrow and shook his head in mock exasperation.

My heart softened as I watched Annie in her little cocoon, one plump hand resting on her father's shoulder and her thumb on her other hand firmly implanted in her mouth. During our climb, I could occasionally hear frenzied sucking coming from the little bundle on Michael's back, and it made me smile. She was worth every visit to the fertility clinic, every poke and prod from doctors, every ounce of despair. Even after all we had gone through, we almost lost her to placental abruption in the delivery room. Only an emergency C-section had saved her life. And mine. We longed for another child, but I wasn't quite ready to accept the risk again.

We reached the crest in about thirty minutes. I quickly took off my backpack and rifled through it for Annie's blanket. I laid it on the ground by the side of a pine tree and gently lifted the still-sleeping Annie. She stirred slightly and raised her ruffle-covered rump in the air. Her thumb found her mouth again and she settled back down.

I walked toward the edge where a coin-operated telescope was mounted, unnecessary for reveling in the beauty of our secluded spot. The twinkling skyline of Atlanta lay to the south and I could pick out the Bank of America tower rising higher than its sister skyscrapers. A halo of light, outlined in the purple tinge of dusk, surrounded the skyline in a gentle benediction. Genetti's Comet glowed dimly on the horizon.

Michael approached and pressed his bare chest against my back. I reached behind me to grasp hold of him. His expert hands quickly unsnapped my bra and then slid around to cup my breasts. I laid my head on his shoulder as he planted lingering kisses on my neck.

"You taste salty," he said as his lips traveled down to my shoulder.

I sighed, enjoying the caress of goose bumps as they traveled down my spine. "Michael, not here. Someone might see." I made no move to step away.

Annie grunted in her sleep, and I shifted around in Michael's arms. "Can you hold that thought until later?"

He touched my cheek, his fingers slowly traveling down to my neck. "If I have to." He reached behind me and refastened my bra.

"I have something to cool you off." I stepped back and walked toward where we had dumped our gear. "We should drink something so we don't become dehydrated. I learned that in my new-mommy CPR class." I squatted in front of my backpack and pulled out two bottles of water.

We sat next to each other, leaning against a scrubby tree trunk, and drank our water in companionable silence while waiting for night to fall completely. A soft snore came from Annie, and the rhythm of it lulled us both to a semiconscious stupor. Michael's head sagged forward and I reached my hand up to wake him, only to find myself seemingly paralyzed. I willed my limb to move, but it lay limp and useless at my side. I struggled to keep my eyes open, but an unseen force seemed to be dragging me into a deep, dark slumber. I made an attempt to wiggle my toes, recalling how doing that had brought me out of bad dreams when I was a girl. Nothing moved; I was completely immobile. The last thing I remembered was reaching for Annie.

I dreamed I was running through darkness. My legs were leaden weights and would not propel me toward a dim light shining though the murkiness. A pervading sense of loss enveloped me, and I knew escape was neither imminent nor possible. A loud whirring sound buzzed in my ear and I turned my head from side to side to make it stop.

I woke up to find a cicada screeching loudly on the tree trunk next to my head. I struggled to orient myself for a moment until I remembered where I was. It was too dark to see my watch, but the sunlight filtering around the earth's edge had turned the moon a vivid red. A black shadow had already hooded a quarter of the moon, causing me to recall the Mayan myth of a jaguar wolfing down the lunar orb.

I reached over to feel for Annie and my hands found the warm tangle of her hair. I moved my palm to her back to feel her strong rhythmic breathing and the heat of her body. Michael's outline slumped asleep against the tree trunk next to me, and I decided not to disturb him just yet. I wanted a private moment with the comet alone before I had to share it. Standing, and trying to recall how much wine I had had at dinner, I walked to the clearing to get a better view of the eclipse. I caught a strong whiff of gardenias, which surprised me, as I didn't remember seeing any on our climb up.

Genetti's Comet hovered brightly in the darkened sky. A chill swept down my spine, raising the hair on the back of my neck. I shivered involuntarily and wrapped my arms around me. It was then that I realized that the insects had ceased their nocturnal chorus. I couldn't hear the traffic anymore. Silence hugged the hilltop, enshrouding us. A strong wind began to blow, whipping my hair about my face, but the sound it made wasn't the gentle whooshing noise that precedes a storm. Instead, the wind howled loudly and then softly, swirling around my head so I couldn't determine the direction. The strong scent of gardenias assaulted my nose again, and I trembled with an unseen fear. My head pounded and the blood rushed through my ears, the pressure so intense that I fell to my knees.

Annie. Something was wrong and I had to get to Annie. I panicked, trying to reach the spot where I had left her in the dark. I stumbled on something hard and rough and fell to the ground. I cried out Michael's name, but I couldn't hear anything over the din of the wind. I crawled on my hands and knees, crying out their names. Only the wind answered me. My fingers grasped the edge of the blanket where Annie had been sleeping, and I began to sob with relief. I crawled over it until I realized it was empty. The bile of pure terror crept up my throat and I threw up. I was still gagging when a hand touched my shoulder.

I screamed and leapt up. I felt the reassuring touch of Michael's embrace and the soothing words of his voice. "Laura, it's me. Are you okay?"

I struggled in his arms. "Michael, do you have Annie? I can't find her!" My voice sounded frantic and I worked hard to bring it under control.

"No. Isn't she on the blanket?" Michael knelt down to feel for her blanket.

"No, Michael, she's not here! Oh, God! We've got to find her."

The shadow slowly swallowed the moon. I threw my shirt back on, grabbed a flashlight, and went flying down the path in search of my daughter.

Neither the police nor we found any trace of her. Huge search groups swarmed the area for days, despite the heat and torrential rains. After a week, they had given up. The police said it was still an open case and they were still looking, but I knew they had given up. Nothing was found—no clothes, no blood, no signs of anything. It was as if she had been absorbed into the moonlight. I know the police suspected us, but no evidence ever surfaced to incriminate either one of us, or anyone else. Annie was just . . . gone.

In the days that followed her disappearance, guilt gnawed at my conscience. I had been the one to insist we bring her rather than leave her with my mother, as Michael had suggested. My grandmother's warning spun around inside my head. Was this what she had meant? Why hadn't I listened? I wanted Michael to lash out at me, blame me. His silence was worse than any accusation could have been.

When the doorbell rang two weeks later, I was in the middle of mending one of Annie's dresses. The tear in the seam at the bottom had come from her stepping on the hem as she tried to stand. She kept doing it again and again, thinking it enormously funny. I had joined in, for her silly giggles were hard to resist.

The needle jabbed and plunged into the yellow fabric, closing the hole sure and swift. The smile on my face faded when I realized the doorbell had rung at least three or four times. I laid my hand on Michael's shoulder as I passed him, his eyes blankly staring at a rerun of *Quantum Leap*. The old clock in the hallway announced the hour, the Westminster chime echoing throughout the still house. I opened the door, still clutching Annie's dress.

A woman and a man stood on my front porch, looking uncomfortable in the heat.

The man spoke first. "Mrs. Truitt?"

I stared at them for a brief moment before finding my voice.

"Yes, I'm Laura Truitt."

"Mrs. Truitt, I'm Detective Peterson from the Roswell Police Department, and this is my partner, Detective McGraw." He indicated the woman with his chin. "We have some news for you."

He paused. I could hear the sounds from the TV inside and Michael coughing. A car passed by on the street in front of our house. Loud music from the radio evaporated as the car sped away.

"Mrs. Truitt?"

I must have said something.

"Mrs. Truitt. We've found a child's body."

The yellow dress fell from my hands, puddling on the floor like crumpled sunshine. "Annie?" My voice sounded a lot stronger than I expected.

"The body is unidentified, but it matches the description of your daughter." The woman's voice was kind, and she took a step toward me.

"A body . . . And you want us to . . . You need us to come down . . ."

I looked behind me and into the parlor at Michael. Angry red marks of exhaustion marred the skin under his eyes. His sun-streaked blond hair looked gray against the pallor of his skin, and for the first time since the beginning of our ordeal, I knew his pain was as great as mine. I recalled how he had wept when Annie was born, and I suddenly wanted to slam the door shut and erase the choked sound of the detective's voice from my memory. I had the impulse to run into Michael's arms and pretend that everything was normal again and our dear, sweet Annie was upstairs in her crib. But Michael's arms lay powerless and empty beside him on the sofa, his palms turned upward in silent supplication.

The man swallowed, and I turned back to face them.

"Mrs. Truitt, we need you and your husband to come to the morgue for identification." More firmly, he said, "You should have someone bring you. If— Well, sometimes, afterward, it's not easy to drive. . . ."

"We'll be fine," I said.

He gave me the information I needed; then I shut the door silently, wondering how I would tell Michael. I forced myself to breathe. I sat on the stairs and took as many deep breaths as I could.

As we hurtled south on I-85, the huge and shimmering Atlanta skyline beckoned from the horizon. The giant peach structure rose on our left, and I fleetingly thought of how Annie always pointed at it and said "apple" when we passed by. I stole a look at Michael and saw a tear escaping down his cheek, and knew he was remembering, too.

We clung to each other as we walked through the fluorescent-lit halls of the Fulton County Medical Examiner's Center. The unnatural light made the hollows and shadows of Michael's face more prominent, and I knew if I bothered to look in a mirror I'd see the same devastation.

We walked ahead as a unit, my husband and I, and stopped before the metal slab. The doctor pulled down the top of the sheet that covered a small form. Two little feet barely stuck up high enough to make the sheet rise.

My gaze traveled to the top, where the doctor held the cover open. Dirty blond hair was matted to the delicate forehead, partially obscuring a large plum-colored bruise. Translucent skin stretched over the small bones of the face, and dark lashes on the closed eyelids fanned the pale cheeks. It could have been Annie; there were so many similarities. But it wasn't my daughter. It wasn't Annie. I broke down then. I don't know if it was from relief that it wasn't our baby or for this loss of gentle life. Maybe it was for all the empty years I knew lay before us.

CHAPTER TWO

——◆——

Press close bare-bosom'd night—press
close magnetic nourishing night!
Night of south winds—night of the large few stars!
Still nodding night—mad naked summer night.

—WALT WHITMAN

The loss of Annie had been the beginning of the unraveling of my life. The end of it came five years later.

Shortly after Annie's disappearance, Michael took up flying. I remembered the heated argument we had when he told me how he was going to deal with his heartache.

"Laura, I've signed up for flying lessons." Michael continued to read the paper as if he had just mentioned that he was going to plant a bed of daffodils.

"You're what?" He had never mentioned such a thing to me before.

"One of the partners at the law firm pilots his own plane, and I thought that might be what I needed." He sipped his coffee and continued to peruse the paper.

"What you need for what? To kill yourself? Or to spend even more time away from me?" I cringed at the shrillness in my voice. I went over to him and knelt beside him. I rested my head in his lap, blinking away tears.

"I miss you," I mumbled into the striped wool of his pants. "I need you. Please come back to me." I looked up at him, uncaring of my tears that soaked into his pants.

He looked at me with shadowed eyes and sighed, pushing his newspaper away. "You're so strong, Laura. You've picked up the pieces of your life and have learned to live with your grief. But I'm falling apart inside. I need to see Annie again. When I'm here or at work, all I see are the memories. I need to go where I can create new images of her and feel her close to me again." He ground the heels of his hands into his eye sockets and rubbed them harshly, as if to clear them of whatever image he couldn't bear to see.

I wanted to argue with him that I wasn't so strong. I had managed to survive by compartmentalizing my grief into a tiny box in my heart and only allowing myself to peek inside when there was no one around to witness the devastation.

I stood, kissed him softly on the lips, and left, a tight ball of fear growing in my stomach.

Later, as I sat and tinkled halfheartedly with the piano keyboard, Michael sat down and put his arm around me. He apologized, but didn't back down.

I could feel the tension in him, felt his need, and knew I couldn't tether him to me forever. "Okay, Michael. If this is what you want to do. Just please be careful. I don't think I could stand to lose you, too."

So Michael searched for Annie in the cumulus clouds and soaring winds while I remained earthbound, but with my eyes toward the heavens. By the time I got the dreaded late-night phone call, I had already prepared myself. I had been down this route before. The voice on the other end of the line mentioned something about engine failure, but I listened with only half an ear. Whether it had been engine failure or a lightning bolt, the end result was the same. I was a widow at the age of thirty-five.

For almost a year after his death, I strived to remember the feel of Michael's touch on my skin. I lay awake at night in my empty bed, trying to feel his presence beside me, the encroaching warmth that would draw me toward him during sleep. The thick air of a Georgia summer settled around my ghosts and me. If sleep did come, it was only to dream he was there. I would breathe deeply and smell his warm, slumbering breath and hear his quiet murmurings in the stale morning air. Then I would open my eyes and know I was alone.

The never-ending search for Annie kept me moving in the halls of the living. And I had my house. It sustained me through that time, its walls seeming to enclose me in an embrace.

I vaguely remembered something my grandmother had told me long ago about a connection between heartache and the moon, and I knew the answer lay high above me. So I remained looking and searching, but no answer came.

I found great solace in my music. I returned to work full-time as an elementary-school music teacher and continued to teach private voice and piano lessons from my home. Instead of finding the constant presence of children depressing, it was what kept me living.

My mother was concerned about me, but she lacked the ability to truly comfort me. I knew she grieved terribly over Annie and, perhaps, blamed me a little for her disappearance. I never forgave her for that. I longed for my grandmother's wisdom, but she had died years before.

I was surprised, therefore, when my mother made an impromptu visit on an early summer evening in June. Reclining on the watered-silk sofa in the parlor with Henryk Gorecki's *Symphony of Sorrowful Songs* flooding over me, I heard a hesitant knock on the front door. My mother's habit was to simply breeze in unannounced, so I was amazed to see her tall, elegant form standing on the porch when I opened the door. Impeccably dressed, as always, with her glossy black hair pulled back in a neat chignon at the back of her head. A warm smile sat on her lips.

"Hello, Laura. I hope this isn't a bad time." Her gaze scanned the house and interior—to either check on their condition or to make sure we were alone, I didn't know.

"Not at all, Mom. Come in. I'll order out for some Chinese if you're hungry," I said, noting how my stomach was rumbling.

My mother gave me a wry grin as she stepped through the doorway. "I see you still don't cook."

"There's no one to cook for, and I can't see going to all that trouble just for me."

She looked a little chagrined, and I regretted being harsh, but I had detected a hint of criticism in her voice and it had reduced me to a chastised adolescent once again.

"I'm sorry. I wasn't criticizing you. Sure, why don't we order takeout? There's a new place that just opened on Canton Street that everybody is just raving about."

As I Googled the restaurant on my phone, my mother took a tissue-wrapped object out of her purse. I did a little start as I recognized it. Putting my phone down, I reached for the picture.

"Mom, I'd almost given up ever getting this back from you," I said as I pulled the picture from its wrappings.

"I'm sorry for keeping it this long. It got misplaced after we moved to the new house, and then I guess I forgot about it with . . . well, with everything that's happened." She smoothed her already perfect hair behind her ears. "I still can't figure out who she is. And it's obviously somebody we're related to." She looked directly at me and failed to suppress a shudder.

I stared at that all-too-familiar face and felt a cold, unseen finger on the back of my neck. Who was she? I moved to put the picture on the hall table, but slipped it into a drawer instead.

Later, sitting at the dining room table amid little white cardboard boxes, my mother and I shared a bottle of wine. She had raised her eyebrows at my extensive collection on the wine rack in the kitchen. I wanted to explain that a glass or two of wine every night was the only way I could shut my eyes and enter oblivion. Otherwise, I would lie awake in my bed and feel the darkness encircle me. I would imagine Annie calling out for me or feel Michael's gentle caress. My solitary torment would be my only companion if I did not have the wine to chase away the ghosts. I didn't want to worry my mother or suffer through a lecture, so I offered no explanation.

Dabbing at the corners of her mouth with a napkin, she said, "Laura, I met the nicest man yesterday at my doctor's office. He's new in the practice, very nice-looking, and . . ."

I held up my hand. "Stop it, Mom. I'm not interested."

"But you haven't even met him!" She started digging in her purse until she came up with a business card and slid it across the polished surface of the table. "Here's his card. I gave him your number, too."

I left the card untouched in the middle of the table. "Then you'd better call him and tell him I'm not interested." I pushed my plate away from me and took a long sip of wine.

"Laura, isn't it time to restart your life? I know you miss them. But life goes on."

I closed my eyes in an effort to control my temper. "You don't understand. Unless you've been here, you couldn't possibly understand. Michael and Annie weren't just a man and a child, easily replaced by the next available candidates. They were *mine*. I can never get them back. And I could never love another man like Michael. So just forget about your matchmaking. Love only brings me grief, and I'm through with it. Forever."

Her mouth became two thin strips of disapproval, but she said nothing. But when she stood to clear the table, she left the business card.

As my mother was helping me rinse the dishes and put them in the dishwasher, she finally broached the subject she had come over to discuss.

She made a big production of scrambling around in the cabinet to find storage containers for the leftover food. As she was leaning down with her head in the cabinet she said, "Laura, have you been reading the papers lately?" She stood to compare sizes of Tupperware, then leaned down to put one back.

"Not really. I haven't had an interest, I suppose."

I turned on the hot water and let it run until I saw steam rise and condense on the window above the sink. I looked through the steamy haze and saw my mother's reflection. She was looking at me with a perplexed frown, as if pondering whether to tell me something. I began to meticulously poke bits of food down the disposal. When my mother still didn't speak, I glanced up to find her still looking at me. I shut the faucet off and turned around to face her.

"Why? What is it?" I asked.

She began to empty the contents of a white carton into the plastic container. She slammed it down a little too hard on the counter and said, "There's going to be another total lunar eclipse in two weeks. The first one in five years."

Something akin to panic began to creep on little bird's feet into the pit of my stomach. "Oh, really?" I tried to keep my voice calm.

"Yes," she continued. "And there will be another comet visible at the same time."

"Genetti's Comet?"

"No, a different one."

I started to tremble and could feel my knees go weak. I hastily sat down at the kitchen table. My mother snapped the container's lid closed and then burped it before putting it in the refrigerator and closing the door with her back. She leaned against it and drew in a deep breath as if to gather her strength.

"It's almost the same conditions as when baby Annie disappeared. I was thinking that maybe whoever took her might come back to the same spot again."

An icy hand began to claw at my insides. I knew what she was going to ask me, and I didn't know if I could do it.

"Laura, I'll go with you if you want. But don't you think that if there's even the slightest chance of getting Annie back, we should try it?" My mother's voice pleaded and her eyes were moist from emotion. I sensed the love she held for my daughter and I softened toward her.

"I want her back more than anything. But I just can't imagine that whoever took her five years ago would return her to the same spot just because there's another eclipse." I averted my eyes so she could not see the fear in them and stood and walked over to the sink.

My mother came to stand behind me and caught my gaze in the reflection of the window. "I know you're afraid. Remember that I was the one who spent the first few days with you after Annie's disappearance. I knew there was something else."

I drew a deep breath to steady my voice. "Mom, that place is evil. I felt as if my soul was being pulled from my body. I don't know if I'd have the will to survive it again." I looked down at my hands, where the knuckles had gone white from gripping the edge of the counter.

"Please think about it." Her words held desperation in them. But I couldn't offer any assurances. She silently picked up her purse and let herself out the front door.

When I heard the latch click into place, I sank down on the floor and stared ahead numbly. I rubbed my eyes with the heels of my hands, trying to think more clearly. Images of my daughter flashed before my eyes and I felt the pull of longing as fresh as ever. I knew I would give my life for hers or to even just see her again. Whatever it took, I wanted her back.

When I stood again, I felt stronger. And I knew what I had to do.

Chapter Three

———◆———

Why I came here, I know not; where I shall go it is useless
to enquire. In the midst of myriads of the living and the
dead worlds, stars, systems, infinity, why should I be
anxious about an atom?

—LORD BYRON

I brought no sunscreen or blankets on this trip—only a grim determination to see a task through. I considered bringing a weapon but had pushed that thought aside. I was completely ignorant of guns and knives and how to use them for defensive purposes, and the results could have been disastrous if I had attempted any sort of forced rescue. I figured my flashlight could be used as a pummeling device if needed. I had no idea what to expect. Only my mother's words and an unexplainable force propelled me to the hill.

Throughout the day and evening, fat gray clouds hung heavy in the sky, leaking out a constant drizzle. Not enough to get soaked, but just enough to be annoying. The tires of my car squished over the wet asphalt as I looked for a place to park. I was startled to find a beat-up Volkswagen Beetle illuminated by my headlights.

As I parked my car next to it and glanced in the windows, my heart skipped a beat. No dolls or coloring books or other signs that a child had ever ridden in the car. I laughed nervously at my imaginings and turned toward the path. Droplets of rain spotted my jeans as I climbed. I looked up at the dimness of the evening sky and pulled the hood of my rain jacket over my head.

As I approached the top, my heart hammered, but not from exertion. A blanket and a few tall branches had been converted into a makeshift shelter for a teenage couple. A small campfire illuminated their faces, while the pungent aroma of burning wood and leaves wafted over to me. The boy quickly adjusted his shorts, stood, and offered his hand to his girlfriend. I smiled awkwardly at them and averted my gaze.

The thick cloud cover blocked any possible view of the eclipse or comet, but the telescope would give me something to do. I fished through my pocket for a quarter and put it in.

A wave of dizziness engulfed me before I could hear the clank of the coin hitting its target. I gripped the telescope to regain my balance and was hit by the sudden smell of gardenias, which brought a fresh recollection of the night Annie disappeared. A man's voice and the whinnying of a horse broke the silence. I whirled around to see who it was. The young couple was absorbed with each other as if they hadn't heard a thing. I saw no one else.

I was about to dismiss it all as the product of my overactive imagination when I distinctly heard the crying of a child. It wasn't the fretful cries of a baby, but the screams of a child who fancies himself injured.

I ran over to the couple. "Did you hear that?"

They looked at me with irritation. "Hear what?"

Turning around, I clearly heard the voice of a man. "Don't run away from me when I'm talking to you. It's dangerous in those woods."

A young child answered back, "You're not my father and I don't have to listen to you!"

"Annie!" I shouted, thinking that maybe those voices would know where she was.

The couple quickly rolled up their blanket, scooped up mud to throw on their campfire, and scurried for the path leading down to the parking lot.

The pinpricks of a severe headache began to work themselves up from the base of my neck. Looking upward, I saw a partial moon through an opening in the cloud cover, a shadow taking a bite out of the edge. The murky sky obscured any view of the comet but I knew it was up there, trailing its mark through the sky, just as another comet had done five years previously.

The earth seemed to tilt at an odd angle, and I lost my balance. This had to be an earthquake. *They aren't totally unheard-of in Georgia,* I reassured myself. My limbs trembled uncontrollably so I lay down, curling up in a fetal position. I heard more voices, closer this time, and I nearly choked on the overwhelming smell of gardenias as I lost consciousness.

The feel of a rough, wet tongue lapping my cheek woke me. Opening my eyes, I found a strange-looking dog of questionable parentage. It was undoubtedly the ugliest mutt I had ever seen, but certainly the friendliest if his pleasure at waking me was any indication.

I sat up quickly and was rewarded with dizziness and spots before my eyes. I put my hands on either side of my head to keep it steady. The dog climbed into my lap and lay down, his tail thumping against the ground.

Absently patting the dog, I looked around. The scenery was new but offered an uncanny familiarity. I realized I must have staggered down the hill in my confusion. The gloomy cloud cover of night had blossomed into a sky of glaring blue, and the ground around me appeared bone-dry. Wanting to see how much time had passed, I lifted my arm, but was dismayed to find my watch gone. It had been a gift from Michael, and I felt another stab of loss.

Seeing no sign of the asphalt parking lot, I determined that I had managed to roam to the other side of the hill in some kind of delirious state, because I couldn't remember anything. I stood, pushing the dog gently off of my lap. The ground appeared to pitch violently, so I sat down again. I searched unsuccessfully in the overgrown vegetation for my purse, with my phone inside it, and then shrugged out of my rain jacket as the sweltering sun bore down on me. When the earth stopped spinning, I stood again slowly to make my way back to the parking lot. With no key or phone, I wasn't sure what I would do when I got to my car, but at least I had a direction to head in. Maybe there'd be more cars in the parking lot and I would just wait until somebody came.

There were no marked paths, so I was forced to walk very slowly. I had to continually brush aside green stalks and blades with my hands, which cut the skin on my palms. I paused to rest and wipe the sweat from my face. It then occurred to me that except for the insistent humming of insects, it was totally silent. No planes flying overhead; no traffic on the highway.

Something pounding through the underbrush on my right shattered the silence. My mouth went dry as I recalled that panthers could still be found in the wild in this part of the state.

I turned as a small boy, age seven or eight years, emerged hurtling through the underbrush and running smack into my middle. I staggered backward. He looked up at me with wild brown eyes and pointed behind him.

"It's a catamount! Help—he's gonna get me!"

I had no need to ask what a catamount was, as the object of the boy's terror slowly sauntered its way out of the thicket, its body low to the ground as it moved toward its prey. Instinctively, I shoved the boy behind me. As if to make his intentions clear, the large cat darted its tongue out and flattened its ears. The feral eyes glinted in the sunlight, and I wondered if it could smell my fear. Something moved outside my peripheral vision, but I dared not look. A deep growling began in the depths of the cat's throat, and I turned and threw my arms over the boy. He trembled, his sweat sticking to my own on my bare arms. I bent my head, prepared for the gouging of sharp claws through the thin cotton of my blouse. The beast hissed and sprang from the ground. I squeezed the boy tightly, his small bones sharp under my hands, anticipating pointed teeth in my flesh. The crack of a rifle shot at close range split the air.

The feline dropped down like a leaden weight, hitting my shoulder and knocking us to the ground. Tasting dirt, I turned my head and spat. I scrambled on my hands and knees away from the cat, dragging the boy with me.

Coming to a spot about ten feet away, I stopped. Clutching me wildly, the boy sobbed incoherently. I gathered him in my arms and made soothing sounds while keeping a wary eye on the panther for any signs of movement. The acrid odor of gunpowder stung my nostrils.

A shadow fell on us, making us both look up. The boy scrambled to his feet and tried to unobtrusively wipe the tears off his cheeks with the backs of his sleeves. His clothing gave me a start. I couldn't remember the last time I had seen a boy his age in anything but jeans and a T-shirt, but this child wore a white cotton shirt with loose knee breeches and suspenders. His dirty feet were bare.

The dog bolted out of the bushes and leapt on the boy with a joyful yapping. I made a move to stand to greet our rescuer, but instead felt two firm hands grab me by the arms and hoist me up. I found myself looking up into eyes that suddenly reminded me of the Caribbean. I had a flash of recognition for a moment, and then it was gone. He was about my age or perhaps a little older, but I was sure I would have remembered this man had I met him before. He was looking at me just as closely, his gaze almost intimate. I lowered my eyes.

"Thank you," I managed. "You . . . you saved my life." His hands trembled on my arms and I realized I was shaking.

"Are you all right?" His look of concern warmed me, and I was ready to say yes, until I felt the pain in my shoulder from where the cat had landed on me. I winced.

He released me gently. "I think you need to see a doctor. Do you live around here? I will take you home."

I blushed when I realized that he was staring at my jeans.

"You are not from around here, are you?" He averted his eyes, then looked at my face.

I paused at the formality of his speech, so unlike what I usually heard at school where I taught or on television. "I live in Roswell. My car isn't far from here. I'm sure I could drive home if you could help me find my purse. It has my car keys and my phone in it." I brushed the dead grass off of my pants and shirt and then noticed he hadn't moved or spoken.

"There are no railroad cars around here, ma'am." He looked at me as if I were speaking in a foreign language. "But it would be my pleasure to escort you back to Roswell. We are heading that way, as well."

Confused, I opened my mouth to reply when I noticed his peculiar costume. He wore a long-sleeved white cotton shirt, a pullover variety with three wooden buttons at the neck. His pants were light brown, almost yellow, and held up with suspenders. A wide-brimmed hat, darkened around the brim with sweat, sat on his head and hid his hair, but his eyebrows were almost black. And then I noticed his rifle. It was huge—almost five feet long—and looked exactly like an antique Civil War Enfield rifle that my history-buff father had hanging in his study.

"Is there a battle reenactment going on?" I asked, hoping that his explanation would soothe the growing worries I felt tickling the back of my brain.

"No, ma'am. Only battles going on 'round here are the real thing."
He looked closely at me with a furrowed brow. "Did you hit your head
when you fell?"

I had begun to wonder the same thing and reached up with both
hands to feel for bumps on my skull. No such luck.

"No. I don't think so. But I heard a child's voice. I . . . I thought it
might be my daughter."

"Your daughter?" He searched the immediate area with his eyes, a
look of growing concern on his face. "Willie and I have not seen anybody at all since we left the house this morning." He took a step closer.
"Will you be all right if I leave you here with Willie while I go look for
your little girl?"

I shook my head. "No. That won't be necessary. Annie—my daughter—
she's . . . she's been gone for five years now. I guess it was only wishful
thinking when I heard that voice. It was probably Willie's." I looked away
from his intense gaze, feeling once again the crushing weight of sorrow and
afraid I might end up crying in front of a perfect stranger.

"My condolences. I am very sorry for your loss."

I looked at him and knew that he was.

"Please just get me back to Roswell. I'll be fine."

He nodded slowly, then turned his attention toward Willie. The boy
stood as still as a tree trunk and looked as if he wanted to blend into the
scenery. The tall, lean man limped as he walked, his pants leg sporting
several patches.

"Willie, you are in for the biggest whipping of your life. You could
have been killed." The man limped over to the fallen animal and
nudged it with the butt of his rifle.

"This here cat would have had you for supper if I had not been here
in time. Sort of what your mother would do to me if I let anything
happen to you."

"You are not my pa. I do not have to do anything you say." Despite
his defiant words, the boy's lower lip trembled. He stuck his chin out
and added, "Anyway, my pa says you are a traitor and should be in
prison. I am not listening to no traitor."

The man paled. He knelt in front of Willie, keeping his left leg straight out to the side. He grasped the boy by the shoulders and said, "Did he really say that?"

Willie stood still, examining his feet, but I could see his jaw trembling. "Yes, sir. And he said that I needed to protect my ma from any secesh claptrap you might be scooping out." The boy's voice was barely audible, and a tear hit the toe of his shoe.

Despite his reaction to the boy's words, the man gathered the child in his arms and hugged him. "No matter what is between your pa and me, it is not going to change the fact that you are my nephew and I love you as if you were my own son." He stood and added, "And that means that it is my duty to protect you as a father would, in your own father's absence. I am sorry, Willie, but I am going to have to give you the switch when we get home."

The boy stood there meekly, with a few stifled sobs racking his small body. My heart went out to him. I went over and put my arm around his bony shoulders.

The man looked at me with dark blue eyes. "My apologies, ma'am, for involving you in our little family disputes. Please allow me to introduce myself." He hastily pulled his hat from his head, confirming that his hair matched his dark eyebrows. "I am Mr. Stuart Elliott of Phoenix Hall, Roswell, and this is my nephew, William Elliott Junior."

I smiled at his gallant bow and introduced myself, mimicking his formal tone. "I'm Mrs. Laura Truitt. I live on Mimosa Boulevard in Roswell."

He gave me a quizzical look. "Where is Mimosa Boulevard? I have lived in Roswell all my life and I have never heard of it."

My confusion, the heat, and buzzing flies made me snap. "Well, that makes us even, I guess. I've lived in Roswell for seven years and I've never heard of Phoenix Hall."

He raised his eyebrows. "I think you have had a bit of a shock." He gave a shrill whistle and the ugly mutt came bounding out from behind a tree. "Charlie, get Endy."

I watched in amazement as the dog ran into the thicket and then emerged with the reins of a horse in his mouth and the horse itself bringing up the rear. It was a huge animal with big eyes and a slobbery mouth. The thing sneezed as it approached, spraying us all with God knows what and showing me a mouth full of teeth. Two rabbits hung by their feet on a length of twine stretched across the back of the beast. I had apparently interrupted a hunting expedition.

Stuart grabbed hold of the reins and firmly patted the jet-black flank of the horse. "Mrs. Truitt, would you mind sharing Endy with Willie?"

I looked the man straight in his eyes to make sure he was speaking to me. I had to look up several inches, as he was a good deal taller than my own five feet seven. "There is no way I'm getting on that horse. Besides, you're limping. You ride that thing—I'll walk." I took a few steps backward to put as much distance between myself and Endy as I could and fell over a fallen branch, landing soundly on my backside.

Stuart stifled a laugh, but Willie had no such compunction and laughed outright.

"That's the last time I save you from a vicious animal attack," I snapped at Willie.

That sobered him up sufficiently. Stuart reached down to me, for the second time that day, and hoisted me up. "You sure are a stubborn woman. But I am not going to ride a horse while a lady walks. Would not do for my reputation as a gentleman at all."

Instead of releasing me, he put one arm under my legs and picked me up like a baby. His touch seemed somehow familiar, and I studied his face intently, aware of his own close scrutiny. Neither one of us said anything as he swung me up onto the horse's back. Too petrified to move, I clung to the saddle. He reached behind the saddle and pulled out a long gray uniform coat with black collar facings and handed it up to me.

"You might also want to wear this, so as not to shock the gentle citizens of Roswell."

I stared at the coat as if it were a snake he had asked me to wrap around my neck. I longed for the rain jacket I had inadvertently left behind.

"It is at least ninety degrees out here, and if you think I'm going to wear a wool jacket, much less release my grip on this saddle to put it on, you've got another thought coming." Sweat saturated my cotton blouse, making it cling tightly to my chest. His eyes widened as they rested on my shirt a little too long, and I hunched forward, having contracted a sudden case of modesty.

"Mrs. Truitt, I really must insist. I do not want to be grist for the Roswell rumor mill and I am sure neither do you. It just would not look right for me to bring you into town wearing, well . . ." He looked me up and down as if trying to decide what to call my outfit. "Well, whatever it is that you are wearing."

Still feeling a bit dazed and confused, and not in the mood to argue, I took the coat and threw it over my shoulders. He lifted Willie up on the saddle behind me, shouldered his rifle, and began to pull the reins and lead the way.

The terrain seemed vaguely familiar but we never came near enough to a main highway for me to get my bearings. I assumed we were sticking to horse trails. After about an hour, we approached a large wooden gate. A hint of recognition pressed on my memory as we passed through the gate onto a long dirt drive. I knew what I would see before I saw the house looming up in the distance. A buzzing sound ran through my head as we approached, and the front door swung open. A petite but very pregnant woman wearing a long, full dress waddled down the steps toward us. From her fingertips, a squeaking mouse dangled by its tail.

"Stuart! Is everything all right?"

I had come home. The one thing I was sure of was that this was my house. I didn't know who these people were or why they were in my house, but I had my suspicions. The thought of it all made me very light-headed. I looked at the little creature, suspended by its tail, and suddenly I felt that time had me suspended, too, helpless in a world I knew and didn't know. Feeling my head swim, my eyes transfixed on the swinging rodent, I promptly slid off the horse in a dead faint.

Chapter Four

—◆—

For time is the longest distance between two places.
—TENNESSEE WILLIAMS

I opened my eyes and found myself staring at close range at a rough cotton shirt. I moved my head and realized I was being carried up the stairs. Stuart stumbled, and my arms shot around his neck. I remembered his limp and attempted to get down.

"You shouldn't be carrying me—I can walk. Please put me down."

Ignoring my request, he crossed the upstairs hallway, entered one of the bedrooms, and laid me gently on a small spindle bed. My hands remained locked behind his neck as my head reached the pillow, and our gazes met. I had definitely seen those eyes before, but the wisp of memory floated beyond my grasp.

His breath felt warm on my cheek, and I blushed realizing I was still holding on to him and keeping his face close to mine. Slowly, I let my arms fall to my sides.

"I did not figure a woman who could face a catamount without a scream would faint at the sight of a mouse." A wry grin touched his face but I could see relief there, too.

"I didn't faint." I ignored his raised eyebrow. "I've never fainted in my whole life and I have no intention of starting now."

I looked around me to get my bearings. I recognized Annie's room but a small bed and stark white walls now replaced the crib and pale pink wallpaper. I sat up with a start as I suddenly remembered where I was. I scurried out of the bed, ran past Stuart and out of the room to the balcony. The sight that greeted me confirmed my suspicions. Not an electrical pole in sight, nor any of the familiar streets and buildings that had surrounded my house. The urban blight of strip malls creeping their way up Highway 9 had been replaced by a red-clay road shaded by trees. But there was no doubt in my mind that this was my house.

The sound of children's laughter and a dog barking brought my attention to the backyard, where a little girl wearing high-topped black boots chased a boy I recognized as Willie. Stuart approached to stand beside me.

"If you will excuse me, ma'am, my sister-in-law will be up in a moment."

With a brief nod, he headed down the stairs, not completely hiding a grimace of pain as he bent his leg to descend the steps.

I looked back at Willie and the little girl. It was obvious he had forgotten all about the promise of a whipping from his uncle.

Heavy footsteps climbed the wood stairs and I turned to see the pregnant woman who had been holding the mouse. She carried a small box and a stack of clean linens. The memory of me fainting at our first meeting made my face flush, but her gentle smile quickly put me at ease.

"I am Julia Elliott, Willie's mother. Thank you so much for what you did today." She smiled, hiding some of the exhaustion on her face. "I brought some of my herbs to make you feel better, but I can see you do not need them." She stopped at the top of the steps, breathing deeply. "I am sorry to have startled you with that little creature. It is only that I had just caught him when I heard Stuart ride up." Her voice was soft and fell easily on my ears as I recognized the gentle inflections of a true Southern accent. It reminded me of my mother's voice, and a twinge of nostalgia made me suddenly wish for her.

Her brows furrowed as she took in my outfit. Taking my arm, she gently guided me back to my room.

"I'm not afraid of a mouse. I've just had a heck of a day and I think I finally succumbed to the exhaustion." I allowed myself to be led and sat back down on the bed.

She bent her head closer to study the sleeve of my blouse. "I have never seen such a weave—it is truly amazing. Where did you find such a thing?"

I couldn't think of a thing to say, so I stood mutely staring at her.

Changing the subject, she asked, "Stuart said he found you on Moon Mountain. Do you live around there?"

My mind seemed to be working at half speed, the seeming reality of my situation butting heads with the impossibility of it. I wanted to believe that I was dreaming, but my sore shoulder and the scent of herbs from the woman's basket told me that this was all too real. The house and the surrounding fields, these people and their odd costumes all pointed in one direction: all pointed to the fact that I had somehow accomplished the impossible. *I had traveled through time.*

I forced myself to answer. "No, I live in Roswell. At least, I think I do."

Her delicate brows knitted together as she studied me before speaking again. "Why don't you rest some and then we will talk." I decided the woman was probably in her mid-twenties, although her manner made her seem much older. Her light brown hair was pulled off her face into a bun, which couldn't quite conceal the curls that popped out around her forehead.

"Yes. I'd like that, if you don't mind." I wasn't tired but I needed some time to devise a plan. I couldn't tell these people that I had come from another century. I would wind up in an asylum for sure. I wasn't completely convinced that I didn't belong in one.

"I will send Sukie up in a little while with a tray and some things for you to wear." She studied my face closely. "You look pale but you do not seem to have a fever," she said, placing the back of her hand to my forehead. "You are exhausted. Rest will be just the thing you need."

She glided out of the room and shut the door softly behind her.

I lay down on the bed and stared up at the ceiling. A breeze blew inside the tall windows, stirring the white lace curtains and moving the hot air around the small room. I needed to use the bathroom and was halfway to the door before I remembered that the hall bath had not been installed until 1921. I went back to the bed and looked under it. I reached to pull out the chamber pot and then decided it could wait. I was in no hurry to discover the inconveniences of the nineteenth century.

The faint ticking of a clock in the hallway lulled me into a doze. I dreamed of Annie—not as an infant but as the young girl of seven she would now be. She was talking to me but I couldn't make out what she was saying. She handed me a flower, and I bent to smell it and realized that it was a gardenia. I awoke suddenly with the potent aroma still in my nostrils. I got out of the bed and followed the scent to the window. Leaning out slightly, I discovered an entire row of gardenias growing below, their pristine petals luminescent in the late-afternoon sun.

A soft rapping on the door preceded a middle-aged black woman entering while balancing a tray piled with food.

"Good evening, ma'am. Miz Julia figured you might be starving by now."

She set the tray on a small table and turned to stare at me as I walked toward it.

Her voice was thickly accented, her English embellished with unfamiliar phrasing and emphases. It was pleasing to the ear but hard to understand at first. "What kind of clothes is that? I never seen a lady wear such a thing. Now I see why Miz Julia wants some new clothes brought up to you. I be right back."

The rich fragrance of the food reminded me that I hadn't eaten since breakfast. Despite the turmoil going on in my head regarding my apparent trip through time, my appetite, absent since Annie's disappearance, came back with a vengeance. I smiled to myself at the thought of Scarlett O'Hara's Mammy admonishing her to eat like a bird because gentlemen didn't like ladies with big appetites. Luckily, I didn't have to worry about squeezing into a corset.

I was just polishing off the last slice of ham when Sukie returned. Her arms were overloaded with flounces and fabrics and what appeared to be enough clothes to dress me for a month. She dumped the whole pile on the bed.

She stared at the empty plates. "My, you sure was hungry."

I guiltily laid aside my knife and fork. "It was delicious. Thank you for bringing it."

"Miz Julia asked me to help you get dressed. This here should fit you." She pointed to the pile on the bed, and I stared at it for a long moment. If I put it on, I'd be agreeing to continue with this charade, that I'd convinced myself this was all *real*. But maybe this was my reality for now. Because it certainly didn't appear that I had any other options.

I began to disrobe while Sukie sorted through the clothing and laid it out in an orderly fashion.

First came the chemise and calf-length cotton drawers. I was a little disconcerted to find that the drawers were split in the middle from the front to the back and only attached at the waistband. After viewing the piles of clothing that would go on top, I quickly figured out that the split drawers would show their usefulness when it came to utilizing the chamber pot.

The chemise and drawers were very comfortable and I would have been fine wearing just these all day, but I knew there was more to come. A pair of white cotton knee-length stockings with ribbon garters followed. When Sukie next held up what I recognized to be a corset, I adamantly refused.

"No way am I wearing that thing. I won't be able to breathe. Please put the rest of the stuff over me and we'll just forget about the corset."

Sukie's eyes widened in surprise. "But all ladies wear corsets!"

I took the offending garment from her hand to examine it. My fingers kneaded the unbending whalebone stays and I quickly thrust it back at her. "Thank you for your help—it's greatly appreciated. But I really would prefer not to wear a corset. If anybody complains, just tell them that I refused. Besides, I don't have enough curves for a corset to hold in. Nobody will even notice."

She shook her head slowly while clucking her tongue but complied with my wishes.

The next part of the ensemble was almost as bad as the corset. It resembled a cage with a framework of flexible steel hoops joined by vertical bands of fabric tape. I stepped into it and Sukie tied it at my waist. On top of this came two white cotton petticoats. I was heavily perspiring by this time and I longed for a tank top and shorts.

Finally, a simple long-sleeved cotton blouse with a matching skirt in a light green floral pattern was put on me, and Sukie deftly buttoned up the front. I felt completely confined and amazed at how heavy the whole ensemble was. But at least I was done. Or so I thought.

Sukie looked at my straight shoulder-length hair and shook her head. But after suffering for what seemed like an hour of her brushing and pinning my hair, she had arranged it in a neat coil in the back of my head, a severe part bisecting my scalp. Nodding with approval, she stood back to get a better view. "You have beautiful hair. And that dress match your eyes. Don' know why you dress in them men clothes."

While adding two decorative combs to my new hairstyle, she caught my reflection in the mirror. "Mr. Stuart say he found you up on Moon Mountain. What you doin' up there?"

Something flickered in her eyes as I looked at her. "I was looking for my daughter, but I couldn't find her. I . . . lost her on Moon Mountain when she was just a baby, and I hoped . . ." My voice drifted off, and I stared at her reflection again.

"She die?"

I shook my head. "I don't know. She just . . . disappeared."

She quickly reached for something around her neck. It appeared to be a small red flannel bag attached to a thin cord. She touched it briefly and then tucked it back into the neck of her dress. "Moon Mountain's a mighty strange place. I know only one other lady who would go up there by herself," she said, patting the lump inside her dress.

"That's really all I remember. I think I hit my head. I'm sure it'll all come to me eventually."

She nodded and smiled approvingly at my new hairstyle. "That look nice. I'll tell Miz Julia you dressed."

I gave up trying to sit down on the bed and just leaned against it, assuming it would be a short time before the mistress of the house found me. I looked at my wrist, forgetting again that my watch was gone. A half hour passed before I finally got up and opened the door.

Craning my neck out of the doorway, I looked around the hallway. As far as I could tell, I was alone in the house. All the sounds of people going about their daily business seemed to be coming from outside. My surroundings greatly unsettled me. I was familiar with it, yet it was different. The hardwood banister beneath my hands was the same, as was some of the furniture. But the knickknacks and wall hangings all belonged to another family, making me a stranger in my own home. I looked closely at a needlepoint on the wall. It was an elaborate sampler with all the letters of the alphabet in an uneven line and a small Bible verse at the bottom. *For what is your life? It is even a vapour, that appeareth for a little time, and then vanisheth away.* The bottom right contained the stitcher's signature, *Margaret Elliott, May 14, 1814, age twelve years.*

I descended the stairs cautiously, the voluminous skirts hampering every step. I should have practiced walking and sitting down in the privacy of my own room before venturing out, as my skirts threatened to throw me headfirst down the stairs. I couldn't see my feet, so I hovered precariously over each step as I felt my way down. In the main hallway below, a cool breeze flowed through the passageway and alleviated a little of the mugginess that clung to my skin. I thought of the central air-conditioning that Michael and I had installed, and longed for the cold blast of air from a vent and an ice-cold Diet Coke from the fridge.

Ghostlike, I flitted through the rooms, examining every detail. There was no kitchen and that puzzled me at first, until I remembered that it would have been separated from the main house to protect it from fire. In the front parlor the upright piano stood in the same spot I remembered. The dark wood was polished to a gleam, and the G key above middle C still had its ivory veneer top. The smooth keys beckoned me and I itched to feel them under my fingers, to touch something hard, solid, and real.

After quite a lot of maneuvering, I arranged myself on the bench by tucking all my skirts under me and began to play Debussy's "Clair de Lune." I was soon lost in the magic of the music and my surroundings faded from my sight, to be replaced by images of my grandmother whispering her warning to me and, surprisingly, of Stuart. I felt the heat rise in my cheeks. I had never fainted in my life, and it irked me to think that he might have thought that I was some damsel in distress who needed rescuing. I had survived on my own for more than a year and I had long since outgrown the need for Prince Charming.

As the last note died, solitary applause sounded behind me. Startled, I swung around on the bench and neatly clipped the edge of the music stand with my elbow. My injured shoulder ached at the movement, and I winced as the stand crashed down on the keyboard. The sheet music fluttered to the floor and scattered throughout the room. I unceremoniously scooted off the bench, my skirts held high, to face my audience and found myself staring into the mirth-filled blue eyes of Stuart Elliott.

"You could have given me a heart attack! Do you normally sneak up on people with the intent to scare the living daylights out of them?"

Without waiting for a reply, I bent down to start picking up the music and my large skirts tipped the bench so that it came crashing down on the hardwood floor. Stuart righted it, then leaned over to help me with the music. His thick black hair fell over his forehead as he bent down, and he impatiently brushed it away.

"What's this?" he asked. He was holding what looked like a piece of ivory. I looked up at the keyboard and found that the ivory veneer on the G key was missing. A small tremor went up my spine, as well as a foreboding sense of déjà vu.

My voice shook as I reached for the ivory. "I am so sorry. I'm not usually so clumsy." I looked up into his face again and saw him struggling not to laugh. I not too gently thrust the ivory back into his hand. "Usually only when people sneak up and startle me."

"Pardon me, Mrs. Truitt. I stepped into the house to tell my sister-in-law the doctor was riding up and heard the piano. I did not mean to startle you."

He didn't look the least bit sorry as his mouth kept twitching into a smirk. I started to say something else when I heard a throat cleared.

The tall, thin man standing in the doorway looked down his slightly beaked nose at Stuart and me on our hands and knees, scrabbling around the floor, picking up music. He appeared not to be amused. I wasn't sure about the habits of dress of the times, but the collar of his shirt could not have been stiffer. Head movement seemed nearly impossible. His eyes were a soft, liquid brown and they regarded me with cool condescension. He had elaborate sideburns that made me think of Elvis Presley, and I grinned involuntarily. His soft chin wagged back and forth as he stared at my silly grin, and that made me grin even more.

Stuart must have guessed that the appearance of this strange visitor was the object of my merriment and rose suddenly to intervene before I began to laugh outright.

"Dr. Charles Watkins, allow me to introduce Mrs. Laura Truitt."

The young doctor bowed stiffly and murmured, "My pleasure, ma'am."

The appearance of the mistress of the house interrupted the pleasantries, even more of her light brown curls escaping from her bun and framing her oval face.

"Hello, Charles. I see you have already met our guest, although I do not believe that she and I have been properly introduced. She was exhausted when she first arrived, and somehow my manners abandoned me temporarily."

Julia must have been working outside, because her face was beaded with perspiration, but her manner was cool and collected as she approached me with outstretched hands. With a warm smile she said, "I am Julia Elliott. Welcome to Phoenix Hall."

"I'm Laura Truitt, and thank you so much for taking me in."

Julia turned to the doctor and explained, "Mrs. Truitt saved my Willie's life today when he was attacked by a wildcat. She hurt her shoulder, and I would like you to take a look at it to ensure nothing was broken."

"Oh, really, that's not necessary. It's fine now—just a little bruised. I have full range of motion in it." I demonstrated this by moving my arm as if preparing to serve a tennis ball, and involuntarily grimaced as the pain shot through my body.

The doctor frowned and walked toward me. "Yes, I see, but Mrs. Elliott would like me to examine it anyway."

I unbuttoned the top button of my blouse but stopped before I unfastened the second one, as the doctor's face turned the color of a cherry tomato.

"I would not dream of impinging upon your modesty, Mrs. Truitt. I will do my examination through your clothes."

With a slight cough, Stuart excused himself and Julia from the room, closing the door behind them.

The doctor motioned for me to sit on the piano bench. Remembering how lethal my uncontrollable skirts were, I ignored his suggestion and instead sat down on a more stable-looking wingback chair, which appeared to be covered in horsehair.

He placed his left hand firmly on my back while he palpated my shoulder with his other. He stared at a spot over my head to avoid eye contact with me. In the course of his ministrations, he must have noted the absence of a corset.

"Mrs. Truitt, I cannot help but notice that you are not wearing a corset. Do you have some sort of breathing affliction?"

"No, Doctor, I don't—but I would if I forced myself into one of those contraptions."

He stopped in his muscle manipulations of my arm and dropped the limb as if he couldn't bear to touch it any longer. "I see," he said in a tone indicating that he did not. "A follower of Catharine Beecher. The thought that corsets restrict a woman from exercise and deform her body is balderdash." He stepped back and closed his black doctor's bag. "Nothing seems to be broken, just bruised. I suggest restricting your movement of the shoulder, and it should be better in a few days."

"Thank you." I wanted to contradict his opinion on corsets, but kept my mouth closed. If this really wasn't a dream from which I'd be waking soon, I needed as many friends as I could get.

"Where are you from, Mrs. Truitt? Your voice has the inflections of the South, but your mannerisms are more reminiscent of the North."

His question caught me off guard, so I blurted out the first thing that came to mind.

"To be honest, I think I hit my head or something, because I don't seem to remember much. I remember my name and that I'm a widow, but not much else." I had watched enough soap operas in my day to know that amnesia was a good explanation for just about anything.

"Oh, really?" His expression told me he didn't believe a word.

His examination apparently over, he walked to the door and opened it. Julia appeared in the doorway, an expression of concern on her face. "Is everything all right? No broken bones?"

The doctor's stern features softened as he looked at Julia. "No. Physically she seems to be fine."

Julia smiled. "Wonderful. Now, Charles, would you like some coffee? And I insist that you stay for supper."

"Why, yes, thank you, Julia. That is kind of you."

Stuart reappeared and the two men found seats while Julia went to see about the coffee. I remained where I was to avoid any further embarrassment.

Stuart turned to me. "Mrs. Truitt, when I met you, you said something about a Mimosa Boulevard here in Roswell."

I set about straightening my skirts to cover my long pause as my mind raced about for an explanation. "Yes, I do remember. I live on Mimosa Boulevard. I thought it was in Roswell, but you told me there's no such street."

"No, there is not," interjected the doctor. "Your case is very interesting, Mrs. Truitt. I know a woman's mental health is weak at best and, when put under the least bit of strain, tends to suffer greatly. I am sure after a period of bed rest your memory will return." He stressed the word "memory," making it sound as if it wasn't my memory that was the problem, but something more akin to my character.

I opened my mouth to make some retort about the insufferability of male chauvinists, but closed it quickly. I needed their help, and offending them would not advance my cause.

Softly, Stuart said, "You also mentioned something about your daughter."

I nodded and looked at the doctor hopefully. If what I believed had happened to me had also happened to Annie, then maybe this was a chance to find her. Surely if a child had been found abandoned she would have been brought to a doctor for medical attention. "Yes—she was only a baby." I paused, wondering if the five years that had passed in my own time would be the same in this time. "Perhaps you treated, or heard of, a child found on the mountain?"

He tucked his chin into his neck and shook his head vigorously. "No. Not ever. And how does a mother misplace a child?"

My eyes stung and I ducked my head, but not before I saw Stuart reach over and grab the doctor's arm.

Julia arrived, followed by Sukie carrying a large tea tray. I looked closely at the tray, recognizing it as the one Mrs. Cudahy had used to serve Michael and me tea on the first day I had seen this house. Despite the heat, I shivered, and remembered something Mrs. Cudahy had said about how the family's treasures had been saved during the war. Something about being forewarned.

Julia poured and handed everyone a cup. I noticed her hands as she bent to her task: small and well-tended but somehow capable-looking, too. Finished, she sat down next to me on the sofa.

I brought the cup to my face and noticed a peculiar aroma. I took one sip and was rewarded with a taste so bitter and so awful that I literally wanted to spit the vile stuff out rather than swallow it. I could feel three pairs of eyes on me and I made my throat swallow.

"What kind of coffee is this?" I asked politely. "It doesn't taste like any I've ever had before."

"Actually, it is made from a recipe that Stuart brought back from the army. It is parched and roasted acorns with a little bit of bacon fat. I don't believe it is so bad once you get used to it." Julia smiled feebly. "Thanks to the Yankee blockades, we have not seen a real coffee bean since 'sixty-one."

The doctor cleared his throat. "Well, wherever you are from, it would appear that you have been drinking real coffee." The doctor stared openly at me, as if I were Abe Lincoln himself sitting in that parlor. "Perhaps William has sent you down here to spy on us."

Julia's cup slammed into her saucer. "Charles, you are being rude to our guest, a woman who saved my son's life, and I demand an apology."

Charles looked chagrinned at her reprimand, but continued to eye me warily. "My apologies, Julia, if I have offended you. But she has not denied it."

"Who's William?" I asked, feeling nervous at the mention of the word "spy." As if I needed these sorts of accusations to further complicate matters. Spying during wartime was no light matter.

Julia turned to me. "He is my husband; Willie's father and Stuart's brother."

I turned to the doctor. "I promise you that I've never met William before. And I'm certainly no spy." I took another sip of my coffee, hiding my grimace, and wondering why Julia's husband would spy on his own family.

The mention of the year prompted me to ask, "What is today's date?"

The doctor paused briefly before replying, "June second."

The thought had barely crossed my mind before I voiced it. "Was there a lunar eclipse seen with a comet last night?"

The room grew silent, with only the sound of the ticking of the hall clock. Dr. Watkins narrowed his eyes at me. "Yes, there was. Why do you ask?"

I ignored his question, my mind already racing in another direction. "What year is it?"

The doctor didn't try to hide his exasperation. "It's 1863."

My mind spun back to all the history lessons I had ever sat through at the side of my father, a self-described history buff, and all of my studies in school. I remembered a biography of General William T. Sherman I had done in honors history in tenth grade but nothing specific about the year 1863.

"Please help me refresh my memory. What's happening in the country right now?"

Either he didn't believe a woman could actually be a spy or he'd forgotten that he'd just accused me of being one, because the doctor proceeded to tell me everything I would want to know if I were, indeed, a spy. "This is pure conjecture, mind you, gleaned from listening to our wounded heroes and reading between the lines of the newspaper, but I believe that our General Lee has finally taken the initiative and is attempting to bring the war into Lincoln's backyard. I imagine he will be crossing the Potomac any day now and heading north toward Harrisburg, Pennsylvania. Smack-dab in the middle of Yankee territory. I wish I could be with them, but I know this town needs a doctor more than General Lee needs one more soldier." The doctor crossed one skinny leg over another and settled back in his chair.

Keeping his stiff leg out in front of him, Stuart balanced his coffee cup on his other knee and turned to look at Dr. Watkins. "Yes, Charles. It is also convenient that you had to pull your two front teeth—the ones a soldier needs to tear open a cartridge with in the heat of battle. Unfortunately, that will also keep a man off the battlefield."

The doctor stiffened. "If you were not such an old friend, Stuart, I would call you out for that. You know as well as I do that those teeth were rotten and that I am needed here."

"I am sure you are," Stuart said as he took another sip of the rancid brew, and grimaced.

The mention of Pennsylvania and Lee's initiative pricked my memory. "Gettysburg," I murmured. The one piece of trivia that stuck in my mind was that following the battle, Lee's train of wounded stretched for more than fourteen miles.

"What do you mean by Gettysburg?" The doctor looked at me with irritation, his hand waving my comment aside. "No, Mrs. Truitt, it is rumored that General Lee is going to the state capital of Harrisburg—and will hopefully do to them what Grant's army is doing to those poor suffering people in Vicksburg."

I knew nothing of Harrisburg, but the name Gettysburg and its bloody aftermath would be etched on the minds of the American people for centuries to come. Not wanting to get into an argument, and perhaps reveal more than I should, I let his remarks go without comment.

I looked at Stuart, a soldier in this conflict. Although I didn't really know him, I was comforted in the knowledge that here was one less soldier whose bullet-ridden body would be lying on the field of battle in a war that was to me a foregone conclusion.

Stuart stood and limped over to the window. "Julia, Mrs. Truitt seems to have suffered a blow to her head and cannot remember much more than her name and the street she lives on. I would like to offer her our hospitality until her memory returns or we find out who she is."

Julia turned to me. "Of course. You may stay as long as you like. I am beholden to you for what you did for my Willie." She placed a warm hand on my arm and squeezed it gently.

"Thank you both. I'll do my best to help you with the house and children, Julia. And I'll find some way to repay you for your kindness."

"You already have. Do not think any more about it." Julia patted my arm gently.

"I'd also like to ask your friends and neighbors to see if they know anything about a baby being found on the mountain. I don't know where else to look."

Julia's hand on my arm tightened and I winced. Her face blanched and she clutched her rounded belly with the other hand.

"Are you all right?" My voice seemed higher than usual. "Is it the baby?"

She nodded, her face contorted with pain. My first impulse was to rush to a phone to let the hospital know we were on our way. But this was 1863; no hospitals, no high-tech birthing rooms, and no epidurals. A woman was left to her own devices.

"Where is your husband?"

She took a gasping breath. "I am not sure. He is off fighting with the Yankees out west. I have not heard from him since last September, when he was here on furlough."

If this were a dream, this would be the moment for me to wake up. I clenched my eyes, but when I opened them again, I was still there and Julia's hands were clutching her abdomen as the two men hovered behind me.

"What can I do?" I asked, trying to push the panic out of my voice. I knew next to nothing about natural childbirth, but I did know the presence of another woman would be comforting.

"Just help me walk. It is not my first baby so it should not take too long. And somebody go get Sukie."

I put my arm around Julia's shoulder and gently led her to the stairs. She stopped suddenly and shook her head.

"No, not in my bedroom. The birthing room has been prepared down here."

Before we could proceed, Julia gasped and a small puddle pooled at her feet. She looked back at the two men standing in the parlor doorway and her cheeks burned red.

Feeling her discomfort, I said, "Don't pay any attention to them. They know that if childbearing were left to men, it would be the end of mankind."

I caught a scowl on the doctor's face but a quick smile from Stuart as I led Julia to the little birthing room at the back of the house.

Chapter Five

— ◆ —

In sorrow thou shalt bring forth children; and thy desire
shall be to thy husband, and he shall rule over thee.

—GENESIS 3:16

The birthing room, which would become part of a modern kitchen addition in about one hundred and fifty years, was sparse and clean. There were no beeping monitors, no running water, and no television to while away the time. I had been left alone with Julia, and it dawned on me that I had somehow been elected to be the birthing coach. I assumed being a woman was my best qualification. But my own child-birthing experience in 2007 bore no resemblance to the episode unfolding before me.

Sukie came in with a clean cotton nightgown and helped me dress Julia. She was so petite and her burden so large that I was concerned, until I remembered that this wasn't her first child. If she had already survived childbirth before she stood a greater chance.

"Julia, is there a midwife here that I can fetch for you?"

She squeezed her eyes shut and shook her head. "No, our midwife died last year. But Dr. Watkins is here."

Her words offered no consolation. As if on cue, there was a light tapping on the door and the doctor strode in. He walked over to Julia and picked up her hand. The gentleness with which he touched her surprised me. The look of devotion was plain on his face, revealing the extent of his feelings for the patient. I was quite certain his feelings weren't returned.

"Julia, I will need to examine you now to see where the baby is positioned."

A small groan escaped through Julia's clenched lips as another spasm swept through her. She struggled under the sheet, her covered mound roiling as if it were a ship on a stormy sea.

Dr. Watkins looked up at me expectantly. "Madam, I require your assistance. Please hold up the sheet for me."

Things were happening so fast. The day before I had been in my car, listening to the radio in the year 2014. And now I was standing in an un-air-conditioned room in 1863 and being asked to help deliver a baby. I stood staring at the doctor, unsure how to respond.

"Is there a problem with your hearing? Have you never been present at a birth before?"

I nodded. "Just once—but I was the one giving birth."

"Surely, then, you can hold up this sheet. But only if you don't think you might faint. I have smelling salts in my bag if you require them."

I stumbled forward and grasped the sheet while the doctor began his examination. I immediately had a flashback of my own birth experience, of doctors and nurses garbed in sterilized gowns, with masks and rubber gloves. Everything had been coated in a reassuring antiseptic smell. I knew that modern technology was out of reach, but I also knew enough about the basics to realize that Dr. Watkins didn't understand the first thing about germs.

"Excuse me, Dr. Watkins. Don't you need to wash your hands?"

He regarded me with complete disdain. "Madam, I am the doctor here. If you would like to assist me, I will accept that. But please leave the doctoring to me."

I bristled under his dismissive attitude. I was tired, cranky, and thoroughly confused with the situation I now found myself in. My temper sparked. "I'm sorry, Doctor, but your unsanitary methods are not acceptable. Haven't you ever heard of germs? Not sanitizing your hands could kill both Julia and her child." I remembered how "childbed fever" had been one of the leading causes of death among women in the nineteenth century and now I knew why. I didn't really know the woman in the bed, but there was some kind of a bond between us. Whether it was a bonding of two mothers was immaterial. But it was suddenly very important to me that she and her baby survive this birth.

I bent over the form writhing in the bed and laid my hand on her arm. "Julia, I know I can help you here. Please ask Dr. Watkins to follow my instructions, or it could be a matter of life or death for you and your child."

Julia looked up at me with my fear mirrored in her eyes. But I also saw trust in them, and a woman's bond was formed.

"Charles, please listen to Laura. Do it for me and for William's baby."

The doctor put the sheet back down slowly and stood at the other side of the bed. "I will do this for you, Julia, and for the baby. But not for William. Not anything ever again for William."

"Thank you." Her voice weakening, Julia stifled a shout as she ground her teeth.

I went to the door and called out Sukie's name. She appeared quickly and listened attentively as I gave her a list of items I thought we would need: clean towels and sheets, alcohol, whatever kind of soap she could find, and lots and lots of boiling water.

My mind raced as I tried to think of what kinds of anesthetics they used to have. I faced the doctor. "Do you have anything to help with the pain?"

He turned on me with harshness in his voice. "Madam, suffering in childbirth is not only dictated by God, but is also necessary to induce maternal love. Her mind needs to be unclouded now to realize and appreciate this blessed event. I would say that using anything to lessen the pain would be sacrilegious."

"Obviously spoken by a man who has never had to suffer through childbirth!" I snapped. "If you care anything for this woman, you will find something for her. The contractions are taking away her strength—and if her labor continues for a long time she won't have the energy needed to push the baby out." I was almost choking on my anger and anxiety and I might have actually laid my hands on the man to physically send him on his way, but Stuart's entrance stopped me.

"You two step out of this room immediately so you can discuss whatever it is without disturbing Julia. I could hear your voices outside on the porch."

A sudden groan brought everybody's attention toward the bed, where Julia struggled to prop herself up on her elbows. Through gritted teeth, as she staved off yet another labor pain, she managed to gasp, "Stuart, it is all right. Charles knows . . . what he needs to do and he had better do it pretty soon. . . . This baby is not . . . waiting much longer." She squeezed her eyes shut and then managed to say, "Now get out!" Her burst of strength disappeared as she dropped back down to the mattress and another labor pain assaulted her small body. The doctor left the room.

Her spirit made me smile, and I went back to the bed. Dipping a cloth in the washbasin that Sukie had placed on the nightstand, I wiped Julia's forehead.

"You're an original steel magnolia, aren't you?"

She smiled weakly and I turned to Sukie, who had returned with the requested items.

"Can you stay with her for a few minutes while I talk to Mr. Elliott and the doctor?" Without waiting for a reply, I grabbed Stuart's elbow and led him out the door.

The doctor spoke first. "Mrs. Truitt, you are probably unaware that the South is surrounded by a Yankee blockade. Even if I wanted to give Julia some laudanum, I couldn't. We have not seen laudanum or morphine in a long, long time."

"Is there nothing we can do to help her pain?"

The doctor shook his head. "No. There is not. Just comfort her. It is not her first, and they do get easier."

"I've got to get back to Julia. Go wash your hands, Dr. Watkins—and don't forget to scrub under the fingernails."

The doctor glared at me as he turned to go.

Stuart turned to face me. "What, exactly, is a steel magnolia?"

"I'll explain later. Could you bring me some whiskey? Not for me—for Julia. It might help calm her nerves."

He nodded, and I returned to Julia's side to begin my vigil. Sukie washed Julia and placed towels under her hips. I washed my hands up to the elbows in preparation and sat down to wait, and wondered what I was supposed to do when it was time for the baby to be born.

The sun dipped low on the horizon, sending a bright sliver of yellow light through the window. I'd given her a little whiskey, but it had made her choke and she wouldn't take any more, no matter how hard I tried. Every once in a while Julia would moan but she never cried out. I finally turned to her and said, "It's okay to scream. We all know it hurts—there's nothing to be ashamed of."

But still she lay quietly, her drenched face a mask of pain. The grandfather clock in the hall ticked on, marking the minutes of Julia's labor, its solemn ticking interspersed occasionally by the groans of childbirth.

As the clock struck nine, the doctor reported that Julia was ready to deliver. I tried to remember anything I'd learned in Lamaze, but my mind came up blank. Julia screamed, and I put my hand in hers as she began to bear down. The bones in my hand ached from the pressure, but I hardly noticed as the baby's shoulders appeared and were gently turned and guided out by Dr. Watkins.

The baby was laid on top of Julia as the doctor cut and tied the umbilical cord. Wet membranes covered the child, but the startling blue skin underneath shone through clearly. Sukie handed the doctor a cloth that he used to wipe the child. The doctor looked strangely agitated and started to gently slap the baby on the bottom. It was then I realized the baby wasn't crying. The doctor tried a few more slaps and movements to revive the child, but the baby lay still and blue, ethereal and peaceful. Solemnly, the doctor shook his head and handed the still form to Sukie, who wrapped the small boy in a blanket.

"Charles? What is it? Why isn't the baby crying?" Julia's feeble voice called out from the bed. I moved to her side and reached for her hand.

I stared dumbfounded. This couldn't be happening. All that pain and effort for nothing. The doctor directed Sukie to press on Julia's abdomen to deliver the placenta and then took the baby from her. "I'm sorry, Julia. Your son has been born dead. There is nothing I can do."

Her sob brought me out of my stupor. As the doctor started to walk from the room, I remembered the infant and child CPR class I had taken when Annie was born.

I quickly walked over to the doctor. "Dr. Watkins, please let me have the baby. I think I can help." I reached for the swaddled baby but the doctor eluded my grasp.

"Woman, the child is dead. He has been delivered unto God and we cannot reach him. Cease your squawking right now so this family can mourn their loss."

Out of desperation, I tugged at the blanket. "Damnit, give me the baby!"

Startled, he relinquished his grasp. I took the limp bundle from his arms and laid the baby down on the floor and knelt down by his side. I tried not to think how much this child resembled the little girl in the morgue with the translucent skin and dark lashes. I put his head in a neutral position with one of my hands on his forehead and the other hand under his chin, just like I'd been taught. Placing my mouth over his nose and mouth, I gave two slow breaths, and watched his tiny abdomen rise and fall. I checked for a pulse in his upper arm and couldn't find one. With my two fingers on the child's breastbone, I methodically began to do cycles of chest compressions and mouth-to-mouth breathing, periodically checking for a pulse. My knees ached from kneeling on the hardwood floor and my fingers felt as if they would break, but I continued. I was aware of other people in the room but I focused on my task. I was about ready to collapse with exhaustion when a feeble pulse beat in the baby's arm. I put my face down and felt warm air coming out of the baby's mouth. Quickly, I picked the baby up and shook him gently, causing a startled cry to come out of him. In my relief, I fell back, slid down against the wall, and sat there, cradling the child. My shoulder ached from my exertions, but it didn't matter. The child was alive.

Two hands reached out to take the baby from me and I resisted until I realized it was Stuart. He took the child over to Julia, who seemed dazed.

I couldn't move. I didn't know whether it was from the physical exertion of the past few hours or the realization of the power I had over these people. I had just altered history. This child would not have survived if I had not been there to save it. Would this event change the course of history's path? I didn't know. And I was too tired to care.

At that moment, a large dark-skinned man, his black hair streaked with gray and running down past his shoulders, pushed open the door and walked in. In his broad hands he carried a delicately carved wooden cradle, which he placed at the side of Julia's bed. At his heels followed the dog, Charlie. I looked at Charlie, and his features somehow seemed familiar to me. I glanced up at the doctor and immediately saw the resemblance: the droopy brown eyes, the perpetual frown. Someone had obviously given the doctor a namesake. Looking between the two, I burst out laughing and continued to howl until the tears ran down my face.

Chapter Six

◆

Wailing pierced the silence and I shot straight up in darkness. Disoriented, I leapt out of bed, only to crash against the chest of drawers. Steadying myself, I gradually remembered where I was and what the noise was all about. I groped my way to the door and pulled it open.

After the birth of Julia's baby, whom she had named Robert and immediately shortened to Robbie, I had gone up to my room to sleep and collapsed, unaware of the time. I had no idea how long I had slept, but it was still dark outside. After a futile search for a light switch, I trailed my hand on the wall and followed the shrieking to the master bedroom. Tapping gently on the door, I walked in. This room never ceased to startle me, as the furniture and its placement were identical to the way it was in my own time. The candle on the bedside table cradled the two occupants of the bed in a soft, glowing light.

Julia leaned against the headboard, her head propped on a pillow and the baby nestled in the crook of her arm, mouth open wide and still bawling. Her dark, wavy hair spilled over the white pillow like a spider's web. Her eyes were sunken with exhaustion, the lids heavy.

I leaned over and gently lifted the baby from her arms. "Did he eat?"

Julia nodded. "And I changed him. But he still won't settle."

"Sometimes they do that. Let me take him for a little bit while you get your sleep."

She nodded, her eyes already closing as I blew out the candle.

The full moon outside shone through the hall windows, bathing everything in its gentle radiance. I made my way down the stairs and entered the front parlor.

I stood by the window, absorbed into the tranquillity of the moonlight-flooded room. The baby fretted, so I took him off my shoulder and cradled him in the curve of my arm. He focused on the great orb filling the sky and he gurgled, raising a fist as if to grab a moonbeam and bring it back to earth. I leaned down to kiss his cheek and saw the moonlight reflected in his eyes.

Oh, moon, where do you shine tonight? Is my Annie looking at you now, as I am, and wondering where her mother is?

I began to sing softly, swaying the child gently in my arms. Without thinking, the words flowed automatically from my lips. "You are my sunshine, my only sunshine. You make me happy when skies are gray."

A splash of moisture landed on Robbie's chin and I realized I was crying. A door opened and an arc of light appeared on the wall next to us. It grew larger in circumference until the room seemed swallowed by it. At the sound of approaching footsteps, I faced the window again, hoping not to draw attention to myself.

Someone coughed quietly behind me. I pivoted and saw Stuart. He was still dressed, but his dark hair was tousled, as if he had been running his fingers through it.

He set down the lamp and took the baby from me. I had neglected to put on a cover over my nightgown and was painfully aware of my undressed state.

"Did you hurt yourself?" he asked.

"Pardon me?"

"I thought a herd of cows was trampling you in your room, from the sound of it."

"Oh, that," I said, rubbing a bruised elbow. "No, I just decided a midnight waltz with my chest of drawers would be a good idea." I smiled. "What are you doing up so late?"

Patting the baby's back, he whispered, "I have been going over the plantation books. They are in a bit of a mess. I am afraid my brother did not have much interest in record keeping." He swayed with the baby snuggled onto his shoulder, as if he had done it many times before.

He stopped abruptly, narrowing his eyes as he stared at my face. "Why are you crying?"

I wiped the remaining tears off my face with the sleeve of my night-gown. "It's just the moonlight. It always makes me think of Annie." I walked closer to the window and pressed my forehead against the cold glass, my breathing making circular patterns and obliterating my re-flection. "She disappeared when she was almost two. She'd be seven now. I don't even know if I would recognize her if I did find her."

"How did she disappear?" he asked quietly, still swaying with the drowsy baby on his shoulder. Soft sucking sounds filled the room.

I took a deep breath. "My husband and I took her up to Moon Mountain to view a comet during an eclipse. When it was over, Annie was just gone. She was sleeping, you see, so I had placed her on a blanket where I thought she would be safe. . . ." My voice broke and I stopped.

He rested his free hand on my shoulder, offering comfort. His touch was warm through the fabric of my nightgown, and I had the bizarre impulse to lay my head on his hand.

"Don't blame yourself. No matter how good a mother you are, things often happen that are out of your control."

I turned to face him. The baby was finally asleep and Stuart had stopped swaying. He looked at me intently.

"Thank you for trying to help. And I know you're right. If only I had a grave to visit or some knowledge of what happened to her, I'd feel better. But I have no closure."

His brows furrowed in his forehead. "Closure?"

I smiled at my careless use of twentieth-century psychobabble. "It just means that my grieving has no end. I'm not sure if I should be mourning her or searching for her."

He nodded silently and I was struck, not for the first time, by how handsome he was. Not in the fair, evenly chiseled good looks that made women turn and stare at Michael, but in a dark, powerful way that made my eyes seek him out when we were in the same room to-gether.

"Do you think Annie might be in Roswell?" His words brought me out of my examination, and I flushed when I realized I had been staring at him.

"I really don't know. It's been five years. She could be anywhere. Or she could be . . ." I couldn't bring myself to finish the sentence.

"If she is here, I am sure we will find her. But I will tell you that it is a small community. If anybody here or in the neighboring towns had found a child on the mountain, we would have heard about it. I do not remember anything—but Julia might." He shifted the baby on his shoulder. "And then we need to find out where you belong."

I swallowed, the sound audible in the quiet room. His expression changed, and his eyes flickered briefly in the dim lamplight. "Why do I feel as if you know more than you are saying, Mrs. Truitt?"

My palms moistened and I quickly swept them through my hair. I couldn't tell him the truth. I could never allow myself to forget he was on the losing side of this conflict, nor the fact that I had knowledge that could possibly change the outcome of the war. I wanted to find my daughter, if she was here, and return home—my home with its host of memories. That was all I had left, and I wanted it back. I had no desire to get embroiled in these people's lives. I just wanted to go home.

I shook my head slightly, not meeting his eyes. "I don't know. But I appreciate your opening your home to me. I promise to be gone and out of your hair as soon as I can find a way home—or at least find where home is." I reached for the baby, and Stuart placed him gently in my arms. "Thank you. You have a way with babies, I think." I smiled. "Good night, then."

Before I got to the bottom of the stairway, I turned around with a question. "Who was that Indian man who brought the cradle for Robbie?"

Stuart limped over to me. "That was Zeke Proudfoot—my grandfather. He lives in a small cabin in the woods behind the house and only comes up here on special occasions."

I nodded, then glanced down at his leg, where he was rubbing the knee joint. "Where were you wounded?"

"In the leg," he said, a smile creeping across his face.

I grinned back. "Obviously. But which battle?"

"At Champion Hill, back in May." He straightened and took a deep breath. "I am lucky to still have my leg. But Zeke rode out to bring me back and have Charles take care of me. Those army sawbones just want to chop everything off. Zeke and Charles saved my leg, and probably my life, too. We are lucky to have Charles—just look what he did for Julia today."

I bristled with that last remark and paraphrased my favorite song under my breath, "Yeah. And Oz never gave nothing to the Tin Man that he didn't already have."

Stuart looked up at me with a quizzical expression. I explained briefly, "Remind me to tell you a great story when you have time. The main character and I have a lot in common."

"In what way?" he asked, his mouth tilting upward. "Are you both steel magnolias?"

"No." I smiled back. "She and I figure out that we're not in Kansas anymore."

He looked perplexed. "I will look forward to hearing that one."

I put my foot on the bottom stair and commented, "I hope I get to meet Mr. Proudfoot."

"Mrs. Truitt, I would be happy to take you out to his cabin to meet him. He might be able to help you with your memory. He is sort of a medicine man, though not like Charles."

I paused on the bottom step. "I'd like that." As an afterthought, I added, "Please call me Laura."

He paused briefly before replying, the hall clock ticking in the silence. "I do not think that would be proper."

Continuing my ascent, I said over my shoulder, "I promise I won't be offended."

Halfway up the stairs, he called out softly, "Good night, Laura."

I stopped, grinning to myself, and replied, "Good night, Stuart." I reached the hallway and went to tuck little Robbie into his cradle. Then I lay down in my bed and fell asleep before my head hit the pillow.

I awoke the following morning to the rolling sound of thunder and the beating of rain against my windows. Sukie was already in my room, drawing the curtains back and laying clothes out for me on the fainting couch. I smiled every time I thought about a fainting couch. As if anyone around here had time to faint. I was relieved to find no cagelike contraption to wear under all the skirts, assuming I was dressing today more for housework than for show. The smell of hot food wafted over to me from the tray resting on the dressing table.

"Good morning, Miz Laura," she said as she poured fresh water into the water pitcher.

"What time is it?" I asked, rubbing the sleep out of my eyes.

"It be after eleven."

I bolted straight out of bed in a panic. "Oh no! I told Julia that I would help her with the children, and all I've done is lie in bed all morning!"

"Don't fret. Miz Julia told me to let you sleep, seeing as how you was up with the baby last night."

"How long has she been up?"

"Since before six. Miz Julia has lots to do, with all them slaves having gone off with Mr. William."

"Stuart's brother took slaves? Why?"

Sukie gave a derisive snort. "Who know what that boy thinkin'. He said President Lincoln freed the slaves and it was breakin' the law to keep 'em. So when he left to go back and fight with the Yankees last September, he took a whole pile of 'em. The ones that were too old or just didn't want to leave stayed here."

"I guess that makes sense, seeing as how they'd been freed. But didn't he think of how hard it would be for Julia to manage—especially without him being here to help?"

"Mr. William don' usually think of anyone but hisself." As if to herself, she added, "Hard to believe that he an' Mr. Stuart be brothers."

"Sukie, if you don't mind me asking, why didn't you go?"

She shrugged. "Miz Julia, she said I was free to go. But this my home and the only family I got. Where would I go?" She fluffed the pillows and arranged them on the bed.

I stood there contemplating what she had just said as Sukie handed me clean undergarments. I was still pretty shy about having somebody help me dress, so I turned my back to take off my nightgown and slip on my underclothes while she busied herself making the bed.

As soon as I was finished dressing, Sukie attempted to make my hair presentable.

She held a thick lock of it between two dark fingers. "Why you cut it? You sick? Such a shame—so pretty and thick."

I shook my head. "No. Just easier to take care of, I guess."

Clucking her tongue, she led me to the dressing table. The breakfast tray was directly under my nose now and my stomach let out a growl. I recognized grits and hastily stuck my finger in it to give it a taste.

I could see Sukie's reflection in the mirror, shaking her head in disapproval. Whether it was over the shortness of my hair or my appalling table manners, I didn't know. But I felt as if my mother were judging me, and I made a mental note to begin scrutinizing my words and actions. Or else explain that I had been raised better, but that I'd grown accustomed to living by myself.

After eating, I went downstairs to seek out Julia and offer her whatever assistance I could. Seeing as how I didn't garden, cook, or sew, I knew that child care would be my best bet.

I heard the sound of an ax striking wood and followed it out the back door. The morning rain had stopped and the air was thick with the fallen moisture and the heady scent of moist dirt and saturated flower petals. Standing on the back porch, I paused to admire the view under leaden skies. Instead of the row of lofty pine trees separating my backyard from the highway, long rows of cotton plants and other crops that I didn't recognize stretched as far as I could see. The dark shapes of five or six people leaning over hoes and several mules working in the fields stood out in bold relief, like a painting from a history book. Stuart watched me approach as he stood near a large pile of wood and rubbed his wounded leg. His skin had an olive cast, making his blue eyes stand out under the dark hair.

"Good morning, Laura," he said, with a touch of a smile on his lips.

"Good morning, Stuart." I stopped a few feet in front of him. "What are you planning on doing with all that cotton?" I indicated the furrowed field behind him. "I would think the market's a bit slow these days."

He raised an eyebrow, as if he wasn't used to those sorts of questions coming from a woman. "The Roswell mills will take most of it, and I'm hoping to sell the rest to a blockade runner bound for England." His gaze scrutinized me as he spoke.

"What are you staring at?" I asked, feeling a touch self-conscious at his appraising look.

"To be honest, I was just wondering to myself whether it would be better for you to go back to wearing your men's clothing or to find someone besides Julia to borrow clothes from."

Julia was a good size smaller than I was, and I did feel the uncomfortable pull of the dress across my chest, not to mention that the skirt barely brushed the tops of my shoes.

"Wouldn't do for me to burst my buttons in front of Dr. Watkins, would it?"

Serious now, he replied, "No, it would not. I'll talk to Julia about it."

"Really, there's no need. These will do. I don't plan on staying here forever. But I did want to talk to Julia about my daughter."

He leaned on the ax handle, taking the weight off his leg. "I asked Julia this morning at breakfast. She doesn't recall hearing anything, but promised to ask around town." He narrowed his eyes. "We also need to ask if anybody recognizes you. I know that if I had seen you before, I would remember."

I looked away, uncomfortable, and unsure what to say. Searching for Annie here, in this place and this time, might be fruitless. I had no idea how the powers that had brought me here worked. Annie could be anywhere. In any time. Or this was some horrible dream and I couldn't wake up.

Turning, I saw Julia with a large basket brimming over with an assortment of vegetables hanging on her arm. Her face was shaded by a large straw hat, obscuring her expression. It was hard to believe that she had given birth so recently.

"I'm sorry to have slept so late. I promised to help you, and I'm afraid I haven't done much more than lie in bed. Tell me what I can do."

The back door opened and Willie and the little girl I had seen on my first day stepped out on the back porch. Charlie yapped excitedly at their heels, his droopy eyes making me grin.

"Hi, Willie. Is this your sister?"

They both stood there, shuffling their feet until Julia approached.

"Willie, Sarah, this is Mrs. Truitt. Mrs. Truitt, this is my daughter, Sarah. You've already met Willie."

Willie gave me an exaggerated bow and Sarah curtsied. Sarah was taller than her brother by a good two inches. Her blond hair was sun-streaked white in places and hung in two heavy braids on each side of her head. A smattering of freckles decorated the bridge of her nose, and clear green eyes stared levelly out at me.

"It's a pleasure to meet you," I responded with a curtsy of my own.

"Mrs. Truitt has kindly offered to help me take care of you and the baby until she is ready to return to her own home. I expect you to treat her as an honored guest."

A loud rumbling in the sky made us crane our necks upward. An ominous black cloud hovered overhead and I knew it would be only a matter of seconds before the sky opened up.

"I'll check on the baby," I said to Julia. Turning to Willie and Sarah, I said, "Quickly, children. Let's go inside before we get soaked. How would you like to hear a story?" I herded the children in through the back door.

"What kind of a story?" they asked in unison.

"Well, it's about a little girl and her dog who get lost, and an evil witch is chasing them. So she makes friends with a lion, a tin man, and a scarecrow, who help her find her way home."

"Is this the girl from Kansas?" Stuart asked as he shut the door behind us.

I nodded. "And she's a long, long way from home," I added, as we all headed into the front parlor just as the sound of rain began pelting the windows.

CHAPTER SEVEN

---◆---

Whoso desireth to know what will be hereafter, let him
think of what is past, for the world hath ever been in a
circular revolution: whatsoever is now, was heretofore; and
things past or present, are no other than such as shall be
again: Redit orbis in orbem.

—SIR WALTER RALEIGH

The summer rainstorm lasted for more than an hour, saturating the fields and yard. Muddy puddles of red clay beckoned the children outside, but I restrained them with the promise of another story.

I left the children arguing over who was going to be the witch and went in search of Julia. Both children had bright minds, and I wanted to ask permission to teach formal lessons. I heard a fretful Robbie and I followed the sound into the back library.

Julia and Stuart were speaking in a low whisper, so I paused before knocking on the partially closed door.

Julia's voice was soft but I could hear her desperation. "I don't know how much longer we can survive here. Flour is already forty dollars a barrel and salt is one hundred and twenty-five dollars a bag. And the dollars we have are worth less and less each day." The wooden cradle creaked as it rocked from side to side. "I hate to think of it, but we might be forced to leave. Perhaps my aunt in Valdosta will take us in until the war is over."

There was a brief silence while Julia made soothing noises for the fretting baby, and then she continued. "I think we can make it through this winter, but if the army keeps on provisioning itself with our food, we will be hard-pressed to make it through until spring. They have just about cleaned out my root cellar." Julia's voice was filled with resignation.

There was a slight pause before Stuart answered. "Julia, I am sorry. You are right, of course. Leaving might be the best thing for you and the children. I have been selfish wanting to somehow hang on to Phoenix Hall at all costs."

A mosquito landed on my forearm and I squashed it, splattering blood on my pale skin. Stuart continued, his voice heavy. "As long as our dividends from the mills continue, we should be able to manage financially, whether or not the plantation is running."

Julia's voice was soft. "I am sorry, Stuart. I know how much this land means to you. Much more than it ever meant to William."

I heard a soft grunt of agreement from Stuart and the irregular cadence of his boot heels on the wooden floor. "The only things that have ever meant anything to William were things that were not his."

The creaking cradle stopped. "Oh, Stuart," Julia said quietly. "I know how much we hurt you, and for that I will always be sorry. But you have been a good brother to both of us, and I only hope you can find it in your heart to one day forgive us."

I imagined Stuart running his hand through his hair. "That's all in the past. It really does not matter anymore. You are part of my family now, and it is my duty to take care of you and your children in William's absence."

At the personal turn in their conversation, I started to back away from the door, when I became aware of Sukie standing behind me in the hall. She raised her eyebrows but made no comment. Rather than appear to have been eavesdropping, I knocked on the door and entered.

Gone was the smell of musty books I had become accustomed to. The bookshelves that lined the wall were full, but I could see no torn or moldy bindings.

"I hope I'm not disturbing you."

Julia was seated at the mahogany secretary while her foot methodically pumped the cradle back and forth. She leaned over the baby as I entered and murmured something unintelligible to all but mother and child.

Shaking her head, she looked up at me. "No, not at all. Stuart was just helping me with the books, and I think my head has had just about all the facts and figures it can take for the moment. Would you like some coffee?"

"No," I said a little too vehemently. "I mean, not right now, thank you." My tongue burned with just the thought of the acid brew.

Julia smiled. "Well, I do think Sukie is making some of her strawberry tea, if you would like some of that."

"Only if it is made with real strawberries. No roasted acorns or shoe leather, please."

She laughed. "I'll be right back, then." She picked up the baby and walked out of the room, leaving the door wide-open.

Stuart stood at the far wall, absently pulling books from the shelves. "Are you finished with the tales of Dorothy?" he asked as he firmly shoved a brown leather-bound volume in its slot.

"For now, at least. I've got at least a dozen more where that came from, so I should be able to keep the children occupied for the next year of rainy days."

He quickly looked at me. "Do you mean to stay that long?"

The four walls of the room seemed to suddenly close in on me. "I don't know. I want to find my daughter and go home. I just don't know how."

"Wherever that is. Your speech is Southern, but . . ." He paused. "It does not sound familiar to me." He examined me closely, his eyes never wavering. "Is that really why you are here—to find your daughter and return home?"

"If you're asking if I have ulterior motives, no, I don't. I apologize for eavesdropping, but I heard you and Julia talking. I'm sorry if I'm a burden."

Brushing aside my apology, he said, "Please don't think you're a burden. In fact, I'm beginning to think of you as a godsend."

"A godsend? Don't you mean another mouth to feed?"

He came to stand in front of me. "Not at all. You are a wonderful help with the children, and I will feel better when I leave knowing Julia has you with her—for however long that might be." He paused briefly. "There is a quality of strength about you. But quite a bit of mystery, too."

I lowered my eyes, eager to change the course of our conversation. "When do you think you'll go back to the fighting?" I asked.

"As soon as I can walk without my leg paining me too much. My men need me and I need to get back to them as soon as possible."

"Your men? Are you an officer?"

He raised a dark eyebrow. "Yes. I am a major in the Forty-Second Regiment, Georgia Infantry. Not that such an elevated position means much anymore. So many talented soldiers and leaders have been killed that they will look anywhere to fill a vacant saddle."

I looked past his shoulder and out the window toward the rows of cotton. "Don't you think you're needed here more than the battlefield?"

He shook his head adamantly. "No." He turned from me and resumed his perusal of the books on the shelves. "To quote our General Lee, 'Do your duty in all things. You cannot do more; you should never wish to do less.'"

He slid a book back and faced me. "I long to resume my life in peace. But I cannot. Not until this conflict is settled."

Julia interrupted us as she returned with the tea. While she busied herself with pouring out the drinks, I surreptitiously studied her. Yes, she was pretty, in a very delicate sort of way. Petite and slender, with dark hair contrasting starkly with her white skin. Large hazel eyes added to her air of innocence. I felt a small twinge when I recalled the personal aspects of her conversation with Stuart, and it made me wonder why I cared.

As we sipped our refreshment in silence, I pondered their earlier conversation. Knowing that General Sherman's federal armies would be invading Georgia and heading directly for Roswell in a year's time, I thought Julia's decision to leave town to be a prudent one. But I remembered something Mrs. Cudahy had told us when Michael and I had first seen the house. Someone had been here to meet Sherman's army and save the house from destruction. If I convinced Julia to leave, who would be here to prevent that?

I cleared my throat before speaking. "Julia, I have to tell you that I overheard you and Stuart talking about your financial matters. Since I have inadvertently become another mouth for you to feed, perhaps I can offer some advice."

Julia and Stuart looked up at me. I continued. "If you haven't already converted all your greenbacks to Confederate dollars, don't. Keep as many greenbacks and gold as you can. Then go into the woods and mark a spot and bury all your money and any other valuables that could be carried away. Most of your livestock is already gone—courtesy of the Confederate Army, I would assume—but you might want to try to hide what you've got left in a pen in the woods. The Yankees will surely take anything that is not bolted down."

Julia looked at me in disbelief. "Surely you do not think the Yankees could get this far?"

I took another sip of my tea and nodded. "Oh yes. Not only do you have the mills here, but you also have a bridge across the Chattahoochee on the way to Atlanta. Trust me—Roswell is circled in red on General Sherman's map."

I was about to say more when Stuart stood abruptly. His teacup slipped to the floor, splattering china and tea in all directions. No one moved to clean it up.

"What a cool liar you are, Mrs. Truitt."

Julia stood, too, her usually composed face a mask of anger. "Stuart! How dare you be so rude to our guest."

He stayed where he was, immobile, hard blue eyes—soldier's eyes—scrutinizing me. "I will not. What I will do is turn her in to the proper authorities and have her arrested as a spy."

My hand trembled as I replaced my cup in the saucer, the delicate china clinking wildly. How could I have been so stupid? "No, Julia. It's okay. I understand why he's upset—"

Stuart cut me off. "Upset? You have just given me information that could only come from somebody associated with the Federals. And you are sitting in my parlor and drinking tea. Believe you me, I am a good deal more than upset. I have no choice but to turn you in."

Julia strode to him and put her hand on his arm. "No, Stuart. She is trying to help us—regardless of who she is or where she got the information. She has already saved the lives of two of my children. Do we not owe her at least for that?" Looking at Julia, her delicate features contorted in anger, I was once again reminded of a soft flower petal reinforced with steel.

Stuart turned to me, his eyes narrowed. "Why are you here? To spy on the mills to find out if they are supplying the Confederate Army? Surely there is an easier way to do that than making up a story about your lost daughter. What was that for—to gain our sympathy?"

Tears stung behind my eyes, but I dared not show them to him. I stood, my voice trembling. "I *did* come here looking for my daughter. I wish to God I were making that part up. And as for how I know all that, I . . . I'm not sure. But I do know I'm not here to cause any harm."

Julia came to stand next to me and put her arm around my shoulder. "Please, Stuart. I believe her. Just look at what she has done for us already. How can you turn your back on her?" She straightened her shoulders and lifted her chin. "And if you do, I will go with her."

Dark blue eyes darted from me to Julia. He shook his head, then looked down at his boots surrounded by shattered china and drops of red tea. His words deep and slow, he said, "I cannot fight you, Julia. I have never been able to, have I?"

Julia's hand tightened on my arm.

He raised his eyes and spoke to his sister-in-law, his gaze never leaving my face. "I will not turn her in—but my good conscience will not allow her to stay here, either. I want her gone first thing tomorrow morning."

With a nod to Julia, he limped across the floor and left the room. Julia dropped her hand from my arm. "I will talk to him. Do not worry—I will not have you thrown out." With a reassuring glance, she followed Stuart out the door.

I bent to pick up the shards of china and wipe up the spilled tea with a linen napkin, then sat silently in my chair, running over the conversation in my head and wondering what I would do if the Elliotts forced me to leave. Unable to sit still, I began pacing the room. I pulled a book off a shelf and stared at it for a while, letting the words blur on the page. Replacing it, I glanced out the window to see Julia striding purposefully toward the side of the house where I knew her garden was. Her eyebrows were puckered together and she seemed lost in thought.

Not willing to wait any longer, I decided to seek out Julia or Stuart to learn my fate.

Charlie's barking drew me out the back door. Willie and Sarah were attending to their chores of fetching water and feeding the chickens. They stopped when they saw me approach.

"Did either one of you see your uncle Stuart come this way?"

Sarah looked at me and shrugged her shoulders, which made me pause. That one movement brought all sorts of memories of Michael flooding back to me. It must have been one of those things a person does and others don't notice it until somebody else mimics the movement. I knelt in front of her, my hands on her shoulders, and stared into her thin face. It had been over five years since I had seen my Annie—a plump little toddler barely able to walk. I searched for that baby in this little girl's face and could not find it. Patting her gently, I let her go.

Willie pointed out toward the cotton field, and I spotted Stuart astride Endy. A tall man stood next to him, and as I walked toward them, I recognized Zeke Proudfoot. I stayed to the side of the turnrow, not wanting to trample the plants underfoot. Some of the creamy white blossoms had already turned red. Soon they would be sprouting burst bolls stuffed with a fluffy white mass of cotton fibers.

Stuart had climbed off his horse and was squatting on his haunches, his long fingers manipulating the leaves on one of the plants. Both men looked at me as I approached. Zeke's rich chocolate brown eyes were edged with deep creases. I had the odd sensation that I had been the object of their conversation.

Stuart stood slowly when I stopped before them, the footprints behind me in the sticky red mud marking my passage. Stuart's eyes were cold as he looked at me, and my stomach lurched. The last time I had felt this way was when I had worn my mother's favorite scarf without her permission and ruined it. I looked up at him, prepared to do battle. I didn't know what I would tell him, but it had to be something good to keep me here. I had no place else to go.

Stuart tipped back his hat to glare at me. "Well, Mrs. Truitt. It seems you have an ally in my sister-in-law. I think she is too trustworthy. But she wants you to stay."

Relief flooded me, but his words made my relief short-lived.

"Just realize that I will not let you out of my sight. And one wrong move from you, and I will personally escort you to the proper authorities and see you tried as a spy."

I moved closer. "I am not a spy, Yankee or otherwise." I met his blue gaze unblinking.

Zeke walked toward me and placed his hand on the top of my head, his brown eyes softening slightly as he stared into my face. Too stunned by his actions to move, I remained still. "You travel in the shadow," he said softly. It wasn't a question.

"What do you mean?" His eyes were warm and I felt a familiarity with his presence.

Removing his hand and turning to Stuart, he continued. "She will not harm you. Her heart is good and her powers are strong. Listen to her and trust her. Salvation will lay in her hands." Without another word, he turned on his heel and began walking toward the woods.

"What does he mean?" I asked, half-afraid of the answer.

"Zeke tends to talk in riddles. But I think he is wrong here. He wants me to trust you, but you are holding something back. I have an odd way of not trusting people who are not honest with me." He paused briefly to call for Endy. "Laura, I can only hope that you will tell me everything in due course." He hoisted himself into the saddle, wincing slightly as he put his wounded leg in the stirrup. "But I will find out everything. Sooner or later, I will find out who you are. And if your motives are to cause us harm by spying or otherwise, then you will wish you had never come here."

Without another word, he galloped away from the field, Endy's hoof-beats muted by the soft, damp earth.

Chapter Eight

———◆———

There is something haunting in the light of the moon; it has
all the dispassionateness of a disembodied soul, and
something of its inconceivable mystery.
—JOSEPH CONRAD

I stood motionless, watching Stuart ride off, feeling more hurt than I cared to admit. I slowly walked back toward the house, my thoughts in turmoil. I hadn't asked to be dropped into their lives, and I certainly didn't want to be there any more than they wanted me. I kicked a hapless cotton plant as I walked by. I wanted nothing more at that moment than to just find Annie, if she were even within my reach, and then go home. I certainly didn't want to care about Julia, her family, this house. Or Stuart. I only hoped it wasn't too late.

At the thought of home, I looked up. The sweet aroma from the Osage orange trees drifted in the rain-soaked air. They had been planted when the house was built to discourage flies and rodents. The ancient oak tree with its sprawling limbs was still rooted to the same spot in the backyard, looking a great deal smaller than in my own time. There was even a swing on a lower branch, just as Michael had made for Annie. I slowed my pace. How was I going to find her? I stopped completely when I considered my next thought. How was I going to get home?

I felt utterly alone. The children were nowhere to be seen, so I turned the corner of the house in search of Julia. I found her amidst cucumber plants and potatoes, furiously pulling weeds. Not seeing me approach, she appeared startled when I spoke her name.

Shielding her eyes with her hand, she looked at me with a frown. I knelt down beside her in the sodden ground among the ridges and began pulling weeds, the moist earth crumbling easily off the roots and the smell of freshly turned soil reminding me of an open grave. I wrinkled my nose and turned to Julia.

"I can do this, Julia. You just gave birth two days ago—shouldn't you be resting?"

She wiped at a piece of dirt clinging to her forehead, smearing it across her skin. "I do not mind, really. It keeps my mind off . . . things. Besides, there is so much work to be done and only a few pairs of hands."

I sat on my heels, watching her attack the weeds. "I wanted to thank you for what you said to Stuart. I promise you that your trust hasn't been misplaced. I swear I'm not a spy." She yanked up more weeds, throwing them with a vengeance into a pile. I continued. "I have only known you for a short time, but I feel as if I really know you—you're almost like a sister to me."

A small smile crossed her face. "I feel it, too. We have certainly been through quite a bit since we met, have we not? It is terribly selfish of me, but I would want you to stay here as long as possible."

I looked down at my hands. "But this isn't where I belong. As soon as I find my daughter, assuming she's even here, I'm going to bring her back home."

She paused and looked at me, her hazel eyes suddenly cool. "What if you cannot find her?"

"I can't allow myself to ever believe that, because then I am lost. I will search for her until my last breath. You're a mother. You understand."

Children's laughter carried over to us from around the corner of the house, and we turned to watch Willie chasing Sarah, her blond pigtails flying. I remembered again that shrug she had given me that was so much like Michael's, and I stared at her fair hair, my mouth suddenly dry.

I swallowed thickly. "Julia, Sarah is around the same age my Annie would be now."

Her clear eyes studied me, the breeze stirring the curls around her face. As if hearing my unspoken question, she said, "Sarah is mine." Her gaze never wavered. "Her birth is recorded in the family Bible, and Dr. Watkins was present at her birth. He will verify everything I have told you."

Silence settled between us as she resumed her chore, and I joined in, hoping I was pulling the weeds and not the vegetables. Suddenly, without looking at me, she said, "I gather such strength from this garden." She grabbed a handful of dirt and let the thick muddy clods fall slowly from her fist. "It is not much, but it is the only buffer my family has against starvation." A crooked grin settled on her lips. "Before the war, I never would have dreamed of sticking my hands in dirt. It is amazing what one will do to protect one's family." She looked directly at me. "I do not know if there is anything I would stop at to protect mine."

A cloud drifted across the sun, creating large pools of shadow. I shivered and rubbed my hands over my arms. Was she warning me? Did she really think I was a spy? She gently placed a gloved hand on my forearm and smiled. "Laura, you have already saved the lives of two of my children. I am in your debt and I will do all I can to help you."

I dropped the weeds clenched in my hands on the pile and looked down at her as I stood. "Thank you, Julia. I appreciate that. But I don't know if anybody can help me." I brushed at weeds clinging to my skirts, ignoring the mud. "If the children are done with their chores, I'll go see about starting their lessons."

Leaving Julia, I trudged to the house to search for the children, who had mysteriously disappeared, as if they knew I'd be looking for them. I went inside and noticed a piece of the broken teacup left in the middle of the library floor. I picked it up, then moved to the window to see if I could spot Willie and Sarah. I saw them by the kitchen, and, forgetting the broken piece of china, I squeezed my hand into a fist to hammer on the window. I cried out, dropping the china, and watched the blood ooze from a thin line bisecting my palm. I stared dumbly at my seemingly disembodied hand, wondering absently what I should do.

A movement from the doorway made me look up. I turned away from Stuart's scowl and looked back at my hand, my eyes tracing the path of blood as it dropped down my wrist and landed in spots on the dark wood floor.

"What happened?" He strode into the room, lifted my arm, and looked at my cut.

"I cut my hand on your broken teacup." I looked into his eyes to see if my barb had had any effect. "If you just want to close the door, I'll be happy to stay in here and bleed to death."

He frowned, but I allowed him to lead me to a sofa. His voice was brusque. "Sit here for a minute."

He came back quickly with what looked like sewing scraps. He retrieved a bottle of whiskey from the cabinet and sat down next to me. "Since you believe alcohol cures all things, we will use this. It might hurt a bit."

I gave an unladylike snort. "Like that would bother you."

He ignored me as he bent to his task of pulling a small shard of china from the wound. His hands were gentle as he soaked a cloth with whiskey and began to bathe the cut. Waves of pain shot up my arm, but I bit my lip, resisting the urge to scream.

"Go ahead and scream. I know it hurts."

I kept my face turned away. "I wouldn't give you the satisfaction."

He had stopped cleaning the wound but still held my hand. I turned back to him and found him scrutinizing me. I tried to jerk my hand out of his grasp, but he wouldn't let go.

"Despite what you might think, I do not relish inflicting pain on you or anybody else. Unless, of course, something of mine is being threatened." His hand tightened on mine, but I refused to wince. "I would like to suggest a truce between us. If we are going to be living under the same roof, we will have to learn to be civil toward each other—at least for Julia's sake. But do not be mistaken." His blues eyes narrowed. "I will still be watching your every move. I will also be accompanying you every time you leave the house. So you had better get used to my company."

I seethed inside but knew that I had no choice but to agree. "All right, then. A truce. Just promise me one thing."

He raised an eyebrow.

"When you discover that you are wrong about me, I want an apology from you."

His eyes widened, mocking me. "Agreed."

He put a piece of material in his mouth and bit it, tearing it in half. "Why are you hiding something from us? You have nothing to fear from us here—unless you really are a Yankee."

I looked down to where he was wrapping the bandage around my hand. Denying that I was holding something back would only make his suspicions worse, so I said nothing.

He looked at me, his eyes solemn, as if awaiting an answer. Shaking his head, he continued his bandaging.

I had always hated the sight of blood and tried to distract myself by looking at the bookshelves. A single title grabbed my attention. *General History of Nature and Theory of the Heavens* by Immanuel Kant.

"What do you know about astronomy?"

He raised his eyes to my face, his expression curious. "Not a lot." Following my gaze, he saw the book. "Oh, those are Julia's mother's books. She had a feeling Nashville would fall to the Yankees and sent them down here for safekeeping."

I studied the thick brush of dark hair as his head bent back to his task. "Would it be all right if I borrowed one to read?"

He looked at me, his face unreadable. "Of course. But if you really want to learn about astronomy, you should speak with Zeke. He is known as an expert on such matters."

As he knotted two ends of the bandage together, I asked, "Is Zeke's house far?"

"No, not far at all if you ride. It is quite a bit of a walk, though."

"I would prefer to walk, if you can show me the way."

"You want to go now?"

Deciding the children's lessons could wait, I nodded. "Yes, so if you could just—"

"You are not going without me, remember? I will accompany you."

I gave him my patient-teacher smile. "I assure you, that is not necessary."

"And I assure you, madam, that it is. I must protect my family."

I exhaled, then stood and walked briskly to the back door. Charlie yelped with excitement when he saw Stuart and happily followed us, trotting at our heels.

Despite the tense moments earlier in the day, my step was lighter. This visit with Zeke could be the first move toward finding Annie and the way home.

The path through the woods was well worn, the damp earth compacted by passing feet and littered with fallen pine needles. A weak sun filtered through the high canopy of pines, sprinkling the ground below with pinpricks of light.

I had deliberately walked fast, knowing that Stuart's limp would make him trail behind. But when I came to a fork in the path, I stopped, unsure of the direction. While I waited for Stuart to catch up, I lifted the hair off the back of my neck and wiped the sticky sweat with the palm of my hand. I unbuttoned the first two buttons on my dress, welcoming a cool breeze.

Feeling guilty at making a wounded man walk briskly through the woods, I slowed my pace to his and walked beside him, searching for a neutral topic of conversation.

"I've been wondering about something."

He looked at me expectantly, probably curious at my civil tone.

"Where did Charlie get his name?"

A smile cracked his stern face. "So you have noticed the resemblance between Charlie and Dr. Watkins?" He stopped briefly to rub his leg. "So did Sarah. When she was four she called the dog Dr. Watkins. We made her change it but she insisted on Charlie. Luckily, Charles has not seemed to notice."

I had suspected Sarah was a smart little girl and that confirmed it. I laughed, thinking about her astuteness. "It's a good thing she didn't think he looked like the rear end of a horse."

Stuart made a strangling noise in his throat as if he were choking. When he recovered, he said, "Yes, our Sarah has a very active imagination. She is always making up stories."

As we approached a clearing, I saw a small log cabin, a wide covered porch surrounding it on three sides. Zeke sat on the porch in a rocking chair, nodding at us in greeting. Charlie bounded off, running around Zeke and barking happily. The old man leaned over and stroked the dog's back.

Thinking of Zeke's last words to me and feeling suddenly shy, I allowed Stuart to approach first. He climbed the stairs of the porch slowly, nodding a greeting to his grandfather. They both turned to look expectantly at me.

I smiled and approached the porch. The rudimentary aspects of Zeke's house didn't surprise me. Despite his family status, I wouldn't have expected him to live in anything grand.

Zeke broke the silence. "I see you two have made peace with each other."

Stuart cleared his throat, and I looked down at the ground. Stuart spoke first. "We have called a truce, yes. No reason why we cannot be civil to each other."

The old man looked over at Stuart and his lined face crinkled slightly into a smile. He picked up a large jug by the side of his chair and offered it to Stuart. After Stuart took a swig, Zeke offered it to me. "Drink some. It will help the pain in your hand."

I realized that my hand was throbbing. Not wanting to appear rude, I walked up the steps and took the proffered jug.

Liquid fire best describes the contents that coursed down my throat. Stifling the reflex to gag, I swallowed it stoically. A small wince escaped me and I quickly took in three gulps of air. I felt the heat all the way from my throat to my stomach and my head suddenly felt light. The throbbing in my hand decreased to a dull ache.

My walk was unsteady as I climbed the remaining stairs to the porch to return the jug. Stuart wore a look of surprise but Zeke's impassive face remained unchanged. To show them what a real woman I was, I took another swig, almost staggering this time with the effects of the contents on my muscle coordination.

"That is enough, Laura," Stuart said with concern, and grabbed the jug and sat down.

I took a seat on the top step to steady myself. The rustic setting reminded me of camping, and I began to hum a favorite camp song. Nobody said anything or asked me to stop, and it wasn't long before I was belting out "Rocky Top." I felt two pairs of eyes on me and quieted.

Stuart stopped rocking. "So you sing, too. Where did you learn that?"

I avoided his eyes. "Oh, it's just something I picked up along the way. My grandmother, mostly."

"Julia would love you to teach music to the children. Especially Sarah—she seems to have a natural gift for it."

I smiled. "That would be more than fine with me. I'll talk to Julia when we return."

I turned to Zeke. "Stuart tells me you know a lot about astronomy. I was hoping you could answer some questions for me."

He nodded slightly, and then, without a word, stood and beckoned me to follow him into the one-room cabin. Stuart stood but made no move to enter. Sparse furnishings accented with brightly colored throw rugs and wall coverings added an unexpected coziness to the room. Despite the heat of the day, a cooling breeze blew through the open doorways. A heavy scent of wood ash clung to the log walls.

Bookshelves covered an entire wall of the cabin. Zeke approached the shelves reverently, letting his fingers glide over the bindings until they stopped. Pulling out a volume, he carried it over to me and gently placed it into my hands. I glanced down and read *Astronomical and Commercial Discourses* and the author's name, *Thomas Chalmers*, on the binding. Opening its pages, my gaze picked out the words ". . . to shoot afar into those ulterior regions which are beyond the limits of our astronomy."

I looked up at Zeke. "I want to go home. Do you know how to help me?"

He looked at me impassively and reached for my arm. Without any thought to stop him, I allowed him to roll the sleeve up to reveal the lower part of my left forearm and the crescent-shaped birthmark. "Ah," he said, staring at it, as if something baffling had just been explained.

"What is it?" I asked, more intrigued than frightened.

"The sign of a Shadow Warrior," he said, pulling the sleeve back over my arm. "A traveler."

I pulled the sleeve back up and stared at the mark I had had since birth and never even noticed anymore. My Annie had the identical mark on her upper arm. "What does it mean?"

He looked at me with hooded eyes. "It is what will bring you home."

"But how?" I shifted the heavy book in my arm impatiently, eager to hear the secret of finding my way home.

"You will learn—keep your ears and eyes open." He paused to examine a lower shelf, then continued. "I will do what I can. But I do not think you will need my help. I see the strong light that surrounds you. I sense we have need of your strength now. Perhaps that is why you have been sent to us."

He turned back to the bookshelves. "Stuart tells me he found you near Moon Mountain. That is a very sacred place to the Cherokee, you know. Stories of its magic have been passed down for generations. Stories of distant travelers sent here by the moon."

His eyes turned toward my face and stared at me intently, but I didn't flinch.

"Some of these travelers were bent on evil and destruction and had to be hunted down and then killed by other Shadow Warriors." Chill bumps ran up my spine as I listened to his words and his eyes continued to bore into mine. "Most of them were."

I swallowed thickly. "I don't know why I'm here. It was purely accidental. If my daughter is here, I need to find her and bring her home."

"Yes, Stuart told me about your Annie." Turning back to the shelves, he plucked out several more books. "Then you will need to read these," he said, and he piled three more heavy volumes into my arms. "These will tell you when the moon disappears and its powers are at its strongest. As for the rest, it is up to you."

I could feel my anxiety rising. "I don't know how I got here or why I'm here. I have no idea where Annie is. She could be here or anywhere. This was an accident. I don't belong here and I'm certainly not needed or wanted. I just want to go home."

Zeke touched my arm. "You have survived many hurts. But your life is not over. Perhaps that is why you are here." Our gazes met. "I had dreams of you before you came. I saw you standing in front of Phoenix Hall, staring at a flying machine in the sky and watching it fall to pieces on the ground."

My mind spun in circles. "No. That's not possible. How could you know?"

He shook his head. "Just know that your secrets are safe with me."

"Thank you," I said, not sure what else I could say. I gathered the books tightly to my chest and stepped out on the porch to find Stuart. I spied the jug and took another long swig, needing to obliterate my thoughts for a while. I ignored Stuart's raised eyebrow and stepped off the porch, Charlie yapping at my heels. My gait was not a little unsteady.

I attempted to walk a straight line when I spotted Julia on the back porch. I could not. Dr. Watkins and an unknown lady stood next to her. I felt the waves of disapproval from the doctor and his companion and detected an almost imperceptible head shaking from the woman.

"Laura? Are you all right?" Julia approached me, her skirts rustling.

"I'm fine." I punctuated my words with a hiccup.

Her brow furrowed as she got close enough to smell the alcohol on my breath. "Let me take you inside and get you cleaned up and put to bed. You can meet Miss Eliza Smith another time."

She sent Stuart a severe look and then gently took me by the shoulders and led me inside.

CHAPTER NINE

♦

Time past and time future
What might have been and what has been
Point to one end, which is always present.

—T. S. ELIOT

I leaned my tired head against the railing as I sat on the back porch steps. I glanced at the almost-empty basket of peas at my feet with a sigh of accomplishment and stretched. Robbie gurgled happily in his cradle next to me, and I itched to pick him up and revel in his sweet babyness. My relief was short-lived, as Sukie approached with another full basket.

She plopped herself down next to me with a pile of the unshelled peas in the lap of her skirt, and we resumed our work.

Willie staggered out from the side of the house, a wooden yoke resting on his shoulders and a large bucket attached to each side.

I indicated the boy with my chin. "What's Willie doing?"

Sukie rolled her shoulders back. "He be carrying out all the wood ash from the house. Makin' lye soap tomorrow." She glanced up at the distant moon on the horizon. "The moon has changed. I never boil my soap on the wane of the moon—it jus' never thicken."

I sighed. Another chore. I was glad that I could be useful, but I was quickly finding that the running of a nineteenth-century house and cotton plantation was a never-ending process. I struggled to find the time to read the astronomy books. In the three weeks since Zeke had given them to me, I had had the opportunity to open them once, and had promptly fallen asleep.

Not that it mattered. I couldn't go home yet; I needed time to find Annie. I sometimes found myself wondering if I were deceiving myself, that I really didn't believe she was here; that this whole experience was fabricated by my grief, a dream to give myself hope. But when I looked down at the peas in my hand or touched the rough wool of my skirt or heard Robbie's cries, it seemed all too real. I had no choice but to continue to forge ahead, believing that Annie and I had traveled through time and were trying to find our way back home.

After relieving himself of his burden, Willie approached the porch. His face and hands were smeared with soot but he seemed oblivious to the fact as he reached for the door handle.

"No, sir! Don' you be touchin' nothin'! Go get yourself cleaned up first 'fore you go inside." Willie rolled his eyes at Sukie and then stomped back down the porch.

"Oh, and, Willie," I called after him. "When you're done washing up, please find your sister, and the two of you go and practice your scales on the piano."

"Yes'm," he mumbled.

His shoulders slumped as he continued walking toward the springhouse, where the cool stream flowed around the property. His mother wanted them to learn music, and I was trying my best. Unfortunately, in the two weeks that I had been teaching them, Willie had shown a remarkable inability to get beyond even the rudiments of piano knowledge. He was very different from Sarah, who showed quite an aptitude for the instrument despite her young age.

I snapped more peas, my thumbs and forefingers slowly becoming stained green.

"Miz Eliza brought some dresses over for you yesterday." Sukie's head stayed bent over her task, from which bright popping sounds came from the breaking pea pods.

"Miss Eliza? Who's that?"

"Miz Eliza Smith. She the lady was here with the doctor when you came back from Mr. Zeke's. She lives with her mama and sisters at Mimosa Hall. Can't say I care too much for her, but you have somethin' respectable to wear now."

I remembered the rather dour-faced young woman I had seen on the back porch with Julia. I could only imagine what stories the doctor had told her about me and why I needed clothes.

"She done need some music lessons herself. She play the organ at church—what a howling mess!"

I smiled. "She didn't look the type to take kindly to my suggestions, Sukie."

"I don' think it matter much what you say to her. I don' think she like you."

I stopped shelling. "What? How would you know? She and I have never met."

"True, but she sure is powerful sweet on Mr. Stuart."

"Oh? And what does that have to do with me?"

For the first time, Sukie paused in her task and looked at me. "Jus' look in the mirror, Miz Laura. An' you and Mr. Stuart be about the same age. Make you a threat to her dream of walkin' down the aisle with him."

Blushing furiously, I kept my head bent toward my lap. "I couldn't imagine why. Besides, I think she would be more threatened by Julia."

Sukie surprised me with her sudden vehemence. "Don' even think it. What was between Mr. Stuart and Miz Julia was over when she say 'I do' to Mr. William. She always been faithful to her husband and has suffered 'cause of him bein' a Yankee. People talk 'bout who that sweet baby's father is jus' about kill her. She stay at Phoenix Hall for jus' about a year—not even goin' to church." She shook her head.

I stared at her, dumbfounded. "You mean there's some doubt?"

"No, ma'am. There no doubt. Just bad talk by mean people. Mr. William here last September. He kept quiet, on account of people 'round these parts not liking the color of his uniform. But when Miz Julia showed up in the family way, people started talking. Especially since Mr. Stuart was back home."

Sukie fell silent as Willie approached us again, his face rubbed pink. He stomped past us and shouted Sarah's name as the back door slammed. Feet clattered on the wooden stairs, and shortly thereafter the interminable piano scales began.

Sukie stood and brushed off her skirt. "I best go and see about making supper and gettin' a fresh nappy for this little one." She gave a wary glance at my lack of progress, picked up Robbie and his cradle, and went inside. Darkness was still a couple of hours away but the early-evening sounds had already started. The cicadas and crickets creaked duets, and at least one bullfrog bellowed from the nearby woods. I closed my eyes and leaned against the porch railing, inhaling deeply the rich aroma from the boxwoods that lined the side of the house. It reminded me so much of my own time that I was temporarily transported back. Approaching footsteps made me open my eyes. I was caught off guard by the sight of Stuart standing not two feet away from me, one booted foot resting on the bottom step.

"Well, if it isn't my prison guard." I hadn't been off the property since my arrival, and I blamed Stuart. I was aching to go with Sukie when she ran errands so I could ask about Annie, but I needed more time to build Stuart's trust before he would allow it.

He ignored my comment. "Mind if I join you?" He smelled of sweat, horse, and leather—a combination I found peculiarly enticing.

"Help yourself," I said, indicating the bottomless basket of peas.

He reached over and grabbed a handful. "Our hospitality must be lacking if you are finding your stay here comparable to a prison sentence."

I shook my head. "That's not what I meant. Everyone, with one exception, has been more than hospitable. But I'm never going to find Annie if I'm not allowed to go look for her."

His long fingers efficiently broke open the pods and emptied their contents into the basket. "I have been asking around town myself. No one recalls a little girl being found up on the mountain." He paused for a moment. "Nor has anybody ever heard of a Laura Truitt." He threw a handful of peas into the basket with more force than was necessary.

Our eyes met, and all was quiet except for the monotonous drone of the insects. Finally, I spoke. "You may choose not to believe me, but I have told you the truth. If you would just give me the benefit of the doubt—"

He finished, "Then my family and this entire town could suffer the consequences."

"Fine. Believe what you want—but when you realize you're wrong and it's time for your apology, I'm going to make you grovel."

He bit his lip, as if trying to hide a smile. "I will be looking forward to that, ma'am."

I gave him an exaggerated sigh and continued the never-ending job of shelling peas. I knew I would never look at the color green the same way again.

We worked in silence, listening to the serenade of the dusk creatures. To break the quiet, I asked, "Why are you fighting for the South while your brother fights for the North?"

He narrowed his eyes, as if trying to determine the motivation behind my question, continuing to pop peas out of their pods. "Georgia is my home. Protecting her is in my blood—almost as much a part of me as my own family." He straightened his wounded leg to stretch it. "I am also a firm believer in states' rights. It irks me no end when the federal government interferes in state government." He put his foot down hard on the step and looked at me. "My brother is fighting for the North only because I am not."

"I see," I said, though I didn't. I had no idea sibling rivalry could be this intense. "What about slavery? Aren't you fighting to uphold it?"

"No." He paused briefly and glanced up at the sky, the stars just beginning to make their appearance. "I hate slavery. I wish Georgia had kept it unlawful to own slaves. But without slavery, our crops could not compete in the marketplace with slave-holding states. Unfortunately, I see no other way to survive on cash crops. That is why I studied architecture at Oglethorpe University. I figured I would leave this plantation for my brother to mismanage while I found a respectable living." He paused in his work and grunted. "Life does not always turn out as one expects it to, does it?"

Our eyes met, the silence broken only by the cicadas. Quietly, I said, "No. It doesn't."

Willie plunged through the back door, carrying a chamber pot. Sukie called after him, "Make sure you put that downwind this time, Willie!"

I grinned as Willie trudged along toward the cotton field to dump his burden.

Stuart cleared his throat. "I am accompanying Julia to church this Sunday. You are welcome to join us."

I turned my attention back to Stuart, trying to see through his offer. "Why do you want me to go? Are you afraid I'll do some spying on the hens if you're not here to watch me?"

He looked genuinely hurt. "Not at all. I thought you would like to mix with some of Roswell's citizens. Maybe somebody will recognize you. Or know about Annie. That is what you want, right?"

I stared back at him, my gaze level. "Yes. Of course it is."

He scooped peas out of a pod and reached for another. "Well, then. Have you never heard about looking a gift horse in the mouth?"

I gave him a derisive snort. "I don't consider my personal freedom to be a gift from you. But, yes, I'd like to go. I take it that Julia hasn't been out in public much lately."

The muscles worked in his jaw as he clenched his teeth. "No. And it is making her look like she has something to hide. It is high time she showed her face again."

"I agree. I'll be happy to lend moral support."

Scurrying out of the house, Sukie opened the door of the detached kitchen, which allowed the aromas of baking corn bread to waft over to us. My stomach growled in response.

"Hungry again?" Stuart asked as he stood and held a hand out to help me up.

Stacking the full basket inside the finally empty one, I responded unapologetically, "I'm always hungry. I seem to have the appetite of a horse."

"You certainly do not look like you eat like a horse."

I gave him a sidelong glance to see if he was giving me a compliment or not. He grinned, and I noticed how his gaze took in the stretching of the fabric of Julia's dress across my chest.

"Maybe you should curb your appetite a bit until we can find you clothes that fit a bit better than . . ."

I didn't give him a chance to finish as I gave him a little shove to make him stop. To my horror, he fell over my perfectly stacked baskets, losing his balance and taking my precious peas with him. I hesitated for a moment, wondering if I should rescue him or my peas first, when I heard him laughing.

"Laura, if you want to pick a fight, pick on someone who is not already wounded."

He lay flat on his back, and I leaned over to help him up. He grasped my hands tightly and pulled to hoist himself, but instead toppled me over on top of him. He grunted as his arms went around me, effectively locking me in place, our noses almost touching.

His breath was warm on my face. "If you are not a Yankee, you should be."

I struggled to get off of him, but he held me tighter. "What do you mean?"

A small grin touched his lips, so close to mine. "Because you are more lethal than a Yankee bullet."

"Let go of me."

He complied, but as I tried to move off him without touching him more than necessary, my right knee collided with his injured leg, making him groan in pain. I quickly rolled off and knelt beside him.

"I'd like to say I'm sorry, but you have to admit you deserved it. And if you're so afraid I might injure you further, why don't you return to the front lines? You'll be safer there."

His eyes were shadowed as he answered. "I am beginning to think that myself." He sat up unassisted and then hauled himself up to a standing position.

He held his hand out to me. "Come on. It is time for dinner."

Ignoring his hand, I stood by myself. "In a minute. I've got to clean up this mess first."

Without a word, he righted the overturned basket and began picking up peas.

Following dinner, the children were put to bed and the three adults retired to the parlor. Julia brought her sewing basket, and her slender fingers pushed the silver needle with lightning speed. By the end of the evening she had completed a pair of pants for Willie.

I volunteered to mend some of Sarah's stockings. After struggling to thread the needle in the dim candlelight and then ripping out most of my uneven stitches, Julia suggested I play the piano. I opened sheet music for the sad Confederate ballad "Lorena" and began to play, losing myself in the music while I concentrated on reading the unfamiliar notes.

A gentle sob came from behind me as the last note faded and I turned to look at Julia, whose head was still bent to her sewing. Stuart walked over to her and put a hand gently on her shoulder.

I quickly turned back to the piano. "How about something livelier?" I asked as I broke into a Scott Joplin medley. I was halfway through "Maple Leaf Rag" when Sukie entered to announce Dr. Watkins.

"What is that music?" he demanded. "It sounds like music from a New Orleans brothel."

I lifted my hands from the keys. "And just how would you know what kind of music they play in a New Orleans brothel, sir?"

The doctor turned an interesting shade of red and glared at me.

Stuart intervened. "Now, Charles. Laura was only trying to lift our spirits—which she did marvelously. Sit down and tell us what brings you here this evening."

Placated for the time being, the doctor turned to Julia, took an envelope out of his coat pocket, and handed it to her. "I was at the company store today and took the liberty of getting your mail."

We all stared at Julia as she excused herself to open the envelope and read the enclosed letter. It took her a long while, and I realized she was reading it twice. She quickly dropped the letter on the table. Her mending slid onto the floor, but she didn't pick it up. Her voice was higher pitched than usual when she spoke. "My mother is coming from Nashville for a visit." Lines of worry creased her forehead. "I do not know how safe that would be for her."

Stuart leaned forward in his chair. "She will be fine. As I recall, she is a formidable force to reckon with. I would not want to be the one to stand in her way, and I pity the person who does." Stuart grinned, but something else showed in his face that made me wonder what his true feelings were regarding Julia's mother. "When should we expect her?"

Julia glanced at the top of the letter and her eyes widened. "Oh, dear. This letter was written five weeks ago. She could be here any day now. There is so much to do." She hastily folded up her sewing and shoved it back into the basket.

"Please excuse me," she said as she stood. Anticipating my offer of help, she turned to me and added, "Laura, please stay here and play hostess for the gentlemen." Not waiting for an answer, she left the room.

Turning toward the two men, I said, "I won't be offended if you two want to retire to the library for something stiffer than coffee."

"Thank you, Laura. I think we will. But please continue to play the piano. Dr. Watkins has yet to enjoy your playing."

The doctor raised an eyebrow. "Only if she will choose something genteel this time. A lady should never consider anything else."

Stuart sent me a warning look over the doctor's head, and I kept my smile plastered in place. As soon as the sliding doors between the parlor and library were shut, I spun myself around on the piano bench and started banging out another Scott Joplin rag. I hoped that it was shaking the starch out of the doctor's stiff white collar and annoying the hell out of him.

CHAPTER TEN

———◆———

The Past—the dark unfathom'd retrospect!
The teeming gulf—the sleepers and the shadows!
The past! the infinite greatness of the past!
For what is the present after all but a growth
out of the past?

—WALT WHITMAN

The following Sunday, after donning one of Miss Eliza Smith's highly serviceable but barely fashionable dresses, I was ready for church. The muslin dress was a sedate brown, with small green flowers striping the skirt and bodice. A prim white collar and white under-sleeves completed the ensemble and made me feel almost Puritan. Sukie coerced me into wearing a corset, explaining that without one, I could cause considerable embarrassment to the Elliotts. My ribs creaked as she pulled the laces tight. After walking two steps without being able to expand my lungs, I readily understood the need of a fainting couch.

I donned the requisite bonnet and kid gloves, then walked downstairs and out of the house, beads of sweat already forming on my forehead.

Stuart stood clutching a wooden cane beside the four-wheeled buggy.

I did a double take, as I had never seen him use a cane. "Is your leg hurting today?"

He made a big production of fiddling with the horses' harnesses. "No, the leg is fine. Doing much better, actually."

"Then why do you have a cane? Any young ladies at church you're trying to impress?"

He sent me a withering glance. "Yes, I guess it is for show, but it is not what you think."

Trying to tread lightly on the subject, I asked, "I don't mean to intrude, but is it to make the other citizens of Roswell feel sorry for you so that they won't be so hateful to you and Julia?"

He stopped his fiddling and looked me square in the eye. "Since you seem to thrive on directness, I will be direct with you. There are some nasty rumors about who Robbie's father is, and I am hoping that if they see how badly I was incapacitated by my wound, they would not think that . . . well . . . that I could have done such a thing."

I could tell how hard it was for him to put those thoughts into words and I had a strong impulse to hug him, but I refrained. I also hid my smile as I considered a fault in his reasoning. "Stuart, I don't know how much you know about making babies, but a wounded leg wouldn't interfere in the process at all."

He stared at me for a long moment and opened his mouth as if to say something, but closed it instead. Narrowing his eyes, he tossed the cane in the grass by the side of the drive and turned to greet Julia as she and Sukie emerged from the house, Sukie holding Robbie. Willie and Sarah appeared behind them, temporarily clean and presentable for church.

Stuart handed us all up into the buggy. Because of the tight fit, Sarah and Willie had to use an adult lap for a seat. Sarah chose mine, giving me the chance to study her closely. She looked like a cherubic angel, but having spent more time with her at her piano lessons, I knew better. She was full of mischief, but had an innate talent for music. I wondered which parent she had inherited that from and assumed it had to be from the absent William, who was growing in mythic proportions in my head every day.

This was my first time outside the boundaries of the plantation. Although I had lived in Roswell for seven years, almost nothing I saw on the short ride to the Presbyterian church was familiar. Only the church— the same church where my Annie had been baptized—remained relatively unchanged. An air of surprise greeted us as we entered through the massive front door. Julia kept her back straight, nodding to acquaintances on both sides of the aisle. I was relieved to see people nodding back. Stuart walked behind us, holding Sarah's hand, and calling out "Good morning" as we made our laborious journey to the front of the church and took our seats.

I spent the remainder of the service surreptitiously scanning the congregation, hoping to find a girl that resembled the image I had created of an older Annie. Following the service, and after some particularly horrendous organ playing by Miss Smith, we all gathered in front of the church. I smiled at all the curious glances aimed in my direction and made myself busy by holding Robbie. Julia stayed close by my side, introducing me to the other churchgoers. Mostly they gave me curt nods and a "How do you do?" Oddly, no one questioned my sudden appearance in the Elliott household. I raised my eyes and caught Dr. Watkins looking at me. He must have already told the townspeople everything they needed to know about me—and I wondered if it had to do with mental illness.

Out of the corner of my eye, I caught sight of Eliza Smith walking toward Stuart. He stood talking to Dr. Watkins and an older man with mutton-chop whiskers that I identified as the Reverend Pratt. She linked her arm possessively through his and smiled at him. While no one could ever accuse her of being beautiful, her face was transformed when Stuart smiled back at her.

Stuart caught my gaze and nodded. Eliza gave me a cold stare and grabbed his arm to capture his attention. Robbie whimpered, and I gladly turned back to him.

"Pardon me, ma'am, but I seem to have missed out on the introductions."

I looked up into baby-blue eyes, clear and wide but not at all innocent.

"You must be Miz Truitt."

Robbie burbled and I shifted him in my arms. "Yes, I am."

The man appeared to be in his early twenties, with a thin covering of blond peach fuzz on his chin that I assumed passed for a beard. His dirty, fair hair was parted in the middle by a line that looked like a crooked mountain path, and hung down in straggly strands on each side of his narrow face. The stale odor of alcohol permeated his brown wool coat. I took a step back.

He grinned, revealing a jack-o'-lantern smile of missing teeth. I searched for Julia to rescue me, but she had left my side. The man's slow drawl brought my attention back to him.

"I apologize for my manners. Allow me to present myself." He touched a dirty finger to his forelock. "I am Matthew Kimball. Mostly known around these parts as just Matt."

Robbie began to fret and I bounced him up and down in my arms, hoping he would start squalling and I could excuse myself. The man stood too close, his foul breath wafting over me. He reached a mud-encrusted fingernail up to Robbie's soft cheek. I jerked the baby away, and his nail scraped the skin on the back of my hand.

"It's nice to meet you, Mr. Kimball."

"Matt." He gave me a wide smile.

"Right. Matt." I turned my lips up in the hopes they'd approximate a smile. "It's been nice talking to you, but I need to change the baby."

"Where are you from, Miz Truitt?" The intense gaze of his eyes belied the casualness of his question. "I was wondering if we might perhaps have some mutual acquaintances."

I examined him closely, wondering if he had mistaken me for some-body else. "I'm quite sure I wouldn't know any of your friends, Mr., ah, Matt. Why would you think—?"

Strong arms pulled Robbie from my grasp. "Time to go, Laura."

Stuart held Robbie with rigid arms, his face stern as he regarded Matt.

Matt's face blanched slightly. "Now, Stuart, we wuz only having a little conversation. No harm in that, is there?"

Ignoring Matt, Stuart grabbed my elbow. "Come on, Laura."

He pulled me away before I had a chance to say anything else. I looked back at Matt and found all traces of politeness gone.

I stumbled, but Stuart didn't even slow his step. "Let go of my arm. You're hurting me."

Stuart ignored my protests, as well as the curious stares we were receiv-ing. Finally, he stopped on the fringe of the group and dropped my arm.

He bent his head close to mine, his voice low and serious. "Do you know that man?"

"I've never laid eyes on him before this morning when he intro-duced himself to me. I don't think he's a person one could easily forget, no matter how addled one's memory is. Why? Who is he?"

Stuart's eyes searched mine, as if trying to decipher a puzzle. Slowly, he straightened. "He used to be a boyhood friend of mine—his father was even a preacher at a church outside town. But he is a deserter. Claims he is on medical leave, but it has been more than a year now without any outward symptoms of a physical handicap. There are rumors about his loyalties." He looked closely at me. "Such as how they can be bought by the highest bidder."

Anger flamed in me. "Is that what you think of me? That I could be associated with a person like that? I would have hoped by now that you would know me better than that."

He raised an eyebrow. "No, Laura. I do not know you very well—but not because I have not asked. You have left me with no choice but to make assumptions."

He was right, but my anger refused to let me acknowledge it. I turned on my heel and ran right into Miss Eliza Smith. Her eyes were bright with curiosity.

Stuart stepped forward and made the introductions.

She nodded brusquely in my direction and I imitated her action. Knowing I needed more allies than enemies, I said, "Thank you so much for the clothes. They're very much appreciated. And your organ playing today was very heartfelt. You must practice an awful lot."

Two blotchy spots of red appeared unbecomingly on her cheeks, an apparent blush. I could feel her thaw a few degrees as she digested my compliment. "Thank you, Mrs. Truitt. Stuart mentioned that you are also musical."

"Well, I try. I'm teaching Sarah and Willie the piano. Sarah is especially gifted. Willie tries, but I know he'd rather be outside, chasing Charlie."

Robbie let out a loud howl, announcing it was his dinnertime. Stuart made our excuses, then found Julia and the children to return home. I sat across from Stuart in the buggy, our knees almost touching. I studiously ignored him, but I caught his gaze on me more than once.

Sunday as a day of rest was strictly adhered to in the Elliott household, and I was looking forward to immersing myself in Zeke's astronomy books. Instead, as we pulled into the long dirt drive, a mud-splattered coach was being led around the side of the house.

Julia leaned out of the buggy. "It must be my mother."

I stole a glance at Stuart, who was looking at the coach, the muscles working in his jaw. Something about this visitor made him tense.

As soon as we pulled to a stop, Julia jumped from the buggy, not waiting for assistance, and ran into the house.

I gathered the children and we followed. Julia's voice came from the parlor, and I ushered the children into the room, pausing on the threshold. A diminutive woman with gray streaks threading through her hair turned toward us. I couldn't see any resemblance between this woman and Julia. Her small dark eyes were cold, and when I first walked into the room, I felt something akin to a frigid wind blowing through me.

Her eyes flickered over me before her gaze settled on the children. Sarah's hand tightened in mine and she buried her face in my skirt. Willie was no less obvious as he took a step backward as she approached, as if to put as much distance as possible between them.

She gave Sarah a brittle smile before turning to Willie. "Willie, will you not give your nana a hug?" Her voice was surprisingly deep for such a petite woman.

With a prod from Julia, Willie dutifully stepped forward and gave her a preemptory hug. I expected her to ask one from Sarah, too, but instead she stepped toward Stuart, who held baby Robbie.

"So, this is my new grandson." She reached to take the baby from Stuart. A strong maternal instinct made me want to knock her away. I knew I was being irrational, but the feeling that I should keep the children away from her pulled hard at me.

As she tried to jiggle the baby to find a comfortable position to hold him, Robbie screamed. I quickly reached for him and plucked him out of her arms. Immediately, his cries were extinguished as I held him snugly on my shoulder.

Giving me the brunt of her harsh gaze, she stood in front of me. Her petite stature in no way diminished the full force of her character. I could feel the maelstrom created by her personality in the air she breathed out.

"And who is this?" Although looking directly at me, she directed her question elsewhere.

"Mother, this is Laura Truitt. She is a good friend and is staying with us for a while. I am eternally grateful to her because she not only saved Willie from a catamount attack on Moon Mountain, but also saved Robbie's life." Julia walked over to me and put her arm around my shoulder. It seemed as if she were trying to protect me.

"Oh, really? And just how did she accomplish this?" Her gaze finally left my face as she turned to Julia.

"It was the most peculiar thing. When Robbie was born, he was not breathing. So Laura laid him on the floor, pushed on his little chest to make his heart beat, and then breathed the air into his mouth until he started doing it on his own."

Her head snapped back to me, her eyes narrowing slightly as they considered me.

Julia squeezed my shoulders. "We are very much indebted to her."

The older woman stepped closer to us. "Really. I suppose that I am also in your debt."

I finally found my voice. "No. I'm indebted to the Elliotts' hospitality. They've opened their home to me."

"Where are my manners?" Julia gushed. "Laura Truitt, this is my mother, Mrs. Pamela Broderick."

I was grateful for Julia's intervention. I don't think I could explain my sudden appearance on Moon Mountain to one more person, for I was sure that was the older woman's next question. I smiled. "It's a pleasure to meet you."

She inclined her head slightly. "Likewise."

"Stuart." She held out both hands to him, which he grasped, and kissed him on both cheeks. "I am so glad to see you safe. We are so lucky, you know. Most families in the county have lost a son, father or brother. And you and William are still in one piece."

Julia interrupted. "Mother, have you news of William?"

"Yes. Did I forget to mention that to you in my letter? He has been assigned to General Sherman's staff. He has been in Nashville these last few months. Has he not written?"

Julia's face fell. "No. I have not heard from him since last September." She pointed her chin at Robbie, who was busy sucking noisily on his fist.

Turning her full attention to Julia, Mrs. Broderick reached for her and cupped her face in her hands. "Daughter, do not fret. There is a war going on, and William has very important duties to attend to for General Sherman. He would have come with me if he could—you know that."

Julia kept her eyes down, hidden from her mother, and nodded solemnly. Forcing a smile on her face, she looked up at her mother and added, "You must be exhausted. I had Sukie prepare a room for you so you have a place to rest, if you would like."

"Yes, thank you. That would be nice." She slipped her arm through her daughter's and slowly ascended the stairs. Stuart and one of the field hands, Elbert, followed with a large trunk and smaller bags.

Feeling the need for fresh air, I left the children with Sukie and stepped out onto the front porch. I took deep gulps, filling my lungs and wondering why that woman had seemed to take the oxygen out of the room.

The sound of the door shutting behind me and the jangling of keys told me Julia had joined me. I knew her storeroom keys never left her side—being keeper of the food stores of the plantation was one of the myriad duties of the mistress of the house.

She came to stand next to me, looking directly out in front of her toward the front drive. "My mother can be a difficult woman to get to know. I hope she did not offend you."

I sat down in one of the white wooden rocking chairs. "No, I wasn't offended."

Julia sat in the chair next to mine and slowly began to rock, her feet gently slapping the wooden boards of the porch floor. "She is from Savannah—that is why her ways are much more formal than they are here. It can be very off-putting to people who do not know her well." She turned her head to face me. "Pamela is my stepmother, but she is the only mother I have known. My mother died when I was three. My father died when I was five years old, so I did not know him very well. He was born and raised here in Roswell and this is where he brought Pamela after they were married. She and Stuart's mother were the best of friends. Very different people, though. I suppose that is why they got along so well." She continued her rhythmic rocking, her face and eyes focused on the past. Her rocking was contagious, and I copied her back-and-forth motion.

"What's your mother doing in Nashville?" Somehow, knowing that Julia was not Pamela's flesh and blood made it harder for me to understand the affection she had for a woman whose very name made me so apprehensive.

She looked down at her hands gently folded in her lap. "My mother enjoys a more cosmopolitan lifestyle. She likes to be among the politicians and policy makers. She has even invested in several businesses there and made her home in Nashville to oversee her interests."

Julia sighed and then pulled herself to her feet. "I do not know what I was thinking, dawdling out here. I have a thousand things to do before dinner. I know this is our day of rest, but I suppose God would understand that we have a guest to entertain. Would you mind, Laura, picking the pole beans from the bean patch?" Her mind already elsewhere, Julia walked toward the door. Stopping, she turned abruptly. "Could you see if you can hunt down Sarah and have her bring in the eggs from the chicken house? I am going to have Sukie make some corn bread with the little bit of cornmeal we have left." Without waiting for an answer, Julia sailed through the door, her steps making a rapid tapping on the floors inside.

I gave one last leisurely rock and then stood. The first halting notes of "Greensleeves" told me in which direction to go to find Sarah. She was seated on the piano bench, her eyes glued to the black-and-white music in front of her.

She smiled when I walked in the room and hastily scooted over to one side of the bench to make room for me. As soon as I sat down, she started plunking out a new tune I had taught her, "Heart and Soul." I added the treble accompaniment and struggled to keep up with her as she raced faster and faster through the repetitions. We ended up collapsing in laughter when the music reached an inescapable end.

Julia peeked in, her finger raised to her mouth. "Sshhh. Nana's sleeping."

I looked up guiltily and nodded. "Sarah, your mother wants you to gather eggs. Come on, I'll go with you. And then you can show me what a pole bean is."

We stopped in the detached kitchen first to pick up a basket and then went to the chicken house. A pitiful rooster strutted his way across the backyard, perhaps lamenting the loss of the rest of his harem. The Elliotts were down to three laying hens, courtesy of the Confederate Army. Using the few eggs we could find so extravagantly on the corn bread was a rare treat.

I held the basket for Sarah as she reached into each nest. She counted them out slowly to me as she laid each egg gently into the basket. Five. I hoped it would be enough, as I had my heart set on corn bread, and so did my ever-grumbling stomach.

Studying the girl as she stood on her tiptoes to reach into another nest, I grew curious. "Sarah, how old are you?"

Concentrating on her task, I could see her shrug a shoulder. "Seven."

"Really? But you're so much taller than Willie and he's eight. When's your birthday?"

She turned around to look at me, clutching one more egg in her hand. "June. It is written in the Bible. I cannot read it, yet, but Mama says it is there."

I surreptitiously approached a hen, her plump roundness filling the circular cavity she had made to lay her eggs. I attempted to remove her prize and was rewarded with a nasty peck.

"Ouch! That hurt!" With my hands on my hips, I gave mother hen my most threatening look. Her small glassy eyes continued to dart back and forth, as if I were nothing more than a kernel of corn.

"Let me do that one, Miz Laura. She tends to get a bit broody."

Sarah approached the offended hen by talking softly to it and then silently, stealthily, slid three eggs out of their warm home, one by one.

As we stepped back into the yard, Stuart approached, his ax held tightly in his hand. My eyes widened. "What are you going to do with that ax?"

He looked at me in surprise. "It looks like we are going to have chicken for dinner." I knew where those neatly wrapped, skinless, boneless chicken breasts came from that I bought at the supermarket, but I had never known the animals personally before consuming them.

He walked past us into the chicken house. The desperate squawk-ings of the unfortunate victim reached our ears, and Stuart emerged holding up his feathered prize.

"You ladies might not want to watch this."

Not really sure that I was up to witnessing the rudiments of meal preparation, I turned to Sarah. She rolled her eyes at her uncle's words and put down her basket. "I ain't scairt. Besides, I seen it lots of times."

"Well, I'm not scared, either, but I don't want it to spoil my dinner." Seeing the stubborn jut of her little chin, I knew she couldn't be budged. I resigned myself to learning more about nineteenth-century rural life.

He laid the chicken in the dirt, holding the struggling body down with one hand. With the forefinger of his other hand, he drew an imaginary line in the dirt from the chicken's beak out to about a foot. The chicken immediately halted all movement and lay as if hypnotized. The shadow of the ax brought my attention away from the still chicken, and I turned my face away at the last minute. A solid *thunk*ing sound told me it was over.

Glancing at Sarah to make sure her young mind hadn't been damaged in any way, I looked back at the scene of the carnage. The headless body of the chicken busily stumbled its way through the yard, its wings propelling the corpse and blood squirting in neat arcs.

I grabbed Sarah and backed up so we wouldn't get sprayed. She placed her small hand into mine and said, "Mama says the blood's good for keeping the bugs away and making the garden grow."

Squeezing her hand, I looked down on her blond head. I felt a surge of affection for this child and her sturdy little character.

Stuart scooped up our dinner, who had since run out of steam and had flopped over in the yard. "I hope this hasn't affected your appetite, Laura."

"Not a chance. I'm so hungry right now, I could eat it with the feathers still attached."

Sarah looked up at me, wrinkling her nose. "Ewww!"

I rumpled the top of her head. "Oh, Sarah, I was just teasing. I'd at least remove the feathers first. But I might not pause long enough to cook it," I said, winking.

I hugged her shoulders as she grinned up at me, and my eyes were drawn to a movement from a back bedroom window. A dark shape stepped back out of view while I looked. I didn't see her clearly, but I knew who it was. A cold tremor swept up my spine and I shivered in the hot summer sun.

CHAPTER ELEVEN

*The moments of the past do not remain still; they retain in
our memory the motion which drew them toward the
future, toward a future which has itself become the past,
and draw us on in their train.*

—MARCEL PROUST

The sound of approaching hoofbeats made me glance up. I shielded my eyes with a hand to block the glare of the summer sun and watched Stuart approach astride Endy. The sweat ran in rivulets down my back, making my chemise stick to my skin. I adjusted the egg basket on my arm and waited for him to approach.

I had gradually settled into my new life on a nineteenth-century plantation. I never stopped looking for Annie, but I knew I had time. According to my own calculations gleaned from Zeke's astronomy books, the next total lunar eclipse wouldn't occur until September first, 1864. Even then, the possibility of a comet being present, or even needed for my purposes, remained a mystery to me. I could only wait and see— and continue asking everyone I met if they had heard of a lost little girl on Moon Mountain.

The work was hard, but I reveled in the simplicity of it. No background noise of traffic, phones, or televisions. No texts or e-mails to distract me. At the end of each day, I eagerly anticipated the quiet evenings in the parlor spent with Julia and Stuart. Julia's mother joined us most of the time, and we eyed each other warily. Since she never asked about where I was from, I assumed that Julia had filled her in with as much as she knew. Perhaps this was the source of her coldness toward me. There was no overt hostility, but it was clear that she somehow considered me a threat, and she continued to fill me with apprehension. About what, I couldn't say.

I spent the majority of my days with the three children, either at lessons or assisting them with their chores. And I was learning as much from them as they were from me.

The approaching hoofbeats came louder as Stuart drew near, slowing Endy's pace and finally stopping in front of me. My greeting died on my lips as I looked up and saw his scowl.

"I just came back from town. Matt Kimball's been asking a lot of questions about you."

"About me? Do you think he knows anything about Annie?"

He shook his head. "No. Those are not the sorts of questions he is asking. He wants to know where you are from and why you are here. Why do you suppose he is so curious about you?"

I put my free hand on my hip. "Why are you asking me? Why don't you ask Mr. Kimball? I think he'd be better able to judge his own motivations. I told you I've never met the man before." I took a deep breath, my frustration with the situation nearing the tipping point. "What do I have to do to make you trust me?"

He stayed high atop his black stallion, looking like a knight in butternut-stained wool. "You could start by telling me the truth."

A dull wind stirred the dust around us, sending grit into my eyes. I blinked hard. How could I explain to him that I didn't want to get involved in their lives any more than I had to? That my only goal was to return home with my daughter before I became inextricably immersed in this time and these people? Becoming emotionally attached could only bring me more pain, and I had had enough of that to last me two lifetimes.

"I am here to find Annie and bring her home. That's all you need to know. I would never hurt you or your family. You should know that by now." My eyes smarted, but I didn't turn away.

Endy snorted loudly in my ear and I involuntarily stepped back. Stuart caught the movement and reined the horse in tightly. He dismounted, then reached into a saddlebag, bringing forth an apple like a peace offering. His face softened, his eyes almost apologetic.

"Perhaps you can gain Endy's trust. He does not need truth, just kind and fair treatment."

I moved closer to Stuart, trying to get away from Endy. "If you're going to kill me, couldn't you just shoot me? It would be a good sight easier than setting your horse on me."

Stuart's voice was soothing, close to my ear. "The only reason Endymion would ever hurt you is if you threatened him or something he considered his. Not very far from human nature, is it?"

I shook my head, my anger giving way to fear tinged with curiosity. Besides our trek down Moon Mountain, I had never been this close to a horse in my life.

"Endymion? What kind of a name is that?" I stared warily at the black beast, its huge eye examining me as it shook its massive head.

"William named him after the Greek god Endymion. Are you familiar with the story?"

"I'm afraid not. My Greek mythology is a bit rusty." I continued to eye the big horse, hoping that Stuart had been joking when he had mentioned me developing some sort of relationship with this animal.

Stuart gave Endy a vigorous scratch behind an ear, making the horse nod with pleasure. "Endymion was the husband of Selene, the goddess of the moon." A wavering grin split his face. "He was quite the talented fellow."

I took a step back from the great nodding head. "Oh, really. How so?"

Polishing the apple on his pants leg, Stuart looked away, as if he shouldn't be telling me. "He fathered fifty daughters by Selene, all while he was reportedly asleep."

I smirked. "You're right. He was pretty talented. Not to mention fertile. I hope your Endymion is equally as prolific."

Slowly, Stuart shook his head. "No. Endymion's children were all pale like their mother and sleepy like their father. Hopefully, Endy's offspring will be a mite more vigorous."

Stuart gave the beast a resounding pat on the side of the neck, apparently a gesture of affection. He pulled off his hat and wiped the sweat off his forehead with his sleeve, then handed the apple to me.

I stared at the fruit in my hand, nervously twisting the stem off the top. "I hope you don't intend for me to feed him this apple. I'm afraid he'll take my whole arm off if I get too near."

The object of our conversation seemed oblivious to our presence as his thick, bushy tail swooshed back and forth in a vain attempt to rid himself of the nuisance flies that flitted about.

"Endy has never bitten anyone." Stuart looked down at his feet and kicked sand at a small lizard scurrying about in the cool shadow created by the horse. "Not seriously, anyway," he added with a twitch of his lips. "Of course, if you are scared . . ."

"I'm just not used to being around horses. Especially not one as big as that . . . that Goliath." I wanted to take him up on his challenge, but the thought of getting near Endy's numerous, and probably very sharp, teeth or his clublike hooves made me want to crawl away like the coward I was around horses. Even small ones.

"Let me take that." He took the basket, then gently nudged me toward the horse's mouth.

Stuart's arm went around me, his other hand forcing my own open so that the apple lay flat on my palm. "You do not want him to think your fingers are little carrots. Would not do to get him liking the taste of human blood."

Darting a quick glance at him, I saw him biting his bottom lip, but he couldn't hide the merriment in his blue eyes.

I stretched my hand out toward the gigantic head, trying to keep my body as far away as possible. The horse seemed to eye me speculatively, determining if I were friend or foe. Then he opened his mouth and took the proffered apple.

I expected to feel the grazing of teeth against the skin of my palm and was surprised with just the gentle touch of soft lips delicately picking up the apple.

The thick jaws worked back and forth, the loud crunching sounding like the crushing of bones. Small bits of apple and a great deal of slobber formed around the horse's mouth, spraying me and the vicinity. Instead of spitting out the core, Endy swallowed the entire thing.

The big head then looked at me, as if waiting for another morsel. Determined not to be the next item on the menu, I looked to Stuart for help, and was astounded to feel a velvet-soft nose coupled with a few juicy apple bits nuzzling into my cheek. Thoroughly disgusted with the messy show of affection, I jumped backward, only to be stopped suddenly by the force of Stuart's body, almost knocking him over. He reached around my waist to steady me and pulled softly on the reins in his other hand to ease the attentions of my equine suitor.

"See? Look at that. You have made a friend." His arm remained around me, and when I tilted my head, I could see the little crinkles at the sides of his eyes as he laughed.

"Are you making fun of me?"

"Certainly not. Just admiring your bravery. And your appeal to males of all types."

I turned to look at him, and he slowly dropped his arm. He stood very close as his smile faded, his gaze never wavering from my face.

Without moving back, he reached in his pocket and pulled out a handkerchief. "You've got pieces of apple on your cheek." He gently swiped at my face with the soft linen cloth. I closed my eyes so I wouldn't have to look into his.

I opened them again when I realized he had stopped wiping but hadn't moved back. The horse snorted to remind us of his presence, but neither one of us seemed to notice. We did, however, notice the small green projectile that suddenly sailed over our heads. Stuart's battle savvy seemed to take over and he quickly forced me down to my haunches.

Before I could ask what was going on, Sarah and Willie emerged running from the side of the house, Willie in the lead. Another green missile landed on the ground in front of me. I reached to pick it up, rolling the hard, verdant bud in my palm.

"Damn!" said Stuart, plucking the object from my hand. "Begging your pardon," he added absently, extending his hand to me to help me up.

"What is it?"

"It's a cotton bud. They're not supposed to be stripping my crop before they have bloomed."

Realizing that it was perhaps my negligence that was causing the children to run wild, I grabbed my basket and hastened after them. "Don't worry. I'll talk to them."

As I approached the rear of the chicken house, I narrowly missed being sideswiped by Willie as he dodged a small projectile.

"Willie, what do you think you're doing?" I asked, picking up the errant missile.

Before he could answer, another torpedo shot through the air. I heard Sarah's giggles before I saw her. She stopped when she spotted me, the avenging hen with arms akimbo.

"Children, stop it! How are we supposed to have a crop when there's nothing left to pick? And, Sarah, don't throw things at your brother. You might poke his eye out." Approaching the unrepentant child, I added, "And shouldn't you be practicing your piano?"

With a mumbled, "Yes, ma'am," she walked slowly to the back door, trailing a line of cotton buds on the ground as they dropped from her opened fist. I spotted Willie out of the corner of my eye, trying to sneak off into the woods. "And you, too, young man. I'll be in to check on your progress in half an hour."

As Willie followed his sister into the house, I turned my head at the sound of hoofbeats and watched Stuart, tall in the saddle, riding out toward the fields. The foot of his injured leg was left out of the stirrup, his well-muscled thighs hugging the saddle. Strong hands held the reins, and I turned away, trying not to remember how they had felt when he touched my face.

With no one looking, I unbuttoned the top three buttons of my dress, pulled the fabric away from my damp skin, and blew inside, hoping to create the slightest cooling breeze. I closed my eyes tightly in a vain attempt to shut out the heat. I succeeded only in stinging my eyes with the salty sweat on my eyelids. Suddenly, an image of plunging into nearby Vickery Creek filled my imagination, and I immediately set off to fetch Willie and Sarah. Surely keeping the children out of Julia's hair would be a big help.

After depositing the basket with Sukie in the kitchen, I walked to the back door. The sound of Sarah's crying greeted me as I stood in the threshold. Hurrying to the parlor, I was horrified by what I saw.

An angry red handprint stained the side of Sarah's face, creeping up her delicate skin like poison ivy. She was crumpled on the floor, but her grandmother held her wrist tight. Willie sat on the piano bench, his shoulders hunched forward as if to make himself as small as possible.

Without thinking, I rushed to Sarah. "Did you hit her?" I knelt by Sarah and put my arm around her. She buried her head in my shoulder, muffling her sobs.

Pamela let go of Sarah's arm. "This child must learn to respect her elders. I will not take any disrespect from a child." Two bright spots of color appeared on her cheeks. "And how dare you speak that way to me. You both need to be taught some manners."

I glared up at her. "I don't know how you were raised, but I am quite sure that striking a child is a very ineffective way to teach her anything."

Fuming and unable, or unwilling, to control the deep flush of anger that rose to her face, she hissed at me, "I do not know who you are or why you are here. But you are out of place in your interfering with the way I discipline my grandchildren." Her hands shook with fury.

Sensing the children's fear, I attempted to lighten the situation. "I think somebody's grumpy and needs a nap."

Sarah's head snapped up to look at me, her eyes wide with surprise. Her look was echoed in her grandmother's expression.

Pamela bent her face toward mine, her beady eyes narrowed. "Do not think that I do not know what you are up to. And you will not get away with it. Not while I am around."

She walked out of the room, almost militant in her stride.

I brushed aside the tinge of fear that had begun to grow inside me and gave Sarah a hug, wiping her tears with the sleeve of my dress. "What did you say to her?"

Sniffling, Sarah explained, "She told me that I had no emotion for the music I was playing on the piano." Pausing to hiccup, she continued. "And I told her she was wrong."

I was unable to see the error in Sarah's reasoning and unsure of how I should approach the situation. Wiping the damp tendrils of hair off her forehead, I whispered conspiratorially, "Well, you were right. But perhaps next time, you should just agree with your grandmother. After all, it's apparent that she appreciates music as much as a rock would."

I was rewarded with a small smile. Then I added, "How about a swim?"

A loud whoop from Willie was a clear answer for both of them.

We took the same path that led to Zeke's cabin, but turned at a different fork in the trail, hoping that Willie really did know where he was. I welcomed the cool shade of the tall pines and longed for the water of the creek.

The children immediately stripped to their undergarments and stood on the edge, their bare toes wiggling among the stray strands of grass and rocks. Where we were, the creek was neither wide nor deep, but it filled our criteria of being wet and cool. With a nod from me, their gleeful cries filled the air as they flung their young bodies into the refreshing wetness.

My first impulse was to strip down to my chemise, but I hesitated. I was sure the children wouldn't have noticed, but I didn't want to be discovered by someone else standing in the middle of the creek, in nothing but a sheer piece of wet cotton. Resignedly, I pulled off my ankle boots and peeled down my stockings. Glancing around to make sure no one was lurking, I hoisted my skirts above the knees and sighed loudly as I waded into the stream.

The children splashed me in their exuberance, but I declined to chastise them. The spattering of water droplets on my face was too refreshing. I eyed the children enviously, their bare arms and legs glinting in the sunlight. Sweat still poured down my face, so I scooped a handful of the moving water and splashed it over my head.

The whinnying of a horse jerked me upright. I dropped my skirts in the water as I hastily turned around. I eyed my soaking clothing with dismay and quickly picked my skirts up again as I waded back to the shore. Charlie bolted past me and landed with a loud splash, his presence greeted with happy squeals from the children.

I faced Stuart as he gingerly dismounted from Endy. "Not to sound discourteous, but what are you doing here? Making sure I don't bolt?" I wiped a stray water drop off the tip of my nose. "I hate to tell you this, but the only covert activity I'm guilty of is trying to cool off in this creek without showing too much skin."

Raising his eyebrows slightly, Stuart replied, "I was paying a visit to Zeke. I have not seen him since Julia's mother arrived. But I heard all this caterwauling and I came to see what had got caught in a trap." He loosely tethered Endy to a tree and walked over to where I stood dripping.

"I thought the children could use a nice respite from the heat." I picked up the edge of my hem and squeezed it tightly, the water droplets scattering dust as they fell.

"The children, hmm?"

"Oh, all right. I was about to melt. And I'd just about give my left arm to be able to take off these clothes and go for a swim."

He looked as if he couldn't decide whether to be shocked or amused. "I see." He sat upon a large rock at the edge of the stream and began to remove his boots. "As much as I might enjoy the spectacle, I would not recommend it. You would scandalize the town."

He was struggling with the boot on his injured leg so I went over to help him. He held up his hand to stop me. "Laura, that is really not proper. . . ."

"Stuart, you need help. Believe me, bare feet have never gotten anybody into trouble."

His eyes widened, but he wordlessly handed me his foot and I pulled off the boot. He winced slightly but nodded his thanks as he pulled off his socks.

I waved my hand in front of my face. "Well, the sight isn't scandalizing me, but the smell sure is. Is that a secret weapon to kill more Yankees than a single bullet?"

Leaning back, he shook his head and laughed. "You know, Laura, I can always depend on you to say what is on your mind. A rare but admirable trait."

"Thank you. I think." I carefully picked my way back into the water and found a seat on a partially submerged tree trunk.

Sobering slightly, he said, "Why such a mystery, Laura? What is so dangerous that you have to keep it hidden?"

I didn't dare look at him. Staring down at the bright reflection of the water, I shrugged. "I hit my head, remember? I don't recall much more about my past life than you don't already know."

He didn't say anything for a moment. "You must think me quite stupid."

"No, I don't. And if I've kept anything from you, it's merely self-preservation. You have nothing to fear from me."

A welcome interruption came in the form of Charlie bounding through the water toward me, inviting me to play. Grasping hold of the bottom of my skirt, he began tugging.

"Charlie, stop it! I can't go in. Willie! Sarah! Please come get Charlie and make him stop." I wrinkled my nose at the smell of wet dog as I vainly tried to remove my dress from Charlie's clutches.

I stood, prepared to retreat to the safety of the water line, when I found footing on a deceptively slippery rock. One moment I was standing; the next I was sitting on my backside, partially immersed in the water.

Once I had recovered from the shock, I politely refused all offers of help in righting myself. Instead, I lay back in my impromptu bath, allowing the water to wash over my face.

I sat up and shouted, "Oh, that feels wonderful! I wish I had thought of that to begin with." And then I promptly lay back again, feeling my hair move with the soft current.

Opening my eyes under the water, I was surprised to see two dark, wavy figures on the bank. I immediately sat up and was relieved to see Zeke with Stuart.

"Hi, Zeke!" I called out, waving my hand and creating an arc of water, and acting as if sitting fully dressed in the middle of a creek was something I did all the time.

He raised his hand in greeting, his face stoic but a corner of his mouth twitching.

I stood and slogged my way over to the bank, my skirts heavy. I did my best to squeeze the excess water out of my hair and dress but felt confident that the burning sun would efficiently do the rest.

I blinked at the two men as a water droplet from my hair plopped into my eyes.

Zeke nodded silently at me. Turning to Stuart, he said, "Julia's mother has come. The dark cloud over your house has told me this."

I looked in the direction of the house and saw only clear sky.

"Yes, she is here. And she has brought word of William. He has been assigned to General Sherman's staff in Nashville."

Zeke grunted. "That is not far enough. Does he know you are here?"

Stuart shook his head. "Not as far as I know. We have had no contact with him for almost a year. Unless Julia mentioned it to her mother in a letter and Pamela told him."

Zeke shook his head. "Then he knows. You should leave as soon as you can."

His words made me start. I knew Stuart was a soldier, but it had never occurred to me that he might actually leave and go back to war so soon.

Stuart's fists tightened at his side. "Am I the only one around here who has doubts that the Yankees could ever come this far?"

Zeke looked at Stuart, his eyes steady. "You are no fool. And you know as well as I do that a well-supplied Yankee army that easily outnumbers Confederates could do as they please with little consequential opposition."

Stuart sat down and began pulling on socks and boots. Brusquely waving aside my offer of help, he yanked them on, oblivious to the pain it caused his injured leg. "I need to get back, regardless of my leg. I am so useless here."

"I wouldn't call holding this family and plantation together useless." I had no thought as to why I felt a sudden panic at the thought of him leaving.

"My regiment is fighting for their country, and I am here, living as if the war is not even happening."

"Don't be ridiculous. It's not like you chose to be shot in the leg, for goodness' sake. And what good do you think you'd be to your men right now? Would you expect them to carry you in a battle because your leg won't let you keep up?"

Stuart and Zeke stared at me with raised eyebrows. Making an effort to lower my voice, I continued. "You are far more useful to your home and family right now than you would be to the Confederacy."

Stuart grunted and stood quickly, almost pitching forward as his leg gave out on him. Zeke caught him before he fell. His face flushed red with anger, and he glared at me. "You are a real enigma, Laura. You do not remember anything about yourself but you know a good deal about what is good for me. Why do you want me to stay? Do you need a reliable informant?"

His soft voice cut the humid air with its vehemence. I took a step forward, my hands on my hips. "I was only trying to help. Fine. Go back to your regiment and get killed. I hope a cannonball lands right on your head." I kicked at a rock and turned away, trying to look as dignified as I could with water dripping from my hair and clothes.

Stuart limped past me without a word and untethered his horse. Ignoring him, I called for the children to come out before their skin grew dimpled like raisins.

Drying themselves as much as possible on the linen towels we had brought with us, they then threw their dry clothes over their wet underclothes and trudged after Stuart, leaving me to follow behind. Zeke sent me a look of understanding and nodded goodbye as we passed the fork in the trail that led to his cabin. We took a separate path from the one I had been on previously and soon came upon the black gates of a small cemetery. I passed through the gates, hoping Stuart would take the children home and leave me to sort out my thoughts alone. I stood in the quiet, realizing I'd been here before.

White headstones dotted the quiet, shady knoll, the grass meticulously cut short. From this vantage point I could see two of the cotton mills of the Roswell Manufacturing Company and a sawmill that lay between the two. Seen from afar, all was a picture of the hustle and bustle of activity. But from where I stood amid the gravestones, a welcome breeze brushing my face and lifting the wet tendrils of hair off my forehead, it was curiously silent.

A prominent white marble monument towered over the other gravestones and I walked over to it. It had been erected in memory of the town's founder, Roswell King. I had seen this marker before when I had visited what was then known as Founders' Cemetery with my father. Besides being a bit whiter, there had been little change through the years. I touched it with both hands, my anchor in the sea of time.

I listened to the hum of insects as I strolled through the tiny cemetery, glancing briefly at each rounded headstone and marker. Kneeling down in front of a small stone, I traced my fingers lightly over the carved letters of a child who had died at age two years, nine months.

I strolled slowly through the cemetery, examining every headstone, conscious that I was looking for the grave of a child with no name. I squinted to see the small lettering on the tombstones and felt a cold chill in my heart when I saw the large number of children who had been buried in the cemetery between the years of 1840 and 1841.

Feeling a light touch on my shoulder and realizing it was Stuart, I stifled a scream. Sensing my question before I asked it, he explained, "Scarlet fever. There was almost no family in Roswell that did not lose a child."

I nodded in silence, not yet wanting to speak, my anger toward him still strong. A small relief passed over me as I realized that whatever dangers Annie might encounter in the nineteenth century, childhood disease would probably not be one of them. As an infant, she had been immunized against diphtheria, measles, polio, and a small assortment of others. Assuming Annie was in the nineteenth century, this was no small comfort.

"Are you thinking of Annie?" His voice was low, concern replacing his anger.

"Yes." I paused for a moment to kneel by another tiny tombstone. "I'm also thinking of all the parents of these children. There can be no greater pain than the loss of a child." Thoughts of Annie consumed me and I began to cry. I stood and furiously tried to wipe the tears away, ashamed to have anyone see me fall apart. He tried to put an arm around me, but I pushed him away and tried to walk back to the gate.

His footfall sounded behind me as his hands grabbed me and spun me around. Wordlessly, he gathered me in his arms and held me against him.

It had been so long since I had felt the warmth and compassion of someone's arms around me, and it made me cry harder. The smells of horseflesh, leather, and sweat pervaded his shirt, and I found them oddly comforting. His chest was hard and solid but made a remarkably soft pillow for my head as I soaked his shirt with my tears. Long minutes later, I was cried out, with only soft hiccups remaining. I felt Stuart's hands on the sides of my head as he tilted my face upward. With his thumbs, he wiped the tears off my face. He brought his lips close to mine and paused for a moment. I closed my eyes and felt his lips gently brush mine.

His words barely audible, he said, "You are not alone anymore. Let me help you." He let go of me and took two steps backward. Small clouds of tiny flying insects began to hover about us in the dwindling twilight. "But you have to be honest with me and tell me who you really are. And why you are here."

My hand closed over my mouth. What had I done? This was not allowed. "Don't. Please don't."

He stepped closer. "What are you afraid of?"

I looked down at the ground, my hair dripping into the dirt around my skirts. I searched for what truth I could tell him. "Of more loss. I could not survive it."

He tilted my face back up to his. "You are strong."

My gaze rested on his lips and I knew I wanted him to kiss me again. I tried to turn away, but his hands held me captive. "No. I'm not. You've misjudged me."

His eyes darkened. "There is something else—I see it in your eyes. What is it? What is it you cannot tell me?"

I could do nothing but look at him and then lower my eyes.

He dropped his hand. "Why do you make me feel as if I am consorting with the enemy?"

"I'm not your enemy. I wish you would just trust me."

"I wish I could." Walking past me, he left the cemetery and grabbed Endy's reins, which had been dragging in the red dirt. He paused momentarily. Without looking at me, he said, "I am not a patient man, Laura. I will find out. And if I discover you have been playing with our affections and deceiving us, you will live to regret it."

Tugging on the reins, he walked on ahead of me, leaving a trail of red dust.

Chapter Twelve

—◆—

We do not know the past in chronological sequence. It may
be convenient to lay it out anesthetized on the table with
dates pasted on here and there, but what we know we
know by ripples and spirals eddying out from us and from
our own time.

—EZRA POUND

The three red drops on my drawers alerted me to the fact that my body was functioning as normal, despite the abnormal circumstances of my life. My father, a Civil War history buff, had dragged me to the Atlanta History Center about one hundred times, the Cyclorama just as many times, and Civil War battle reenactments more times than I could count. But nothing I had ever learned could have prepared me for the realities of being a woman in the 1860s.

Knowing by instinct that a woman's monthly cycle would be a delicate subject, I had to consider who would be the best person to ask how to deal with it. Asking Stuart would be out of the question. Julia would probably be able to give me an answer, but only after a few horrendous moments of utter embarrassment.

There was a brief tapping on my door, and Sukie entered with a pile of clean linens. My muscles ached as they remembered helping to wash the linens the previous day—lifting, turning, and squeezing constantly—and I was pleased to see the fruits of my labor.

I gave her a bright smile. "Sukie, I need some help."

She paused in the middle of the room. "Ma'am?"

I decided the direct approach would work best. "I need something to protect my clothing. I'm having my period."

She squinted at me for a moment before she realized what I was saying. "You be havin' your monthly bleeding." She set the laundry down on the bed and patted my sleeve. "I be right back."

And that was the easy part. Figuring out what to do with the cloth belt and mounds of rags that Sukie brought for me was another. Staring at the strange ensemble, I suddenly realized where the expression "on the rag" came from. Sighing to myself, and saying a quick prayer of thanks that I ovulated sporadically and nowhere near twelve times a year, I set about folding the rags in a thick bundle and inserting the ends in loops on the belt. I said another prayer of hope that the thing would stay in place.

Walking down the stairs, I heard the soft murmur of voices. Hoping to find Julia to enlist her in teaching me about some of the plants in her garden, I approached the library. I hesitated in the hallway when I realized it was Pamela's voice.

"It does not matter where I got the information. It is from Sherman's headquarters and could do the Confederacy a lot of good." I heard the rustle of petticoats and the tapping of heels against wooden floor. "Here—take it. Use it." Her voice was low, the word "use" coming out with a hiss. "And if you get caught, I have brought some quinine with me. You could say it is the medicine you are smuggling and nothing else."

Stuart's voice was also low, but I heard enough to understand what the conversation was about. "How can you betray your own son-in-law? Does Julia know?"

I pictured Pamela waving her hand through the air, dismissing any inconvenient thoughts. "During wartime, one must forget one's personal loyalties and concentrate on the needs of the greater good. I am not betraying anyone. I am only doing what I can for the South."

The cabinet door opened, followed by the clinking of glass. I pictured Stuart pouring himself a drink. After a slight pause, he said, "And if William finds out whose side you are really on, what then? What will happen to Julia?"

Pamela chuckled softly. "Do not worry about William. I will contend with him if the need arises. And as for Julia, I am sure you will take care of her."

I heard Stuart slam down the glass. "That is enough. There is nothing between Julia and me. And if I take that piece of information from you it will be for the Confederacy and not for some petty cause like thwarting William. Despite our many differences, he is still my brother, and Julia is his wife."

Another pause was followed by Pamela's voice. "There is something else we need to discuss. That man, Matt Kimball, approached me yesterday in town. He wanted me to pass on a message to Mrs. Truitt. I thought I would tell you first."

I held my breath to better hear her words.

"What is it?" Stuart's words were clipped.

"He says he has information regarding her daughter."

My heart tightened in my chest, and I barely heard Stuart's voice. "I do not trust him. I will speak to him myself. Do not tell Laura about it. If it is anything, I will let her know."

Pamela's brittle laughter came through the door. "Is it him you do not trust—or is it her?"

"Never you mind, Pamela. I will handle it."

The stamp of his boots heralded his departure from the room, and I quickly ducked into the parlor just in time to see Stuart cross the hallway and crash out the front door.

I jumped, startled, at the sound of pecking from the parlor window. I walked slowly toward the sound, peering cautiously through the glass. I stepped back as a large black crow, its raven wings a startling shadow against the brightness outside, brought its beak against the glass. The staccato taps broke the silence of the room as the black head of the bird continued to thrust its beak at the windowpane.

The hairs on the back of my neck stood on end, and I abruptly turned around.

Pamela was staring at the crow, her eyebrows raised and her face a pasty white. Without looking at me, she said, "A crow tapping on one's window is a very bad sign."

"What do you mean?"

She turned toward me, her black eyes as cold as marble. "It is an omen of death." Without another word, she turned and left the room.

My body shivered, and I hugged my elbows to give me warmth.

For the next several weeks, I waited for Stuart to approach me with information about Matt Kimball. When he didn't, I knew I'd have to take matters into my own hands and seek out Matt myself. I just preferred to do it when Stuart wasn't around to catch me doing what I was sure he would consider covert activity.

The news of General Lee's devastating Confederate loss at Gettysburg in Pennsylvania cast a somber pall over the town, and there were considerably more women dressed in head-to-toe black in church on Sundays. I didn't see Matt Kimball in church again, and wondered how I would ever find a way to approach him.

As we moved into September, the overwhelming heat of summer began to dissipate and the oncoming autumn was evident in the turning leaves and cooler evenings. Since the scene in the cemetery, Stuart had been avoiding me, his attitude cool when we did cross paths. But sometimes as we all sat at the dining table or in the parlor, I would look up suddenly and find him watching me, his eyes brooding. I began to feel like a mouse nibbling at cheese set in a trap.

Julia was busy in her garden, harvesting the fall vegetables and planting turnips. She explained to me that the turnips would have a sweeter taste if they were planted in time to experience at least one frost. From the amount she planted, I assumed the turnip would have a starring role on our winter dining table.

One evening I sat on the porch before supper, rubbing my knees, made sore from helping Julia in her garden. The door opened and Stuart hesitated in the threshold.

"I am sorry to disturb you. I thought you were Zeke."

I stopped rocking and frowned. "I must try harder to stay out of the sun if you're mistaking me for a man more than three times my age."

Stuart sent me a sheepish smile. "No, you misunderstand. Zeke was supposed to meet me on the porch for a game of backgammon, but he sometimes forgets the time when he is immersed in one of his books." He held out a board, a bag of playing pieces clinking in his other hand.

I sat up. "Backgammon? I love that game, but I haven't played in a very long time."

He walked closer to me. "May I challenge you to a match, then?"

"Only if you're not a sore loser."

He cocked an eyebrow without comment as he slid a small table over and pulled up a chair. "Perhaps we should set up stakes for this."

"Stakes?" I smiled nervously.

"If I win, I get something. And if you win, then you get something."

Worry grew in the pit of my stomach. "But I have nothing to give."

He leaned close to me, his eyes narrowed. "Oh, but you do." His mouth spread in a thin smile. "If you lose, you have to answer truthfully any question I ask."

My throat felt thick. "And if I win?"

He settled back in his chair and began setting up the game. "That would be your choice. You could have your freedom to come and go as you please."

"I should have that anyway," I said. I finally saw a way to seek out Matt Kimball. "Whoever wins the best of seven." I picked up the dice and rolled them. Double sixes. "I go first."

We began playing and I quickly discovered we were evenly matched. Soon we were called in for supper, and afterward we moved the set indoors to the parlor. A crisp snap had invaded the air, and the ladies were all wrapped in thick shawls. The clicking of Julia's knitting needles and the popping of the wood in the fireplace punctuated the cozy silences in the conversation lulls.

I found myself furtively watching Stuart as he contemplated a move. He had the habit of running his hands through his hair when he was concentrating, causing the thick black bristles to stand on end. When he growled as I rolled another pair of sixes, I offered a polite suggestion that he smooth it back down so as not to scare any visitors.

Dr. Watkins had taken to calling most evenings now that the cotton harvest was over and Stuart had more free time, and he had perched on a chair between Julia and her mother. I watched him as he looked at Julia, his eyes softening like a puppy's, and I knew that his feelings for her hadn't altered since Robbie's birth.

I had been almost unbeatable in backgammon when I had played my father or Michael, but Stuart was a formidable opponent. I won three in a row, and then my luck seemed to run out. Unfortunately, I was not as gracious a loser as he was. By the middle of the sixth game, he was resoundingly whopping me. I looked in dismay at the large number of my counters still on the board and the piles of his pieces resting on the table.

He tossed the dice onto the board and chuckled slightly with the result. I brought my hand down on the table with a thump, making the pieces jump. "That's not fair," I shouted in mock dismay as I stared at the double sixes. "If you win this game, it will be from sheer luck and not due to any skill on your part, that's for sure."

I realized that all eyes rested on me and I offered, "The man gets doubles every time he rolls," as a feeble explanation for my outburst. The three gave polite smiles in my direction before resuming their conversation.

Stuart rapidly picked up two of his counters and began moving them home. He looked up at me, a small smile framing his lips.

"Do you really think that's the best move?" I asked, pretending to study the board.

He shook his head slowly. "That is not going to work on me, Mrs. Truitt."

I gave him a look of false innocence. "Pardon? I'm sure I don't know what you mean."

"Hmm," he murmured, and he threw the dice again. Double fours.

I put both elbows on the table and made a frown. "I don't think it's gentlemanly to beat a lady at backgammon."

Quietly, he said, "If I did not think I would win, I never would have agreed to our little wager." He leaned forward, as if to make sure nobody else heard him. "But if you continue with your distractions, you might still win this match."

I saw his gaze directed at the low neckline of my dinner dress, one of two from Julia's wardrobe that had been modified to fit me. I quickly yanked my elbows off the table and sat back as far as my hoop skirt would allow, which was approximately two inches. I felt myself blushing as I hastened to roll the dice. Snake eyes. "Whoop-de-do," I said unenthusiastically.

"Never say you do not roll doubles," Stuart said, and he rolled again and completed moving his counters off the board. His blue eyes gazed steadily at me, making the blood run thick and heavy through my veins. "One more game, and the winner takes all."

I chewed on my inner cheek, wondering how I would answer the question he was bound to ask me. I looked down at the board and began setting up my pieces one last time.

The wind outside picked up, alerting us to the signs of an early autumn storm. Dried leaves and other debris were tossed carelessly at the window, mixed with the louder *pat-pat* of water droplets against the glass. The crackling of the fire in the fireplace joined the chorus, and I breathed in deeply the homey smell of the pine logs. I absently fingered the smooth polished wood of a counter in my hand, remembering games I had played with my father and with Michael.

"Your move," Stuart said, his voice low.

I jumped, startled into the present, and gave him a weak smile. "Sorry, I was just daydreaming. Calling up ghosts, actually."

We began to play in earnest, the dice rolling quickly, and the click of the pieces on the board drawing us further into the game. We were neck and neck as we pulled our remaining counters into the home stretch. He had three on the first space, and I had four on the fourth space. All I needed was at least a double four and I would win. I picked up the dice and brought them slowly to my lips. I blew softly on them, Stuart's eyes never leaving mine, then let them drop. They rolled as if in slow motion before coming to rest. Double fives.

I stared at them in shock. "I won," I whispered.

Stuart sat back in his chair, a bemused expression on his face. "This time. But do not think I am through trying." He rolled a counter between long fingers. "Name your prize."

The tempting thought of claiming another kiss crossed my mind, but it was all whimsy. "I want my freedom to come and go as I please."

He nodded slightly. "So be it. Unless you do something to jeopardize our trust."

Julia spoke up. "What a wicked night. I was just sitting here calling to mind a night just like this. The night Willie was born." A dreamy smile touched her lips as she paused. "The wind was blowing something fierce, just like it is now, but we thought it might be a hurricane coming in from the coast. All the shutters had been nailed shut over the windows, and the house was very dark." Her soft hazel eyes grew still and dark, looking at me but past me, seeing another autumn night.

She put her hand lightly on her abdomen, smoothing the fabric of her dress. Her voice sounded as if it were coming from a far-off place, barely audible against the violence of the wind outside. "I felt the baby stretching, pulling my skin so tight that I thought it might burst, and I knew that my time had come. But I had no fear. Zeke had told me that everything would be all right." The firelight flickered over her face, casting a portion of it in shadow but illuminating the other half in a soft, radiant light. The undulations of light and darkness mimicked the surges of an unborn child in the womb, making me grieve afresh for the emptiness of my own.

Julia blinked, as if seeing me for the first time, and smiled. "And he was right. Willie was born in the early-morning hours, chubby, pink, and bawling."

The mood broke as Julia laughed softly, and the click of her knitting needles began anew.

"You're very blessed, Julia. All three of your children are so beautifully healthy." The words tasted sour on my tongue, and I hoped that no one had detected the bitterness. "So, now I know the story of Willie's birth, and I was there for Robbie's. Tell me about Sarah's."

Dr. Watkins stood and moved to the window. He crossed his arms on his chest and leaned back. "That was frightening—remember, Julia? It was summer, June if I remember correctly, and she was a good two months early. So small. We did not think she would make it."

Julia kept her head down, the needles clicking vigorously. An ear-splitting scream broke the silence of the house. Stuart stood immediately but was held in place by a gesture from Julia.

"Let us see if she quiets down by herself."

I looked around me for some sort of explanation, but all faces were turned to Julia in mute awareness. A minute passed in silence, my heart beginning to beat at a normal rate again, when the same horrifying scream began again.

Julia stood abruptly and her knitting needles, still attached to the stockings she had been working on, slid from her lap. "I will go," she said, and left the room. Suddenly realizing that it was Sarah who had screamed, I followed Julia upstairs.

Muffled sobs reached me as I crossed the landing and entered Sarah's room. She shared a room with Willie, whose curved form I could make out in the dim light on the opposite twin bed. In true male form, he had not been awakened by the shrieks.

Julia sat on the edge of the bed, her arms around her daughter, murmuring unintelligible words of comfort. I heard her hand thudding gently on the back of Sarah's nightgown.

Sarah brought her head back abruptly and pointed toward the window. "Mama, make it go away!" she screamed, and then pushed her face onto her mother's shoulder.

The curtains had been pulled back, revealing nothing but pitch-black darkness. The wind still whipped against the house, but the rain had stopped. I approached the window cautiously and peered out. Nothing could be seen in the yard below, but a small brightening of the night ceiling brought my gaze upward. Thin strips of cloud slid quickly across the sky, alternately exposing a round, full moon and casting it in shadow. As the bright moonlight flooded the room momentarily, Sarah screamed again.

"Close the curtains." It was Julia's voice, soft as usual but commanding nevertheless. I quickly grabbed the two panels and brought them together.

Julia began to sing quietly, and Sarah's sobs lessened. I felt like an intruder in this maternal scene and softly crept out of the room. As I started to walk down the stairs, Julia left the room, closing the door behind us.

I turned to Julia. "What was she afraid of? Was it the storm?"

Her face was in shadow, dark and unreadable. "No. She is afraid of the full moon." She stepped past me and walked down the stairs, her dress rustling as it brushed the steps. A chill covered me in goose bumps, and I shivered.

I didn't follow her. Instead I went to the library and to the shelf where the family Bible was kept and pulled it from its place before opening the front cover. There, the next-to-last entry under a long list of births and deaths: *Sarah Margaret Elliott, born June 16, 1856.* Quietly, I closed the book and pushed it back on the shelf.

Feeling restless, I crept quietly past the parlor to the front door and stepped out onto the porch. The storm was passing but leaving trailing shifts of wind in its wake. My skirts billowed out around me and I slapped my hands down at my sides to try to keep them from making me airborne. The sound of buggy wheels and the brisk trotting of horse's hooves came from the front drive, and I assumed the good doctor had taken his leave. The cloud cover had thinned and the bright moonlight streamed down on the front yard, reflecting itself in the sporadic puddles and illuminating the scattered debris of twigs and leaves.

I walked slowly toward the edge of the porch and leaned on a column, its hard surface a comforting support. The smell of wet clay and damp animals assailed my nose and I breathed it in deeply, as if to convince myself of the new reality of my life.

A different scent caught my attention, and I turned slowly around to see Stuart at the other end of the porch, drawing on a cigar. He walked toward me, his face hidden in shadow but briefly illuminated by the end of the cigar as he inhaled.

I remained where I was. "I'll leave if you want to be alone."

He stopped and stood several paces away from me and blew the smoke to the side. "I find your company refreshing."

I laughed. "That's mighty big of you to say, since I pummeled you at backgammon."

He smiled down at me, but his eyes were serious. "Are you sure you will not change your mind about your prize? Is there anything else you might like?"

My gaze traveled down his face and settled on his lips before quickly glancing away. "No. I like the idea of being a free woman again."

He tipped ashes over the railing, his eyes never leaving my face, and I watched them scatter in the night air. "You won the match, which is why I will allow you a bit of freedom. But do not think it is because I trust you."

I bit back my anger, suddenly realizing how much I wanted to gain his trust. I grabbed the railing with both hands, my back to Stuart. "If you're standing on a river's edge, just looking at the water, not touching it, do you have to wade in to find out that it's wet?"

He didn't say anything, so I turned to face him. "These people—Julia and the children—do you really think I would do anything to harm them? And this house—it's more of a home to me than you would ever realize."

My voice quivered as I remembered standing in front of the house for the very first time with Michael and feeling the powerful force of being home. I shivered as a gust of cool wind worked itself down the front of my dress.

Stuart took a step toward me, still unspeaking, his face unreadable. Smoke from the cigar danced up between us like little ghosts, vanishing with the wind's whim. "These are dangerous times, Laura. Things are not always as they appear to be. People, too. I have met men and women since this conflict began who will risk anything to promote their cause. I have learned to withhold my trust until my boots are completely submerged in the river. Then I will believe it is wet."

I threw my hands up. "Fine. Just allow me to write the inscription on your headstone. 'Killed by a bullet he did not believe would hurt him.'"

He leaned close enough that I could smell the soap on his skin. I pressed my back against the rail, unsure of the light in his eyes. "The only thing that sustains me when I am in the heat of battle is the picture in my mind of this house and my family—and knowing they are safe. But now you are here, living with us. I do not know who you are, where you are from, or what you want. You have secrets. You have never denied it. And I have a strange way of not trusting people who are not completely truthful with me."

I straightened, my anger brimming like static electricity. "What if . . . What if the truth was so insane—so unspeakable—that you wouldn't even recognize it as the truth?" I slammed my fist on the railing. "I don't even know what the truth is anymore—and I really don't care. I just want to find Annie and go home. I just want to go home with my daughter."

"Where is home? And what is there that is so important to you—more important than staying here, where so many people have grown to care for you?"

I didn't realize I was crying until he reached up and brushed a tear from my cheek. Pushing his hand aside, I used my sleeve to wipe my cheeks. "My memories—of my husband and our lives. Of our perfect little life with our daughter."

Stuart's voice was low and measured. "I have watched my boyhood friends die for this cause. I held the head of my best friend while his brains drained into my haversack, and all I could think of was my rations being spoiled."

His words drew me toward him and I faced him again. He threw down his cigar and ground it out with the heel of his boot.

"Why are you telling me this?"

His eyes were dark pools of still water. "Life goes on, Laura. Memories will not keep you warm on a winter's night." He inhaled deeply. "And I also want you to understand what is at stake. We have sacrificed so much, and I do not want to give away what is left so easily."

"I won't take anything from you. I just need shelter until I can go home."

"It is too late for that."

My hand clutched his sleeve. "Too late to go home?"

"No. Too late to leave without taking anything with you. You have already captured hearts, Laura. You could not leave without taking at least one casualty."

I knew he wasn't talking about Julia or the children. The moonlight lent his face an eerie blue cast, giving him the appearance of a ghost. I felt the goose bumps on my arms when I realized that, to me, he was a ghost—at least somebody who had lived in my own distant past. He saw my shiver and slipped off his coat, placing it gently on my shoulders.

His eyes were clouded in shadow as he looked down at me. "I might as well tell you this now. Charles has told me that I will not be fit for combat duty for a few months yet, but I have some business to attend to and will be making several short trips before I return to my regiment."

I opened my mouth to mention the conversation I had overheard between him and Pamela, but stopped. He would never let me go into town if he realized I knew Matt Kimball wanted to speak with me.

"Will you miss me?" he asked suddenly.

I was glad of the darkness. "Yes, I will. A lot," I answered, without hesitation. With a trembling voice, I added, "There's nobody else here who can play backgammon."

He chuckled lightly as he placed his hands behind my neck and tilted my face toward his. He leaned down and kissed me softly. His lips lingered over mine, and a faint sigh escaped me as I tasted cigar smoke and whiskey.

"This might be considered by my superiors as consorting with the enemy, you know."

I kept my head back in the hopes he'd kiss me again. "I'm not your enemy, Stuart."

"This coming from the woman who said she wanted a cannonball to land on my head."

His lips were so close, I shut my eyes. My voice sounded languid in the night air. "I didn't really mean that, you know. I might even be upset."

His kiss this time was anything but gentle, his lips bruising mine. His mouth traveled to my ear and he whispered, "Memories cannot compete with flesh and blood, can they?"

The front door opened and we stepped apart. Julia looked at us knowingly, a tight smile on her face, and I was glad again for the darkness to hide the stain of red creeping up my face.

"I was wondering where you two had gone off to. Laura, we were hoping you might play something for us on the piano."

We followed her inside, but she stopped me before I entered the parlor so she could adjust my hair. With a raised eyebrow at Stuart, she swept past us and settled herself onto the sofa, waiting demurely as I sat at the piano and began to play.

Much later, as I lay in my lonely bed, I tossed and turned, unable to sleep. The full moon turned the blackness in my room to gray, reminding me of how my life was no longer black-and-white but instead had fallen between the colored cracks of reality. Finally, in the last stages of wakefulness when the world tends to blur its edges, I imagined I heard the *tap-tap*ping of a black crow's beak against a windowpane, and my blood chilled with dread.

CHAPTER THIRTEEN

—◆—

The past is only the present become invisible and mute;
and because it is invisible and mute, its memoried
glances and its murmurs are infinitely precious.
We are tomorrow's past.

—MARY WEBB

I walked in the henhouse with authority. I had found that this worked with even the most stubborn chicken. Let them know you were afraid of their pesky little beaks, and the result would be something out of an Alfred Hitchcock movie. Not that I was in a mood to care about being pecked—I was going into town alone. Stuart had left on his trip to deliver whatever information Pamela had given him, and Julia needed me to go into town to fetch cloth at the company store for new pants for Willie. They no longer accepted Confederate money, and we had to rely on what we could trade.

I thrust my hand under chicken number one, whom I had dubbed Cher, and snatched away a lone egg, placing it in the folded-up skirt of my dress. Number two just as easily acquiesced, until I got greedy and reached for the second egg. She responded with a resonant squawk and a well-aimed peck of her beak on my forearm.

Despite her protests, I unceremoniously removed her from her perch and found yet another egg. I left the henhouse ignoring the squawks of disapproval and feeling a bit smug.

Hastily depositing the eggs in a basket, I changed clothes and headed for the buggy. I had received informal training on how to maneuver the thing, and I was fine just as long as I didn't have to get too close to the horse. I'd been assured it was an old and docile horse—too old and docile to have been confiscated—but I still planned to keep my distance.

Julia ran out of the house and handed me an empty basket and a list. She shielded her eyes with her hand as she looked up at me. "Good-bye, Laura. And thank you."

She looked so forlorn, I felt the need to reassure her. "Don't worry, Julia. I'm not running off. I'll be back shortly."

She waved a hand at me and stepped back from the buggy. "I know that, Laura. It is just that . . . Oh, never mind."

I slapped the horse's rump with a whip, and we trotted off in the cool afternoon air. I recognized the brick facade of the company store, remembering how I had eaten several times at the restaurant that would eventually be housed in the building.

The door was propped open, allowing the fresh, crisp air inside and lighting the dim interior. Waiting a moment for my eyes to adjust, I soon made out a counter at the end of the room with a man standing behind it.

The thick smell of dust, presumably from the sacks of grain propped against the counter, permeated the room, making me sneeze. Tall, empty glass jars lined the top of the counter. I imagined them filled with assortments of fudge and gumdrops. A little girl walked over to one filled with honeyed popcorn balls and touched it gently, but, with a firm shake of her mother's head, she retreated to the back of the store. I knew how dear sugar had become at this point in the war, and the prices for the candy were exorbitant.

"Good afternoon, ma'am." The tall, lanky shopkeeper wore a loose apron over his shirt and pants and had long wisps of sparse hair creeping across his scalp like spider legs. "Mr. Northcutt, proprietor, at your service. Is there anything I can help you with today?"

"Nice to meet you. I'm Laura Truitt. I'm staying at Phoenix Hall." I handed him Julia's list. "Julia Elliott sent me to pick up a few things." I lifted the egg basket. "I've brought eggs."

He settled bifocals and regarded the list. "I will get these things together for you, if you care to wait."

A woman I remembered vaguely from church leaned across the counter next to me. "Is that coffee on the shelf behind you, Mr. Northcutt?"

"Yes, ma'am. I have five pounds of it. Brought to me yesterday by

Samuel Baker, who is on leave on account of an injury to his arm. Says he got it off a dead Yankee."

"How much are you asking?"

"It is worth about thirty dollars for a pound. Or half a hog."

The woman slowly shook her head. "You tempt me, Mr. Northcutt. But I just cannot afford it." She sighed and gave me a brief nod, then left the store.

While Mr. Northcutt gathered the items for Julia, I strolled around the store, my feet kicking up the sawdust scattered on the floor, and examined the mostly empty shelves. I was surprised to see a few cans of corn and other vegetables, and thought that this was mostly a modern technology. I wondered if their source was the same as the coffee beans.

Empty hooks hung from the rafters with a few batches of tobacco leaves hung upside down on them. The fading stench of raw meat told me what had been hung previously.

My toe struck something hard and I turned to see a wooden barrel on the floor. Lifting the lid, I was met with the biting smell of pickles that wafted up, and I could see the dark green pickles floating within. Every available shelf space and much of the floor was littered with all sorts of baskets, most empty but some full, and sacks and barrels filled with a few things I recognized, like eggs and molasses, and many items I didn't. The tempting aroma of baked goods led me to the front of the store again, where an assortment of fresh-baked pies sat suggestively on a low shelf. The Elliott house had not had sweets for some time because of the scarcity of sugar, and my mouth watered as I looked at the flaky edges of the piecrusts.

My heels tapped across the oak floor planks, echoing in the small room. A shadow blocked the light from the doorway, and I turned to see who had entered.

The woman was dressed in head-to-toe black mourning. The severity of her costume was not even alleviated by a single jet brooch or other piece of jewelry. A little girl of about seven or eight, also dressed in black, followed her, her eyes never leaving the floor.

Stepping into the shop, the woman raised the black veil that had covered her face. Piercing gray eyes alighted on me momentarily before moving on toward Mr. Northcutt. The woman seemed to be in her early forties, but the signs of strain under her eyes and stretching across her forehead added years to her face. I remembered seeing her at church but had not been introduced. Her only son had been killed at Gettysburg, and for this reason she had snubbed Julia. Despite the hours Julia spent rolling bandages and knitting socks for the Confederates, and all the food stores she had given to the Southern armies, her marriage to a Yankee branded her.

My attention was drawn to the little girl, who was now standing facing a wall full of shelves. A doll with a porcelain face and exquisite clothes was propped up on the lowest shelf, and the girl was staring at it.

My heart jumped at the sight of the strawberry blond hair. It had been pulled back in a single braid running down her back. It was the shade of Annie's hair, although I had always assumed it would darken, as most children's did, as she grew older.

One small hand reached up to stroke the lace skirt of the doll, and I noticed the smattering of freckles on her hand and wrist. My heart thumped wildly and my mouth went dry as I slowly walked over to stand next to the girl.

She looked at me with wide eyes, withdrawing her hand guiltily. Her large brown eyes answered my question: She was not my Annie. My heart sank in disappointment, but I smiled at her and returned to the front counter to settle the account with Mr. Northcutt.

As he handed me the items, I asked, "Would you by any chance know where I might find Matthew Kimball?"

The shopkeeper looked at me with tight lips, and the bereaved mother sent me a withering glance. "No. I am afraid not, Mrs. Truitt," he said, his clipped words effectively informing me that even if he had, he wouldn't have shared the information with me.

Embarrassed, I thanked him and stepped outside. I was immediately confronted by a blast of wind sending an icy chill up my skirts. I loaded the baskets into the buggy and was contemplating driving around the town in the hopes I might catch sight of Matt Kimball when I spotted the man crossing the town square.

Recognizing that yelling to him wouldn't be appropriate, I followed him with my gaze until he disappeared inside a two-story brick build-ing on the east side of the square.

Making sure the reins were tethered properly, I turned and walked toward the building.

I stopped in front, under the painted sign that read AUNT CLAIRE'S ROOMING HOUSE. I knew this was a bad idea, that if Stuart, or even Ju-lia, found out that I had followed Matt Kimball into a rooming house my credibility would be gone. But I'd been searching for Annie for so long, and my desperation erased any second thoughts. I knocked, and when nobody answered, I turned the knob.

It swung open into a deserted hallway. Tall, narrow stairs led up-ward against the wall on the right, and a short corridor stretched out in front of me on the left. A baby cried somewhere above me but was quickly drowned out by a man and woman shouting. Two closed doors, old brown stain faded to gray, could be approached by the hallway. There were no mailboxes, signs, or anything else to tell me who lived in the house. With shaking hands, I knocked on the first door.

I stood in the still hallway, listening to the hushed sound of other people's lives around me and trying to hear any movement behind the door. I knocked again for good measure before moving on to the next door.

Before my fist struck the wood panel, the door flew open. A hatless Matt Kimball stood in the doorway, a darkened room behind him.

I forced a smile. "Hello, Mr. Kimball. I'm Laura Truitt. We met at church."

"Of course. Not a person I am likely to forget." He separated his lips, showing the bottom edges of his teeth, in an apparent smile. "What brings you to my door?"

I decided to be blunt, not really wanting to prolong any conver-sation with him. "I understand you have information regarding my daughter."

He nodded. "Ah yes. I am surprised it took you this long." He re-mained in the doorway, making no move to invite me in.

"I wasn't able to come any sooner." I deliberately shifted my gaze over his shoulder. "May I enter so we can talk?"

He raised his eyebrows, and I knew I had crossed the boundary of propriety. But I didn't want to think about that. I needed the information about Annie and would get it any way I could.

With a mocking grin, he moved back. "Why, of course."

The stench of sweat and unwashed sheets hit me and I immediately regretted my decision. Resisting the impulse to cover my nose with my hand, I glanced around for a place to sit and was horrified to find the only furnishings consisted of a bed and a chest of drawers. A scrawny black cat sat upon the grimy pillow and acknowledged my presence with a bored yawn. The back of my nose tickled, calling to mind my cat allergy.

I stayed with my back against the closed door and tried to appear calm. He didn't step back, but remained directly in front of me, so close I could see specks of food on his collar.

"Mr. Kimball." I swallowed hard, trying not to sneeze or choke on the filthy air. "I heard you had news of my daughter."

He looked confused for a moment and then a grin slipped over his face. "Oh yes. Now I remember. Your daughter." He leaned toward me with an outstretched arm, bracing his hand on the door behind me.

I didn't flinch but surreptitiously felt behind me for the doorknob. I looked up at him expectantly. "My daughter disappeared on Moon Mountain when she was two and I haven't seen her since. I heard you might know something about that."

He leaned nearer to me, his stale breath washing over me. "And just what did you have in mind as payment?" His gaze shifted to my chest and insolently traveled back to my face.

I had had my doubts about Mr. Kimball, but I had never once anticipated this turn of events. "Payment? You want payment for telling me about my own daughter? Believe me, Mr. Kimball, I have no intention of paying you for anything in the manner you are insinuating." I pressed my back against the door, my hand clutching the cold brass knob.

"Why else would a woman come alone to a man's room?"

My fists clenched in rage, and I struck out without thinking. I managed to clobber him on both sides of the head, making him reel backward. I was sure it was more from the shock of a woman hitting him than from any pain I might have caused. Regardless, it gave me the opportunity to twist the knob and run out into the foyer. He had made it to his doorway by the time I reached the outer door. I yanked it open and ran outside and down the short flight of steps to the pavement. I looked back at the rooming house in time to see the front door slam shut.

My breath came in deep gulps of air, and I noticed to my dismay that a thick strand of hair had fallen from my upsweep and dangled in front of my face. I raised my hands to fix it, and at that moment noticed Miss Eliza Smith on the sidewalk, stock-still and staring directly at me.

Her pinched face had the eerie resemblance to an apple that had been on the ground too long. I would have laughed if I weren't so shaken, and if I hadn't realized that whatever she thought she had seen would be quickly transported back to Stuart.

"Eliza, it's not what you think. . . ."

But before the words were out of my mouth, she had turned without acknowledging me and walked quickly away, her wide skirts billowing around her like a circus tent.

A gust of wind struck me as swirls of leaves danced around on the sidewalk. I glanced at the front window of the rooming house and saw the black cat watching me, its feline eyes blinking slowly. I stared back, despair mixed with determination. I wasn't through with Matt Kimball. If he did indeed know something about Annie, I would find out. I had to.

I drove back to Phoenix Hall as quickly as I could. I needed to do a great deal of damage control before Eliza had a chance to wag her tongue. Thankfully, Stuart was away. At least I had time to get Julia firmly on my side before he returned. I pushed those thoughts aside, and as I sped through town, my mind drifted to thoughts of a little girl with strawberry blond hair and freckles across her nose, and of the daughter that seemed so near but so far away.

The house was deathly silent as I entered. I called for Julia but received no answer. I was about to head out back toward the kitchen when the sound of singing came from the dining room. I dropped the baskets on the floor in the hall and went in search of the voice.

Sukie was in the dining room, standing on one of the chairs while attempting to swipe the dust off the crystal chandelier with a feather duster.

"Do you know where I might find Julia?"

She nodded and pointed with the feather duster. "She be out back in the kitchen, messin' with her herbs."

I thanked her, but before I walked away, I thought of something else. I turned around to make sure we were alone in the room and then walked toward her, keeping my voice low.

"I was wondering if you could help me with something."

She peered over a chandelier stem at me. "Yes?"

"I need to know how I'm supposed to manage these hoops without embarrassing myself. I swear I just about show everything under my skirt every time I attempt to sit down."

She raised her eyebrows but nodded as she stepped down and pulled out another chair.

"Stand right here."

I moved myself into position.

"Now back yourself up slowly. Now sneak your hand on top o' the metal hoop at the top of your leg. That right, you doin' real good, Miz Laura. Now pull it up gentle-like and sit. There?"

I was amazed that I had managed to sit in the chair without mishap. I smiled my thanks and stood. As she leaned over to pick up my chair and replace it under the table, the chain around her neck with the red flannel bag I had noticed before slipped out of her dress.

Sukie must have realized what I was looking at, because her fingers immediately flew to the bag. She covered it with her hand as if to protect it.

"What is that?" I stepped toward her.

She took a step backward as I approached. "Ain't nothin', Miz Laura."

I stopped, confused at her reaction. The sound of footsteps from behind caused me to turn around. Pamela lurked in the doorway, her arms folded in front of her.

"It is a charm necklace, Laura. Sukie has powers, apparently. That little pouch carries all sorts of things, like frog bones, snakeskin, ashes. Right, Sukie?"

Sukie stared down at the floor while she hastily stuck the bag back into her dress.

Pamela continued. "Such foolishness, what these people bring with them from Africa. I really do not understand how Julia can allow it. I have tried to talk to her, but she has a mind of her own."

Sukie excused herself and left the room without looking up.

Pamela's dark eyes coolly appraised me. "I would be careful around her. That is a powerful charm around her neck."

I couldn't tell whether she was being serious. "I'll be sure to be very careful, then." I hoped my words would placate her, as I had no desire to get into an argument with her regarding superstitions. I had it on good authority that magic was very real. I made a move to leave.

"Yes. You be careful, Laura. Be very careful. Your hold on the Elliotts is tenuous at best. I would behave myself if I were you."

I stopped and stared at her, waiting for her to say something else. Instead she swept past me in a rustle of silk and climbed up the stairs.

An uneasy feeling settled in my stomach as I wondered if Pamela had somehow already heard about my visit to Matt Kimball. Slowly, I walked out to the kitchen house in search of Julia.

Julia had removed her hoops and donned a work dress and was busily crunching something with her mortar and pestle. Without looking up, she greeted me by name.

"Hello, Julia." Eager to get this conversation over with, I blurted, "I'm afraid I've done something that might be deemed . . . inappropriate."

She bent to rub her chin on the shoulder of her dress, and continued her work with the mortar.

I continued. "I met with Matt Kimball in his room at this boardinghouse."

She stopped, the mortar paused in midair. "You did what with Matt Kimball?"

I shook my head quickly. "It's not what you think. I overheard Stuart telling your mother that Matt Kimball had information on my daughter. But when Stuart never approached me with it, I figured I had to do something on my own. I used the opportunity today to seek him out."

Her hand shook slightly, her face now the color of the pestle. "Did he tell you anything?"

"No. He wanted . . . payment."

She laid the mortar down and gripped the table with both hands. "I see. Did anyone see you enter or leave?"

I bit my lip, feeling like a scolded child. "I'm afraid so. Eliza Smith saw me as I was leaving. I'm sure I appeared disheveled—"

Julia interrupted, her expression worried. "Did he . . . hurt you?"

"Not that he didn't try, but no. I guess it was foolish of me to go into his room."

She closed her eyes and shook her head. "And Eliza of all people." She looked at me again. "I understand how desperate you are for information about your daughter, but you must be more careful with your reputation in future. Do not worry. I will speak to Eliza and try to undo any damage that she might have already caused." She pursed her lips together. "My main concern at the moment is how we should tell Stuart. You know he will be furious."

"Furious enough to arrest me? He'll believe I went to see Matt for other reasons."

Julia's voice was quiet. "I do not know if he would do that. The man has feelings for you, Laura. You would have to be blind not to notice." She returned to the mortar, rhythmically crushing its contents in an even, circular motion, and slipped a quick glance in my direction. "But I have known him to put duty and obligation over his heart before. I will see what I can do."

I tried to ignore the flush of heat creeping up my cheeks. "Do we need to tell him at all?"

She nodded without looking at me. "Yes. Most likely he will know before he returns. Gossip travels swiftly, I am afraid."

I stepped closer to her, the sharp smell of the crushed herb stinging my nose. "I'm telling you the truth about why I went to see Matt. I wasn't passing on information or anything. I just wanted to make sure you knew that."

Her left hand reached out and settled softly on mine. "I know, Laura. I believe you."

She put down the mortar and began scooping the contents into a glass jar. Turning to me, she added, "Besides, we need to tell Stuart so he can get the information from Matt himself. Stuart has means of persuasion not available to us that he can use if he needs to."

Julia reached for some dried herbs hanging upside down from the ceiling. "Matt's been a troublemaker for years. I cannot help but wonder where he got information about your daughter." She paused to look at me. "Have you remembered anything more yet? Anything about where you came from or how you ended up here?"

I met her eyes, surprised at how easy lying had become to me. "No. Nothing more."

She nodded, and then with a large kitchen knife she chopped off small chunks of the root portion of one of the herbs and placed these into the mortar. She picked up the pestle, but I stopped her.

"Julia, let me. Perhaps I might even learn something." She smiled and let me take her place. "How did you ever learn all you know about plants and herbs? I can hardly tell the difference between rosemary and a rose."

Her cheeks pinked with a becoming show of pleasure. "Pamela taught me everything I know. She started teaching me when I was still very young."

"Hmm," I murmured. "I somehow can't picture Pamela communing with nature."

"Mama is a wonderful healer. I think she derives pleasure in the power it gives her."

"Yes, I can certainly understand that."

I crushed the plant with the pestle, quickly grinding it into a powder. The rhythmic thumping was like a soothing mantra, and I could feel the calming effects.

The powder smelled strange, and I took a pinch to bring it to my nose to get a better sniff.

Julia moved so fast, I didn't know what was happening until it was all over. She hit my hand, knocking it out of the way and causing me to tip over the mortar. It somersaulted through the air, throwing out powder in great puffs, and landed on its side with a solid *clunk*. I stared at her in surprise. She was already kneeling on the kitchen floor and trying to salvage what she could of the white powdery substance.

"I'm sorry," she said. "I thought you were about to taste it. It is hellebore root—very poisonous."

I bent down next to her and began to scrape up as much of the elusive powder as I could.

"I did not mean to hit you so hard. I apologize. And I certainly did not mean to knock this over, either. It grows in the North Georgia mountains, and I have to wait for a peddler to come around with it. But I think I have enough for the tea I was going to make for one of the field hands. He has a bit of a sore throat."

I stared at her. "You're going to poison him because he has a sore throat?"

"Oh no." She almost laughed. "Using a tiny bit in a tea has wonderful soothing properties. Anything more would kill a person. And I know the difference."

"Good, then I'll let you make the tea."

I left her to her own devices and went in search of the children. I tried to have a regularly scheduled lesson time for them, but between their chores and the haphazard nature of my responsibilities, it usually came down to whenever the three of us weren't doing anything else.

Charlie's barks led me to the side yard, where I found them busily engaged in a pinecone fight. I herded the children into the library. Because my nerves couldn't handle it, I had decided to dispense with a strict lesson and instead have story hour. We stopped abruptly in the threshold, and I felt Sarah's hand tighten in mine. Pamela faced us, and I recognized some of the astronomy volumes in her hands. I remembered how Stuart had told me that they were hers, left here when she moved to Nashville.

"Sorry. We didn't mean to disturb you."

She gave us a brittle smile. "No, you did not disturb me. I was just choosing a few books to take up to my room and read. But I am done now."

The children followed me into the room and sat down on either side of me on the green velvet sofa. They sat rigid and silent until Pamela had left the room.

"Miss Laura, can you tell us the Dorothy story again?" Sarah's green eyes pleaded.

"Well, I guess that can be arranged. But as soon as I'm done, we're going to work on writing our letters. Without any complaints. Agreed?"

The blond head and the dark brown head nodded quickly in agreement.

"But first, can you sing us that song again?" asked Willie.

I knew this was more of a stalling tactic, but I went along with them. "Sure. Which song did you have in mind?"

"The one Dorothy sings about the rainbow."

"Oh yes. That's a favorite of mine."

I cleared my throat and began belting out "Somewhere over the Rainbow" in my best operatic rendition, sending both children into giggles.

I halted, the words "Why, oh, why can't I?" dying in my throat when I saw the darkening at the doorway. Pamela had returned.

Her chest rose and fell rapidly, her face a pasty white. I jumped up and grabbed her arm to bring her to the sofa. The children quickly moved away.

She allowed me to sit her down, but she knocked my hands away as I tried to unbutton the top of her dress. "No, really, I am all right. I think I just climbed the stairs too quickly." Her eyes were wild but did not leave my face.

"I think we should call the doctor. You're not looking well at all."

"No. I am fine. Really." She leaned her head back against the sofa and closed her eyes.

After a few minutes of allowing her breathing to return to normal, she stood and shakily made her way to the door. As if in afterthought, she turned around and asked, "Laura, that was a beautiful song. Where did you learn that?"

I quickly searched my head for a plausible answer. "Somewhere in my childhood, I think."

She nodded and slowly walked from the room.

The light from the window suddenly darkened, and I looked outside to see dark swells of clouds rolling in and obscuring the sun. A small smattering of raindrops hit the window as the children snuggled up next to me again. It felt so natural to be sitting there with them, in that house made for families. My thoughts turned to Stuart, as they often did, and I stared out at the storm, seeing him in it. "Be safe," I whispered, hoping that the scattering wind would carry my thoughts to him, wherever he was.

CHAPTER FOURTEEN

---◆---

Time flies over us, but leaves its shadow behind.

—NATHANIEL HAWTHORNE

During the cold, blustery evenings of December, Dr. Watkins continued to call and would sometimes bring the paper and read aloud any news of the war. This was how we found out about the fall of Chattanooga and the retreat of General Johnston's Confederate forces to Dalton, Georgia. I knew this was the beginning of the end of the war and that in the spring, Sherman would rout Johnston's army and chase them all the way to Atlanta. I looked at the faces around me, their eyes reflecting the firelight, and wondered what would become of us all when Sherman's army reached us here, as I knew they inevitably would. But Pamela would meet my gaze with her eyes' own fire, her jaws clenched. Her expression quickly returned to its controlled placidity before resuming her sock knitting—badly needed socks for Johnston's ragged army.

Zeke no longer came up to the big house—and I suspected Pamela's presence had something to do with this—so I took the children to see him at least once a week. I let down my reserve when I was with him, and it was refreshing to be out from under Pamela's watchful gaze.

On an unusually warm December afternoon, Zeke and I sat out on his front porch. The children's laughter could be heard nearby in the woods as they played hide-and-seek with Charlie. I snuggled down deeper into my shawl to keep out the chill caused by the dipping sun.

Zeke looked up at the sky where the circle of the moon near the sun could be seen. "It will be a full moon tonight."

I shivered again but not from the cold.

His face remained bland, chin tilted upward to view the sun and moon in close proximity. "Stuart is safe."

I stared at him. "How do you know? Have you heard from him? Where is he?"

"I know. The rest is not important. But he will return to you."

"To me? Don't you mean to his family and home?"

"No. To you."

I felt no embarrassment at his cool appraisal, for I recognized the truth in his words.

"Be patient with him, Laura. He understands even less than you do. Try to look past his anger and help him to trust you. He will need that trust in the months to come."

"I don't know what else I can do to win his trust."

"You will find a way. You must." He didn't say anything else, but continued to rock.

Several nights later, I tossed and turned in my bed, thinking of Zeke's words. The furniture in my room hovered about me like great hulking beasts, the room partially illuminated by the bright moon outside. I was slowly drifting off to sleep when I thought I felt a breath on my neck. I sat up abruptly, my eyes scanning the darkness. A horse whinnied outside.

I sat still until I heard the sound again. *Stuart.* I got out of bed and grabbed a shawl and silently crept down the stairs and out the front door. The night was still, bathed in the cool glow of the moon. A shadow moved near the barn, and I walked toward it.

At first I thought it was an apparition or a trick of my eyes. But when he started walking toward me, I began to run through the damp grass.

I stopped when I reached him, my breath loud and labored in the still night. I wanted him to reach for me, but he remained where he was, hands at his sides.

"You're back." My voice was winded from running.

"So it would appear."

Belatedly, I realized how ridiculous I must look. "I've been worried. I . . ." I stopped, wishing I could read his face, but it was hidden in shadow. "I'm happy you're home safe."

"Not as happy as I am sure Matt Kimball was to see you walk across his threshold."

My gut clenched. "I made a mistake."

He took a step toward me. "No. I am the one who made the mistake. I trusted you, Laura." He coughed, a dry, racking cough most likely caused by nights sleeping outside in the cold rain. "I am only surprised to find you still here."

I looked at him calmly, pushing away the growing anger. "If you will just give me the chance to explain . . ."

He coughed again. "Explain how you and Matt are working together? And then you went to his rooms unaccompanied? Your reputation in this town—"

"My reputation?" I no longer tried to keep my voice quiet. "Who cares about my reputation? I only went to see him to get information about Annie—information you were supposed to find out about and never did. I overheard you talking with Pamela. Didn't you think it important enough to tell me?"

He moved quickly, placing his hand over my mouth, his other arm reaching around me. He smelled of leather and wood smoke, and I tried desperately not to notice how good it felt to be close to him again.

His voice caressed my ear. "I went to see him about it, but he had left town. Why do you think I took so long to go on my trip? I was waiting for him to return. But I needed to leave. I wanted to talk to him myself before I told you. I do not trust the man and believe that he is merely thinking of a reason to talk with you." He dropped his hand from my mouth. "Assuming, of course, that you were unaware of his motivations."

I pulled away from him. "Of course I was unaware of his motivations. Do you think I would have willingly put myself in a position to be . . . ogled by that man?"

Stuart gripped both my shoulders, the scratchy wool of my shawl digging through the thin nightgown. "Did he touch you?"

"No. But I'd be lying if I said I hadn't considered it if I truly believed he knew anything about my daughter."

He shook me none too gently. "Don't ever say that again. Not ever. I do not want you to even glance in his direction; do you understand?

I will deal with him." His hands tightened on my arms. "I will find out why you went to see him, Laura. And I hope, for all our sakes, that he has information about your Annie."

I balled my hands into fists and pushed against his chest. "I don't answer to you, Stuart Elliott. And I will find my daughter with or without your help."

He released his grip on me. "So be it. But do realize that there will be consequences if you disobey me again. I have told you before. These are dangerous times."

I bowed my head, staring at my bare feet beneath my nightgown, their whiteness like glowing rocks in the sea of grass. "Yes, they are."

He touched my chin and brought my face up again. "What are you afraid of, Laura? Why will you not let me help you? I could take hearing that you are a Yankee spy. It is the not knowing that is killing me in small measures."

I wanted to tell him then, to ease the tension between us. But the less I told him, the thinner the bond between us, and the easier it would be to say goodbye. I shook my head, missing the feel of his touch as he moved his hand away.

His words were curt, abrupt. "Go back to bed, Laura. You will catch your death out here."

I turned to leave and felt the shawl slip from my shoulders. He bent to pick it up, then moved nearer to drape it on me again. He wrapped his arms around me as he settled it over my back, but he didn't move away. His breathing was warm and heavy on my cheek and I made the mistake by turning to see him clearly in the moonlight.

His lips covered mine before I had a chance to read what was in his eyes. His arms tightened behind me until I felt the buttons of his jacket pressing against my chest. My arms, seemingly of their own accord, went around his neck as I stood on my toes for a deeper kiss, feeling the rough stubble of his unshaven chin. The shawl slid again onto the grass as Stuart's hands moved over the cotton of my nightgown, molding to the curves of my back and hips.

He pulled back suddenly, his eyes wide, a question stalled on my lips. "I am sorry. I am so sorry." He rubbed his hands over his face. "I am no different than Matt Kimball."

I stared back at him, the blue shadows from the moon accentuating the planes of his face. "Yes, you are." My fingertips brushed the stubble on his chin. "I wanted you to touch me."

His breath grew white in the night air, and I watched it rise toward the sky. "Not as much as I wanted to touch you."

Two worlds separated us, his and mine, and suddenly I was afraid of what might happen should they collide. I felt for a moment as if I held the country's fate in my hands.

A horse whinnied from the barn. I turned away and scooped up my shawl, my fingers fumbling as I attempted to tie the ends in a knot. "Good night, Stuart." I didn't look back.

I started for the house, listening for his words, but he remained silent. But I knew his eyes followed me until I entered the house.

Heedless of my wet footprints, I ran across the foyer and up the stairs. As I reached my bedroom door, I heard a soft *click* from somewhere in the house. I knew it wasn't Stuart, or I would have heard him follow me. I silently opened my door and slipped inside. Still chilled by the night air, I left my shawl on and crawled into the cotton sheets, shivering as their coolness touched the bare skin on my legs.

I stretched out, hearing my spine pop as I pointed my toes and reached my hands over my head, yawning in the process. My foot hit something in the bottom of the bed, something that hadn't been there before. I reached down and pulled it out from under the covers. I didn't need a candle to see what it was. The smooth pouchlike feel was enough. A pungent herbal odor emanated from the soft cloth, almost making me nauseous. I hastily threw it on the floor, eager to get it away from me. What was Sukie's charm bag doing in my bed? I had no idea, but would certainly find out in the morning.

I awoke to the feel of someone bouncing on my bed. Full daylight flooded my room, telling me it was at least midmorning. Sarah was eagerly jostling me awake, and enjoying it immensely, to judge by the grin on her face. I had no idea what time I had finally fallen asleep, but from the numbness of my head, I hadn't been asleep for long. Still, I was embarrassed to have slept so late.

"Miss Laura, Miss Laura! Time to get up! We are slaughtering Mr. Porker today!"

I glanced at her, dubious of the apparent joy at something that I was a bit apprehensive about. I threw the covers back and slowly slid out of bed.

"And Uncle Stuart's back, too. Mama told me to come up here and let you know." I felt my face redden at the thought of him and turned quickly to the washbasin.

Someone had already brought in fresh water in my pitcher, and I hastily splashed my face with the lukewarm water, hoping to make myself more alert. It did not.

"Stop bouncing, Sarah. It's hurting my head."

She stopped and gave me her most endearing smile. "All right. But if you are not downstairs in two shakes, I am coming back up to bounce on your bed and make your head hurt again."

I pretended to threaten her with my hairbrush as she raced from the room, her mock squeals descending with her down the stairs.

As soon as she left, Sukie came in. Seeing her, I immediately thought of the pouch I had found in my bed. I raced over to the side of the bed where I had thrown it. The floor was empty.

"Where is it?"

"Where what is, Miz Laura?"

I scrutinized her face, but her bland expression hid all thoughts.

"Your charm bag," I said, starting to feel annoyed.

She reached for the rope around her neck and pulled out the familiar red pouch. "It be right here. I never take it off 'cept when I sleep."

"Well, it was here last night—in my bed. I threw it on the floor and now it's gone."

Her eyes widened and her hands tightened on the bag. "No, ma'am. Not this one. It be where I left it last night."

"Then someone must have taken it and returned it. Who would have done such a thing?"

Her gaze darted around the room, looking at everything but me. Feeling nervous, I approached her and took her arm to make her look at me. "What does it mean, Sukie?"

Her warm brown eyes stared levelly at me. "It mean you be careful."

"Careful? Careful of what?"

"Careful of someone who do you harm."

I was losing patience with this line of conversation. "I don't believe that. One of the children must be playing a prank." I waved my hand in dismissal, wishing I could dismiss my uneasy thoughts just as easily. "I don't want to talk about it anymore. What does one wear to a pig butchering?"

Later, dressed in the simple floral cotton dress that had become somewhat of a uniform for me, I descended the stairs just in time to see Pamela leaving to go into town. She made these trips at least once a week. She always insisted on going alone, and would return humming with an electric energy. I had no doubt that she was deeply involved in espionage. I had even seen her unrolling a piece of paper, presumably a secret message, from her coiled hair once. I did wonder who she went to see and if Matt Kimball were involved. Regardless of where she got the information from or who her cohorts were, it was clear that Stuart would again be needed to transmit to the Confederate Army whatever information she had gathered.

I found Stuart with two male slaves outside near the pigpen and was slightly relieved that we weren't alone. As I walked into the backyard, I saw one of the men deliver a stunning blow to the pig's head with the business end of a mallet. A bench had been set up with buckets beneath it to catch the blood, and Stuart and the other man held the animal down on top of it. The pig lay still, allowing Stuart to reach around and neatly slice its throat.

The heavy smell of fresh blood permeated the area as the animal bled to death, the thick gush of fluid in the buckets slowing down to a final drip-drop. Quickly tying the hind feet together, the two men hoisted the pig up over a kettle of steaming water. I knew this was in preparation for scraping the bristles off the hide before the animal would be disemboweled and halved. No part of the pig would be wasted. From using the bristles for brushes to stuffing the small intestines with sausage, every last morsel would be utilized in some way.

Knowing that my Christmas ham and the fresh roast pork for the following day's party was in the process of being made, I had no intention of spoiling my appetite. I wanted to go, but I was reluctant to leave. Despite the chill of the day, Stuart removed his jacket, though he kept his shirt on. He sweated in his exertion, and dark hair stuck to his forehead. He swiped his face with his sleeve, leaving spikes of hair framing his face like a crown. I grinned at his porcupine look.

He caught sight of me and approached, his face giving nothing away. "Good morning, Laura."

I swallowed quickly, my throat dry. "Morning."

"I went to town this morning to see Matt Kimball. His landlady says he has gone north to Dalton. She does not expect him back."

I met his gaze. "I guess that must mean I gave him information so important, he had to rush right off and share it." My voice cracked, but I continued. "And I bet you didn't stop to think that anything he might know about my daughter is gone with him."

Two dark eyebrows shot up. "I am not giving up on finding him. We are not done with Matt Kimball, you and I." He swiped his face with his forearm again; then, with a short nod in my direction, he returned to the business at hand.

Turning my back on the activity, I made my way toward the house. The door crashed open as I reached the steps, and Sarah catapulted into me.

"Whoa, Sarah. Slow down. What's the rush?"

"Sorry, Miss Laura. Mama sent me to find you. She wants you to help her hang the mistletoe and some other decorations for the Christmas party tomorrow."

She made to move past me, but I firmly grabbed hold of her shoulders. "Just a minute, Sarah. I don't think you need to be out back right now."

Sarah looked up at me, her eyes pleading. "But, Miss Laura, Mama's let me watch before. And I ain't scairt one bit. Besides, Uncle Stuart promised I could have the pig bladder."

"The pig's bladder? What on earth for?"

"Me and Willie like to fill it with water and throw it at each other."

"And your mother says it's okay?"

Her head bobbed up and down, her green eyes bright with excitement.

If Julia approved, I couldn't exactly stand in her way. "All right, then. But don't make a nuisance of yourself, and stay out of the men's way."

She turned to go, but I stopped her again.

"By the way. Did you or your brother take anything of Sukie's and put it in my bed?"

Her eyes stared at me with clear confusion, and I knew that she was innocent. "No, ma'am. Me and Willie would never take anything that did not belong to us."

I nodded. "Okay. You can go now." Wordlessly, she pounded down the steps.

Julia stood in the hall, a large pile of greens and white berries overwhelming the circular table in the middle of the foyer. She offered me a smile as I approached.

"I was thinking you would be the best person to tell me where to hang some of this mistletoe."

I tried to look nonplussed. "I suppose I'm as good as any."

She dropped her hands in her lap. "You can say what you want, Laura, but I happened to see two people out by the barn last night. And it did not look like they were watering horses."

"Oh." I studied the intricate pattern on the wallpaper, not wanting to face her. "I . . . We . . . That was a mistake."

Julia's eyes were warm as they regarded me. "I wanted you to know that I have spoken with Stuart. To be honest, I think he is angrier over the fact that Matt tried to touch you rather than any information about the mills you might have passed on." She picked up a clump of magnolia leaves, their shiny coating glowing dully in the dim foyer light. "But he is giving you the benefit of the doubt until he speaks with Matt." She gave me a meaningful glance. "And he does not want you going anywhere on your own again."

I leaned down and gathered a few sprigs of mistletoe. Holding one up over the door, I said, "We can hang this here for when Dr. Watkins arrives and you answer the door."

"Laura! How could you say that about Charles? He is a dear old friend."

"Ha! And you call me blind."

She shook her head as she slid a chair to the middle of the hallway. "No, Laura, I am not blind. I just prefer not to recognize it. That way, he and I can still be good friends. And besides, I am a married woman."

"Maybe we can get Charles and Eliza under the mistletoe together."

Julia laughed softly and shook her head. "What did we ever do without you?"

We spent the next hour in contented silence, with only the occasional comment as to the perfect placement of magnolia leaves on the mantels or holly arrangements on the tables. As an afterthought, I hung some of the mistletoe in the library, on the inside, over the door. I hummed to myself, trying to remember the last time I had felt any joy at Christmas.

CHAPTER FIFTEEN

———◆———

The Road goes ever on and on,
Down from the door where it began.
Now far ahead the Road has gone,
And I must follow, if I can. . . .

—J. R. R. TOLKIEN

I stared at myself in the mirror, quite pleased at what I saw. Julia had unearthed a gown that had belonged to Stuart's mother, Catherine, and, with Sukie's help, had altered it for me as a surprise. I was touched at their efforts, not to mention the fact that the dress was breathtakingly beautiful. The two women had updated the style to make it fashionable again and made the necessary adjustments so that it would fit. The bloodred velvet accentuated the darkness of my hair, which Sukie had left down with lots of loose curls and tendrils, only anchoring the sides with mother-of-pearl combs. The off-the-shoulder neckline revealed more décolletage than I thought appropriate. I kept trying to hoist the dress up until finally Julia slapped my hand away. I acquiesced to wearing a corset, and Sukie cinched in my waist to a size I was sure it hadn't been since I was eight. I felt like I was playing dress-up. And I loved every minute of it.

As Sukie was putting the last touches on my hair, a slight tapping sounded on the door. At my request, the door opened and Stuart hung back in the threshold, his expression unreadable.

"Have you come for a Christmas truce? Or are you going to just stand there and gawk?"

Sukie quickly grabbed a shawl and threw it over my shoulders while she whispered in my ear, "You don' want to spoil the surprise."

"I suppose you may call this a truce of sorts." He entered the room and placed a small black box on the dressing table in front of me. "These were my mother's, and when Julia told me you would be wearing that dress, I knew you had to wear these, too. I remember my mother wearing them together."

Curious and touched, too, I reached for the box and opened it. The beaded onyx earrings sparkled in their nest of black velvet, every bead glistening and reflecting the candlelight. I picked them up and jiggled them to catch them in full effect. I swallowed deeply and searched his eyes in the reflection of the mirror. "Stuart, these are wonderful. Thank you." I slipped the posts into my pierced ears and shook my head at the mirror, hearing the slight clicking as the beads bumped into each other.

"Allow me." Sukie stepped back as Stuart leaned over and plucked the matching necklace out of the box and placed it on my neck. The cool beads chilled my throat, but his hands were warm where they rested on my skin while he fastened the necklace. I caught his reflection in the mirror, making me think of a parallel universe. Perhaps Stuart, and these people who now filled my life, had always lived behind the glass, their warm flesh blocked by its coldness and only accessed by the most inexplicable of events.

"You look beautiful, Laura."

"Thank you." I turned my attention to his clothes, the same ones I had seen him in earlier. "Shouldn't you be getting dressed yourself?"

"Yes, ma'am. I will see to it right away." Bowing formally, he walked out of the room, almost bumping into Julia on the way in.

"Laura, you look absolutely stunning."

"You're not so bad yourself," I said, admiring her powder blue silk with the noticeably higher neckline covered with a lace fichu.

Julia caught sight of my earrings and touched one delicately with her fingers. "These were Catherine's."

"Yes, I know. I hope you don't mind me wearing them."

"Of course not. They are not mine, anyway. They were given to Stuart by his mother before she died—not to William. His mother intended that they should go to Stuart's wife."

"Oh," I said, unsure of what that meant. I looked at Julia's expression in the mirror and caught a slight grin.

Sukie excused herself and then reappeared with a tray and two glasses of red wine. "Miz Catherine always say a glass of wine afore a party to soothe the nerves," she said, handing Julia and me a glass of what I knew to be from one of the quickly diminishing bottles from the wine cellar.

I took a sip and immediately felt the warmth traveling through my veins. "This will help my nervousness."

Julia sat on the edge of the bed. "You will be the belle of the ball. Do not allow any mean-spirited people to spoil your fun. You have been through a lot, and I daresay you deserve to have a little fun."

She drained her glass and reached for my empty one. "And it is time for our guests to arrive. Would you be so kind as to receive with me?"

I nodded and stood on shaky legs. I caught Julia eyeing me with a worried expression. "Maybe you should not have any of my punch, either. You will need every ounce of strength to fight off all the men tonight. Well, maybe not all of them," she added with an uncharacteristic smirk.

I smirked right back at her. "Oh, I think I hear the good doctor downstairs. I will make sure to shove you both under that bough of mistletoe in the dining room."

Julia looked genuinely shocked. "You would not dare!"

Seeing my smile, she gently took my arm in hers and led me out the door.

There was a murmur of male voices that conspicuously stopped as Julia and I appeared at the top of the stairs. Stuart and Dr. Watkins openly stared. Feeling self-conscious, I glanced behind me to see what they were looking at, only to have Julia elbow me in the ribs.

We descended slowly, my hand gripping the banister to steady my wobbly legs. I made a mental note to avoid any further alcoholic beverages for at least another hour. At the bottom of the steps, Stuart took my hand and bent over it, kissing it gently. I felt a small electric shock, and wondered if anybody else had noticed.

"Are you all right, Laura? Your face is all flushed." His broad grin belied his concern.

"It's just the wine. And the realization that what they say is true."

He quirked a dark eyebrow. "What who says is true?"

"About men in uniform." I was brazenly appraising him now, my boldness empowered by the wine. I had never seen him in full dress uniform and it was indeed a magnificent sight. His tall, lean form was well suited to the gray knee-length frock coat with black facings and trimming. The gilt buttons gleamed in the bright light of the foyer but did not outshine the resplendence of the braided trim of his rank on the cuffs and collar. Around his slim waist he wore a narrow red silk sash under his waist belt, and his broad shoulders accentuated the masculine line of the coat. My knees felt weak, and I wasn't sure if it was from the wine.

"It must be the jacket," he said, straightening both arms in front of me so I could admire the handiwork. "Julia made it."

I felt a quick pang dimming the excitement of the evening for just a moment. Before I could respond, Sukie opened the front door, allowing in a cold blast of air and the first guests. I recognized Eliza Smith along with her mother and sisters from the endless meetings of the Ladies' Aid Society. These meetings consisted mostly of interminably rolling bandages and listening to idle gossip about other townspeople. I had found no information there about Annie and would just resign myself to two hours of fending off questions from the well-meaning ladies.

All four women nodded to me, Eliza staring at my neckline, her lips pursed in a show of displeasure. Stuart fussed over her and took her wrap and gallantly kissed her hand. She bristled with the pleasure of it and blushed becomingly.

I recognized most of the guests from the Presbyterian church and from my excursions into town. They were all exceedingly polite to me but slightly aloof, for which I did not blame them. Most of them had lived in Roswell all their lives, as had their parents. I was an outsider, a stranger of unknown origins.

Pamela appeared, her eyes raking over my outfit without comment, before turning on her social face and becoming the gracious hostess with Julia.

The mingled scents of perfume, smoked ham, and fresh pine danced eagerly through the rooms, delighting the senses. All the faces reflected a genuine gaiety, obliterating all thoughts of war and suffering, at least for one evening. Eliza and I took turns at the piano, and I was quite impressed at her repertoire, if not her habit of thumping on the keys.

The furniture in the parlor and hall had been pushed against the wall, and several of the guests used the space for dancing.

Stuart claimed me for a waltz and, despite my protests of not knowing how to dance, swept me up in his arms. I managed to stay off his toes and follow his lead, most likely due to the fact that he was an accomplished dancer. His leg had nearly completely healed, his limp almost imperceptible as he effortlessly led me through the steps. He waltzed me down the hall and into the library, where a single candle glowed, its reflection softly illuminated in the glass of the window.

"I believe we just passed under some mistletoe," he said, his lips close to my ear.

I pulled away slightly. "You wouldn't want to be accused of consorting with the enemy."

"Shh," he whispered in my ear. "Truce, remember?"

He bent his head nearer mine, then stopped. "May I kiss you?"

I answered by standing on my toes and touching my mouth to his. His lips were warm and full, his tongue pushing my own lips apart. Immediately my arms went around his neck, and his arms around my back, his fingers splayed wide.

His hands caressed my back through the soft fabric of the dress. "I have been waiting all evening to find you under the mistletoe." His lips traveled to the bare skin of my shoulder, causing gooseflesh to ripple up my skin.

"Me, too," I murmured as I tilted my head back farther. "But I was afraid you wouldn't. Now I'm afraid that you'll stop, like you did the last time. And I'm afraid . . ." I wanted to say "afraid that you'll mean too much to me," but I stopped.

His fingers lingered on my neck as his eyes searched mine. "What is this between us, Laura?" He paused for a moment, the music, laughter, and disembodied voices flooding the space between us. "Since the moment I first saw you, it was . . . as if I have always known you. As if there was not a time in my existence in which I did not know you."

I remembered the feeling of familiarity I had felt when I'd first looked into his eyes on Moon Mountain and knew that no matter how I tried to push him away, there was a connection between us. A connection that had nothing to do with linear time.

I thought I heard someone calling my name from outside the room and Eliza's voice saying I was in the library, but I quickly dismissed them from my mind to concentrate on the feel of Stuart's lips on mine and the thickness of his hair under my fingers.

"Miss Laura!" My head snapped up and I quickly disengaged myself.

Sarah stood in the threshold, her eyes wide. "Mama needs you right now. There's something wrong with Robbie."

After a reluctant look back at a slightly disheveled Stuart, I followed her out of the room and up the stairs to the master bedroom. Julia sat on the bed, Robbie cradled in her arms. His weak cries sounded like a wounded puppy's, not like his usual lusty wails. His face was flushed slightly, with pinkened cheeks and glazed eyes.

As I approached the bed, she pulled the baby's gown up over his abdomen and lifted a pudgy leg. "Would you please take a look at this, Laura?"

I stared at the round mark on the back of Robbie's thigh. "Did something bite him?"

"I am not sure. I thought you might know."

I examined the mark more closely and determined that it wasn't a bite because there seemed to be no holes marring the surface of the skin. "Me? Why would you think that?" I sat down next to her on the bed, my hand stroking Robbie's warm cheek. His fretting subsided slightly.

Julia looked at me. "You are so smart." She lifted her hand to halt my objections. "No, you do not know much about sewing and gardening. But you always seem to figure out the right thing to do."

"Have you called for Charles to come up?"

"Not yet. I called for you first."

"I really think we need a doctor here." Turning to Sarah, who had brought me upstairs, I said, "Go get Dr. Watkins, please. And ask him to bring his bag, if he has it with him."

I placed the back of my hand across Robbie's forehead and felt the fever burning his skin.

There was a soft tapping on the door and the doctor entered, followed by Sarah. With a brief nod to Julia and me, he took the baby from Julia's arms and laid him on the bed. Robbie started whimpering again as the doctor lifted his gown and prodded his abdomen. Robbie emitted a hoarse howl as the doctor tried to pry his mouth open to examine his throat and then continued to protest as Dr. Watkins ran his fingers over the glands in Robbie's neck.

Pamela appeared at the door. "Julia, what is wrong?" She glided into the room, her black silk gown swooshing across the floor and trailing the scent of a musky perfume.

Her gaze not leaving the baby, Julia answered her mother. "Robbie has a fever. I just want Charles to have a look at him."

Pamela leaned over the doctor while he examined Robbie. "He is flushed. I will go prepare some wintergreen tea to bring down the fever." She left as suddenly as she had appeared, her heels tapping across the hallway.

Turning the baby over, the doctor paused as he caught sight of the mark on the leg, and he stretched the discolored skin between his thumb and forefinger.

"What is it, Charles?" Julia asked, reaching for Robbie.

The doctor scratched his chin and looked at Julia and then me. "It appears to be diphtheria. Little Rosa Dunwody has also come down with it this week."

I knew eight-year-old Rosa and her mother from the Ladies' Aid Society meetings. Rosa and Sarah were great friends. But I was even more familiar with the name diphtheria.

"Are you sure?"

"Yes, I am sure. But with good care, we can make him well." He pulled Robbie's gown back in place. He continued. "The best way to treat it is give him plenty of rest, keep him comfortable, and try to get his fever down. I suggest a camphor rub on his chest to help him breathe, and for those tending him to wear a lump of camphor around their necks to ward off the vapors of the disease." He started to close his bag. Then, nodding in my direction, he added, "Make sure everyone who comes in contact with him washes her hands thoroughly. And that includes all of you here before you return to the party. I have heard talk from battlefield surgeries about these germs. Perhaps there is some truth in your theory."

Almost shocked at the doctor's concession to my obsession with clean hands when tending the sick, I let his Dark Ages comment about vapor-killing camphor pass unremarked. But I certainly had no intention of wearing the foul-smelling stuff anywhere on me.

"Most importantly," I interjected, "we need to keep him separated from the other children."

Dr. Watkins bristled. "I really do not see the need—"

"Please, Charles," Julia said softly. "Do as Laura says. Remember how she saved Robbie." Julia handed the baby to me. "I am going to go help my mother. I will also find Sukie and have her keep an eye on him, because I want you to return to the party and play hostess for me."

"Actually, I should let everyone know that Robbie has diphtheria so they can be on the alert for symptoms in any of their own family members. I'm afraid with such a contagious sickness in the house, we should ask the guests to leave."

Julie studied me for a moment, then nodded. "You are right, of course. Would you please take care of that for me?"

"Are you sure I can't be more help here?" I asked, cradling the baby and feeling his sweat-soaked gown.

She smiled, although I saw the strain around her mouth. "This is not the first child I have ever nursed through a fever. I just need to give him some of the tea Pamela prepared to lower his fever and get him settled. I will be fine."

I thought I caught a glint of something in her eye, but she gave me a warm, comforting smile. "Really, Laura, Robbie will be fine. All children get sick. Between Charles, my mother, and me, we will have him crawling like a june bug in no time."

My tongue seemed to thicken in my mouth. In my time, most children were vaccinated against diphtheria. I knew I had been inoculated, as had Annie. But here, in this time, there was no such protection. Children and their parents were subject to the whims of virulent diseases that randomly plucked children from their parents' arms and laid them in small graves.

Turning, Julia opened the door, and the sounds of garbled voices and laughter could be heard from below, climbing the stairs and pulling me toward them. The doctor followed her out, and the sound of their footsteps descended the stairs. Shortly afterward, Sukie came to take Robbie.

I handed him over just as Sarah, who had remained silent in a corner of the room, approached. "Will he be all right, Miss Laura?"

I laid my hand on her blond head. "Your mama certainly seems to think so. We'll just have to do everything we know how to get him better, and that would include playing quietly when you're inside so you don't wake him up. The doctor says he needs his rest."

She looked down into the little bundle cradled in Sukie's arms and then kissed him.

I pulled the baby away. "No, Sarah. Please don't. You could get his germs and get sick, too."

Her eyes widened with fear.

"I'm sorry, Sarah. I didn't mean to scare you. But I want to keep you healthy." I gave her a hug and propelled her out of the room. "I think it would be best if you stayed away from other people until we know you're not infected. Go ahead and get ready for bed and I'll come up to say good night." She gave me a somber look and then walked slowly down the hall to her room, her feet dragging in an exaggerated way with each step.

I wanted to give the partygoers a few last minutes of peace and joy, so I slipped out the back door and walked toward the fallow cotton fields, the earth cold and brittle in the December winds. Bright stars and a quarter moon brought relief to the inkiness of the night and I moved my face toward the frigid wind.

"Laura."

I turned to see Zeke, who had been standing in the shadow of the oak tree as I approached.

"Good evening, Zeke. Why aren't you with the party?"

"Too many people for me. I have made an appearance for Julia's sake, and now I think I will go back home. I need to make a root poultice for Robbie's neck."

But still he stood, not making as if to leave. He pointed toward the sky. "Can you see the Little Bear?"

I tilted my head back and stared up at the icy black sky. "Do you mean the Little Dipper?" I asked, recognizing one of the few constellations I was familiar with.

"Yes. If you let your eyes follow along the handle, you can see the polestar."

"It's the very bright one, isn't it?"

He nodded slightly, still looking upward. "The polestar has been used throughout the centuries by navigators for charting their routes." He was now looking directly at me, as if to convey a meaning to his casual conversation.

"Zeke, are you trying to tell me something?"

"Nothing that you do not already know. Just reminding you to use the skies and your heart to guide you home." Very silently, he said good night and began to walk toward the woods.

"Good night, Zeke," I called after him. I saw him raise an arm and wave before he was enveloped in darkness. My nose hairs froze as I breathed in the winter air.

My hands felt numb from the cold so I turned to go back in. I heard the faint notes of the piano tinkling "Dixie." Despite the liveliness of the tune, I felt a deep and abiding sadness. The lives of these people would soon be irrevocably altered. History had already decried that their way of life would be gone forever, as would many of their sons, brothers, and husbands. But what if I could change that, save one life? I shook my head, focusing on my house and Annie. I had to get back soon, before it was too late and I foolishly interfered with fate.

The wind carried scattered voices past my ears, and I listened as if I were hearing them across the passage of time. The back door opened, and I recognized Stuart's form silhouetted against the light spilling from inside. I could feel his eyes on me, like a beacon on the dark sea, guiding me home. He waited for me as I picked up my skirts and walked toward him.

CHAPTER SIXTEEN

And thus the whirligig of time brings in his revenges.
—WILLIAM SHAKESPEARE

I awoke to the smell of smoke. Jumping out of bed, I ran to the door and was relieved to find it cool to the touch. I cracked it open and stuck my head out to investigate but found no flames, only the pervasive smell of smoke.

I hastily returned to the bed to wake Sarah, who had been moved into my room when Willie had come down with swollen glands and fever. Despite her children's illness, Julia continued to stay unalarmed and infuriatingly calm, but her face now held a pinched, strained look. But it must have worked, because I did not feel panicked. Robbie didn't seem to be getting any better, but he didn't seem to be getting any worse, either. Dr. Watkins had told us that the disease would climax in about ten days and then we should see a change.

Every night I remembered to close my curtains tight, just in case there would be a full moon to scare Sarah, so I stumbled in the dark to the window and threw open the curtains to peer out. I didn't see anything, but smelled the heavy scent of smoke in the air. "Sarah. Get up," I said as I knotted a shawl around my shoulders. She groggily rolled back over into her pillow, and I had to pick her up and get her off of the bed so I could remove the blanket. Just in case.

I ushered her out into the hallway. "Fire!" I shouted, deciding to err on the side of caution, even if no flames were detected. Julia emerged from the sickroom, the bundled form of Robbie in her arms.

"Can Willie walk?" I asked. She shook her head as I strode past her and picked up Willie. He had a slight frame and I estimated he could weigh no more than fifty-five pounds. Light enough to carry—if not for very far.

"Sukie! Stuart!" Shuffling feet sounded from downstairs and the flickering light of a candle illuminated Sukie as she poked her head up the stairwell. Stuart's door opened from the other end of the hall and he emerged, hastily buttoning up his shirt. Pamela ran out of her room, her hair unbound and flying wildly about her thin face.

Heavy wisps of smoke now floated haphazardly in the air, infusing everybody with a show of alarm. We all clambered down the stairs, Julia with Robbie in the lead, the baby protesting with thick, croupy coughs.

Sukie ran ahead and opened the front door, allowing the rest of us to take refuge on the front lawn. Leaving Willie with Julia and the children, I followed Stuart around the side of the house, in search of the smoke source.

"Damn!" I heard him swear and then I echoed him as I saw the kitchen house and the adjoining storehouse engulfed in flames. Smoke from the burning wood coated my throat while the heat licked at my face, making me step back. The surprising aroma of bacon cooking filled the air.

Three dark forms ran toward us from the direction of the slave cabins on the other side of the field. Turning abruptly, Stuart said, "Run to the barn and bring every bucket you can find. It might be too late to save the kitchen, but we might be able to salvage the storehouse."

I ran as fast as I could, ignoring the chill as I stepped away from the heat of the flames, the hem of my nightgown heavy from the moisture on the grass.

The five buckets I found were readily pressed into service as we formed a system for bringing water from the creek near the springhouse. Stuart told me to go back with Sukie and Julia, but I ignored him, knowing that every arm helping could make the difference between starvation and having enough food to get us by until the spring.

Sparks flew in every direction, and I caught Stuart's worried gaze as a stray one would shoot near the house. My muscles ached from the hoisting of the heavy buckets filled with water, but we all struggled on, black and white, fighting the common enemy.

A loud splintering split the air as the roof over the kitchen crashed down, blowing puffs of flame rolling toward us. We all ran back until

I heard Stuart's voice shouting, "The meat box! Get the meat box!" He rushed forward, disappearing in a wall of smoke and flame. My heart stuck in my throat as I stared at the spot where he had gone.

Within minutes he reappeared, dragging the meat box. One of the other men rushed to help him, pulling the precious store of food with them.

Stuart shouted at me over the din to get the other women and children to the relative warmth of the barn, which was far enough away from the flames as to pose no danger. As they ran back to the kitchen, a rumbling sounded overhead. All faces turned upward in open appeal, and were quickly rewarded with the splattering of icy-cold raindrops.

Stuart's face, awash with the light from the flickering flames, wore a crooked grin as the clouds started their onslaught, washing the black smudges from his forehead and jaw. A cry of delight went up as the flames diminished, the hissing and popping slowly dying to a low steam.

I threw my arms around Stuart, our drenched clothes sticking to each other, and I was grateful for the shawl that granted me a modicum of modesty. A bolt of lightning illuminated the sky briefly and was soon echoed by more rumbling thunder as sheets of rain fell on us, saturating hair, clothes, and earth.

Placing me gently to his side, Stuart turned to the others. "You men go on home. There is nothing else we can do tonight while it is still smoking. We will see what we can salvage in the morning." Slowly, the other men walked away, back to the dryness and warmth of their cabins. Stuart grabbed my arm and led me to the shelter of the back porch.

Growing worry gnawed at me. "Do you think there will be anything left to salvage?"

His profile was a mere shadow in the dark, but his warm breath licked at my cheek.

He shook his head. "Not much. We had just about everything in that storeroom—salt, syrup, tallow, lard, potatoes, turnips—everything. It is all gone. Luckily, most of that hog we butchered is still in the smokehouse." He lifted a hand in the darkness and wiped his dripping hair off his forehead. "But I doubt it is enough."

"Enough?" I hated that word. Although there hadn't been any Confederate requisitioning parties to deplete us further of our already-low food stores, there never seemed to be enough cornmeal, eggs, flour, meat, and medicine for the sick children. Somebody was always hungry. But when the Yankees came, in less than a year's time, there would be even less.

"Stuart." My voice cracked. "You need to send them away."

His callused fingers rubbed my skin as he cupped my face, his fingertips delicately brushing my temples. "Why? What do you know?"

A sob escaped my throat. "Because it's true—Roswell isn't safe for them. The Yankees will be here, Stuart—don't ask me how I know, but I do. You need to trust me just this once."

His fingers tightened on my skin, pushing on the hard bones of my skull. "What are you trying to tell me?"

I couldn't see him, but the tense urgency in his words gripped me like claws. I paused, knowing already the choice I had to make. My tears mixed with the rain on my face, and the pressure of his fingers increased. "The Yankees will be here, Stuart—in less than a year. Atlanta will be theirs by September. And then they'll push through Georgia to the sea, destroying everything in their path. They'll be in Savannah by next Christmas. Take Julia and the children south—to Julia's aunt in Valdosta. They'll be safe there until the end of the war."

My hands covered his and forced them away from me. He stood, facing me, his eyes glittering in the dim night. "How do you know this?" He pulled away from me. "Why are you telling me this?"

"Don't you know? I love them, too. Julia, the children, Zeke. Even . . ." I was going to say, *You, you thickheaded, stubborn man*, but I stopped, not wanting to complicate matters further. Instead, I said, "I want you all out of harm's way. I couldn't live with myself knowing that I did nothing to protect you."

His voice carried softly to me on the night air. "Tell me, then. Who are you, Laura, really? Where do you come from? How do you know these things?"

I shook my head and turned from him. "I've told you enough. I can't tell you any more. Just let me help you."

The silence between us grew heavy, the hissing of the dying fire filling the emptiness.

I shivered in my damp nightgown, my teeth chattering. Coldly, he said, "Go to bed. We do not need you catching your death out here."

Without waiting for a reply, he turned and walked off in the direction of the barn.

I was asleep before my head hit the pillow. But I didn't stay asleep long before I heard a little voice beside me. "Miss Laura? Are you awake?"

I opened my eyes to see a pair of green ones staring back at me, a warm body pressed up against mine. "Sarah?"

"Are Robbie and Willie going to die?"

I sat up, wide-awake now. For a child so young, Sarah was incredibly perceptive, and I knew better than to try to gloss over the truth. I gave her a reassuring pat to her arm.

"They're both very sick right now, but we're doing everything we know to make them get better."

"Oh." She paused for a moment. "I ain't scairt of dying, Miss Laura. I done it before."

I remained completely still, willing her to continue. When she didn't say anything else, I prompted. "You think you've died before?"

She nodded. "It was dark for a long time, and then I was here."

I stared at her in the darkness and recalled Stuart telling me about Sarah's imagination. Having no idea what to say, I just put my arm around her and hugged her.

She turned her head on the pillow and I tucked the blankets under her chin. On impulse, I kissed her forehead. "Sweet dreams." She smiled sleepily, and as I drifted off to sleep, I heard the reassuring rhythm of her breathing beside me.

The following day was Christmas Eve. Despite the war shortages, Julia had done her best to find presents for the children. She had even helped me make a few things, including a pair of socks for Stuart. With paper being such a rare commodity, the socks were tied only with a hair ribbon and hidden under my bed. I recalled the extravagant gifts that Michael and I had exchanged and knew that these socks were more a labor of love than anything I had ever given.

Sarah was already gone when I awoke, and I hastily washed and dressed. The door to the sickroom was open and I peered around the door. Sukie sat in the rocking chair, holding a gasping Robbie, and Willie was sitting up in his bed, his neck swollen, but with a big smile for me. A dry, raspy wheeze came from Robbie as his chest sucked in to get air.

Sukie looked at me, her eyes shadowed. "Miz Julia's gone get Dr. Watkins. Robbie took a turn for the worse over the night."

I laid a hand on the burning cheek. "But Dr. Watkins said that the disease will get worse before it gets better."

She nodded. "Miz Julia want the doctor here."

"Sukie, why don't you let me hold him for a while." I reached for the swaddled form. A dark-colored liquid oozed from both of his ears and nose, producing an almost overwhelming stench. Sukie handed me a wadded rag and I wiped his little face. She dipped another rag in the washbasin and laid it on his forehead. Walking over to Willie's bed, she tucked the covers snugly around him and then left the room.

A thin, grayish white membrane had grown weblike over Robbie's tonsils and was getting thicker every day. It interfered with his breathing and swallowing, making it almost impossible for him to suck milk. It was with painstaking care that we were able to feed him a drop of liquid at a time from a spoon, and even that was mostly spit back. Willie had the same thing, but perhaps because of his age, he had been able to cope with it better and was managing liquid foods. Trying to dislodge the membrane only caused it to bleed, and we realized that there was nothing we could do about it until the sickness passed and it expelled itself.

The sharp stench of camphor wafted up to my nose from the hot bundle in my arm. It was supposed to help him breathe, but I don't think it had much effect. I tried to hold him upright in an attempt to help get air in his lungs, but nothing seemed to matter. Every breath was a struggle, and he strained and kicked in his efforts but he didn't cry. It seemed almost as if he knew he needed to save his energy. I held him close and sang to him. It was the only thing I could do, and it seemed to soothe him.

Sarah hovered in the threshold, not daring to enter. It had been a week since Willie and Robbie had become sick, and Sarah still did not show any symptoms of the disease. But that didn't mean she was immune, and was kept out of the sickroom and away from her brothers. She slid down the doorframe and sat in a heap on the ground, her elbows on her knees and her chin in her hands. She smiled wanly at me, her green eyes uncharacteristically subdued.

I leaned back in the rocker, patting Robbie softly on his back, and began singing my favorite nursery song, one that I had sung to my

Annie when she was a baby and one I had not sung since the night Robbie was born.

"You are my sunshine, my only sunshine. You make me happy when skies are gray. You'll never know, dear, how much I love you. . . ."

A little voice sounded from across the room, clear and compelling, "Please don't take my sunshine away."

I stopped rocking, frozen. Robbie fussed, but I couldn't move. "Sarah, where have you heard that?"

Her clear green eyes, so much like mine, stared back at me. "From before."

My arms shook so much, I was afraid I would drop the baby. I tried to concentrate on holding him steady, but my mind turned furiously, putting all the puzzle pieces in place.

"From before?"

She nodded. "From before I died."

Robbie had fallen into a restless sleep, and I carefully carried him over to his cradle and lifted him inside. With shaking legs I walked over to Sarah and crouched in front of her. My hands cupped her cheekbones, solid and real underneath my fingertips.

Green eyes fringed with black lashes looked at me. "Why are you crying, Miss Laura?"

"I need to see your arm. Can you pull up your sleeve?" I helped her with the small buttons, then pulled up the muslin. I knew what I would see before I gently turned her arm, but it still shocked me. Her crescent-shaped birthmark was paler than mine, almost indistinguishable from a blemish except for its peculiar shape, and nearly hidden on the inside of her forearm. I thought of the times I had seen her swimming in the creek and I had never noticed. Most likely because I had never thought to look for it. I thought of Julia lying to me when I asked her if Sarah was her daughter. *She is mine.*

I hugged her tightly, so tightly that she cried out. "I'm sorry. I'm so sorry. I'm just so happy to see you." I hugged her again, gently this time, feeling her sturdy body in my arms.

The sound of horses' hooves and buggy wheels on the front drive reached us. "Julia," I said out loud. The name made me flinch, her betrayal almost more than I could stand. I looked anew at Julia's face for any signs of duplicity as she entered the room. But all I saw was her look of concern as she reached for Robbie. She laid him on Sarah's empty bed, and the doctor began his examination. He loosened the bandage that had been covering the skin ulcer on the baby's leg, wrinkling his nose at the foul odor. Eventually, he straightened and closed his black bag.

"Charles, what are you doing? There must be something you can do." Julia's voice held a frantic note in it, her fingers clutching at the doctor's sleeve.

His whole face dropped as he regarded her. Taking her hands in his, he slowly shook his head. "I am sorry, Julia. All we can do is wait and pray for a miracle."

Julia bent her head and let go of the doctor. He gave her a tender look she didn't see, then picked up his bag. "Rosa Dunwody's parents asked me to see her. I am afraid she is not doing well. I will be back here afterward."

With a brief nod to me, he left, his boots clattering on the wooden steps. Sarah scrambled down the stairs behind him. Rosa was Sarah's best friend. Children in this time learned about death much too early. I listened as Sarah called out the doctor's name, wanting to call her back but knowing I couldn't protect her from grief.

Julia sat down in the rocking chair and began the incessant rocking that all mothers of sick babies are familiar with. I sometimes even felt myself rocking in my sleep. Her expression softened as she looked at Robbie's pale face. I had seen that look before when she gazed upon Willie and Sarah. She loved all three of her children. There could never be any doubt about that. Perhaps she hadn't lied; perhaps in her heart, Sarah *was* her daughter.

I slowly rolled up my sleeve, then hesitated, unsure if she could handle my revelation. But then I thought of all the times we had spoken of my daughter, and her betrayal stung anew.

I knelt by her rocker, the smell of camphor heavy from the bundle in her arms, and spoke her name. She looked at me, her eyes like dark smudges on the white canvas of her skin, and I felt a moment of pity. Wordlessly, I held up my arm, the crescent-shaped birthmark like an island on the smooth skin of my forearm.

"My Annie has the same mark. But you know this, don't you? You've seen it before."

She continued rocking but bent her head to Robbie's. His labored breathing slid against my conscience, but still I pressed on. My pain was like a piece of fabric caught on a nail, and I kept tugging until something ripped loose.

"You knew," I whispered. "All this time you've watched me searching for my daughter, yet you knew where she was the whole time. Why?"

Tearstained hazel eyes looked at me. "You already know the answer to that, Laura. Because we both know what it is like to lose a child."

Wailing came from downstairs as the back door slammed and little feet ran up the stairs. My daughter rushed into the room, tears streaming down her cheeks, and holding her elbow.

"Mama! I fell and hurt myself real bad. It think it might be broken."

I opened my arms to her but she rushed to Julia's side, burying her face in an available patch of lap. My stomach curled, as if it had just been punched. I was just a woman she called Miss Laura. I had been relegated in her memory to a shadowy image singing her lullabies. Julia was the only mother she knew.

I stood watching Julia comforting both children while also telling Sarah to leave the room because it wasn't safe.

"She can't get diphtheria, Julia. Let her stay." Without waiting for an answer, I left.

Julia stayed in Robbie's room for the rest of the day, and I was glad, as I was not sure what I would say to her. I kept myself busy, avoiding Stuart, too. I was unsure of his complicity in Sarah's true identity, and I wasn't yet ready to face him. Not that I needed to avoid him; he was doing a good job of that on his own.

I skipped the midday meal, having no appetite, and instead ensconced myself in the parlor with a book. I had no idea what the book was, as my eyes kept blurring over the words. Sarah came in at one point, and all I could do was stare at her. She played something on the piano for me; then, after a brief peck on my cheek, she skipped off to sit in the sickroom.

I sat down at the piano, my fingers poised over the keys but unable to play. I brought my fists down on the keyboard, my raw nerves impervious to the sound. Robbie was dying, and my daughter was as gone from me now as if she, too, were being taken away from me for the second time.

"Julia has asked me to solicit your help in filling the children's stockings."

Jerking around on the piano bench, I found Stuart, a grim smile on his lips. I had forgotten it was Christmas Eve. I remembered Julia telling Sarah and Willie that although Santa would try his best to run the blockade, he might not be able to bring them very much this year. I pushed my somber thoughts aside and stood to join Stuart. I would not ask him about Sarah, not now. I needed a respite from my thoughts, and preparing Christmas for the children was all I wanted to think about.

He hammered three nails into the mantel, and then we got down to the business of playing Santa.

Zeke had carved a wooden doll with jointed limbs for Sarah. Julia and I had made two little dresses for it, and I was quite proud of my handiwork. Stuart had made a stick horse for Willie with a rare piece of tanned leather for a bridle. Robbie's stocking held only a stick of plaited molasses, and I tried to think of him enjoying it once he got better. I stepped back and smiled at our efforts, knowing how delighted the children would be. But my smile could not warm my heart.

We both turned as we heard a noise from the doorway. Julia stood in the threshold, holding Robbie and looking at me with hollow eyes.

"Is he better?" My breath stuck in my throat.

Slowly, she shook her head. "No." Her gaze circled the room, then focused on me again.

The string of popcorn I had been holding fell to the ground, scattering the white puffs to roll soundlessly on the floor. I walked over to Julia and looked down at Robbie. I imagined I heard the beating of wings and a soft brush of feathers on my cheek, and I knew he was gone.

I stroked his still-warm cheek and bent to kiss his forehead. "He looks like he's sleeping," I whispered, my voice sounding loud in the hushed room.

"He is, Laura." Julia's voice was deceptively strong, until it broke on the last word. "Would you like to say goodbye?"

I nodded, touched that she would release him to me. She kissed the smooth forehead and then handed the bundle to me. I took it, holding it gingerly at first, and then clutched it tightly to my chest.

I turned and walked out of the house to the front porch, not expecting Julia to follow. I had given him life as much as she had, an understanding between mothers.

I sat in the rocker and rocked, staring up at the unforgiving moon. The inert form in my arms felt lighter than the child I had known, as if his little life force had held all his weight and with it gone, only bones and flesh remained. The chair slid back and bumped into the house. I stood hastily, covering Robbie's head with the blanket, and then let it slide off again, realizing the foolishness of keeping the cold air off the small head. The door opened and shut behind me.

Stuart stood beside me and touched my arm. I flinched and moved away.

"Don't. Please don't touch me."

He stayed close but didn't make another move to touch me. "Julia told me about Sarah and how she came to live with us. I promise you, Laura, I did not know—not before tonight." He laid a hand on the baby's head, caressing the delicate skin. "It seems we are both capable of believing the worst about each other."

I walked away toward the railing, my footsteps hollow on the wooden floorboards. "I was thinking that maybe it would have been better if I had let Robbie die when he was born. Then you and Julia and the rest would have been saddened, but not as much as now. Now, after we've known him for so long. Now that there's something to miss."

Naked branches swayed in the December wind, and I summoned their shadows for a place to hide my heavy heart.

"But then I thought if it would have been better to have never known Annie than to stand her loss, and I realized that I would never give up one precious minute of knowing her. No matter what happens, we will always have our memories of Robbie and Annie, and no one can ever take those away from us."

He came to stand behind me, and I felt his lips on the back of my head. "Promise me one thing, Stuart. Promise me that if I go away and Sarah is still here, that you will make sure she is taken to Valdosta. Then I'll know she'll be safe."

His hands gripped my shoulders, then relaxed. "I will keep her safe, Laura. I promise you."

Turning, I buried my face in his chest, cradling the baby between us and feeling the rough wool of his coat against my cheek. His hand stroked my hair, soothing me as if I were a child. Eventually, he took the baby from me and I laid a hand on his cheek. "Thank you." I again looked at the serene white face, luminous in the light from the window, his pale lashes closed in restful sleep. I shivered, remembering Michael's face in his coffin the moment before the lid was closed.

"Did the real Sarah die?"

Stuart nodded. "Yes. Sarah had never been strong—she was born too soon and never seemed to gain any strength. Julia took her to the mountains, to a healing spring there, but she died. Shortly afterward, before Julia sent word of Sarah's death, Pamela discovered a child about the same age as Sarah on Moon Mountain, and she bore a striking resemblance to Julia's daughter. Pamela brought the child to Julia, and Julia took her in. She knew if she told the townspeople she had found an abandoned child, people might not be kind to her—perhaps speculate that she was illegitimate or unwanted." He sighed softly in the cold air, his breath gently rising in the night. "So she buried Sarah quietly and raised your Annie as her own."

He held me for a while, his body warming mine. Letting me go, he said, "It's time to go inside." Pulling out a handkerchief, he wiped my face, then led me back into the house.

I lay awake for most of the night, listening to Willie cough and straining to hear a baby's crying. But the house remained still and hushed, while the insistent ticking of the hall clock continued to mark the time minute by minute and hour by hour.

CHAPTER SEVENTEEN

The present is the ever moving shadow that divides
yesterday from tomorrow. In that lies hope.
—FRANK LLOYD WRIGHT

The black-clad figures huddled under umbrellas, the hems of skirts and cloaks liberally splashed with red clay mud. With the war now in its third year, there was no lack of black mourning clothes in Roswell.

Despite the heavy downpour, most of the townspeople gathered around the small pine coffin at Founders' Cemetery. Willie, not yet fully recovered, was the only member of the household not present. I stood back from the immediate family, uncomfortable with my place and not quite sure where I should stand. Even the dog Charlie was there, unusually subdued, and sticking close by Sarah. Zeke stood separated from the crowd and as far away from Pamela as he could get. Pamela stayed with Julia, her back rigid, her eyes dry.

Julia turned around, her eyes searching the sea of faces until they alighted on me. Walking past the other mourners, she pulled me over to stand next to her, never releasing my hand. The wind blew hard droplets of rain against our faces, and we snuggled deeply into our hooded cloaks, but Julia kept her face level, her expression set like ice, listening to Reverend Pratt's short eulogy. I would have thought she was calm except for the tight grasping of my hand and the slight trembling of her arm.

Stuart and Charles lowered the tiny casket into the dark, muddy hole, the rain thudding against the lid. Sarah wept openly as they began to shovel the rain-drenched clay over the box. I reached for her, but she buried her face in her mother's skirts, her tears mixing with the torrential rain as she shivered with the cold.

As everyone began to file out of the cemetery, I remained behind in the shelter of an oak tree, needing to be alone and gather my thoughts. The pungent aroma of wet leaves and moist earth seeped out of the ground. I sat on a cold stone bench under the tree, heedless of the wind whipping my cloak away from my body, welcoming the frigid splash of rain on my face.

If I had been sent to this place to find Annie, I had accomplished my goal. But could I, should I, bring her back home if I ever figured out how to accomplish it? She had a new family now and shared memories. The brief time she had spent with me was all but forgotten. I might do her more harm than good by bringing her with me and forcing her to leave all that she knew and held dear.

The rain stopped and only the occasional drips from the oak leaves overhead interrupted my thoughts. I heard a footfall behind me and turned to see Stuart taking off his cloak and throwing it over my shoulders. He sat down next to me, making sure our bodies did not touch.

"We were wondering where you were."

"I needed time alone to think."

"About Sarah?"

"About everything. About whether I will ever find my way home, and how I could possibly leave my daughter behind, knowing now where she is."

He regarded me calmly, his dark blue eyes still and unreadable. "Why leave, Laura? Why not stay here?"

I recalled the pictures and stories of the devastation and starvation of Reconstruction, and knew then that at the very least I had to save my daughter from that. I would take them all if I could, but I knew that wasn't possible. Besides, by virtue of the time they were born, they were made of stronger stuff than I. They would survive.

"Because I don't belong here. This was never meant to be permanent."

He stiffened next to me. "The way you pillage and burn, Laura, you must be a Yankee. You have come into our lives, our home—our hearts. And yet you would leave us without a thought."

His words were so far from the truth that I couldn't think of an answer. Instead I took his hand and brought the palm to my lips and kissed it. "I will leave with more regret than you could ever know."

He brought my hands to his own lips and kissed the tops, his fingers resting on the gold wedding band I wore on my left hand.

"Memories are not flesh and blood, Laura."

I bent toward him, seeking out his warmth in the blustery day. "No. But they're safe. They can't hurt me."

Stuart bent and plucked a sodden oak leaf from the ground and began examining the delicate veins. He tore the leaf into small pieces and then let the wind pick them off his hand, scattering them across the cemetery. "All love does not lead to loss." He picked up another leaf and held it in his open palm.

"It's certainly been my experience. I think I'll cut my losses and retire." I tried to smile but failed miserably.

He leaned over and kissed me lightly on my forehead, his breath warming my cheeks. "What has not killed you has certainly made you stronger. It has made you a lot more resilient than you would like to believe. Sooner or later you will realize that what you had with your husband and Annie is gone, never to return, no matter how much you wish it, and it is time to move on with your life."

I shook my head gently. "Even if I do, I still can't stay. I'm not meant to be here."

His face was close enough that I could see the fine lines at the corners of his eyes. "How do you know? What is it that pulls you from us?"

"There are things I cannot explain, even to myself." I looked up, as if the answers were written in the sky. "I'm still not completely convinced that this isn't just a dream."

His fingers tightened on his thighs, then relaxed. We sat in silence for a while until I reached out my hand and touched his arm, no longer able to hold in my doubts and not entirely sure I was strong enough to hear the answer.

"How could you have not known about Sarah? Surely you or her father noticed it wasn't the same child."

He raked his fingers through his hair, the rain plastering it to his head. "I was away at university, and William . . ." He shook his head.

"William never looked more than twice at his daughter. Even without the uncanny resemblance, he would never have noticed."

He let go of the leaf and we watched it drift to the ground, its tender edges buffeted about by the strong breeze. "But I promise you I never knew the truth until yesterday. And I had no reason to doubt Julia. Please do not think ill of her. She thought the child abandoned and unloved. She has never loved her any less than she did her own children."

We continued to sit and listen to the rain drip off the trees and onto the ground covering of leaves. Finally, Stuart spoke. "I have to go away again for a few days. But when I return, I am moving everyone down to Valdosta."

I reached for his hand and squeezed. "Why are you trusting me on this?"

He cupped my jaw with one hand, his fingers tight on my jawbone. Troubled blue eyes searched my face, his brows knitted together as if deciding between answers. Finally, he said, "Because of Sarah. You would keep her family safe."

I moved his hands away. "Is that the only reason?"

A shadow fell over his face, closing his gaze off from me. "It's enough of a reason."

He stood, grabbing my hand and pulling me up. His cloak fluttered about me like a big gray bird flapping its wings. His voice was quiet, the wind pulling the words toward me. "Stay with us, Laura. Make this your home."

I looked down at our feet, his worn boots half-hidden by leaves. "I can't. You don't understand."

His voice changed, his words pressing, insistent. "Then make me understand. Tell me what you are afraid to tell me. You have asked me to trust you. And I am asking you for the same."

I forced myself to look at him again, seeing his gray uniform and remembering what it stood for, understood his loyalty to a lost cause. I could see how easily he could convince me to play with history and tip the scales. By saving Robbie's life, I had already played that game and had lost. I cared too much about Stuart, about the Elliotts, to tempt fate again. "It is bigger than you think; bigger than both of us. Please, Stuart. Please don't ask me again."

He moved away abruptly, taking the warmth of his body with him. "Damn you, Laura. Damn you." Turning on his heel, he walked away, his footsteps swallowed by the soaked earth.

The wind began to blow again, bringing thick blobs of rain with it, and I shivered, feeling more cold and desolate than I ever had in my life. I turned my face to the rain, impervious to the cold wetness on my skin, and began to walk home, imagining Stuart's cloak was his arms wrapped around me.

With little food in the house and Willie still sick, the mourners had not lingered. The last buggy was pulling away as I walked up the front drive. A form rocked on the front porch, a dark smear against the white paint of the house. As I approached, I recognized Julia. She raised her head and smiled. I sat in another chair and rocked in silence, ignoring the weather, the floorboards creaking in rhythm.

She surprised me by reaching for my hand. "Thank you for my Robbie, Laura. You saved him when he was born, remember? You gave us six wonderful months with him."

I studied her face, so calm and serene, and felt only deep shame. Shame at all the times I had cursed my fate, hated having had a child so I could know what I missed.

I couldn't speak and looked at our hands clenched together, her capable fingers rubbed red and raw from the constant cleaning of the sickroom.

"Will you be taking Sarah home with you?"

Dropping her hand, I stood and walked toward the railing. "I don't know. It's all so mixed up, isn't it?" Facing her, I said, "I'm not going anywhere for the time being, so we both have time to think. To figure what's best for Sarah."

According to the astronomy books, September 1, 1864, was the next date for a comet and a lunar eclipse. That gave us nearly nine months to figure out the impossible.

"That's fair." She kept her head down, staring at her hands. "What I wouldn't give now for some cream for my skin. My grandmother would be mortified to see my hands. . . ." Her voice trailed away.

"Should we tell her?" I asked.

She stood and I saw how straight her back was, how calm her hands. But she could not hide the grief from her face. "I think we should wait. Robbie has just died, and I think it would be too much."

She tilted her head. "When Robbie and Willie were so sick, you said that Sarah couldn't get sick, too. How did you know?"

I almost told her then, how in 150 years children would be protected from diphtheria and smallpox and polio. But I stopped, my burning secret left to smolder on my tongue. "She had it before. When she was a baby."

She nodded and I watched her walk inside, the cold breeze drying my tears on my cheeks.

After a while I followed her, remembering the Christmas gift I had made for Stuart. I wanted to give it to him before he left. I raced up the stairs but paused before going into my bedroom at the sound of gagging coming from Willie's room. I rushed in to find Sukie pounding Willie on the back, a breakfast tray on its side in the middle of the bed.

"What's happening?"

"He tried to swallow some johnnycake and he started choking."

"Stop pounding him—that will only make it worse." I rushed to the side of the bed and put two arms around his middle, preparing to deliver the Heimlich maneuver. But before I could, Willie gave one last cough and a white, thick membrane shot out of his mouth, landing on the edge of the tray.

Sukie swallowed, probably to keep herself from throwing up, and I did the same. Picking up the cloth napkin, I wrapped the offending tissue in it. "Willie, I think this means you are firmly on the road to recovery. And I doubt you will ever be able to face a johnnycake again."

I retrieved Stuart's gift from under my bed, then went searching for him, half expecting that he had already left without saying goodbye. I found him in the library, facing the window. He turned as I entered, looking handsome in his uniform. His face remained blank as he regarded me, but his eyes brightened.

I stepped toward him. "Merry Christmas." I handed him the barely wrapped present.

He took it, but instead of opening it, he laid it on the desk. Reaching into his coat, he pulled out a tiny brown parcel and handed it to me. "You go first."

I sat down on the sofa and pulled open the paper. A gold filigree chain lay inside. I held it up, the intricate work reflecting the light in the room. "It's exquisite." Slowly, I lowered the necklace down on the paper. "But I don't know if I can accept it."

"I apologize if it seems too forward, Laura, but I wanted you to have it—especially now, before I leave."

I looked him in the eye. "Why?"

"You seem so reluctant to take anything of ours, or to make your mark on us. You want to vanish from our memories as soon as your back is turned. Perhaps this necklace will make you think of me when you are gone, and remember me."

I fingered the chain, the metal cold to the touch. "I won't need a necklace to remember you." I swallowed, forcing myself to keep my voice steady. "I'll never forget you."

He turned suddenly to face the window, his back to me, and rubbed his hands through his hair, the static electricity making it wild. "You are speaking as if you are already gone."

"No. I have a few months yet, I think. I just thought it was only fair to let everyone know that I won't be here indefinitely."

He walked to me and took the necklace from my fingers. Standing behind me, he placed the gold chain over my neck and fastened the clasp. I closed my eyes to better feel the nearness of him and the accidental touch of his fingers. My head turned toward him, my cheek brushing his hand. Slowly, his hands dropped to my shoulders, then deserted me completely.

Shaken, I stood and stepped away. "It's your turn." I indicated the package on the desk.

He untied the ribbon and held up the gray wool socks to examine them. "They are not even square," he said, referring to my first few failed attempts at knitting socks.

"If you're going to be ungrateful about it, you can just give them back." I stepped forward to grab them out of his hands.

"No, Laura, they are perfect. And thank you. I shall definitely be needing these." He rolled the socks into a ball, examining them as if they were a rare jewel. "I have been told that Sherman's amassing troops in Chattanooga, making preparations for a huge campaign. Like striking south into Georgia."

I focused on the buttons on his coat. "Just keep your family safe."

He grabbed both of my shoulders in a tight grip. He clenched his jaw, and for the first time, I was aware of his sheer strength as his fingers dug into my flesh. "What about me, Laura? Do you care what happens to me?"

"Oh, Stuart." I touched his cheek. "I care more than you know, more than I want to."

His voice shook as he spoke. "I knew it the minute I saw you here, when you fainted on the front lawn. You belong here—with us. With me." His kiss was hard, brutal, and I tasted blood in my mouth. It was as if by sealing his words, it would make them true.

I pulled away, my tongue running against my cut lip.

He released his grip, but his strength of will kept me standing. His voice was very low, coming from between clenched teeth. "When all this madness is over, I will come back for you. Wherever you are, I will find you, and you will tell me the truth."

He grabbed his hat off the desk and walked out of the room, taking my heart with him and leaving the socks I had given him resting on a chair.

I walked out into the hall and almost ran into the black-clad Pamela. Her eyes blazed as she looked at me. I had no idea if she had overheard my conversation with Stuart, and I didn't care. I walked past her without speaking to find Julia. I was desperately in need of companionship.

I found Julia in the dining room, a large basket resting in the middle of the table, its contents spilled out on the polished mahogany surface. She looked up as I entered.

"It was surely an act of Providence that my herb basket was not in the kitchen the night of the fire." She picked up a jar to examine it and then put it back on the table. "I had wanted it nearby in case Willie or Robbie needed something in the night." Her voice caught, but she averted her head, hiding her eyes.

"Stuart's leaving now."

"I know. He already said goodbye to the children and me. He does not like long goodbyes, preferring to ride off on his own. Stubborn man," she said, almost as an afterthought.

I pulled out a chair and sat down next to her. "What are you doing—anything I can help you with?"

"There will be—there is so much to do. Stuart said he had mentioned it to you, that we are going to have to take refuge in Valdosta."

"Yes. He mentioned it. For the record, I think it's a very good idea."

She went back to perusing the contents of her basket, continuing to arrange jars, bottles, and pieces of dried herbs back in the basket. "I cannot decide if you are a coward or just plain stubborn."

"What do you mean?"

She placed her hands neatly in her lap and looked at me, her chin tucked slightly, as if preparing to give a scolding. "Laura, life is never easy—especially for us women. We are the ones left behind to pick up the pieces, to make the men whole again or to comfort our children when they ask for their fathers." She lifted a stray piece of hair off her forehead and attempted to tuck it into her bun. "But when life gives us something and our heart tells us it is something good, we need to grab it with all our strength, regardless of what our head is telling us. What is a life without risk? If the seeds in my garden did not risk the cold winter snow, we would never see their glorious blooms in the spring. Stuart loves you, Laura, more than he has ever loved anyone before, I suspect. Open your heart to him. It could erase all those shadows in your eyes."

I felt foolish as the tears started to flow. I wiped at them impatiently. "Julia, you're the one who just lost a baby. I should be comforting you, not the other way around."

She grabbed my hand as if to emphasize her point. "We have all lost something, Laura, and giving comfort is just as good as receiving it." She squeezed my hand before letting go, the warmth in her eyes genuine.

Reaching into her pocket, she pulled out something I immediately recognized, something that made my heart lurch at the sight. I reached for the small stuffed giraffe, its one eye missing, its fur matted and rubbed off in spots. Annie's giraffe.

I bent my head into its fur, sniffing the musty toy, any scent of the little girl it had once belonged to long gone.

Gently, she said, "I thought you would have guessed the truth. Did you not have any suspicions? She looks so much like you, you know."

I shook my head. "No. I guess I believed that if you had known anything about my missing daughter, you would have told me. I trusted you like a sister, Julia. I would never have expected you to deceive me. I understand why—I do. And I know eventually I will forgive you. But there's still a lot of hurt and anger."

"I know," she said softly. She put a hand on my forehead. "You are looking a bit pale. Are you feeling all right?"

I had been nursing a throbbing headache all day, and since my confrontation with Stuart, it had grown progressively worse. "I've just got this dreadful headache. I think I'll go lie down."

"Let me make you a soothing tea and I will send it up to you."

"Thank you, Julia." I stood to leave, clutching Annie's giraffe.

Julia held me back. "Stuart's no fool, Laura. And he can be a very determined man once he sets his eyes upon something he wants."

"He didn't get you—he let William take you away from him."

She flushed slightly. "So you know the story. But, no, I do not think Stuart ever really wanted me. We would have had a happy marriage— a marriage between friends. But you and Stuart have something else. Something many of us live a lifetime without ever experiencing."

I shook my head, feeling the blood rush through my skull. "I can't think about it right now, Julia. All I really want to do is go home. And I can't do that and have Stuart, too."

She looked at me, her eyes wide. "Where is home, Laura?"

I gave her a wry grin. "You wouldn't believe me if I told you. But it's closer than you would think." I rubbed my fingers on my temples to soothe the incessant pounding. "My head is just killing me," I said, wishing desperately for some aspirin.

She nodded and let me go. "I will send that tea up in just a bit."

I climbed the stairs and heard quiet voices as I passed Sarah and Willie's room, but resisted the impulse to peek in.

I was sitting at the dressing table and pulling the pins out of my hair when someone tapped on the door. Sukie entered, holding the cup of tea.

"Miz Julia said for you to drink this."

"Thank you, Sukie," I said, warming my hands on the china cup and smelling deeply of the rich aroma.

She left, and I moved to the bed with my cup, sipping it and enjoying it in a rare moment of leisure. The throbbing at my temples soon began to dissipate and my eyelids grew heavy. I pulled back the covers and lay down.

Vivid dreams hurled themselves at me, full of color and overblown, with monsters in the dark lurking around every corner. I heard babies crying amid the overwhelming smell of gardenias. I felt the wetness on my cheeks but could not move my arms to wipe them away. Michael emerged from cold darkness and bent to kiss me goodbye, his brittle lips icy against mine. Great balls of smoke hovered around me, twisting their way around my body and between my limbs, obscuring my vision until Stuart emerged, holding his drawn saber. The wrenching pain in my gut as he stabbed me finally woke me. But the pain was still there. I rolled out of bed and reached my washbasin just in time to vomit. I collapsed on the floor, still retching and sure that I would die from the pain. I tried calling out for Sukie or Julia, but no one heard me. The last thing I remembered was calling feebly for Stuart as I finally succumbed to blissful unconsciousness.

Chapter Eighteen

Evil is unspectacular and always human,
And shares our bed and eats at our own table.
—W. H. AUDEN

I knew I was going to die. I lay on the floor, unable to move and urgently wishing for death. I stared at the dust balls under the bed and smelled the musty rug beneath my cheek and made more feeble attempts to call for help. I threw up again and barely had the energy to turn my head. Eventually, I slipped into unconsciousness once more.

A cool washcloth stroked my forehead, and I turned a bleary gaze to the figure hovering at the side of my bed. Tiny droplets of water tickled down my face as the washcloth was squeezed over my mouth. My cracked lips opened gratefully as I accepted the nourishment.

I tensed at Julia's voice. "Laura? I am here. I will take care of you."

I vaguely remembered the tea that she had sent up to me and her basket of secrets on the dining room table. Flinching from her touch and using what remaining strength I had left, I pushed at her hand. My arm fell boneless back to the bed.

"Go away," I croaked through parched lips.

A dark form appeared next to Julia and I saw black hands take the washcloth and dip it in the washbasin. Julia disappeared from the side of the bed and I heard Sukie's voice, speaking in a strange tongue I had never heard before. Guttural clacking, oddly soothing, reverberated throughout the room and in my head. She opened the pouch around her neck, extracted something from it, and made sprinkling motions over my head. I recalled, in my semiconscious state of delirium, that it had been Sukie who had brought the tea. I tried to move away and was startled to find myself paralyzed. I opened my mouth to scream, my lips moving with soundless words. I wanted Stuart, but my lips wouldn't form his name.

"Here, drink this. This should help your stomach." Pamela's face hovered within my short field of vision. The wrenching pain in my abdomen had never ceased, the agony knifing through me constantly. I felt her cold fingers on the back of my neck as she held up my head and opened my mouth. I felt the tepid liquid slip through my lips and spill down my chin.

With as much care as one tending a newborn, she wiped up the spill with a clean cloth, shaking her head and murmuring, "There, there, do not worry. This will all be over soon."

I remembered seeing Julia in her kitchen, making medicines and telling me she had learned everything she knew from her mother. I knew Pamela had the power to make me better, and I clung to the slim glimmer of hope and opened my mouth again for more of her healing tea.

She pulled up the sleeve of my nightgown, exposing the crescent-shaped birthmark. Her fingers tightened on my arm before she slid the sleeve down again. Her breath brushed my cheek, her face hovering only inches above my own. Her words came to me in an urgent whisper. "Who is Michael, Laura? You keep calling out his name, telling him you are a traveler. What does that mean?"

I tried again to speak, but only guttural noises came from my throat.

"Do not fret yourself, now. We can discuss this when you are better. Let me make you some more tea."

I don't know how long I lay in that bed, moving in and out of consciousness, unaware of what I was saying and to whom I was saying it. I was unable to keep anything down except for Pamela's tea. But the pain never left me, and I knew that I was going to die.

A deep voice at the side of the bed brought me out of a deep slumber. "Stuart," I croaked, but was dismayed when I recognized Dr. Watkins's voice.

He lifted my wrist and held it gently. I felt almost disembodied in my complacency, and I lay limp as the doctor finished his examination.

"Laura, can you answer some questions for me?"

I could hear him quite clearly, but wasn't sure if I could answer him. I nodded.

"Do you remember if you ate anything unusual—something that only you ate?"

I nodded. A dark shape stood beside the doctor, but I couldn't see the face clearly.

"Can you tell me what it was?"

He bent his ear close to my mouth and I tried speaking, my voice raspy. "Tea. From Julia. Sukie . . . brought . . . it."

The shape next to the doctor seemed to materialize closer to me, and I recognized Sukie's voice as she spoke. "No, Doctor. Miz Pamela give me the tea and I brung it up like she ask."

Slow trickles of realization eased their way down my spine.

The doctor straightened and turned to Sukie. "What was in that tea? And has she had any more of it?"

Sukie's agitated voice replied, "I don' make the tea so I don' know. And Miz Pamela's been fixin' some of her healing teas to make her better. But nothin's workin'." She wrung her hands, the movement making my stomach roil. "I try to warn her, I did. I put my magic pouch in her room. There be an evil power here, an' I can't fight it."

A fit of uncontrolled trembling possessed my limbs. With my last ounce of energy, I forced out the word, "Stuart."

The doctor's cool hand rested on my forehead. "Are you calling for Stuart?"

I nodded.

"I am going to get Zeke. He might be the only person who can help you."

He disappeared from the side of my bed, his voice sounding dim. "Sukie, stay with her. Do not let anybody else near her."

Sukie's warm hands brushed my face, her rhythmic chantings once again soothing me into a deep, dark sleep. I don't know how long I slept, hovering through life, watching the sun's pattern glow and fade on the floral wallpaper. Sukie bathed me and changed my nightgown, and then I slept again.

I opened my eyes, the yellow flame from my bedside lamp creating a hole in the darkness. Voices and heavy footsteps sounded on the stairs outside my room and then my door was flung open.

"Laura?"

Stuart. I wanted to cry from sheer relief, but I was so dehydrated that nothing came out. With all my strength I lifted my hand to him. He grabbed it and squeezed it tightly, his warm breath burning my cheek as he leaned closer. "I will not let you die, Laura. I will not. We are bringing you to Zeke's. Can you move at all?"

I struggled to move my limbs but succeeded only in breaking out in beads of sweat.

"I will carry you."

He spoke to another person, but I couldn't make out the face in the shadows.

Strong arms lifted me off the mattress while someone else tucked blankets around my body. I turned my head to see Sukie holding the lamp, its flame creating hollows of her eyes as she stared at me. My head collapsed onto the scratchy wool of Stuart's jacket.

The flickering light from the lamp illuminated our way down the steps. I closed my eyes as dizziness assailed me, and I said a quick and fervent prayer that I wouldn't throw up on Stuart.

Biting air hit me as the door opened but I breathed it in greedily, glad to be rid of the fetid smell of the sickroom. A soft whinnying forced my eyes open. "No," I croaked.

Despite the grimness of his face, I saw his mouth soften slightly in a smile. "Laura, you and Endy are friends now, remember? He is going to take you to Zeke's as fast as possible."

I nodded, too weak to say any more.

He handed me over to another pair of arms, and I heard the quiet tones of Zeke's voice.

"Is Pamela still here?"

Stuart answered, "Yes, Charles is with her, and we will decide what to do with her in the morning. Right now, I only want to get Laura away from here."

Zeke nodded, his long hair brushing my face, and then handed me up to Stuart sitting astride Endy. He held me tightly with one arm as he gathered the reins in his other hand. All strength now completely gone, I leaned against him and let him hold me on the saddle.

The moon in the clear sky guided our way through the woods. As I began to drift into unconsciousness again, lulled by the slow rocking of the saddle, I felt the light brush of Stuart's lips against my hair. I gave his hand a quick squeeze before sliding off into a deep sleep.

I vaguely recalled being brought into the cabin and bundled into a warm bed. A roaring fire cast an amber glow throughout, soothing me until I succumbed to darkness once more.

The night began to blend into daylight, and I found myself existing in a twilight, unable to distinguish between reality and dream. I saw Michael many times sitting on the edge of the bed, his face cold and pale. He beckoned for me to go with him, but I resisted. Something held me bound to the place where I was, and I could not abandon it.

I held Annie, as a baby, and I spoke to her and sang to her until Michael took her from me and left, leaving me bereft in the twilight once again.

And then I heard a voice, piercing the darkness around my mind, and I reached out to it, seeking deliverance from the overwhelming sense of loss that had settled over me like a blanket.

"Laura!" I heard my name shouted by a voice, a voice I recognized as being of the living.

"Stuart," I mouthed, not yet able to make a sound.

"Hold on to me." I felt a strong, callused hand grab mine and squeeze tightly. I seemed to draw strength from it as I turned my head toward the sound of his voice. And then I slept, this time without dreams.

I awoke to the crackling sounds of a fire, the warm orange tones of the firelight illuminating the room. The rounded logs by the side of the bed I was lying in told me that I was in Zeke's cabin. I snuggled down deeper under the warm down coverlet, the feeling of being safe, protected, and loved overwhelming me.

A movement next to the bed caught my eye and I turned my head. Stuart stood from a chair and leaned over me. "Thank God. You're awake."

Another person emerged from the shadows and I recognized Zeke, holding a cup with steam rising over the edge.

"Have faith, Stuart. All will be well."

He took Stuart's place by the side of the bed, holding out the cup to me. "If Stuart helps you, do you think you can sit up to drink this?"

My dizziness, although not completely gone, was beginning to fade. And while I still felt queasy, I also felt the first pangs of hunger. I had no idea how much time had passed since I had last eaten. I nodded.

Stuart hoisted me gently to a reclining position, then placed a pillow behind my back. The room seemed to spin suddenly as my lightheadedness returned. I began to slump and immediately felt Stuart's arm around me again.

"Do not worry, Stuart. She is only weak from lack of nourishment. Charles said that it has been almost a week since Pamela was allowed near her, so most of whatever poison she had been administering is out of Laura's body. We just need to build up her strength."

Zeke brought the cup nearer and I smelled a strong apple scent. I took a sip, feeling the warmth of it slip into my stomach.

"Can you drink more?" he asked.

I nodded and took another sip.

"If you can hold this down, I will make you some chicken broth."

I managed a weak smile. "Oh, joy. Just what I was hoping for."

Stuart's face softened, the creases in his brow disappearing. "I think she is feeling better."

Zeke indicated the chair next to the bed. "Stuart, stay here and help her finish the tea. I need to get more firewood."

A small burst of cold air hit me as the door opened and closed. I eagerly took more sips from the proffered cup and then lay back on the pillows, completely exhausted.

The china clinked as Stuart sat the cup and saucer down on the nightstand. I looked into his face and saw the dead seriousness in his eyes. His sharp-cut features were softly hidden by a scraggly beard, and the dark circles under his eyes told me it had been days since he had slept.

"You look terrible," I said.

He ran his hand over his stubbly jaw. "I imagine I do. I was worried about you."

"Oh, so that's it. And I thought you had come back for your socks."

"My socks?"

"Yes. The ones I gave you for Christmas that you left behind."

Smiling, he nodded. "Oh yes. That was the main reason."

He leaned closer to me, his penetrating eyes inches away from mine, his face serious. "I thought you were going to die with all that was unresolved between us." He paused briefly, as if unsure what to say next. He seemed to relax a little before saying, "I was determined to keep you alive until you could apologize for being so hardheaded."

Despite my weakness, I struggled to sit up. "Apologize? For what?"

He sat back with a big smile. "Your fighting spirit is back. You must be on the mend."

"You could have just asked me, you know. But I still feel as if I've been hit by a truck."

"A truck?"

Realizing my error, I quickly said, "Oh, just a manner of speaking. It means to be trampled by a large horse."

He regarded me steadily. "You said a lot of interesting things in your delirium."

Feeling a pinprick of unease, I answered, "Oh, really? Like what?"

"You were talking with Michael. And you talked a lot about Annie."

"I think I remember that part. Anything else?"

"A lot of it I did not understand. You mentioned a Mrs. Cudahy a few times, and you kept asking for a Diet Coke."

He looked at me expectantly, but I conveniently smothered a yawn and slumped back down on my pillow. "I'm really tired. Could we talk about this later?"

His eyes narrowed, but all he said was "Of course," and leaned down to kiss my forehead, his beard rubbing my skin.

"Go shave," I muttered as he straightened.

"Yes, ma'am. But we have some serious talking to do when you are better."

With my eyes closed, I nodded and snuggled deeper into the pillow.

For the next four days, Zeke nursed me back to health with his teas and simple meals. My appetite returned on the third day, but he wouldn't let me eat anything solid—and he showed an amazing lack of compassion by eating his meals in my vicinity, the tantalizing smell wafting toward me. On the fourth day, in desperation, I climbed out of bed. With unsteady feet, I made my way to the table and snatched a piece of corn bread from his plate.

"Feeling better, Laura?"

Spots swam before my eyes and he quickly stood and helped me into a chair. "I'll feel a lot better as soon as I can eat some decent food."

The door opened, and Stuart appeared. Zeke threw a blanket over my nightgown, making me smile. Stuart had definitely seen me at my worst, and I don't think the sight of me in a state of undress would have shocked him at all.

I suddenly realized that I hadn't seen anyone else since I had come to Zeke's cabin. "Where are Julia and Sukie?" I asked, stuffing another bite of corn bread in my mouth.

Zeke and Stuart exchanged glances. Stuart answered, "When you were sick, you kept screaming for them to keep away from you. I wanted to talk with you first before bringing you back to the house."

"Oh." I recalled Sukie's face and the powder from her pouch as she had sprinkled it over me. "I thought Julia was trying to poison me. Because of Sarah."

Stuart pulled up a chair to the table and sat down. "I am sure in your delirium you might have believed that. But now, with rational thought returning, I hope you know that Julia loves you like a sister, and would never harm you. You know that in your heart, don't you?"

I looked down at the corn bread, my appetite deserting me. I knew he was right. I'd known Julia for only a short time, but I had seen her resilience and strength of spirit through dark periods, witnessed her kindness and compassion. She was not a killer, regardless of motive. I met Stuart's eyes. "But who else would want to hurt me?"

Stuart held me with a steady gaze. "Zeke and Charles are convinced it was Pamela. The tea Sukie brought to you was given to her by Pamela, and not Julia. Do you know why Pamela would want to harm you?"

"I promise you I don't know. I'm aware that she uses you and others to ferry information to the Confederate Army, but I have never done anything to thwart her." I swallowed thickly. "I have no interest in this conflict. I'm an innocent bystander, I assure you." Dots danced in my eyes again, and I leaned back in the chair. Zeke shook his head at Stuart, staving off any more questions for the time being.

I sat up suddenly. "Where is Pamela now?"

Stuart glanced at Zeke before saying, "She is gone. She left the night we brought you here. Hit poor Charles over the head with her washbasin and made her escape on one of our two remaining carriage horses." He raked his hand through his hair. "What she has done she has done for a reason, Laura. And you are the key. So think hard—why would she want to kill you?"

"I promise you—I really don't know." Angry tears formed in my eyes, and I turned away.

Zeke spoke. "Enough, Stuart."

With a screeching of wood on wood, Stuart slid his chair back and stood. "I will go heat up some water and bring it in for you to wash."

Zeke stood and cleared the dishes, and then I helped him remove the sheets from the bed and replace them with clean ones. When we were done, he considered me with a gaze I couldn't decipher.

"I will go check my traps now and see what we are having for supper today." He pulled on his coat and added, "I am also going to pay Julia a visit. Would you like me to bring Sukie here to help you?"

"No, thank you. I don't think I need her. Besides, I think I'm feeling well enough to go back. I'm sure I've been a big nuisance to you, invading your home."

He didn't refute my words and I grimaced inwardly.

"I want you to stay here at least one more day. I want to make sure you are fully recovered. I am not sure of the poison she used on you. Enjoy the rest. The women will put you to work packing up everything as soon as you cross the threshold."

"They've already started?" I asked with some surprise. I knew it was coming; I just hadn't expected it so soon. But with the kitchen and storehouse gone, along with most of our winter food, it was a foregone conclusion.

"Yes. Willie is fully recovered, and they will be ready to leave soon."

I nodded, having mixed feelings. With Phoenix Hall empty, Stuart would return to the army. And I would have to go with Julia to Valdosta, leaving Moon Mountain and my chance to return behind me.

Stuart returned with buckets of water and began heating them over the fire in the fireplace. He pulled out two large wooden buckets and poured the steaming water into them. "Zeke uses the creek to bathe," he offered in explanation.

"Even in the winter?" The thought made me shiver and long for the convenience of hot water coming through the tap at the twist of a hand.

"All year round. He claims that it is not so bad because he is used to it."

"Yes, I'm sure after you lose circulation in all your extremities, you don't feel a thing."

Eager to wash, I shrugged off the blanket Zeke had thrown over my shoulders and began to rummage around for anything resembling soap and a towel.

"Over there," Stuart said, pointing to a rocking chair. "Julia sent them back with me."

"Thank you," I said, holding aloft the two items. He stood between the two buckets, his gaze darting about the room, looking at everything but me.

Realizing I was wearing nothing but my white cotton nightgown and standing before a window to boot, I immediately understood his discomfort. I moved the towel in front of me.

"I should be going now. We need more wood." He didn't move.

"Yes. And thank you for the hot water."

"You are most welcome." He picked up his hat from a chair and began backing up toward the door. He grabbed his rifle and left with a short nod before shutting the door firmly behind him.

With my stomach no longer empty, I felt invigorated and almost whole again. Not enough to run a marathon, but at least I was regaining my energy. I stripped out of the nightgown as soon as the door closed, shivering as the chilled air touched my flesh. He had placed the buckets in front of the fire, so I kneeled and gratefully dipped my hair into one, enjoying the sensation of the still-hot water on my scalp. I reached for the soap and ran it through my hair. I was glad Zeke didn't have any mirrors in the cabin, because it had been some time since I had bathed and I must have been a sight worthy of a Stephen King novel. After rinsing, I twisted my hair up in a towel turban and continued.

Dipping the washcloth into the water, I squeezed out the excess, allowing the coolness of the water to spread over my skin. Droplets snaked their way down my spine and I closed my eyes, enjoying the sensation. Prickly gooseflesh appeared on my arms and torso, causing me to shiver. I rubbed my arms harshly, making them red, reveling in the fact that I was still alive. Every sense seemed magnified as I continued bathing. The pounding outside of Stuart's ax echoed in the rafters of the cabin. My skin stung where I scrubbed it, and I hastily soothed it with a handful of water. I delighted in the feel of the water flowing over my naked body, standing exposed and alone in the middle of the room. I had grown weary of the confining clothes of the nineteenth century.

Unwilling to put on my soiled nightgown, I took the towel off of my head and wrapped it around my body. I took another piece of corn bread that Zeke had left out and sat in the rocker in front of the fire to finish drying off. My proximity to the blazing logs made my skin burn, but I knew that if I backed up even a little, the icy chill of the room would claim me again.

I stared into the fire, trying to conjure Michael's face. I saw the blond hair and the color of his eyes, but I could not see the face of the man who had slept next to me for almost eleven years.

Instead, deep blue eyes and a shock of dark hair formed in my mind. I saw the fine crinkles at the sides of Stuart's eyes as he smiled, and smelled the pungent aroma of wet wool and horseflesh that hung about him. I hugged my arms around my chest. How could I ever say goodbye?

Drowsiness settled over me, and I closed my eyes to hover in a half-awake state.

Somewhere I heard a knocking on the door. Without thinking or opening my eyes, I uttered, "Come in."

The door swung open, the frigid air making me bolt upright in the rocker. Stuart appeared in the threshold, his face obstructed by the stack of wood in his arms. He crossed the room and unburdened his load by the hearth. As he straightened, he caught sight of me and stopped, his face stricken.

"My apologies," he stammered, and abruptly strode to the open door. "I thought— I am sure— Well. You did say to come in. I will just leave now."

I wasn't quite sure what I wanted. But I knew I didn't want him to leave. Still gripping the towel close to my body, I rushed over to the door and shut it. "Don't go."

Without turning his head, he said, "Laura, I do not know how strong I am, but it is not enough to stand this close to you dressed like that and not touch you. I do not believe I can be expected to act like a gentleman if I stay."

Feeling suddenly giddy, I replied, "If you promise not to act like a gentleman, then I promise not to act like a lady."

He turned toward me, eyebrows raised. "What are you saying?"

In answer, I stood on my tiptoes to kiss him, then stepped back to wait for his reaction.

Without a word, he turned around and latched the door from the inside, focusing his eyes on the rough wood. "I want you, but I do not want to take advantage of you. If you ask me to leave, I will."

I slipped in between him and the door and pulled his face down to mine. "I want you to stay." Yellow light from the fireplace warmed the side of his face as he regarded me with darkening eyes. I felt the tension ease out of the thick muscles in his neck.

He closed his eyes for a moment as he touched his forehead to mine. "I never thought I would hear you say that to me."

My teeth chattered in the icy air around the door.

"You are cold."

"Then warm me." My chattering teeth prevented the seductive smile I tried to give him.

Scooping me up in his arms, he walked me over to the bed and placed me gently on the clean sheets. He leaned over me, a hand on either side, and whispered, "Are you sure?"

"Yes. I'm sure." A quick image of Michael flashed in my mind, then faded as I said goodbye to old memories and opened my heart to an uncertain future.

Stuart sat down next to me, his eyes serious. He took one of my hands in his, entwining our fingers. "There have been no promises between us yet. You have been holding on to something that you were not quite ready to give up. If you are still not ready, I will understand. But do know this: I want you. Not just now. I want you forever."

He kissed me, his lips tentative against mine. He leaned back and slipped off his coat, letting it fall to the floor. I leaned forward to kiss him back, his lips tasting of salt and fresh air.

I slid the suspenders off his shoulders. Keeping one hand clutching the towel closed around me, my other hand began undoing the three wooden buttons at the top of his shirt, our gazes locked. I tugged the shirttails out of his waistband and then slid my hand up his chest, gliding over his smooth skin, feeling his blood warm at the surface. Gooseflesh rippled under my fingers.

"Your hands are cold."

"Sorry," I said, as I kneeled on the bed, facing him. I leaned to kiss him again, but he placed firm hands on my shoulders.

"Just a moment."

I stopped, paralyzed. "Stuart, please don't tell me no again. I don't think I could stand it."

He shook his head. "I could not tell you no even if I wanted to." His gaze scanned the room until it settled on the brown jug on the hearth. He retrieved it and brought it to the bed. "I just needed something to calm my nerves."

"Your nerves?" I sat back on the bed, breathing heavily, wondering how to ask the question. "Do you mean . . . ?"

He took a long swig from the jug and then eyed me warily. "I am no novice." His glance swept over me, and he reached to smooth the hair behind my ear. "I have never had anyone warm my blood the way you do."

He removed his shirt and sat again on the edge of the bed. His hand stroked my cheek, his callused fingers rough on my skin. "We should speak of marriage. I do not want to dishonor you, Laura."

I allowed the towel to slide from my body and put my finger to his lips. "Don't say anything else. We'll think about tomorrow later."

I smelled the whiskey on his breath as his fingers gently traced the line of my collarbone, like a blind man committing me to memory. More firmly, his hands, warm and knowing, spanned over my waist.

"Thank you," I said.

His hands stopped. "For what?"

"For this—for wanting me."

He ducked his head, his shoulders shaking.

"Are you laughing at me, Stuart Elliott?"

He looked back up, serious again, a strange light in his eyes. "No, Laura. It is just that you certainly know how to surprise a man. Thanking me, indeed." He leaned over to kiss me and whispered quietly, "Now, let me show you how thankful I am."

He stood and untied his waistband from behind then slid his pants over his slim hips. I stared in open admiration at his lean, muscular body, toned from hours in the saddle and the day-to-day work of the plantation. Dark hair covered the small hollow in his chest, and I longed to nestle my head there and hear his heart beating beneath me.

I reached my hand out to him and he lay beside me, only our breaths separating us. I saw the hesitation in his eyes but stilled the question on his lips with a kiss. He moved on top of me, and the solidness of him anchored me here, to this place. He rose on his arms, then slowly rolled me over.

Dazed, I complied, feeling the soft pillow against my cheek. His breath burned my neck as he lifted my hair with trembling fingers. "I have always wanted to kiss you here." His lips pressed against the base of my skull. Small bursts of heat traveled down my spine, searing away the last of my resolve to keep my heart protected from this man. "When you wear your hair up, it is all I can do not to touch you. Here." He kissed me under my ear, ignoring the tiny explosions going on under my skin. "And here." His lips traveled lower, to the top of my spine, my resolve now lying in charred ruins along the way.

I turned into his arms, my mouth eagerly seeking his, my palms desperately searching for his solid flesh. I had been brought from near death, and the journey had been fought for this man, for this moment. I bit him on his neck, tasting the realness of him, and let my head fall back upon the pillow as his lips found mine again. Goose bumps lifted my skin, stretching it tight across my bones.

His warm breath kissed the hollow between my breasts, his words vibrating against my sensitive skin. "I thought I would die from wanting you." He closed his eyes, the dark brows knitted in concentration. He opened them again, his gaze piercing me. "And now I might die from losing you."

I shook my head, afraid to speak lest I cry. I lifted the quilt over us, creating a pocket of warmth, and pulled him to me. His voice came deep and tremulous in our dark cocoon. "I feel as if I have touched you before, as if my hands and body have loved you forever." His fingers moved against my skin, then stopped, and I gasped, wanting to beg for more or for mercy, but not finding the place inside me from where words come.

Sharp teeth bit my earlobe, and I twitched under him. His fingers feathered over my thigh, and I sighed, melting into the pillow as his face pressed against my hair and his breath wrapped around my neck. "I have known your scent all my life, it seems. Why do you think that is, Laura? Have we always been lovers? Not here, but in some other place?"

I had no words to offer, so I pulled him toward me, showing him my answer while the lonely moon rose in the sky, and battles raged and lives were lost on the other side of our horizon. And outside our warm cocoon, with the flames crackling in the fireplace, the answers to questions that could not be easily answered waited in the dark corners of the room.

CHAPTER NINETEEN

---◆---

'Tis all a Chequer-board of nights and Days
Where Destiny with Men for Pieces plays;
Hither and thither moves, and mates and slays,
And one by one back in the closet lays.

—OMAR KHAYYAM

I drowsily opened an eye. From the dim light in the cabin I realized it was late afternoon, the slanting sunlight from the windows reaching out silent fingers toward the bed. My head nestled on Stuart's arm; our legs entangled, his rhythmic breathing the only sound.

I shifted my head slightly to admire his profile: the straight nose; the high, broad cheekbones. In sleep he was beautiful, reminiscent of a marble effigy I had seen on an old tomb on a visit to England. I shivered. Embers glowed in the fireplace, but I resisted the impulse to leave the comfort and slow, steady heat of Stuart's arms to restart the fire.

A deep rumbling began in Stuart's chest and I raised my head to see if he had awakened. His eyes remained closed, but his head twitched on the pillow, his eyebrows furrowed together. His muscles stiffened under me as he wrestled with the demons in his dream.

He bolted upright in bed, a warrior's cry on his lips, the sound echoing off the rafters. His broad shoulders shone with perspiration as he bent forward, his head in his hands. "Oh, God," he whispered, grinding the heels of his hands into his eye sockets.

I couldn't see the assaults of men in blue and gray, rifles lifted, bodies falling. Nor hear the blasts of angry artillery as it blew bits of horses and men across a battlefield. But I could see the tension in his back and the desolation in his eyes, and I knew Stuart did see.

He startled when I touched him but quickly drew me to him and buried his face in my hair. "Laura." His voice was muffled but the tone of affirmation in his voice clear.

I lifted my head to look in his eyes. "I'm here, Stuart." I smoothed the hair back from his forehead and then rested my hands on his neck. His pulse skipped and raced under my fingers, and I knew his battles were still raging. "I'm here," I said again as I leaned forward to kiss his neck. He tasted of warm sleep and salt, and I kissed him again.

He took my head in both hands. "Yes, Laura, now. But will you always be?"

"Isn't now enough?"

The pressure of his hands on my head increased. "No."

The fear and desperation of his dream filled his eyes, the eyes of a soldier. They were foreign to me, and I felt a flash of alarm.

"You're hurting me. Please let go."

He began shaking, and the pressure eased as he removed his hands, staring at them as if they didn't belong to him. "Forgive me. This war dehumanizes us."

"I know." I grabbed his hands and turned them over to kiss each roughened palm. I had felt how gentle his hands could be. Wanting to erase the haunting images in his mind's eye, I held his shoulders and pulled him down on the pillow once more.

His gentleness was gone this time, his lips hard on mine, his body rough and demanding. His lovemaking left me feeling like a shattered and fallen star, splintering down toward earth, then coming to rest on the barren winter grass.

The last sliver of light disappeared from the floor, leaving only the dim glow of dusk from the windows illuminating the room. Slipping on his pants, Stuart walked across the room to rekindle the fire and then returned to the bed with me.

I rubbed my hand against his cheek. "You shaved."

"I was ordered to." His cheek creased as he smiled.

"I didn't order you. I'm much more subtle than that."

"Subtle, hmm? I do not think I noticed that about you."

I elbowed him in the ribs, making him grunt.

"Why hasn't Zeke come back?" My fingers were busy entangling themselves in the black thickness of his hair, brushing it off his forehead.

"He will not be back for a while—he might even spend the night in the woods." Stuart cocked an eyebrow. "He knows. He always knows things that are not always apparent to others."

"Won't he and the others be scandalized?"

"Not Zeke, and I doubt anyone else would find out. I think that the citizens of Roswell are too busy worrying about their next meal to worry about who is going around unchaperoned."

"But it's freezing outside. It's making me feel incredibly guilty."

"Zeke prefers to sleep outside. He once told me that the stars were the eyes of those not yet born. He takes great comfort in sleeping under them."

I smiled, resting my head on his shoulder. "That's beautiful. I'd like to think it was true." I thought of the eyes of my parents, not yet born, watching over me.

I ran my finger over a scar on his chest that I had noticed earlier. It was about the size of a quarter, but it must have been deep, because the skin was purpled and puckered. "What's this?"

His hand rested over mine. "William. He shot me with an arrow when we were boys. It was an accident."

From what I had heard of William, I somehow doubted it.

He turned to me and touched his lips to mine. "They are the color of moss, I think."

I looked at him questioningly.

"Your eyes. It will always be your eyes that I will think about when I am away from you."

I held a finger to his lips. "Don't. Don't talk about us not being together."

"Then stay, Laura. We could—"

"Sh," I said, and leaned forward to kiss him and silence the next words from his lips. Words that I expected to be my undoing.

A booming shot filled the room, echoing from the nearby woods. Stuart had scrambled from the bed and pulled on his shirt by the time I realized it had been the sound of a shotgun.

"Wouldn't that be Zeke hunting?" I was reluctant to move from the comfort of the quilt.

Looking down to button his shirt, his reply was muffled. "Most likely. But he said he was checking traps. He would only use his gun if he ran into trouble. I had best make sure he is all right."

"What kind of trouble?" I wrapped the quilt around me and walked over to him as he buttoned up his coat and buckled his belt over it.

"If a catamount became interested in Zeke's trap, there might be a fight. Zeke could probably take care of it, but I would like to make sure."

He avoided my eyes as he settled his hat on his head. I grabbed his elbow as he reached for the rifle. "There's something you're not telling me."

Pulling a sidearm from its holster, he handed it to me. "Do you know how to use this?"

Reluctant to touch it, I stepped back. "Why would I need that?"

He opened the gun, checked it for ammunition, then snapped it shut. "These are uncertain times. I cannot leave you here unprotected."

I straightened my spine. "Then you had better show me how to use that thing."

It was the first gun I'd ever held, and I found this Colt Navy to be surprisingly light. Stuart showed me how to cock the hammer and quickly moved aside as I pointed the gun at him. "Watch where you aim that. It has an easy trigger."

He took the gun from me, released the hammer, and laid it on the table. "I want you to keep the door latched and only open it when you hear our voices. Do you understand?"

I nodded, feeling numb. He wrapped his arms around me. "It is probably nothing. I just want to make sure."

I reached my arms around his neck, letting the quilt fall, and kissed him solidly.

"We will talk when I get back." Stooping, he picked up the quilt and handed it to me. "And you might want to get dressed, just in case Zeke gets back before I do. Not that I think he will be surprised, but he is my grandfather."

"Be careful." I couldn't think of anything else to say.

"Yes, ma'am," he said softly, and let himself out the door.

Drops of rain spotted the wood planks of the porch, blown by a strong wind. I latched the door and stood there briefly, my hands flat on the hardwood, and whispered a little prayer.

The cabin suddenly seemed vast and empty. I walked over to the fire to stoke it, making the wood pop and crackle, the homey scent of pine filling the room. I found a clean nightgown Julia must have sent with the soap, and I slipped it over my head and began to wait.

The thick silence of the evening woods filled the air with a palpable heaviness. A discernible feeling of expectation lingered on the darkened windowsills. I peered out into the emptiness and saw only my reflection, my eyes wide. The wind battered the small cabin, the rain falling heavier as the night progressed.

I paced the room until my gaze rested on the full bookshelves. I pulled out Victor Hugo's *Les Misérables*, smiling to myself as I thought of Zeke reading about the French Revolution.

Propping myself up in the bed, I placed the gun on the bedside table within easy reach and began to read. My eyelids grew heavy as the fire burned low, and I quickly fell asleep.

The gray tones of dawn sent a tentative light into the darkened cabin. The fire had long since gone out, explaining the numbing cold that permeated the room. I sat up abruptly, the heavy book sliding off my lap. I had no idea how long I had been asleep.

I crept out of bed. The early light lent a muted quality to the colors of the room, as if I were still dreaming. But the sharp poke of the table corner told me I was indeed wide-awake.

Gnawing worry invaded the morning peacefulness. The men had not returned, and I had no idea what to do next. I walked to the window, my footsteps sounding oddly muffled. Peering out, I was met by thick, swirling puffs of fog. I leaned my forehead against the glass but could see only the hulking shadows of trees near the house.

A shout in the distance made me jump. It had definitely been a male voice. I sprang to the door, unlatched it, and opened it wide.

The crisp smell of morning and wet pine straw greeted me as I stood on the porch and strained my eyes to see beyond the steps. I took a few hesitant steps before stopping, the hairs on the back of my neck standing

212 · *Karen White*

at attention, a primordial sign of warning. The soft whinnying of a horse came from nearby. "Stuart?" I called.

A footfall came from behind me. "Turn around slowly."

Despite the frigid morning, sweat ran under my armpits. I turned to face the double barrel of a rifle not two inches from my face. I could not see them through the thick mist, but I felt two dark eyes boring into me.

"Why are you doing this, Pamela? I've never done anything to you." I amazed myself with my calmness. Inside, my stomach churned with terror.

"I am afraid I must disagree." She nudged me in the arm with the barrel. "Let us go inside. We have a little talking to do."

She followed me into the cabin, closing and latching the door behind me. "Sit down."

I allowed myself to drop into the rocker, not taking my eye off the rifle. I had seen the gun before in this cabin. I knew it was Zeke's.

"Where's Zeke?" I asked, trying to keep my voice calm.

Without turning her back to me, she examined every detail in the room, her eyes registering surprise as she took in the well-stocked bookshelves. Her gaze drifted to the tousled bed. "Ah. So you have seduced Stuart. I warned him, but he would not listen. Just like a man. I have found that the best way to deal with a man is to eliminate him—just like Julia's father." She chuckled lightly.

"Where is Zeke?" I repeated, refusing to be goaded.

Pamela hooked a chair leg with her foot and dragged it out from under the table to sit. "Somewhere in the woods." She paused to give me a wide grin. "With a bullet in him. And I hit him in the head with the butt of my rifle for good measure."

"Why?" I started to stand up, but her rifle motioned me back. "What has he ever done to you?"

"He helped you. That makes him my enemy."

My mouth went dry and I could almost hear my heart thumping. "I don't understand."

Her look softened slightly as she raised a quizzical smile. "Do you really not know who I am?"

I shook my head, then forced myself to ask the next question. "Where's

Stuart?" I clung to the chair like a lifeboat. No matter how much I wanted to get up and run, I knew just as strongly that Pamela would have no problem with shooting me before I reached the door. She had already tried to kill me once before.

"He is alive—for now. I find that keeping the two of you alive would be a most prudent move on my part. You are far more useful to me living. Right now, anyway."

I tried to reason with her. "Pamela, I think you are a very sick woman. I know you didn't mean to hurt Zeke—or me. Perhaps there are doctors who can help you. Just put down the gun so there are no more accidents."

She stared at me, amazement spreading across her face. "I know who you are. Do you not know who I am?"

Where is Stuart? I glanced at the window, white wisps of fog still stroking the glass. "I know you're a spy for the Confederates, if that's what you mean. But I am not a Yankee spy, as you probably think. I don't think I'm even capable of choosing sides in this conflict." I kept talking, hoping it would buy me time until Stuart returned.

The sound coming from her sounded like a bark, making me cringe. "I am not stupid, Laura Truitt. I know you are a traveler."

The blood seemed to evacuate my body, leaving my extremities to tingle with dread. "A traveler?" My voice sounded foreign to my ears.

"When I heard that you had been found on Moon Mountain, I suspected. And then you sang that rainbow song. When you sang it when you were sick, then I knew for sure. What I do not know is who sent you."

"Who sent me?" My mind reeled. How could she know about the traveling?

Her face narrowed into a tight pucker as she walked closer to me, the rifle barrel prodding me in the chest. "I will not be toyed with. And I would be happy to shoot you if you do not cooperate with me."

Realization, white-hot as lightning, struck me. "Are you a traveler, too?"

She cackled again. "Of course. From 1953, to be exact. I'm here on a mission, and you are going to help me succeed."

I remembered her astronomy books that she had sent down from Tennessee for safekeeping, and her ever watchfulness of me. But she was here for a purpose. "No. That can't be," I whispered. "You mean other people know about this?"

Her lipless grin showed small, even white teeth. "Oh yes." She looked at me with hooded eyes and pulled up the sleeve of her dress. A dark crescent-shaped birthmark marred the whiteness on her forearm. I sucked in my breath.

"How did you get here?" I couldn't move my eyes away from her arm.

"The same way all Shadow Warriors travel: wrapped in the atmosphere of a comet intensified by a lunar eclipse."

"Travelers," I whispered.

"Yes, dear. Like you and me. And your daughter. I saw her mark when I found her on Moon Mountain. I knew I needed to keep her close by to see who came after her. It was so convenient when Julia's daughter died. Otherwise, I would have had to help her along."

I felt sick. "Surely you wouldn't harm an innocent child."

Her face was serious. "I will do whatever it takes."

I swallowed my fear, eager for answers. "Are there many of us?" I began to shiver. Pamela grabbed the quilt off the bed and tossed it at me. Picking up my gun from the nightstand, she returned to where I was, pulled out a chair, and sat down opposite.

Still keeping the gun aimed at me, she began talking. "Not many—usually just one or two every generation. I thought I was the only surviving Shadow Warrior, but now I know I am wrong. I am a Southern Loyalist, and I am here to make sure the South wins. The South will rise again." Her voice shook with vehemence.

I wanted to laugh at the absurdity of it. "You can't be serious. You're only one person—you can't win a war single-handed."

She leaned back in her chair. "You know, Laura, for a young woman of obvious intelligence, you can be dense at times." Sitting up straight, she continued. "It is like playing the lottery, only you know the numbers beforehand. I am not alone. I have a group of loyal followers. And now I have you." She drummed her fingers on the rifle butt. "Now, why are you here?"

I swallowed and took a deep breath, trying to clear my brain. "I really don't know. It was an accident. I was just trying to find my daughter on top of Moon Mountain and I ended up here." My eyes widened as I considered another possibility. "Do your loyal followers know who you really are?"

"Of course not. Who would believe anything like that? No, they have all been handpicked by me to be slow of brains but quick on the trigger. And a little low on morals. Money talks with these men, and I have got lots of that. I came here prepared."

She laid the rifle behind her chair, but kept the handgun still trained on my chest.

I tried to reason with her, if only to keep my panic at bay. "I am not here for any purpose, and I refuse to help you do something that will deliberately change the course of history. Aren't you concerned that anything you change now might not have the repercussions you're planning on?"

Her eyes sparkled with energy as she leaned forward, elbows resting on her knees. "This war will bring the South to her knees, forever tying her to the yoke of Yankee dominance. These things will happen if I don't intervene. If I succeed, I can relieve the South's suffering by eliminating Reconstruction and lessening the effects of the Great Depression. I will be the South's savior." Her eyes flashed with a fanaticism that chilled my skin.

"I will not help you. Even if the South wins now, it's only a matter of time before they're fighting again. The South cannot win, now or later. It doesn't have the resources. It's ludicrous."

She leaned forward and hissed. "I am not asking for your opinion. It does not matter to me anyway. And besides . . ." A feral grain crossed her thin face. "If you ever want to see your daughter again, I suggest you listen very closely to what I ask of you."

My heart tightened in my chest. "What do you mean? Where's Sarah?"

"She is with my associate, Matt Kimball. We tried to get rid of you before, remember? But Matt wanted to have a little fun with you before he killed you, and missed his opportunity. It is just as well, because now I have a better idea."

"Why is Sarah with Matt?" My fingernails bit into my palms.

She smiled almost maternally. "That is my better idea. Matt is holding Sarah until you do what I ask of you. And if you do not . . ." The smile vanished from her face. "Matt will not think twice about cutting her throat."

I stood, feeling as if I were high on a tightrope. "She's only a child. You can't do this. Please. Think of Julia—of what you'd be doing to her. I won't say anything, I promise. Just tell me where Sarah is."

She smiled gently at me. "Now, where would be the fun in that?" She pushed the barrel of the gun into my chest and shoved me back in my chair.

"I want you to understand something. All it will take is a word from me, and you will never see your daughter alive again. But do as I ask, and I will release her to you. It is up to you, my dear."

"Laura!" It was Stuart. He was getting closer, probably at the edge of the woods.

I gripped the seat tighter, willing myself to remain where I was instead of wrapping my hands around her throat and choking her to death. Only the cold steel barrel of her gun prevented me from moving.

"What do you want me to do?" My voice croaked, my breath vaporizing in the chill air.

"I need you to kill General William Tecumseh Sherman." She paused, as if waiting for the enormity of her request to sink in. "We cannot let him take the city of Atlanta. If he is repulsed and forced to retreat, then the Northern war effort will crash. Our Northern neighbors are sicker of this conflict than we are—it will not take much to make them give up. Without a strong victory here, Lincoln will not be reelected in the fall. His opponent, McClellan, will win and sue for peace with the South. The nation will be torn apart—permanently. The Confederate States of America will be her own sovereign nation, never to be held in bondage by the Yankee oppressor again." She tightened her hold on the gun. "I would do it myself, but I am much too valuable."

I shook my head. "You are certifiable. There are a lot of ifs involved here. . . ."

She brushed my words aside with her hand. "Stuart's getting closer, Laura. All I have to do is shoot him through the door with my rifle. What are you going to do?"

I heard Stuart's voice outside again, coming closer. "Damn you! I can't—"

She picked the rifle off the floor and trained it on the door. "You can bury him next to Sarah."

My mind reeled in a sickening kaleidoscope of bloodred fear. "All right. I'll do it." My voice reverberated throughout the room.

Lowering the rifle, she smiled at me. "Good choice. I knew you were smart." She stood, leaving the handgun behind on the chair. "Do not tell Stuart about this. I will find out, and I will kill him and Sarah both. And find an excuse not to go with them to Valdosta. I need you here." She strode to the door. "Pack a carpetbag with whatever you will need for traveling, but keep it hidden. Make sure you include the red dress you wore at Christmas—General Sherman is sure to find you irresistible in it." She paused, then added, "Be ready at a moment's notice." She unlatched the rear door and let herself out, quickly disappearing in the swirling mists. The muffled sound of hoofbeats faded into the fog.

Dots danced before my eyes and I realized I had been holding my breath. Filling my lungs with great gulps of air, I stood and ran to the door, calling Stuart's name.

CHAPTER TWENTY

—◆—

So many worlds, so much to do,
So little done, such things to be.

—LORD TENNYSON

I flew blindly out the door, only stopping when I realized I stood in the middle of a wall of fog and could see neither the cabin nor the woods, although I knew the cabin was somewhere behind me. My breath came hard and fast, my lungs pressing on my ribs.

"Stuart!" I screamed, feeling the panic rise and struggle to choke me. Pamela was out there with her gun. "Stuart!" The swirling haze sucked up my voice, evaporating the sound.

A dark form emerged from the mist and I struck out in an automatic reflex. A strong hand grabbed hold of my wrist, but another scream died in my throat when I recognized Stuart.

"I have Zeke—he has been shot. Help me get him back to the cabin." A thick shadow hovered behind Stuart's shoulders and I realized it was his grandfather.

"This way," I said, leading him the way I had come.

Stuart laid Zeke on the bed and pulled a knife from his belt. Bright crimson spotted Stuart's jacket in an incongruous rose pattern as the coppery taste of blood lingered in the air. Stuart cut through Zeke's pants, peeling back the blood-saturated material. A hole in his right thigh, about the size of a quarter, oozed red, surrounded by black tissue. It looked surprisingly like a black eye in the middle of his thigh. Congealed blood spilled down his forehead, making his hair stick to his skin. A soft groan emerged from Zeke's cracked lips, letting us know that he was alive. But from the gray pallor of his skin, I wasn't sure for how much longer. A large loss of blood would lead to shock. He needed a massive infusion of fluid.

I raced to the cold fireplace and took down the kettle, luckily filled with water. Using a ladle, I began feeding him the fluid his body needed.

"Give me your nightgown." I hardly recognized Stuart's voice.

"What?"

"I need it to staunch the flow of blood." Stuart reached for the hem of my nightgown.

He tore a hole in it with his knife, and, with a heavy jerk, made a large horizontal tear.

I reached over to the bed and snatched the sheet off of it. "Use this instead." I had already realized that one of us had to run for help, and I certainly didn't want to do it naked.

Stuart and I began ripping at the sheet, aided by the knife.

"It was Pamela, Stuart. I saw her."

Stuart didn't pause. He vigorously ripped the fabric and then moved to Zeke's side to apply it with pressure to the gaping wound.

He looked at me, blue eyes blazing. "She was here?"

I paused, not knowing how much I could tell him. "Yes. I heard your shout, so I opened the door and she was there. She had a gun, but she ran when she heard your voice."

I couldn't look at him, afraid he'd see the lie in my eyes. I went over to Zeke and lifted his arm. The skin on his forearm felt clammy and cold. "One of us needs to get help."

"I know." He looked at me closely. "But I have experience with gun-shot wounds." Our eyes met over Zeke's still form. "Endy knows the way blindfolded and can get you to Phoenix Hall quickly."

I swallowed. The thought of riding Endy at a trot in full daylight was harrowing. The thought of riding him through the woods in heavy fog at breakneck speed was unthinkable. I looked down at Zeke, whose shallow breath barely made his chest rise and from whom the stench of blood rose thick in the air. The thought of him dying under my un-skilled hands was worse. "All right. I can do it."

He nodded. "You will be fine." His voice held all the conviction I lacked.

I stayed with Zeke, applying pressure to the wound, while Stuart saddled Endy.

The fog had begun to lift and hovered amid the higher branches of the trees, the murky sun making an effort to penetrate the cloud and illuminate us below.

Stuart wrapped me in his warm coat and strapped his holster and gun around my waist. I knew I had nothing to fear from Pamela, but accepted the gun without comment. As he lifted me into the saddle, he said, with a weak grin, "Do not shoot the horse."

I couldn't make my facial muscles return his grin. "Yeah, sure." I grabbed hold of the pommel. My voice shaking, I said, "Okay. I'm ready."

He gave me the reins, patted the horse on the rump, and shouted, "Go!" The earth slid out from under me as the great beast lurched forward, his speed steadily climbing as he began to cover the distance. All the riding tips and pointers that Stuart had given me during my informal lessons fell by the wayside. The only thing I could think of was holding on for dear life to avoid being thrown off and trampled. The thought of Zeke's pale body on the bed spurred me on, and with renewed fervor I kicked the sides of the horse, making him gallop harder.

The outlines of Phoenix Hall appeared, and I leaned over the horse's neck, giving him the lead. The air was sucked out of my lungs, my fingers numb from gripping the saddle so tightly.

Endy stopped at the back porch, and I was relieved to see Julia at the door, as I had no idea how to dismount from the horse by myself.

"Julia, Zeke's been shot." I left out the detail of who had shot him. That would come out soon enough. "He might be dying, and he needs help."

"Where is he?"

"He's at his cabin with Stuart."

She stepped forward, grabbing my arm. "Sarah is missing. Have you seen her?"

"Yes." I swallowed, trying to still the shakiness in my voice. "She's fine right now. We'll talk about it later."

She didn't release her grip. "Did you say anything to her to make her run away?"

"No, Julia. I promised you I wouldn't, and I didn't. We'll talk about it later—we've got to help Zeke now."

Too distracted to notice my dress, or lack thereof, Julia turned around to go back up the porch steps, her skirts swirling around her. "I will get my medicine and take Endy back to the cabin. You go get Charles and bring him there."

Within minutes, we had exchanged places and I watched her disappear into the woods, her skirts flying around the black flank of the horse, her long hair streaming unbound behind her.

Charles's office and residence were only about one mile from Phoenix Hall, and I ran all the way. I was out of practice, but the adrenaline pushed me down the dirt lanes and brick road to his house.

A rumpled Dr. Watkins was busily trying to erase the sleep from his eyes when he finally answered my banging on the door. His robe was belted over his nightshirt, and his face registered shock at my appearance. His eyes took in Stuart's coat thrown over my torn nightgown and my bare toes peeping out from under the ragged hem.

I pushed open the door. "I am sorry to bother you so early, Dr. Watkins, but we need you. Zeke has been shot."

The disapproving frown disappeared from his face as he sprang into action. "I will be down in a moment." He paused on the top step, looked at my disheveled appearance once again, and opened his mouth to say something. He closed it, then ran up the rest of the flight of stairs.

Knowing the buggy wouldn't fit through the path in the woods, we rode the doctor's horse. I kept pulling my nightgown over my legs as best I could, but eventually gave up, hoping Dr. Watkins had more important things on his mind than my alarming lack of modesty.

The cloying aroma of brewing herbs struck me as we entered the cabin. A soft groan came from the bed, and I sighed with relief knowing Zeke was still alive. Realizing I could only get in the way, I approached the now rekindled and blazing fire, my frozen fingers and toes aching with cold.

"Thank you again, Laura." I startled at the soft voice behind me and whipped around to see Julia, her hands caked with blood and droplets spattered on her dress in a macabre pattern.

"For what?"

"For once again coming between my family and disaster."

I waved my hand at her, feeling guilty for my part in this particular disaster. "I haven't done anything but be a messenger. I feel quite helpless, actually."

She sat down next to me in the rocker. Nodding in the direction of the bed, she said, "He is in good hands now. I have faith that Charles can save him."

Julia began to tuck stray ends of hair behind her ears. Then, in a barely audible voice, she said, "It was Pamela who did this?"

I answered simply, "Yes."

Her shoulders slumped and she looked down at her lap. "I blame myself, then. I knew she was not in her right mind. I should have had her committed long ago." Her hands rested in a tight ball in her lap. "But she was the only family I had left. I never thought she could do something like this."

I stared into the fire and saw two dark eyes staring back at me over the muzzle of a rifle. "She has Sarah."

She stood so suddenly her chair would have crashed to the floor if I hadn't steadied it. "What? Where is she? We have to find her." Her eyes widened as the color drained from her face. "She is not safe with Pamela."

"Sit down," I said, forcing my voice to stay calm.

After a brief hesitation, she did as I'd asked. I leaned closer so as not to be overheard. "She's blackmailing me. If I do something for her, she'll keep Sarah safe."

Her fingers gripped the chair arms. "What does she want you to do?"

I shook my head. "I can't tell you—it would put all of us in jeopardy. And you can't tell anyone what you know, either—especially not Stuart. She's threatened all of you if I whisper a word. We already know what she's capable of." I glanced at Zeke. "I will do whatever it takes to get her back. Do you understand?"

She buried her face in her hands, her shoulders shaking from silent sobs. I knelt in front of her chair. "Do you understand, Julia? You're not to tell anyone. You need to trust me."

She nodded, then raised her head, her eyes rimmed with red. "When will this war be over and we can resume our lives again? Nothing is as it should be anymore, and I am starting to doubt that we can survive it."

I grabbed her with a hand on each shoulder. "Listen to me. This war will be over in slightly more than a year. You've already made it through almost three years of hardship and worry. I know you can go a little bit more. And I can promise you that you will not lose your house." I wondered if I had said too much, but I couldn't bear to see her give up now.

Her sobs had stopped and she stared at me. "How do you know these things, Laura? How could you possibly know?"

I glanced at the two men by the bed, tending to Zeke and out of earshot. "You're going to think I'm crazy, Julia, but I swear it's true. I don't know why or how—all I know is that it really happened and I'm as sane as I've ever been."

She leaned forward, her swollen eyes open wide. "What are you talking about?"

I took a deep breath and blurted out everything before I could change my mind. I didn't leave out any details, as if by including everything, it would seem more believable to us both.

I paused briefly and finished. "I was born in 1979. Technically, I haven't been born yet and won't be for another one hundred and sixteen years from now." I could now see the whites all around her irises.

"Ouch! You're hurting me." Her fingers had become clawlike as they gripped me.

She immediately released her grip. "Sarah, too?"

I had to lean closer to hear her, her voice was so quiet. I nodded. "And Pamela. But I don't know how long she's been here. She said she was from the nineteen fifties." I felt the burden of my secret release a bit of its hold on me.

Julia blinked, as if she were trying to focus on something she couldn't quite see. "How is this possible?" she whispered.

"I don't know. All I know is that there's some kind of a connection between Moon Mountain and the dual specter of a lunar eclipse and a comet. And this." I showed her my birthmark. She sucked in a deep breath, and I knew she was recognizing it from Sarah's arm. "Besides that, I don't know. But I suspect Pamela does. It was no accident that found her here in this time."

I looked closely at her. Her face blanched, her eyes dark circles of color in her white face. "Are you okay?" I rose to be able to catch her if she decided to fall out of her chair.

She nodded, but I remained unconvinced. "This is a bit of a shock." She stood shakily. "But this is the least of our worries right now," she said, indicating the tableaux by the bed.

"I don't know why I'm here—if there's even a reason for it. And I don't know what repercussions there could be. No one knows but you. And Pamela. She knows about Sarah, too."

She gave me a weary nod of her head and stood. "I want to argue with you, to force you to bring me with you to save our daughter. But I do trust you. Just as much as I understand that you must do this alone. I do not like it, but I cannot fight it." She took a deep, shuddering breath. "Please bring Sarah back safely, Laura. Without her . . ." She looked away, unable to finish her sentence.

Slowly, she returned to the bedside. I stole a glance at the still figure on the bed and felt a sinking feeling in my belly. The sheets were stained a deep crimson, creating a dramatic backdrop to the pale leg lying on top. A white bandage, startling against the grayness of his hair, now covered most of Zeke's forehead. Charles probed into the leg wound with a long metal instrument, while Stuart poured the amber contents of Zeke's beloved jug over the hole, making Zeke's body twitch. I swallowed quickly and turned away. I felt helpless in my inactivity, but I knew there was nothing more I could do.

I awoke to the sound of a log falling in the fireplace. Stuart prodded the fire with a poker, his face grim. I sat up with a start, my stomach grumbling. "What time is it?"

His face creased in a slight smile. "Time for you to eat."

I glanced toward the bed. A white bandage had been wrapped around the wounded leg, but there was still no movement from Zeke. "How is he?"

"Better. Charles managed to remove as much of the bullet as he could, and Julia has dressed the wound to prevent it from festering. Now we just wait and see."

"Where are Charles and Julia?"

"They have returned to Phoenix Hall. We are to bring Zeke there later. He is not safe here."

"Stuart." A weak voice sounded from the bed.

Zeke's teeth chattered together, his whole body shaking. I pulled the quilt up on the bed and tucked it in around him. He had always appeared tall and imposing, but now it was as if his body had left a mere shadow of the man on the bed. Instinctively, I laid a hand on his forehead and brushed the hair out of his eyes.

His eyes bored into mine, emphasizing his words. "We have to get you away from here. Pamela . . . It was Pamela."

"We know," said Stuart. "We are going to bring you back to Phoenix Hall to keep you safe." He dipped a ladle into the water bucket and held it to Zeke's lips.

Zeke pushed it away angrily. "Listen," he said, his voice hoarse. "It is Laura who is in danger."

He began to rise off the bed, but I gently pushed him back. "It's okay. Pamela won't hurt me. We reached a truce. We're safe."

I felt two sets of eyes on me and could not meet either one.

"What kind of a truce?" Stuart's voice held a hint of anger, but I managed to meet his eyes.

"I need you to trust me again. A lot more than you know is at stake." Zeke groaned, and I saw that his eyes had become glazed. "Do you have anything for his pain?"

Distracted momentarily, Stuart answered, "Yes, Julia left some wintergreen tea." He walked toward the fire. "We are not done with our discussion."

Nothing more was said as Endy was saddled and we prepared to vacate the cabin. We rode back to Phoenix Hall near dusk in a somber procession. I sat behind Zeke on Endy's saddle, clutching tightly to the older man to prevent him from slipping off. His mind was clouded over with pain. He spoke in a tongue I had never heard before—probably Cherokee. I was surprised when Stuart answered him back in the same language. The soothing inflections of his voice told me he offered words of comfort to his grandfather.

While Stuart brought Zeke inside, I raced upstairs to put on some clothes. It felt strange to be in my room again, as I remembered the last time I had been there and was in a haze of poison and near death. I shuddered but entered, the cheeriness of the room pushing back the dark thoughts of Sarah with Matt Kimble. And what might happen should I fail to do the impossible.

I dressed hurriedly, skipping the corset and hoops, but at least remembering three petticoats. My mind raced as I buttoned up the coarse muslin, weighing my options.

When I had entered the house, I had noticed all the little things that were missing: pictures from the walls, knickknacks from the tables. I had nearly tripped over a trunk of children's clothes and linens that lay open at the bottom of the steps. It was apparent that Julia was ready to move her household to Valdosta.

Pamela had told me to stay. But I could not endanger Sarah's life by telling anyone why. I had to think of another reason.

I followed voices into the parlor as I came down the steps. Stuart stood by the window, drinking from a glass. Dr. Watkins stood next to him, his eyes on Julia, who was sitting on the sofa. All heads turned as I entered.

"You are leaving for Valdosta tomorrow." Stuart took a deep swallow from his drink.

I bristled under his authoritative statement. "I don't think so."

He raised a questioning eyebrow.

I turned to Charles. "Surely Zeke shouldn't be moved yet."

"Yes, you are quite correct." He looked at Stuart and shrugged. "But the news from up north is not good. The Yankees are amassing a huge army just north of our border, and Captain Clark of the Roswell Battalion has informed me that they will be making defensive preparations in case of an attack on Roswell. He is advising that women and children leave."

"And it is doubtful my mother will follow us all the way south to Valdosta." Julia's quiet voice was almost lost in the din of the blood pounding in my temples. I had thought of a plan.

"I will stay here with Zeke. When he is well enough to travel, we will follow you."

Stuart and Charles began their protests at once. But Julia's voice drowned them out. "Laura is right. It could kill Zeke to move him. The Yankees are not coming tomorrow—they will be safe for the time being. If she wants to stay, then let her stay."

My gaze met Julia's, and she gave a quick nod before glancing away.

"But what about Pamela? She tried to kill you and Zeke both." Stuart rubbed his hand through his hair. "And I could never leave a woman alone here with only a sick old man." He stopped his pacing to stand in front of me. "What kind of a truce did you make with Pamela?"

Charles stepped in. "You cannot trust Pamela. Her mind is obviously unhinged."

"I can't tell you—I gave her my word." I stared into two sets of eyes, one brown, the other blue, and saw the same expression in them. Like I was some recalcitrant child that needed to be persuaded into something that was for her own good. "I know I have said this more times than you've wanted to hear it, but you have to trust me. There is too much at stake for me to tell you any more."

Julia's voice sounded loud and clear. "Think of everything that Laura has done for this family. She has never betrayed our trust in her. I believe her and will do as she asks. I am asking you both to do the same."

I could see Stuart wavering.

Julia stood, imposing despite her small stature. "Would you rather we abandoned your house to looters and put your grandfather at risk?"

The two men looked at us as if we had lost our minds. Stuart scooped his hat off the table, and glowered at Julia and me. "I have met mules who were less stubborn than you two women. God help the Yankees if they ever pick a fight with you." Excusing himself, he left the room, with Charles following in short order.

Julia faced me, her false bravado gone. "Have you any news of Sarah?"

I shook my head. "Not yet. But I won't go anywhere until I know she's all right, and I will let you know. Somehow I will get word to you."

She surprised me by hugging me. "I don't know how we have survived without you." Pulling back, she said, "I need to see to Zeke. Before I leave tomorrow, I will have to show you how to make his dressings and how to prepare his medicine. I will also need to come up with a plausible reason why Sarah isn't with us." In a rustling of her skirts, she also left the room.

All through the night, the slamming of drawers and trunk lids and the sounds of heavy furniture being dragged across wooden floors shattered the night. I was relieved to see the piano remaining, assuming it was too big to be moved anywhere and thus also safe from the Yankees.

The following morning, I stood staring out the sidelights of the front door, watching Stuart load one of the wooden farm wagons. Soft footsteps approached behind me, the light fragrance of lavender surrounding me.

"He's almost done," I said. Julia stood beside me and nodded. "What did you tell the men about Sarah?"

She turned and placed her valise on top of a trunk. "I told them she had been invited by Ruth and Josiah Reed to ride to Valdosta with them and their family. They left yesterday." She took my hand and squeezed it. "Godspeed, Laura. And bring Sarah home." Her voice cracked, her eyes pooling with tears.

I ignored her reference to home, as if the very word wasn't in dispute.

She let go of my hand and reached into a pocket of her cloak. "I want you to have this. It goes to the secret compartment in the armoire in my bedroom. I am taking the family Bible with me, but I've copied all the family records in here—of births and deaths." Her eyes bored into mine, and I reached for the object she was handing me. I knew which armoire she was speaking of: the same one that would sit in my bedroom more than 150 years in the future. But I had never known it contained a secret compartment.

"I will put some personal family letters and documents in it. If you do return to your home, you will be able to find out what has become of us all." Her eyes were misty as she dropped a small, heavy object into my hand. I looked down, my palm burning. Lying in my open palm was a key. A key identical to the one worn around the neck of the woman in the portrait Mrs. Cudahy had given me. "I have one just like it and will keep it locked after I have put everything in it."

I swallowed to ease my suddenly dry throat. "Thank you, Julia. But

I hope that I can give it back to you in person." She embraced me tightly, the top of her head resting under my chin and her hair smelling of lavender and wood smoke.

Stuart came in the front door and hoisted the last trunk onto his broad shoulders, his limp no longer discernible. He avoided looking in my direction and left again to put the final piece of luggage on the wagon. From the corner of my eye, a gleam of silver caught my attention. Mrs. Cudahy's tray, forgotten on a hall table. Easy pickings for the marauding army. I grabbed it up and ran out of the house, clutching it to my bosom.

"Wait! You forgot this!"

Stuart jumped down from the wagon. "One of the few unsold pieces of my mother's wedding silver. Thank you."

Our eyes met in the watery reflection of the smooth silver. "I don't suppose I can change your mind about staying," he said.

"No. You can't." I stepped closer. "Do you remember what Zeke told you right after I came here? Something about how you needed to trust me because I would be your salvation? This is the time, Stuart. Regardless of where you think my loyalties lie, you need to believe that I have your and your family's best interests at heart. Staying here with Zeke is something I need to do. I'm not helpless, and I certainly don't need a man around to protect me. Don't worry about me—I can take care of myself. You taught me how to shoot, remember?"

His eyes narrowed into blue slits. "There is an army of about a hundred thousand men who are thinking about heading in this direction, and you are telling me not to worry about you. It is all I can do not to tie you up and throw you in the back of this wagon. Maybe all the jostling on the road to Valdosta would knock some sense into you."

"I wish we could stop arguing about this. My mind's made up and I won't budge. Can't we just leave it at that and say a proper goodbye?"

He leapt onto the wagon and secured the tray in one of the trunks. I wondered briefly if I would ever see it again in this century.

I thought again of telling him everything, and just as quickly dismissed it from my mind. Sarah's life hung in the balance, as did Stuart's and everybody else's, and there was no doubt in my mind what

Pamela would do if she found out I had confided in him. I looked up at his stormy face and knew that no matter what I said, he didn't really trust me enough to leave this alone.

The gray sky overhead held the chill of the air close to the earth, and the heavy cloud cover threatened rain. I wrapped my shawl tightly around me as Willie ambled out of the house, his eyes downcast. Even the horse seemed subdued. I had said goodbyes many times in my life, but none as painful or as permanent as this one seemed to be.

Julia had gone to the cemetery to say goodbye to Robbie one more time. I wanted to reassure her that she would come back to Roswell at the war's end. All I knew was that her beloved house would survive, but not who would come back to claim it.

"Laura."

I turned to see Stuart with his arm outstretched. I took his hand and allowed him to lead me across the winter-browned grass to the side of the house. The deceptive dark green of the boxwoods made it seem like spring, but the drab browns and grays of the rest of the fauna reminded me that this was the darkest part of the year.

"No, I am not going to ask you again. I know your mind is made up. But I cannot leave you, in good conscience, without means to protect yourself. I have asked Charles to keep an eye on things here. Let him know if there is anything you need." He stopped walking and turned to me, his blue stare melting something inside me. "And there is something else."

He lifted my left hand and I felt cold metal on the tip of my third finger. A gold filigree ring with a stone of black jet slid easily over my knuckle, resting next to Michael's plain gold band.

I stared at it, the smooth surface reflecting the clouds overhead. "What is this?"

"My father gave this to my mother when he proposed to her." His eyes studied me, as if measuring my reaction. "I am giving this to you for protection."

My gaze traveled back down to the ring, dark against the paleness of my skin. "How would this protect me?"

His gaze never wavered. "That would depend on which army you have the most to fear. If you marry me, you would become not only the wife of a Confederate officer, but also the sister-in-law of a Federal officer on General Sherman's staff. You would be covered on all sides."

I blinked hard. "Are you asking me to marry you?"

"Well, yes."

"To protect me?"

"Yes—among other reasons."

"Like what?"

He paused, scrutinizing me. "I will tell you everything when you do the same."

I touched the ring with my right hand, shaking my head. "I am glad that is the main reason. Otherwise, I could not say yes in good conscience."

His arms went around me, pulling me close. His lips touched mine briefly before he pulled away. "I will be back as soon as I know Julia is settled. When I return, we will have the Reverend Pratt make it official."

I clutched the ring tightly, trying to hold on to the smallest glimmer of reality. How could I marry him and then disappear? Could he remarry, not knowing what had happened to his wife?

He kissed me again and held me against him for a long time, until we heard Julia's voice calling for us. With a final kiss, he led me back to the wagon to say my final goodbyes. As I kneeled one last time in front of Willie, he clutched at my skirt. "Miss Laura. I am going to miss you so much!"

I shut my eyes tight and hugged him to me. "And I'm going to miss you, too, Willie."

He looked up at me with his tear-streaked face, and I brushed the drops aside with my fingers before planting a kiss on his freckled nose. I said goodbye one last time and helped him up to the bench seat of the wagon. "Mind your mama now, you hear?"

Stuart mounted Endy and suddenly there was nothing more to do. They were ready to leave Roswell and their home for the duration of the war, and perhaps longer. It was time. I hugged Julia one last time before Stuart helped her up and she took the reins, and then I forced myself to wave as the wagon pulled out, Endy following closely behind.

I watched them until they were nearly at the end of the long drive before I couldn't take it anymore. "Wait!" I shouted. I ran to catch up with Stuart, my skirts held shockingly high. I reached him all out of breath and, before I could protest, he leaned down and pulled me up on the saddle in front of him.

"Did you forget something?" The side of his mouth quirked up slightly.

"Yes, I did." I swallowed deeply, trying to regain my breath. "I forgot to tell you to be careful." Something flickered in his eyes, his hands tightening on my waist. I threw my arms around him, kissed him soundly, then quickly slid off the side of the horse.

Julia gave me a wan look as the loaded wagon trundled past, and I knew she was thinking of Sarah. I mouthed the words, "I'll bring her back," and she nodded as she passed me. Willie's dark head bobbed beside her, his brown eyes filled with tears. I sucked in my breath and held it, afraid to let it go. Afraid to let them hear my shrieking out my grief at letting them go, and my fear of staying behind and not knowing what was to come.

Sukie sat on the other side of Willie, hugging him. A wheel hit a soggy rut, and there was a moment when we thought that their trip would be delayed, but the straining of the horse pulled it out and they continued down the front drive.

Stuart sat atop Endy, his eyes fixed on me. Finally, as the wagon drove through the front gates, he tipped his hat and turned the horse around to follow. I raced after them and stood leaning on the gate, bent over while I sucked in my breath in deep gulps, my gaze anchored to Stuart's back until he disappeared around the bend.

I lifted my muddy skirts and trudged back to the house. I felt the unfamiliar weight on my finger and stopped halfway to examine the ring. The overcast sky clouded the jet, giving it only a murky gleam. I felt the tears coming and knew I couldn't hold them back much longer. I stared at the house as I got nearer and felt a surge of pride and, for the first time, what compelled Stuart and so many others like him to risk their lives for their homes and all they represented. There had always been a connection between this house and me ever since I had first seen it with Michael. Phoenix Hall had become my home and my daughter's, just as the Elliotts had become my family. Perhaps I had been sent here to save them both from destruction. Or maybe I had been sent here to find happiness in my life again. And, maybe still, the two were connected.

A black crow flew overhead, cawing loudly. A feeling of someone walking over my grave settled on me, making my skin tingle with dread, and I thought of Sarah and where she might be. I climbed the porch and entered the house, closing the door soundly behind me.

CHAPTER TWENTY-ONE

———◆———

Between two worlds life hovers like a star,
'Twixt night and morn, upon the horizon's verge.
—LORD BYRON

During the remaining cold weeks of January and February, my thoughts were never far from Sarah. I grieved anew for my daughter, and knew there was nothing that I wouldn't do to bring her back. So I tended Zeke and the garden, watching them both stir in the last embrace of winter, and I waited for Stuart. And Pamela. Every noise in the night and every shadow at the window sent my heart racing. After the first week, I stopped tiptoeing about the house, expecting her around every corner. After three weeks, I had relaxed enough to be able to sleep through most of the night, waking only a few times in the darkest hours with an edgy wariness.

On a warm afternoon, I was rocking on the front porch, enjoying the hint of spring in the air and taking a much-needed break from nursing. Dr. Watkins's familiar buggy appeared at the front gate and ambled its way down the drive. Too tired to stand and greet him, I waved.

Clambering down, Charles tied his horse to the hitch, then lifted his hat to me before joining me on the porch.

"Mind if I sit?"

"No, of course not." I waved my hand in the direction of the chair next to mine.

"How is Zeke?"

"Much better—no headaches for three days now. And he can manage walking with the crutch without my help."

Grunting, he sat back and began to dig in his vest pocket for his pipe and tobacco.

"I'm starting to see something green in the vegetable garden. I might need some help in identifying whatever I'm growing."

Charles nodded and then took a puff from his pipe, slowly letting the smoke leak out of his mouth. The tobacco perfumed the air and I was suddenly reminded of my father.

Without looking at me he said, "Mrs. Truitt, may I call you Laura?" He pinkened under his whiskers.

"I'd like that. But only if I can call you Charles."

The color in his cheeks deepened, and his gaze continued to focus across the front lawn. He nodded. "Yes. Yes, of course."

He began fidgeting with his pipe and cleared his throat three or four times. Not knowing how much of his discomfort I could bear, I asked, "Is there something you'd like to say?"

The stricken look on his face reminded me of Charlie when I had had to pull a large splinter from his rear paw. "Um, ahem. Yes, there is, as a matter of fact. Of course. Yes."

I stopped rocking and glanced over at him with anticipation. He looked back at me and moved his lips, but no sound was forthcoming. He was beginning to worry me.

"What? Is it about Stuart?"

He stood abruptly, making the back of the rocking chair bang against the front of the house. "Well, yes, in a way, I suppose it is."

I stood next to him, one hand on the railing. "Is he hurt? For Pete's sake, would you just spit it out before we both grow old and gray?"

He blinked his eyes quickly. "I would like to move into the preacher's room. I would be out of your way, and I could help take care of Zeke."

I narrowed my eyes at him. "What's wrong with your house? The preacher's room is barely big enough for a bed and a Bible. Why on earth would you want to do that? And we both know Zeke is on the mend and I am more than capable of nursing him back to health."

He shifted on his feet, looking down at his boots, seemingly examining every scratch.

"And what has this got to do with Stuart?"

He finally looked at me, his watery brown eyes full of embarrassment. I had to strain my ears to hear him. "Stuart thought that you, um, might need my protection. I told him you would not like it, but he insisted. So here I am."

The echoing honks of geese flying overhead in their V formation brought my gaze heavenward. I turned back to Charles and placed my hand on his forearm, the brown wool of his coat rough under my fingers. "There is no need for you to move in here, but the fact that you would be willing to do that for my sake is admirable. And appreciated."

He pressed his lips together. "I beg your pardon, Mrs.— I mean, Laura. But for your safety, you need a male on the premises."

"I appreciate your concern, but there really isn't any danger. The Yankees are still up in Tennessee and no immediate threat. Just because I'm a woman doesn't mean I don't know how to protect myself. And Stuart himself showed me how to use this." I reached into the pocket of my housedress and pulled out the gun Stuart had given me.

Charles stepped back, his eyes widening. "Be careful with that—it's liable to go off."

"Not very likely, Charles. I'm not an idiot." I turned away from him and started to shove the gun back into my pocket when my ears were split with a sudden explosion. I looked down at the front of my dress and saw a large, smoldering hole decorating the pocket edge.

"Are you all right?" The concern in his voice was genuine, but I was too embarrassed to soften toward him.

"Of course I am. But my dress certainly isn't." I stuck my fingers through the hole and was dismayed at the extent of the damage. My whole fist could have fit through the opening.

Charles straightened. "I will move my things into the preacher's room this afternoon."

I looked at his determined face and hoped against hope that Pamela wouldn't object to his presence. But I had no doubt that when she was ready to speak to me, she would have no trouble avoiding detection from anybody else.

"Fine, Charles. If you think it best." I shrugged. "You Southern gentlemen sure are stubborn."

The corners of his mouth turned up slightly. "And so are our women."

I gave him a grudging smile, and then we said our goodbyes before

I turned to go into the house. I opened the door and went into the hallway, the sight of a figure at the top of the stairs startling me.

"I heard a gunshot." Zeke held a precarious foothold on the top step, one arm clutching his crutch, the other one holding an enormous musket of ancient vintage.

I rushed up the stairs toward him, before he could pitch forward and do more damage to his leg, or worse. "Zeke, what are you doing on the stairs?" I took the musket out of his hands, placed it on the floor, and grabbed him securely by his arm. "It was only me being stupid. I accidentally fired my gun."

He nodded, making the fine beads of sweat on his forehead run down his face.

"I'm sorry for scaring you." I led him to his room and settled him onto his bed. He leaned his head back, his skin ashen against the stark white of the pillow.

His eyes didn't leave my face. "You are in great danger, Laura. My dreams show me a dark shadow hovering behind you. Leave here. Leave while you still can."

I sat down on the edge of the bed and saw the challenge in his eyes. "I can't, Zeke. There's a problem." Restless, I stood and went to the window, looking out at the gray landscape of naked trees. A few stubborn leaves clung to branches, unwilling to let go. Buds covered the tree limbs, promising a new spring. I pressed my hand against the window, the glass cool against my palm. I knew I could take him into my confidence, and the strain of keeping my worry about my daughter a secret pulled at me. "Sarah is in great danger. Pamela's taken her and won't release her unless I do something for her."

He grunted softly. "Sarah is well, Laura. I would see in my dreams if she were harmed."

I shook my head. "I want to believe you, but we both know what Pamela is capable of. And she isn't working alone. I know Matt Kimball and others are involved, too."

His eyes, glazed with pain, regarded me gently. "Sarah is safe. Now, tell me: What is it that Pamela has asked you to do?"

"I'm not going to tell you. It could put you in grave danger. I don't know if I can do what she asks, but I've got to do something. I cannot lose my daughter again."

"Does Stuart know?"

"No. He would most likely want to do something that could put us all in danger. He can't know."

I walked over to the bookshelves and pulled out the backgammon game and began setting it up on the flattened bedclothes next to him. "I must find Sarah and bring her back soon. According to your books, the next time a comet will appear in conjunction with a total lunar eclipse will be September first, 1864. That gives me seven months. Seven months to sell my soul."

A strong hand grabbed my wrist. "Do what you must, Laura. But remember the legend: The ancient travelers who journeyed with evil spirits were always hunted down and slaughtered. They must not be allowed to walk in this plane."

His grip tightened, and I shuddered. "What would you have me do, Zeke?"

He let go and placed his hand on my head, just as he had done when we first met. "Sometimes we are called upon to do something greater than ourselves, against forces we might not understand. It is a gift." He pulled my sleeve up over my forearm. The crescent-shaped birthmark looked like a bruise on the pale skin. "You have the mark. It is a very rare mark—I have never known of more than three people born within a century to be blessed with it."

Again, I shuddered. I saw his eyes droop and his mouth soften. His hand fell to my arm and he muttered, "Be careful," before succumbing to sleep.

I settled him, then gathered up the game and left the room. I faltered at the top of the steps, the game board slipping from my grasp and somersaulting down each stair. The markers danced on the wooden treads, their eventual destination determined by the hands of fate.

I sat down on the top step and rolled down my sleeve. A spark of light caught my attention and I reached over to a corner of the step. I picked up a marble and rolled it in my hand, feeling the cold smoothness. Fresh grief flowed through me as I recalled Sarah playing with them, lying close to the floor and flicking them with her little fingers toward Willie. I ached for my child with the same intensity I had felt when she went missing on Moon Mountain so many years ago. Her life was in my hands, and I wouldn't fail her again. I stood and began gathering the round markers as I descended the stairs.

The days passed in almost nerve-jangling precision, and still no word from Stuart or Pamela. I prayed for Sarah, for there was precious little else I could do, except wait. And then in mid-April, Stuart came back to me. I was in the chicken house, battling with the hens. My skirt was full of eggs, which were quickly forgotten when I heard his voice.

"Hungry again?"

I whipped around, the eggs jumbling against each other in the corner of my skirt.

"Oh," I said, letting go of my dress and listening to the muffled crashing of the eggs in the hay. "You're back."

He stood silhouetted against the henhouse doorway, a tall, dark shadow. "Is that the way a bride-to-be greets her groom?"

I walked toward him, a nervous smile teasing my lips. I looked into his eyes and saw my reflection. "You should have called first. My hair's a mess and I haven't a thing to wear."

With a quizzical look on his face, he stilled my chattering by bringing his mouth to mine. "Hush, woman, and allow me to give you a proper greeting." He kissed me again, his skin moist and smooth and smelling of soap.

I broke away, laying my hand on his cheek. "You shaved."

"Yes, ma'am. I know how you feel about beards. And I did not want to offend your delicate sensibilities."

I snorted. "I didn't know I had any."

His mouth tilted at the corners. "You might have a few, but not too many. That's what I find so attractive about you."

His expression became serious. "Is there something wrong?" He reached out a thumb to smooth the frown lines over the bridge of my nose.

I blinked, trying to get rid of the sting in my eyes. "I miss Sarah— and the others. And you, too. I missed you."

He bent to kiss me, his firm body pushing me against the side of the building. I pressed myself against him, showing him how much I had missed him.

Stuart broke away, his breathing heavy. "I am riding into town first thing tomorrow to talk with Reverend Pratt. I have two more days of leave, and I would like us to be married before I go."

"For my protection, right?"

A dark eyebrow bent over a blue eye. "Yes. For your protection."

We walked toward the peach orchard, the new buds just beginning to emerge on the branches above us. Despite the warmth of the day, a chill breeze brushed through the neighboring pines and settled cool air on us. I wrapped my shawl closer to me.

"I wish things could be different, Stuart."

I felt him still, the air bristling between us.

His voice, with its studied antipathy, stung. "I do, too. And they could."

I turned away from him, not able to stand the hurt in his eyes. The sky cast deep shades of gold through the trees as the sun set in the distant sky.

I looked down at my shoes peeping out from under my frayed hem, the cracked brown leather coated with red dust. "I want you to promise me something. If something should happen and we are separated forever, I want you to get on with your life. Nobody should go through life alone. I've tried it and I don't recommend it."

I felt his fingers on my shoulders, turning me around gently to face him. A stray breeze lifted the hair off his forehead. "You always have the choice of going to Valdosta—you will be safe there. When this war is over, I will come for you there."

The earnestness in his eyes stopped me from saying more. "Just promise me."

Slowly, he nodded; then I reached for him in the twilight and held him close.

We were married the following afternoon at the Roswell Presbyterian Church—the same church in which my Annie would be baptized in the future. I stood silently clinging to Stuart's arm, feeling like I was having an out-of-body-experience. Charles was our witness, as was a perturbed Eliza Smith, who also doubled as organist. I shivered throughout the ceremony, wondering if there should be an added clause concerning unexplained disappearances.

Stuart kissed me, his lips warm, thawing the brittle ice on mine. He took my hand and led me down the aisle as Mrs. Stuart Elliott. I halted halfway down and looked at my husband. "Wait. I don't know what your middle name is."

He stopped next to me, his expression puzzled. "Did you not hear Reverend Pratt say it?"

I shook my head. "I wasn't listening. Too nervous, I suppose."

"Are those your teeth chattering?"

"It's either my teeth or my knees. But I really must know—what's your middle name?"

"Couper. Why do you want to know?"

I slid my arm through his as we continued down the short aisle. "I don't really know. I guess I thought that I couldn't know you well enough to marry if I didn't know your full name."

He stopped to lean down and whisper in my ear. "Laura, I would say that we know each other better than most couples on their wedding day." He gave me a sly wink.

I averted my head with mock prudishness. "I'm sure I don't know what you mean."

He chuckled quietly as he led me out into the warm April sunshine.

We spent our wedding night in the room and bed I had shared with Michael in another place and time. I had at first protested, not wanting to add an unwanted memory into our marriage bed. But Zeke had insisted, and I couldn't refuse when I saw all the brightly colored blooms strewn over the coverlet, smelling of spring and new beginnings. Stuart and I lay under the half tester bed, filling our lungs with the heady aroma and lush petals of violets, azaleas, and roses, the stately mahogany posts bearing witness.

I thought suddenly of Mrs. Cudahy, and a bubble of déjà vu floated through me. *Most of my ancestors were conceived on this bed.* I stared into Stuart's eyes, and it occurred to me where I had seen them before. A tall, elderly woman with glorious skin and eyes the color of the Caribbean.

We lay together in the cool night air, our bodies chilled. I impatiently kicked off the covers, letting them slide into an ungraceful heap on the floor. Stuart's fingers slowly traced circles on my skin. A rough finger slid from my collarbone to my navel, pausing on my C-section scar. He hadn't mentioned it the last time we'd been together.

"What is this?"

"It's the scar from an operation I had as a child."

He bent to kiss it, his lips warm on my bare skin.

"Did it hurt?"

His lips traveled to my side, reaching my ticklish spot. I squirmed. "I don't know, Stuart. Did it hurt when you got shot?"

He looked at me, his head cocked to the side. "You certainly have an odd sense of humor, Mrs. Elliott." A warm tongue licked at the curve of my waist, flooding me with liquid heat. "But I like it." He nibbled at my skin and I clawed at his back, to make him stop or continue, I couldn't tell.

He took one of my hands and moved it over my head, his face now over mine. I felt his wanting me, but he held back.

His voice was hushed but fueled with urgency. "Now you know what it has been like to be me these past few months. The endless needing of you—without you giving me what I want. It is a little bit of torture, is it not?" He pulled my other arm over my head and bent toward my lips, biting me gently.

"I have wanted to break you, bend you to my will so many times, but I cannot. Your strength is what I love most about you, Laura. You are killing me little by little, but I will not take your strength from you. God help me, I will not."

I wrenched my hands from his grasp, sliding them down his back to his hips, pushing him against me, my need too urgent to put into words.

His breath caught. "I will leave my mark on you."

My eyes stung as the tears ran heedlessly down the sides of my face. "You have, Stuart. You already have."

I reached my arms around his neck and pulled him down toward me. Afterward, I stayed awake while Stuart slept, watching the distorted shadows dance across the walls. I thought again of Mrs. Cudahy and her words, then drifted off to sleep, dreaming I was floating in a sea of spring blossoms and seeing a pair of startling blue eyes.

CHAPTER TWENTY-TWO

———◆———

The woods are lovely, dark and deep.
But I have promises to keep,
And miles to go before I sleep.

—ROBERT FROST

I awoke before sunrise, the hint of a word whispered in urgency lingering in the cool morning air. Moonlight illuminated the room, etch-
ing vague outlines of the furniture. Stuart slept on his back, his face
turned toward me, soft and innocent as a child. His even breathing
told me he had not spoken.

Carefully lifting the covers, I rose from our bed. A flower petal, disturbed by my movement, floated to the ground, its blackness against the
wood floor like a drop of blood. I went to the window and looked out.

The dark shadow rose like an obelisk on the lawn, the hidden eyes
catching the misty morning light. My breath caught in the back of my
throat. It was time.

From under the bed I grabbed my carpetbag, already packed with a
few belongings, including the red dress and the necklace and earrings
Stuart had given me. Stopping by the bed, I leaned forward to feel his
soft breath on my skin. I closed my eyes for a brief moment, remembering the previous night, then stood. I wished I had had time to write
him a note, but anything I could have said would have made him come
after me.

I blew him a silent kiss, then took the chain he had given me, with
Julia's key on it, off the dressing table and slipped it over my head. I
escaped to Julia's room, where I had stashed a few things on the day
Stuart returned. I shimmied out of my nightgown and threw a blouse

and skirt on, skipping the underpinnings. I had no idea how we were traveling, but I wanted to be as comfortable as possible.

The front door squeaked as I opened it and I paused, listening for any stirrings in the silent house. Hearing nothing, I opened it farther and stepped out. Matt Kimball waited for me on the porch.

I smelled his fetid breath in the early-morning air. "So, Laura. We meet again. I cannot tell you how much I am looking forward to our little trip together." I turned my face, trying to escape the stench of him. "Come on. We have a train to catch."

"Where's Sarah? And where are we going?" I cursed my voice for wavering.

His teeth appeared gray in the twilight. "Do not bother your pretty little head about all that. You will find out soon enough." He reached out a hand, but I ignored it, stepping past him.

He left the steps of the porch and began to lead me across the front lawn. We had barely reached the drive before I heard the shout behind me.

"Laura!"

Matt spun around, ripping a gun out of his belt and pointing it at Stuart. "Stop where you are or I will kill you."

Stuart made a move to come toward me. I took a step backward. "No, Stuart, don't. He means what he says. Just let me go. I have to do this."

"Do what? Where are you going?"

I put up my hand to stop him from moving forward. "I'm leaving with Matt. I can't tell you why, but this is something I have to do."

He started walking toward us again, and Matt cocked the gun. Stuart stopped. "What do you mean? You cannot go with him—you are my wife!" He raked his hands through his hair and threw his arms out in a gesture of impotence.

Matt stepped closer, and a veil of fear fell on me. "It is not what you think. Let me go now, and nobody will get hurt." My eyes burned, and I said the only thing I knew that might ease his hurt. "I love you, Stuart. I wouldn't leave you if I didn't have to."

"You love me? Then how can you go with him?"

He walked toward me, his eyes growing darker until they appeared ebony in the obscure predawn light. "Goddamnit, Laura. I will not let you leave."

I ran to him to halt his progress. "Stop!" I screamed, suddenly aware of the Colt Navy he had kept hidden behind his leg. If he shot Matt, I would never see Sarah again. "Stop!" I screamed again, pushing his arm up and away from its target. But my voice was drowned by the loud report of a gun. I jerked around toward Matt, his smoking gun lowered at his side and a sneer on his face.

As if in slow motion, I turned back to Stuart. I saw more than pain flash through his eyes. I saw betrayal. Incredulous eyes stared at the blood quickly spreading on his shirt right below the collarbone. His knees buckled and I reached to catch him, but succeeded only in breaking his fall as he crumpled to the dewy grass.

"Stuart—no!" I knelt and touched shaking fingers to his neck, feeling his pulse skitter under my fingertips.

"Leave him."

The cold barrel of a gun pressed into the back of my neck. I ignored it, leaning forward to push on the wound and stop the bleeding that had saturated his shirt and now dripped into the grass. Blood oozed between my fingers, mixing with my tears. "Don't die, Stuart—please don't die. I do love you—I do. God, Stuart, don't you die." His eyes flickered, then closed again.

The pressure from the gun became more insistent. "Leave him, or I will kill you, too. And if you die, there is no more reason to keep Sarah alive."

"But I can't . . . leave him here. I've got to get Charles."

As if he heard his name being summoned, Charles appeared at the front door. I stood quickly, my hand firmly on Matt's arm. "Don't shoot— I will go with you willingly now."

Charles ran to Stuart, his eyes full of questions as he stared at my bloody hands. "What happened?"

I shook my head. "Save him, Charles. Please don't let him die."

Before the doctor could respond, Matt pulled on my arm, and we ran together down the dirt drive and out to a buggy waiting on the other side of the gate.

The wheels of the buggy crunched over the dirt road, the pounding of the horse's hooves matching the throbbing in my heart. I stared at the dried blood on my hands, my tears washing white streaks through the rivers of red. "What have I done?"

I didn't look up when I heard the brittle laughter from my companion. "You just saved Sarah's life." Matt moved his hand to my lap and squeezed my leg. "Do not worry about not having a husband no more. I am available, and I am kinda partial to widows."

I gagged, moving my head to the side of the buggy just in time. I looked back, like the biblical Lot's wife, and half wanted to be turned into a pillar of salt. I saw nothing but the tall oak trees that lined the front drive, their branches sweeping toward the earth, the dew-laden leaves weeping. And on an uppermost branch, a crow rested, its black feathers an ominous blob against the cerulean sky. It cawed loudly, then descended in one fell swoop, still cawing, until it disappeared from sight.

The buggy rumbled over the rocky road, jostling my bones. I clenched my teeth to prevent them from shattering every time we tumbled in and out of a rut. Bright dogwood blooms heralded spring all around us, the scent of new life heavy in the air. I would have reveled in the beauty of the day except for the image penetrating my thoughts: the look of betrayal in dark blue eyes, and the spreading stain of blood on a white shirt.

Midmorning, we approached a mangy-looking pair of mules pulling a wagon. The gaunt man in front of the rickety vehicle stared at us without comment, his eyes as empty as his right sleeve and as sad as the pants leg pinned up at the hip. The woman next to him barely lifted her head to notice us, her skin hanging in loose folds, her dress baggy on her emaciated frame. A baby's weak cries came from the back of the wagon, and I turned around as we passed them to see seven children of varying ages, as dirty and hungry-looking as their parents, thrown in the back like sacks of flour. A little girl about Sarah's age sat against the side of the wagon, clutching a bundle of rags. A squawking began and a small hand thrashed out of the bundle. The girl placed the armload over her shoulder and looked at me with deep brown eyes, her wan little face showing no emotion.

Matt stopped the buggy and looked at me. He pointed to the departing wagon, the dry red dirt swirling in the air between us. "She reminds me of your little girl." He shot a stream of tobacco juice out of the side of the buggy; not all of it made it over the edge. He swiped a grimy sleeve across his mouth, then used the same sleeve to wipe the sweat dripping from his forehead. Brown streaks of tobacco juice marked his skin, and I turned away, unable to look.

"When do I get to see Sarah? I need to know if she's all right and to let Julia know. She's worried. We both are."

He shrugged. "I dunno. But she is safe just as long as you follow orders." Air pushed through his nostrils in an assumed attempt at a snicker. "She is real safe—heck, they are keepin' her in an old abandoned church, if that makes you feel any better. It is a nice place, not far from where I was born, as a matter of fact. But I am just bringing you to Miz Broderick. She will let you know when you can see your daughter." Leering, he added, "We will have a bit of time in between to get to know each other better."

I swallowed thickly. "Where are we going?"

"To the train depot in Atlanta. And from there we are to take the Western and Atlantic railroad to Dalton to see our fine boys in gray, and to a Mrs. Simpson's boardinghouse. Not sure how Mrs. Broderick plans on getting you to Chattanooga from there, but I am sure she has got it all worked out." He looked down at my hands. "First we got to find you a stream to wash that blood off your hands. People might start asking questions."

I didn't answer, but rested my head on the back of the seat and closed my eyes. But the bruised memory of Stuart kept coming back to me, and my eyes shot open again, my heart filled with dread. I pressed my fist to my heart, his name on my lips as I prayed that Charles had reached him in time. Failing to save Sarah was not an option. I had already lost too much, and Stuart was beyond my help. I approached my task with a single-mindedness, allowing no other thoughts to cloud my objective.

We reached Atlanta around noon, and Matt had to struggle to steer the buggy through the pandemonium of the city. People bustled throughout the streets on foot and in every kind of conveyance. The dirt roads had been reduced to muddy ruts, but the hurried pedestrians and wagon drivers carried on as if they were asphalt. They all shared a singular look of panic.

Matt stopped the buggy at the side of the street in front of the train depot. Lines of red dust caked the creases and folds in my dress. I had no mirror, but I knew my face looked equally as dirty.

We each grabbed a carpetbag and went in search of the ticket window inside. I startled at the bundle of gold coins Matt pulled from his jacket. He winked at me. "There's plenty more where this came from." I remembered what Pamela had told me about her followers, about how they would do anything for money.

I sat on a bench to wait, and Matt walked down the platform as far away as possible. The hands on the station clock seemed to move in slow motion, each minute seeming more like ten, and an hour like a whole day. The platform grew more and more crowded during the three-hour wait, the din of people's voices rising as the sounds of a distant train came from down the track.

Someone tugged on my arm. "Come on now. Time to get on the train."

I followed Matt, who was now affecting an exaggerated limp, presumably for an excuse to explain the fact that he wore no uniform. I paused to read a broadside on a pillar:

> NOTICE!! All able-bodied men between the ages of 20 and 50 are earnestly called upon to join the Southern Army. Rally to the call of your countrymen in the field. One united effort, and those Northern hirelings will soon be driven from our sunny South.

I hurried to catch up, brushing by two soldiers reeking of cheap whiskey, and moved to the steps of the train, where a soldier stood, examining traveling papers. He looked at Matt, who nodded; then he looked in the other direction as I mounted the steps and boarded the train. I began to understand the reason for carrying so many gold coins.

As I settled on the seat next to Matt, he stared straight ahead, not acknowledging me.

In a low voice, he said, "Do not sit next to me. Nobody needs to know we are traveling together." He then turned toward the window and gazed out in silence. I stood and grabbed my carpetbag and looked for another seat. The press of bodies in the car was enough to tell me that finding another seat would be almost impossible. As if hearing my thoughts, a man across the aisle stood and pushed his way through the milieu. Before anybody could spot the vacant seat, I plopped myself in it.

A woman with a little boy and girl sat next to me. An attractive woman with dark eyes and black hair, she didn't look much older than me, but lines of worry and exhaustion streaked her face. It was all she could do to keep the little girl from squeezing past me and toddling down the aisle of the car while holding on to the screeching infant in her arms. Finally, I turned and offered to hold the baby boy. With no hesitation and a look of deep gratitude, she handed him to me.

I looked down into enormous blue eyes and my heart jumped. He looked so much like Stuart's child, a child I knew I could never have. His sobbing subsided as he studied my face and stuck a chubby finger in my nose. I laughed and he laughed back, forging a tender trust.

The mother excused herself and left her seat to retrieve her daughter from the other end of the car. After settling back down, she said, "Thank you so much. You seem to have the mother's touch."

I smiled back. "So it would seem. He's really adorable."

"Thank you." She tucked the little girl behind one arm and stuck out her hand in my direction. I touched her gloved hand, warm and soft in mine. "I am Mrs. Elizabeth Crandall. This is my daughter, Alice, and my son, Reid."

"It's a pleasure to meet you. I'm Laura Tru . . . I mean, Elliott."

She nodded at the wedding ring on my finger. "Are you going to see your husband?"

I shook my head. "No. What about you?"

"I hope to. Isaac does not know I am coming—he actually told me not to, that it would be too dangerous. But I know General Johnston will never let the Yankees into Georgia. I hope to reach my husband so we can celebrate a Confederate victory together." Her voice sounded forced, and her sad eyes belied her true feelings.

I smiled broadly. "I'm sure he'll be happy to see you and his children."

Reid arched his head back and I lost my grip. He slipped from my arms just as Elizabeth let go of Alice and extended her arms to catch him. Seeing her chance, Alice headed straight across the aisle and landed smack in the middle of Matt's lap. Matt's head rolled forward groggily as he awoke from his nap, and his eyes focused on the plump toddler in his lap. Alice looked solidly up into his face, let out a loud hiccup, and began to scream. I grabbed her before she could catch a second breath and began patting her solidly on the back.

We rode for several hours, chatting about children and recovering her wayward toddler from other parts of the car. In midsentence, I was jerked from my seat by the sudden screeching of the train's brakes. People left their seats and raced to the windows, straining their necks to see what the problem was. Leaning my head out the window, I spied three soldiers in gray galloping alongside the train. We continued to slow until we came to a complete stop. Two of the men dismounted and entered the engine.

A man standing next to me, wearing a long duster coat and a straw hat, stuck his head out the window and shouted to the remaining soldier on horseback. "Why have we stopped?"

The soldier rode up to our window and called back, "We have orders to search for a passenger. She is believed to be a Yankee spy and might be on this train."

"Who is she? And under whose orders?"

"Her name is Laura Elliott, and she is traveling with a man. Major Stuart Elliott has issued the orders to search the train."

My breath came in deep little gasps. Stuart was alive, and I couldn't shout with joy at the news. Instead I felt my blood flood my skin, warming it. I glanced at Elizabeth and found her staring at me, her eyes wide. Then I looked over to where Matt had been sitting. He was gone.

The man in the long jacket continued. "Will this take long? I am headed for Dalton to take a photograph of General Johnston. I do not want to be late."

"Sorry, suh. We are under orders. We will have to detain this train until we can examine every passenger on it."

"Damn," the man said, as he slid his hat off and wiped his forehead. "Begging your pardon," he said, indicating Elizabeth and me.

The engineer appeared at the door to our car, followed by the two soldiers. I caught Elizabeth's eye, and she gave me an almost imperceptible nod.

"Everybody off the train. We are under orders to have every person on this train interrogated. Everybody off the train."

Children screamed and people grumbled as we all piled off. Great puffs of smoke climbed over the people, and the hot smell of steam and metal filled the air. I spotted Matt standing near the passengers from the first-class compartment. He didn't acknowledge me.

The soldiers started with the people from the first car. Knowing it would be a long wait, we sat down a distance away from the other passengers, Alice on my lap. Elizabeth sat next to me, cradling a sleeping Reid. "Do not worry," she whispered to me. "I will take care of it."

"Why would you risk yourself for me? How do you know I'm not a Yankee spy?"

"Are you?"

"No."

"Well, then. I did not think so. But you are obviously in trouble and need help. You have been an enormous help to me. Let me repay the favor."

"Thank you." I didn't know what she had planned, but I knew it couldn't be any worse than the reason I was on the train in the first place.

The man with the long duster coat and wire-rimmed spectacles approached us. "Pardon me," he said, doffing his hat. I stared at his face, with the dark, pointy beard and unkempt brown hair. He looked vaguely familiar. "Would you two ladies like to sit for a photograph?"

The last thing in the world I wanted at that moment was to call attention to myself. But Elizabeth yanked me to my feet and said, "Yes. We would be delighted."

"Forgive my manners, ladies. Allow me to introduce myself. I am

Mr. Mathew Brady, photographer. And if you will allow me and my assistants to fetch and set up my equipment, I would like to capture your images for the sake of history."

I had to forcibly keep my mouth from hanging open. Now I knew why his face seemed familiar. My father had several books of his famous Civil War photographs, one with his picture emblazoned on the front cover.

Elizabeth introduced us, giving me the last name of Crandall, and I stepped forward to see the man up close. "I'm familiar with your work. I'd be honored."

While I kept a stealthy eye on Matt for any signal, and the soldiers worked their way down the line of passengers, Mr. Brady's two assistants hauled a large trunk out onto the grass and began setting up the equipment. The famous photographer made a big fuss about ensuring a sleeping compartment inside the train was set aside for a darkroom. One assistant was sent racing back to the train with large sheets of dark cloth.

They set a large wooden box camera atop a tripod and began adjusting it while I kept my eyes on the approaching soldiers and Matt.

A soldier began talking with Matt, and he pulled out a white envelope and handed it to the soldier for inspection. He scanned it briefly, showed it to his companion, and then handed it back before stepping toward the next person in line.

"Ready, ladies, when you are." I turned back to the famous photographer, who had taken off his hat. The children began to fuss, so Elizabeth left my side to see about them. I absently fingered the chain around my neck, feeling the rises and falls of each link, the metal warm in the afternoon sunshine. My hand fell to the key at the bottom of the chain, and I grabbed it to tuck it into my dress. As the metal object slid smoothly down the skin on my neck and chest, I froze. The image of a sepia-toned photograph of a woman in nineteenth-century clothing flashed across my memory. The woman, who bore a strange resemblance to me, had been wearing a large key on a chain.

"Ready? Do not move!" I stood still, not daring to breathe and feeling my body temperature sink. I stared at the hunched shape under the dark cloth and wanted to laugh. The pieces in this unbelievable puzzle were starting to fall into place. My only hope now was to finish the puzzle without losing any of the pieces. I pulled the necklace back out and placed it in the middle of my bodice. An exact replica of the old picture.

A fly droned past my ear, but I remained still to allow for the long exposure time of the film, and thought wistfully of my iPhone, which took pictures with the press of a button.

The soldiers had reached our group just as the shutter clicked. Elizabeth came to stand next to me, a squalling child under each arm. "Here, take one," she said, thrusting Reid at me.

I grabbed him, the odor of baby spit-up and milk filling the air. I looked up as a soldier approached. "Ma'am," he said, tipping his hat.

I looked into somber brown eyes, trying to enlist his sympathy.

"Sorry, ma'am, but I have to ask you a few questions."

Reid gurgled and burped in response. Something wet and warm drizzled down my wrist and under my sleeve. "I understand. But please make it quick," I said, holding Reid out in front of me to illustrate my point.

"Yes, ma'am," he said, wrinkling his nose. "What is your name?"

"Laura Crandall," I lied, without hesitation.

"Are you traveling alone?"

I glanced at my small companion. "Not exactly."

His weary expression didn't change. "May I see your traveling papers?"

"She is with me." Elizabeth came and stood next to me, a finally still and quiet Alice perched on her hip.

His gaze took in Elizabeth from head to foot. "And what is your relationship with this woman?"

She looked him in the eye. "She is my sister-in-law. We're going up to Dalton to visit my husband, her brother, who is fighting for our glorious cause."

She straightened herself to her full height, which was all of about five feet, and stared at him down the length of her nose.

"May I see your traveling papers?"

Elizabeth unfurled a piece of paper from Alice's hand and gave it to the soldier. He glanced at it quickly and looked back at Elizabeth.

"It does not mention a traveling companion."

Elizabeth stared back at the man, unblinking. "No. I am afraid it was all last minute. This dear woman insisted on accompanying me to help me with my precious children. I just do not know what I would have done without her."

To prove her point, I knelt down, laid the baby on his back, and began to unwrap his diaper. "Elizabeth, do you have a clean nappy? He really needs to be changed." I looked up at the soldier, who was busily looking at everything but us. "Any more questions?" I asked.

"No, ma'am," he said quickly. "I think I have heard all I need to know. You are both free to reboard."

Hastily rewrapping Reid in a fresh diaper, I then scooped him up and followed Elizabeth and Alice back to the train. As I stood on the bottom step, somebody grabbed me from behind. I gasped and turned around. Matt stood there, holding my carpetbag. "We need to go."

Elizabeth looked down at me with a sad smile, and I handed Reid to her. "Goodbye, Laura." She studied my face for a moment. "I hope you find what you are looking for."

Our hands touched for a moment before Matt pulled me off the step. Then, with one last look at Elizabeth and her children, I ducked and followed Matt under the train to the other side.

I brushed off my skirts, not having had the time to pull them up before being made to crawl on all fours under the train. "Why are we leaving?"

Without answering, Matt pulled on my arm and began running across an empty field toward the cover of a forest approximately one hundred yards away. Turning his head toward me, he spat, "Because your damned husband is at the other end of the train."

I yanked my arm from his grasp and stopped. "Stuart's here?"

"Damnit, woman. You are sorely trying my patience. Do you want him to find you? You ain't never going to see your daughter if we do not get away from here real quick-like."

The train blocked my view of everything on the other side of the rail cars, effectively blocking their view of us, too.

Matt grabbed my arm again. "Come on—it is only a matter of time before somebody on the train sees us."

With one last look at the train, I lifted my skirts as high as I could and began running to the edge of the woods. Matt quickly overtook me. As I neared the scrubby pines, I stumbled on a root and sprawled on my stomach, the wind knocked out of me.

The ground rumbled, and I rolled over and stared at the sky in confusion. It wasn't until Matt towered over me and began dragging me toward the forest that I realized it was hoofbeats. Dizzily, I scrambled to my feet, half dragged by Matt, and looked back toward the train. I recognized Endy first, and then the man sitting astride him, a bright white bandage holding one arm immobile against his side, his body leaning heavily over the horse's neck.

Matt shoved me, face forward, toward a tree. I braced my hands against the trunk, tripping around it, and then ran as fast as I could into the dense forest, Matt close behind me. We headed toward a small hill, the pines and overgrowth covering it so completely that it looked like the hump of a great beast. When we reached it, he pushed me down to hide behind a scrub of bushes and then crouched next to me.

My cheeks stung from the whipping of branches, and small gnats danced around the small trickles of blood, but I dared not move.

We sat in absolute silence for a long while, listening. Our breathing had resumed a normal pace and my legs had begun to ache, and still no sound from Stuart. Mixed with my joy at finding him alive was my fear that if he found me, I would lose Sarah forever. I closed my eyes and listened, but heard no more than the wind through the leaves.

From a distance, the sound of the steam engine starting and moving vibrated against the old trunk behind us. The chugging dissipated down unseen tracks, then silence again. Finally Matt shifted and lifted his head. Satisfied that we were alone, he stood.

A booming sound clouded my ears and Matt seemed to jump, then sprawl backward against the tree behind us. He bounced against the trunk and came to a rest next to me, his hand sliding across my cheek as he fell. I recoiled, seeing the gaping wound in the middle of his chest, white bone visible like a maggot in decaying meat.

I struggled to my feet, my hands held over my head. "Stuart, it's me, Laura. Please don't shoot!"

"I would not shoot my own wife."

Startled, I whipped around, finding him only a few yards away, his hunting rifle now pointed at the ground. I hadn't heard him approach, and wondered if Zeke had taught him how to move like a Cherokee. Relief and fear flooded me, making my knees shake.

He took a step forward. "But I would certainly like to wring her neck."

I moved backward against a slender sapling, alarmed at the pallor of his skin and the way his eyes darkened as he looked at me.

He took another step forward and stopped. I watched as his eyes rolled up into his head and his knees buckled as he slid to the ground.

Chapter Twenty-three

*The wind goeth toward the south, and turneth about unto
the north; it whirleth about continually, and the wind
returneth again according to his circuits.*

—ECCLESIASTES 1:6

I dropped to my knees and bent my ear to his face to feel the reassuring warmth of his breath on my cheek. Realizing he had fainted, I unbuttoned his jacket and the top of his shirt, feeling the bulk of bandaging under the thin cotton. Blood had begun to seep through the bandages, making me aware of how serious his wound was.

"You damned fool," I said to his closed eyes. "You should have stayed at Phoenix Hall, where Charles could care for you properly."

Blue eyes opened briefly. "I am a damned fool—but not for this." His voice sounded strained, as if it took all his effort just to speak. "It's not so bad. Bullet passed clean through." He took a deep breath, his eyelids fluttering. "I am . . . here to take . . . you back with me."

I reached under my skirt and began ripping the cotton ruffle around a petticoat. "I can't go back with you, Stuart." I had to make him understand, and the only way I could was to tell him the truth. "Sarah's in great danger. Pamela is holding her hostage unless I help . . ." I could barely say the words. "Unless I help her assassinate General Sherman."

He struggled feebly to sit up, but I pressed him down. Gasping heavily, he squeezed words between each breath. "I will not . . . allow you . . . to put yourself . . . in danger."

He winced as I struggled to sit him up against the tree. "You don't have a choice. You can barely breathe, much less chase me through the woods."

Narrowed eyes regarded me solemnly. "But my men could."

I'd forgotten all about the other soldiers. My hands stilled. "Don't. Sarah's life is at stake. And I'm the only one who can help her."

I raised his shirt and wrapped my petticoat ruffle around his chest, tightening the pressure on his wound to staunch the flow of blood, like I'd seen Julia do for Zeke.

He grabbed my wrist and our gazes locked. "Damnit. Why will you not let me help you?"

I shook my head, fighting the sting of tears in my eyes. "Because if Pamela finds out I've told you or solicited help, she will kill Sarah. I don't doubt it."

He winced as I pulled him forward to reach around him. "Do you have any idea where Sarah might be?"

With a glance over at Matt's body, I leaned Stuart gently back against the tree. "Only what Matt told me—that she was being held in an old, abandoned church. I have no idea where—except Matt did say it was near where he was born."

His forehead was beaded with sweat. "Matt's father was a preacher." He winced, closing his eyes. "It could be that church. In Alpharetta— about a day's ride from here."

I sat back on my heels, my heart heavy. "Will your men find you?"

Panic crossed his face. "You cannot go alone. I will . . ." He struggled to stand, but collapsed against the tree, his eyes admitting defeat.

"Will your men find you?" I asked again.

He paused, then nodded. Between gritted teeth, he said, "Endy will show them."

Thunder rumbled overhead, as fat blobs of rain pelted the leaves and branches, dribbling their way down to where we sat. He lifted his good arm, reaching for me, and I leaned toward him. His fingers brushed my cheek, then cupped my jaw, sliding around to the back of my neck. He pulled me to him, then kissed me deeply, and I lost myself in it. The smell of the rain and wet wool brought me back to awareness and I pulled back, worried I might hurt him.

His eyes were dark with pain and something else, his words low as he spoke. "I am half out of my mind with pain and with anger, yet still I want you. This wanting of you—it is sure to kill me if nothing else does."

I gently laid my head on his chest, and his fingers found my hair. "I'm sorry, Stuart. I'm so sorry." I buried my face in his neck, kissing him softly, then lifted my head and stood.

He grunted, trying to sit up. "Laura, please. Do not go alone. We can find Sarah together." His eyes burned into mine. "I love you."

I swallowed my tears, my heart battling with my head. Telling him the truth of my feelings for him would bind us forever; would keep him searching for me long after I had gone. My head won, and I swiped away my nonexistent tears like I could swipe away my feelings. Matter-of-factly, I said, "If Sarah is not where you think she is and I don't show up to see Pamela, they will kill her. I will not fail my daughter again."

He crumpled back against the tree, and I turned to retrieve my carpetbag that Matt had dropped as we flew into our hiding spot. It was stuck under one of his legs, and I shuddered as I moved it to retrieve my bag, the rain hitting it with solid *thuds*.

I faced Stuart, clutching the red carpetbag. "There's a bag of gold coins in Matt's coat. Take it. You'll need it after the war's over." I ducked my head. "Go home, Stuart. If I know you're being taken care of, that's one less thing I have to worry about."

His voice was barely more than a whisper. "Do not go."

Swallowing hard, I shook my head and turned away, then headed up the hill in the dense underbrush.

The rainstorm ended as quickly as it had begun, and I was grateful that I didn't have to slog through mud. I was a poor navigator, despite my four years as a Girl Scout. All I knew was that the train I was on had been headed north to the town of Dalton. So I stayed in the woods but kept close to the edge, where I could follow the bends of the rail tracks. I listened for a while for the sounds of pursuit, and when none came, I relaxed a bit. I hoisted my skirts and knotted them as high as I could to make walking easier, only lowering them when the woods gave way to sparsely populated farmland. A road grew out of the fields, and I followed it for a while until a wagon ambled by piled high with lumber. The old man holding the reins showed no surprise at my disheveled appearance when I asked him if the road would take me to Dalton. He nodded solemnly and then offered me a ride. I didn't need any persuasion to accept his offer, and climbed up onto the running board before he could change his mind. The man did not utter a word, and for a time, I thought he had drifted to sleep. I took off my shoes to examine my blisters, startling as the man shouted and slapped the reins at a bumblebee.

He dropped me off at the Dalton train depot, for lack of anywhere else to go. I thanked him, and he rode on, a single hand held up in farewell.

At the ticket window, I asked for directions for Mrs. Simpson's rooming house, the place Matt told me Pamela was staying. Dreading every step, I headed off for the short walk.

Full dark had settled over the town, the streetlamps coloring the clusters of Confederate soldiers in a faded yellow. Women, many wearing black, scurried across streets with baskets over their arms or holding on to small children. I wondered if there might be a curfew, and quickened my step.

Pamela answered my tapping on the door. When she looked past me into the hallway, I told her, simply, "Matt's dead. Confederate soldiers stopped our train and chased us into the woods. He was shot, but I managed to escape."

I kept my voice steady and my gaze firm, knowing I couldn't mention Stuart's involvement. Her eyes flickered over my appearance, and then she held the door wide to allow me in.

"Does anyone know you are here?"

I shook my head slowly.

"Let us hope you are right." She closed the door behind me with a final *thud*.

I gave myself a sponge bath behind the screen in the room and slipped on a nightgown, pleased to finally rid myself of my torn and tired traveling dress. If it weren't for my growling stomach, I would have been too tired to make it to one of the two single beds.

To remain inconspicuous, we ate our dinner of chicken dumplings, yams, and corn bread in our room. Tight knots clenched at my stomach, but I still found my appetite and cleaned my plate, chewing slowly while my mind digested my thoughts.

Pamela's teeth ground her food, her jawbones jutting out from the colorless skin on her face. As I studied her, my mind skittered in all directions. I hoped Stuart's injuries ensured his return home to Phoenix Hall where he could completely recover. A part of me wanted him to stay weak for several more months, to keep him out of the war.

We placed our trays outside the door; then Pamela began to dress for bed. As she removed her clothes, I heard the distinct sound of rustling paper. I turned and watched in amazement as she relieved her petticoat of its unusual fullness at the sides and rear by drawing out three newspapers.

On her bed she laid out the *Cincinnati Enquirer*, the *New York Daily Tribune*, and the *Philadelphia Inquirer*. I approached the bed and glanced at the dates—all recent editions.

"What are these for?" I asked, thumbing through the Philadelphia paper.

She snatched it out of my hands and stacked them on the floor next to her bed. "They are for our army, of course. To give General Johnston and his staff some insight on the status of Yankee morale and some such. Our neighbors to the north are worried about Grant's losses in the east. One more staggering defeat of Federal forces and I do believe the Yankees will be ready to sue for peace." She grinned widely at me. "The death of Sherman and the resulting loss of morale among his men will be the turning point in this war—you mark my words." She practically beamed as she pulled the bedclothes from the bed. "Mrs. Simpson is a friend of mine and will be sure to deliver these to General Johnston tomorrow."

I watched as she placed a revolver under her pillow and lay down. "Go to sleep, Laura. We have a very busy day ahead."

Pamela turned down the lamp, and as I watched the flickering shadows disappear from the walls, a thought occurred to me. "How will we get to Chattanooga? It's held by the Federals, and I can't imagine them letting us walk right in."

Her voice was sharp in the quiet night air. "We will have to depend on our own resources and the fact that you are related to an officer on General Sherman's personal staff."

I sat up straight in the bed, my eyes squinting in the dark in Pamela's direction. "What do you mean?"

I heard the smile in her voice. "Your new brother-in-law, dear.

Captain William Elliott, aide-de-camp for General Sherman. Stuart's older brother."

I recalled the arrow scar on Stuart's chest and all the things I had heard about William. Knowing William's relationship with his brother and Julia, I was unsure if he could be relied on to be an ally. "And he's supposed to help us get rid of General Sherman?"

"No. And I know you are smart enough not to enlighten him on the matter. He believes me to be a Yankee spy. How else do you think I have been able to get the information to pass on to Stuart? William is merely our passage into the general's company. And then you will take it from there."

I thought of the red velvet dress with the low neckline I had brought with me. "You're going to have to be more specific than that, Pamela. I haven't a clue how to be a seductress."

"Then you had better start practicing. But I do not think you will have to do much; men seem to flock toward you regardless." I saw a dark shape against the whiteness of the wall, like a shadow in a nightmare, and realized she was also sitting up in bed, looking directly at me. "I will arrange for you and the general to be alone, to get to know each other. You will suggest a secret rendezvous and your complete discretion. When he meets with you, I want you to blow his head off."

She's insane. The thought struck me again as an owl hooted in a tree not far from our window, and I suddenly wanted to climb up the tree with him and watch all of this from a safe distance. Instead, I found myself an actress in the middle of this macabre play, with only one way off the stage. I placed my hand on my heart and felt it fluttering rapidly. I willed it to slow by taking deep breaths. What if I succeeded in killing General Sherman? Would the war continue longer and the blood of thousands be on my hands? It was immeasurable, unfathomable, and certainly unpredictable. Then I thought of Sarah, scared and alone, her fate now an unknown, and knew I didn't have a choice.

I lay back down on the cool cotton sheets, and eventually fell asleep in the early hours of the morning.

We left the rooming house before dawn, sneaking down the back stairs and out the door without detection, and headed north through the woods. I shivered in the dark air, trying to make out the moonlit-backed shapes in front of me. My long skirts caught on brambles and dead twigs, so I eventually hoisted them up over my knees, exposing stockings with more holes than fabric. After a couple of hours, I stopped from near weariness, cool prickles of sweat beading my forehead. I dropped my carpetbag, opening hands that had been clutching the handle and the skirts, and painfully stretched the small bones and muscles. The bloodred sun appeared low in the sky, bleeding light into the dark forest.

"Do you have any idea where you're going, Pamela?"

She stopped about ten yards ahead of me. "Of course. I have studied this terrain for years. Now pick up your bag and keep going. We have a lot of ground to cover."

I stayed where I was, swaying with exhaustion, tiny gnats flitting about my face. "How many miles from Dalton to Chattanooga?"

"About thirty. But do not worry—we will commandeer a horse as soon as we see one."

I grabbed my bag and hurried up behind her. "You want us to steal a horse?"

She didn't answer, and we plowed on. We followed closely to the railroad tracks of the Western & Atlantic, trying to stay out of sight of the tracks while using it to direct us. A few miles west of town, we had to walk on the tracks through a narrow gap in two facing rock walls, which Pamela called Rocky Face Ridge. I said a silent prayer that no trains would come, as there would be no room for us to escape.

By midmorning we reached a clearing. Pamela motioned me back, and I peered from behind her to see a wooden rail fence enclosing a large pasture. The morning breeze carried the pungent aroma of horse manure, and I knew we had reached the right place. A saddleless horse stood on the far side of the pasture, its head buried in the tall grass. I looked past the horse to the farmhouse with fading whitewash, where a woman stood next to a wood pile, her ax raised before she drove it into a log. Two little boys ran around barefoot in the dirt, causing the mother to stop her chopping and bark at them, with little to no effect.

A husband was nowhere in sight—a familiar occurrence in these times. I worried about her vulnerability, perched as she was between two opposing armies. My eyes traveled down the side of the house until I saw her only protection, a long rifle leaning against the brick chimney.

"We can't take this woman's horse," I said. "It looks like it's the only piece of livestock she's got left."

Pamela snorted. "If we do not take it, the Yankee Army will. Probably kill it, too, just to prevent the rebels from getting it. It is well past its prime, but it will do."

"But she's got a gun."

Pamela patted her pocket. "So do we."

I turned to see if she was bluffing, but could tell from the glint in her eye that she wasn't.

"Follow me to the other side of the fence to the gate."

She led me to the edge of the woods before ordering me to crawl. I longed for my jeans. Maneuvering in long skirts on this journey had been the hardest part so far. We reached the other side without incident and stopped by the rail fence, not ten feet away from the horse. It regarded us with lazy eyes and resumed munching.

"What now?" I whispered.

"Give me your bag."

I complied, not sure what my other options were. She reached inside and pulled out a carrot, one of several we had taken from a root cellar earlier in the morning, and handed it to me.

"Go show this to the horse and make him come to the fence so we can mount him."

I still hated horses, even though I had eventually learned how to get along with Endy. But even mild-mannered horses like this one made me jittery. I knew it was hopeless to argue, so I took the carrot and entered the fenced-in area.

The horse showed only mild curiosity as I approached, but at least raised his head from the grass. I showed him the orange vegetable and he began walking toward me. The reverberating *thwacks* in the distance told me the woman was still chopping wood and hadn't noticed that her only form of transportation and plow pulling was being stolen right from under her nose.

I backed up, the carrot raised in front of me, until I felt the fence at my back. Pamela had climbed to the top rail and easily slid her leg over the back of the horse. I flattened my hand, as Stuart had shown me, and gave the entire carrot to the horse. While he busily munched, I handed up the carpetbags, climbed the fence, and settled in front of Pamela.

It was then I noticed that the chopping sounds had ceased. We both turned in time to see the woman race toward the side of the house and grab the rifle.

I dug my heels into the sides of the horse just as I felt a ripple of air to my right and the resounding report of a gun behind me. The horse lurched forward, nearly toppling both of us off his back, and then began what passed for a gallop. Luckily, the horse wore a halter, which gave me more of a grip. I leaned forward over the neck, Pamela clinging tightly to my middle, the carpetbags tucked securely between us. I felt us listing to the right but maintained a tenacious hold as I heard another shot fired from the house. I threw one last look behind me and saw the woman standing in the middle of the pasture, her arms loose at her sides, staring forlornly at us as we disappeared with her horse into the woods.

We slowed our pace once we were within the shadow of the woods. We found a well-worn dirt road through the forest and headed north. Soon after, we heard hoofbeats in front of us. Quickly guiding the horse off the road, we hid among the tall trees and underbrush as a detachment of Yankee soldiers rode by, their navy blue uniforms a marked contrast to the well-worn and varying uniforms of the Confederate soldiers we had seen in the previous days. As the last soldier passed us, Pamela whispered, "We are almost there. Be prepared to be stopped by the Yankee's advanced guard. Do not protest—they will shoot."

We pulled back on the road and resumed our ambling pace, the old horse frothing slightly at the mouth. I felt sorry for it, and tried hard not to shift my weight too much.

I swiped my forehead with my sleeve. "How did you come here to this time?"

"The same way all of us marked as Shadow Warriors travel. Wrapped in the atmosphere of a comet intensified by a lunar eclipse." The droning of a fly interrupted her and she swatted it away with her hand. "Every comet has a set orbital time period. For instance, Halley's Comet reappears every seventy-six years. It has been doing this since the beginning of time and will continue until the end of time. And a Shadow Warrior, being in the right place and the right time, can be swept up in the tail of the comet and moved within the comet's orbital time period." She took a deep breath. "With practice, one can navigate within any orbital time period."

"What do you mean, 'navigate'?"

I glanced back at her, and she gave me a look with the exaggerated patience of a teacher talking to a slow student. "If I want to travel back two hundred years, I do not necessarily need to find a comet with a two-hundred-year orbit—just one in which the time period between now and then is divisible into two hundred. Like a fifty-year comet. One would just need to navigate to arrive in the correct time."

"But how does one learn to navigate?" I asked, more confused than ever.

She touched my forehead with a long, pale finger. "You use parts of your mind that are usually ignored." A thin smile appeared on her lips. "But sometimes it happens accidentally. Just like you and Sarah with Genetti's Comet."

The name startled me. "How did you know about Genetti's Comet?"

She laughed, a dry and brittle sound. "I know the orbits of every comet that have been and will be. And I also know the places where the powers are strongest. Moon Mountain is one of only three."

My heart beat faster. Finding the answers to my questions would allow me to control my own future—assuming I had one. "One of three? How did you learn about this phenomenon? It's not exactly science-textbook material."

She pulled out a handkerchief and wiped her face, then placed it back in her skirt pocket. Taking a deep breath, she continued. "For centuries the Cherokees and other native people around the world have passed down legends. As a history major at Vanderbilt, I became fascinated, obsessed almost. And when I found a picture of an ancient Cherokee carving that matched my birthmark, I knew there had to be some truth to the stories. The legend of the dragons on Moon Mountain that would mysteriously appear and disappear certainly fascinated me. There seemed to be a void or a warp there that would trap ancient, or perhaps future, creatures in this place. But they were always hunted down and killed. As were the people who were caught traveling through time. They were an aberration of nature and needed to be destroyed." She shrugged. "The one thing I have not been able to ascertain is how many there are of us. I suspect the number is quite small—perhaps one every generation—otherwise we would not be alone."

I shifted, her words making me uncomfortable. "Don't you miss your family, your friends? Aren't they worrying about you?"

She snorted. "People disappear every day. My disappearance certainly would not be beyond the usual. Besides, there was no one to miss me. I made sure of that."

I thought of my parents and my friends, my coworkers and students, and wondered if they were still looking for me and how long they would continue searching before they gave up. And then I thought of Stuart, and I knew in my heart that he would search for me forever.

The plodding pace soothed me, each step lulling me closer to sleep until I felt myself fall over the horse's neck. Pamela yanked me up by the back of my dress. It was then I noticed that the sounds around us had changed. The birds had stopped twittering in the trees; even the sound of chirping crickets had ceased. I looked up through the thick canopy of trees and saw clouds creeping over the sun and casting us in shadow. But there were no storm clouds; nothing to cause the rippling of flesh up my spine.

I stifled a scream as a man in a dark blue uniform stepped out of the trees in front of us, his rifle pointing at my chest.

"Halt!"

Leaves above us rustled and I craned my neck to see another soldier roosting on a branch, his weapon trained on a spot near my head. I pulled on the horse's mane, assuming it would know to stop. A speckled yellow leaf drifted down on my lap as the tree climber swept down to stand in front of us. He was at least a head shorter than the other soldier, with light blond fuzz covering his cheeks. He looked no more than nineteen.

The taller soldier walked over to us. "What have we got here, Johnny? A couple of rebs, if you ask me."

Johnny took his hat off. "Looks like a couple of women, Corporal." His rifle wavered but remained fixed on us.

Without lowering his gun, the tall corporal asked, "Who are you and what are you doing here?"

Pamela shifted the carpetbags, which seemed to have made a permanent wedge in my back, and reached for her pocket.

"Stop!" The corporal approached the side of the horse and, without apology, stuck his hand in Pamela's pocket. I forced myself to remain calm and reminded myself that Pamela was smart enough to have removed her gun.

My heart sank as he pulled out a folded letter. I stole a glance at Pamela, but her eyes were on the soldier, staring at him expectantly. "Open it."

He did, and then looked back at Pamela, while Johnny reached for the letter. "Are you Mrs. Pamela Broderick?"

She nodded, her eyelids downcast in mock servitude.

He indicated me with his rifle. "And who is this?"

"This is Laura Elliott, William Elliott's sister-in-law."

"And you are Captain Elliott's mother-in-law?"

Again she nodded.

"Is he expecting you?"

She shook her head. "No. But I am carrying important information for him to pass on to our General Sherman. Once I obtained it, it was too late to notify Captain Elliott—and far too dangerous. The information I am carrying is much too sensitive for it to fall into enemy hands."

I peered down at the letter in his hand. I recognized the handwriting from an old letter from William that Julia had shown me.

"Why is this young lady with you?" The shorter soldier spoke to Pamela but stared at me.

"I needed her for protection. I am an old lady—not as strong as I used to be."

The boy raised his eyebrows and looked at me. "Are you armed?"

Pamela answered, "No, but she is a lot stronger than she looks."

I sat quietly on the horse, my hands clenched tightly in front of me.

The older soldier ordered us to dismount, taking a step backward as I reached the ground. His gaze traveled up and down me while he spoke. "Ladies, we will escort you to our sergeant. He will bring you to the provost marshal, who will decide if you will see General Sherman."

He turned his head slightly and spit a long stream of dark brown juice out of the side of his mouth, then wiped the remaining bits clinging to his lip with his sleeve. "And if you ain't who you say you are, Uncle Billy will probably string you up, women or not."

The younger soldier led the way and we followed him down the path. I saw more shadows in the woods and knew we were being watched by other soldiers on picket duty. Our two guards no longer pointed their rifles at us but still held them where they could easily be aimed and fired. The taller one led the horse by his halter.

"Why do you call General Sherman Uncle Billy?" I asked.

Johnny answered with a shy smile, "On account of him being one of us. Real personable. Me and the corporal been with him since Shiloh—and there just ain't a better soldier." He paused for a moment. "But he don't much like women, preachers, or newspaper people in his camp, that's for sure. I recommend telling him what you need to and then getting out of the way."

For the first time in this odyssey, I was nervous. I remembered pictures I'd seen of the sour-faced Sherman, and his reputation in Georgia as being the Nero of the nineteenth century. This was the man I was supposed to seduce. Being shot sounded like a fine alternative.

We walked in silence, our footsteps punctuated by the occasional wet slap of tobacco juice and spittle against dead leaves. We crested a ridge, and I felt a tightening in my chest. Below me lay the South's destruction. White canvas tents, filled with men in blue uniforms, covered the green slopes and hills. I sighed into the breeze as I eyed the show of strength before me. Soldiers filled the ground between tents like ants at a picnic, scurrying from one place to another. Horses and artillery crowded the far rise, and I sucked in my breath, imagining the force behind these placid pieces. History said that all the pride and patriotism of Johnston's Southern army would be laid low in the deep grass of Georgia's hills, bowed down in the face of the awesome power of lead and the sheer numbers that lay before me. But the ink in the history books was apparently not indelible.

Our procession attracted stares and downright leers as we were led deeper into the encampment. Campfires littered the ground, and the smells of bacon fat and burning coffee made my mouth water. I hadn't eaten since dinner the previous evening. I was acutely aware of my status as a female in a sea of males who were prepared to die. I gathered my skirts closely around me and hugged the carpetbag over my chest.

Our horse had been left on the outskirts of the camp. I wanted to ask someone to take it back to the woman we had stolen it from, but thought again that perhaps the woman wouldn't welcome the soldiers on her isolated farm with only her single rifle to protect herself.

It was late afternoon before we found our way into Chattanooga. We had been given horses to ride and escorted from the encampment by four soldiers from 7th Independent Company, Ohio Sharpshooters. I could feel my hair springing loose from its pins and straggling against my neck. My skirt had a jagged tear up to the knee, exposing my ripped petticoat and holes from my two days of walking through the forest, and I was sure dark circles of exhaustion ringed my eyes. I hoped my brother-in-law would have pity and take us in without question.

We entered a large house at 110 East First Street. I was told that the house had been commandeered from the wealthy Lattner family, who had fled from the city when the Yankees had first captured it in 1863.

Rich carvings accented the tall ceilings, and crystal chandeliers glittered light into the rooms. Our feet tapped on the black-and-white marble floors, heralding our arrival. We were shown into the parlor and left alone to wait for my brother-in-law.

Pamela seated herself on a red velvet sofa and stared at me with level eyes. Desperate for a mirror, I searched the room for anything reflective. I noticed a mirror at the bottom of the buffet, a petticoat mirror for the ladies to unobtrusively check to see if their underskirts were visible under their dresses. Being unobtrusive wasn't a current concern, so I knelt on the floor to inspect the damage to my hair and face.

I licked my fingers and began to remove a dirty smudge from my chin. I was in the midst of scrubbing when I heard a throat being cleared, too deep to be Pamela. I stood, hitting my head on the bottom of the buffet and knocking a dish to the floor, shattering blue and white china into tiny pieces.

Rubbing my head, I stood and found myself staring into familiar blue eyes. My heart skipped a beat as I looked at his face and saw the beloved similarities. The hair was the same, straight and dark, and parted to the side. The nose a trifle longer, a bit haughtier. The same strong jawline. But there was something else—a fundamental difference. No light shone behind these eyes. I peered into them and saw something cold shivering in the icy blue depths.

I forced myself to smile at him. "You must be William."

He looked at Pamela in confusion. "What is going on here?" He looked back at me and let his gaze travel up my costume—from my mud-encrusted shoes to my dirty face and wayward hair. He narrowed his eyes. "Who are you?"

"I'm Laura Elliott. Your sister-in-law." I couldn't stop myself from staring.

"My sister-in-law?" Without preamble, he grabbed my left hand to examine my ring. "This was my mother's." An angry flush stained his cheeks.

I could see the effort he made to smile back at me. "Then let me welcome you into our family, sister." He embraced me, crushing me to his chest. I felt his moist lips linger on my cheek and I resisted the impulse to wipe his kiss off my skin.

I studied his face again and knew that I could never count on this man to be my ally.

Our attention was turned by a commotion in the foyer and several loud voices reverberating throughout the hallway. One in particular caught my attention. Deep and clear with staccato accents, it seemed to be a voice of authority. "Tell those busybodies that my trains are for supplies for my army. I have no room, and I repeat, no room, for do-gooders and those damned newspaper people."

Footsteps approached the parlor, and I waited expectantly for the owner of the voice to appear. He walked in and stopped abruptly, taking us in with a bold appraisal. The elusive aroma of cigar smoke entered the room with him.

He was tall and very thin, his weathered face lined with deep crevices. His dark red hair, standing up as if at attention, somehow did not make this man a comical character. The stars on his shoulders belied the stained and sloppy appearance of his dark blue uniform. There was no doubt who this man was. I had heard him referred to by various names— from Nero to Satan to Georgia's Nemesis. And, recently, as Uncle Billy.

This man was without a doubt no other than the man who would coin the phrase "War is hell": General William Tecumseh Sherman.

He blinked rapidly at us before turning his attention to William. "Captain Elliott. Who are these women and why are they here?"

William snapped to attention and began introductions. "General, you have met my wife's mother, Mrs. Pamela Broderick, at a dinner in Nashville at the home of Andrew Johnson. And this is my brother's wife, Mrs. Laura Elliott."

The general peered at me through narrowed eyes and then turned back to William. "Captain. I believe your brother is with the rebel army."

"Yes, sir. As much as it pains me, he is."

"I see." General Sherman scratched his short beard. "And your sister-in-law. Is she a rebel, too?"

"That would depend," I interjected, smarting at being treated as if I weren't in the room.

The general raised his eyebrow at me. "I see. And what would that depend on?"

"On who is asking the question."

Pamela stepped forward. "I beg your pardon, sir. Mrs. Elliott and I are both staunch supporters of the Union. We are here to pass on information that might be of some use to you."

On our long journey she had divulged the information she was speaking of. Direct from Confederate General Joseph E. Johnston's headquarters in Dalton, she had a list of the full strength of the Southern armies—down to the last mule. She handed the small stack of papers to him without pause, knowing it would be of little use to him or his army once he was dead.

He took the papers from her and examined them, the crease between his brows deepening. "Where did you get these?"

"I beg your pardon, sir, but I must keep my sources secret. Suffice it to say the gentleman in question is a member of General Johnston's own staff."

He nodded and folded the papers in half. His hands were callused and spattered with dark brown freckles. "Very good. I will, of course, verify these figures. But your efforts are greatly appreciated. I hope the two of you will do me the honor of dining with me and my staff this evening."

Not pausing to wait for an answer, Sherman faced me, his eyes flickering over my appearance. "Madam, have you traveled far?"

My knees nearly buckled with fatigue, and my weariness pushed all thoughts of politeness and the purpose of my visit out of my head. "No. I always look like I've been in a train wreck."

There was a stunned silence to punctuate my remark. I heard the passing of a carriage outside and someone shouting. He raised an eyebrow.

"I see. And does your husband approve?"

One knee did buckle, and I tried to estimate how many steps backward I'd have to take to make it to the nearest chair. "I don't think my appearance is a major concern of his, General."

He coughed into his hand, but I could see he was grinning. "Actually, I meant does he approve of your Unionist sympathies."

"Uh, not exactly."

He rubbed his beard, the rasping sound grating on my nerves. "Are you still on speaking terms?"

"Yes, you could say that." I took another step backward and felt the backs of my knees at the edge of a chair. I dropped into the seat without looking. The cushion vibrated in startled movement and erupted with a loud meow.

I jumped out of the chair. "Shit!" I exclaimed, as the black-and-white feline escaped through the doorway. All eyes were on me as the blood rushed to the tips of my ears and a small gasp came from Pamela.

Ignoring my outburst, General Sherman said, "You must be tired." He turned to William. "Captain, please see that these ladies have a room." He emphasized the word *ladies*. "Dinner is at eight o'clock." He bowed sharply and left, but not before I saw the grin through his beard.

I plopped back down in the empty chair. William came and stood before me, offering his hand. "My, my. Where did my brother find you?"

Ignoring his hand, I stood. "You wouldn't believe it if I told you."

He threw his head back and laughed—Stuart's laugh. Tears sprang to my eyes. I needed him now. I needed him to tell me I was doing the right thing. I turned my head away.

"What I need now is a room and a bath. Perhaps after that I will be in the mood to chat about Julia and your family, since I'm sure they're your primary concern." It hadn't escaped my notice that he hadn't mentioned Julia's name once.

"Yes, I would like that." His face registered annoyance as he picked up our bags and indicated with his hand that we precede him through the door. "Ladies."

With a heavy sigh, I followed. Low voices carried toward me from the library, like murmurs of ghosts from the past. I felt eyes on my back and I turned to see General Sherman and another officer watching our progress. I inclined my head slightly, then turned back, my feet tapping against the marble floors. The sound made me think of footprints in history. I wondered if my own would be indelible, with thick, deep impressions in the soil, or fade with time, like yellowed pages from an old history book.

CHAPTER TWENTY-FOUR

———◆———

They cannot scare me with their empty spaces
Between stars—on stars where no human race is.
I have it in me so much nearer home
To scare myself with my own desert places.

—ROBERT FROST

A large beetle crawled across the toe of my satin slipper. Hearing my intake of breath, Pamela turned in time to see the insect scurrying under the puddled draperies. She stooped to pick it up, its shell shiny in the thin light from the lamp, then tightened her fingers around it until it crunched. She stepped to the window and discarded the remains into the garden below.

Wiping her hand on the skirt of her dress, she walked back to me, studying my red velvet dress with a critical eye. She reached up with both hands and tugged at the short sleeves, exposing as much chest and shoulder as the dress would allow without being obscene. My hand twitched, wanting to pull the sleeves up to my neck, but I was resigned to the fact that I would need to do whatever it took to get Sherman's attention.

Pamela had done a decent job on my hair and I thought, as I fastened the jet earrings in my ears, that I was more than passable. The smell of cooking drifted up the stairs, making my stomach rumble. Pamela crooked an eyebrow at me. "Perhaps we should go down for a drink before dinner, hmm?"

I turned to face her, my fingers clutching at the fabric of my dress. "I need to see proof that Sarah is . . . alive." I had promised Julia that I would send her word. Even if I couldn't, I owed it to her to find out.

She gave me a condescending smile. "I am sorry, dear. But that is not possible."

"What if I refuse to . . . to cooperate unless I know she's all right?" Her smile evaporated. "Then she will be killed. Any more questions?" I stood, frozen, then shook my head and walked toward the door.

She stopped me with a hand on my elbow. "One last thing. When this is all over, you will not implicate me or anybody else. You are acting of your own accord, because of your hatred for the Yankees. This is part of the bargain, Laura. Follow it through, and there will be enough people to risk their lives to save you. And then you will be reunited with your daughter."

I swallowed heavily. "How do we know this will all turn out as you plan? This is all very risky, isn't it?"

"No different from life, Laura. We can only do what we can. Now go downstairs. I will follow you shortly."

Pamela closed the door behind me. The stilted strains of a Beethoven sonata drifted toward me. I followed the music to a room across from the parlor I had been in earlier. I remembered floor-to-ceiling books from my brief glance inside—books left behind by the previous tenants. I stood tentatively on the threshold, one hand pressed to my collarbone where the blood pounded under my fingertips.

My eyes were immediately drawn to the grand piano in the corner, the highly polished mahogany lustrous in the yellow light. A bone-thin woman sat on the bench, her jawbones working as she plunked on the keys in an attempt to re-create Beethoven. I gravitated toward the instrument before I realized there were other people in the room and all were watching me. The music stopped abruptly as the woman looked at me, pale gray eyes staring coolly out from under ash-blond hair.

"I do not believe we have been introduced." Her voice was flat and nasal, straight out of a New England town.

William emerged from a cushioned sofa and came to stand beside me, his long fingers, so much like Stuart's, holding on to a short glass filled with amber liquid.

"Please, allow me. Mrs. Mary Audenreid, my sister-in-law, Mrs. Laura Elliott." I inclined my head slightly in acknowledgment while she sat motionless, her expression cold. She was several years younger than me but her bearing was much older than she looked.

I saw three other gentlemen by the bookcase on the far wall, and each was introduced in turn. One was Mrs. Audenreid's husband, Captain Joseph Audenreid, the officer I had seen General Sherman speaking with earlier. He was tall and fair, like his wife, but his eyes were warm as they appraised me. The other man on the general's staff was Captain James McCoy, a man whose girth pressed his uniform taut, threatening to send the brass buttons into orbit. He bowed slightly, his graying hair falling forward over his forehead. His physical likeness to St. Nick belied the grimness of his eyes as he contemplated me.

William continued. "And you have already met General Sherman." I gave him a warm smile, and wished fervently for a drink.

"Are you a rebel, Mrs. Elliott?"

I looked at Mrs. Audenreid, surprised to hear such a direct question.

Before I could respond, General Sherman stepped forward. "That would depend—would it not, Mrs. Elliott?" The creases in his face deepened as he regarded me, amusement apparent on his face.

I smiled back tentatively. "Yes. And since it is a Union captain's wife who is asking the question, I would have to say no."

The woman sniffed in response, holding a hanky to her nose. "Honestly, I do not see why we are fighting them. Let them have their miserable climate and torturous springs." She sneezed loudly into her hanky.

I loved spring in the South, and I figured something had to be wrong with somebody who thought otherwise. "Oh yes. Cold and damp springs are much preferable to warm ones full of abundant blooms with a few sneezes. Perhaps you should speak to a few more generals, Mrs. Audenreid. To think that you have had the answer to ending the war all this time and have been keeping it to yourself."

The tomblike silence was broken by Pamela's entrance. She was dressed all in black, like a crow, and greeted everyone stiffly as introductions were made.

Mrs. Audenreid resumed her playing, this time a barely recognizable Chopin scherzo. A black manservant appeared with sherry for the ladies. I gulped mine quickly to still my nerves.

Mary Audenreid stopped playing. There was a small smattering of applause as she stood to take her glass of sherry. She came to stand next to me, a slight frown on her face. "That was Chopin, Mrs. Elliott. I am not sure if civilized music has made its way south yet. I am trying to

educate these poor unfortunates with every bit of culture that I can."
She took a sip of her sherry, a pink tongue darting out to lick her lips.
"It is to be expected, though, from a people who subjugate others and
whip them to within an inch of their lives each and every day."

I glanced over at William, who wore a tight smile on his face. "How
very kind of you. Let me speak for all my unwashed brothers and sisters
of the South and give you a heartfelt thank-you for all your selfless efforts. It is a wonder, isn't it, that the North would want our participa-
tion in this country at all, with us being so backward and evil and all."
I let my accent slip into a redneck impersonation, eliciting a laugh from
a male voice behind me.

I welcomed the anger that flushed through me, settling my nerves.
And I had never been known to back down from an argument. I set my
glass on a table and walked slowly over to the piano. "My. So many
keys. Would you mind if I tried?"

With a condescending glance, she fluttered a pale hand at me. "Of
course. But not too loudly, please."

Pulling out the bench, I sat down and did a few short finger exer-
cises to warm up my hands. Next came a few arpeggios, my hands racing up and down the length of the keyboard. Mary Audenreid's mouth
pursed itself into a perfect O. The color red appeared high on her cheekbones, then spread over her entire face. Enjoying the effect, I continued
with the floor show.

"This is Debussy. He's from France. That's a big country across the
Atlantic where they speak French. Have you heard of it?" I asked as I
played a few bars of "Clair de Lune."

"This is Mozart. He was from Salzburg—a beautiful city if you
don't go during the winter. He died tragically young but what a gift of
music he has given to the world. Not that uneducated people like myself would ever realize." I played a page of a Mozart sonata, my fingers
frantic on the keys. Mary Audenreid sat as still as a piece of furniture,
her cheeks and nose a bright pink.

"Have you ever heard of Beethoven? His 'Für Elise' is a bit over-
done, as is his 'Pathétique,' but they are some of my favorites," I said as
I quickly ran through a sample of each.

I felt all eyes on me, but I was on a roll and couldn't stop. I quickly broke into Scott Joplin's "Heliotrope Bouquet" and pounded out the entire thing in record time. My spontaneous recital ended without applause.

Mary stood and walked slowly over to me and stated simply, "You, madam, are common and not fit to be in this room with us."

I stood, careful not to knock over the bench with my skirts.

"And you, madam, are an insufferable boor. You prance around with your high ideals about Southern women and their atrocities to their slaves. But I'll have you know that I speak to the slaves with a great deal more respect and kindness than you have just shown me." I said this with great control, enunciating every word.

Her jaw was shaking as she regarded me, but she said nothing and turned and left the room. My corset stopped me from taking a much-needed deep breath, so I found myself gasping in tiny puffs of air. "I'm sorry," I said, to no one in particular. "I usually have better manners."

Her husband stepped forward, coughing into his hand. "No, she provoked you. Perhaps you would better understand it if I told you that her brother was killed at Gettysburg by a Confederate bullet."

I studied his face and noticed a scar that started at the left jaw and neatly bisected his cheek. "It explains it, but it certainly doesn't excuse it. My husband was shot with a Yankee bullet in his leg. But I can't seem to hate all Yankees because of it."

He set his face with a grim look. "Apparently. Or else you would not be here."

I heard a grunt from Captain McCoy. I turned to find him closely examining his boots.

The manservant interrupted by announcing that dinner was served.

William offered me his arm, and I reluctantly placed my hand on it. As he closed his hand over mine, I repressed a shudder, much as I would have done if a large and hairy insect had been crawling up my arm.

We filed into the dining room, and I felt not a little guilty knowing a family had been evicted from the premises, that a family that should have been sitting around the dining table, talking about their day's events.

I sat on General Sherman's right, with Captain Audenreid to my right. His wife sat in stony silence across from me. Conversation was stilted, owing as much to the fact that I was a Southerner as to the fact that there were women present. At one point, a courier came in, and I could see General Sherman's eyes alight with excitement. He ate faster, as I was sure he was anxious to share the news with his officers. No doubt it had something to do with his imminent plans to move his massive army southward toward Atlanta.

We eagerly turned our attention to the food—the abundance of which was truly amazing in this place and time. An entire chicken and roast beef occupied the center of the cherry pedestal table. They were surrounded by countless other dishes, including three different kinds of vegetables and all sorts of sauces. Eyebrows were raised at my heaping plate. I shrugged and took another helping of the honey-glazed yams.

Mrs. Audenreid appeared to be enjoying the spread as much as I was. "This is truly the most delicious food I have had since our honeymoon in Paris."

Captain McCoy shifted in his seat and swallowed a mouthful of savory rice. "I shall take credit for that, Mrs. Audenreid. I brought my chef from home. Monsieur Fortin is indeed French."

I eyed the captain's girth and knew he spoke the truth.

Mary Audenreid continued. "I would truly like to thank him, but I do not speak a word of French. My mother thought it was pretentious, so it was never taught to us."

"I speak French." I smiled at her, an innocent enough expression. "I'll be happy to give you an appropriate phrase to show your gratitude."

She smiled primly. "Really? I am surprised. But thank you. I would appreciate that."

I hid my grin by giving my attention to the chocolate torte, stabbing my fork into the rich, creamy layers. I washed it down with real coffee, savoring the taste and smell of it.

As we left the table, I approached Mrs. Audenreid and whispered in her ear. She gave me a quizzical look and repeated it back to me quietly. I nodded, assuring her it was perfect. When Monsieur Fortin appeared in the doorway to satisfy himself that all the guests were contented, she said, with an amazingly good French accent, *"Monsieur Fortin, voulez-vous couchez avec moi ce soir."*

Pamela began coughing, choking on her last sip of coffee. Somewhere behind me a china cup dropped onto the wooden table, but I was unable to look anywhere else but the unfortunate chef's face. Mary Audenreid looked around the room, from the beet red face of the chef to the mortified look on the officers' faces. "What did I say? Was my accent wrong?"

A flash of lightning illuminated the night, followed shortly by a loud crash of thunder. Accepting the interruption as a sign that I should leave, I promptly excused myself and headed up toward my bedroom. I had hoped to feel amused and somewhat vindicated, but all I could feel was a sick feeling that I had done something wrong. She hadn't deserved that. My only excuses were that I was exhausted and worried about Sarah and what I was here to do, and not a little bit drunk from the wine at dinner.

As I ran up the stairs, I heard hastily spoken French with a tone of righteous indignation from Monsieur Fortin, and a loud exclamation from Captain McCoy. The last thing I heard before slamming the door behind me was Mary Audenreid shrieking at her husband, and a gaggle of male voices speaking in a mixture of French and English.

I lay down on the bed and stared up at the intricately carved ceiling medallion surrounding the crystal chandelier. How could I shoot a man in cold blood? How could I not? Images of Annie sustained me—images of her as a baby and then as the little girl she had grown to be. I had made my choice, and there was no turning back. Reluctantly, I sat up, smoothing my hand absently on the pillow. I rolled off the bed and began pacing, waiting for an opportunity to present itself.

For a while, I heard the excited murmur of male voices, and then the house grew still. I stopped my pacing to listen to the leftover wind blow against the house. I pulled the curtain aside and saw only scattered debris on the deserted street. I longed to loosen my corset, but I needed help to do it. Pamela was nowhere to be seen. Surely she didn't think I'd need our bedroom for a purpose other than sleeping. I rubbed my hands together and was startled to find that they were moist. I wiped them on my skirt and resumed my pacing.

I found myself standing in front of the dressing table, peering at the reflection of a woman I didn't know anymore. My skin flushed pink against the glaring red of the gown, my dark hair an elegant contrast.

I took a deep breath and almost laughed at the show of cleavage I revealed. At least I knew I had it if I needed it.

A whiff of cigar smoke tickled my nose. General Sherman must still be downstairs. Without thinking about what I was doing, I dug Pamela's carpetbag out from under her bed and thrust my hand inside. My hand closed around the cold steel of the revolver. I pulled it out and examined it with an impartial eye. I pulled off my stockings, placed the garter around my calf, and tucked the gun in my garter. I straightened, smoothing my skirts. Giving the woman in the mirror a backward glance, I left the room and carefully made my way down the steps.

My skirts trailed behind me on each rise, until they pooled elegantly around me as I reached the bottom. The aroma of cigar smoke was stronger in the foyer. A triangle of light illuminated the floor outside the partially opened door to the library. I walked toward it, my steps purposeful, like a hunter stalking its prey. I heard the scratch of pen against paper as I gently pushed open the door.

I was relieved to find the general alone. He looked up as I entered, a new cigar clenched between his teeth. He sat at the desk, arm poised above a ledger. I could feel the gun rubbing against the skin on my leg. His jacket was completely unbuttoned and opened at the chest, displaying a dirty white shirt underneath. The red hair stuck up like a porcupine, as if he had been rubbing his hands through it as he pondered how to feed his troops off fertile Southern land.

I stopped in front of the desk, not sure how to proceed. I had the urge to perch myself on the edge but knew that with my voluminous skirts and hoop, I would cause considerable damage to the items on top.

He did not stand. "Good evening, madam. Are you looking for French lessons?" A flicker of amusement crossed his face.

I felt my cheeks flame and shook my head. Before speaking, I retrieved the whiskey decanter from the sideboard and refilled his glass to the top.

He studied the tiny rivulets running down the side of his glass and forming a small puddle on the desk. Pushing with both hands, he leaned back in his chair, quirking one ruddy eyebrow.

"Mrs. Elliott. Are you trying to get me drunk?"

I reached for an empty glass and sloshed whiskey into it. "No. I just don't like drinking alone." I took a long swallow, then came up for air, gasping.

He stood and came from around the desk, taking the glass from my hand, his callused fingers touching mine briefly. "Mrs. Elliott, why are you here? You do know I am a married man."

My face heated again as the whiskey began to work its magic and swim through my head. His face was a mere foot away and I stared into gray-blue eyes, intelligent eyes and not nearly as cold as I would have expected. And that was when I knew. I couldn't kill him. Nor could I jeopardize the outcome of the war. I was diminished in the grand scheme of things, and my wants and desires were merely grains of sand on the great beach of history—of no more consequence than an ant facing an army of soldiers.

"I need your help, and I'm trying to figure out the best way to ask you so that you'll believe me."

He placed the glass on the desk and led me over to the sofa. "Sit," he commanded, his voice soft but stern. I sat, and he looked me over from head to foot before speaking again. "You will find that the best way to deal with me is to speak plainly. You are an intelligent woman, Mrs. Elliott. Please do not waste my time with social niceties."

I took another drink from my glass and eyed him levelly. "There is a plot to assassinate you. And I'm supposed to pull the trigger."

He stood stock-still, his widened eyes the only clue that he had heard what I said. "I see." He raised his hand to scratch his face, the rasping sound loud in the quiet room. "And can I assume you have changed your mind?"

I stood and faced him. "You don't think I'm serious. Look." I leaned over, jerked my skirts up, and pulled the revolver from the garter at my calf. He didn't move.

"Do it, Laura. Now."

I turned to the doorway where Pamela stood, pointing a small silver pistol at me.

Sherman showed no fear as I raised the revolver. I heard a buggy pass by on the wet street outside, voices dying as it drove away. I saw Sarah's face and Stuart's, and wondered if I had lost everything again.

Calmly, I pivoted, aiming the gun at her shoulder. Before I squeezed the trigger, I heard another blast and my arm exploded in fire. My arm jerked and my gun went off, the force knocking it out of my hand. I was thrown against the bookcase, toppling several volumes down on me as I slid to the ground.

I clutched at my upper arm in a semilucid state. General Sherman was leaning over me, his voice frantically calling out for help. I turned my head to find Pamela. I had seen her fall, but I needed to be sure she was still alive. I kicked myself along the floor toward the placid figure on the ground, the pistol still clutched in her hand. Blood and thick clots of tissue oozed from a ragged hole in her neck. It dripped onto the powder blue rug, saturating it and giving it an eerie shimmer in the lamplight. I remember thinking absently that it would ruin the Oriental carpet on the floor, and I stretched my hand toward it to stop the flow. Her eyes twitched and I realized she was still alive.

The general raced to the door, flung it open, and again shouted for help. I looked back at Pamela. Her lips moved, as if in slow motion. "Sarah's dead." The sound gushed from her mouth, the words bubbling with blood.

The last thing I saw before slipping into unconsciousness were dark, unseeing eyes, as cold as ice and still as death.

CHAPTER TWENTY-FIVE

———◆———

The Angel of Death has been abroad throughout the land;
you may almost hear the beating of his wings.
—JOHN BRIGHT

I awoke in shadows, the forms of people around me dark ink stains against the pale wall. I groaned and tried to sit up, only to be held down by strong arms and the flaming pain in my arm. I thought of Sarah and of Pamela's last words to me and I stopped struggling.

"Mrs. Elliott?"

I opened my eyes wider in an attempt to focus on the features looming over me. I recognized Captain Audenreid's face as he leaned closer. "The doctor has given you a bit of morphine, so your head will be rather unclear, I am afraid." A soft pillow cushioned my head, and I realized I was back in my bedroom.

Hands gripped my shoulder, and white bandages were being wrapped around my upper arm. A soft shawl that smelled gently of lavender was placed over me. Pain snaked its way back into current memory and I winced.

"You have been shot," he said matter-of-factly.

I grimaced. "Yeah. I know." My lips felt like paper, cracked and stale.

"But you are a very lucky young lady. There are no bone fragments to worry about. The wound has been cleaned thoroughly and I expect it to heal without incident. I have found a local physician to continue with your care." He went to the door and whispered something to someone on the other side.

"Why isn't an army surgeon taking care of me? I would think they would have more experience with bullet wounds." I shifted, trying to ease the pain.

He paused by the side of the bed. "Mrs. Elliott, General Sherman has ordered all troops to move from Chattanooga tomorrow morning. He has been very strict with his orders—we have been stripped to our barest essentials, and no extraneous persons will be allowed. You will stay here and be under the care of a very good doctor."

I dug my heels into the mattress, forcing myself to sit up against the headboard, heedless of the pain that radiated through my body. "I can't stay here. I need to go home."

The word "home" came easily to my lips, softening the ragged edges of my memories. Stuart would be there to comfort me, to help me. "I have to get back to Roswell. I need to find my daughter." I refused to believe what Pamela said was true. I grabbed at the captain's arm. "Please. I can't stay here."

A shadow emerged from the back of the room and William came to stand next to the captain. "As your closest male relation, Laura, I cannot allow it."

"I want to speak to General Sherman." I kicked the bedclothes off, then slid from the bed, the wall of pain pressing on my senses and making me light-headed. I hastily pulled the shawl over my nightgown, then stumbled for the door, but was restrained by a light hand on my uninjured arm.

"Mrs. Elliott. Wait. If you want to speak to the general, I will arrange it for you." Captain Audenreid gave a stern look to my brother-in-law, who stood silent, his lips pursed. "But may I suggest changing your clothes first? I will send my wife in to help you."

My legs gave out and I eagerly sought the floor, my bottom landing firmly on the rug. I held up my hand. "I'm all right—just a little light-headed." I brought my knees up and rested my forehead on them. My voice sounded muffled but I couldn't seem to raise my head to speak. "But I'm afraid that your wife might just finish the job Pamela started."

I heard a smile in his voice. "No, you are wrong. We all know what you did. We are very much in awe of your bravery and are indebted to you for saving the general's life."

I put my head back between my knees as the room began to swim before my eyes. "But at what cost?" I whispered. I squeezed my eyes shut to keep the room steady. I wouldn't allow myself to think about it.

Captain Audenreid and William helped me back to the bed and then the captain excused himself to get his wife.

I lay back on the pillow, exhausted from the physical exertion, and closed my eyes. I felt a tentative touch on my cheek. I lay still, not yet having the energy to open my eyes. The touch grew stronger as the unseen hand stroked my jaw. My eyes flew open. William's face leered into mine, a mere few inches between us.

"You are an exciting woman, Laura. My brother is a fool to let you go so far from home."

I moved my head back as far as it would go, recoiling from his touch.

His hand fell to my neck, and my body went rigid. "Stuart never did know how to control a woman. You need somebody stronger, Laura. Somebody who knows how to handle a woman."

"I am your brother's wife," I said, trying to move away from his touch.

He leaned his face closer to mine, his blue eyes sparkling with malice. "Come away with me, Laura. We will go west—together. Build a new life away from this war. Let me show you the difference between a real man and a boy." Light, feathery strokes caressed my collarbone. I cringed back into my pillow.

He continued, his voice low and teasing. "Besides, Laura, I doubt you will be welcome back at Phoenix Hall once Julia discovers what you did to Pamela. I do not think you have much of a choice."

With my last effort, I gathered saliva onto my tongue and spat in his face.

He wiped his jaw with the sleeve of his coat as the door opened and Mary Audenreid entered, a steaming pitcher of water in her hand. William straightened and excused himself without a backward glance.

Mary Audenreid stood in front of the closed door, her eyes focused on the steam rising from the pitcher. "Mrs. Elliott. It would appear that I owe you an apology. I was hoping that even if we could not be friends, perhaps we could be civil to each other."

I nodded. "If you help make me presentable enough to meet with General Sherman, I will make you my best friend."

She gave me a hesitant smile and began pouring the water into the washbasin.

She helped me wash and then rigged a dress to fit over my bandages. My head still didn't feel steady, and we needed her husband to help me down the stairs for my meeting with General Sherman. I froze at the threshold of the library, remembering what had transpired in there.

"It is all right, Mrs. Elliott. There's nothing in there to disturb you." Captain Audenreid gave me a gentle push on my back.

I was relieved to see the carpet had been removed, as had every trace of Pamela. I shuddered involuntarily as I moved to stand before the general's desk.

He stood and regarded me with strong eyes, the ever-present cigar smoking in an ashtray on the desk. "Mrs. Elliott. It is good to see you on the road to recovery from your ordeal." He indicated the chair behind me and I gratefully collapsed into it. "Tell me what I can do for you."

I leaned my elbow on his desk for support. "I need to get home to Roswell, Georgia. I can't do it on my own, especially since I know I would have to cross lines of battle. I would like your permission to travel with your troops."

He stared at me as if I hadn't spoken, then picked up his cigar and began pacing the room. "Mrs. Elliott, I am not sure you understand what you are asking. My troops will be traveling fast and light. We will be engaged in battle—a dangerous situation for anybody, even by-standers. I will have more than one hundred thousand men on this campaign—no women. Not even laundresses. I cannot think of a single reason why I should permit an injured woman to join us."

Spots began dancing before my eyes again and I drew in a deep breath. I leaned heavily on the desk as I stared into his eyes and said, "Because you owe me your life."

He paused, blowing a puff of smoke into the still air. He nodded once. "Yes. That I do."

I closed my eyes and put my head on my arms. The general called for Captain Audenreid, and I felt myself being gently lifted from the chair. I held to the chair for a moment. "General?"

He sighed. "I will have my men prepare space for you on a medical wagon."

I nodded my thanks, then allowed myself to be led away. As we crossed the foyer, the front doors were thrown open and two blue-clad soldiers struggled in, each of them clasping the arm of a man wearing a tattered gray uniform. The man's head was slung forward, as if he were barely holding on to consciousness, blood and bruises covering the part of his face I could see. He had been beaten, and badly.

"What is this?" William's voice came from the top of the stairs as he descended.

One of the soldiers saluted, almost losing his grasp on the prisoner, and addressed William. "Begging your pardon, Captain. The man claims to be your brother."

I looked back at the soldier, not completely comprehending until my gaze fell on the prisoner's hands. Bruised and torn, and tied together at the wrist with a hemp rope, I recognized the strong, long fingers. The filthy and blood-encrusted bandage across his shoulder. Blood rushed to my head. I pulled away from Captain Audenreid's grasp and ran. "Stuart? It's me—it's Laura."

Slowly he lifted his head like a marionette being pulled by a string. Dried blood and grime caked his face, and one eye was swollen shut. But the eye that did shine out at me was a deep blue, and I recognized him. I wanted to throw my arms around him, but knew of no place where I could touch him where it wouldn't hurt.

Instead, I turned to William. "He's badly hurt and he's got a bullet wound under his shoulder. Can we move him to a room upstairs and send for a doctor?"

Ignoring me, William strode over to Stuart. "So, little brother. We meet again. What brings you here?"

The dry, gravelly voice was almost that of a stranger. "I have . . . brought . . . Sarah."

The strangled sound came from my own throat. As if my wish demanded it, the door opened again and another soldier entered, pushing my daughter ahead of him. She seemed taller than I remembered and much thinner, but the light in her green eyes was the same.

I fell to my knees, my strength finally deserting me, and opened my arms to her.

"Papa!" she shrieked, as she rushed by me and flew into William's arms.

She nearly toppled him over in her exuberance, and he quickly put her aside, his face a mask of anger and confusion.

"What in the hell are you doing bringing a child here, Stuart?"

One of Stuart's captors stepped forward. "We found them walking down the road from Dalton, just as plain and easy as you please, as if there ain't no damned war goin' on." He coughed before continuing. "We, uh, didn't give him a chance to talk first—sorry, sir. But later he said he needed to reach you, that he was your brother and this was your daughter."

Stuart's eyes fell on me. "Am I . . . in time?"

I nodded, seeing him through a blur of tears. He had somehow found Sarah, then risked his life to bring her here to prevent me from fulfilling my bargain with Pamela. My joy at seeing Sarah was clouded by my fear over Stuart's predicament. He was in the enemy's camp.

Softly, I told him, "Pamela's dead."

He nodded in understanding.

"Miss Laura?" Sarah stood by herself, and I reached for her and she came to me. My fingers searched out her bony shoulders and thick head of hair, and I cried with relief at the solid presence of her in my lap. "I missed you, baby—I've missed you so." I lifted her head and wiped the hair away from her eyes, studying her face. "Are you all right? Did anybody hurt you?"

She shook her head, her hair whipping around her face. "No." Her eyes blinked; then she leaned forward to rub her face in my neck. "Is my mama here? I miss her."

Her words were like a blow. I patted her back, ignoring the hollow feeling in my chest. "No, sweetheart. But I'll take you home. Your mama will be so happy to see you."

William stepped forward and looked down at me. "Am I to understand that my brother knew about the plot to assassinate General Sherman?"

General Sherman stepped out of the library. "What in the hell is all this commotion?"

William addressed his commander. "I believe we have in custody another member of the group who planned your assassination."

I made to stand, but my foot caught on the bottom of my skirt and I ended up on the floor at his feet. "No, William. He's your brother— don't do this." I hugged Sarah close, not wanting her to witness the scene.

William shot me a cold look. "Are you denying that he knew about it?"

"No, but . . ."

He cut me off and spoke directly to the two guards. "This man is a prisoner. Take him someplace where he can be held under lock and key."

"No!" I screamed. "He needs immediate medical attention." I turned to the general, on my last leg of strength. "Please— Please don't let them send him away."

His face was closed to me. "I am sorry, Mrs. Elliott. But until we can ascertain the truth, we need to hold him as a prisoner."

Dots spotted my eyes again, and I heard myself shouting for Stuart. Warm air rushed at me as the door opened. I didn't hear Stuart struggling, but I knew he was gone when the door slammed shut. Sarah squeezed my hand and I held on to it as I stared at the closed door for a long, long time.

Woodenly, I headed up the stairs to my room and lay down on the bed with Sarah, willing sleep to come if only so I could forget what I'd just seen.

When I awakened, I was in my bed and Captain Audenreid sat next to me, a look of concern creasing his face. I sat up, wincing at the pain in my bandaged arm. "Where's Sarah?"

"Mary is with her. She is giving her a bath and a fresh change of clothes—not to mention a hot meal."

I lay back, my mind not completely at ease. "But what about my husband? He's wounded—he needs medical care." I turned to him.

"Please. I beg of you. Can you see to it that he at least gets medical attention?"

He rubbed his jaw, as if needing the movement to make a decision. "I most likely can, Mrs. Elliott. But that is all. He is a rebel officer, and he will have to face charges."

"But he's innocent." I tried to sit up in bed, but the captain held me back.

"Then he can defend himself on those grounds. In the meantime, I will see what I can do to get him a doctor."

I nodded, then lay back in the bed, staring at the ceiling again and praying for a dreamless sleep.

We left before dawn on the morning of Thursday, May 5, 1864, after saying goodbye to Mary Audenreid and the other officers' wives. The throbbing pain in my arm masked any trepidation I should have felt at being one of only a few women on this march. William ignored us as he rode out in front of the column of men, leaving Captain Audenreid to help get Sarah and me settled. We had originally been placed in the back of a covered medical wagon, but the jostling over the rough terrain was causing more injury to my person, so I begged to sit up front with the driver.

I didn't know where Stuart had been taken, and nobody would answer my questions. I tried not to think of him in a dark cell somewhere, starving to death. At least I knew his wounds had been tended, thanks to Captain Audenreid. As I hugged Sarah close to me, I made plans to petition General Sherman for his release. I was out of bargaining chips, but I had to try.

The long column of men stretched out on either side of me in an uninterrupted wave of blue. The dust rising from the ground in their wake wafted over to me, and I could feel the grit settle in my hair and clothes. I longed for a bath.

The soldiers' methodical marching was interspersed occasionally by singing. I recognized some of the songs, and Sarah and I would join in for lack of anything better to do and to take my mind off of Stuart. I vacillated between utter joy at having her with me, close enough to touch and hear her laughter, and the pain in my heart over Stuart. I tried to be angry at him for not returning to Phoenix Hall. But then that would have meant I wouldn't have Sarah.

Captain Audenreid pulled up on his horse to ride next to the wagon.

"Good morning, Mrs. Elliott," he said, tipping his hat. "And you, too, Miss Elliott." Sarah giggled, then hid her mouth with her hand as she stared up at the handsome officer. Strands of reddish blond hair peaked out from under his hat. A single dimple punctuated his smile and his light gray eyes appraised me openly. The scar on his face did nothing to lessen his handsomeness. It might have even added to his appeal.

Smiling, I nodded in his direction.

"I hope you are not finding this trip too unpleasant."

"Not too much. It's bringing me home." I had long since lost any feeling in my lower extremities, and I squirmed on the hard wagon seat to bring the blood flow back.

Noticing my discomfort, the officer said, "You might be more comfortable in a saddle. I would be more than happy to find you a horse."

The captain smiled affably at me, sitting easily astride his mount. I had come to the conclusion that one must be born to the saddle to truly be comfortable. Judging from my sudden jitteriness at the mere mention that I should ride a horse, there was no hope for me.

Sarah squealed with delight. "I want to ride a horse. Can I? Can I?"

I turned to her with worry. "No, Sarah. You might get hurt. . . ."

She was already pushing herself to my side of the wagon. "Please, Aunt Laura? Please?" It took me a moment to realize that she'd called me Aunt Laura.

The captain reassured me. "I will be careful with her."

I nodded and he reached down to lift Sarah onto his saddle. He smiled at me. "You are like a mother to her."

Sarah interjected. "She is my aunt Laura. We are going to see my real mama in Georgia."

I looked down at my lap. "Yes. We will be home soon." I had explained to Sarah that Julia and her brother were in Valdosta, but that I would write to them as soon as I could to let them know we were on our way home.

We continued riding in a companionable silence, moving relatively quickly over the bumpy terrain. I wanted to get down and walk, to get the blood flowing again in my posterior, but was unsure I could keep up with the grueling pace.

I began humming to myself to keep my mind off of the painful thoughts racing around my head. I started to enjoy the scenery, admiring a Southern springtime in full bloom. Suddenly, my humming stopped.

I recognized the area immediately—the small farmhouse tucked inside the clearing with rows of wilted plants stretching out from the house like sunbursts. Clothes still hung on the clothesline outside, dancing a jig with the breeze.

The officer at the head of the column raised his hand, and the lines of soldiers stopped behind him. The driver of my wagon pulled off to the side, allowing me a full view of the farm from the slight rise we were on. Only the soft whinnying of the horses and the jangling of their harness penetrated the silence. I immediately saw the woman's rifle against the side of the house and felt the first ripple of apprehension course through me. From my brief experience with her, she would not have gone far without it.

I strained my ears for the shouts of her little boys, but could hear only the dry clothes snapping on the line.

"Jenkins, Duffy, Lee—you men head down and check things out. This is rebel territory, so be careful." The officer eyed the brown and cracked leaves of the newly sprung plants and the wilted stalks in the kitchen garden. "If there are any provisions to be had, take them."

"Wait." I leapt from the wagon, wincing as I jarred my arm. The officer looked at me and halted his men. "I know the woman who lives here. She has two small children and might be inside and scared. Perhaps I should go, too."

Captain Audenreid rode up beside me and lifted Sarah back onto the wagon seat. "Only if I accompany you." He dismounted and gave the reins to another soldier. He came with me behind the three infantrymen, their rifles raised in readiness.

With a word to Sarah to stay where she was, we walked through the field and over the dead plants, plowing them into the earth from which they had sprung, and halted outside the porch. A wooden train lay upended on the floorboards, waiting for little fingers to play with it. A mending basket sat expectantly next to the white rocker, a piece of brown thread trailing down the side. The door stood open in invitation.

It was then I noticed the smell. It had been hovering around me like an unpleasant memory, but I had pushed it to the back of my mind. Only as I stood looking at the farmhouse, the breeze teasing my hair and separating the odor in the air, did it hit me in the face. I had smelled that smell before when I was a child. I had been walking through the woods behind our house with my father on a hot July afternoon. The odor had appeared suddenly, permeating my clothes, hair, and the inner lining of my nose. It burnt with sickening ferocity and I couldn't escape it. Even after I had heaved my guts out, I couldn't stop gagging. My father had left me, choking on empty air, to investigate and had found a female deer. Its abdomen had been slit, exposing its entrails and creating a veritable feast for all the beasts and insects of the forest. My father had picked me up and brought me home. But I had never forgotten that smell.

I grabbed the front of my skirt and held it against my nostrils. Captain Audenreid motioned the other men back, then pulled his sidearm out of its holster. I walked up the porch steps, close behind the captain. "Hello," I called to the dark space behind the door.

The wind pushed at the wooden door; it sighed quietly, allowing a fresh outpouring of the stench to wash over me. I swallowed thickly as my stomach churned.

"Hello," I called again, walking slowly to the open door. The captain shoved it gently with his arm. It yawned wide, and we stepped in.

It took my eyes almost a minute to adjust to the darkness. Only two windows illuminated the entire one-room house, creating a murky interior in shades of gray. My eyes squinted in the dimness until they rested on the shape of a double bed.

Swarming flies hovered over me as I approached, the buzzing of the insects growing louder. The two small boys lay on their backs, heads touching and arms folded neatly over still chests. Empty eye sockets stared up at me, and the light reflected off something white and twitching. I leaned forward and saw the maggots swimming in and out of the dark holes. I lifted a hand in an age-old maternal desire to smooth the hair back on a troubled brow. My hand stilled when I noticed what was left of the ear on the child nearest me. A jagged tear ripped the ear in half, dried blood outlining the wound. A pillow lay at the foot of the bed, and I guessed how the children had died. Gingerly, my hand shaking, I put the pillow aside and pulled the quilt over the two bodies, the buzzing of the flies now screaming in my ears. I felt their mother close by, but I wasn't afraid.

I heard heavy breathing behind me and turned to put a hand on the captain's arm. I was surprised to find it trembling.

A loud rustling erupted from a corner of the room. The bushy tail of a fox darted out through the open door, dust rising in its wake. Shots from outside followed its progress.

Captain Audenreid coughed and held his hand up to his face.

I took another step backward, my foot sticking to the floor. I bent to investigate the dark pool and I saw her hand. Two slits bisected her wrist, and gnaw marks from an animal had nearly severed the hand from the arm. She lay on her side by the hearth, her skirts settled purposefully around her, like she was posing for a portrait. Her face was mostly gone, but all I could see when I looked at it was the expression of lost hope I had seen as she stood in the middle of her empty pasture.

"Oh, my God," I mumbled, staggering to my feet and stumbling through the door. I walked blindly ahead, away from the soldiers. I needed to be alone. To grieve for this woman and her lost children, and for whatever part I may have played in her final, desperate act.

Quick footsteps approached me, but I kept walking, breathing in the sweet April air in a futile attempt to eradicate the vile stench of death.

"Mrs. Elliott, stop! We have to move on now."

I continued walking, almost running, calling back over my shoulder, "You go on. I want no more part of your war."

The captain quickened his pace and I soon felt his hand on my shoulder, stopping me. "I am sorry you had to see that. But that had nothing to do with this war—surely you could see it was a suicide."

I turned on him in fury, knocking his hand off my arm. "How can you say that? Didn't you see? She was alone here on this farm with two small children. Where was her husband? Most likely obliterated by this war." I swallowed back the tears that threatened on the surface. I thrust my arm out in the direction of the little house and spat out my words. "Those are just three more victims of this war. You men who speak of glory and victory. Tell me this: Can you look at the faces in there and tell me that anybody can truly win?"

The tears won and spilled down my face.

I struck out at him with my good arm, and he allowed me to pummel him in the chest. He pulled me to him and patted my back, murmuring words of comfort until my tears subsided.

Too embarrassed to raise my head, I mumbled into his dark blue jacket, "Can we at least bury them?"

He paused, weighing Sherman's orders for haste with the scene inside the farmhouse.

I felt him nod. Leaving me where I stood, he walked to the crest of the ridge to speak to the officer there. Orders were given and two soldiers appeared with shovels, walking toward the little house.

Each sound of shovel hitting dirt felt like a physical blow. I had known loss before, but not this devastation of the heart. What had sent her there? What final blow to her spirit? And if Sarah were dead, would I be looking at the same desert places?

"She was a good mother, you know." The soldier looked up at me, then resumed his digging. I spoke louder. "It would have been much worse to leave them, abandoning them." I closed my eyes tightly, not wanting to see the young mother's look of desperation.

The children were laid on either side of their mother, and I knew I would never be able to smell freshly dug dirt again without thinking of them. There was no minister, so Captain Audenreid said a simple prayer. And then the dirt was sprinkled back into the open grave, obliterating the sun forever from sightless eyes.

I climbed back into the wagon, careful not to wake Sarah, who had fallen asleep. We resumed our frenetic march, faster this time to catch up with the rest of the troops. I turned around in the seat and watched the small farm disappear slowly from sight, streams of early-morning sunshine warming the newly turned earth.

I felt a sharp stab in my lower abdomen that took my breath away. And then nothing else. I placed my hand on my stomach, feeling its flatness. I had had that sensation only once in my life, when the thought of conceiving a child had seemed like an unobtainable dream. But now I had proof that it wasn't. I smiled with a mother's knowing, and looked down at the sleeping face of my firstborn.

The wheels of the wagon rolled onward like the never-ending cycle of life, death, and rebirth. I placed my hand on my abdomen again, willing some sort of sign from the child I knew grew inside. But all was still.

CHAPTER TWENTY-SIX

——◆——

Cry "Havoc!" and let slip the dogs of war,
That this foul deed shall smell above the earth
With carrion men, groaning for burial.
—WILLIAM SHAKESPEARE

We had been brought to Meadowland, an antebellum mansion in Tunnel Hill, about ten miles north of Dalton and the Confederate Army. Sherman had made this imposing Greek Revival structure his temporary headquarters, and Sarah and I had been sent to a room and unofficially told to stay out of the way.

She and I talked about her kidnapping, and she seemed to have suffered no long-term ill effects except for an aversion to being left alone. A woman with a child Sarah's age had been sent to care for her, and Sarah regarded the whole thing as a sort of adventure. William had come to see her only once since their reunion, and I told him the truth of my relationship to Sarah. He had reacted to the news with only a shrug and a "Poor Julia" before casually changing the subject. I still hadn't told Sarah, my reasons for my hesitation not clear to even myself.

My first sounds of war came from far away, almost as an afterthought. I sat in a rocker on the upstairs balcony, reading aloud to Sarah. I had paused to look at her and was admiring the way the light made her green eyes shift colors when a soft boom vibrated the air. I stood, the book sliding off my lap. Another boom percolated in the distance as puffs of smoke rose on the horizon and disappeared into the blue morning sky. The soft strains of "The Star-Spangled Banner" crept over the hills and trees to tease my ears. The staccato beats of drums reverberated across the hills.

Sarah ran to look over the railing, her eyes alight with excitement. "Are those soldiers?"

I stood paralyzed, my legs shaking and my arm hurting again. I wondered where Stuart was and if he was safer in a prison than on a battlefield. Or if he was even alive. "Yes, Sarah. Lots of soldiers."

We stayed on the balcony the entire day, my nerves frayed and my imagination running wild. But I couldn't leave the sounds of battle.

Eventually, a young Irish maid called me to dinner. She brought Sarah down to eat in the kitchen, and I went to the dining room, where I was once again surrounded by Sherman and his staff. This was the first time I had seen the general since Stuart had been taken away, and I vowed not let the night pass without speaking to him alone.

Midway through the meal, a courier rushed into the dining room and handed the general a telegram. He read it quickly, a large grin splitting his face. "It is from McPherson," he said, referring to General James B. McPherson, commander of the Army of the Tennessee. Sherman slammed his fist on the table, making the china and crystal shimmy. "I have got Joe Johnston dead!"

I demurely took another spoonful of soup while the men did a lot of back clapping and other congratulatory gestures. I glanced up to find William staring at me, his eyebrow raised. I put my spoon down and lowered my gaze.

I couldn't share in any jubilation. I longed for word of Stuart, my fears for him growing with each passing day. I swallowed my food and bided my time.

I lay awake in my bed for a long time that night, waiting for the last of the guests to say their goodbyes. Then I slipped from the room with a shawl thrown over my nightgown.

I found the library in the darkened house, only to be disappointed that it was empty. I helped myself to a glass of Scotch, then brought it out to the foyer. I smelled a freshly lit cigar coming from up above. Stealthily, I crept back up the stairs and walked out onto the upstairs balcony. The pale moonlight shone through the banister slats, creating a line of dark soldiers marching in formation across the wooden floorboards.

The balcony appeared to be deserted. I leaned over the railing, taking deep breaths of the cool evening air, trying to swallow my disappointment. I knew I could convince General Sherman of Stuart's innocence if I just had the opportunity to speak to him alone. My palms grew moist as I thought of my plan to convince the general if my words failed to sway him. I stood and started to take a sip of the Scotch but stopped, my lips pursed over the rim, my other hand resting on my abdomen. I moved my head, the distinctive odor of fresh cigar smoke drifting over to me. From the corner of my eye I saw the unmistakable end of a cigar glowing red in the dark.

"Madam."

The suddenness of the sound caused me to drop the glass, sloshing liquid over my bare feet and bouncing the glass off the porch. I heard the delicate sound of shattering crystal as it hit the brick steps below.

"You startled me." I bent to wipe the dripping Scotch off my legs with the hem of my nightgown.

"Apparently." I heard the smile in the general's voice. "I hope our talking did not keep you awake."

I shook my head. "No. Actually, I was waiting for everyone to leave so I could talk with you." I hid a yawn behind my hand. "Besides, I haven't been sleeping well lately. Too many scary thoughts." I straightened, feeling the sticky liquid drying on my bare skin.

"Scary thoughts," he repeated after me. "Well put." He took a long sip from his glass. I heard him swallow in the stillness of the night. "What did you want to talk to me about?"

I knew he would expect my bluntness. "My husband. He's as responsible for saving your life as I am."

"Really?" He brought the glass up to his lips and took another sip.

"Pamela Broderick kidnapped my niece. She threatened to kill her unless I followed through with her plan to murder you. Stuart found Sarah and brought her to me so I wouldn't have to go through with it. He risked his life to save me—and you. He doesn't belong in a prison camp."

He paused, and I could hear his deep breathing. "Yet he is still a rebel officer, and he was captured. Why should I release him so he can return to his army and fight against me?"

I ground my toe into the floorboard. "He risked his life to save me.

I will do anything to save him. Anything." I let my shawl fall to my elbows, looking at him sharply.

His hand with the cigar froze midway to his mouth. I stepped closer to him, near enough to smell the Scotch on his breath. He appraised me boldly. "Madam. Are you making me an offer?"

I forced myself to hold his gaze. "I will do anything you ask in return for the release of my husband."

He took a slow drag on his cigar, his eyes never leaving my face. "You are an attractive woman, Mrs. Elliott. And I am honored that you hold me in equally high regard." The warm breeze stirred my nightgown around my feet, cooling my flaming skin. "But I am afraid I cannot accept your generous offer."

I bit my lip, holding back my disappointment. My desolation. "Why?"

Half of his mouth turned up. "Madam. I am in command of the Military Division of the Mississippi with more than one hundred thousand men. I pull a bit of weight in the ranks."

"Then why? Why won't you help me?"

"I did not say I would not. If your story is true, which I suspect is the case, then, despite your husband being a rebel officer, he is innocent. I owe you my life—releasing your husband is the least I could do."

The air seemed to have been sucked out of my lungs. "Do you mean you were willing to release him before I even opened my mouth? And yet you let me make a fool of myself?"

He took a slow drag from his cigar. "On the contrary, Mrs. Elliott. I had yet to hear a complete accounting of your husband's involvement in the assassination plot." He slowly blew out the cigar smoke. "Besides, you have shown me how much you love your husband. Any man whose wife loves him with such devotion deserves a second chance."

"Oh," I said, for lack of anything better.

"Do not be embarrassed, Mrs. Elliott. War does things to people—it changes us. You were merely doing what you thought you had to do to ensure your husband's safety."

I turned away from him, staring out over the railing and into the night. "I'm not that type of woman, and I appreciate your understanding. On behalf of my husband and me, thank you."

We were silent for a few moments before the general spoke again. "I would like to try to convince you to stay here, in safety. It is going to be rougher from here on out, and I think you would be more comfortable staying put."

"No." I shook my head, my loosened hair swinging about my face. "It's very important that I get home. I'm going to have a baby, and I need to get home."

A flash of white appeared above his beard. "Congratulations, Mrs. Elliott. My wife and I welcomed six children into our lives, soon to be joined by number seven." He stopped to stare out at the darkened sky, both hands gripping the railing and the cigar clenched in his teeth, trailing smoke. Quietly, he said, "It is almost hard to imagine a new life amid all this destruction."

I closed my eyes on the darkness, seeing a deserted farmhouse in the middle of a barren field. "War is hell, isn't it, General?" I said, opening my eyes and noticing the bent shoulders on the tall frame silhouetted against the moonlit sky.

"That it is, Mrs. Elliott. That it is." He flicked cigar ash over the railing, then watched the particles filter through the night air.

I turned to leave. "I suppose I should try to get some rest. Good night, General."

He turned his head toward me. "Good night, Mrs. Elliott. I will see to your husband's release."

"Thank you," I said again, then closed the door behind me. As I stood in the darkened hallway, I heard the light tread of feet moving quickly down the stairs and across the foyer. I dismissed an uneasy feeling, then went to my bedroom.

As it turned out, despite his proclamation over dinner the previous night, Sherman did not have Johnston dead. General McPherson had neglected to push his advantage at the little town of Resaca, and was now facing a growing Confederate Army. And so we moved south, toward Atlanta and General Joe Johnston's army. The Southerners were now digging into defensive positions around Resaca, about ten miles south of Dalton and a mere fifty miles north of Atlanta.

Sarah and I were left with the entire army wagon train at Snake

Creek Gap while the separate divisions took their places around Resaca. The sound of cannon began in the early-morning hours of May 14, shaking the earth with their bombardments and creating a heavy cloud of smoke across the valley and over the bald hill that stood as the blind sentry over the battlefield. I began pacing and biting my fingernails. I even tried reading a book to Sarah. But the battle sounds permeated the air around me and could not be escaped.

By the second day of battle, I refused to be a bystander any longer. I had at least one working arm and I had every intention of putting it to good use. I left Sarah in the care of the cook, whose bosom was as ample as her helpings of corn bread, then trudged along the wagon train, asking for the field hospital. Men pointed and stared, but none tried to stop me.

The smell of burning flesh hit me first. The flaming piles of severed limbs stacked outside the surgeons' tent told me I had reached the right place. Gritting my teeth, I walked inside and entered hell.

Surgeons in blood-splattered aprons sawed into wounded flesh, oblivious to the screams and moans around them. Two doors, ostensibly ripped off of nearby farmhouses, served as makeshift operating tables. Scalpels, saws, and horsehair sutures were laid out on a blanket and hastily replenished as they disappeared.

As soon as one limb had been lopped off, the patient was whisked away on his litter and another one would be brought forward. Using the same bloody saw, the surgeon would again attack a wounded limb, allowing it to plop into a quickly filling basket.

I stood still, being shoved in every direction from the fast-moving people around me, unsure where I could step in and help. Someone grabbed my arm. "Are you a nurse?"

Numbly, I nodded.

"Good. Come make yourself useful."

He brought me to an operating table. "Hold him down," I was instructed. The man speaking had dried blood spattered in his beard and across his forehead. Tiny glasses perched on the bridge of his nose and his eyes appeared overly large as he looked up at me.

Not willing to make excuses for my shoulder, I stood behind the wounded man's head, my hands on his shoulders, and held firmly. The young sergeant stared up at me, panic plain in his eyes. "Ye can't let them take off me leg. It's an imported leg, it is. Straight from Ireland."

The surgeon probed at the open wound with his index finger, studying it intently. A minié ball had shattered part of the bone, spreading pieces of lead, dirt, and torn uniform through the leg. He shook his head.

I looked back down at the patient, trying to keep my voice steady. "You will die if you don't allow the doctor to take it off." He struggled slightly, but I held firm. "Do you have a wife?"

He stopped struggling and nodded. "And six wee ones."

"Well, then, I expect she'd rather see you return from war with one less leg rather than not at all."

A medic stood by, a towel and bottle of chloroform at the ready. "Will it hurt?" The man's eyes were wide with terror, beads of sweat marking their way down gunpowder-stained cheeks.

"Not as much as giving birth six times, I shouldn't think."

He looked temporarily shocked, then gave me a weak smile. "All right, then. Let's get on with it."

I squeezed his shoulder reassuringly as the chloroform-soaked towel was lowered over his nose and mouth.

And so the procession of wounded men and boys continued. The ones with gut shot were triaged to the rear. They were given water and pain medication, but there was nothing else to be done for them. Eventually, they would be taken out behind the tent to await burial, their stiffening bodies already covered with flies.

The sun rose high in the sky, making the inside of the tent an inferno, but we kept working. The fused stench of sweat, blood, and death filled the confined area, permeating my hands and clothes, but I wouldn't allow myself to stop. I would hold hands and talk or give water. I no longer noticed the colors of their uniforms. It simply didn't matter.

By late afternoon, the bombardment of the cannon had subsided, leaving only the moans of the wounded. An orderly approached me with about ten canteens and instructed me to go out on the battlefield to help more wounded until they could be brought in.

I stared numbly out onto the scarred field, the branchless trees like sentinels guarding the dead. The field sloped down into a miry creek choked with felled men, trees, horses, and an upended flat-bottomed boat. Soldiers in blue and gray lay side by side along its banks, drinking the dirty water. The canteens strung around my shoulders bounced and clanged against each other, the water sloshing inside. Examining the murky depths of the filthy river, I didn't want to know where the water in the canteens had come from. I no longer felt the pain of my wound— the sights and smells around me were too overwhelming.

A thin pall of smoke settled over the ground, the sickly sweet smell of sulfur and gunsmoke thick in my nostrils. I coughed, my throat and nose stinging.

Men lay strewn across the battlefield like the discarded toys of an angry child. Elbows and knees bent at odd angles, faces contorted with the expressions of life. I picked my way across corpses, looking for a dry mouth croaking the never-ending litany of "Water."

I knew it had been a Federal victory, but as I stared out at the broken bodies, I could not feel anything but regret.

I knelt by a soldier, his light brown hair matted with blood and dirt. "Mama," he whispered, looking directly at me. He looked about sixteen— barely old enough to shave, much less wear a uniform and carry a rifle. I gingerly slid my hand under his neck, lifting his head up to drink from a canteen. The water dribbled into his mouth, leaking down his chin and blackened face.

"Mama," he said again, light brown eyes staring sightlessly at me.

"Yes," I said, easing myself down to the ground next to him and placing his head on my lap. I stroked the dirty hair, its strands slick between my fingers.

"I'm . . ." He stopped, gasping to fill his lungs. "I'm . . . I'm sorry . . . for . . . leaving."

I paused, not quite knowing what to say. "It's okay. Don't worry any more about it. You're forgiven."

I gave him more water and looked to see if there was anything to be done with his wound. My eyes stopped when they reached his abdomen. His jacket and shirt had been pulled out of his pants and hunched in disarray over his prostrate form. The grass between us was drenched with dark red blood, already humming with tiny insects. His entire side was missing, exposing bone and torn tissue and vital organs. I looked back at his face, now still and peaceful, his vacant eyes reflecting the open sky.

I put his head back on the ground and closed his eyes with shaking fingers.

I stood and looked out over the sea of gray and blue. A coppery taste settled on my tongue, making me gag. I took a swig from a canteen to wash it away, but to no avail. The putrid taste was in the air. I shuddered, realizing it was blood. Collapsing to my knees, I began to retch. I dug my fingers into the dirt and touched my forehead to the grass, breathing in the sweet smell of it. I hadn't eaten since breakfast and could only gag on dry air. I wanted to expel the vileness in the air that seemed to saturate my body.

But still the croaks for water continued, bringing me to my feet again. Medics rushed to place the wounded on litters, racing to the rear those who could be helped and leaving those with no hope on the ground where they had fallen.

By dusk my canteens were empty and the cries of the wounded had stilled. I saw a large rock by a tree and walked toward it. My foot stepped on something hard, and I bent to retrieve whatever it was. It was a small pocket Bible, no bigger than my hand, the binding worn as if it had been opened many times. It fell open to a page upon which a dried rose lay. I picked up the rose and it crumbled in my hand, its withered petals scattering in the wind. A single verse had been underlined with thick, black ink, and I read it aloud.

"To everything there is a season,/ and a time to every purpose under the heaven:/ a time to be born and a time to die;/ a time to plant, and a time to pluck up that which is planted; a time to kill, and a time to heal."

I stopped, the words blurring before my eyes. My shoulders sagged, the canteens sliding off into the well-turned earth. The field was scattered with personal effects of the dead: eyeglasses, letters, and diaries. I couldn't look at them and not see the mothers, wives, and daughters who would be waiting for news. I placed the Bible back on the ground by the large root of the tree. The breeze picked up slightly, blowing vanished voices away on the wind.

I looked up at the sound of hoofbeats and recognized Captain Audenreid astride the horse fast approaching me. He tipped his hat as he drew close. "Mrs. Elliot."

I stood quickly, my head light from the effort. I steadied myself on the tree.

The captain dismounted, holding the reins loosely in his hands. "Your husband's sent a courier. He left a missive with General Sherman."

I stared at him mutely, his words not quite registering. "Oh," I said, not quite sure what my next course of action should be.

"I thought you would be pleased to hear your husband is no longer a prisoner."

"Yes, thank you," I said, suddenly springing into action as I gathered up the empty canteens and raced toward General Sherman's tent, the captain doing his best to keep up with me.

The general was seated in a camp chair outside his tent, holding a piece of paper. William sat next to him in stocking feet, polishing his boots. They stood as I approached.

"Mrs. Elliott, I have some news for you."

"Yes, I know. Captain Audenreid told me. When can I see him?"

A glance passed between William and the general. "Your brother-in-law and I were just discussing it. We cannot allow you to go into their camp. You are somewhat of a heroine here, and your capture could be used as quite a bargaining point. I would like to suggest a meeting in the middle of the field, on neutral ground."

I stood close to the general, noticing the smattering of freckles on his nose, a marked contrast to the stern expression on his face. "All right. When?"

"I have arranged for tomorrow at dawn. Can you be ready?"

I gave a faint smile. "I'll be there."

Dawn came early. I shivered from cold as I stood to dress, the walls of my tent damp with morning dew. I gasped as I threw icy-cold water from the washbasin onto my face.

In my joy at learning Stuart had been released, I hadn't yet thought of what I would say to him. My hand slid to my abdomen, my thoughts unsettled. For my child and me to both survive, I could not stay in this time. But if what Pamela said was true, maybe I could learn to navigate time, holding on to the tail of a comet's orbit. I kissed the still-sleeping Sarah, then left my tent. I shivered again, but not from the cold.

I was surprised to see William waiting for me and holding the reins of two horses. He handed one to me, a mock smile on his face.

"It has been decided that I will accompany you, little sister. After all, he is my brother."

I stilled my protest, not wanting a confrontation to spoil my reunion with Stuart.

He assisted me into the saddle, his hand sliding casually down the length of my leg. He then pulled a wooden pole from the ground, a rectangular white flag tied to it, and mounted.

The sky had an ominous red cast to it. *Red sky at morning; sailors take warning.* I crouched lower in my saddle, trying to warm myself and stop my teeth from chattering. Campfires roared throughout the field as men bustled about, preparing their breakfast. My stomach churned at the thought of food, while at the same time grumbling from hunger, another sign of impending motherhood.

I didn't have time to be nervous about riding the horse; I was too busy scanning the far side of the field for a familiar figure. We trotted slowly out onto the tortured ground, scarred from the mortars and trampling feet of the previous day. My horse shied away from the decapitated body of another horse, sidestepping quickly, its hooves slipping on the dew-moistened dirt. I held on tightly, following William, who had not paused.

A lone figure emerged from the dusk-shadowed woods on the far side. I heard the thin echo of hoofbeats vibrating the ground beneath me. I recognized Endy first, his black coat fuzzy in the morning dimness. Clinging tightly to my reins, I dug my heels into my horse's sides, heedless of William's shouted warning.

The wind stung my eyes but I refused to close them, lest I lose sight of the tall figure in gray atop the large black horse. He, too, broke into a gallop, clods of dirt flying behind him. I reined my horse in tightly, making it rear. I slid off the side, my skirts catching on my saddle and giving any and all spectators a brief and complete show of my undergarments.

I ran as fast as I could, the sounds of William's horse close behind me. Stuart had also dismounted and he stood next to Endy, waiting for me. He started walking, and then running as I neared, catching me as I flung myself at him. He swung me around to regain his balance, my skirts flying and his arms wound tightly around my waist. I buried my face into his neck, feeling the unfamiliar fuzz of a new beard.

"Thank, God," I mumbled into his beard.

His voice searched for sure ground. "You are still as beautiful as the first time I saw you." His fingers traced my face, caressing my jaw. "This is the face I see each night before I sleep."

I smiled, tilting my head back to look into his face for the first time, and keeping my uninjured arm around his neck. His face, still showing signs of his beating, was thinner and a jagged scar showed through the beard on his jaw. I kissed it first and then kissed him full on the mouth. He responded, his lips hard against mine.

He rested his chin on the top of my head, his arms wrapped tightly around me. "It will be your face I will be searching for when this war is over." He cupped his fingers around my skull, his eyes searching mine, a hint of danger hidden behind the dark blue recesses.

I jerked my head back, my gaze touching his jaw. My hand drifted to my abdomen and I thought of the child that should be bringing us together but was the one thing that could separate us forever. "I have to go away for a while. But if there's any way in this universe that I can return to you, I promise you I will." There had been no decision for me to make. The truth had been in my heart for a long time, and all I had to do was look and find it.

His hold on me tightened. "You still have secrets, Laura. How can you not trust me after all we have been through together?" His eyes were cold, but I could feel his craving for me in the touch of his hands and the smell of him. I was nearly breathless in my wanting of him, yet he held me away.

I touched his face, in the sensitive part below his ear, the place that made him moan when I touched it with my lips. "You've earned my heart and my life, Stuart. I can't keep any more secrets from you."

He stepped back suddenly, his hand touching upon the revolver in his belt as he looked behind me.

"Hello, little brother. So, we meet again." William put his arm around my shoulders, giving me a little squeeze. "We did not get to talk much last time we saw each other, but I wanted to say that I have found your wife absolutely delightful."

I jerked away from William's hold and stepped toward Stuart. "Go away, William. I have things to discuss with my husband."

He shook his head in an exaggerated way. "I do not think so, sister. You have been privy to too many discussions involving our General Sherman. I do not believe it would be wise of me to allow you to converse any more in private." He smiled broadly. "Besides, I wanted to have a chance to talk to my brother."

Stuart's jawbones moved under his cheeks. "I have nothing to say to you, William. I can scarce believe you are actually my brother."

"But I think you might want to hear what I have to say anyway."

I suddenly remembered the stealthy footsteps I had heard following my conversation with General Sherman. Dread filled me as I waited for William to speak.

"Were you not surprised to be released from prison so quickly? And let us not forget your medical care. Did you ever stop to wonder how that was all arranged?"

I turned on William. "Shut up! Everything you say is a twisted lie. Don't listen to him, Stuart—he's trying to make things sound worse than they are."

Stuart slid a glance in my direction. "Just a moment, Laura. I want to hear this."

"She does not want you to hear it, Stuart. Or you will find out what kind of a woman she really is." William turned to me. "Tell him about your conversation with General Sherman. Tell him what you offered the good general in return for Stuart's release." He faced Stuart again. "And it was not our mother's jewelry, little brother. Oh no. Your wife offered him the most precious thing of all."

Stuart moved closer to me. He looked into my eyes, and I met his gaze. "What is he talking about?" His eyes widened as comprehension hit him.

I looked closely at him, at the beloved lines and soft skin of his neck, wanting to be away from this place with him, and all this behind us. Our gazes clashed and all sounds seemed to disappear; even the small insects in the grass lay still, waiting for my answer.

"Tell me he is lying."

I looked away, then back at his accusing eyes. "It is true, but nothing happened. I promise you nothing happened."

He stepped back. "But you would have."

I squeezed my hands into fists, wanting to strike out at William—at Stuart. "Yes, damnit, I would have. I would have sold my soul to the devil to save your life."

Shock registered on his face and he shook his head as if trying to erase a thought. "Is this the kind of secret you have been holding back from me all this time?"

"No. No! Of course not. Oh, God, Stuart. I love you. I need to tell you everything so you'll understand."

He walked up so close to me that I could feel his heat. "Then tell me."

I wanted to blurt out everything, to erase the look of hurt on Stuart's face, but William's presence stopped me. He couldn't be trusted with the truth. I shook my head.

Stuart turned and began walking back toward Endy. I couldn't let him leave. William held me back by my wounded arm as I tried to go to Stuart.

"Tell him our news, Laura."

I pushed William away and rushed after Stuart, grabbing hold of his jacket. His eyes were bright with anger as he glared at me.

"I'm going to have a baby."

His gaze flickered down at me and then over to where William stood. Then he looked me level in the eyes. "And who is the father?"

For a moment I couldn't breathe. And then I slapped him as hard as I could across the face.

He didn't flinch. He simply mounted Endy and rode out to the edge of the field, disappearing into the dim shadows of the woods.

Chapter Twenty-seven

◆

I have been a stranger in a strange land.

—EXODUS 2:22

"I brought you and your little girl something."

I sat back in the wagon, feeling the heat of the late-June afternoon press down on me. I smoothed my hand over my dress, feeling the slight swelling of my abdomen. Looking at the private walking toward me, I cocked my head.

The soldier pushed a black-and-white cow forward, its large brown eyes lazily browsing the crowd of men who had gathered near the wagon train after setting up camp.

I recognized the man as one of Sherman's bummers, one of the many swarms of soldiers assigned to forage for food. Generally, these men gleefully stripped the land and its inhabitants of anything valuable and anything edible. But as Sherman drove deeper and deeper into enemy territory, foraging was the only way to supply his army. Still, I felt guilty as I ate three square meals a day, knowing from where the food had come. My pregnancy meant I was hungry constantly, and several of the soldiers, knowing my condition, would always make a point of saving the best pickings for me.

Someone shouted from the crowd, "Hell, O'Rory, if I thought you was that lonesome, I would have loaned you some money to come inta town with me."

The shouting was met by catcalls and a loud moo from the cow. The soldier faced the growing crowd. "Aw, you all shut up. I thought Mrs. Elliott would like some steak."

"Yeah, O'Rory. And if she don't, I bet you'll take ole' Daisy May back to your tent."

More ribald laughter and comments followed this remark, and the young man's face grew stern. He turned back to me.

"Please accept this gift, ma'am."

I glanced over the cow, noticing the very full udder and the panicked look in the cow's eyes. I looked back at the soldier. "Well, she certainly does have nice calves."

The group of men exploded in laughter as the man's face turned a deep red. I climbed off the wagon and put my hand on his arm.

"I'm sorry. It's been a while since I've made a joke and I couldn't resist. But I can't accept this cow. This is a milk cow. Where did you get it?"

He looked down at his boots, scuffing the dirt with his toe. "From a farm not two miles from here. Stupid rebs left her all alone in the pasture."

I felt the blood drain from my face. "This cow is full of milk—somebody's been milking it regularly. Probably a mother with young children. I think she needs it more than we do."

He stepped between the cow and me, as if to protect his prize. "No, ma'am. They's just rebs. They deserve to starve to death."

I was a good head taller than he was and I stepped closer to him to take full advantage of the difference in stature. I leaned over him and said, "Women and children are not your enemies. They're just trying to survive. Imagine if it were your wife and children."

He gave me a defiant look. "I ain't got no wife."

My retort was interrupted by the arrival of Captain Audenreid. Since my meeting with Stuart, he had stayed close to my side as much as possible. He never asked about Stuart, and I would not talk about him, but the captain seemed to know that all was not well. I had seen him closely regarding William as Stuart's brother doggedly pursued me, and Captain Audenreid would put himself between my brother-in-law and me when he could.

He took one look at my blanched face and ordered a camp chair for me. "Are you ill, Mrs. Elliott?" His solicitous look was warming.

I shook my head. "No. It's just that, well, I want this soldier to take the cow back from where he stole it."

The captain was apprised of the situation, and ordered the soldier to return the cow.

With much grumbling, the private retreated, the cow faithfully in tow.

I reached out and squeezed the captain's hand in gratitude. He looked at me, startled. "I'm sorry, Captain. I apologize if I was being forward. But I wanted to thank you for that."

His face softened as he regarded me in the hot sun. "Remember, I was in that farmhouse, too. I shall never forget it, nor shall I ever forget you."

I turned away, flustered, not knowing what to say.

"I apologize. I did not mean to cause you discomfort. I just wanted to let you know that I hold you in high regard. And that you can rely on me to get you home safely."

I looked back at his face, my hand shielding the sun from my eyes. I could see a slight flush under his sunburn. "Thank you, Captain. I shall treasure your friendship."

Smiling warmly at him, I watched him remount and ride away, his hand raised in farewell.

I had traveled with Sherman's troops through the hot months of May and June as his massive army continually flanked the Confederates and forced them to retreat farther and farther south toward the inevitable confrontation at Atlanta. I kept myself busy in the hospital tents, doling out what little mercy I could. I enjoyed the time I had with Sarah, and we spent it becoming better acquainted. I found that her favorite color was blue and that she loved most vegetables but especially corn. I learned the name of her best friend, and the way she liked her mother to plait her hair. But I didn't know what it had been like when she lost her first tooth, nor what gifts she had received for her last six birthdays. Nor did I know what songs her mother sang for her at bedtime, or the words of comfort she listened for when she had nightmares. She still called me Aunt Laura, for I had not yet told her otherwise.

I refused to think about Stuart. If I did, the tightness around my heart would tear at me, making it almost too hard to breathe. Instead I made plans. I had been alone before, and I knew I could do it again. The next conjunction of a lunar eclipse and a comet would be on

September 1. I would leave the same way I had arrived—borne on the wind of a speeding mass of celestial particles. Stuart would assume whatever he wanted, and I would disappear from his world forever.

By July 3, Sherman had entered Marietta, some fifteen miles west of Roswell. I was summoned to Kennesaw House, the town's most fashionable hotel, where Sherman had set up his headquarters.

I left Sarah on a bench outside the office. As I entered the room, the general stood by the window, caught in a fit of coughing. As soon as he finished, I heard the strident wheezing that reminded me of Michael's asthma. To my astonishment, he picked up a cigar from the desk and began puffing on it.

"General, do you think you should be doing that?"

He frowned at me, his brows knitting together. "Pardon me?"

"Smoking. It won't help your asthma."

He continued to stare at me and puff on his cigar. "I will take that under advisement. Sit down, please."

He indicated a seat by the desk, then reached into a drawer and pulled out a letter and handed it to me. "This is a letter from me granting you and your possessions immunity from Federal authorities." He came around the desk to stand in front of me. "Mrs. Elliott, for your protection, I have sworn to secrecy all who know about what happened to Mrs. Broderick. It might not go well for you if it were known by your fellow Southerners." He smiled warmly at me. "But please do not think I am not grateful—I am. You did save my life. If there is anything that I can ever do for you, please do not hesitate to call on me." With a sly grin, he added, "And there will be no payment required."

I ignored the flush rushing to my face. "I understand, and I thank you for this," I said, indicating the letter. "I know of your men's propensity for burning houses." I shuddered, recalling the smoldering ruins we had passed on our way to Atlanta. All that remained of once-beautiful plantation homes were the lone chimneys—Sherman's sentinels, as they were called.

"I am sending you with Brigadier General Kenner Garrard, the commander of the Second Cavalry Division, to Roswell. It has been a real pleasure knowing you, Mrs. Elliott, and I wish you godspeed."

He moved back behind the desk and I knew I was being dismissed.

I began walking toward the door but hung back, wishing to say one more thing. "General, I have a strong feeling you will be giving Savannah to President Lincoln as a Christmas present."

He leaned forward with both hands on the desk. "Really? Well, I certainly appreciate your vote of confidence." He began shuffling papers on his desk, and I knew he had lost interest in the topic.

"Goodbye, General. And thank you again." I turned and shut the door behind me.

I almost ran into Captain Audenreid as Sarah and I hurried down the stairway. He was coming up, his hat in his hand, and a small hatbox in his other. "Mrs. Elliott. I am glad to see you. I hope you do not mind, but I have brought something for Sarah. I thought she could use a bonnet to protect her skin in this hot Georgia sun. I love her freckles, but her mother might not."

Sarah squealed and took the box from the captain with a shouted thanks and immediately opened it. She slipped a straw bonnet on her head and asked me to tie the lilac ribbon under her chin.

I smiled at the effect. "Captain, thank you so much—you shouldn't have. But I'm glad I ran into you. I'm afraid this is goodbye. I'm returning to Roswell today in the company of General Garrard."

He looked genuinely sad as he reached for my hand and bent to kiss it, his mustache tickling my skin. "It has been an immense pleasure, Mrs. Elliott. I shall not easily forget you."

Despite his words, I did not feel uneasy. "Thank you, Captain. Thank you for everything."

He looked at me intensely. "Mrs. Elliott, please be careful. There are those whose intentions toward you aren't completely honorable."

I knew to whom he was referring. "I will. I promise. And you continue to dodge bullets, okay?"

He sent me a sad grin as I reached out and squeezed his hand. "Goodbye," he said softly. He chucked Sarah under the chin. "And you take good care of your aunt, you hear?"

Sarah nodded and gave him a hug.

We turned and walked across the street toward Marietta Square, amid the hustle and bustle of civilians and soldiers.

On Tuesday, July 5, General Garrard and his forces arrived in an almost-deserted Roswell. The Confederates had abandoned the little mill town, burning the bridge across the Chattahoochee as they left. Crossing the river would bring the troops closer to the prize of Atlanta, and I knew the burning of the bridge would be a sore point with General Sherman.

So many of Garrard's men suffered from heatstroke in the broiling Georgia sun, they were falling out of their saddles by the handful. One of the first things General Garrard did was set up hospitals for them on the front lawns of the Dunwody and Pratt houses, and also the Presbyterian church where I had been married. Anger rose in me as I saw the ripped-out pews tossed on the front lawn of the church, to be used as firewood, but I was helpless to stop them.

I yearned to see my house again. I didn't know what shape Phoenix Hall would be in, but I knew without a doubt it would still be standing. I was eagerly waiting to be told I was free to go home and to be offered an escort there, but they seemed to have forgotten us.

While the impromptu hospitals were being set up, Sarah and I took the opportunity to join several of the soldiers in picking our fill of blackberries. We seemed to have been forgotten, and easily settled ourselves on the side of the road in the middle of town while the soldiers went about the business of setting up camp. I laughed at Sarah with the blackberry juice dripping down her chin. I was busily popping berries into my own mouth when I saw the flames. From the direction they were coming, I realized it was the cotton mill, burned under General Sherman's orders. I knew the Elliotts' main source of income was as stockholders of the Roswell Manufacturing Company, and this would make them destitute.

The flames licked at the sky, large particles exploding into the air. I thought of Phoenix Hall and how a deserted house would lure looters, and I itched to get there as soon as possible. I assumed Zeke had long since joined Julia in Valdosta, but a part of me wished he were still there to greet us when we returned home.

I stood and glanced around me to be sure no one watched. I took my carpetbag from the back of the wagon, as well as Sarah's hand, then began walking the three miles to the house. I had barely crossed the town square when I heard my name being shouted. I turned to face William Elliott.

I hadn't seen him in the trek from Marietta, and I had assumed he had stayed with Sherman. Knowing his deviousness, however, I was sure he had managed to come here, where he knew I would be. I knew without a doubt that his being in Roswell had nothing to do with him wanting to see his home and family.

I continued walking, barely pausing long enough to shout over my shoulder, "I'm free to go, William. And we really need to get home." I patted the pocket in my dress to reassure myself that General Sherman's letter was still there, then turned back and resumed walking.

He raced to catch up with us, falling in step beside us. "It is my home, too, Laura, and I have offered the grounds as an encampment area. It certainly would not be proper for you to be staying there with all those men without being chaperoned by a male member of your family. Besides, I wanted to be near my daughter." He ruffled Sarah's hair, causing her to smile up at him.

I stopped to stare at him. "A bit like the fox watching the chicken coop, wouldn't you think?"

He threw his head back and laughed, the sound grating my nerves. I turned and continued walking with Sarah as William watched us go, our pace quickening as we neared my destination. My heart fell when I reached the gate. The top hinge was broken, the gate hanging drunkenly by the remaining hinge. The grass grew high around the post, and a tiny green lizard poked its head out from the grassy base. We walked through the gate, noticing the weeds pushing up through the rocky dirt of the drive. Sarah let go of my hand and began running. I dropped my bag and followed her, grabbing her hand and running together.

My breath caught in my throat when I saw the chimney appear as we crossed the bend in the drive. As the entire house loomed into view, I began to shout. I shouted people's names: Julia, Willie, Sukie, Zeke. But the shutterless house stood silent, its windows vacant.

I barely noticed the peeling paint and missing floorboards on the porch as we climbed the stairs and turned the doorknob. It opened without resistance, and hot, dusty air blew over me. I stepped into the empty hall and stood in the stillness, letting the familiarity settle around me. A slight breeze from the open door danced around me, making the dusty crystal chandelier tinkle a greeting. We had come home.

Sarah darted in and out of rooms, slamming doors and shouting names. I walked around the house more slowly, my fingers making crevasses in the thickly heaped dust atop the furniture. Besides the dust and dirt, everything seemed intact. I collapsed onto the piano bench and ran my fingers across the keys. I wept with joy as I banged out familiar tunes on the horribly off-key piano, my only audience Sarah and the mice and insects that had been inhabiting the house in our absence.

I retrieved my carpetbag from the end of the drive and soon settled down to practical matters. We had no food to eat. The kitchen garden had long since been taken over by weeds, and the root cellar stripped clean of everything Julia hadn't been able to fit in the wagon. We would have to return to camp and beg for our dinner.

At the sound of horse's hooves, I stepped outside to peer into the sun-speckled lawn, squinting my eyes to see who approached. I stayed in the shade of the porch until William drew nearer. Clouds of red dust told me more soldiers were on their way.

He doffed his hat as he stopped in front of me. "Mrs. Elliott. How kind of you to offer your home to us, the conquering army. I apologize for impinging on your hospitality at such short notice." He swiped at the sweat dripping off of his forehead. "A few of my troops will be camping out in the yard."

Sarah came out and stood next to me, her hand clutched on my skirt, and tilted her head at the man she called her father, as if she no longer recognized him. I leaned against a pillar, my arms crossed in front of me, and watched the soldiers march toward us on the dirt drive. "I don't know what kind of hospitality you're looking for, but you won't find it here. The house is empty of all food and the garden is dead. Even if there were food, there would be little we could eat." I couldn't resist a small smile. "I don't cook."

William sent me a brief glance before sliding from his horse. "Not to worry, Laura. We have brought enough provisions, and I am sure one of the men can do the cooking."

He walked up the steps toward me. I stepped back, giving him a wide berth to walk past us and into my house.

We settled into a familiar routine revolving around mealtimes. Happily, this was the only time I was forced to endure his company.

The rest of the time I spent in my room or in the library, reading to Sarah. We took long walks in the woods and visited Zeke's deserted cabin several times until Sarah asked that we not go anymore. She said it made her too sad. I wrote to Julia in Valdosta, letting her know of my return with Sarah, and I waited each day for her reply.

I didn't have the heart to play the piano, as it reminded me of happier times with Stuart. And I made sure my door was bolted every night, knowing that William was in the house and watching me like a cat would a mouse. Mostly, I bided my time, knowing September quickly approached.

The second week after my return, the nights turned suddenly cool, offering a brief respite from the sticky heat of the day. I threw my windows open wide, allowing the bright moonlight to illuminate the room, and drifted to sleep listening to the cicadas and other night creatures.

The hand over my mouth startled me and brought me to the edge of sleep, not quite awake. When I tasted salty sweat, my eyes flew open to stare at the dark form hovering over me.

"I will move my hand if you promise me you will not scream, little sister. And if you break your promise, you will be sorry." His other hand rested on my neck, and he applied enough pressure to make me choke. I silently nodded.

William removed his hand but kept hold of my arm so I couldn't escape as he sat on the side of the bed. He smelled strongly of alcohol, and his hot breath stung my eyes. I backed myself against the headboard as far as I could go.

He reached out his hand and caressed my cheek. "Surely you find me more attractive than General Sherman." I saw a flash of white in the darkness and could picture the leer across his face.

I bent my knees back and kicked him in the chest with both of my feet, loosening his hold on my arm, then lurched for the other side of the bed. I became entangled in the bedclothes and tumbled to the hard floor. He leaned toward me. In panic, I scooted away from the bed and felt his hand grab hold of the hem of my nightgown. My feet managed to find the floor, and with a loud tearing sound, I ran for the door.

"You bitch!" he roared, grappling to his feet.

I reached the door and pulled. It was locked. I turned around, my hands pressed against the door, and saw him lunge at me. I did the one thing that I remembered from my self-defense course. I raised my knee and brought it in direct contact with his crotch.

The effect was immediate. He dropped to his knees, his forehead against the wood floor. I turned the key and opened the door wide. Leaning over him, I hissed, "Get out of here. And if you ever try a stunt like that again, I will personally tell General Sherman. I would do it now, except for the disgrace you would bring to this family."

He tilted his head up to me, his eyes glittering in the moonlight. "You will pay for this, Laura. You sanctimonious little whore." He swiped at his mouth with his sleeve, his breathing ragged. "You have not seen the last of me."

He staggered to his feet and left the room without a backward glance.

I stood in the doorway long after I heard the latch to his door click into place. I slammed my door, then raced to the windows, shutting them tightly one by one. I should have realized that any boy who had been raised in this house would know which trees to climb.

I didn't see William for several days. I knew that there was a flurry of activity around the burned bridge as the Yankees worked diligently to rebuild it. I assumed William was thus occupied, and breathed a sigh of relief. Still, I spent most of my hours in my room or Sarah's, spending as much time with her as I could, as if my mind realized something my heart couldn't yet see. We read a lot, and sometimes I just stared out the window, thinking of Stuart whenever my mind would catch me off guard.

On the evening of July 14, I sat in my room after Sarah had gone to bed, watching dusk gather in the sky, one hand resting on my abdomen. Despite being nearly four months pregnant, I barely showed, the rise under my nightgown hardly noticeable. The sounds from the men encamped around the house changed subtly, and I got up to look out the window. Holding the curtain aside, I peered out at the dozen or so campfires dotted around the yard. In the field beyond, a colony of fireflies glowed and dimmed, glowed and dimmed in a primal mating dance. A movement by the side of the house caught my attention. Three uniformed men staggered together, one of them holding a lit torch. Their drunken laughter carried up to me, and it didn't take me long to figure out that they were heading for the smokehouse. The grass was dry and withered and it wouldn't need much of a fire to burn everything up, including the house.

Grabbing my shawl, I unbolted the door and flung it open. I had reached the top of the steps when the front door flew open and two men on horseback rode into the foyer, sabers raised, slashing at the walls and upholstered furniture, bringing to mind Mrs. Cudahy's words. Soldiers stood outside with torches. I ran back to wake Sarah, then grabbed Sherman's letter and raced down the back stairs and out the back door.

I left Sarah on the porch with the letter and with instructions not to move and to scream if anybody came near her, then flew across the backyard, my bare feet gripping the cool grass as I ran toward the torches, realizing too late that in my haste I hadn't grabbed a weapon.

I reached them just as the taller soldier was opening the door to the smokehouse, preparing to toss the torch inside. All three soldiers swayed, apparently in no condition to walk a straight line. Lunging myself at the soldier, I knocked him out of the way. The torch flew from his hands and landed in the brown grass several feet away.

I took the shawl in both hands and beat furiously at the torch and small fire feeding itself on the dried grass. My arms pumped at a frenzied pace and I continued to beat the helpless ground until only dust rose to drift out over the field.

Finished with my task, I turned my fury on the three soldiers swaying on their feet and staring at me with disbelief and anger mingled on their faces.

"What in the hell do you think you're doing? You idiots! You could have burned the whole house down—with me and my daughter in it. You have the combined brains of a pea!" Having no weapon, I stuck my toes in the dirt and kicked it at them.

Stooping to gather up the smoldering torch and take it out of harm's way, I turned around and began to walk back to the house. I felt rather than heard the rush of air behind me.

The impact knocked me facedown in the dirt and temporarily took the breath from me. Someone was lying on my back and I could smell his stale whiskey breath while his rough beard stubble chafed my cheek. I felt my assailant get off of me and roughly grab hold of my shoulders and flip me over on my back. My almost-healed wound screamed in pain, but I had no time to think about it.

I tried to scramble to my feet but his hands held me down.

"Look here, boys. See what I got." His hat had fallen off in the scuffle and the sweat dripped down his forehead and cheeks.

His hands groped at my breasts and I started fighting him in earnest. Drunk or not, the man was too strong for me and was able to pinion both hands above my head with one hand while the other one tried to reach under my nightgown. Luckily, the other two were either too drunk or too stunned over what was happening to join their companion in his obscene dance.

Fighting panic, I struggled with renewed vigor. I opened my mouth to scream, only to have a callused hand smother any sound. He moved his hand off my breasts and began to fiddle with the top of his pants. He shifted his weight and rose on his knees. Seeing my chance to knock him off balance, I sat up, shoving both hands at his chest. He fell backward.

No longer captive, I clambered to my feet and began stumbling toward the house. I hadn't gone very far when I heard the distinctive sound of a pistol cocking. I stopped and turned around slowly. My attacker was on his knees and was unsteadily pointing his pistol at me.

"It takes a brave man to shoot an unarmed woman in the back!" I shouted with false bravado as I turned around and began walking slowly toward the house.

An officer on horseback raced around the corner of the house, but I continued walking, not wanting to stop until I had reached the sanctuary of my room, with the door bolted securely behind me.

The sound of a gun firing made me jump. I could hear the blood rushing in my head, but I forced myself to remain calm. Without turning around I shouted over my shoulder, "You missed!" and kept walking.

The officer dismounted and walked quickly toward me, shouting at the soldier to drop the gun. He grabbed my arm as I tried to make my way past him. "What is going on here?" he barked.

I knew this face—I had seen it many times in history books. The broad forehead, dark wavy hair and beard, the affable Scottish looks. General James B. McPherson.

I looked him squarely in the eye. "Three of your gallant soldiers just tried to set fire to my house. Failing at that simple task, they then decided that a good game of rape would be a fun thing to do. Luckily, for me at least, they failed at both attempts. Now, if you would be so kind as to let me go, I would like to go inside. I'd appreciate it if you could keep your men under control while they are on my property."

Other soldiers had run to restrain the man that had attacked me. General McPherson examined my disheveled state, the charred shawl flung over my shoulders. "My apologies, madam. But these men have been given orders to burn this house and its surrounding buildings. The owners are not only major stockholders in the Roswell Manufacturing Company, supplying the Confederate Army, but they are also known rebels."

I yanked my arm from his grasp. "No, that can't be! Who gave those orders?"

"I did, ma'am. And I received my information from a reliable source— Captain William Elliott on General Sherman's staff."

I began to shake. *How could he do this to his own family?* "That son of a bitch," I muttered under my breath.

"I beg your pardon?"

I looked back at him and shook my head. "Never mind. It's not important." My mind began to race, conjuring up possible solutions to this nightmare.

"I will need you to evacuate this house as soon as possible."

"Wait!" I felt my face crease into a wild smile. "I have a letter from General Sherman himself, protecting this property. Hold on." I ran to the back porch and took the letter from Sarah, then handed it to General McPherson.

He held the deeply wrinkled letter up in the fading light, scanning the words. He lowered it slowly. "My deepest apologies. I do not know how this misunderstanding could have happened. I will ensure you are protected. When my troops depart, I will leave a guard."

He handed the letter back to me and I clutched it to my chest. "Thank you. I'm going inside now. I trust you will see to it that the man who attacked me is duly punished."

"Yes, ma'am. Again, my deepest apologies."

I started walking but turned back, thoughts of lost love heavy on my mind. If my memory of my history book was correct, this man had less than a week to live. "General McPherson."

He stopped, surprise registering on his face that I should know his name.

I continued. "I have a strong feeling you should write your fiancée soon. Perhaps tonight before you retire." He opened his mouth to say something, his expression quizzical, but was interrupted by shouts behind him from the man who had attacked me and who was now being restrained. I walked to the house without turning back and collected Sarah from the porch.

The foyer was in a shambles. Feathers from chair cushions floated about the floor like snow. Deep gashes marred the wallpaper, leaving it to hang in large sags. But the soldiers were gone and the house had been saved. From the bottom of the stairs, I saw an orange glow in the sky from the upstairs hallway window, and I knew someone else's house had gone up in flames. Again, I heard Mrs. Cudahy's voice in my head. She was saying something about how no one knew why Phoenix Hall had been spared destruction. And now I did.

I put Sarah to bed and she soon fell sound asleep, untouched by the nightmare of the world around her. I stared at her sleeping face, this child that was mine but not mine. This was her home, her time, her people. How could I take her with me? Yet how could I leave her?

I bolted the door and crawled under the covers with Sarah, listening to her soft breathing, as I fell asleep.

Chapter Twenty-eight

———— ✦ ————

Love knows not distance; it hath no continent;
its eyes are for the stars.

—SIR GILBERT PARKER

Less than a week later, the soldiers were gone—creeping ever south-ward toward the prize of Atlanta. The end was near. General McPherson was true to his word and left a guard and plenty of food to get us through the next several months. He also mentioned that William had disappeared, probably deserting the army. I hoped that he had fled west and that I would never see him again.

I was out by the well, drawing water, when I heard the unmistak-able sound of wagon wheels. I had grown accustomed to this sound as refugees continued to move out from Atlanta and seek shelter from the invading army in the Georgia countryside. But this wagon was ap-proaching the house, coming to a halt on the front drive.

Dropping the bucket, I walked quickly to the side of the house to see who my visitors might be and wondering why I hadn't heard the guard.

Turning the corner, I spotted the guard sitting on the front porch steps, busily munching on hardtack and oblivious to the wagon that had pulled up in front of the house.

I opened my mouth to speak when I heard my name. I stopped in disbelief as Julia and Zeke appeared from the other side of the wagon.

"Zeke! Julia!" I ran to them, my arms outstretched.

Sarah bounded out the front door, her small legs almost flying as she threw herself into Julia's arms. "Mama!" she shouted. Their heads bent together, and they cried and laughed at the same time. I turned to Zeke, unable to watch the reunion between mother and daughter.

He embraced me, and it felt good to have somebody's arms around me again. I wept on his shoulder as he stroked my hair.

"You are leaving us."

I nodded, wiping my eyes with my sleeve.

Julia stilled, her arm around Sarah. "Please, Laura. Stay with us."

I shook my head. "I can't, Julia. I'm going to have a baby."

Julia gave a shriek of delight and threw her arms around me, catching me off guard. "Zeke told me you had married Stuart. I am so delighted for you. Now there is even one more reason for you to stay."

Tears, which always seemed near the surface every time I thought of Stuart and of leaving this place, spilled down my face. "I have to go back. I can't survive childbirth here. Besides, Stuart doesn't think the baby's his." My voice hitched on my last words.

Zeke and Julia both wore stunned expressions. "It's a long story—but of course it's his. Suffice it to say that William contributed to the seed of doubt in Stuart's mind."

Julia grabbed my arm. "You've seen William."

I looked into her warm brown eyes and knew she could handle the truth. "Yes, Julia, I have. And Pamela, too." I saw the panic in her face just as I realized that we were missing someone. "Where is Willie?"

"I left him with the Holcombs. I didn't want to bring him until I knew it was safe. I will send word to let them know they can come home now."

I threw my arms around her and Zeke again. "Why don't we go inside and have some coffee—the real stuff—and we'll talk about everything?"

We talked long into the afternoon until the low rays of sun faded into dusk. Sarah sat at Julia's feet, never letting go of Julia's skirts, as if she were afraid they would be separated again. Eventually, the little girl fell asleep, and I was able to speak more freely about what had happened in the months since we had seen each other.

As darkness grew, Zeke lit the lamps while Julia and I prepared supper. Julia had listened in silence as I told her about Pamela's death. She had not thrown accusations at me, but I still needed her forgiveness.

I broached the subject amid the clatter of china and silverware. "Julia, I'm sorry for your loss. But I can't say that it wasn't for the best."

She let the remaining silverware in her hand drop on the mahogany table and walked over to me. "I owe you so much. I am not one to question your motives. You have shown incredible strength and courage, and I shall always be grateful for that." Her hand swept the hair off my forehead in a maternal gesture. "You rescued Sarah and saved my house—there is nothing to forgive. You did what few of us would have had the courage to do." I felt an inner peace as she reached for my hands and squeezed them. We returned to our chores and didn't speak of it again.

Zeke and Julia stayed with me through the long days of August. Julia and I talked of babies while Zeke whittled or just sat in comfortable silence next to us. I half hoped for word from Stuart, but none came, and I buried my hope deep inside me.

On the last day of the month, I put Sarah to bed, and the three of us sat on the front porch, watching the fireflies dance across the lawn. Julia told me that Eliza Smith and many of our Roswell neighbors had also taken refuge in Valdosta, making the desertion of their homes a bit easier. Charles had joined the Roswell Battalion and hadn't been heard from since. I told them a little about the twentieth and twenty-first centuries. Except for washing machines and air conditioners, they weren't too impressed. I somehow agreed with their sentiments. As we talked, my fingers clutched the key around my neck, thinking of things to come.

"Julia, I've been doing a lot of thinking. When this war is over, times will be really tough." I continued rocking, my toes tapping lightly on the floorboards. "And I want to try to make things easier for you." I took a deep breath, trying to decide where to start. "First, forget about cotton. Try peanuts instead. You may have to buy some land farther south for a better growing area, but peanuts should make a profitable crop. Peaches, too."

She looked at me like I had lost my mind. "Peanuts?"

"Yeah, peanuts. You know, goober peas. Haven't you ever heard of peanut butter?"

She shook her head.

"Well, I'll tell you about that later." I slapped at a mosquito on my forearm. "But you also need to find a man in Atlanta by the name of

Asa Candler. In about twenty years he's going to get a patent for a non-alcoholic drink that will make him and all of his investors millionaires. Invest everything you can afford with him. You won't regret it."

"Asa Candler, peanuts, and peaches," she murmured. "I'll remember that."

"Good," I said, reaching for her hand. "I'll feel better knowing you're all taken care of."

I didn't let go of her hand, nor did I look at her. "And I'm leaving Sarah here. With you."

She continued rocking and I felt her eyes on me. "I know."

I turned to face her. "How did you know?"

With a soft smile, she said, "Because she still calls you Aunt Laura. You have never told her the truth. And besides." She squeezed my hand tightly. "You love her."

"I do." Tears sprang from my eyes, but I did nothing to wipe them away. "I can't believe that after all I've been through to find her, I can't bring her home."

Julia left her chair and kneeled before mine. "Come back, then, Laura. Come back after the baby's born. We all want you here. With us."

I shook my head. "But Stuart doesn't want me."

"Of course he does. I do not know what went on between you two, but whatever he said to make you believe that he did not want you is a lie. He must have been hurt or confused, but I know the man loves you." She placed both her hands over mine. "Come back, Laura. Come back and stay."

I pulled my hands away, unable to look at her, remembering the hateful words Stuart had said. "No. I won't."

She stood and sat back down in the rocking chair.

I looked out at the red dirt of the drive, committing it all to memory. "Take care of Sarah. Don't let her forget her aunt Laura."

"We will never forget you. Or stop hoping that you will return to us."

We continued rocking in silence, until dark descended and the crickets began to cry.

The morning of September 1 dawned gray and misty. The fat clouds hovered in the sky all day, finally breaking out into huge thunderclouds by late afternoon. It had been decided that Zeke would accompany me back to Moon Mountain, so I said my goodbyes to Julia and Sarah at Phoenix Hall near sunset.

"Goodbye, Sarah." I knelt, and she walked into the circle of my arms. I hugged her to me for the last time, transferring to her all my love and hopes for the child I had lost and found, and then given up. "You keep up your piano practicing, okay? And don't fight so much with your brother."

She sniffled into my shoulder. "I will." She pushed herself away. "I have something for you."

She handed me a sprig of rosemary, the silvery gray of the leaves almost glowing in the dim light of the day. "Rosemary—for remembrance. So you will remember me."

I took it from her reverently. "I'll treasure it always—not that I'll need it to remember you." I hugged her again, feeling one more time the solidness of her small body next to mine.

I then hugged Julia, who was dabbing at her eyes with a handkerchief. "What shall I tell Stuart?"

I felt a tremor at my temples. The hurt and anger were still very much alive. "I don't care. Let him always wonder what happened to me."

"I cannot do that, Laura. It would be too cruel. He does love you, you know."

"He couldn't. He so easily believed the worst of me. Just tell him . . . Tell him that I've gone back home."

Her fine eyebrows knit together. "I will try, Laura. But I think he deserves the truth." She gave me another tight hug. "Do not forget your key. I promise to write everything down and leave it in the secret compartment. I will let you know about the peanuts, all right?"

"You do that," I said, my voice cracking. With one last goodbye, I turned away and began the long walk to Moon Mountain with Zeke.

By the time we reached the base of the mountain, the skies had unleashed their fury. Electrical bursts kept the heavens in constant illumination while the thunder rolled ceaselessly. We could see no comet or moon, but I felt the tingling on my skin reminding me of the time before. They were up there, all right, working their magic and pulling at me.

Then, mixed in the roll of thunder, the sound of heavy hoofbeats. I turned my ear toward the sound, imagining I heard my name shouted. A flash of lightning opened up the sky and the heavens, making all around us as bright as day. Standing close to me, I saw Endy and Stuart astride him. Stuart slipped off the horse and came to me without a word.

We stood in the rain, watching the play of light on each other's faces.

I turned from him, but he pulled me back. He had to shout to be heard over the din of the storm. "I was a fool, Laura. William always brings out the worst in me—that is my only excuse."

My skin tingled. I didn't have much time. "Why are you here?"

He moved closer to me. "To ask your forgiveness." His hand tightened on my arm. "I am risking being shot as a deserter. The least you can do is forgive me."

He touched my cheek and I put my hand over his. "I love you, Laura—I will never stop."

I hesitated for a moment, feeling the changing atmosphere around me. There was no more time for anger between us. I fell into his arms, the rain cleansing us in its harshness, Stuart's lips bruising on mine. His hands swept over my back and then to the rising mound of my abdomen. The child kicked, and Stuart jerked back, his eyes wide with amazement. I brought his lips back down to mine, pushing my body into his, the proof of our union guarded between us.

A crash of thunder rolled high above us and Endy screamed, his front hooves pawing the air. Zeke moved to stand before us. "It is time, Laura."

I smelled gardenias again and quickly reached out to Stuart. He grasped for my hand, but his fingers seemed to pass through mine.

Zeke held his hand up, the rain pouring over him and sticking his long hair to his head, like two wet snakes on either side of his face. The rain seemed to part on his face, miraculously circumventing his eyes. He stared straight at me, unblinking. "May the spirits of the ancient Shadow Warriors be with you, Laura, in all your travels."

I opened my lips to speak to Stuart, but the rain flooded my mouth, making me choke. The aura around me became electric, and I could almost see the burnt ions splitting the air in front of me. Bubbles of air burst in my head and I felt myself sink to the rain-soaked earth. Stuart's voice reverberated in my head, but I could no longer tell where it was coming from. "Laura, come back! I love you—please come back!"

I remember shouting Stuart's name, and then nothing more.

I awoke in a hospital. Not the dirty mayhem of a field hospital in the middle of a battlefield, but an antiseptic white world of stainless steel and hushed voices.

I blinked suddenly and tried to sit up in the bed.

"John, she's awake!"

I recognized my mother's voice as I focused my eyes on my parents by the side of the bed.

A nurse hurried toward my bed and checked the readout on a machine by my head, then rushed from the room.

"Laura? Do you know who I am?"

I stared into my mother's familiar face and I reached for it. "Oh, Mom. Of course."

Her tears drenched my cheek as she gathered me to her. She smelled of Colgate and Chanel No. 5, and I clung to her silk blouse. "Laura, what happened to you? Where have you been?"

I had no desire to spend countless hours with therapists questioning my sanity. I blurted out the first thing that came to me. "I don't remember."

My mother leaned over me and whispered, "But you're pregnant, Laura. Surely you remember something?"

I shook my head, and my father, who had been hovering in the background, came to the other side of the bed.

He held my hand, his palm warm and rough. "Laura, it doesn't matter to us. You're here now, and we'll stand by you. We'll be ready to listen when you're ready to tell us."

I nodded, not sure if they'd ever be ready to hear the truth.

"Did I have something in my hand—like a sprig of rosemary?"

My parents glanced at each other, and my mother spoke. "We wondered what that was. We had it put with your personal effects—including an unusual ring we've never seen before. But it must be an antique, because it looks very old."

I said nothing.

I spent the first week at my parents' house being coddled and fed. My mother scheduled an appointment with an obstetrician. He must have been coached beforehand, because he didn't mention anything about the baby's father. He poked and prodded and pronounced me fit, if a bit undernourished. He sent me home with instructions for my mother to put some weight on my bones.

My parents had kept Phoenix Hall, not willing to accept the fact that I might not come back. It still stood, the paint a little worn and dust sheets over the furniture, but still glorious in my eyes. Amid huge protests from my parents, I moved back in to the house that held so many memories for me.

My mother hired a housekeeper, Mrs. Beckner, to cook and clean for me and, I'm sure, report back to her if I wasn't taking care of myself. My father brought in the suitcases of all the maternity clothes they had bought for me and set them inside the foyer. I tentatively walked up the steps and hovered in the doorway.

I took a deep breath and walked inside. I examined the polished banister, the gleaming wood floors, the electrified chandelier. I heard the central air shut off and the hall clock steadily marking off the minutes. The piano stood in its same spot in the parlor, the veneer still missing from the G key. I smiled, remembering how it had happened. I half expected to turn and see Stuart standing behind me, his blue eyes smiling. I slammed my hand down on the keys, making my father jump.

"What's wrong?" He rushed to my side, his hands firmly on my upper arms.

"Nothing, Daddy. Nothing that can be fixed."

He put my head down on his chest and patted my back. "In time, sweetheart. In time."

Mrs. Beckner left at five o'clock, leaving me blissfully alone to enjoy the long shadows creeping along the floor. I resisted turning on the electric lights, finding their glare too bright, as if they might illuminate things in the corners I did not wish to see. So I walked slowly through the darkened house, imagining I could hear the brush of long skirts against the wooden floors, and listened for a footfall.

I woke in the middle of the night with a furious kicking from my womb. I sat up and placed my hand on my swollen belly and felt the roils of limbs pressing at me from inside.

"Mama's here, little one. You're not alone."

My voice seemed to calm the baby, for the kicking ceased. I looked across the moonlit room, gazing at the familiar furniture. It was then that I noticed the strong scent of lavender. I sat straight up in the bed, wondering where the smell was coming from. The windows were all shut, and I could hear the humming of the air conditioner. I slid from the bed to look out onto the front lawn. My throat went dry when I realized there was no moon. The glow was coming from inside my room.

I turned, my back against the window, and heard the distinct sound of rustling skirts. The glow began to shrink and take on the vague form of a person. It undulated with small light bursts until it bore the unmistakable resemblance to a woman wearing an old-fashioned long dress.

"Julia," I said, my voice barely a whisper. The temperature had dropped by at least fifteen degrees and I began to shiver, despite the sweat trickling down my spine.

She stood at the foot of the bed, and I saw her smile. She then turned, and with a glowing hand pointed to the armoire.

I left the window, no longer afraid, and stood next to her.

"What, Julia? What are you trying to tell me?" The smell of lavender was stronger now, as if I were in a field full of it.

She looked directly at me and then pointed at my chest. My fingers flew to my neck, and I realized the chain holding the key was gone. And I suddenly knew what she was trying to tell me.

"The secret drawer?" I whispered.

She nodded. I reached out my hand to touch her, but my fingers only grasped cold, empty air. The apparition faded into nothingness, and I could almost hear a whispered goodbye as the room closed in on darkness.

I flipped on every light switch in the house as I raced downstairs to the foyer table. I remembered my mother putting my few personal effects in the drawer when I had moved back in. With shaking fingers, I pulled it open. Light from the chandelier glinted off the metal key still attached to the chain Stuart had given me. Gingerly, I picked it up, then clasped it tightly in my palm.

As I began to slide the drawer back in place, the corner of a picture frame caught my attention. I lifted the picture from the drawer and stared at it. It was undoubtedly the picture Mathew Brady had taken of me on my journey to Dalton. With trembling hands, I shut the drawer, and, clutching both the picture and the key, raced back up the stairs.

I threw open the doors of the armoire, sneezing at the faint aroma of cedar mixed with lavender. I knelt in front of the massive piece of furniture and my fingers, like spiders, crept along the inside wall to the back, where I felt the outline of a drawer in the false back.

The overhead light barely reached to the back of the cabinet, and I had to use my sense of touch to open the lock with the key. I grew frustrated feeling the key slip at the outside of the keyhole. I was about ready to give up and wait until morning when I felt the key slide home. I turned it and heard a click. Pulling on the key, I heard wood slide out. I grabbed the entire drawer and lifted it out into the light.

Old papers, their edges yellowed and ragged with age, had been placed inside the narrow drawer. They had all been rolled together to allow them to fit inside the tight compartment. I spread them on the bed, using various items from my dressing table to hold the pages flat.

Many of the documents appeared to have been removed from ledger books. My eyes widened as I stared at the numbers reflecting dividends from the Coca-Cola Company. The handwriting wasn't Julia's. Instead of her small, flowery style, this was much tighter and bold. I didn't believe I had seen it before. I smiled to myself, realizing Julia had heeded my advice and had indeed invested in Asa Candler's fledgling company.

There were more documents pertaining to peach orchards and peanut production and even a recipe for peanut butter. I sat back for a moment to rub my eyes. Julia had obviously prepared this drawer with meticulous care to let me know what had become of them all. It struck me then that they were all dead now—even my Annie. I hastily wiped back the tears, not wanting the wetness to smudge the ink on the pages. The baby kicked again, and I was once more reminded of the endless cycle of life and death. It was through this child that these people I

loved could live again. I picked up another page, unrolled it, and began
to read.

August 21, 1867

My dearest sister,

*It has been three years now since we have last seen you, and a day
does not go by that we do not think of you or wish that you were
here.*

*You would be so proud of the children. Willie and Sarah
continue to grow strong and sturdy—due mostly, I am quite sure,
to their great fondness for peanut butter. Sarah promises to be a
great beauty, although most of the boys here are a bit humbled by
her brains and wit.*

*As you can see by the enclosed papers, we are surviving, thanks
to you. It is still a bit of a struggle, because nobody has anything,
much less any capital to invest in a new farming venture. Matt
Kimball's gold has helped considerably. But we are managing, and
the future of our new ventures seems most promising.*

*We have not heard from William. I assume he is either dead or
in the western territories. Either way, I have no husband and my
children have no father. But I am not sure if it isn't for the best.*

*Stuart returned home from the war thin but otherwise healthy
in body—but not in spirit. It is heartbreaking to see him, Laura.
On the night you disappeared, we told him the truth. I know you
didn't want that, but I don't think we had any choice. He wanted
to know if you planned to return, and when we told him no, he
has not asked about you since. But I know you are never far from
his thoughts. His eyes are so sad. Fighting in this war nearly killed
him, and I almost think he wishes it had. He moves about his
daily business, but his heart isn't in it. He loves you desperately,
Laura, and if he could see you but once again, I know that the
wonderful spirit of him would return.*

*Laura, I also told him about the armoire, and he asked if I
might include a letter from him. It is contained herewith. I have*

338 · *Karen White*

*not read it, as I am sure the private matters between husband and
wife should remain private. I hope it somehow heals your heart.*

*I cannot bear to think that we may never lay eyes on you
again. You will forever remain in our hearts. May God go with
you, Laura, wherever you may be.*

*With great affection,
Your sister, Julia*

A tear dripped on the bottom right corner, and I hastily brushed it
aside with the sleeve of my nightgown. I turned back to the drawer to
find Stuart's letter. After sorting through several pages, I saw the familiar handwriting, and my heart leapt. I unrolled it carefully and anchored the corners.

April 28, 1867

Dearest Wife,

*How much longer am I expected to live through this torture of not
knowing where you are? Julia has told me why you had to leave,
but I know that I am solely to blame for your reluctance to return.
I begged for your forgiveness on the night you left, and I am
begging for it now.*

*I have no idea how the mechanism of the thing that took you
away works, but because you have not returned to us, I can only
assume that you have no desire to see me again—and for this I
cannot blame you. You think that I have believed the worst of you,
but I have always known in my heart that you would never betray
me. It was only my stupid male pride. And for that, I have lost the
most precious thing in the world.*

*How is our child? I do not even know if I have a son or a
daughter. If it is a daughter, I hope she is like you—full of fire and
spirit. And if it is a son, I hope he will grow strong and proud and
be there to watch over his mother since his father cannot.*

Come home to me, Laura. I will wait for you until the end of time and even beyond, for my love for you is deathless.

> *With all my love,*
> *Stuart*

I lay down on the bed and stared up at the ceiling fan and its ceaseless rotation. The tears rolled down from the corners of my eyes to my ears and hair, saturating the sheets beneath my head. I could never forgive myself if he had gone to his grave believing I had stopped loving him.

I rolled up all the documents and put them back in the drawer. Except for Stuart's letter. I held it close to my chest and fell asleep clutching it between my arms and our baby.

When I finally awoke the next morning, Mrs. Beckner was knocking on my door with a steaming tray of eggs, bacon, and homemade biscuits. She poked her gray head through the doorway, her pale blue eyes expressing concern as I saw her register my puffy eyes and dark circles.

"Bad night, was it?" She clucked her tongue like a mother hen. "I remember being pregnant with my last child."

She continued chattering as she bustled about the room, opening curtains and placing my tray in front of me. As I smoothed the blanket down on either side of me, my hand touched something hard and cold. It was the picture frame. I stared at the image for a minute and then reached for my iPhone to look up a name and phone number.

She was the only Margaret Ann Cudahy listed. Her address was on West Paces Ferry Road in a posh condo building in Buckhead.

I introduced myself as Laura Truitt, and she recognized my name immediately. She didn't seem in the least surprised that I had called.

"Mrs. Cudahy, I hope you don't take these questions as too personal, but I've been trying to do a bit of history on this house and was hoping you might be able to help me."

"I'd love to help you, dear. Ask away." I heard the sound of opera music playing from a stereo in the background.

"All right. Are you by any chance related to the Elliott family?"

She chuckled into the mouthpiece. "My maiden name was Elliott. Until you, Elliotts have owned Phoenix Hall since it was built."

My hand shook a little as I held the phone. "And your great-grandmother, the one that gave you the picture of the woman that looked like me, what was her name?"

"Oh, these are too easy, Laura. You should find her name very simple to remember since you have the same first name. Her name was Laura Elliott."

I had to clutch the phone with both hands, I was shaking so hard. "I see," I whispered. "And do you happen to remember your great-grandfather's name?"

"I certainly do. It was Stuart. Stuart Elliott. But I don't remember what his middle name was."

"Couper," I choked into the phone.

"Yes, dear, I do believe that was it. As a matter of fact, were you aware that Stuart and Laura's son is a direct ancestor of our last president?"

"No. I wasn't." I was finding it very difficult to talk. "Mrs. Cudahy, thank you so much for your information. But I'm not feeling well at the moment and I think I'll need to call you back later."

I dropped the phone on the floor and lay on my bed for what seemed like hours, listening to the ceiling fan whir and the incessant beeping of the phone off the hook. The elephant that had been sitting in the middle of my room since the day I returned finally stared me in the eye. This was my house, but it wasn't my home. My home was with my husband and the people who loved me. This realization strangled my mind, bringing with it as much anticipation as it did apprehension. My travels through time were not yet over.

EPILOGUE

---◆---

Journeys end in lovers meeting.
—WILLIAM SHAKESPEARE

My son, Couper, was born on a cold January morning. He came into the world kicking and screaming, convincing me that he was ready for whatever life would bring him. I knew without looking that he would carry the identical birthmark on his forearm—like his mother and sister. The doctor asked me if I wanted it removed. I shook my head fiercely and told the doctor it was part of my son's heritage and that he would keep it for life.

I spent most of his first two years preparing. I diligently took Couper to the pediatrician for his checkups and vaccinations, and spent a good portion of my afternoons in the library in the astronomy section, charting the different comets in their orbital time periods until I found the right one.

I prepared my parents as best I could, telling them that my son and I would be going on a long trip and not to worry about us. They were instructed to keep Phoenix Hall in good shape, always in readiness for our immediate return. Just in case.

By the autumn of his third year, I was ready. I left Sarah's sprig of dried rosemary on the dressing table in my room for my mother. I carried with me two bottles of Children's Tylenol and a recent edition of the *Atlanta Journal-Constitution*. But that was all. Everything else I needed was there, waiting for me on the other side of time.

We found Stuart outside the barn, brushing Endy's gleaming dark coat. We stood in the shadow of an old oak tree, our feet crunching on fallen acorns. The horse whinnied in greeting, and I put my finger to my lips. The sound of children's laughter and a dog barking carried to us on the crisp air, and I closed my eyes for a moment, feeling the tug of the wind on my hair and smelling a wood fire burning in the distance. I shivered with cold, the air seeping through my cotton sweater and jeans.

Stuart didn't look up but bent over the horse's legs, examining the shoes. A brisk wind struck us, making Stuart's hair dance and scattering leaves about our feet. I stared at the mass of dark hair, realizing how much like Couper's it was.

Couper slid down off my back and stood beside me. He looked up at me with piercing blue eyes and I nodded. Slowly, he walked toward Stuart and stood directly behind him. My heart skipped a beat as I saw them next to each other for the first time, father and son.

Stuart picked up a bucket of water and began emptying it into the grass.

"Excuse me." Couper's little face looked up at Stuart as Stuart swung around, splashing his boots and pants with the water.

I stepped back behind the tree, leaning out only enough to see.

Not expecting to find anybody behind him, Stuart nearly tripped over the little boy. He caught himself and looked at the child, his brows knitted tightly together. "Who are you?"

"I'm Couper." He peered out from around Stuart's legs. "Is that your horsie?"

Stuart's eyebrows lifted. "Couper?"

"Yeah. Can I pet your horsie?"

Stuart kneeled in front of the child, a hand on each shoulder. "Couper, who are you?"

He wouldn't take his eyes off the big black horse. "I told you. I'm Couper. Now can I pet your horsie?"

Stuart lifted him up in his arms and approached Endy. "Be very gentle. You can pat him right here," he said, and indicated the neck with the mane blowing in the breeze.

Stuart moved his head back to get a better view of Couper's face. "Where are your mother and father?"

Couper's pudgy fingers were busily entwining themselves in the thick horse's mane. He tilted his head as if he didn't quite understand the question. "I don't know about my daddy, but my mommy's over there." He stuck out a sturdy arm in the direction of the oak tree.

I stepped out from my hiding place as Stuart turned, his son in his arms. I saw the color drain from his face, and then he started to shake.

I rushed forward to take Couper, afraid Stuart might drop him. Stuart moved away, shaking his head, clutching the child tightly.

"Laura." His voice was barely more than a whisper.

"Hello, Stuart. It's been a while." My voice was barely stronger than his.

His eyes widened, but I saw a ghost of a smile around his pale lips. "Yes, you could certainly say that." He looked at Couper and his expression changed suddenly. It was as if he were looking in a mirror for the first time. "Are you this handsome young man's mother?"

I gave a small laugh. "Yes. I'd like you to meet your son, Stuart Couper Elliott the Second."

Stuart glanced from me to Couper and back. His face was still handsome, but there were deep creases in his cheeks that hadn't been there before. "I can't believe this."

I walked closer to him, my eyes searching his. "Believe it. We're here to stay."

He opened his arms to me and I walked into his embrace, smelling the autumn air in his clothes and feeling the beloved scratchiness of his cheek.

Couper squealed, his active three-year-old body rebelling at being hugged so tightly. "Hey, stop! You're mushing me!"

Stuart squeezed us even harder as I felt his tears on my head.

The wind picked up momentum, whipping my hair around my husband and my son and sending the fallen leaves airborne once again in the direction of the beautiful white house. It stood, strong and silent, still beckoning me. The sun made shadows of the front columns on the lawn, like arms welcoming me back.

I had come home.

Whispers of Goodbye

CHAPTER ONE

———◆———

Grief cannot be apportioned as if measuring flour for a cake. But when Jamie died, my husband claimed the lion's share of it, leaving me with only a handful to mull over and sift through my fingers. I was not entitled, he insisted, because I had killed our beloved son.

What was left of my husband after the war was quickly destroyed by Jamie's death, and I watched the destruction with pitied frustration until his final act of obliteration and revenge. I found him in his gray uniform, his sword still in its scabbard, his revolver lying next to him on the pillow in the bedroom. The blood seeped crimson into the white sheets of the bed, hiding their purity in a gruesome display. I gathered the sands of my grief and held them close to me, tucking them inside, where I would never allow anyone in to see.

My anger and the gnawing of hunger pulled me from my bed each morning. My fields, where the finest-quality Sea Island cotton had once grown, now lay as barren and trampled as my soul. The old house, the house in which I had lived first with my parents and then with my husband and son, lay in heaps of ashes. The odd fragment of brick or china shone like bone in the scorched earth, the only remains of my once-happy life.

There were fewer friends and neighbors huddled around Robert's casket at Christ Church Cemetery than had been at Jamie's memorial service. I supposed that many, facing the same devastation as I, had left our beloved island of Saint Simons to seek refuge inland. Even as the pastor's words droned on to their inevitable conclusion, I knew I could not leave. My anger was as fresh as the newly turned dirt, and my leaving would be like forgiveness—and anger was something with which I was not yet ready to part. But the hunger pains gnawed on.

I thought often of joining Jamie in the surf off our island, of feeling the shifting sand beneath my bare feet as I walked slowly into the dark depths of the ocean. But, perhaps akin to the stubbornness of my fellow countrymen who would not recognize defeat, I held firm to life. I would stare out over the ocean, the salty air stinging my cheeks, and refuse to look behind me. Whatever lay ahead did not frighten me. I had nothing left to fear.

I had sought shelter in the overseer's cottage. Mr. Rafferty had abandoned it in the first year of the war, leaving in the middle of the night. The Yankees who had encamped on Saint Simons had left it intact, finding the simple furnishings not valuable enough to steal. But to me, it was a roof over my head and a place to lie down at the end of each day.

Two weeks after Robert's funeral, while scrounging around the overgrown vegetable garden for a forgotten or only half-rotten potato or onion, I heard the sound of approaching hoofbeats pounding down the road.

Will Benton took off his sweat-soaked hat when he saw me, then gingerly slid from the saddle, his wooden leg not seeming to hamper him overly much. His gaze flickered over me, and I was surprised to see sadness instead of the pity I was used to. Perhaps he, too, was remembering the old days, when we were not too much younger, days when we danced in the ballroom of the old house; he with two legs, and I in a satin gown with ribbons in my hair.

I wiped my cheek with the back of my hand, realizing too late that dirt had crusted on my knuckles. "Hello, Will. This is a pleasant surprise."

A ghost of a smile haunted his face, an apparition of the boisterous smiles of his carefree youth. The youth he'd had before the war had come and robbed us all. "Hello, Cat. That is nice of you to say."

Will looked behind me at the crude structure of the tabby cottage and then back at me, his eyes focusing on the faded black cotton of my dress. "I brought you a letter. I did not know the next time you would come to our side of the island, and I thought it might be important. It is from Louisiana."

My heart constricted slightly. I had not heard from my elder sister, Elizabeth, during the long four years of the war. Three months after the firing at Fort Sumter, she had been bundled and packed away to her husband's home state of Massachusetts, leaving behind the beautiful home on the Mississippi that had been left to her and her new husband by our grandmother. I had not even sent news of Jamie and Robert, not knowing if my words would ever reach her.

I tried not to look at my dirty hands as I opened the envelope, too starved for news of my sister to worry about my bad manners in making Will wait.

My dearest Cat,

My situation here is intolerable, and I have no one with whom I can share my thoughts and feelings. There is something evil here that I do not understand, something heavy in the air.

Oh, Cat, you have always been my constant, the one who helped steer me from trouble. It is hard to imagine sometimes that I am the eldest! I am afraid I may have made quite a mess out of things, and I need your guidance.

Please, if it is at all possible, do come to me. You can have your old room, and I will grant you as many favors as you request if you will just come. If your Robert is back from the war, I would welcome his presence, too. He has always given a feeling of strength and security, as have you, and I need that now, more than you can know.

I have taken the liberty of sending a coach and funds for your journey. It should arrive within a week or so of this letter. I know how you hate to leave your precious island, but I have nowhere else to turn.

I need you, dear sister. I am so afraid.

Affectionately,
Elizabeth deClaire McMahon

My gaze met the concern in Will's. "Everything all right, Cat? You look like you have been spooked by a ghost."

I shook my head. "Yes, I am fine. It is from Elizabeth. She wants me to come for a visit."

Will's face was grim. "About time, if you ask me. No offense to your sister, but it is just not right for you to be living out here alone like this. Not right at all." He turned toward his horse, then vigorously closed up the mailbag. "I am sure that Yankee husband of hers has been holding her back from asking you to visit."

I did not know much about John McMahon other than that he was the second son of a wealthy Boston merchant. On a business trip to Saint Simons, he had taken one look at my sister and decided that he had to have her, along with the bales of cotton he was purchasing from our father.

Elizabeth had been transfixed by the dark brooding eyes and the tall stature of the Northern stranger. I had caught those eyes watching me several times, an unreadable emotion lingering in their dark depths, but he always turned away whenever I would acknowledge him. I believe I hated him on sight with all the fierceness a fourteen-year-old girl could muster. It was not for anything he had ever done to me directly, but for the simple reason that he had decided that he needed my sister more than I did. It did not matter that his inscrutable face softened and his cold ebony eyes warmed when he gazed upon her. She was as much a part of me as the island, yet John McMahon separated us for the first time in our young lives when he married Elizabeth and took her to Louisiana.

Too hungry and tired to disagree with Will, I said goodbye and watched him ride off in the late-afternoon sun. Buttery light pierced the trees and the veils of Spanish moss, and I sighed heavily. How could I ever leave this place? I stilled for a moment, straining to hear the quiet murmur of the ocean. I began walking toward it, needing to feel its tranquillity and contemplate whether my sister's letter would be my salvation or my ruin.

Puffs of dirt sailed out from under the wheels of the coach like little whispers of goodbye. I stared down at my hands, not wanting to watch my life pass by outside the window. My mother had once told me that if you stared after somebody until they disappeared, you would never see them again. I refused to think of this parting as permanent, and so I kept my gaze fastened on the worn black leather gloves.

My sister's words traveled with me each day of the long, arduous journey. I knew in my bones that something was dreadfully wrong, and I had to reach Elizabeth as soon as possible. The driver, a Mr. O'Rourke, deferred to my comfort, frequently asking whether I needed to stop. But I urged him on, conceding to stop and rest only when the horses were near exhaustion. My aching bones and muscles protested each mile, but my sense of urgency pressed us on. If I were not worried about the driver needing his sleep, I would have demanded that we drive day and night, not stopping until we reached the welcoming arms of my sister.

My mother would have been scandalized by my lack of a chaperone, but my circumstances had changed. I simply did not have the resources left to worry about social niceties. Patrick O'Rourke, a ruddy Bostonian, was courteous and protective, and I felt quite safe in his presence.

As we drove farther and farther inland, the heat and humidity pressed in on us, and I found myself missing the cool breezes of the ocean. The prick of tears began behind my eyelids, but I willed them away by pulling at my anger like an old wound, making it swell again inside me.

Twilight fell on us as we neared the outskirts of New Orleans and the final leg of our long journey. A spattering of rain slapped the roof of the coach, as if small hands urging us on. The coachman pulled up on the reins and stopped on the road near a muddy swamp visible in the dim light. He climbed down from his seat and opened the door of the coach to speak with me. Something screeched high in a tree.

"The road is very wet, and I do not want to risk going farther in the darkness. If it has been raining for a while, the river could have overflowed its banks and washed out the road. We would do best to find a place in town to stay and start off again tomorrow morning."

I sat on the edge of my seat, listening to the croaking tree frogs and creatures of the night. I sniffed deeply but raised my hand to my nose when I smelled the murky miasma of the muddy river instead of the salty air of home. It had seemed so familiar for a brief, heartbreaking moment.

The rain fell harder as something screeched again, beseeching, pleading, crying. My skin tingled with the sound of it, hearing in it a spoken plea for help. *I need you, dear sister. I am so afraid.* It was as if Elizabeth spoke to me through the wild animal, begging me to continue on.

Facing Mr. O'Rourke, I said, "No, we must go on. I am afraid this is a matter of the utmost urgency."

His face, mottled with dark shadows and yellow light from the coach's lanterns, looked down at me. "No, madam. We are turning back."

I grabbed at his sleeve and leaned toward him, not caring about the rain soaking my traveling gown and cloak. "No. It is urgent I see my sister—tonight. And if you will not take me, then I shall rent a hack and complete the journey on my own."

He stepped back as if to gauge my seriousness. I grabbed my carpetbag from the seat across from me and stepped out of the carriage, nearly tripping on my skirts.

"Please be so kind as to tell me the way to the city."

The rain pelted on my bonnet and dripped onto my face, but I stood resolute.

The man shook his head. "Mr. McMahon will have my skin if I let you do such a thing. Please, madam, it is for your own good. Please get back into the coach."

I jerked my arm away from him, the night sounds pressing close, the pulsing beat a rhythm of urgency. "I will only get back in if you promise to take me to Whispering Oaks. Otherwise I am walking."

He turned around to face the darkness that eluded the small circle of lantern light. A guttural growl echoed in the distant swamp, pressing an unseen finger of fear at the base of my skull. *I need you, dear sister. I am so afraid.* I made a move toward a lantern to remove it from its hitch.

Mr. O'Rourke stared at me, then pressed his lips together. "Fine, then. But do not say I did not warn you if we get stuck on the road."

"Thank you, Mr. O'Rourke." Without waiting for his assistance, I stepped back into the carriage, afraid he would see the abject relief on my face.

The rain continued its steady pace, making the carriage sway to and fro more violently than before as the mud greedily sucked at the wheels.

I closed my eyes in a futile attempt at rest and to still the chattering of my teeth. The humidity weighed on my person like a log, but my body shivered uncontrollably. From what, I could not say.

It happened before I had time to realize I was in danger. Mr. O'Rourke shouted, but before the sound had even reached my ears, a sickening *thud* came from the front left of the coach, followed quickly by the splintering of wood. The coach lurched to the side as the lantern light disappeared, sending me in a spiral through total darkness. I hit my head, disorienting myself momentarily, and then realized I was lying on the roof of the carriage, my skirts and feet under about a foot of water.

I shouted for Mr. O'Rourke, but only the incessant patter of rain and the interminable night sounds of the river answered me. Something splashed in the water outside the half-submerged carriage, and I called for Mr. O'Rourke again. This time, I heard his voice very faintly. I struggled to the side of the coach and fumbled with the upside-down door handle. It turned, but the door could not be opened.

"Help me! I cannot swim!" Mr. O'Rourke's voice sounded stronger.

My blood stilled. It was as if I were hearing my Jamie's voice again, crying for help from the water. I remembered jumping in to save him, feeling the pull of the water on my skirts, my arms cutting through the waves, strong and sure. But I could not save my son. And now the water taunted me, daring me to try again and surely fail.

The two horses whinnied, stamping their feet in the water and trying to pull away from the waterlogged coach. Something was out there. Something they did not like. I willed myself to move. I had to get to Mr. O'Rourke. With trembling fingers I removed my cloak and hat, then tore at my skirts.

Relieved of my cumbersome clothes and wearing only my underpinnings, I slipped easily through the window and found myself in water up to my knees. Tall grass reached up to my shoulders, brushing against me with deceptive sweetness. A faint light shone above me, and I looked up what appeared to be an embankment. The light seemed to be coming from one of the coach's lanterns that had fallen during our plunge downward.

The plaintive cry of the driver came again. "Help me!"

I struggled through the tall grass, the blades tearing at my skin, then up the embankment. I used my hands to claw my way to the top, the dirt caking under my nails. "Mr. O'Rourke, where are you?"

The rain had slackened, and I listened closely for his voice. Something moved behind me, and a large splash broke the silence. I ran for the lantern and held it high over my head. The light picked up something white in the darkness, and I realized it was a leg waving from a scrubby tree high on the other side of the flooded road.

I clamped down on my teeth to cease their chattering, then spoke. "I will come get you—do not move." My confident voice almost deceived me.

The earth reverberated with a muffled thudding coming up from the ground, racing up my legs, and matching the pounding of my heart. I strained my eyes in the darkness, my mind tricking me into seeing would-be rescuers.

Rushing water and swishing reeds sounded from below the embankment to where the carriage lay upside down. The horses screamed, stamping up and down in the water. Thundering hoofbeats bore down on me as something slithered outside the realm of my lantern. A movement skittered past me and I startled, dropping the lantern, the light disappearing as suddenly as if a hand had closed on the flame. The water tugged at me, pulling at me, rendering me useless, just as it had once before. The water had beaten me yet again and I could not save Mr. O'Rourke.

The rain lessened as heavy clouds shifted above, uncovering a three-quarter moon and lending the tall reeds and scrubby oaks a blue cast. Bobbing lights attached to the thundering hooves grew larger, and I forced my legs to move, my feet slipping in the mud and mire as I ran toward the sound and lights.

"Elizabeth!" a man's deep voice called out as the large form of a horse and rider took shape.

I reached toward him and felt strong hands grab me under the arms and lift me onto the saddle in front of my rescuer. The horse snorted and reared as other men on horseback arrived. A gunshot and then another rent the air. I struggled against the hard chest that seemed intent on smothering me.

"We must get the coachman—he is in a tree. He cannot swim." I pointed to where the white of Mr. O'Rourke's shirt shone in the darkness.

The man stiffened, then pulled me against his chest again and began barking orders. More shots were fired up in the air as a horseman rode across the submerged road to rescue Mr. O'Rourke.

His voice was hard and deep, as if used to delivering orders. The men followed his directive without question. My face was pressed against a smooth linen shirt, the smell of starch mingling with cigar smoke, leather, and the smell of a man—a smell I had once enjoyed and now pulled away from like a skittish horse. But muscled arms held me fast, and I sat rigid, trying to limit the contact between our bodies. He twisted in his saddle and I found myself enveloped in a large wool cloak.

Another horseman pulled alongside. "It does not seem to be robbery. The coachman is our Mr. O'Rourke. Is the woman Elizabeth?"

My rescuer grunted. "No." His fingers worked their way around my jawbone and tilted my face to his. He raised a lantern and his breath hissed as he sucked it in, his face wearing the shock of a man who had seen a ghost. "Who are you?"

I recognized him then, the coal black eyes glittering in the lamplight. John McMahon, my brother-in-law. A small tremor passed through me. "I am Catherine, Elizabeth's sister. Where is she?" Running water moved under us, the small rippling teasing my ears as I waited for his answer.

He lowered the light, casting his face in shadow. "She is gone."

I gathered the cloak under my chin. "What do you mean, gone?"

His warm breath brushed my cheek, making me shiver, and I felt those dark eyes on me again. "She has disappeared, with no indications as to where she might be. No one has seen her for four days. She is simply . . . gone."

He reined in his horse and turned it around. Holding me tightly against him, he urged on his mount, the thundering hoofbeats resonating like a distant nightmare.

Chapter Two

———— ◆ ————

Either the chill of the humid night or the slowing of the horse woke me from a brief doze. The rain had stopped, leaving a pungent scent of wet mud and grass in the air. I jerked awake with a start, aware of the hushed feel to the air. My grandmother's house loomed ahead like a brilliant ghost through the alley of live oaks. The eight Doric columns along the front of the structure gleamed in the moonlight. Long fingers of Spanish moss reached down toward us, the storm-born breeze causing them to undulate like a hand beckoning us onward.

The darkness came alive as we neared the house, torches on poles illuminating the night and making it as bright as day. Despite the late hour, small groups of men approached on horseback, and small campfires brought the smells of coffee and food to us.

"Are they searching for Elizabeth?"

My brother-in-law said nothing, but continued to move toward the house, coming to a halt at the foot of the wide steps. A young boy appeared and took the reins of the horse as my captor slid to the ground with me in his arms. As if I were a baby, he effortlessly carried me up the stairs and through the wide set of mahogany double doors and into the foyer I had not seen since I had been a young girl in plaits.

But I was no longer a helpless girl. Life had certainly stamped her out of existence, and I refused to be treated as one. I struggled against him. "Please put me down. I am more than capable of walking."

Without a word, he approached the wide, elegant staircase and proceeded to carry me up the stairs two at a time. With a booted foot, he pushed open a door at the top of the stairs and unceremoniously dumped me in the middle of the bed. I recognized this room—along with the tall four-poster with red velvet hangings—as the one I had stayed in as a child.

I scrambled off the side of the bed. "How dare you, sir! I am not a child. And I demand to know what has happened to my sister."

He stood in the doorway, the breadth of his shoulders nearly filling the space. "I will send Marguerite for you."

With that, he closed the door neatly behind him.

I flew to the door, flung it open, and stifled a scream.

A woman, perhaps twenty years my senior, stood close enough that I could smell the cooking smoke in her hair. Pale green eyes stared out of a face of light brown skin. Hair the color and texture of dried moss was pulled off her face and wrapped in a scarf, showing a cluster of gray at the temples. Her eyes widened in surprise when she saw me, as if she recognized me.

I did not know this woman, nor did I expect to. In letters from my sister, she had explained that her husband had freed our grandmother's slaves and brought in hired Irish help from Boston, and a few local, freed slaves to work the sugar plantation.

"I am Marguerite," she said. "Mr. McMahon has asked that I see to you."

Her voice, low and soothing, surprised me. It was not the voice of a servant, but rather that of an educated white woman.

I tried to see past her, but she gently led me back into the room and closed the door. "We need to get you cleaned up and fed. After a good rest, Mr. McMahon will see you."

For the first time I became aware of the heaviness of John McMahon's cloak around my shoulders. Looking down, I saw with dismay the muddy condition it was in and the unmistakable white of my undergarments showing beneath.

Reluctantly, I allowed Marguerite to help me bathe. She brought in a white cotton nightgown for me to wear, and I caught the familiar scent of lavender on the robe as I put it on. It was my sister's scent, and I felt a stab of panic and worry course through me. *Where is Elizabeth?*

A steaming tray of food was brought to me, and I ate from hunger. I should have refused it on principle. My brother-in-law had been a major in the Federal Army, his rank no doubt protecting his land and property from the marauding armies of the North. But I had survived far worse than starvation thus far, and I was not about to succumb to something as unworldly and impractical as principle. I speared a steaming forkful of ham and stuck it in my mouth.

Marguerite reappeared as soon as I was finished and whisked the tray away with a promise that Mr. McMahon would be in to see me as soon as he could. I crawled under the sheets and lay against the white linen pillowcases, a luxury I had not indulged in within recent memory. I closed my eyes to rest and soon sank into peaceful oblivion.

When I awoke, I blinked in confusion. The candle by the bed was barely more than a wick, the sputtering flame wreaking havoc on the walls in the forms of shadowed beasts. I sat up suddenly, aware that I was not alone.

John McMahon sat in the wooden rocker by the fire, his coat gone and his white shirt lying opened at his neck. His black hair, just brushing his collar, was swept off his forehead, as if by agitated hands. Long legs encased in knee-length black boots were braced on the floor, and in his hand he held a glass of spirits. He stared at me with something akin to revulsion. An unseen energy seemed to hum around him, crossing the room to where I lay. My skin tightened, and I pulled the covers up to my neck.

"This is not acceptable, sir, for you to be in my bedchamber. Please leave. I will speak to you in the library after I have properly dressed."

"Why are you here?" He acted as if he had not heard me speak, his eyes never leaving my face.

"My sister sent for me." I almost mentioned to him about her fear and the sense of urgency I had felt, but I did not. Something about his demeanor alarmed me, and if there had been something for Elizabeth to fear, I had the suspicion that it very well could have been the man sitting across from me. "Did she not mention it to you?"

He took a long sip from his glass, his eyes glittering in the faint light under stark brows. "No. She did not. That is why when I saw you I thought . . ." He lowered his gaze to stare into his glass, his brow furrowed. He turned to stare into the flickering flame. "Do you realize how much you resemble Elizabeth?"

Despite our four-year difference in age, people who did not know us well would mistake us for twins when we were children. But as we grew, our faces and demeanors seemed to evolve into that of two quite distinct people: Elizabeth, the otherworldy beauty excited by new dresses and parties, and me, the reserved sister, the one satisfied to sit on a beach for hours, her bare feet stuck contentedly under warm sand. As we had reached womanhood, people no longer considered us to be quite so similar.

"Not anymore," I said. "I have not seen Elizabeth in nearly seven years. Perhaps we have grown alike again."

He tilted his head back against the rocker, staring at the undulating images on the ceiling. "You could be one and the same." He took another sip and in the still room I heard him swallow.

"Do you have any idea where she could have gone? Did she leave a note?"

He stood abruptly, the chair rocking in his wake. "No. We have searched the area and questioned our neighbors. Nobody has seen her." He strode to the door. "As for a note, there were none. At least none for me."

He opened the door, but I held him back with a question.

"How did you know I was not Elizabeth when you found me on the road in the dark?"

He contemplated me for a moment, then took another swallow of spirits. "Because you showed kindness and concern for Mr. O'Rourke's welfare." He paused. "My wife would have shown neither."

As he closed the door, the draft extinguished the small flame on my candle, throwing me into complete darkness. I lay back on the pillows, listening to his footsteps disappearing down the stairs and wondering at his words.

Brittle morning sunshine crept through the windows when I next opened my eyes. The sound of jangling horse harnesses and the low murmur of male voices brought me out of bed and to the window.

I looked out at the expanse of front lawn leading toward the alley of oaks and saw several men and horses milling about, tin cups grasped in hands. John McMahon stood in the middle of one group, and my gaze was irrepressibly drawn to him. He struck an imposing figure even from a distance. He stood a good head taller than the next man, his form solid and lean but pulled taut like well-honed leather. As if sensing an unseen audience, he stopped speaking and twisted around, looking directly at my window. A current moved through me like a flash of light, filching the wetness from my mouth. I stepped back, aware that I was not only staring, but also wearing only a thin nightgown. I held tightly to the curtain panel, willing it not to swing and hoping I had not been spotted.

A dress had been laid out for me, and the pitcher filled with clean water. The dress was a soft blue silk, and I felt a guilty spark of pleasure at wearing something other than black cotton. I wondered whether this meant they had not been able to recover my bag from the submerged coach. I could not deny that I would not miss any of its contents overly much.

I picked up the gown, wondering if any scent of my sister might still linger. It was faint but still there, and I closed my eyes, remembering the times of our childhood we had spent in this house. It had been one of the first plantation houses built on the River Road. Despite the threat of the ever-encroaching Mississippi River, it had remained intact since its original construction in 1800.

Our mother had been born here, as had our grandmother. But deaths outweighed the births at Whispering Oaks, and I always wondered what we had done to be so cursed. Yellow fever had taken my mother's five brothers and then returned for another visit two years later, taking my grandfather when it left. The names on the mausoleum in the small cemetery in the woods behind the house were all that remained of my aunts and uncles. When we were children, Elizabeth told me stories of how the dead would rise from the crypt and come into the house to watch the living. I would lie awake, far into the night, never doubting the veracity of her story.

Grandmother Delacroix had faced the withering sun of her grief, the petals of her strength refusing to shrivel and die. My mother said that I reminded her a lot of her mother, but I had my doubts. Grandmother's heart had remained soft and loving, a constant in my and Elizabeth's lives until the day she died. But my own grief had turned my heart into a cold, hard orb in the center of my chest, and I doubted I would ever find the warmth to nourish it back to health.

I laid the dress back on the bed and went to the washstand to clean my face. As I poured the water into the basin, a peculiar sound reached my ears. I held the pitcher tightly, listening closely. It sounded as if a small child were humming a tune—a tune that was hauntingly familiar to me. I knew it yet I did not. Perhaps it was a song from my distant past, long since forgotten.

I walked to the door and opened it a crack. There it was again—that humming. It was definitely a child and it was coming from the L-shaped corridor to my right. I stepped out into the hallway, my bare feet padding gently against the wood floors, and followed the sound. The low murmur of a female voice accompanied the humming, and I followed the sound until I stopped at a closed door at the end of the corridor.

Curious, I pressed my ear against the door and listened. The humming became more frantic now, faster and higher-pitched. I recognized Marguerite's voice, soft and soothing, as if attempting to comfort a child. A sudden crash came from inside the room, and the humming turned into a loud and piercing scream. I jumped back and found myself pressed against a warm, firm body.

I jerked around and stared into the unreadable eyes of John Mc-Mahon.

His voice was gruff. "What are you doing here?"

"I . . . I heard a sound. I wanted to see what it was."

He released his hold on me. "This was Elizabeth's room. There is nothing in there that might interest you." I noticed his use of the past tense, and I took a step backward.

Straightening my shoulders, I attempted to still the shaking in my voice. "But perhaps there is. I am Elizabeth's sister, and I ask that you allow me to help find her. There might be letters or a journal or something that might give us a clue as to where she might be." I turned toward the door, my hand on the knob. "And there is somebody in there with Marguerite, and it sounds like a child."

His hand closed over mine, and again I felt the current ripple from my fingertips and surge through my blood. "Please let go of me." My voice shook.

His gaze flickered over me and I was made aware once again of my undressed state.

"Go get dressed. I will send Marguerite to help you. Breakfast is waiting for you in the dining room." His eyes were hard, making it clear that opposition to his wishes was not recommended.

Slowly, his hand slid away and I dropped mine from the doorknob. Being in a somewhat precarious situation, I decided not to press the matter. Not yet. I began to walk away, but turned back when I heard the door open without a knock. Inside I spied Marguerite on her knees, picking up small porcelain fragments, and a blond, wide-eyed child staring up at the man in the threshold. The door quickly shut, blocking the scene from my view.

I sat alone at the foot of the long dining-room table, mounds of food heaping the polished surface. A young woman with red hair and freckles and a thick Irish accent introduced herself as Mary. She stood at attention by my chair and waited until I was seated before beginning to pile food on my plate.

I wanted to turn away in disgust at the wasteful abundance, remembering my recent months on Saint Simons, relying on the charity of friends and neighbors and whatever I could find in the abandoned gardens. Every waking thought had concerned itself with where my next meal would come from.

Such thoughts had no place in my life anymore. I had to eat to survive, and survive I would. I lifted my plate and allowed Mary to serve me.

As I worked my way through my second helping of grillades and grits, my brother-in-law strode into the dining room. Without a greeting, he moved with a panther's grace to the server and poured himself a cup of coffee. The small china cup looked out of place in his long, lithe fingers. I saw the power in the muscles and bones in the back of his hand, and pictured them shattering a cup with very little effort. I lifted my gaze to meet his.

"I have sent some of my men to salvage what they can from the coach. As soon as we can get all your things cleaned and dried, we will have you on your way back to Saint Simons. There is nothing you can do here."

I dropped my fork with a clatter. "I beg to differ."

Mary, who had been in the process of pouring my coffee, began to shake so badly, the teacup rattled in the saucer. I took them from her with a look I hope passed for understanding. She left the room with small, hurried steps.

He placed his cup back in the saucer with forced control. His gaze darkened as he regarded me. "You, madam, are in no position to argue with me. You were invited by someone who is not here, making you an uninvited guest. I will be more than happy to see you taken safely home."

I slid my chair back, heedless of the scraping on the wood floor. I fairly shook with emotion as I faced him. "How dare you, sir? My sister is missing and she may be in grave danger. I cannot—nor will not—return to my home before I know that she is safe." Tears stung my eyes, but I refused to give him the satisfaction of seeing me cry. "If I have to sleep on the front lawn, I will not leave." I swallowed thickly, forcing back the anger, and turned to reason. "I have no one else, sir. I have lost everything. Even my home. I will not easily give over my sister, too."

Something passed over his face—pain? Regret? It softened his features for a moment, allowing me to see inside him, and what I glimpsed did not frighten me. For that brief moment, I recognized something as cold and barren as my own soul, and I connected with it. I made a move to leave the dining room, but his words made me halt.

His voice was almost kind. "Do not go. Please finish your breakfast. You are too thin." I drew in my breath as he placed his cup and saucer on the sideboard. "You may stay—but you must keep to yourself as much as possible. I do not want you interfering in the search, nor do I want you making the servants nervous with any questions. If you do have questions, you are to bring them directly to me."

I lowered my head. "Agreed." I looked back up at the sound of his retreating footsteps. "Who was that child upstairs with Marguerite?"

He stopped without turning around. As if holding his breath, he said, "That is Rebecca, your niece." He began walking away from me again toward the front door.

"My niece? Elizabeth's child?"

His only answer was the slamming of the door.

CHAPTER THREE

———◆———

For the remainder of the morning and most of the afternoon, I was left to my own devices. I wandered through the house, noticing the dust on the dark wood of the furniture and the scuff marks on the floors. The black marble on the fireplaces looked pasty, as if the mantels had not been polished in quite some time. I tried to listen for the voice of the child Rebecca or that of servants, but I heard none inside the house.

The windows were covered in a thin coating of dirt, muting the sunlight that tried to eke its way in through the cracks of closed velvet draperies. In the front parlor I had opened them, only to find myself choking on the dust I had stirred up with the movement of fabric.

Despite my love for my grandmother, I had always hated coming to this house as a young girl. The light here was full of shadows, never quite making it inside the dark corners of the large rooms. It made it seem as if the house had no soul, only lurking secrets.

Elizabeth said it was because our great-grandfather had built the house on the highest piece of land he could find this close to the Mississippi River. Legend said the rise in the land was due to an ancient Tunica Indian burial mound. Some said he knew the legend but built the white-columned mansion anyway, piling any bones they found in a heap and burning them. I had been told by my sister that an Indian woman carrying a crying baby was seen many times walking across the grass at the back of the house, toward the pond, then disappearing into thin air. I peered out the dirty window of the library at the murky water of the pond, wondering if my sister had shared the same fate.

Mary called me in for supper, and I ate in complete silence, noticing again the piles of food. I wondered where it would go when I finished with my portion, and if the master of the house would be joining me.

But my meal progressed without interruption, and when I finished, Mary cleared the table.

I wandered out into the foyer, my hands fidgeting against my skirts, frustrated at being idle when so much needed to be done. The front door opened and I turned, surprised to see a man in the doorway.

He was slightly taller than I, with light blond hair and a heavy mustache. His clothes were simple but well tailored, his black boots polished to a high sheen. He clutched a black felt hat to his chest as he slammed the door behind him. When he spotted me, he seemed to sigh with relief, then strode toward me.

"Elizabeth," he said, his voice more of a breath than words. As he neared, his steps slowed as he regarded me with curiosity. He stopped, examining me closely, his head tilted to the side.

"Elizabeth?" he said again, this time as a question.

His eyes were dark gray with black specks in them. They were kind eyes, and I warmed to him, in desperate need of a friend. Pale lashes blinked as if to clear my image.

"No," I said. "I am Catherine deClaire Reed—Elizabeth's sister." I stared at him for a moment, wondering if I had seen him before. "Have we met?"

He took a step back. "No, I do not believe so." He gave me a deep bow. "Allow me to introduce myself. I am Daniel Lewiston, country doctor, gentleman farmer, former Yankee, and friend and confidant of John McMahon." A deep dimple appeared on his right cheek as he smiled at me. He took my hand and kissed my wrist, his mustache tickling the skin on the back of my hand.

I felt an unfamiliar smile creep to my lips. "It is a pleasure to make your acquaintance, Dr. Lewiston. But I am afraid that if you came to see Elizabeth or John, neither of them is here at the moment."

A shadow seemed to cross his face before disappearing as quickly as it had come. "Then perhaps we should use this opportunity to become better acquainted. Shall we, Mrs. Reed?" He offered his arm.

I paused for a moment, looking closely at his friendly face. Needing someone to talk to, I took his arm. "Yes. Thank you, Dr. Lewiston."

He led us outside to the front porch, where we settled into wooden rockers and eyed each other politely. Leaning toward me with his elbows on his knees, he looked up at me, his gray eyes lighter in the bright daylight.

It felt good to be outside the dreariness of the house. A cerulean sky had replaced the dark clouds and rain of the previous night, bringing with it a hint of temporary coolness, not uncommon for late spring in the Delta. I stared past the lane of oaks toward where the great Mississippi River lay, breathing in deeply to catch the brackishness of it. I had hated the smell as a child, a constant reminder of how much I missed my faraway home.

To the east lay the wide fields of sugar cane and the sugar mill. I remembered my father saying it took a very rich cotton planter to be a very poor sugar planter. I wondered at my brother-in-law's success. He had known nothing about planting until he had moved here with Elizabeth to take over the running of the former cotton plantation. My father said he had brought with him the luck of the Irish. Years without flood or frost, and protection against enemy invasion, certainly made John's success appear lucky. But if Elizabeth's disappearance was any indication, it would seem his luck had finally run out.

I turned toward my visitor. "I assume you have heard about my sister."

He nodded, a dour expression on his face. "I did. I could not come sooner because I was with Mrs. Brookwood, delivering her twins. I am afraid I might not know any more about the situation than you do, however."

I rocked steadily in my chair. "Mr. McMahon will tell me nothing. All I know is that my sister disappeared from here five days ago and has not been seen or heard from since. It would appear my brother-in-law has sent out search parties, but no one has found any trace of her."

Dr. Lewiston looked toward the ancient oaks and spoke almost absently. "That would have been Thursday. She came to my office that day."

I sat up. "Was she ill?"

He did not look at me. "I am really not at liberty to say. Everything between a patient and her doctor should be kept in strictest confidence." He turned to me with a smile that evaded his eyes. "I am sure she will tell you all you need to know when she returns."

I placed my hand on the arm of his chair. "Do you really think she is coming back?"

He smiled reassuringly as he patted my hand. "Yes, I am certain of it. And I am sure there will be a good explanation for all of this. You will see." He sighed heavily. "She has to. It would kill John to lose her. He loves her so much."

I wondered at the strange tone of his voice. When he did not say any more, I settled back in my chair and diverted the subject. "You said you were a former Yankee. How did you come to be here?"

His mustache bristled as he smiled. "John and I were boyhood friends in Boston. We have known each other since we were still in the nursery. Shortly after his marriage to Elizabeth, I accepted an invitation for a visit down here, and while at Whispering Oaks, I met my wife. Clara and her father were visiting from their cotton plantation in Saint Francisville and were invited to dinner." His pale eyes looked down at his hand and the band of gold on his third finger. "I suppose it must have been love at first sight, for we were married within three months and I had become a Southern planter."

He sent me a rueful grin. "To be honest, I am not much of a planter. Clara's father had more than thirty thousand acres in cotton and people to run just about all of it. Most of it survived the war, too, largely due to John's influence. But, as far as I could see, my father-in-law did not really need me. Besides, medicine is my calling, and I continued to practice in my field up until the war. I was conscripted into the Confederate Army and became an army doctor. Which is a good thing, since I could not see myself taking up arms and firing on my own countrymen. I am surprised John still speaks to me." There was no mirth in his voice.

Dr. Lewiston seemed kind and affable, but his voice was so forlorn, I took pity on him. It had been so long since I had been able to give comfort, and I reached over and placed my hand on top of his.

A dark shadow fell over our hands. My brother-in-law stood towering over us, a cool expression on his face.

I released Dr. Lewiston's hand and he stood to greet his old friend. "John," he said, extending his hand. "Your lovely sister-in-law and I were just discussing this business with Elizabeth. I am here to offer whatever help I can."

John took his hand and shook it. "Thank you, Daniel. But I do not think there is anything else anybody can do right now. I have got my men going all the way to New Orleans and Baton Rouge. I can only wait here for word of her." He concentrated on pulling the riding gloves off his fingers. "Clara tells me that Elizabeth came to see you last week."

Dr. Lewiston's eyes widened in surprise. "Well, yes . . . Yes, she did. But you could have asked me, you know, instead of my wife. I would have given you the same answer."

John appraised his friend with narrowed eyes. "I am sure you would have. But you were with Mrs. Brookwood and I did not want to disturb you."

"Yes. I was." The doctor clamped down on his teeth, and I could see his jaw muscles working.

"Was my wife ill, Daniel?"

The doctor looked his friend squarely in the eye. "I am not at liberty to say. Elizabeth can tell you herself when she returns."

John took a step forward, but the doctor refused to step back. "And if she does not come back?"

The doctor squared his shoulders. "Then we will discuss it. But she will return. I know it."

John's eyes clouded as he stared out across his sugar fields. "I wish I were as confident as you, Daniel. But I have my doubts."

Despite the heat of the day, I shivered. I stood, ready to confront him with his reasons for doubting Elizabeth's return. I paused in midbreath as the front door swung open with a crash and a young girl, about four or five years of age and clutching a doll that was nearly as big as she was, ran out onto the porch, neatly colliding with Dr. Lewiston.

Unbound blond hair, reaching almost to the child's waist, hung limp and wet with sweat, the girl's cheeks reddened with exertion. Marguerite followed her closely out the door but pulled up abruptly when she saw the three adults.

"My apologies, Mr. McMahon. I am trying to get Miss Rebecca to learn her letters, but she keeps running away from me."

The girl clung to the doctor's knees, refusing to relinquish her grasp. Dr. Lewiston stroked her hair and murmured comforting words while keeping a wary eye on his friend.

I watched as John's face softened, resembling the look I remembered him saving for Elizabeth when they had first met. He knelt, bringing his tall frame down to a more approachable level for a child, and held out his arms. Rebecca lifted her face, then ran with her doll to John with outstretched hands.

His transformation from a brooding ogre was completed as he kissed the bright blond head and lifted her into his arms. She put her head down on his shoulder and stuck a thumb in her mouth.

"Perhaps, Marguerite, you should attempt to make the lessons more stimulating for a child. For heaven's sakes, she is running away from you, not her lessons. Play with her. Make her laugh. God knows there is not enough of it around here."

Marguerite's mouth tightened. "You are undermining my authority, Mr. McMahon. I have raised children before, and I know what is best." She stepped forward as if to take the child, but John held tight.

"Please do not touch her—can you not see she is upset? It is time for her nap. I will take her upstairs."

I raised my hand to stop him. "Please wait. I would like to see her." I walked toward the child and brushed the blond hair away from her face. Her coloring was so different from Elizabeth's, but the eyes, almond-shaped and a vibrant blue, were identical. I touched the back of my hand to her cheek, then jerked it away. They were also Jamie's eyes. If her hair and brows were darker, it could have been my child.

She stopped sucking on her thumb, those eyes regarding me closely. And then she began to scream.

I stepped back, astonished at her reaction, wondering if she had sensed any of my sadness and disappointment that she was not the child I wished her to be.

John pulled Rebecca away from my reach, then entered the house without a glance back. I sat down in my chair, trying to catch my breath.

Dr. Lewiston spoke softly to me. "Do not worry, Mrs. Reed. Rebecca is a high-strung child and is overtired at the moment. I am quite sure it had nothing to do with you."

I nodded, still unable to speak, and wondered if my own animosity toward the child was a random event or a personal reaction to a child who resembled my son so much that I could feel nothing but resentment toward her.

I rocked in silence as Dr. Lewiston approached Marguerite. "It is good to see you again, Marguerite. Clara still misses you and sends you her best."

Marguerite gave him a tight smile. "Thank you, sir. She knows I feel the same. But we do manage to see each other often enough, I suppose."

A subtle change flickered over the doctor's expression. "Really? Clara has never mentioned it to me."

Lids lowered over pale green eyes. "You were most likely too busy tending to your doctoring to notice such things." She reached for the door handle. "I must see to my duties. It was good seeing you, Dr. Lewiston."

With a small swish of her skirts, she disappeared inside.

The doctor leaned against a column, his arms crossed over his chest. "She raised my wife from birth. Clara considers her almost her mother." He pulled a gold watch out of his watered-silk waistcoat and looked at it for a moment before replacing it. "Had to sell her during the war—needed the money—and Elizabeth certainly needed the help. Your sister was not as . . . strong as she would have liked to be, and she needed another female here at Whispering Oaks. Soon after purchasing Marguerite, John freed her." He took a deep breath, his face sad. "I suppose she will stay on for Rebecca's sake. Until Elizabeth returns," he added hastily.

I rubbed my temples with the pads of my fingers, the start of a headache beginning to pound behind my eyes.

The doctor's voice was soothing. "Will your husband be joining you?"

I blinked at him in the sun, unable to find the words. Finally, I managed, "He will not be. I am . . . I am in mourning." I took a deep breath, needing sympathy from a kind soul. "For my son, too. He drowned."

He stood, swallowing, and I saw the kindness in his pale gray eyes. "I am sorry, Mrs. Reed. You, well . . ." He looked down at the celery green gown I had borrowed from my sister. "You are not dressed in mourning."

"My clothes were ruined in an accident. This is Elizabeth's dress."

"Yes, I just realized." He stood near me. "I am sorry for your loss." I looked into his eyes and saw that he meant it. He took my hands and squeezed them.

"Yes, well . . ." I dropped my gaze and stared at his pale hands covering mine, the skin as soft and smooth as a girl's. Gently, he let go.

"I must be leaving. Would you please do me a favor?" He reached into his coat pocket and pulled out a short rope of licorice. "Rebecca loves these. I always give her one when I see her. Would you be so kind as to pass this along to her?"

I did not want to, but I realized I could not avoid the child forever. Perhaps this would serve as a sort of peace offering. I nodded and took the piece of candy.

"Thank you, Mrs. Reed. It is greatly appreciated." He bowed, placed his hat over his head, and descended the steps. As an afterthought, he turned toward me as he reached the bottom. "Do call on us soon. My Clara would love to meet you. She and Elizabeth were great friends. We are straight down River Road in Saint Francisville. Barely thirty minutes by horse."

I smiled, ignoring his past-tense reference to my sister. "I will. Thank you."

He waved as he walked toward the stables, and I turned back to the house.

I paused in the dim doorway, hearing the strange humming again. The tune vibrated against my own lips, so taunting in its familiarity, yet its identity still beyond my grasp. With the licorice held tightly in one hand, I slowly ascended the stairs, following the haunting melody hummed with such sadness by a young voice.

The door to Elizabeth's room stood open and I approached it with caution. Quietly, I peered in, not sure what I would see.

Rebecca sat on a small chair in front of a dressing mirror, wearing nothing but her camisole and bloomers, her large doll leaning against her legs. I remembered that she was supposed to be napping, and wondered what she was doing in her mother's room.

She sat brushing her fingers through her long, fair hair as she stared transfixed into the mirror. The lingering scent of lavender made me turn my head, as if my sister had just walked through the room. Only dark corners and rose-colored satin bed linens met my gaze.

The humming ceased, and I focused back on the little girl. Her blue eyes widened with fear as she spotted me, and she scrunched her shoulders as if trying to disappear into the dressing table. *Oh, Jamie,* I thought, and breathed, the crushing sadness upon me again. I turned to leave, then stopped. She was only an innocent child, my sister's child. Perhaps she needed comfort now as much as I did.

Slowly, I turned to face her. Not quite managing a smile, I approached, the licorice held in front of me. When I stood before her, I knelt, remembering her father's action.

"Dr. Lewiston asked me to bring this to you. He says it is your favorite."

Her head was down, dimpled hands folded on her lap. I touched the back of a hand with the piece of candy. Without looking up, pudgy fingers opened up and took it.

I was so close, I could smell the sweetness of her. My heart broke again as I remembered holding Jamie and burying my face in his little neck and crying with the joy that he was mine.

My voice faltered but I swallowed, clearing my throat. "Do you know who I am?"

She shook her head, still looking down.

"I am your aunt Cat. Your mama and I are sisters."

That brought her head up as two piercing blue eyes stared at me intently. I forced myself not to look away.

I patted the yellow yarn hair of her cloth doll. "What is her name?"

"Samantha." Her voice was clear and high-pitched. So much like Jamie's.

"She is beautiful. Where did you get her?" I lifted the doll to get a better look and noticed the painted-on bright blue eyes.

"My papa. She is my friend." She grabbed the doll and hugged her close.

Abruptly, she slid from the chair and ran past me and out of the room.

I stood to follow her, then halted. Turning around, I looked down at the dressing table. Except for a nearly empty bottle of perfume, it was bare. Dust outlined where a hand mirror would have lain, and long, dark strands of hair littered the top. But there was no sign of my sister's comb, brush, or mirror.

I walked toward the large armoire and threw it open. Ruffles and flounces of every type of silk, satin, and linen filled the entire space, hiding the back of the armoire. It would have been impossible to determine if something were missing. I pushed two dresses aside and peered into the back of the armoire. An empty brass hook, made to hang a dressing gown, winked at me. I looked on the floor of the armoire to see if it might have fallen, but there was nothing there except a pair of evening shoes. The scent of stale lavender permeated the small space, almost gagging me.

The humming commenced again, so I closed the armoire behind me and followed Rebecca to her room down the hall. She stood before a tall chest and was tugging on a bottom drawer. I knelt next to her and helped her open it. She looked at me with grateful eyes, imparting a tender thread of trust in me.

I gasped in surprise as I looked at the contents of the drawer. It was filled with licorice ropes identical to the one I had just given her. With little aplomb, she dumped her latest addition to her collection.

"Are you saving them?" I asked, curious.

She shook her head, blond hair swinging. "No. I do not like them. But Mama says I will hurt Dr. Lewiston's feelings if I say no. So I keep them here."

"I see," I said, brushing hair off her face. She didn't flinch.

We both turned at a sound from the door. Marguerite stood there, a frown on her face.

"Mrs. Reed, it is time for Rebecca's nap. It would be much better for the child if you would leave and let her rest." She came over and took the doll from Rebecca's arms and tossed it on the bed.

I opened my mouth for an explanation, then closed it. She was right: The child needed her rest.

I rose, resisting the impulse to pat the little girl on the head, and left. The door shut abruptly behind me, and as I walked down the hallway to my own room, I heard the haunting melody drift through the house once more.

———◆———

CHAPTER FOUR

Marguerite had laid a deep blue silk gown on the bed for me to wear to the evening meal. I walked past it and opened the armoire, where the cleaned and dried clothes from my trunk had been hung.

I stared in dismay at mended spots and uneven dye color, my gaze straying to the silk gown on the bed. With a sigh, I pulled the faded black cotton from the armoire and called for Marguerite to help me dress before heading down to dinner.

The smell of food drifted into my room, enticing my long-starved appetite. I paused in the gloomy hallway, the dusty lampshades mellowing the yellow flames, breathing shadows onto the walls. I descended the stairs, listening to the tread of my slippers, the only sound in the tomblike silence.

The dining-room table had been set with three places, with Rebecca and her father already seated at one end of the table. Samantha must have been left in the nursery. John's gaze flickered over me, and he frowned as he eyed my dress. He stood and indicated the chair to his right.

He pulled the chair back for me, his presence somehow unnerving to me.

"Was there something wrong with Elizabeth's gown?"

I shook my head, embarrassed that he had noted the condition of my clothing. "No. But I am in mourning."

He took his seat, then filled my goblet halfway with red wine, a drop staining the white linen tablecloth and spreading like a drop of blood. "I assumed you were in mourning from your clothes. I am sorry for your loss." He stared at me, unblinking, for a moment. "The dark blue was the closest I could think of. Elizabeth does not own anything black. Or anything very dark, for that matter."

I looked down at my plate, feeling my face color. It had never occurred to me that he had selected the gown.

Eager to change the subject, I turned my attention toward Rebecca, who sat silently in the chair across from me, thumb in mouth.

"Does Rebecca usually join you at table?" I watched as Rebecca slowly twirled a blond lock around her finger.

"Why do you ask, Mrs. Reed? Do you not like children?"

My host indicated to Mary that she should start serving the food. She came to stand by me with a covered silver dish and lifted the lid. Candied yams, covered in sauce, swam invitingly inside, making my mouth water. I helped myself to a large portion, concealing the fact that his question had stilled my hunger pains.

"That is not what I meant. My husband and I always enjoyed our son's presence at our table. But I know not all parents feel that way." I took a bite full of yams, savoring the sweet taste.

Strong fingers wrapped around his goblet, obliterating the facets of light. "Elizabeth did not allow it. But she is not here, and I like Rebecca to dine with me." The same hand that had been grasping the wineglass so tightly now softened and reached for Rebecca's tiny hand. Palm upward, he closed his fingers around hers.

"Did your son remain on Saint Simons, Mrs. Reed?"

The candied yams seemed to stick in my throat, but I forced them down with a swallow of wine. I took another quick gulp, needing the fortitude to find words to describe the loss of my son without communicating the depths of my grief. That was mine, and all I had left. I would not share it. Especially not with this forbidding man, who would offer brittle platitudes that could never compare to the warmth of my son's hand in mine.

"My son is dead, Mr. McMahon. He drowned this past March."

Ebony lashes lowered over dark eyes. "I am sorry. I cannot fathom the loss of a child."

His voice caught, giving me a start, and I noticed how his hand closed even tighter over his daughter's.

I took my time cutting a piece of ham and then chewing it. "I am sure you can understand my dedication to finding my sister, sir. She is all I have left."

His weary gaze brushed my face. "But surely you two were not all that close. We have not seen you since the wedding."

I pressed my napkin to my lips. After her marriage, Elizabeth had promised to visit, but never had. Even at my wedding, and our parents' funerals, followed so closely one after the other, Elizabeth's presence had been conspicuously absent. We assumed the reluctance lay on the part of her husband, which would also have been the reason why I was never invited to visit her here. And then the war came, and Elizabeth was sent to live in Boston, and all contact had ceased. Until her last cryptic note.

"That was not my choosing, sir." I lifted my gaze to his, expecting to see guilt. But all I saw was confusion and perhaps regret.

A black eyebrow shot up, oddly resembling a crow's wing. "Nor was it mine. You were always welcome in this house, as you are now. Even up North, Mrs. Reed, we are capable of extending hospitality. You are welcome to stay as long as you like." He took a long drink of his wine, his gaze never leaving my face, the sincerity of his words unclear. "I simply expect you to follow my rules in this house. And that would include staying out of rooms I have told you are off-limits."

I recalled Elizabeth's dresser empty of toiletries and her missing dressing gown. I wondered if that was what he did not wish me to see.

Mary stood by my side again with sweetened corn bread, and I helped myself to two large pieces, remembering in time to use the serving utensil instead of my fingers. Starvation had been my companion for so long, I could hope only that my table manners would not desert me completely.

"Take all you want, Mrs. Reed. There is plenty more in the kitchen."

I dropped the serving utensil ungraciously onto the platter, feeling the flush rise in my cheeks.

"I apologize. I did not mean it unkindly. I only meant to imply that we have plenty of food and I would like you to avail yourself of it."

I looked down at my hands resting on the snowy white napkin in my lap, the nails brittle and broken but mercifully now free of dirt. Humiliation simmered under my skin at the need to take this man's charity. He had worn the dreaded blue, and it was his ilk who had brought me so low.

I raised my napkin to the table in an indication that I was through with the meal, but my host appeared not to notice as he cut up meat for Rebecca. The child had sat silently since I had been seated, slowly chewing food her father cut and put on her plate. Her almond-shaped eyes seemed to miss nothing as her gaze shifted between her father and me.

Mary stood behind John with the bowl of yams and took the lid off the dish. He waved her away, and she returned it to the server.

"Do you not care for candied yams, sir?"

His gaze met mine slowly, as if embarrassed about something. "No, actually. I do not."

"Then why have them at your table? Surely, as the master of the plantation, you can dictate what is served?"

He took a long drink of wine, then offered a smile to Rebecca before answering me.

"Elizabeth told me once they were a favorite of yours. I thought they might help you feel not so far from home."

I carefully studied my plate, unsure of my response. I was humbled, but at the same time could not help but think he had an ulterior motive for showing such concern. Finally I said, simply, "Thank you."

Slowly, I slid my napkin back to my lap, lifted my fork, and speared a bite of sliced ham. "Any news of Elizabeth?"

He took his time chewing and swallowing and I wondered if he were stalling for an answer. When it came it was short and abrupt. "No. I am afraid not."

I leaned forward. "Should you not be the one traveling to Baton Rouge and New Orleans to search for her? Why leave such an important detail to others?"

His face appeared set in stone as his eyes narrowed. "I am needed here. If she chooses to return, this is where she will find me."

I slapped my fist on the table, making the wine dance in the glasses. "But what if she is in danger? What if she needs you?"

His face relaxed as heavy-lidded eyes regarded me. "That, my dear Mrs. Reed, is highly unlikely."

I sat back in my chair, stunned. I remembered Elizabeth's letter. *I need you, dear sister. I am so afraid.* What had she been so afraid of? And was it enough to send her away without a word to anybody?

Too late, I remembered Rebecca's presence. She had been quietly eating, but now I realized she had dropped her fork and was listening intently. My heart sank as I tried to recall what we had said and if she would find any of it hurtful.

John picked up a silver bell at the end of the table and rang it. His hands were so gentle when he touched his child, but their breadth and strong tendons told of their hidden strength. I could not help but wonder what those hands were truly capable of. Within moments, Mary rushed in, her freckles prominent in her flushed face. "Yes, sir?"

"Tell Marguerite that Rebecca is done with her dinner and is ready to be put to bed." Mary left as the child slid from her chair and moved to put her head on her father's arm. He reached a hand around her shoulders as she stuck her thumb in her mouth and continued to regard me closely.

"Mama?" she said. I watched as she ducked under her father's arm and came to stand near me.

A warm, sticky hand reached up, hesitated a moment, then touched my cheek. Pain chilled my veins. I wanted so much to comfort this motherless child, to smooth away her fears. But I could not. When I looked into those cursed eyes I was reminded again of what I had lost. I averted my head, afraid she would see the tears welling in my eyes.

Marguerite came and took the child, and only then did I look up. My brother-in-law was looking at me coolly, his hands gripping the arms of his chair. "I see you have more in common with your sister than mere looks, Mrs. Reed."

Without explanation, he excused himself and stood, leaving me alone at the table.

Having no more appetite, I, too, slid back my chair and left the room.

Dusk had settled over the plantation, casting more shadows inside the dimly lit house. I wandered the downstairs, curious as to the obvious lack of house staff. A cloudy chandelier suspended on a velvet rope in the foyer swayed gently in the hot breeze from the open windows. The candles flickered briefly, undulating like lovers in the sticky heat.

I drifted into the front parlor, where a lone hurricane glass offered the only illumination. Long shadows followed me as I sat down at the piano in the corner, an old friend from the days I visited my grand-mother. Sighing softly, I pressed down a few keys. I was surprised to find it in tune. My fingers touched each key, sliding up a chromatic scale and then down again. I began playing a tune with just my right hand, plucking out each note from memory. I realized I was playing the song I had heard Rebecca humming and stopped, the last note echoing in the dark room.

A movement in the corner twisted me around. The tall form of my brother-in-law stepped forward. The light was behind him, casting his eyes into dark circles of shadow. "Please do not stop. This house has not heard music in a very long time." He stepped around me and lit three arms of a candelabra atop the piano. The breeze from his movement brushed my skin, making it tingle with what seemed a thousand pin-pricks.

I turned around on the bench, self-conscious. "I am not that good. Elizabeth was the one with all the musical talent, I am afraid."

"I would not know. She has never played for me. I made sure to keep it tuned, but she never showed any interest."

He stood behind me, and the room began to feel incredibly small. Gingerly, I stroked the keys, my hands finding their homes, and started a Brahms waltz. His presence unnerved me, causing my fingers to stumble like a small child learning to walk. I lifted my hands from the keyboard but did not turn around. "I am a bit out of practice, I am afraid. My piano was demolished by the butt of a Yankee rifle. It made it quite difficult to play."

I regretted the words as soon as they left my mouth, but my anger still burned fresh. I let my hands fall to my sides. "Why was Elizabeth so unhappy?"

Only his soft breathing answered me. Then, after a moment, "She alone could tell you that. She did not make me privy to her thoughts. And I eventually grew tired of asking." He remained behind me, close enough that I could feel his breath on the top of my head. I did not turn around.

"Was it your decision to keep the birth of Rebecca a secret? I cannot believe that was my sister's wish." I kept my gaze focused on the keys, watching the light dance with the shadows upon their surface.

380 · *Karen White*

He shifted away from me. I turned and watched as he walked to the window and stared out through the murky glass. "You were not the only one she kept in the dark. I did not know I was a father until my first furlough during the war. Rebecca was already five months old."

The sadness in his voice was palpable, tugging at my compassion. But I held back, wondering if this man was responsible for Elizabeth's actions. I smoothed the fabric of my dress. "This woman you describe is not the sister I remember."

He stared at me a moment, the house utterly quiet except for the breeze moving through the darkened rooms. "Perhaps. People do change. Or maybe you never knew the real Elizabeth."

I stood. "I assure you, sir, my sister and I were very close. There were never any secrets between us. At least not until she married."

He tilted his head as he regarded me. "You are not the young woman I remember from seven years ago. The first time I saw you, you were dancing barefoot along the beach, impervious to the broken shells. I gather that it has been some time since you have felt carefree enough to do such a thing."

I flushed, embarrassed that he should recall such an intimate detail about me. "I suppose, Mr. McMahon, that a war can change people. I do not believe that girl exists anymore."

I moved to the doorway, and he followed me. Turning to say good night, I found him standing very close. Something akin to panic flooded through me and for a moment I could not find words. He spoke first.

"If Elizabeth never returns, would it be your desire to take Rebecca to her mother's family?" Penetrating eyes stared down at me.

"No." My vehemence showed in the one syllable. I recalled the small cemetery where the rest of my family lay, and the scorched and overgrown land that had once held so much bounty. "There is nothing left of our family on Saint Simons. And I do not think I could care for another child."

His eyes never left my face. "Good. Because I would never let her go."

"The child is yours, sir. I would not consider taking her from you." I looked for an answer to my unasked question in those eyes. "Elizabeth will return. She must."

I waited for a response, but he remained silent. My heart thudded in my ears. Something about this man pushed at my blood, making it rush through my veins in a hurried torrent. I stepped back. "I am tired and will retire now to my room. Good night, Mr. McMahon."

I reached the bottom of the stairs before he spoke. "If you will be staying here for an extended period of time, you might call me John."

My hand flew to my neck, where I felt the heat under my palm. I forced my voice to stay calm as I stared at my hand on the balustrade. "If you wish. And you may call me Catherine."

I took two steps.

"Good night, Catherine."

I paused, then turned around. "Good night, John."

The shadows hid his face, but I was quite sure I saw a glimmer of white. I hurriedly climbed the stairs, feeling his gaze upon my back until I disappeared from view.

My heart pounded as I entered my room. I had to lean against the door to catch my breath and recover from the heat that had suddenly pervaded my body. The bedside lamp had been lit and it threw a circle of light over my bed, illuminating black spots on the coverlet.

Thinking they were insects but wondering at their stillness, I approached cautiously. When I got close enough, I realized they were leaves. Gingerly, I scooped a few into my hand.

They were thin, shiny dark green leaves, about six inches long. I sniffed them, hoping for a clue, but I could smell only the night air.

The hair at the back of my neck stood up and I turned to the closed door, thinking I heard a footfall in the hallway. I flung open the door but saw no one. Immediately, I ran for the bell and pulled it urgently.

I waited for what seemed an eternity, but was most likely only about five minutes, until Marguerite appeared, her eyes heavy with sleep and wearing a cotton wrapper. "Yes, madam?"

I opened my palm to show her the crushed leaves. "I found these on the bed. Do you know what they are or how they got there?"

Green eyes widened and I saw fear in them as she gazed at me. "Those are oleander leaves. They can kill you if you eat them."

My hand shook a little. "How did they come to be on my bed?"

She shook her head. "I do not know. Maybe some of the other servants are playing a trick on you."

"Really," I said, sounding doubtful. "What other servants? I have yet to see any evidence of their existence."

Marguerite crossed her arms over her chest. "They are afraid of you. Those that did not run off because of your sister do not like to show their faces too much."

"What do you mean? Why would they be afraid of Elizabeth?"

Dark lashes lowered, hiding her eyes. "There are some who take their unhappiness out on other people."

"Why do you think Elizabeth was so unhappy? What would make her so miserable?"

She shook her head, then fixed her cool green gaze on me. "People build their own prisons and then do not know how to find a way out. It made her angry—and she would take that out on whoever was about."

I swallowed, not quite believing what she said of Elizabeth was true. "But why should they fear me?"

Her eyes seemed to flicker. "You look so much like her, they think you are one and the same. They think a voodoo priest has you in a spell and you have a nice spirit in you now, but the evil spirit will come back."

I raised an eyebrow. "That is nonsense." She continued to stare at me as if I were the one speaking irrationally. "You may go now. I am sorry to have disturbed your sleep. Good night."

"Good night," she muttered, before leaving and closing the door quietly behind her.

I stared at the closed door for a long while. Then, opening my hand, I let the leaves fall slowly to the floor.

CHAPTER FIVE

———◆———

I slept fitfully, waking throughout the night, sure I had heard a foot-fall nearby. Whispering voices moved from my dreams to my waking, causing me to sit up in bed, my ears straining to hear what was being said. When I opened my door, I found more oleander leaves sprinkled on the threshold of my bedroom. Somewhere in the depths of the house, a door closed, and I shivered in the warm air.

After twisting the key in the lock, I went back to my bed and lay down, not again closing my eyes until the white light of dawn peered through the windows.

I was awakened midmorning by Marguerite knocking on my door. I opened it and she bustled into my room with an armful of clothes. Following her was a young black girl, around fifteen or sixteen years of age, carrying a steaming breakfast tray. I tried smiling at the girl, but she kept her eyes averted from me the entire time she was in my room.

The girl set the tray on the bedside table as Marguerite spoke. "They are starting to harvest the sugarcane today, so you best stay out of Mr. McMahon's way. You will be getting most of your meals in your room until the harvest is over." I nodded, my heart sinking slightly. I was already terribly lonely, and the thought of not seeing another adult for days on end, even if the adult were morose and not extremely pleased with my presence, was stifling.

Staring at the large bundle in Marguerite's arms, I protested. "I am in mourning, Marguerite. I really cannot wear those clothes. But thank you." I looked at the bundle closely. "Did you notice any of Elizabeth's things missing? Things she might have packed if she were going on a trip?"

She continued folding and placing the clothes in the large rosewood armoire—the same armoire I remembered being locked inside as a child by Elizabeth in a game of find the button. She was quiet for a moment, smoothing down fabric and ruffles. Then she said, "No, ma'am. Not that I recall. And I would have noticed. Seems like she just ran off without a second thought."

I swung my legs over to sit on the edge of the bed. "Do you really think she ran off? What would have made her do something like that? She knew I was coming."

She regarded me coolly for a moment. Changing the subject, she said, "Mr. McMahon told me to bring these in for you. He also told me to burn your old things."

She glanced at me from the corner of her eye as I sat up straight with indignation. "They are the only clothes I own, and you will not burn them."

She shook her head. "Mr. McMahon will not be very happy to find his orders are not being carried out. You best just let me have them."

I slid out of the high bed, my feet slapping the wood floor. "I will not."

Marguerite turned toward me, her hands on her hips. "He has ordered new dresses for you." Her green eyes narrowed. "I was not supposed to tell you that, so keep it to yourself. If I were you, I would just accept it and leave it at that. Mr. McMahon does not like to draw attention to himself."

Who did the man think he was, orchestrating something as personal as my own wardrobe? He could order dresses without my knowledge as much as it contented him. But I would never wear any of them.

Marguerite picked up what looked to be a black serge skirt. I raised my hand. "Wait. What is that?"

She held it up for me to see. "Miss Elizabeth's riding habit."

"May I see it?"

I held the soft fabric in my hands, noting the exquisite workmanship. Small grosgrain-covered buttons ran up the front, and a large pocket decorated the left side of the skirt. The collar and cuffs were of fine cream linen. A blue grosgrain cravat completed the ensemble. It was simply beautiful and carried the mark of my very elegant older sister. I slid my fingers over the fabric. It had been many years since I had been privy to such a beautiful thing. Every stitch of clothing I owned had been taken by the soldiers before they burned my home, leaving me with only what I had on my back. I had been given two more dresses by kind neighbors, who helped me dye them black when it became necessary for me to wear the mantle of mourning.

"I will wear this," I said, holding it up to me. "I would like to go riding this morning."

She nodded and helped me dress.

I felt almost foolish wearing such high style. It had been much more my sister's desire to be fashionable than mine. She had waited with anticipation for the day she could put up her hair, lower her skirt lengths, and wear a corset. I had dreaded it, knowing how the auspices of womanhood would restrict me in ways not just physical.

As Marguerite stood behind me, putting the final pins into my chignon, our gazes met in the mirror. "I found more oleander leaves outside my door last night. Do you know how they got there or what they might mean?"

I studied her reaction closely, looking for some clue. There was something about this woman that made it clear she did not like me. Whether it was because of my resemblance to Elizabeth, I could not say.

She studied my hair. "I do not know who would do such a thing, Miss Catherine. It could be bad gris-gris. Or maybe somebody just wants to warn you."

I knew what gris-gris was, having spent time in my girlhood at my grandmother's plantation. There had been a young slave, Rowena, who had been about my age and whose mother secretly practiced voodoo. I had been fascinated, if not wholly convinced, with her potions and charms, but I knew there were more than a few who believed one could be a fixer of a curse and, thus, be crossed by the same.

Marguerite's hands rested on my shoulders near my neck as our gazes clashed again in the mirror. "Maybe somebody's just trying to warn you. Maybe they think that whatever happened to your sister could happen to you if you stay here much longer." She shrugged. "It is not my business to know." She stuck a hairpin firmly into my hair, pricking me in the back of my skull and filling me with a sense of foreboding.

My toilette completed, I went outdoors. The thick odor of the river pervaded my first breath of morning air as I stepped outside. My nose wrinkled, and I wondered if I would ever get used to it. As I walked toward the stables, I looked out toward the sugar mill and the fields, the tall cane swaying from unseen hands. On the outskirts of the field I saw dark men, their torsos shirtless in the heat of the morning, carrying long wooden-handled blades with hooks on the end. They were slicing at the cane near the ground where it grew, leaving patches of bristled cane that resembled the fur on a frightened cat.

I recognized Mr. O'Rourke inside the stable, spreading fresh hay. He looked startled to see me, then visibly relaxed when I spoke.

"Hello, Mr. O'Rourke. I see you have recovered very nicely from our little mishap." I forced a smile on my lips, but it was not returned. "I hope you will accept my apology for getting us into that mess. You were right. We should have stopped. But I knew my sister was in trouble. . . ." My voice trailed off, my fingers fiddling with my riding gloves.

"Can I help you with something?" He closed his mouth, stingy with his words.

A horse whinnied in a back stall. I doubted my host would easily accept my asking the servants about Elizabeth, but I saw no other recourse for solving the mystery of my sister's disappearance. My brother-in-law certainly had no intention of enlightening me further. "I have been meaning to ask you a question. When my sister sent you to me, did she say anything about where she might be going?"

He glanced at me quickly, his eyes resentful, before going back to his job of spreading hay. "No. She gave me my instructions and indicated that I needed to follow them as soon as possible." He paused for a moment, his lips pressed tightly. "I believed that Mr. McMahon knew of her plans, which is why I did not question them." Looking at me with narrowed eyes, he said, "I do as I am told and nothing more."

I nodded, uncomfortable with the news of my sister's deception. I recalled Marguerite's words regarding the servants who thought I was Elizabeth but with a temporary gentle spirit inside. I wondered if Mr. O'Rourke was of the same school of thought. I swallowed, embarrassed, then changed the subject. "I would like to go for a ride. Does my sister have a mount?"

He straightened, dropping a handful of straw. "Yes, she did. But she didn't like to ride her. Preferred to take Miss Rebecca out in the buggy instead. Never wanted a chaperone, she said. Was content with just her daughter."

"Is her horse still here?"

The first smile erupted on Mr. O'Rourke's face. "Oh, she is a fine filly. I ride her myself just to give her exercise. The mister bought it for his wife, but I do not think she has ridden her but once or twice."

"What is her name?"

I was amazed to see a flush appear on his broad cheekbones. He looked at his feet and kicked at the newly strewn hay. "Mrs. McMahon named her Jezebel."

"I see," I said, understanding Mr. O'Rourke's discomfiture. "May I ride her, then?"

"Yes. Just give me a few moments to get her saddled for you."

"Thank you." I moved my hand to my skirt, intent on brushing away a stray strand of straw. When my fingers touched the fabric, I felt something hard and unyielding within.

I thrust my hand into the pocket and pulled out a small brass key. I held it up, examining it closely. The key was too small to be a door key, yet big enough to serve another purpose. Perhaps it was for a desk or letterbox? I slipped the key back into the pocket, intent on pursuing it later.

Jezebel was a bay with smooth chestnut hair and a black mane. A calm horse, she gently nuzzled my neck as I stood near her and rubbed her nose.

"She is delightful," I said, glad to have finally made a friend at Whispering Oaks. I wondered why my sister had not ridden her. Elizabeth had been a fine rider at home on Saint Simons. But even then she had preferred riding in the phaeton. She claimed she could spread her dress prettily and avoid the dust that way. I had preferred the exercise of galloping on the beach and narrow lanes of the island, racing the ocean-born breeze and feeling the wind pull at the pins in my hair.

Mr. O'Rourke helped me mount. "I will return in a moment to escort you. Mr. McMahon would not want you riding unchaperoned. But I can only be gone for half an hour. I am needed in the field to help bind the cane and cart it over to the mill."

"Really, Mr. O'Rourke. That is not necessary—and I hate to cause you any trouble. I promise I will not go far and I will rub Jezebel down myself when I return."

He cupped his hand over his eyes to shield them from the piercing morning sun. I felt drips of perspiration slip down between my shoulder blades as I sat still in the saddle. Finally, he spoke.

"If you promise not to go too far, I do not suppose Mr. McMahon would mind. But stay close, you hear? Go toward the river—you will find bridle paths there. Keep out of the swamp on the other side of the property. It is not safe even for those of us who know it well."

I remembered well the area he spoke of. It had been one of my favorite places until Elizabeth had told me it was haunted by the ghost of the Indian lady and her baby. The horse shifted, and I held tightly to the reins. It had been Elizabeth's favorite place, too, and I wondered if it would hold any clues to her disappearance. I coughed, the cloying smell of hay, horse, and humid air pressing in on me.

Nodding, I pulled Jezebel away. I adjusted the small hat on my head, waved goodbye to Mr. O'Rourke, and headed toward the river.

My own horse on Saint Simons had been a gelding named Persimmon, and our favorite pastime had been riding along the beach at low tide, the spray of water kicked up by his heels shimmering in the island sun. But he, as so much in my life, had been taken from me. Like most of the livestock on our plantation, he had been confiscated as enemy contraband by the Yankees. I missed Persimmon more than I cared to admit. But there was so much to be missed, I dared not think of any of it at all. Otherwise, I would stop in my tracks and suffocate from the thoughts, just as if a heavy blanket had been wrapped around my face.

Jezebel cantered down the dirt lane between the dropping oaks. At the end of the drive, I pulled up and looked back, making sure we were no longer in view of Mr. O'Rourke. Slowly, I turned her to the right, running parallel to the river, and toward what Mr. O'Rourke had referred to as the swamp. It was really nothing more than a bog, with ornamental gardens that had been planted by my grandmother, complete with a grotto and whimsical brick bridges. It had been a magical place for me at first, before Elizabeth had told me about the ghost and I found myself looking for an apparition behind each tree.

I skirted the pond in the back of the property, then headed toward the cover of trees surrounding the bog before anyone in the tall cane fields could spot me.

Nothing looked familiar as I ducked under the shade of the trees. Things were hushed in there, as if I had entered another world. The horse whinnied, stepping back, but I urged her on. The barely discernible path was strewn with sticks and rocks, making it hard to stay on solid ground. Choked reeds of swamp grass hovered in their shifting garden, the alluvial sand moist and sucking. We edged forward until we reached what was left of Grandmother's clearing, and my heart sank with sadness. Nothing here resembled the magical world of my girlhood. It appeared as if my last refuge from my old life was gone.

Moss covered a stone bridge, its color a deep mottled gray. Weeds grew in profusion at the base of the grotto, almost completely disguised by ivy. A small gecko, its tongue whipping in and out in a furious manner, darted its head in my direction, then disappeared over a slime-covered rock.

A cloud of gnats lifted from the still water and enveloped both me and Jezebel, causing her to move her tail with a frenetic swish. I swatted at them with my arms, almost sliding off balance as Jezebel stepped back to get away from her tormentors.

A small splash diverted my attention for a moment. Only swirls of water eddying out toward the path remained of whatever creature had made the noise. I leaned forward to get a better look when Jezebel reared, knocking me completely out of the saddle. I hit the ground hard, my leg landing on a rock and bearing the brunt of my fall. The horse reared again, nearly catching me underneath her panicked hooves. I hunched over, my arms crossed over my head, not looking up until I heard her hoofbeats running down the path from whence we had come.

I sat up, trying to catch my breath, an icy finger of foreboding brushing the back of my neck. A thick black snake lay coiled only inches from my hand. Its tail vibrated as it raised its head, opening its mouth to reveal a white interior.

Cottonmouth, I thought calmly. I did not move; even my breath remained still in my chest. Staring at the snake, its obsidian eyes watching me closely as its head swiveled in the air, I felt no fear. Perhaps the lack was due to a primal act of survival. Or perhaps my life had left me immune to fear. Regardless, all I felt in the first moments after I spotted the serpent was simply, *Let it be quick.*

Leaves crackled on the path behind me but I did not turn my head. As the scaled body reached me, the air was rent with the sound of a shotgun, and the snake exploded into bits of skin and gore. I turned my head away, feeling pieces of it land in my skirt and hair.

A man's harsh voice spoke beside me. "Rufus, go get Dr. Lewiston and tell him to come to the house."

John knelt by my side. "Are you hurt?"

His voice was anything but solicitous. I shifted away from him and tried to stand, but my legs buckled under me. John caught me and lifted me in his arms.

I tried to push away. "Please, let me down. I can walk."

Ignoring me, he pushed his way down the path. He addressed the man Rufus again. "I asked you to get Dr. Lewiston. Now go!"

I lifted my head and stared at Rufus, a large black man whose broad shoulders strained the buttons on his red and white checked shirt. The man's eyes were wide with fear, the whites showing around the round black iris. He stared at me as if he were looking at the devil incarnate.

He spun on his heel and fled down the path in front of us. Shortly after he disappeared, I heard the beat of hooves riding away. My leg throbbed and I began to see spots in front of my eyes. Reluctantly, I laid my head on John's chest, finding the warmth of him cold comfort.

I was vaguely aware of him lifting me onto his horse and mounting behind me. I slumped against him and did not protest when his arm came around my waist to hold me steady.

His voice was low but forceful when he spoke. "Did not Mr. O'Rourke give you explicit instructions to stay by the river?"

I did not lift my head. "Yes, he did. Please do not fault him for this accident. I simply wanted to explore my grandmother's plantation. I am not a stranger to this place, you know."

He stiffened and I shifted my head, pressing it against the linen of his shirt. My cheek brushed against soft flesh, stinging me, and I realized his shirt lay open. I heard his intake of breath and looked up at his unreadable eyes. I ducked my head again, taking care to rest it on cloth.

"If my overseer had not seen you, you would be dead by now. There is no cure for a cottonmouth's bite." He took a deep breath. "I am master of this plantation now, and I expect everybody to follow the rules that I have set. I cannot have people disobeying me. I have got much more important things to take care of than playing nursemaid to a silly woman who will not listen to directions."

I bolted upright, causing him to tighten his hold on my waist. "I am not a child who needs instructions and discipline."

"I beg to differ. Perhaps you are not so unlike your sister after all."

I stayed where I was, not touching him. "It has been more than six years since I have seen her." My voice caught and I looked down at my hands. His hold on me loosened. "And it would seem that there was quite a lot about Elizabeth that I was not aware of." I looked directly into his eyes. "I doubt that we are very much alike at all."

I leaned back against him again as we continued our ride in silence. Finally, he said, "Elizabeth never knew how to give proper thanks, either."

His words brought back the memory of a Christmas when I could not have been more than twelve and Elizabeth sixteen. I had received the gift of my dreams, a rabbit-fur muff to keep my hands warm on chilly winter days. Elizabeth, despite having received an entire room full of gifts, threw a tantrum because she had not received a muff, too. Upset to see her so distraught, I had given it to her. She wore it every Sunday to church during the winter season, and it gave me great joy to see it bring her such happiness. I did not recall her ever offering to me a word of thanks, but, then, she did not have to. She was my sister and I loved her.

"What do you mean?" I asked, too lulled into complacency by the warmth of his hard chest to take affront at his suggestion that I was ungrateful.

He did not speak for a moment. Then: "I understand that your life has been difficult these past few years. If I had known of your plight, I would have offered help sooner. I do not know how much Elizabeth was aware of your situation. She never discussed it with me." He paused, looking out toward the cane field. "I do feel responsible for you, and I would appreciate it if you would accept my help without complaining. It would make it easier for both of us."

"I never asked for your charity," I said, not sure whether I should be angry or grateful. "I fully intend to return to Saint Simons when Elizabeth is found. I doubt I will require your assistance after that." I sincerely believed that I would rather starve than ask this man for help.

"Then you could at least say thank you. Surely your Southern pride does not override common courtesy."

We entered the shade of the oak-covered lane leading to the house. My cheeks flamed, and I was glad my mother was no longer alive to witness my lapse in the manners she had instilled in me from the cradle.

"Thank you," I said, my voice low. "Thank you," I said again, louder this time. "For the new clothes. Marguerite told me not to mention it to you, but I do not want you to fault me again for deplorable manners."

His voice sounded puzzled. "Really? I wonder why she would say such a thing. If something makes you happy, I would like to know about it. If it makes you smile, I would double my efforts to repeat it. I would venture to say that your lips have not smiled much in the recent past."

I bent my head, attempting to hide the flush I felt rising to my cheeks. This man unsettled me greatly, and I did not want him to.

I was spared from saying anything else by our approach to the house. Once again he lifted me from his horse and carried me inside and upstairs to my room. As he placed me gently on the bed, his arms seemed to linger. My skin burned through the fabric of my dress where he touched me, causing an ache I had not felt in years. I looked into his dark eyes, the pain in my leg and the day's adventure making me reckless. I made a stab at imitating Elizabeth's flirtatious nature. "I am starting to make a habit of needing your rescue, am I not?"

He released me and stood. "Yes. It would appear that you are."

His solicitous manner had changed suddenly into one of wariness. "I will send the doctor up when he arrives. In the meantime, I will have Marguerite see to your needs."

I heard a quick swish of fabric and the muffled sound of running feet out in the hallway. John appeared not to have noticed.

Just as sudden as his change in mood, he left the room.

Marguerite came and dressed me in one of Elizabeth's nightgowns and laid me against pillows on the headboard. She examined my leg, pressing on the sore spot, and pronounced it not broken. Then she left, too, and I dozed.

The eerie melody seemed to creep into my brain as I slept, nudging my memory. All I knew for certain when I opened my eyes was that it had something to do with Elizabeth.

I saw the child Rebecca and her doll sitting at the foot of my bed, humming the melody, and I started.

"Hello, Rebecca," I said, yawning. "Where have you been all morning?"

Grass stuck in her hair, and her wayward braids were almost completely undone. A tear in the hem of her dress hung open. Her doll had fared no better, with dusty smudges on her face and pinafore. I imagined she had been attempting to hide from Marguerite again.

I wondered at her sudden appearance at the foot of my bed. Then a thought occurred to me. "Did you know Dr. Lewiston is on his way over?"

She looked at me shyly and her pixie face brightened with a grin. Her blue eyes sparkled, and I caught my breath. I sensed the spirit of my son within her and felt a small portion of my heart begin to thaw.

I recalled the sound I had heard out in the hall when John was placing me on the bed. "Do you like to spy on people, Rebecca?"

Her thumb popped into her mouth as the fingers on her other hand twirled Samantha's yarn hair. She nodded solemnly, as if she expected me to scold her.

"What interesting things you must see."

Before the child could reply, a sharp rapping came from the door. It startled me, as I had not heard footsteps. I called out for whomever it was to enter, then greeted Dr. Lewiston.

He smiled, giving Rebecca an odd look. I wondered how much of our conversation he had overheard. He smoothed Rebecca's hair, then rested his hand on her shoulder as he addressed me. "I understand you have had another accident."

"It was silly, really. My horse got spooked by a snake, and I fell off. I hit a rock and I hurt my leg."

"I see," he said, setting down his black bag on the bedside table and opening it. "Let me make sure it is not broken; then I will have a poultice made to reduce any swelling. You will be as good as new in no time."

I turned my head as he administered to my leg and pronounced it merely bruised. I thanked him and prepared to say goodbye when Rebecca began humming her mournful tune again.

The doctor paled, turning his head toward Rebecca. The child caught his movement and stopped.

I pushed myself up against the pillows. "Perhaps you can help me, Doctor. I am so sure I know that melody, but I cannot quite place it. Do you have any idea what it could be?"

He shook his head, forcing a smile, but his face blanched. "No. I do not believe I have heard it before. It is very beautiful, though."

He snapped his bag closed. With another pat on her blond head, Dr. Lewiston handed Rebecca a stick of licorice. She looked down at the piece of candy, then stole a glance at me, a glance so full of childish humor, that I had to wink at her. The rush of pleasure I received from that one little act healed a small part of the great wound inside me. It would take much longer to heal completely, but I recognized then that the road to recovery did indeed exist, and that I might have found my way to that meandering path.

CHAPTER SIX

⸻ ✦ ⸻

The same young girl who had brought my breakfast came to my room after the doctor had left. She entered, visibly trembling, her gaze darting about and landing on everything but me.

I slid from the bed, limping as I approached her and noticing how she flinched as I neared. "What is your name?" I kept my voice low so as not to frighten her further.

Her jaw shook so badly it was difficult for her to force out the words. "Del . . . phine." Her gaze stuck to the floor.

"Delphine. What a pretty name. I am glad to meet you."

The girl stood quietly shaking, her dark skin matching the cocoa color of her dress. I was beginning to lose patience. Superstitions or not, I could not manage with an entire household of servants frightened of me.

"I am Mrs. Reed—Mrs. McMahon's sister. I understand we look quite a bit alike."

Amber eyes flickered up to my face, then back down again. "Yes, ma'am," she mumbled. Still studying the floor, she forced out, "Dr. Lewiston's stayin' for supper. Mr. McMahon wants to know if your leg's feelin' better and if you wants to join them."

My leg was sore, but walking on it held no difficulty. "Tell Mr. McMahon that I will be there. Please send Marguerite to help me dress."

She gave a quick curtsy, then scurried from the doorway. I hobbled to the window seat and sat down. I moved aside the lace curtains and looked out upon the lawn. This had always been my favorite part of day, the time when the sun gave way to the gathering dusk, its thin fingers of light holding on to the earth as they clawed their way to the edge and disappeared.

Oh, Elizabeth. Where are you? What were you so afraid of? A heavy breeze moved the curtains, brushing them against my face. A soft tapping sounded at the door, and Marguerite appeared with a gown over her arm.

It was beautiful—a midnight silk that shifted from blue to black as the light moved over it. The neckline was uncomfortably low, but I recognized it as a favorite cut of Elizabeth's. Marguerite offered to do my hair, and stood behind me at the dressing table as she brushed out my long dark curls. Her eyes sparkled in her reflection, as if she held something back, something she could not wait to share. But she kept silent, the rhythmic strokes of the hairbrush almost hypnotic.

When she was finished, I checked my reflection in the cheval glass, surprised at what I saw. Years of near starvation had hollowed out my cheeks, adding a bit of mystery to my face and making my eyes appear even larger. The dress, like most of Elizabeth's clothes, fit me well, if just a bit loosely around the waist and hips. After all, she had been well fed in Massachusetts during the long years of the war. But the gown hugged my bosom like a glove, displaying more of my chest than I thought proper. I searched in vain for my shawl, then had to be contented with just tugging at the neckline to pull the dress higher.

I followed the male voices to the parlor and found Dr. Lewiston and John speaking companionably, with little Rebecca perched on her father's knee, giggling as he bounced her up and down like a horse. The doctor, while replying to his friend, never looked away from the child, his face aglow with affection.

The moment I stepped into the room, all movement and words ceased. I stood, hovering on the threshold, unsure. The doctor stared, his voice suspended midsentence. Something sparked in his eyes, then disappeared again. John merely glowered, his lips clamped shut.

Rebecca stopped chortling and began to scream the wailing sound of a banshee. It chilled me to the bone that such a small child could hold that much grief and pain inside. Dr. Lewiston stood, his face devoid of color and his mouth open in abject surprise. "Elizabeth," he whispered, his voice rasping the word.

John stood, too, holding his daughter against him while she buried her streaming face into his neck. "It is all right, sweetheart. It is just Aunt Catherine." He held the back of her head as she ventured a look at me. She stopped screaming, then stuck her face back into her father's neck, still sniffling.

I took a step forward, then stopped. "I am Aunt Cat. Remember?" I spotted Samantha lying prone on the floor and picked her up. Cautiously, I approached Rebecca again, handing her the doll. She took it and buried her face in the doll's chest with a huge sniffle.

I looked at John. "What is wrong?" I felt as if I had walked undressed into the room. I pressed my fingers to my neck, feeling the rapid pulse of my blood. Why had Rebecca acted so frightened? What, or who, had terrified her so in the past to cause such a reaction? I wanted to leave, back out of the room unnoticed, anything to stop the terror in the child's eyes and the shock on the faces of the two men.

Dr. Lewiston approached, his smile warm but his face strained. He offered his arm to me. "Nothing, my dear. I just believe we are all hungry and ready for supper. Please do me the honor of allowing me to escort you to the dining room."

With a glance back at Rebecca, who seemed to have calmed down considerably, I placed my hand on his arm and accompanied him to the dining table.

I do not recall what food I stuck in my mouth and swallowed. The air in the dining room was stifling, despite the slight breeze creeping under the tall windows. Three sets of eyes regarded me intently, as if I were the evening's entertainment.

Dr. Lewiston watched me with a look I imagined a man would give a beloved object he had lost and then found again in the most obvious place.

John left most of his food untouched, but drank glass after glass of wine, his cool dark eyes watching me, then watching Dr. Lewiston's close appraisal of me.

When Mary brought in dessert, I begged a headache and excused myself. Welcoming my escape from the dining room, I ran quickly upstairs. As I reached the landing, I leaned against the banister, trying to find my breath, my heart hammering in my chest from the exertion. I was not used to wearing stays, my life of the last year making them unnecessary and absurd, and I was finding myself constantly out of breath and on the verge of fainting.

The door at the end of the hallway stood open, spilling light onto the dark floor. This had been my grandmother's room, and I knew that it now served as the master bedroom. I faced the door for a moment and spotted a bright splash of color on the wall—a splash of midnight blue.

Slowly I approached the door and pushed it open, the hinges moaning a protest. There, hanging on the wall opposite a huge rice poster bed, was a full-length portrait of Elizabeth. She wore the same silk dress that now clung to my frame. Instead of feeling comforted, the sight made me feel unclean.

The portrait could have been me, except for the eyes. The eyes I saw in my own reflection were haunted and hungry, but still quite human. The ones in the portrait were cold and lifeless. If I had not known the subject of the portrait, I would even have called them malevolent.

A hot breath teased at the back of my neck. I spun around and found myself staring up into the face of John McMahon.

I swallowed. "It was the dress, wasn't it?"

He nodded. Keeping his voice low, he said, "It was quite a shock for us. The resemblance . . . especially in that dress, with your hair done up that way . . ." His voice lingered.

His presence held me to the spot, draining me of the will to move away. "I do not understand. She is your wife! Why do reminders of her bring such terror to not only you but to your daughter as well?"

His gaze flickered across my face as he raised a hand. I did not flinch as he lowered a finger to my neck and gently brushed away a lock of hair. I felt the heat of his touch long after he had removed his hand and half wished he would touch me again. Still, I did not look away.

"You are so much like her, and yet . . ." He stopped, his gaze regarding me openly. "You have such a gentle spirit. I am left to wonder sometimes if I married the wrong sister."

My eyes widened and he stepped back, breaking the spell. He walked toward the portrait and stood before it. "Elizabeth seemed to always be searching . . . searching for something more. Whatever would make her happy. I am afraid that whatever it was she required, I could not supply. It did not matter where she lived. She was miserable in Boston and here.

And when Elizabeth was unhappy, she made sure everybody around her was unhappy, too. Even an innocent child."

My gaze wandered to the looming portrait, but I found I could not look at it. Small snatches of memory came at me, making his story ring true. Even as a child, Elizabeth had been full of mischief, always goading me into one of her adventures. Her mischievous behavior never seemed to take the form of inquisitiveness, but rather stemmed from her desire to experience things new and dangerous. Her vivaciousness always seemed to mask something darker, something unsettled about her. Yet her persuasive charm was something few could resist. I grew comfortable in her shadow, only sharing the center of attention with Elizabeth when I could be dragged along, clinging to her skirts.

He sighed, still absorbed with the portrait. "There is something within me that almost wishes she were gone forever. There were certainly times when my anger at her was so great, I could have . . ."

He stopped speaking and turned, as if he suddenly realized I was there. A cold chill gripped me as I stared at his hands. I had felt how gentle those long, powerful fingers could be. But I wondered at what else they might be capable of. My husband had had gentle hands, too. Yet they had committed such a vile act of revenge, an act tantamount to severing a part of me. The evil that lurked inside a man's heart was rarely visible to the naked eye, yet I knew enough never to put any man above suspicion.

As if sensing my thoughts, his entire demeanor shifted to the cold, brooding one I had grown used to.

I suddenly realized I was in his bedchamber, alone with him. "I should not be here. I am sorry. I saw the portrait. . . ." I backed out of the room. Looking down at my feet before turning and retreating, I stammered, "Good night."

I felt his gaze on my back as I walked down the hallway to my room.

I sat at the writing desk in my room, dressed in one of Elizabeth's nightgowns and my own wrapper, nearly overwhelmed with the cloying scent of lavender that clung to her clothes and stationery. Unable to sleep, I had tried to write a letter to my closest neighbor on Saint Simons, but had held pen poised over paper for nearly an hour with only the greeting spelled out.

I did not want to discuss Elizabeth's disappearance as of yet, nor her enigmatic husband. I was not sure what I thought of him, and certainly could not construe that on paper.

The doctor had left shortly after dinner, and I was disappointed that I had not had the opportunity to talk more with him. I found his company entertaining and peaceful—completely the opposite of my host's.

When I heard his buggy being brought around, I had peered through my window. Dr. Lewiston had not seen me, but as the buggy drove down the drive, I looked down to find John's dark eyes staring up at me from the front entrance steps. I had quickly let the curtain fall.

I laid the pen down and rubbed my eyes, finally ready to seek the comfort of my bed. The room was stifling, with no hint of a breeze coming from the open window. I slapped at a mosquito that had found its way inside, thankful once more for the netting hung around the bed.

I stood and opened my door, trying to catch a cross breeze. As soon as the door opened, I heard scurrying feet at the end of the hallway. I stuck my head out in time to see the bottom half of a small white nightgown disappearing around the corner of the hallway.

Grabbing my bedside lamp, I sped toward the fleeing figure. As I reached the corner and looked down the hallway, I was surprised to find it deserted. Baffled, I raised the lamp higher to see if anyone could be lurking in a corner. This portion of the house contained guest bedrooms that were barely used in my grandmother's day. Elizabeth and I had played hide-and-seek in them, and I had been locked inside more times than I cared to recall. Servants rarely came to this wing of the house, and I had once been left in one of the rooms until supper. Elizabeth had been my rescuer, hailed by our parents as the heroine of the day. I had waited for her to mention that she had also been my jailer, but I do not believe she ever did. I so enjoyed seeing her revel in all the attention that it never occurred to me to mention it.

I called for Rebecca and listened. A clock chimed softly from the depths of the house. I was about to call for her again when I heard the distinct sound of bare feet running upstairs. I recalled the door to the attic was on this corridor and I hurried to it. Flinging it open, I shone my light into the dark space. I thought I saw another flash of white at the top of the steps and raised the light higher. Nothing but uninterrupted darkness touched the circle of light.

"Rebecca?" I called again. Something rustled up the stairs, and I quickly followed the noise into the attic.

I remembered the large space from childhood, exposed beams and stacks of old trunks and furniture pushed against the perimeter walls. It was hot and stifling, a breeze stealing its way through a broken window the only relief. A movement sounded overhead in the rafters, something different and not at all the sound of a young girl's footsteps. "Rebecca?" I said, my voice quiet and not too steady. Something fluttered above by the roof, and I jerked my light to see. Straining my eyes, I could see only the blackness.

A huge crash from behind spun me on my heels. I gasped, spotting Rebecca standing not two feet away holding the ubiquitous Samantha, a heavy shape at her feet. "What are you doing?" My voice was lost in my throat as I regarded her.

Without a word, she dashed away in the direction in which I had come and disappeared down the dark and silent steps.

With my heart knocking loudly in my chest, I bent down to discover what had been knocked over. My hand touched something smooth and solid. *Wood,* I thought. I set the lamp down to get a better look.

It appeared to be a box-shaped object and it was lying on its side, the apparent victim of a fall from a nearby low chest. Using two hands, I picked it up and turned it over, ecstatic at my discovery. It was a letterbox, my sister's initials carved on a brass plate on the top, a matching brass keyhole winking at me in the dim lamplight.

The key! My hand fell to the pocket of my wrapper. The key had been left in the skirt of the riding habit. Had Marguerite taken it to be laundered? Eager to discover if the key and this box belonged together, I lifted it and tucked it under my arm.

I felt a brush of air near my cheek and then a light form touched the top of my head and disappeared into the blackness of the ceiling. I screamed, dropping the box. The sound made the attic erupt into motion as a dozen fluttering objects propelled themselves from the rafters and dove at me, whipping at my hair and touching my clothing. I abandoned the lamp and the box and crawled toward the steps, the sound of small bodies whipping through the air surrounding me. I swallowed the bile in my throat and concentrated on making it the short distance to the stairwell.

I stumbled down the wooden steps, my knees and hips taking the brunt of my fall. Struggling to stand, I fumbled for the doorknob in the pitch-darkness, feeling the relief flood through me when my hand grabbed the cool brass. I turned it and pushed, but the door held fast. I tried again with no success. The door was locked.

The panic spread through my veins like a raging fire as I pounded on the door with the flats of my hands. "Let me out!" I shouted, the air around me roiling with unseen tormentors. High-pitched squealing bounced against my eardrums, reverberating in my head.

The door swung open and I fell through it and into the arms of my sister's husband. He slammed the door behind me, creating an immediate silence. I clung to him with both hands, my body shaking, but my will still strong enough not to give way to tears. No man would ever see my tears again.

His arms fell around me, pulling me against him in the hushed hallway, pressing my head against his chest. He smelled of his own unique scent of soap, cigar, Scotch, and something else. Something raw and powerful and as enticing to me as blood to a mosquito.

His fingers threaded their way through my unbound hair and I felt him bury his face in it, breathing in deeply. I needed to move away, to step back and stop. But, God help me, I could not.

"Are you all right?" His voice vibrated in his chest.

I nodded, not daring to look up.

"Why were you in there?"

I swallowed. "I was following Rebecca, but she ran away. I was attacked by bats, and when I tried to escape, the door was locked."

He did not say anything. Finally his fingers touched the edge of my jaw and brought my mouth to within inches of his. His breath teased my skin, making me tremble anew. *I should go back to my room. Now.* I jerked back, my hand on my lips. He let me go but remained where he stood, his eyes flickering with the light from the wall sconce. I backed away, not able to break his gaze.

"Papa!" Rebecca ran down the hall and past me, into her father's arms.

As he lifted the child, I backed away, finally turning on my heels and disappearing into my room.

I sat on the edge of my bed in the dark, watching the sultry sway of the curtains move in the damp breeze. It was only much later, as I lay half-awake, that I wondered why John had been close enough to the attic door to rescue me so quickly.

CHAPTER SEVEN

———◆———

When I awoke the following morning, it was with the vague feeling that I had forgotten something. The mood persisted as I bathed and dressed in one of my black dresses.

Again, I ate breakfast alone in my room, thankful I did not have to face John. What would I say? I should have been appalled by his behavior and by my own response to it. I had every reason to be, yet I could not. He stirred something long dormant in me, something I had been quite content to leave slumbering within until the end of my days. And he was my sister's husband.

The cane field was alive with people, and I spotted John from a distance, his towering height making him easily visible. Heat teased at my cheeks and I turned away. Marguerite had told me that the harvesting and processing of the cane in the mill would occupy John for a good many weeks, keeping him away from the house. I prayed fervently that Elizabeth would return before then, thus releasing me to go back to Saint Simons.

Idleness did not come easy to me after my years of running a house and plantation and then finding myself responsible for my mere survival. I needed to do something to fill my time. In search of Marguerite, I walked through the back door to find the kitchen at the rear of the house.

I recognized Delphine leaning over to take biscuits out of the bread oven. She dropped the tin on a sturdy wood table when she spotted me. A woman not much older than me and with a clear resemblance to Delphine turned from a mixing bowl to see what was making the young girl's eyes go round.

"Good morning." I watched the woman wipe her doughy hands on an apron, her eyes as wide as Delphine's. "I am Mrs. Reed, Mrs. Mc-Mahon's sister." Inexplicably, she made the sign of the cross.

I thought it odd, but held on to my composure. "I was looking for Marguerite, but I suppose you should be able to help me." I looked around at my audience, suddenly nervous. "In my sister's absence, I was hoping to assist with your mistress's duties. The food has been wonderful since I have been here, but I was thinking I could help with the menu planning. I have also noticed that the housecleaning is not what one might expect and would like to speak with the housekeeper, if I could."

The older woman finally stepped forward, standing between Delphine and me. Her eyes were wary as she spoke. "I be Rose. Delphine's my chile." She looked back at the girl as if to make sure she was still there. "There ain't no more housekeeper. No housemaids neither, except for Mary. Miss Elizabeth done let them all go. Well, all thems that don' leave themselves."

"I see," I said, feeling uncommonly hot even in the heat of the kitchen. Nothing was making sense. My sister hated housework. The Elizabeth I had known could not have cared less about housemaids, just as long as her house was clean. I hardly recognized this person I called my sister anymore.

"Well, then. You had best show me where the beeswax is. The floors are in dire need of attention."

The door to the kitchen opened and Marguerite entered. "Miss Clara is here—Dr. Lewiston's wife. She says she has come with news of Elizabeth."

Before I could turn, I caught Rose doing another sign of the cross. Thanking Marguerite and asking her to bring us tea, I left the kitchen to meet Mrs. Lewiston.

I almost overlooked the small woman sitting on the settee in the parlor. She wore beige, with no other color to accent the drabness. It matched her skin tone and the back of the settee so well that she blended into the scenery like one monochromatic swath of an artist's brush.

She smiled timidly when I entered, her mouth opening only slightly, as if from years of practice at hiding slightly protruding front teeth. I had the oddest urge to ask Marguerite if she had announced the proper visitor, for this woman did not match the doctor's vibrant personality in the slightest. He had told me it had been love at first sight, and I examined her closely to see the same spark he had seen.

Rising, she extended a small, gloved hand to me. At full height she only came to my shoulder, and her voice was so quiet I had to bend my head to hear her.

"I am Clara Lewiston. But you may call me Clara." She studied my face intently. "You look so much like Elizabeth I would have known you anywhere."

I smiled, relieved to have found somebody who did not mistake me for my sister. "Yes, several people have mentioned that." I took her hand. "I have already met your charming husband. I am Catherine deClaire Reed, but please call me Catherine."

Clara nodded. "I shall call you Catherine, then. Daniel has told me so much about you." Her expressionless face left me with no clue as to the content of such conversations.

Marguerite entered with the tea service and set it down on the small table at my side. As I began to pour, I felt Clara's steady gaze on me.

I handed her a cup and noticed her fingers shook as she took it.

She kept her eyes down as she spoke to me. "I actually have a two-fold purpose for my visit. I wanted to meet you, and I also have news for John of Elizabeth. My father has just come from Baton Rouge and is quite certain he saw her there at a party at the governor's mansion." She took a sip from her cup, a rather unattractive position for one with protruding teeth. "I knew that John would be eager for any word."

I sat up quickly, the hot tea sloshing onto my hand. "He saw Elizabeth—he is quite sure?"

She sent me a timid smile. "Yes, he is quite sure." She set her cup down on the table. "Where is John? I would like to tell him in person."

The back of my neck tingled even before I heard his voice. "Hello, Clara. I saw you arrive."

He stood just inside the room, dressed in a rumpled white linen shirt and fawn-colored pants tucked inside black knee-high boots. His face appeared anxious as he patently ignored me, turning his complete attention toward Clara.

I found I could not look in his direction, feeling the heat in my face. Instead I focused on Clara. She did not smile at him, and she held her lips over her teeth primly. "As I was just telling your sister-in-law, my father is quite sure he saw your wife at a ball at the governor's mansion in Baton Rouge." She patted her lips delicately with a napkin. As she lowered her pale lashes, I noticed how her hand shook and I wondered if she was always as nervous as a rabbit.

She looked almost apologetic as she spoke with her quiet voice, her gaze never quite making it to John's face. "She appeared to be in the company of a young man whom my father could not name."

The shock of her words held back my breath. I forced myself to look at John. His skin, bronzed by the sun, had turned a murderous shade of red, his fists clenched at his side. "Is that so?" The words came out practiced and precise. "Did your father approach her?"

Clara blinked, then swallowed, her gaze focused on a chair. "No. You know my father is . . . Well, he has not been well. The shock of seeing her weakened him, and he walked outside to the gardens for a breath of fresh air. By the time he returned, she had vanished."

Thin pale lines showed in the skin around his mouth. "And he is quite positive it was Elizabeth?"

Her small hands twisted in her lap. "As sure as he can be. Again, he is easily confused—he is of that age—but he seemed quite sure."

"I see." He bowed stiffly. "Then I must go see about leaving for Baton Rouge. I have things to take care of first, but I hope to be off tomorrow morning. Please thank your father, Clara." His gaze rested on me for a moment, and I colored again. I lowered my eyes, staring at the blue veins crisscrossing the white skin at my wrist. "Ladies," he said in farewell, then left the room.

Clara shifted in her seat. "My husband told me how much you resembled Elizabeth. He was right." Her light brown eyes met mine. "She was quite beautiful."

"Yes. She is." I did not continue, not wanting to share my thoughts and doubts with a near stranger.

She compressed her lips and appeared to be deep in thought. "I wonder . . . I wonder why she left. I cannot understand why she would leave her husband."

"Or her daughter," I added almost absently.

She blinked rapidly. "Oh yes. Rebecca."

I glanced at her sharply. There had been something about the way she had said Rebecca's name.

Clara continued, her fingers clutching the teacup tightly. "She is an odd child. Difficult enough to raise a child like that, and now . . . this."

"What do you mean, a child like that?"

She smoothed her hands on her skirts and tilted her head. "I know she is a sweet child, but I just recall everything that Elizabeth told me. Rebecca is a bit high-strung, I think. Her mother even called her a clingy, needy child."

I bristled. "Most children her age are. She will undoubtedly grow out of it. All she needs is a mother's love."

Clara shook her head and tucked her chin to her chest, making it even more difficult to hear her. "Elizabeth did not really understand children. She did not spend a lot of time with the little girl, I am afraid."

"How can that be? I understand that they used to go for frequent rides together—just the two of them in Elizabeth's little phaeton."

My question seemed to disturb her, the pallor of her skin lightening one degree. "Well, then. Perhaps I am mistaken."

"Do you have children, Clara?"

Her face grew pinched as she looked down at her fingers busily plucking at the sturdy fabric of her dress. "No. The good Lord has not seen fit to bless us with children."

I softened. "I am sorry. Perhaps you will. You are still quite young."

She did not answer but looked away, her gaze resting on a small daguerreotype of Rebecca sitting on the end table. Picking it up, she rubbed a finger over the glass, brushing off dust.

I cleared my throat. "Why do you think Elizabeth left? Do you know if she was unhappy?"

She placed the small frame back on the table. "We were quite close, you know, and the only thing she ever told me was . . ." Looking up, her gaze met mine, her face stricken. "But perhaps I should not share confidences."

My interest had been raised. I placed my hand on her arm. "If you have any information concerning my sister's state of mind before her disappearance, I think it should be shared. Please. Tell me. What did she say?"

Grabbing hold of both my hands, her fingers cold, her lusterless eyes sought mine. She lowered her voice to almost a whisper. "She was afraid of her husband."

I raised my eyebrows, hoping to encourage her to say more.

Her gaze flickered toward the doorway where John had stood, then back at me. "She was afraid he might . . . he might hurt her somehow."

I gripped her hands tightly. "What did she mean? That he might strike her? Had he struck her before?"

Shaking her head, she dropped my hands. "She did not say." She leaned toward me, her voice earnest. "But I do know he has a fiery temper. They say he shot a man in Boston in cold blood. His family is rather powerful, and they claimed it was self-defense. He never was charged. But I cannot help but wonder what else a man capable of murder could do. . . ." Her voice trailed off, the silence full of implications.

"Why do you think John would want to hurt Elizabeth?"

She pursed her lips as if contemplating the right words. Finally, she said, "I am not privy to what might have transpired between them as husband and wife. But servants talk." She kept her voice hushed in a conspiratorial manner. "They said they had awful arguments—things being thrown and mirrors broken. Even smashed furniture. Lots of shouting and screaming. Foul language, too. They are not exactly sure what all the fighting was about. They never stayed close enough to find out." She sat back in her seat, closing her eyes, her face drawn. "I hope I have not offended you with this gossip." She opened her eyes again. "But I suppose you should know."

"Thank you for telling me." It was hard to force the words out. I felt as if I had suffered a blow to my chest. I could hardly breathe. I recalled how John had courted Elizabeth, the quiet looks, the soft words, the restrained touches. I could not help but wonder if that time had been colored by the eyes of a fourteen-year-old. Perhaps I had seen only what I wanted to see. One striking memory floated back to me: the memory of Elizabeth packing her trousseau before her wedding. Even at the time, I had thought it odd that she made no mention of her soon-to-be-husband. Her biggest excitement was not that she would be getting married, but that she would be leaving Saint Simons. To see the world and have real adventures, she had said.

I poured another cup of tea for the two of us, my thoughts in turmoil. Sitting back to sip the fragrant brew, I studied the room around me with its dark woods and heavy fabrics. I somehow doubted that Elizabeth had found the adventure she craved in our grandmother's plantation in the backwoods of Louisiana.

My guest placed her cup in its saucer with a small clatter. "I hope I have not upset you. It is my sincerest wish that perhaps something I have said to you today might assist you in locating your sister. We all miss her, you know."

I nodded and stood with her. She offered me a tight smile. "I hope that you will do us the honor of a visit. Since the war, we do not get very many visitors, and it would be lovely to have a friend to chat with. Perhaps you and John would care to join us for dinner soon?" Her gaze dropped to my black dress. "My husband has told me you are in mourning, but I think it would be acceptable to a have a small dinner among friends, do you not?"

I wanted to tell her no, that I could not bear the thought of sitting alone in a carriage with John for the distance it would take to reach their plantation. But I could not turn down her invitation without seeming rude. "Yes, I would like that. I will mention it to John."

"Wonderful. Daniel will be so pleased to hear it. He has developed quite a fondness for you, you know."

"That is very kind. It will be nice having friends close by. It can get rather isolated here during the day."

The light changed in her eyes. "Yes. I believe it can."

I watched as she was helped into her carriage, and waved goodbye from the porch as she took off down the oak lane. I felt incredibly lonely all of a sudden.

The sky darkened, swallowing the shadows on the ground. The air reeked of rain, of summer grass, and of the pungent scent of the river. I looked up at the sky to see fat, billowing black clouds moving quickly toward us.

I heard a footfall behind me and I stiffened, knowing instinctively who it was. My skin tingled, betraying me, but I did not turn around.

His voice was close to my ear. "Do not believe everything she tells you. She is a horrible gossip."

"Really?" I said, pressing myself against the front railing in an attempt to move away from him. "Do you give any credence to what she tells us about her father seeing Elizabeth?"

He sighed. "Her father is quite old and very senile. It is anybody's guess as to what he really did or did not see. But I am compelled to find out for myself."

Fat drops of rain began to fall from the sky, exploding in the dry dust of the ground below us. "Then you will be leaving?"

"Yes. I feel I must." He paused for a moment, then: "I am sorry for last night. I should not have touched you as I did."

Heat flamed my cheeks as I recalled every last detail—the feel of his body against mine, the coarseness of his shirt under my hands. It was wrong, and I wanted to be sorry for it. But I could not.

"Turn around."

Reluctantly, I faced him. His eyes mirrored the storm clouds above, dark and roiling and full of pent-up energy. I could not speak.

"Will you accept my apology?"

I nodded, unable to find my voice.

He took a step closer. "I want you to know what I am sorry about. I am sorry that what I did was inappropriate. I am not sorry that I wanted to kiss you."

I gasped, swallowing my breath.

He touched my arm, then dropped his hand as if realizing we were in full view of anybody who chose to look. I lowered my gaze, no longer able to see the lit fire in his eyes. "I can understand how you must miss your wife, and our resemblance must have confused you."

Leaning down, he whispered, "No. I knew exactly who you were the moment you fell into my arms."

"You are my sister's husband." My voice was barely audible.

"There is much you do not know." He stepped back then and walked down the porch steps, his legs lean and powerful in the formfitting pants. He strode all the way to the barn without turning around once.

The sky erupted in a torrent of rain as I went back into the house, echoing the turbulence in my heart.

I stood in the middle of the foyer amid the gathering gloom. I turned this way and that, restless, wondering what I should do. Suddenly, I remembered. *The key!*

I dashed up the stairs, into the darkened hallway to my room. The wind blew the rain at the window with force, the trees outside bowing to its strength. I threw open the armoire, my hands hungrily grasping each fabric, looking for the riding habit. My fingers recognized the soft wool and I snatched it from the armoire and threw it on the bed.

A loud clap of thunder shook the window, making me jump. I lit the lamp with shaking hands, eager to get on with my search. I found the pocket and reached my hand inside, only to come up empty. I stuck my hand inside again, stretching my fingers into every corner, but nothing. It was simply not there.

I remembered Marguerite on the day of my accident, helping me out of my clothes and into my nightgown. She must have found it and put it elsewhere. I would just ask her where it was.

A door slammed downstairs, followed by the distant wail of a child. I ran back down the stairs, looking for the source of the cry. Lamps had been lit in the foyer, casting a yellow light and reflecting off something on the floor. I stooped to look and saw it was water.

Clinking silverware brought me to the dining room and I found Marguerite, her black hair shimmering with raindrops, dropping plates and silverware on the table with force.

"What is wrong?" I asked, still hearing the distant wailing. "Where is Rebecca?"

Marguerite braced her long, slender fingers on the back of a chair. Her green eyes coolly appraised me. "She is being punished. For stealing."

"But she is only a small child. Surely there has been some misunderstanding. What did she take?"

She continued to regard me with brittle eyes. "Something of mine. Something she had no business touching."

I wanted desperately to let the matter rest. This child might be part of my blood, but she did not claim my heart. I would not allow the attachment. I moved to leave the room and had reached the threshold when a flash of lightning threw an eerie blue light into the dim foyer, quickly followed by a loud crash of thunder.

The wailing became a shriek, and I stopped. Jamie had been petrified of storms and would without fail run to my bed at the first crack of thunder. I could almost feel his small shivering body in my arms as I attempted to soothe him. If Rebecca were frightened and alone, I could not ignore it.

I turned back to Marguerite with alarm. "Where is she? She sounds petrified."

She had resumed setting the table. "Leave her be. I will see to her discipline."

I rushed forward, the impulse to strike someone stronger than I had ever felt it. "Tell me where she is!"

The woman looked at me with an insolent smile. "It is no concern of yours." She turned a china plate on the table, making sure the pattern matched the one next to it.

I ran out of the room, listening to the crying to orient myself. It sounded so far away, almost as if it were outside.

I headed toward the back door, then raced off the back porch and into the rain, my ears picking up the sound of the shrieking, this time louder. I ran past the kitchen garden and into the grassy field behind the house and toward the pond.

I saw her then, a forlorn waif in sodden pale yellow, a withered buttercup felled by the rain. She was humped over in the grass, her small hands over her ears, and by the time I reached her, the shrieking had stopped.

I called her name and she jerked her face up. Like a drowning soul, she reached her arms up to me and I lifted her, holding her tightly against my body. She pointed back to the ground and I spotted Samantha, as sodden as Rebecca. I leaned over and handed her to Rebecca. The child hardly weighed more than a puppy, and I easily carried her through the grass and back toward the house, my skirts heavy with rain.

We met John at the back door, his expression questioning. I walked past him into the house and waited for him to shut the door. "Marguerite left her out in the storm as a punishment for stealing. She is just a child." I hissed my words at him, thinking he had somehow condoned Marguerite's behavior.

"Good God," he said, his voice breaking. He stepped toward us and reached for his daughter.

The little girl lifted her head from my shoulder and peered at her father. "Papa," she said, then buried her face again.

"She is still scared. Let me bring her upstairs and put her in some dry clothes and I will bring her to you."

His face darkened. "No. I want her now. I am her father."

I looked at him coldly. "And I am her aunt. She has just had a terrible fright and she wants to stay with me. Unless you want to terrify her further, I would suggest you leave her with me."

He looked taken aback, but did not stop me as I carried Rebecca upstairs and into her room.

I pulled a blanket off the bed and dried her and Samantha with it as best I could before wrapping it around Rebecca's small body. It took a while to calm her, but I sat in the small rocker and sang to her all the songs that I had used to calm Jamie. They were hard to force out at first, but after a few stumbles, the words came more easily.

Eventually, I dried her hair and changed her clothes, hiding my tears from her as I touched her sweet white skin and thought of my son. About the same age as Rebecca, he had just begun to grow out of his babyhood, his bones pushing through the layer of baby fat on his arms and legs, giving him a new angular look. The image of that emerging boy was the only thing I had left.

As I brushed out her hair, I marveled at its silkiness and its blond paleness, so different from Jamie's black hair, but similar, too. It had the same thickness and even the same wave at the back of the head that forced the hair to stick up regardless of what I did with the brush. I impulsively bent and kissed that little part of my son, causing Rebecca to turn around quickly, looking at me with those eyes. It was almost as if she knew I wasn't seeing her, but wishing that perhaps I would.

A nagging question forced itself into my head and I knew I had to voice it. "Rebecca, remember in the attic, how you showed me that letterbox and then you ran away? Were you the one who locked me inside?"

Again, those bright blue eyes studied me carefully, an understanding far beyond her years clearly visible in their depths. She shook her head.

"Do you know who did?"

She shook her head again and buried her face into Samantha's hair, which now smelled like wet wool.

I held Rebecca's hand and led her to the door, preparing to bring her down to supper with her father. She slid her hand from mine and ran back into her room. I watched as she took a china doll off the bed. Instead of bringing it to me, she turned the doll upside down and shook it.

Something clattered on the floor and Rebecca stooped to pick it up. With a mischievous grin on her face, she walked back to me, her arm poised as if she wanted to give me something.

I opened my palm toward her, my curiosity aroused. The small brass key bounced into my hand, the bright metal winking at me again in the lamplight.

Chapter Eight

—◆—

I knelt in the foyer, my sleeves rolled up, my hands covered in beeswax. I had been working for nearly an hour and had yet to cover even a quarter of the floor with wax. My back ached at the thought of then going back over it with a buffing cloth, but it felt good to be busy again, to be doing something useful. It was much more desirable than worrying about Elizabeth or letting my thoughts settle on her husband. Rebecca sat on the bottom stair, mimicking my silly alphabet song. Every once in a while she would stop, and I would look up at her and find those blue eyes watching me intently.

I bent my head back to my task, only to jerk it up suddenly as the child began to hum the old, haunting tune again. I listened for a while, then resumed my task, the little voice repeating the simple melody over and over. Although I still could not put a name to it, I found it strangely comforting, as if I had heard it as a child, during a period of my life where all was well and safe.

The night before I had sat down at the table with John, glad of Rebecca's presence. He had informed us that Marguerite would continue with her household duties and assisting me, but that she would no longer be serving as Rebecca's nanny. That responsibility was being handed over to me. I resented being told rather than asked. Then, peering at Rebecca's waiflike face, I realized the good judgment behind his decision. Anything would be better than leaving her in the care of someone who would put a small child out in a thunderstorm as punishment for a minor infraction.

I questioned him as to why he did not let Marguerite go. He had regarded me with hooded eyes before explaining that Elizabeth was very attached to Marguerite and that they would decide what to do with her once Elizabeth returned. There was also an obligation to the

Lewistons. Marguerite was like a member of the family to Clara, but Clara, like most of the families in the county, could not afford to rehire her if she ceased working at Whispering Oaks. She would have no place to go.

I looked up at the sound of the doors to John's study sliding open and Rebecca's joyful cry of "Papa." John, dressed for traveling and carrying a valise, approached, his dark eyes distracted. He dropped the valise and bent to pick up his daughter, his hand absently stroking her blond plaits.

I stood suddenly, the blood rushing from my head. Dizzy, I put out my hand to steady myself and clutched John's coat sleeve. His strong fingers gripped my arm. "Are you all right?"

Nodding, I pulled away. "I must have stood too quickly."

He and Rebecca stared at me with the same penetrating gaze, one dark blue and one obsidian. "Did you eat enough at breakfast? I have noticed how very thin you are, and I feel it is my duty to see that you get enough to eat while you are here."

"I can take care of myself. I do not need a nursemaid."

"Perhaps you do." He looked at the smudge of wax I had left on his sleeve. I did not apologize.

He glanced at the wadded rags and thick paste congealed on the wood floor. "And Mary or Delphine should be doing this—not you."

"I am used to keeping busy, and this needed to be done. I want the house to be in order when Elizabeth returns."

We shared a moment of silence as I watched his face. He seemed unsure of a response. Finally, he said, "I doubt your sister would want you cleaning floors. Do you not have a hobby or some other ladylike pursuit to occupy your time?"

I crossed my arms. "I did. I used to paint. Before the war. Before the Yankees burned my house and my studio and all my paints and canvases. Besides." I looked down at my hand and scraped a clump of wax out of a fingernail. "There was nothing left to paint."

Patrick O'Rourke appeared at the door, a hat crumpled in his hands. "If your bag is ready, sir, I will pack your horse." His gaze flickered uncomfortably to me, then moved to Rebecca. Slowly, he raised his eyes to John.

"Thank you, Patrick. I believe I have everything . . . except for my pipe. I cannot seem to find it, and I am starting to think somebody may have made off with it." He patted his coat as if hoping it might appear, then handed his carpetbag to the coachman. The man, with a look that was almost like relief, tipped his forelock and left, sliding his hat back over dirty hair.

John kissed his daughter on the cheek and let her slide from his grasp. Addressing me, he said, "I am going to Baton Rouge. I plan to be back with or without Elizabeth in three days. I expect you to keep an eye on Rebecca and see to her well-being."

"That is something I need not be told. She will be well cared for, I assure you."

His mouth turned upward in a smile, and I was amazed at the transformation. John McMahon was a handsome man, despite his brooding, dark nature. But when he smiled, he was devastating. "I am quite sure she is in capable hands."

He picked up his hat from a hall table, then turned to leave.

I squared my shoulders, snatches of my conversation with Clara coming back to me with full lucidity. "But was my sister in capable hands?"

He turned slowly to face me, his black eyes glittering in the morning light streaming from the windows. "That would depend."

I waited for him to continue. Rebecca moved to my side and wrapped her fist in my skirt. I broke the silence. "On what?"

"On whose hands she put her trust in." He placed his hat on his head and opened the door. "Goodbye, Catherine. I will see you in three days. Perhaps Elizabeth can answer your questions better than I can. I am afraid she is as much a mystery to me as she is to you."

He strode across the porch, and I followed.

"Why were you so near the attic the night I was locked inside?"

A dark eyebrow arched over an eye. "My daughter is wont to wander the house at night when she should be in bed." He glanced briefly at the child, who stood as if attached to my skirts. "I went to check on her, and when I found her bed empty, I went in search of her. I heard the noise in the attic, which brought me to the door. If you are asking me if I locked it, no, I did not." His eyes sparked. "If you are done with this interrogation, I must be leaving."

I stepped forward. "What if you do not find Elizabeth? Then what?"

He looked down at his daughter and his face softened. Then a deep scowl covered his features. "Then my daughter and I will resume our lives. I daresay the absence of her mother will not have a detrimental effect on either one of us."

Without another word, he strode down the steps and toward his waiting horse.

I stood, watching him walk away, wondering once again at his words. But the one person who could answer my questions had disappeared. I stopped my thoughts, realizing that I needed her presence more to reassure me that her husband had not harmed her than to be assured that she was safe. I bit my lip, ashamed, then looked down at the little girl who was tugging at my skirts. I wiped my hands as best I could with a clean cloth, then lifted her in my arms. "Come on, little peanut. Let us go find that box in the attic."

I walked up the stairs slowly, trying to get Rebecca to talk to me. She rarely spoke, but I suspected she saw everything that went on in the house. I needed to earn her trust so that she would be more willing to share confidences.

"How did you know that box was in the attic? Did your mama show you?"

Those incredible eyes stared back at me, and she popped her thumb in her mouth.

I reached the landing and headed down the corridor. I recalled the sound of stealthy footsteps in the hall and her confession about how she liked to watch people without their knowing.

"Did you use to see your mother in the attic? And she did not know you were there?"

Without removing her thumb, she gave me an impish smile.

We reached the attic door and I stopped. I put Rebecca down on the floor and knelt in front of her. "I need you to stay here while I go up, just in case there are still bats. I do not think so. Mr. O'Rourke promised me he had chased them all out and mended the window. But I want to make sure you are safe, all right?"

She nodded, her luminous eyes wide.

I opened the door slowly, feeling the ghost of the apprehension I had felt the previous night. Pushing the door as far as it would go, I headed up the stairs.

The new boards in the window had darkened the attic considerably, and I had not thought to bring a light. I waited a moment for my eyes to adjust, then moved to the spot I recalled seeing the letterbox.

It was not there.

I moved forward, my gaze searching the dusty floor, sure I was in the right spot. I saw the trunk it had fallen from and my extinguished lamp—even the dust appeared disturbed on the floor in front of it—but the letterbox was conspicuously absent.

I lowered myself to my hands and knees, determined to find it and refusing to accept the implication if, indeed, it were missing. I crawled among the trunks and old furniture, disturbing years of accumulated dust, making it rise from the floor like a cloudy phoenix, sparkling in the sliver of light from the boarded window.

Worry and a nagging fear tugged at me. I knew where the box had been, and it simply was not there. I stood, ready to give up, when a small object caught my attention. It lay not three feet away from where I searched, its obvious position in the middle of the floor indicating that perhaps it had been dropped rather than hidden. Stooping, I picked it up and held it between my fingers. It was a gentleman's pipe.

I tapped the bowl against my palm and let the tobacco sprinkle into my hand. The scent rose to my nose—a pungent, leaflike smell that suddenly reminded me of my father. A pang of homesickness engulfed me for a moment, weighing heavily on my spirit. I shrugged it off and let the tobacco fall to the floor.

Somewhere in the house a door shut, the sound reaching me almost like a jolt of air. Putting the pipe in my pocket with the key, I walked toward the top of the steps and called down. "Rebecca? Are you still there?"

After hearing no answer, I walked down the steps to the hallway, looking for my niece.

"Hello? Is anybody home?" a female voice called from the foyer. I was quite certain I recognized the voice.

"Clara? Is that you? I will be down in a moment."

I closed the attic door behind me, then brushed the dust off my dress before heading for the stairway. I patted my pocket and felt the outlines of the key and pipe as I descended the stairs.

Clara Lewiston waited for me in the foyer, breathing heavily, as if she had just walked a great distance. She dabbed at her forehead with a handkerchief, blotting away perspiration. Her eyebrows lifted as she caught sight of me with my sleeves rolled up on my forearms like a cleaning woman. Her gaze moved to the wax and rags pushed against the wall and the half-waxed floor. Like any well-bred Southerner, she ignored the implication completely.

I had to still my breath so I could hear her quiet voice. "I apologize for letting myself in, but there does not seem to be anybody here to answer the door. And it is so hot outside." She snapped open a fan and fluttered it in front of her face.

I flushed, taking her comment as an insult directed toward my sister. Before I could stammer out an excuse, she continued.

"Please, you need not apologize for Elizabeth. She told me all about her problems with the servants. Their superstitions are quite silly, but they do take them seriously."

"What do you mean?" I recalled Marguerite mentioning the servants and their beliefs in the supernatural and wanted to hear more.

Her pale eyes shifted as she surveyed the room as if to ascertain we were alone. "Perhaps we should take a walk outside. These walls might have ears."

My curiosity piqued, I excused myself for a moment to find Rebecca. She was in the kitchen, being plied with sweets by Rose. Her doll, Samantha, was conspicuously absent. "Where did you go, peanut? You were supposed to wait for me in the hallway."

Her wide blue eyes stared up at me, a hint of mischief making them sparkle. "It is a secret," she said, taking another bite of peanut brittle.

I felt Rose's gaze on me and dropped the subject. I gave Rose instructions to keep my niece occupied and within her sight until I returned.

I found my visitor on the porch. As we walked, she slipped her hand companionably into the crook of my elbow. Watching her from the corner of my eye, I studied her appearance. Again she was awash in an unflattering, monochromatic beige. She did have beautifully smooth skin, but the sallow color was even further emphasized by the shade of her clothing. Pale eyebrows nearly disappeared into her forehead, and her lashes were almost nonexistent, lending an appearance of a blank canvas on which the artist had yet to apply color.

Again I wondered what had sparked the attraction of love at first sight for Dr. Lewiston. Even Clara's personality seemed timid and droll against his warmth and charm. But I was no expert on what lay inside a man's heart. I had been married for four years to a man I later learned I had not known at all.

We walked in silence down the avenue of oaks, a light breeze teasing the tops of the trees, making the leaves whisper like a hushed conversation. I waited for Clara to speak, but she seemed content to walk by my side, avoiding mud puddles and ignoring the heat that swallowed us as completely as a wave from the ocean.

"Clara, please tell me. What happened to all of the servants?"

She clucked her tongue, reminding me of an old woman I had known on Saint Simons. She had no teeth and had been wont to snap her tongue against her empty gums at the most inappropriate times. "I hope you do not think I am gossiping, but as Elizabeth's sister, I suppose you should know." She squeezed my arm in a reassuring manner, and I nodded for her to continue. "It all started innocently enough." She looked down at our feet, as if wondering if this would be called gossip. "It began at the Blackmores' annual masquerade ball. I suggested she rethink her costume, but I am sure you know how stubborn she could be. Elizabeth dressed up as that Indian princess who is supposed to haunt the pond in the back of your property. She even carried a doll to portray the poor dead baby. Her gown was absolutely shocking—it did not appear as if she wore stays or any petticoats at all. Just a doeskin sheath and her dark hair in plaits with feathers."

She stopped walking for a moment and looked at me, her eyes blinking in the bright light. "She was very beautiful, and the men could not take their eyes off of her. I daresay most of the female population of the county was scandalized. But the servants thought she really was the ghost, and fled the house that night after seeing her."

We paused again, tilting our heads back to gain access to the faint river breeze that moved among the oaks and down the lane. "Of course, that was not the only problem dear Elizabeth had with servants."

She closed her mouth, as if she were done speaking. I cleared my throat. "What other problems did she have?"

Watery eyes looked into mine as a thin line of perspiration beaded her upper lip. "Well, some of them felt the need to approach her husband with problems they had with her. Elizabeth believed that they should do whatever she asked them at the drop of a hat, regardless of whatever other job they were expected to do." She sniffed. "If they complained to John, Elizabeth made their lives so miserable that they would soon be compelled to leave."

I stopped, tilting my head, straining to identify the odd sound coming to us on the breeze. "Elizabeth and I were not raised that way, Clara. I do not know what could have made her change so. But I love her, regardless of what she may have done, and I will welcome her back. And Rebecca needs her mother."

I watched Clara as she pursed her lips and then turned her head, hearing the same sound I was. Her eyebrows knitted together, forming parentheses of wrinkles on the bridge of her nose.

"Do you know what that is?" I closed my eyes, concentrating on the faint musical chiming.

She dropped her hand from my arm and began walking briskly to the end of the lane. I followed her, noticing how the sound grew louder. She stopped under an oak and looked up under the veil of Spanish moss. I came and stood next to her and raised my eyes to the tree.

Five empty bottles, in an assortment of colors, hung by thin twine ropes from a tall branch. The breeze, in its effort to dance through the oaks, would whistle into the bottles before escaping again, creating an odd melody. I found them enchanting and turned to my companion to tell her so, but stopped.

Clara's face had stiffened as she stared at the wind chimes with disapproval. "I would have your man Mr. O'Rourke take this down immediately. It is pagan and should not be allowed on your property."

I looked up again at the bottles, trying to find anything ominous about them. "Do not be silly, Clara. It is just a wind chime."

Her eyes widened to form perfect little circles. "Oh no. They are used to ward off so-called evil spirits." She nodded her head knowingly. "Marguerite told me all about those African beliefs when I was growing up. It is dangerous and sacrilegious and is not allowed on my property. I doubt John knows about it." She placed a trembling hand on my arm. "You do not suppose . . ."

She stopped talking, then looked directly into my eyes but did not speak.

Finally, I spoke, my voice strained. "You do not suppose this has anything to do with Elizabeth's disappearance, do you?"

She glanced away as I looked furtively back at the bottles as they began to moan again in the wind.

She shook her head quickly, causing the thin ringlets on the sides of her head to bounce. A forced smile crept up her face. "No, of course not. I am sure everything is all right and this does not mean anything. Elizabeth will come home. You will see."

The sky darkened suddenly, carrying with it a humid breeze, thick with the scent of rain. The bottles clanked against one another with reckless abandon, the sound filling me with apprehension.

A heavy drop of rain slid against my cheek. Turning around, I grabbed Clara's arm and began to lead her quickly back toward the house, the eerie sound of the lost wind in the bottles diligently following us. As the tall columns of the house came into sight, I turned to Clara to ask her to clarify what sorts of evil spirits at Whispering Oaks might need warding off. I opened my mouth to speak, only to be silenced by an ear-piercing scream from somewhere behind the house.

I lifted my skirts, not caring what kind of undergarments I might be displaying, and ran as fast as I could around the house. I paused near the kitchen and saw Rose and Delphine coming out the kitchen door, their eyes wide with fright.

"Where is Rebecca?" I shouted. My stays pressed tightly into my chest, making it difficult to catch my breath.

They both looked past me, toward the pond. Delphine pointed. "She went to get her doll."

Spots danced before my eyes, but I sucked in as much of a breath as I could and ran in the direction of the pond.

Something floated in the middle of the water. Something with a head and arms and legs. My head seemed to explode in white puffs of air as I reached the edge of the pond, the water just licking at my shoes. Raindrops dotted the water's surface, making it move and sway like a living thing. My lungs refused to expand and I could not seem to breathe in enough air. The body continued to float in and out of my vision, my mind screaming to me to put a foot in the water and to dive under the cool depths and rescue whoever it was.

But I could not move. Huge black circles now hovered before my eyes, obliterating my sight. I fell to my knees and somehow registered the piercing wail again. *Jamie, do not let me fail you again,* I thought, sinking into the grass. The sweet smell of oranges filled my nostrils, so thick I could taste the fruit. Was I in my grandmother's orange grove? The image of the body in the water flitted through my mind again. *Rebecca?*

Another voice cut through my consciousness. A man's voice. "Catherine!"

Strong hands moved under my head. I gulped in air, my breathing calmed enough that I could fill my lungs again, clearing my vision. My eyes flickered open and I stared into John's worried face.

"Catherine?"

I nodded my head to show I had heard him, then pointed toward the pond. "Rebecca." Rain pelted my face, soaking it, dripping inside the collar of my dress.

He bent his head close to mine and said, "Rebecca's fine. Somebody threw her doll in the water—that is all." Warm hands brushed the rain and matted hair from my eyes as the fear gripping my belly eased its hold. But there was something in his eyes that told me all was not well.

"Why are you here? I thought . . . you were in . . . Baton Rouge." I lay my head back against his arms, exhausted, still struggling to breathe, the stays cutting into my skin as I gulped in air.

"I was on my way but had not gone very far. Patrick O'Rourke rode out to call me back." His jaws clenched.

"What is wrong?" I whispered.

His arm trembled beneath me. "They have found Elizabeth." He looked away for a moment, then gazed down at me again, his eyes hard. "She is dead."

CHAPTER NINE

———◆———

The wind moaned through the oaks that surrounded the house and slapped the windows and roof with rain. A full day had passed since Elizabeth had been found, and she now lay in a hastily made pine coffin in the front parlor, lit candles burning at her head and feet and around the room. The house accepted her presence without even a stir, as nothing could make the pall in the old rooms darker.

The pinched, waxlike face of the woman in the pine box bore no resemblance to the beautiful sister of my memory. No wind teased her hair; no sun brightened her eyes and highlighted her hair—nor would it ever do so again. The sister I had known and loved was gone. But she had been gone long before her last breath had left her. The person who lay before me was a stranger, and I had no more grief to give.

I need you, dear sister. I am so afraid. I leaned over the edge of the coffin and whispered, "What were you so afraid of, Elizabeth?"

A hand closed about my arm and I stifled a scream. I looked up into the steel gaze of Elizabeth's husband. He abruptly dropped his fingers. "Why do you think she was afraid?"

I swallowed, the sound audible in the still room. "She . . . wrote me. She said that she needed me. That she was afraid of something . . ." I let my words drift away as my eyes strayed back to the woman in the coffin.

"Do you think it was me she feared?"

My head jerked back to regard him. I paused for a moment, searching for an answer. Finally, I said, "I do not know. She did not say. And now her secrets will be buried with her."

He moved closer and I flinched. Something heavy and foreboding filled the room, not all of it due to the open casket. Leaning toward me, he whispered, "Perhaps some secrets are best buried."

I held my ground, my back pressed against the smooth pine box. "Are you saying that the circumstances of her death are best kept secret?"

John took a step back, allowing me room to move away from him. He looked down at his wife, his face hidden in shadow. "Perhaps they are." His eyes met mine again, and a chill tiptoed up my spine. "But not for the reasons you might think."

I briefly wished for some semblance of fear to hold back the words, but that emotion had long been too elusive. "Did you have anything to do with Elizabeth's death?"

He stared at me and said calmly, "No."

I did not say anything, afraid my doubt would show in my voice. The rain continued to punish the house, reverberating on the windowpanes. I touched Elizabeth's cold hand, the bones small and fragile and so much like my own. "Why is her skin still so perfect? She was left lying in the cane field for so long. . . ."

John turned to stare out the window, the shadows of raindrops covering his face. "I saw Elizabeth there. Nobody would go near her. There was not a mark on her—not even bugs crawling in the vicinity of where her body was found." He turned his head toward his wife for a moment. "It was so odd. And then Rufus became hysterical and had to be taken away, mumbling something about her being fixed with a curse." He faced me, his expression unreadable. "There is to be an inquiry. They will be taking her body tomorrow morning to determine the cause of death before we can have her burial service. I hope that it will not upset you overly much."

I shook my head, mute for a moment, the image of Elizabeth's pale, sightless eyes staring up from a sea of sugarcane vivid in my mind. "No. It will be a relief to be able to find some answers."

A clearing of the throat brought our attention to the doorway. Dr. Lewiston stood, his hat in his hands, his eyes fixed on the dark box in the corner. A candle at the foot of the coffin fluttered, then died, leaving the acrid scent of burnt wax.

"Your man O'Rourke sent for me. My condolences, John, Catherine, for your loss." He seemed to visibly struggle to move his gaze from the coffin to his old friend. "If there is anything I can do . . ." His voice died in the heavy silence.

John turned his back to the doctor and faced the coffin again. "Yes, Daniel. There is something. And I would like to speak to you in private."

I nodded and left the room, closing the door behind me. I stood in the darkening foyer, listening to the murmur of voices behind me and of the windows rattling from the assault of rain. The crystal candelabra above had been lit to chase away the gathering gloom. With a start, I noticed the large mirror over the hallway console had been covered with a white sheet. I moved to stand in front of it and saw Marguerite hovering in the alcove below the stairs. She had been avoiding me ever since I had been given the responsibility of attending to Rebecca's needs, and she must have stepped back in hopes of me not seeing her.

"Why has the mirror been covered?"

Marguerite stepped forward, the whites of her eyes almost glowing in the dimness. "To protect the soul of the dead. If a soul sees her reflection, then she will be trapped in the mirror forever."

A shutter banged against the front of the house like a disembodied shout. The crystal beads jostled one another as the flames on the chandelier sputtered from an unseen breath.

"That is nonsense," I said, trying to keep the edge of unease out of my voice. I reached up to try to pull the sheet off the mahogany acanthus leaves at the top of the mirror. They held fast, and I heard Marguerite's throaty chuckle.

"They do not want you to take off that sheet, Miss Catherine."

My hands stilled. "Who is 'they'?"

Marguerite stepped closer to me, her voice almost a whisper in my ear. "The undead. They do not want you messing with what is theirs."

I resisted the urge to move back. "My sister's soul is in heaven. All of this talk is superstitious nonsense and it will serve no purpose except to frighten Rebecca." I gave another tug to the sheet but it remained unyielding.

Her eyes flickered. "Then you best get down on your knees and pray for her soul. But I think you will be wasting your time. Only repentant souls are saved." She stepped back. "I need to see to supper."

I listened as her soft footsteps padded across the foyer. The men's voices in the room behind me grew steadily louder. John's voice, deeper, more stern, seemed to be asking the same question over and over, while Daniel answered with a strained voice, the volume of his words escalating each time he spoke. The one word I understood was "No."

I left the sheet on the mirror, making a mental note to take care of it later. Quickly I walked toward the stairs, not wanting to be privy to the men's conversation. My fleeting thought of staying and listening flamed my cheeks, and I hurried up the steps, intent on a brief respite of sleep.

As I reached the top of the stairs, a high-pitched keening sound struck my ears. I stopped, my hand clutching the railing as I listened closely. It wasn't keening. Instead it was the old haunting tune that Rebecca favored, and my skin puckered as I heard the odd tune hummed at such a high pitch as to be almost a cry.

The sound stopped almost as soon as it had begun. With hesitating steps, I walked toward the child's bedroom. I pushed open her door slowly and found myself staring into Rebecca's empty room. A lamp had been lit, and I stayed in the threshold for a few moments, listening to the dying rain.

"Rebecca?" I called out softly.

The only answer was the running of small feet and a slamming door somewhere down the corridor behind me. I rushed out of the room and stopped suddenly. The doll Samantha lay sprawled on the floor at the end of the long hallway, her legs caught in the opening of the attic door.

Ignoring the blood thumping in my temples, I approached the attic door with purposeful footsteps. "Rebecca!" I called again. "Come here this instant. This is not the time for playing."

Approaching the door, I picked up the doll, still damp from its adventure in the pond, and peered up the dark steps. "Rebecca! If you are up in the attic, I ask that you come down now, or I will have to punish you."

Somewhere deep in the recesses of the great house, I heard the humming again, faint and liquid, oozing up the walls toward me. It seemed to come from the very plaster. Clutching the doll tightly against my chest, I stepped back and into a rock-hard chest. Strong hands held my arms. With a deep breath, I turned.

John's eyes regarded me calmly. "Catherine, what is wrong?"

I swallowed and kept my voice steady. "I am trying to find Rebecca. I think she is playing tricks on me."

He looked past me and up the attic stairs. "Do you think she may have run into the attic again?"

"At first I thought so, but I just heard her somewhere else in the house." I indicated the doll. "But she had to have been here just a moment ago, because I found this here. She must be very fast, because she was able to run down the corridor and down the steps before I could even turn around."

John took the doll. "I think I will take a look in the attic anyway."

He stepped past me and took the stairs two at a time. The wood floor creaked as he walked overhead and softly called his daughter's name.

I heard him at the top of the steps and watched as he slowly descended the stairs. His brow was furrowed as if in deep thought.

I wondered at his expression. "Is everything all right? Did you see any sign of Rebecca?"

He shook his head. "No. I didn't see anything." He stepped past me, still holding the oversized rag doll. It reeked of wet wool and pond water, and the old feeling of panic settled in my veins again. I placed my palms flat against the wall behind me, trying to steady myself.

John looked at me. "Are you all right?"

I nodded, forcing my breathing to return to normal. I searched for something to distract my thoughts. "I heard raised voices downstairs. Does Dr. Lewiston know anything more about Elizabeth?"

He turned his back to me as if preparing to leave but remained where he was, his attention on the damp doll in his hands. "Yes, actually. He did."

I moved closer to him, my hand raised to place on his arm. I let it drift back to my side. Being this near to him affected my senses in ways I could not control, and to touch him might be disastrous. "What did he say?"

He tilted his head, an ebony brow cocked like a crow in flight. "I told you that some secrets are best buried with the dead. Perhaps this would be one of them." He started to walk away, his boots thudding softly on the carpet runner.

I walked quickly toward him. "If this concerns Elizabeth, then I demand to be told. I am stronger than you seem to think and . . ." My words died in my throat as it constricted, and I thought for one horrifying moment that I might cry. Perhaps it was his brief look of sympathy as he turned to face me, or perhaps it was the shock of my sister's death that suddenly paralyzed me, but I found myself standing in front of John, unable to speak a word.

Inexplicably, he reached a hand to my face, and I did not flinch. He wiped away a tear and let the back of his hand caress my cheek. "My dear Catherine. You have already been through so much." His hand stilled as I trembled at his touch. "I am loath to add to your burden."

I turned my head aside, making him drop his hand. "My burdens are not your concern. Tell me what Dr. Lewiston told you. I need to know."

His eyes darkened as he stared dispassionately at me. "Elizabeth was with child. That was the reason she went to see Dr. Lewiston before she died." He turned from me once more, the doll hanging limply at his side.

I raised my hand to touch his shoulder but let it fall. "I am sorry. This is a double loss for you."

He shook his head and stepped away. "The child was not mine."

His words reverberated in my mind as I watched him approach the stairs.

I followed on his heels and clutched at the railing. "Wait." I nearly screamed the word. "What do you mean?"

I watched his jaw work, as if negotiating a difficult mouthful. "I do not wish to sound indelicate, but you have been a married woman and understand the affairs between man and wife. Suffice it to say that I know, without a doubt, that I could not possibly be the father of her unborn child."

He paused for a moment, as if to gauge my reaction. Seemingly satisfied that I would not faint and take a plunge over the banister, he turned and continued his descent.

I stood at the top of the stairs, looking down on him, my mind reeling from the implications and trying to think clearly. "But, that would mean . . ." My face flushed hotly.

He turned to stare up at me, his eyes hard. "Yes, Catherine. Your assumptions would be correct." He bowed slightly, then turned away. "If you will excuse me, then, I must go find my daughter and return her doll."

I listened until his footsteps faded away. My gaze strayed to the closed parlor door, the stilled body of my sister lying behind it, and I wondered, not for the first time, what other secrets might have died with her. I fled for my bedroom. Lying on my bed, I stared up at the canopy until the beat of my heart had returned to normal and I could fill my lungs with air again. Finally, I turned to my side, my sister's name whispered on my lips. "Was this why you were so afraid? And would this be reason enough for your husband to end your life?" I listened to the dying winds as they blew goodbye to the old house by whistling under the eaves, the sound eerily like that of a crying baby. I blinked, feeling the tears run down my face. "Who were you really, Elizabeth? I do not seem to recognize you at all."

I let the tears fall until none were left. My gaze roamed the room, searching for what, I did not know. Finally I settled on the gown I had worn the previous day. Delphine had hung it outside the armoire to dry thoroughly before putting away. I sat up quickly, the room spinning for a moment. Slowly, I slid from the bed and approached the dress. My fingers crept to the large patch pocket and pulled out the gold key. Reaching in again, my hand closed over something smooth and hard, and I lifted it out. I opened my palm and stared at the pipe, the smell of tobacco still fresh. I recalled John's puzzled expression as he descended the attic stairs and felt with certainty that I knew why.

I need you, dear sister. I am so afraid. The pipe fell from my hand, landing with a small *thud*, and sprinkling dark tobacco on the cream-colored rug like spots of blood.

Soldiers came at dawn the next morning to take Elizabeth away. I did not venture downstairs, but watched from my bedroom window. I saw John speaking with familiarity to the captain. The captain squeezed John's shoulder, and I wondered if they knew each other from the war and if their friendship might bear some weight on the proceedings.

I listened as the soldiers scuffled their way into the parlor and began carrying out the coffin. A man cursed and something crashed to the floor. With a sickening feeling in the pit of my stomach, I raced to the top of the stairs, clutching my wrapper tightly about me.

One end of the coffin had dropped, a deep gash in the freshly polished wood floor bearing testament to what had happened. The lid had slipped, revealing Elizabeth's face, her sightless eyes now open and staring directly at me. I turned my face away, more from respect for the dead than from any fear I might have felt. Despite the vagaries of my life over the last few days, I stubbornly clung to my fearlessness. If war, starvation, and grief had not yet killed me, then surely they had made me stronger. For seeing the corpse of my sister, her clear blue eyes coldly appraising, did not scare me. But what had put her in her coffin certainly did—if not for my own sake, then for that of her child, Rebecca.

I turned back to see John placing coins over Elizabeth's eyes to keep them closed. With impatience, he instructed the soldiers to seal the coffin again. They hesitated, and more than one remarked on the incredible preservation of the body. If not for the still chest, she appeared to be sleeping.

With the cloying scent of freshly hewn pine heavy in the air, they lifted the coffin once more and carried it out the door to the waiting wagon. I stayed where I was at the top of the stairs, listening until I could no longer hear the wheels rolling down the long drive. Before I could turn to go, John reentered the house and stood at the bottom of the steps, looking up at me with a shadowed face.

"You look like an avenging angel." His gaze swept over me, lingering on the almost-transparent white fabric of my wrap that fell over my legs and then moving slowly upward until our eyes met.

Unbidden, my pulse raced faster. I clutched the fabric tightly under my neck. "Perhaps I am."

His eyes darkened as he put one booted foot on the lowest step. "What do you mean?" He climbed another step toward me.

I did not back away. "I meant that perhaps I am here for a reason."

He did not drop his gaze but continued to climb the stairs. When he reached the step below me, we were at eye level. I did not blink under his close scrutiny. "Tell me, then, Catherine. What do you think happened to Elizabeth?"

I dropped a hand from my wrapper and reached for the banister behind me. "I do not know. I think we all must wait until we learn of the cause of death." My pulse raced and skittered, but not from fear. What I felt was much more of a curse.

He was close enough that when he spoke, his warm breath pushed at the fine hairs lying on my forehead. "Do you think I had anything to do with her death?"

I could feel my own heart beating. The need to ask him again pressed down on me. "Did you?"

His black eyes stared directly into mine. "As I told you before, and as I will doubtlessly be forced to say repeatedly, no. I did not."

He stepped past me and into the upstairs hallway. I faced his retreating back. "Clara Lewiston said you shot and killed a man in cold blood in Boston."

Stopping, he turned around. "It was self-defense—which was proven in a court of law. It is public record, if you should choose to question my word. As for idle gossip, you are bound to hear quite a bit. Unfortunately, speaking ill of the dead is not something the people around here shun. I would ignore it all. Although some of the rumors might hold a grain of truth, I will not justify them with any remarks and cause a scandal. I want Rebecca to hold her head up high when she is old enough to care about such things."

As if summoned, a door opened down the hallway, followed by the quick scampering of small feet. "Papa!" John reached for Rebecca and scooped the child up in his arms, holding her close to him. His face softened as he held her, the love and adoration he felt clearly etched on his usually forbidding features. He was undoubtedly the same darkly handsome man who had the disconcerting habit of stealing my breath away, but he was almost unrecognizable when with Rebecca.

He faced me. "You need to get dressed, Catherine. They want you down at the town hall for questioning. I told the captain we would be there before noon."

I nodded and watched as he carried Rebecca back to her room. His broad shoulders cradled her head, his strong fingers gently patting her hair. Could a man who loved a child as much as he obviously did also be capable of the ultimate act of violence?

A movement from downstairs caught my attention and I found my gaze drawn to the large mirror in the foyer. I had taken off the sheet and had heard no more about the subject from Marguerite. Something dark and shadowy flickered in the depths of the glass, and I started. Surely it had been a trick of the eye or the reflection of a bird flying outside the window.

I leaned over the banister to get a better look and spied Marguerite standing in the dining room doorway and watching me with a smug expression. I straightened and went to my room without acknowledging her, the sound of Rebecca's humming suddenly flooding the house with its melancholy and mournful tune.

CHAPTER TEN

———◆———

J ohn helped me into the buggy and then slid in next to me, taking
the reins. The roads were full of puddled ruts from the recent rains,
the air thick and heavy. Navigating the road took most of John's concentration, and I used the opportunity to scrutinize him closely.

He wore an elegant coat of black wool broadcloth and a light gray
silk waistcoat. A gold chain hung from the pocket, and I recalled that
Elizabeth had purchased him a watch for their wedding and wondered
if it was the same one. Being tall and broad shouldered, he wore his
clothes well, his taut muscles discreetly covered but as obvious as if he
were shirtless. I recalled how he had turned heads on his visit to Saint
Simons. As a child of fourteen, I had been immune, but now, as a
woman of almost twenty-two years, the physical force of his presence
was impossible to ignore.

Staying as far away from him on the single seat as I could, I allowed
my gaze to travel the length of his powerful body, watching the shift of
his leg muscles through the fine cloth of his pants. I lifted my gaze to
his hands, bare of gloves. I had felt the gentleness of his touch but knew
also of their hidden strength. The fine muscles moved under the skin as
he handled the reins, and I imagined those same fingers touching Elizabeth as a man would touch his wife. How would those hands have
reached for her if confronted with evidence of her infidelity?

My gaze shifted to his face. Lean and tanned from his daily work
on the plantation, it hinted of brutal strength and unforgiving words.
But I had seen it soften as he looked at his daughter, and fleetingly
wondered what it would be like to be the object of such a gaze. The
brim of his hat covered his black hair and shaded his eyes to such an
extent that I didn't realize at first that he was watching me closely.

Flushing, I turned away, an apology ready on my lips as the wheel hit a rut and sent me skidding over to him, my hands greedily clutching his coat. He used his arm to steady me, my face pressed momentarily into the shoulder of his coat.

I lifted my head with a sudden motion, oddly disturbed by a scent lingering in his coat. I looked into his dark eyes and realized what it was: freshly turned earth. It was not an odor I would ever forget, having buried so many loved ones in such quick succession, as well as tending the barren earth of a garden that would not grow for me. I pulled back and his hand fell from my shoulders.

Flicking the reins, he stared ahead. "Do I repulse you so much, Catherine?"

I looked down at my hands, covered in the soft gray kid of my sister's gloves. Squaring my shoulders, I faced him again. "On the contrary, John, you are much of an enigma to me." I took a deep breath, wondering if I should be thankful for my newfound confidence—a trait hard-won and not without its terrible price. "I have glimpsed a kind and warm soul in you since I arrived. But there is something else in you—something that battles with the goodness. It is like a dark shadow on your soul that you go to great lengths to hide."

His hands tightened on the reins, the skin over his knuckles pulled taut. "I do not recall you being so outspoken the last time we met."

I settled my back gently against the seat. "I was only fourteen when last we met. I have changed a great deal since then. Not that I think you took much notice of me with Elizabeth near."

He faced me for a moment, something flickering in his eyes. He turned away again before speaking. "You wore your hair loose down your back, regardless of your mother's pleas to tie it back or put it up. You would walk barefoot on the beach every day with your sketch pad and your paints, and spend hours painting the birds and ocean. Your smile was open, honest, and genuine, and your laugh was like an ocean-born breeze. I found you intoxicating."

I stared at his broad back for a moment as he leaned forward, imagining the play of muscles under his coat. "I . . . I had no idea. . . ."

"No, you would not have. You were fourteen and completely without guile. Since Elizabeth looked so much like you, it was not hard to imagine that perhaps she held the same blithe spirit."

"And did she?"

He flicked the reins again before settling a dark look upon me. "No. She did not."

I waved away a swarm of gnats that had surrounded my bonnet, hovering in the heavy humidity. "I loved Elizabeth—worshipped her, almost, as only a younger sibling could. Despite our age difference, I always fashioned that we were quite close." I closed my eyes, recalling the look on John's face when he told me the child Elizabeth carried could not have been his. "I cannot help but wonder if I inherited my parents' adulation of her. She was so beautiful, it was hard to imagine her capable of doing any wrong. I . . . I wanted to be more like her."

John reached out suddenly, grabbing my wrist, his expression firm. "Do not. Do not ever say that." His gaze flicked downward toward his hand and he quickly let go. "Elizabeth was very clever and very charming. She only let you see what you wanted to see. Until it was too late."

I turned away and stared at the scrubby trees along the road, not wanting to look at John or hear the truth in his words. There had been times in my childhood where Elizabeth had frightened or hurt me with her sharp words, but her charm and beautiful smile always made her easy to forgive, or at least made one believe that her actions held no evil intentions to harm or deceive.

Finally, I said, "Perhaps we are all like that."

He leveled black eyes on me. "I think you may be right."

The buggy climbed the road to the levee, the murky water of the Mississippi moving thick and lazy below us, chunks of leaves and debris from the recent storm dipping and twirling in a watery dance. It was so different from the salty blue ocean of my Saint Simons. For a brief moment I felt a stab of nostalgia, a deep longing for the way things used to be when I was free from grief and Elizabeth stood high on a pedestal to be admired and adored.

The town of Saint Francisville remained relatively unchanged in the years since I had last seen it. Because it had not been in the direct line of marching troops, it was virtually unscathed by the recent war. However, as was evidenced by the boarded shops and flaking paint on some of the buildings, the changing fortunes of many of the townspeople were clear. Because of the new military rule descending on Louisiana, soldiers wearing the dreaded dark blue of the Federal Army marched around the town square, the weathered storefronts frowning darkly down upon them at the town's new fate.

The Stars and Stripes flew over the town hall, filling me temporarily with dread. I held tightly to John's hand as he helped me down from the buggy, feeling strangely relieved that he was here with me. Our gazes met briefly as he placed me on the ground, and I thought I recognized relief in his eyes, too.

While John was escorted into another office, I was led into the chambers of the town magistrate, an officer named Major Brody who had kind brown eyes and a warm countenance that calmed me despite the navy blue uniform. He waited for me to be seated before seating himself and calling for refreshments. I wondered briefly if John was being afforded the same treatment. I recalled the respectful greetings of the other officers in the building, many who seemed to recognize John and hold him in high regard, and I knew that he was among friends. I wished only that I could feel the same way.

The interrogation lasted almost an hour, each question asked with a gentle regard for my feelings. I answered each as best I could, explaining that I had not been in contact with my sister in almost seven years. I did not imagine I had been able to help much with the investigation, and wondered at my own hesitation to offer possible motives for Elizabeth's death.

As Major Brody stood to dismiss me, he asked one last question. "Mrs. Reed. How is it that you found yourself at your sister's house? I believe you live on Saint Simons Island."

"Yes, that is true. But since I had not seen my sister in so long, I was quite desperate to see her." *I need you, dear sister. I am so afraid.* I shut out my sister's words, seeing instead the dark eyes of John McMahon and listening to his denial that he had anything to do with his wife's death. I imagined him again with Rebecca, his smile soft and warm, and knew I could not tell this man about Elizabeth's letter and turn their attention in the direction Elizabeth might have been planning all along.

Major Brody nodded. "I see. So you would not have known that she harbored thoughts of taking her own life."

I held my breath for a moment. "No. Never. My sister would never have contemplated such a thing." I hoped that my doubts at my own words were not detected. Elizabeth's heart harbored many shadows, and I would never know how dark some of them lay. I held the man's gaze. "She . . . She was expecting a child. Dr. Daniel Lewiston told us yesterday. Elizabeth had been to see him the day before she vanished."

"A double tragedy for your brother-in-law, to be sure."

I could do nothing but nod. Would the mere existence of an unwanted child be enough for Elizabeth to end her own life? Or could having proof of a wife's infidelity drive a man to murder? I could not point an accusatory finger at John. Nor could I sully the reputation of my dead sister. Perhaps John was right. There were secrets best buried and forgotten.

The major showed me to the door. "If you think of anything, please do not hesitate to contact me. I am most sorry." With a gallant bow, he dismissed me.

John stood waiting for me in the corridor, his tall frame nearly blocking the light from the large smudged window at the end of the hallway. Without a word, he offered me his arm and led me down the steps and outside into the hot afternoon sunshine. He helped me into the buggy and then we set off, the silence between us almost palpable.

Just as we cleared the outskirts of Saint Francisville, the buggy jolted over a rock. Something, presumably tucked under the seat and out of sight, was loosened and cascaded into the back of my shoes. I looked down and picked up the object, holding it gingerly between my fingers.

It appeared to be part of a wasp's nest mixed with long strands of dark horsehair. It lay on a small square of red silk, the fabric marred with smudges of dirt. It seemed to carry with it the scent of sun-scorched earth and grass as I held it, feeling the brittle weight of it in my hands. "What is it?"

John's gaze swept from my hands to my eyes before he pulled off the road, parking the buggy behind a live oak, obscuring us from any possible passersby. Before I could question him further, he reached under the seat and pulled out a man's leather glove.

His eyes darkened as he regarded me, and I shivered in the heat as if a dark cloud had covered the sun. "I found it clenched in Elizabeth's hand when I found her. I think that's what made Rufus so crazy—he called it bad gris-gris."

Lowering the bundle into my lap, I began to cover it in the red silk. "Who do you think put it there?"

He paused for a moment before answering. "Elizabeth."

I stared at him. "Elizabeth? Why would she do that?"

He held up the glove. "For the same reason she placed my glove near where her body was found. The red silk is from a handkerchief of mine, and I have no doubt that the dark horsehair came from my horse. She wanted it to look like I had been at least involved in or even responsible for her death."

I blinked in the strong sun, noticing the stillness of the trees around us. No breeze stirred a single leaf nor teased my cheeks. The air sat heavily on my shoulders and I could barely move. "So, you also believe that she took her own life."

He sat as still as the air around him, the heat swirling over his broad shoulders like an aura. "I am quite certain of it. A week before she disappeared, we had one of our arguments. We were standing in Rebecca's room, arguing over something I cannot even remember." He took a deep breath. "She told me she would rather die than live another day here with me. She said she would leave this place even if she had to take her own life to do it."

I thought back on Elizabeth's note to me. Was this what Elizabeth had been so afraid of—that whatever desperation had grabbed her soul was bringing her to the brink of suicide? I clenched my eyes, unwilling to look at the despair that had hovered so close to my own soul since Jamie's death. I could not blame Elizabeth for her desperate act; I knew the temptation far too well.

We sat in silence and breathed in the heated air, watching the gnats flit around us. Finally, John looked down at the red-wrapped bundle and held out his hand to show me the glove. He gave a short bark of laughter. "Her final act of revenge against the man who could never give her what she really wanted—whatever that happened to be.

"It is presumed she took poison—something that is hard to detect and had some sort of preservation qualities to it. This would explain the good condition of her body. Your sister was known to dabble in . . . such things, and would know which one to use." He shook his head. "So vain—even in death. But I would not have expected any less from her." He looked at me closely, and I did not flinch. "I have convinced them to list the cause of death as unknown. That will be easy to accept, since nobody had any real motivation to kill Elizabeth. Except for me, of course."

I swallowed but did not look away. "And what of the father of her child? Would he have had a motive?"

John shrugged, staring off into the distance. "It could have been anyone. Elizabeth traveled to Baton Rouge quite frequently. I was not aware of any one lover in particular. Besides, his secret would have been carefully kept. Elizabeth had too much to lose if the truth were known."

A stab of guilt assailed me. "Why did you hide this from the authorities? Do you not think they should know?"

He raised a dark eyebrow. "Know for certain that she had killed herself and implicated her husband? I could not do that to Rebecca. I believe the authorities know all they need to."

Our gazes met, and I am not sure if what he saw in my eyes was a look of accusation or an offer of collaboration. With a sudden movement, he grabbed the evil charm from my lap and threw it far from the buggy. It landed in a patch of dried brown grass, the red silk glaring with reproach.

I stood, but he pulled me down with his arm. "It is foolish nonsense, Catherine, and I will not allow my family to be tainted with it. It had nothing to do with Elizabeth's death, and I will not give it any credence by bringing it to the authorities." He placed his face so close to mine, I could feel his hot breath on my cheeks. "I have Rebecca's future to consider. I will not let what has happened spoil her chances for a happy life. Her mother is dead. Let us bury her and move on with our lives."

Shaking off his hold, I shot back at him, my words harsh. "You forget, sir, that Elizabeth was my sister. I shall not bury her and forget her as you would wish me to."

His voice softened. "That was not my intent. I expect you to grieve. I am merely thinking of Rebecca's happiness. As her father and as her aunt, I believe we both need to do whatever we can to make things go easily for her. Having it be known that her mother committed suicide would be detrimental. She has not had an easy childhood so far."

I sat back on the seat, recognizing the truth of his words and wondering, too, how easily he allayed my doubts. He grabbed the reins again, and I found myself mesmerized by his hands and unable to turn away. Beneath the bronzed skin lay a gentleness hidden by incredible strength. I hoped I would never be the recipient of either one.

I stared straight ahead as the buggy made its way back onto the road. "You seem to know my weaknesses, do you not? You know that I would do whatever possible to protect a child. How very clever of you."

The buggy lurched, and I found myself again pinned to his side. He reached his arm around me, his hand pressing into my shoulder. "I am not trying to be clever. I am merely protecting my interests, my daughter being the primary one."

I pulled away, strangely reluctant to leave the warmth of his touch. I recalled again the scent on his coat of freshly turned earth, and I wondered at my willingness to so easily place my trust in him.

We rode in silence for a short while before John spoke. "You did not flinch when I showed you the gris-gris. You are not afraid of much, are you?"

Splaying my hands wide on my lap, I stared at the fine leather and perfect seams of Elizabeth's gloves. "Water. I seem to have developed a fear of deep water."

He turned to me, his face compassionate, and I looked away. "My son, Jamie—he drowned, you see. I was with him, painting on the beach. He was not supposed to go into the water. He was too young and not yet a strong swimmer." Closing my eyes, I could almost feel the sand beneath my feet and hear the gentle lap of the ocean. "I had taught him to swim, against Robert's wishes, and Jamie thought he could go by himself." I forced a smile, recalling my beautiful boy with dark hair and vivid blue eyes, so much like Rebecca's. "He was so strong-willed. He thought he would show me himself what a good swimmer he was." I stopped speaking, trying to find my breath, my lungs constricting tightly.

John placed a hand gently on top of mine. The reassurance restored my voice, and I continued. "He was so far out when I heard him shout. I dove in as quickly as I could, but my skirts were so heavy and I could not move. He shouted for me one more time, and then I heard nothing else." I clenched my eyes shut, willing the tears to go away. I wanted to be through with them. They stole my soul and sapped my will for living. John squeezed my hand, and I continued. "We never found his body. The currents can be so strong and . . ." My voice disappeared, caught in the dark undertow of my haunted memory. I focused on the creak and groan of the buggy, waiting to find my voice again.

Quietly, I said, "All I have to remind me of him is a small marker in Christ Church Cemetery in Saint Simons."

I pulled my hand away from John's and stared out over the unforgiving waters of the Mississippi River. "When Robert returned home from the war and found out what had happened, I think he went slightly mad. I almost felt as if his anger at me for letting it happen was even greater than his grief at losing his son." I took a deep breath, seeing again the growing red stain on the bedsheets. "He took his own life."

John swore under his breath, causing me to lift my eyes to his face. It was covered in a dark scowl, and for a moment I believed it to be directed at me. Flicking the reins harshly, he said only one word: "Coward."

The buggy rumbled at the increased pace, and I found myself clutching John's sleeve until we reached the lane of oaks approaching the house. The suspended bottles in the trees sparkled with new meaning as they tinkled against one another in the humid breeze. We came to a stop under the porte cochere, and Mr. O'Rourke came to fetch the buggy.

I found myself weary down to my bones and craving nothing more than to lie down in my darkened room. I stared up at the house, wanting to feel reassurance or, at least, a welcoming, but felt nothing except an unspoken foreboding as I looked up at the empty windows. We climbed the steps, each one a real effort. As we approached the front door, my arm was jerked back and I found myself pressed against John.

I turned to question his behavior and saw him staring at the floorboards in front of the door. There, glistening in sun filtering between the oak leaves and Spanish moss, lay a cross molded out of what appeared to be salt.

I wanted to take a step back, but John held firmly to my arm. With an oath, he swiped his booted foot over the cross, scattering the white flakes. The sound of scurrying feet came from beyond the door, and he jerked it open, letting it crash against the wall. We stood in the threshold of the empty foyer, waiting for our eyes to adjust to the dimness. It was then that I saw her. I blinked, staring at the mirror in the foyer and into the eyes of my dead sister.

CHAPTER ELEVEN

—◆—

"Dear God." John's voice held in check a burning animosity, and I reached for his hand.

He took it, then pulled me close to him, but I pushed away, mesmerized by the frozen image in the mirror. I blinked, marveling at the vivid blue of her eyes—the same shade as the midnight blue of her dress.

Swiveling on my heels, I turned to face the full-length portrait of my sister, now inexplicably leaning against the wall in the foyer and facing the mirror.

John swore under his breath, then moved swiftly across the floor. With both arms he gripped the top of the frame and pulled the portrait from the wall, stepping back to let it fall, facedown, onto the bloodred rug. It landed with such force that thick clouds of dust puffed out of the carpet, rising like a specter in the filtered sun from the open door. A large fissure cut through the gilded wood of the frame, neatly splitting it in half. Yet the canvas seemed undamaged.

"Marguerite!" John's voice bellowed up the stairs and throughout the house, and I prayed that Rebecca was not near to see her father's fury. I had never witnessed such anger, nor did I wish to ever be on the receiving end of it. I thought briefly of Elizabeth and wondered whether she had ever borne the brunt of her husband's wrath. Without being aware of it, I pressed myself against the console, the mirror at my back, as I watched Marguerite approach.

She lowered her eyes as she came to stand in front of John, but not before I noticed those strange green eyes full of knowing and completely without remorse, flouting his anger. Watching him closely, I saw him struggle to curb his emotions. His hands clenched and unclenched at his sides while he took deep breaths, his jawbones working furiously.

A deep red stain on his face belied the calmness of his words as he spoke to her. "I thought I asked you to get Rufus to remove this portrait from the house. Why is it here, of all places?"

Her tone didn't match her apologetic words. "I am sorry, sir. You just told me to get it out of your room, and I did."

John closed his eyes as if calling his anger in check. "I want it out of the house. In a barn or cellar, I do not care—just get it out of this house!"

"Yes, sir. I am sorry, sir." Marguerite bowed her head, but I could see her lips upturned in a smile.

John took a step closer. "And are you the person responsible for the salt cross on the porch?"

She lifted her head, her proud chin raised, her expression blank. "Yes, sir. To keep the evil out of this house." With deliberate slowness, she leveled her gaze on me. "Evil is easily disguised sometimes."

John closed his mouth, his lips a straight, unforgiving line. "You are employed here solely as a favor to the Lewistons. But your refusal to do as you are asked could very well be cause enough to send you packing. Consider this a warning. I will not hesitate to dismiss you should you disregard my orders again."

Marguerite stayed firm, her voice calm. "I do not think so, Mr. McMahon. You and I know it is in both our best interests that I stay here."

His long bronzed fingers clenched and unclenched again, his fury so close to the surface as to make the air palpable. "Get out of my sight. Now."

With a mocking bow, Marguerite left the room.

My fingers hurt, and I realized it was from clutching the edge of the console. Ignoring John, I walked over to the broken portrait and knelt on the floor, my finger tracing the jagged tear in the wood.

"She is not even buried, yet you are erasing her presence already. Have you no compassion?"

I felt his shadow upon me, but I did not look up when he spoke. "I wish I could tell you. . . ."

I looked up then but found his face guarded, the anger dissipating as he regarded me, but his black eyes hid his emotions. "Tell me what? That Marguerite knows something that you do not wish for others to know? You are hiding things from me."

He lowered himself next to me, and our gazes met. "Whatever you suspect my motives to be, be assured that protecting you and Rebecca is my highest priority. I could not save my wife from the demons that haunted her, but perhaps in you and my daughter I have been given another chance."

I brushed my finger against the damaged wood again and stabbed my finger on a long golden sliver.

John took my hand and held it close to his face. His skin was still warm, nearly burning my own. He looked at me with the knowledge of what his nearness did to me, and my gaze retreated to my hand.

Gently, he slid the splinter from my finger and we watched as a small circle of blood pooled on the white surface. "This will stop the bleeding." He raised my finger to his lips and I watched, spellbound, as he placed it on his tongue and sucked. I tried to pull away, but he held fast to my arm.

Slowly, he removed my finger from his mouth and reached in his pocket for a linen handkerchief. With steady hands, he wrapped it around my wound. "Press tightly on it and it will stop bleeding."

I could not speak. I merely placed my hand in my lap and pressed the handkerchief tightly against my finger, waiting for the throbbing of my pulse to return to normal. He hovered near me, and the desire to ask him about Marguerite's words was strong. But I hesitated. Perhaps there were things that were best left unsaid.

John stood abruptly at the sound of the front-door knocker. I stood, too, on shaky legs, while he opened the door to let in a large gentleman who oddly resembled a pear in shape, and who wore green pants and a green jacket to complete the image. When he was introduced as the mortician, I was sure I had misunderstood. The man who had seen to the removal and burial of my parents and of Robert had worn solid black, with a dour countenance to match.

Mr. Cumming greeted me warmly and with genuine sympathy in his eyes. I welcomed his presence and his intrusion. The atmosphere in the foyer had become charged with unseen energy. His gaze raked over the fallen portrait, but he refrained from comment.

I excused myself and went to find Rebecca. The child had just lost her mother and would need comfort. I found her on the back porch with Samantha, having a pretend tea party. I sat on the steps, smoothed my skirts, and watched.

Rebecca didn't acknowledge my presence at first, and I remained quiet, waiting until she was ready. As she poured the tea she began humming the old familiar tune, and the sound teased at the hairs at the back of my neck. I leaned forward on my elbows, feeling the old, familiar sadness as I noted the odd similarity she had to my Jamie. They even had the same hands, small and square, and so unlike mine or Elizabeth's. I wondered absently which ancestor had given them their unique trait.

She stopped suddenly and looked at me, her dark blue eyes wide. "Why do you not like my song, Aunt Cat?"

I drew up, surprised at her astuteness. "Why do you think that?"

She picked up Samantha and held her on her lap. "Because your face looks all sad."

"It is not the song, child. It is just that you remind me so much of . . . of someone. Someone I miss very much." I brushed long strands of blond hair off her face.

Rebecca resumed her tea party, holding a pretend cup to Samantha's mouth. "I do not miss my mama. I am glad she is gone."

I moved closer, wondering at the vehemence in such a small child. "You do not mean that, Rebecca. I know I miss her."

She looked at me with those innocent eyes again, and said, "Maybe you did not really know her."

I straightened, unsure how to respond, and searched for something else to say. "What is that song that you hum so beautifully? It sounds so familiar to me but I cannot quite give it a name."

She said nothing, but began to hum the tune again. I watched as she methodically placed a girl and boy doll next to each other on the small blanket that was being used as a tea table. Abruptly, she stopped singing. "Mama liked it, too. But she told me not to tell."

I moved closer to her. "Told you not to tell what?"

She shook her head, her blond hair flying. "It is a secret. Mama would be angry if I told you."

Gently, I lifted her onto my lap, and she did not resist. "Rebecca, your mama has gone to heaven. There is no anger in heaven." I held her tightly, wishing briefly for the respite of heaven instead of the residual anger and hurt living in those left behind.

"My mama is still here. Marguerite told me so." She stuck her thumb in her mouth and rested her head on my shoulder.

I would deal with Marguerite later. No matter what secret she held over John's head, surely its revelation would pale in comparison to the torment she inflicted on his beloved daughter.

I brushed her silky hair with my hand, feeling the soft slope of her skull, so small and perfect—like Jamie's. I closed my eyes and buried my face in her sweet-smelling hair. "I would like to take you back home with me sometime to Saint Simons. Your mama and I grew up there, you know. It is so beautiful there." I could almost smell the salty air and the incessant rhythm of the waves on the sandy shore. I made no mention of the water. It was no longer a refuge for me, but the sounds and the memories of it were.

"Maybe, when I have found a home to live in again, you can come stay with me for a while. I will show you how to open an oyster shell and where to find the beautiful great blue heron. He is very shy, you know, but I know where he likes to hide." I smiled at the memory of lying in a shallow-bottomed boat on the edge of the marsh with my Jamie and seeing his eyes widen in wonder at the glorious bird.

A footstep sounded on the bottom step, and I jerked my eyes open to see our visitor.

"I beg your pardon, but my daughter is not leaving this plantation. She is mine, and nobody will be taking her anywhere."

Without further preamble, John lifted Rebecca from my lap and held her close to him. She reached in my direction and I took heart, until I realized she was reaching for Samantha. I handed it to her and stood.

"I would never take her without your consent, of course. I simply thought that a visit to her mother's home could be healing. . . ." I stopped, the cold expression in his eyes halting my words.

"It does not seem to me that you found Saint Simons healing in the least. When you arrived here, you were as pale and skittish as a rabbit."

I sucked in my breath at his cruel words, and his eyes softened with remorse. "I am sorry," he choked out. "I did not mean . . ." He closed his eyes briefly. "I should not have been so harsh with you. But when you spoke of taking Rebecca . . ."

I stepped back, feeling the pinpricks of tears. "I . . ." I could not think of a thing to say. He knew of my circumstances, yet he could slap me in the face with them. I slipped past him off the porch steps and ran across the yard toward the orange grove, intent on getting as far away from John McMahon as possible.

Elizabeth's funeral was held on a wet Saturday morning. The family mausoleum was unsealed, waiting with gaping mouth to receive its next inhabitant. I had been inside of it once when I was eleven, during one of our summer visits, on a dare from Elizabeth. It had been opened to inter the remains of a distant cousin who had died overseas. It was cousin Peter's wish to be buried at Whispering Oaks, and so his coffin had been shipped across the Atlantic and down the Mississippi toward its final resting place. Cousin Peter had died in Egypt, and it was rumored that he had been mummified to preserve his body on its long trip home. Elizabeth had had a wonderful time wrapping herself in strips of sheets and frightening me and our friends. She had made amends by allowing me to dress as the mummy while she transformed herself into Cleopatra. That was so very much like her; she always made sure that everyone had what they thought they wanted.

The mausoleum had been built into a sloping hill, covered on three sides by grass and the opening sealed with a heavy metal door and a locked gate. The door had been opened and the gate unlocked in preparation for cousin Peter's burial, and the dark opening seemed to beckon to my sister with a call to mischief.

Elizabeth had given me a small stub of a candle to light my way and then told me to stay inside until the candle burned out. She had shut the door behind me, and I had sat shivering inside the oddly cool cavity, staring at the flickering candle, watching each undulation with breathless fear. When it began to fizzle and burn my fingers, I had dropped it, finding myself suddenly swallowed in suffocating blackness. I waited for Elizabeth to call for me, to congratulate me on my bravery, and to let me wear her red cape to church as she had promised.

But no one had come for me. After waiting for countless minutes, I had dropped to my hands and knees, praying I wouldn't bump a shelf with a dusty coffin, and crawled out of the enclosure. The sunshine blinded me momentarily. When I could see again, I saw Elizabeth and Philip Herndon, from nearby Bellevue plantation, sitting on the ground behind the grassy slope of the mausoleum, and he was holding her very close. When he spotted me, he pulled away and stood, yanking Elizabeth with him. Her clothes were rumpled and covered with grass, and her lips red and swollen. Philip flushed with embarrassment, but Elizabeth gave me only a crooked smile and then merrily announced that I had earned her red cape—an object I had been craving—but only if I promised not to mention that Philip had been by for a visit. I agreed, too excited to have the lovely cape and not realizing the precarious position in which I could have put my sister had I told Grandmother.

And now, as I turned my face to the steady drizzle, Elizabeth would be placed into the crypt herself. All of her beauty and wit to be hidden forever under the green slopes of the mausoleum.

Just a few close friends came to the internment. I kept my somber thoughts at bay by studying the faces of those around me. Rebecca stood solemnly, clutching her Samantha close and holding her father's hand. Clara and Daniel were there, as well as an older couple and an elderly gentleman I thought I recognized from my visits to my grandmother's.

Following the funeral, a larger group gathered at the house for the wake. Daniel seemed drawn and reserved, Clara always at his side. At one point, as I leaned against a dining-room chair for support, Daniel sought me out. I was surprised to find him alone, and he looked relieved.

He kissed my cheek, then held my hand. "I cannot imagine how devastated you must be right now. Please know that my shoulder is always available for you. I . . . had great affection for Elizabeth."

He looked as if he were about to cry, and I patted his shoulder. It was at that moment Clara appeared and promptly claimed Daniel's arm, steering him away from me. Again, it struck me how incongruous the two of them looked together, like a mismatched pair of bookends.

The late arrival of a tall man caught my attention and I studied him closely as he moved behind an older couple. The woman looked at him with surprise and then squeezed his hand in welcome. I still could not place how I knew them. The young man looked vaguely familiar, and his soft hazel eyes flickered in recognition when he spotted me. He dipped his head in a brief greeting before turning his full attention to the reverend.

I spotted him again much later. He stood in a corner of the dining room, scouring the crowd as if searching for someone. When his gaze alighted on me, he approached with a singular determination.

He stood in front of me and looked down at me with soft hazel eyes. "Cat? It is me, Philip. Philip Herndon. An old summer friend."

Now I remembered. And I recognized the older couple as his parents—old friends of my grandmother's. "Yes, of course. I thought you looked familiar. It is good to see you again."

His face sobered. "It was a shock to hear about Elizabeth. My deepest sympathy for your loss."

I studied his handsome face, now fully matured, without the softness of his earlier youth, and saw true remorse. "Thank you, Philip. I shall miss her deeply." I felt better, somehow, speaking to him. Just seeing him brought back memories of my carefree youth, the time of my life when death and loss were not my constant companions.

He looked down for a moment before speaking. "I would . . . If you do not mind, I would like to call on you sometime while you are here. I feel there is so much catching up to do. And I would like . . . I would like to talk about Elizabeth. Perhaps that would bring us both some healing." He smiled a small, faraway smile. "You know, I thought for a long time that she and I might marry. . . ." His voice trailed away and his eyes seemed lost in thought.

His smile faded as he caught sight of something behind my shoulder. I turned and watched John approach, his face a mask of restrained thunder.

"Mr. Herndon," he said brusquely, giving a brief nod. "I must say I am surprised to see you here. I thought I made it quite clear that members of the White League are not welcome at my home."

Philip flushed deeply. "I do not know what you mean, sir. I am here with my parents to show our respects to our closest neighbor and old friend."

John gave him a mocking smile. "I see. Well, consider your duty done, sir, and see yourself out. You may wait outside until your parents are ready to leave. But you are not welcome here, and if you don't want to cause a scene, I suggest you do as I ask."

The red flush in Philip's cheek quickly faded to a pale white. Anger flickered in his eyes and I thought, for a brief moment, that blows would soon fall. Instead, with a brief nod in my direction, Philip excused himself, and I watched as he let himself out the front door.

Angrily, I turned to John. "What was all that about? You just insulted him gravely. He was here with a sincere offer of sympathy, you know. He was a friend of not only Elizabeth's but mine as well."

John gripped my elbow, pulling me close to him so he could speak without others hearing. "The man does not have a sincere bone in his body. If it were not for my personal dislike of the man I would dislike him on principle. He spent the entire four years of the war in Europe, miles away from the battlefields where his friends and neighbors were slaughtered. And now he has involved himself in the White League, whose main purpose is to take the law into their own hands and harass freedmen and Republicans. That group alone is responsible for more than a dozen lynchings in the last year."

We were interrupted by the appearance of the elderly gentleman whom I recalled to be Judge Patterson, a contemporary and old friend of my grandmother's. My heart leapt at the recognition, for this man had been like a grandfather to both Elizabeth and me. We had always suspected more than friendship lay between him and my grandmother, but they had never married. Regardless, he had loved and spoiled us like his own grandchildren, and I had loved him deeply in return.

Leaning heavily on a cane, he bent to kiss my cheek, his lips dry and withered against my skin. The judge offered his condolences, and we spoke of my grandmother for a while, until John excused himself to find Rebecca. I turned back to the judge to find his warm brown eyes examining me closely. His hand, with gnarled fingers resembling claws, grabbed hold of my forearm and he leaned close to my ear.

"I want you to know . . ." His next words were lost in a spasm of coughs. Still gripping my arm, he continued. "I have missed you all these years, my dear. You have grown into a beautiful young woman."

I blushed, but thanked him and smiled.

"I remember you always telling me what lay in your heart—all your wishes and fears. If you ever need someone to tell your heart to, know that I am still here to listen."

I wondered if I should dismiss his utterance as the ramblings of an old man, but when I looked into his eyes, I knew the sentiments were real and sincere. Patting his hand, I said, "Yes, Judge Patterson, of course. It is reassuring to know that I have friends who care about me."

"There might be some unpleasantness regarding Elizabeth's death. I am sure it has been kept from you, but you need to be aware that there's talk that John may have got away with something because of who he is and whom he knows. You and I know this is not true, but the gossip is there. Just remember that I am here to help you if you need me." He squeezed my arm, then left to go. I watched the bent figure of the old man as he walked away and felt no small comfort in knowing that I had a friend.

I seemed to be the focus of attention and braced myself for the inevitable onslaught of neighbors and friends who sought me out to introduce themselves and examine me closely. From their curiosity, I feared that I must have grown three heads. But every so often, I would look up and find John's eyes on me, and he never failed to send me a reassuring smile.

The scrutiny and constant attention left a throbbing headache at my temples. At my first opportunity I slid out of the room and hid myself in John's library. I felt completely numb. I wanted to grieve for my sister in private and to relegate my memories of her to some sort of permanence while allowing the truths of whom she had become to slip through the thin fingers of my memory and evaporate into the firmament.

Taking off my shoes, I curled up into John's desk chair and rested my forehead on my knees. I let my eyes flicker as the droning voices behind the door lulled me into a dreamless sleep, an enviable place where there were no mysteries or unanswered questions.

When I awoke, I noted that the sun no longer shone through the window and the purple cast of dusk had settled into the corners of the room. The guests must have left, because I heard no voices. The house nearly shouted its silence.

I sat up, my neck stiff, and knew instinctively that I was not alone. I slowly lowered my legs and stilled, my eyes struggling to focus on a dark shadow by the door. The steady rhythm of somebody breathing pulsed in the still room as I widened my eyes to see better. The shadow moved closer and my breath caught in my throat.

"Catherine."

John's voice did nothing to still the hammering of my heart. "I have been thinking about you. Your future, to be exact."

I searched my sleep-muddled brain for words. "My future?" Something in the tone of his voice heightened all of my senses.

"Yes, Catherine. Your future. I have been thinking about it quite a lot lately."

I straightened, feeling suddenly that I could read his mind. I wanted to reach up and put my hand over his mouth before he could continue. But I remained where I was.

"I think that you and I should marry."

Chapter Twelve

—◆—

A door slammed somewhere in the house, and I think I must have said something. John approached and leaned toward me, but I did not move. He lit a lamp on the desk and straightened. His black eyes flashed in the lamplight with an emotion that I could not read but that made my skin feel as if I had been burnt by the sun.

I tried to stand but realized my legs could not bear my weight and sat back down.

John raised an eyebrow and spoke. "I know this is sudden, but after talking with my neighbors today, I have found that your presence in my house has led to a great deal of speculation and that your reputation is at stake."

I gripped the edge of the desk. "I assure you, sir, that my reputation does not concern me at this juncture of my life. And I do not plan to remain here at Whispering Oaks, so it does not matter much."

He paused, his eyes raking over me, my every pore tingling from where his gaze touched. I pushed the chair back, putting distance between us.

He took note of my movement and smiled. "There is another matter I wished to discuss with you. It concerns Rebecca. She needs a mother, and it seems that you two are growing fond of each other. I cannot imagine that you would wish to leave and not see her again."

I forced myself to stand, leaning heavily on the desk for support. As much as I wished for solace amid my grief on Saint Simons and to be away from the child who so reminded me of the one I had lost, John was right. I had no wish to abandon Rebecca here in this house of dark shadows. But his proposal was not to be considered.

"You seem to forget that your wife is barely cold in her grave. If your acquaintances are gossiping about my mere presence here, imagine what such a hasty marriage would do to your own reputation."

He studied me with those black eyes that held so many secrets. "It is not my reputation that I care about. I know that there is nothing left for you on Saint Simons. And I want you to stay—for your sake as well as Rebecca's. The only way I see that occurring is if you marry me and live here as my wife."

My heart seemed to stutter, skipping a beat. "I have no desire to ever be married again. I tried it once and found it lacking."

That infernal eyebrow shot up again, lending him a wizened expression. "Then perhaps you were simply married to the wrong man."

I heard myself sucking in my breath before I realized what I was doing. "You go too far."

He stepped around the edge of the desk until he stood directly in front of me. "Robert treated you badly, Catherine. Do you not think that you are due a husband who will treat you with nothing but kindness and respect?"

I jutted my chin. "Like you did for Elizabeth?" I regretted the words as soon as I had uttered them.

He gripped my shoulders, pulling me closer. "You do not know the truth of what was between your sister and me. I hope, for your sake, that you never do."

His eyes burned with controlled passion and I craved, just for a moment, to see it unleashed. This man fascinated me. As much as I wished to pull away, I wanted to feel his touch on me and let his heat burn away the eternal coldness that had resided inside of me for so long. But he was like a fire: uncontrollable, its path unknown, and, for those unwary enough to fall in its path, too easily consumed.

He released me and let his hands fall slowly to his sides. His gaze dropped to my mouth and then, deliberately, to my throat, where he could see my quick breaths and rapid pulse. I raised my hand to hide my traitorous skin, but he reached and took my fingers, his touch creating a spark that snapped in the darkening room.

My palm stung where he had touched, but he would not let me pull away. His voice was low and seductive, the tremulous notes warming places inside me that had not been touched in a very long time. I closed my eyes for a moment, trying to shut him out, but his presence overwhelmed me.

"Catherine, let me take care of you. You will never lack for anything—certainly not food or clothing or a dry roof over your head. Can you honestly tell me that you have any of those things waiting for you back on Saint Simons?" He spoke softly into my ear, his warm breath sending goose bumps down my neck and arms. "Can you?"

I found myself leaning into him and put my hand on his chest to stop myself. "Why would you want to marry me? I have nothing to give you."

His eyes became hooded, his emotions effectively locked away from my view. "I have always held you in high regard, Catherine. You had such a brightness of spirit about you, a joy for life that was very captivating. I . . ." Abruptly, he dropped my hand and turned away toward the window. "And Rebecca needs a mother—desperately. I think you two would be good for each other."

I stared at his broad back, foolishly imagining placing my face against it and finding rest. "Then you . . . you are speaking of a marriage of convenience."

He whirled on his heels, the grace of his move reminding me of an encounter I had once had with a catamount. So sleek and beautiful; so deadly. Back then I had my father and his rifle for protection. Now I had only me.

A flash of white appeared as he smiled. "No, Catherine. I have no desire for another cold marriage bed. I would fully intend to claim my marital rights."

I was glad for the dim light to hide the flush I felt creeping over my face. "I . . . I see."

He walked toward me, his footsteps muted by the carpet. I held my breath and forced myself to look in his face.

"I do not think you would find my bed wanting." He leaned down, his lips hovering over mine. "Let me show you how it should be between a man and a woman."

When I spoke, his lips brushed mine, taking away the intended sting of my words. "Sir, you are being presumptuous."

His fingertips lightly swept down my arms, and for the first time in my life I felt completely and utterly helpless. I hardly knew this man, and what I did know was incomplete. There were too many unanswered questions, too many hidden emotions, for me to want him the way that my body demanded. But when he was near me, even barely touching me, my reason abandoned me.

His lips touched mine gently and I tasted him for the first time. When he pulled away for a moment, I closed the gap between us like a starving person hungering for his touch. Our mouths collided as my body melded into his. His arms pulled me closer and I found myself floating in an ocean of warmth and passion, the waters threatening to suffocate me, but their lure of refuge and heat impossible to resist. I wondered if this was what drowning would be like, and the thought brought a fissure of reason to me. Like a person coming up from a deep slumber, I pulled away.

He did not step back but continued to hold me close. "You are not indifferent to me, Catherine. We have both felt this thing between us since that first night when I rescued you from the swamp."

I shook my head, swallowing thickly. "No, I am not indifferent to you." His expression remained guarded, but I could feel the steady beat of his heart beneath my palm. I was aware of every place on my person that he had touched, and felt a small pulse of anger at myself for allowing him to see how he affected me. Who was this man? What secrets did he hide? I needed to remove myself from his presence to allow myself to think. It was near impossible to do so clearly with him so near. And he was well aware of it.

I pulled back and stepped away from him. "I need time to think." I walked clumsily around the desk, putting it between us, my legs wanting to buckle under me.

He stood rigid by the desk, regarding me intently. "Yes, do think about it. Think about your life these past months on Saint Simons and then think about your life here. I doubt you will have to think much further."

"But marriage! Surely there is another way." I looked at him anew, a glistening thought budding in my brain. "For what reason could you possibly want me as your wife?"

He raised an eyebrow. "I have already mentioned my reasons."

"No, there has to be more to it. What do I have that you could possibly want enough to acquire by marrying me?"

His gaze darkened. "Do not insult me, Catherine. Perhaps in due course you will understand. But for now, suffice it to say that I need a mother for my child and a companion in my bed. And you, my dear, will lack for nothing."

"It is you now, sir, who is being insulting. This transaction you are proposing is slightly better than selling myself. I may have lost everything, but I still have my pride."

"Forgive me. I did not mean to insult you. You know that I hold you in the highest regard." He began to walk around the desk toward me. "And I find your pride one of your most attractive assets. One of many, I might add." His gaze flickered over me before returning to meet my eyes. "I merely meant to imply that a marriage between us would be mutually beneficial."

He now stood within arm's length of me, and I knew I had to escape before I agreed to anything just to have him touch me again. "I need time." Without another word, I turned on my heel and left the room.

I ran to my bedroom, feeling faint from the pressure of my corset as I closed the door. I sat down on a small settee by the window and waited for my breathing to return to normal. My thoughts were in turmoil—torn between grieving for my dead sister and this remarkable proposal from a man I could admit intimidated me as much as he excited me.

I thought of my barren existence on Saint Simons, the constant gnawing hunger and grief, and knew that John was right. There was nothing there for me except for more of the same and with no end in sight. At least if I stayed here, I would have food and shelter and no more worries. And I would have Rebecca. She was not Jamie, but I knew in due course that I would come to love her as my own. She was all that I had left, a final connection, somehow, to the family I had loved and grown up with.

But marriage to John! The thought thrilled and repulsed me in equal doses. The physical intimacies of my marriage to Robert had been rote and painful, but I could only imagine that sharing a marriage bed with John McMahon would be anything but.

I shivered, my body at war with my mind. What did he know of Elizabeth's death? And what was he not telling me? He had sworn to me that he was innocent of any wrongdoing, and I had believed him. It was so easy to believe his words when standing in his presence. But now, away from him, I would have doubts. How could I marry a man I was not sure I could trust?

A niggling thought teased at the back of my mind. Kneeling before my dresser, I pulled out the bottom drawer and reached into the back, feeling with my fingers until I grabbed the pipe that I had found in the attic. I stared at it in my hand and then, without really knowing why, I placed it in my pocket. I supposed I carried it on my person for the same reason I now wore the key on a chain around my neck and securely tucked inside my dress.

I paced the room, unable to come up with any answers to my predicament. I heard John leave the house, and I opened my door, feeling relieved that I would not run into him. My steps took me outside to the back porch, where I heard voices from the kitchen. Hoping to find Rebecca, whom I had left in Delphine's care, I entered the small brick building.

The pungent aroma of old smoke mixed with freshly baked bread touched on my memory and sent a wave of nostalgia through me. I stood in the doorway and waited for my eyes to adjust to the dimness. Rebecca sat at a small table in the corner, Samantha on her lap, eating a thick slice of bread liberally smeared with butter. Delphine and her mother, Rose, stood silently, their gazes watching me with open curiosity.

I smiled. "I am sorry to disturb you, but I wanted to read to Rebecca and put her down for her nap."

Rose knotted her thick, dark eyebrows, staring at me intently for a moment before speaking. "Delphine do that. I needs to speak with you, Miss Catherine."

Rebecca finished her last bite of bread, then willingly took Delphine's hand, allowing the young servant to lead her and Samantha away to bed.

"Is there a problem, Rose?" I had once run a plantation, and I relished the thought of becoming useful at Whispering Oaks.

She placed a cup of tea on the wooden table recently vacated by

Samantha and motioned for me to sit. "Have some of this tea, Miss Catherine, while we chat."

There was something ominous in her voice, and I did as she asked. A sizzling and popping sound came from a large black kettle hanging above the fire, and I jerked around to see Rose throwing a yellow powder into the pot.

"What is that?"

She did not respond, but instead wafted the smoke in her direction, sniffing deeply of the sweet and pungent odor. I looked down into my tea, but doubts assailed me and I could not bring myself to drink it. I should have left then, but I had always had a stubborn curiosity about me and I found that I could not.

Rose dipped a long-handled ladle into the pot and poured it into a tin cup. This she placed across the table from me and stood by it expectantly.

"Sit, Rose, and tell me what it is you need."

She sat across from me, still silent, then lifted the dented tin cup and drank slowly from it, her eyes closed. She sat motionless and breathing deeply for several moments. I was growing impatient but did not want to say anything to break the spell she seemed to be under.

Finally, she opened her eyes, the black pupils in the center enlarged. When she spoke, her voice was foreign to me, the words sounding old and withered and full of thick black smoke.

"You not like the other one. They says she your sister, but blood is the only thing you share."

She looked directly at me, but her eyes did not seem to see me. Rose continued, her words without inflection. "You done suffer much sadness. And it not done with you yet."

I drew in a breath sharply, but she appeared not to notice. "There be two men in your life—two men you share your life with." She shook her head slowly, her eyes still not seeing. "But one of them is not who you thinks he be. He betray you in a terrible way."

She paused, and I used it as an excuse to try to stand, but her hand snaked out to hold my arm, knocking over my tea. It splattered over the table, unheeded, the dark liquid creeping slowly to the edge. It seemed to thicken first before hurtling off into drips and hitting the hard brick floor. I wanted to ask her about the two men but didn't want to give any credence to her words, despite the effect they had on me.

Her grip on my arm tightened, hurting me, but she seemed oblivious to my struggle to free myself. "But there be a great love to be found. A man who love you like you deserve. You soul mates—you be together in a past life and you done found him again." Her gaze settled on my face and her eyes seemed to clear. "Your lives like the roots of an old oak tree—they runs deep and they cross over each other again and again. Don' you fight this love. It save your life."

Slowly, she released her hold on me. Rubbing the spot recently relinquished by her fingers, I asked, "Why would my life be in need of saving?"

Shrugging, she said, "It not for me to see the why of it. I jus' see the way it will be."

I tried to lighten the mood. "But I am sure your prophecies are only meant for those who believe in such things."

She smiled broadly, a gap of missing teeth prominently displayed. "No, ma'am. They's for everybody who listens." She pushed back from the table and walked over to a rough-hewn box sitting by the fireplace. Opening it, she reached in and pulled something out before returning to the table. She spread her palm wide and a shiny black stone rolled onto the table's surface.

"This lodestone be for you. It pull in all the good luck while pushing away the evil. You needs to carry this with you."

I stared at it for a long time with some loathing, not wanting to touch it. But neither did I want to insult Rose. What would be the harm in taking it? With a smile, I reached across the table and took it, sliding the smooth stone into my pocket. My hand brushed against the pipe inside and my skin chilled. There was so little I knew, but so much I had to learn. I thanked Rose and left.

I had my supper sent to me on a tray, unable to face John as yet. Luckily, the cane from Whispering Oaks and those of local tenants needed to be processed at the mill, and John was kept busy for most of the following week. When he was home, I managed to avoid him, but knew he was waiting for my answer.

I had done nothing but think about our discussion. The more I thought about it, the more sense it made. I had nowhere left to go, and he was offering me sanctuary. Surely not a reason I would have hoped for marriage, but I had few options left. I could not admit to myself that the prospect of marrying John excited me. My common sense continued to tell me to leave, run away as fast as my legs could carry me.

And there was Rebecca to consider. My heart remained wary, its scar tissue still raw, but the child had begun to find a place within me. Her sweet smile and joyous laugh touched me in ways I could not name but for which I was grateful. I was a long way from healing, but she was bringing me there, her little hand tucked securely into mine. We needed each other, and I knew I could not bear to be parted from her.

The Sunday following Elizabeth's funeral, I dressed with care for supper. Marguerite selected a dark amber silk from Elizabeth's room for me to wear, and I shed my black and donned the beautiful gown before I had a chance to think about what I was doing. Marguerite swept my hair up, fastening it with tortoiseshell combs, and I sent myself a frail smile in the mirror, pleased with the results.

I felt John's appraising eyes on me the moment I entered the dining room. With a gallant bow, he seated me, his fingers brushing the back of my neck. I pretended not to notice, but I was sure he could see the rippled flush that crept over my neck and shoulders.

Rebecca had eaten her dinner earlier, at my orders, and John did not seem displeased to have my undivided attention. We talked of mundane things, avoiding any topic that was close to the heart. The only reminder of the reality of our lives was the sweet, cloying smell of flowers, left over from the funeral and that littered the house. Most of the blooms had withered and died, dropping their petals on the floor. Lack of direction for the servants had allowed them to remain, their weeping limbs the only sign of grief in the house.

When dinner was over and John stood behind my chair, I wondered if he could hear the thudding of my heart. I knew that the time to tell him of my decision had arrived but I somehow could not find the words. He offered his arm to me, and I took it, our eyes meeting for a brief moment before I turned away.

Stalling for time, I walked slowly toward the parlor. When we reached the hallway console and the old mirror, he stopped, his movement turning me around to face him. The chandelier above cast shadows on his face, only the spark from his eyes visible. "I have waited long enough for an answer from you, Catherine."

My chest rose and fell with each breath. Turning my back to him, I faced the mirror. I could not stand so close to him and look in his eyes and be able to think coherently. "I think I have come to a decision." His hands gripped my shoulders, but I did not turn around. "But I first must ask you something."

I opened my hand where I had been clutching my handkerchief all evening, letting go long enough to let it rest in my lap while I ate. Slowly I unfurled the corners, displaying the pipe I had found in the attic. "Is this yours?" I faced him but stepped back, making sure no part of me touched him.

He seemed unusually calm as he took the pipe from me. "Yes. It is the one I have been missing." Something flickered in his eyes as he raised his gaze to me.

I took a deep breath. "I found it in the attic—the time after I had been locked in when I went back to find the letterbox. The box was gone, but this had been left."

He raised an eyebrow. "And?"

I was taken aback. "I want to know how it got there—if you were the one who removed the letterbox."

A dark shadow seemed to pass over his face and I looked up, expecting to see something large obliterating the light from the chandelier. But all I saw was the ornate crown molding and the brass chandelier, each flame giving a valiant effort to shine light into the darkness.

John laughed. "You have quite the imagination, do you not? It is another one of your admirable qualities." He sobered slightly. "But I cannot tell you how the pipe got in the attic because I do not know. Nor do I know anything about a letterbox. I have been up there quite often in recent weeks, trying to locate papers pertaining to the plantation. It could have easily fallen from my pocket on several occasions. You just did not notice because you were so absorbed in your find."

His words soothed me, but I knew that as soon as I was alone, my doubts would assail me once again. Taking yet another deep breath, I pressed on, my future hanging in the balance. I gazed directly into those black eyes, daring him to look away. "What do you know about Elizabeth's death that you are not telling me?"

He placed his fingers under my chin and lifted my face up to his. "I am only going to say this once more and then I never want to discuss it with you again. I had nothing to do with Elizabeth's death. I am not saddened by her passing, except for any grief that it might have bestowed on you and Rebecca, but I very truthfully believe that she died by her own hand." He lowered his face closer to mine, his scent overwhelming and addictive. "But I will admit that I do not think she could have pushed me much farther before I would have been forced to take matters into my own hand to get what I want."

I turned away again, facing the mirror, trying to find my ability to resist him. But I was like a bee to nectar, and I was afraid I had gone too far already. My voice sounded far away. "What is it that you want?"

His eyes met mine in the glass. "I want you."

I closed my eyes as he bent his head, placing his lips on my neck. A low moan escaped me, and I had the wild fancy of turning in his arms and succumbing to the passion I knew we both felt and letting him make love to me there, on the floor in front of the haunted mirror.

"Marry me," he whispered in my ear.

I opened my eyes and stared at our reflection. My voice sounded breathless when I answered. "Yes. Yes, I will marry you."

Our gazes met again in the mirror, but a distortion in the glass seemed to change John's face into a malevolent mask, and I wondered if the spirits inside were trying to tell me something. I shut my eyes once again to block out the image and surrendered to the passion John's mouth and hands evoked deep inside of me.

CHAPTER THIRTEEN

❖

I wanted a long engagement, to at least give a show of mourning for Elizabeth. But John was impatient and I knew he was a man used to getting his way. I did not fight him on the matter, although I refused to admit even to myself the anticipation I felt. It was anticipation tinged with alarm—not admirable emotions for a soon-to-be bride. I found now that I could not be in a room with him without watching his hands and wondering how they would feel touching me. He would catch me staring and I would flush, causing a devilish grin to spread over his face.

My doubts would consume me once I was out of his presence. I spent many a night tossing and turning, wondering over all the missing pieces in the puzzle of Elizabeth's existence at Whispering Oaks and of her death. John had allowed two weeks before we announced our engagement, and I intended to use that time to truly consider my alternatives.

On a warm afternoon while Rebecca napped, I found myself in the old grotto once again. Despite my deep musings, I kept a wary eye out for snakes, not ready to replicate the disaster of my last visit. I could see that someone had been there clearing out the underbrush and removing debris that many years of neglect had brought. Heavy foliage created a verdant screen from the wilting sun, and I sat down on a crumbling bench nestled against an ancient oak tree, and turned my face up toward the subtle warmth.

A crunching of dead leaves alerted my senses. I looked around, wondering who was near, but saw no one. I heard another footfall and stood, peering through the overgrown foliage. "Hello? Is anybody there?" Irrationally, I thought of the ghost of the Indian lady and her baby, and felt a chill of apprehension creep up my spine.

A tall figure pulled back the thick fronds of a fern and stepped into view. I smiled with relief, recognizing Dr. Lewiston.

He gave me an apologetic grin. "Sorry if I frightened you. I was just riding up for a visit when I saw you coming here, so I followed. I hope you do not mind."

I was genuinely glad to see him. "No, of course not. Come sit over here with me. It is quite cool in the shade."

I made room for him on the bench and he sat next to me, removing his hat. A shard of sunlight glinted off his head, making it shine like gold. I remembered longing for hair like that as a child and grinned to myself, thinking it wasted on a man's head.

With a gallant gesture, he pulled a bloodred tea rose from his lapel and offered it to me. "I brought a beautiful flower for a beautiful woman, hoping it would make her smile in her sadness. She does have the most ravishing smile."

"Thank you," I said, blushing at his compliments. It had been so long since anyone had made me feel pretty, and my mere words of thanks could not adequately describe my gratitude. Instead, I reached toward him and squeezed his hand where it rested on his knee.

He squeezed mine back, then let go quickly. His eyes, so cool and gray, studied me closely. "It is amazing, you know, how much you resemble her."

"Elizabeth?"

He nodded. "Yes. She was so beautiful." He looked away for a moment. "It is hard to imagine her taking her own life."

I studied him. "I have learned, since coming here, that Elizabeth showed a different face to everyone who knew her." I leaned back against the ungainly oak, its monstrous roots rerouted to make room for the small creek that oozed from the bottom of the grotto. "I remember one summer when our grandmother took us to a carnival in New Orleans. They had a house of mirrors, and Elizabeth was captivated by it. I was rushing along the hallways, trying to find her. I would see her face and run toward it, only to find it an image of her." I sighed into the tepid air, the distorted image of Elizabeth haunting my memory. "She was vastly amused by my pursuit. I think that is how she pictured her life: sitting back and laughing at those of us who would try in vain to find the real Elizabeth. I wonder if she is laughing at us now as we try to sort this out."

His eyes hardened to a steel gray, reminding me of the sky over the ocean before a storm. "How different you are from her—but you have that same ethereal beauty. It is almost like . . ." He paused, as if realizing he had spoken aloud. Covering my hand with his, he faced me with a concerned expression. "I hope you do not find this forward of me, but if you should be afraid of staying here . . ."

"Afraid? Why should I be afraid?"

He patted my hand. "Nothing I can really say, but with Elizabeth's death, despite the coroner's verdict and John's suspicion of suicide, there seem to be things here at Whispering Oaks that just are not right. Besides, there is the matter of a lack of a chaperone. In your grief you might not have noticed how . . . improper it is for you to stay here. I really feel, as a close friend of the family, that a move to our home would be the right thing to do under the circumstances."

His concern warmed me, and I placed my other hand on top of his. "Thank you, Daniel. I really cannot express how much your concern for my well-being touches me." I squeezed his hand. "But I do not think—"

"Daniel!"

We both startled at the sound of Clara Lewiston's voice. For such a small woman, her voice was loud and commanding. Standing directly behind her was John McMahon, a scowl darkening his features and his gaze focused on our entwined hands. Not knowing why, I guiltily slipped my hands from Daniel's and stood.

Daniel stood, too, and I could feel the tension in the thick air as he spoke. "Clara, John. This is a surprise. What brings you here?"

Clara's nose twitched like that of a small rabbit, but her voice was level as she answered her husband. "My father told me you had come to call at Whispering Oaks, and it seems that you have forgotten our supper plans with the Herndons. John was helping me find where you might have run off to." She sent a reproachful look to Daniel.

The doctor forced a laugh as he approached his wife. "My dear, I have not forgotten anything nor have I run off anywhere. I was just following Catherine into the grotto. I have invited her to stay with us."

Clara's pale mouth had formed itself into a perfect "O." "I . . . well . . . Of course Catherine is welcome at Belle Meade. And I must apologize for not thinking of it first." She smiled at me, and I judged her offer to be sincere.

John had come to stand by me, and I felt his hot gaze. Without acknowledging him, I spoke. "It is very kind of both of you, but I must decline. With Marguerite and the other servants, I find myself adequately chaperoned. And I do feel that it is best for Rebecca if I stay here with her."

John placed a hand on my shoulder. "I must agree with Catherine. It is best for Rebecca to stay among familiar surroundings, and equally important for Catherine to remain close by."

Out of sight of the Lewistons, John's thumb traced circles on my back, caressing the thin fabric of my dress as if it were my bare skin. I could not pull away without making it obvious, and I was almost glad of it.

I heard the hint of amusement in his voice as he added, "And I promise as a gentleman to behave as one."

Dr. Lewiston flushed. "Really, John, acting as a gentleman has never been your forte. I find I must insist, for the sake of Catherine's reputation, that she return with Clara and me to Belle Meade. And I invite Rebecca, as well, if that is your wish."

John's hand stilled on my shoulder, but he did not remove it. In a very controlled voice he said, "No. Rebecca stays here and Catherine with her. I will hear no more arguments—the matter is settled."

John placed his hand on my arm to lead me along the path out of the grotto, but I held back. I felt uncomfortable with John's dismissal of their offer and felt I needed to smooth any ruffled feathers. "Will you please join us for some refreshments? We would very much enjoy your company."

Clara spoke first. "Thank you, Catherine, but we must be getting back. I left in the middle of doing an inventory of my spices and I hate to leave them out from under lock and key for so long. Not to mention that we have supper plans for later. But thank you very much. I hope to return the invitation as soon as your mourning permits."

I nodded. "Thank you. I shall look forward to it." I found myself frowning and quickly straightened my features. But I could not help but wonder as to why she had not sent a servant to fetch Daniel—and why it was so important to remind him of supper plans now. It was barely past noon. I studied her plain face for a moment and the way it nearly glowed when she looked at her husband, and thought I knew the answer.

As John turned to allow us to pass in front of him, he stopped before the tea rose I had left behind, its brilliant red an odd splotch of color against the cream-colored bench. He retrieved it and held it up. "Clara, this looks like it came from your renowned rose garden." He sniffed it and smiled, but there was nothing pleasant about the gesture. "Here. Let me return it to its rightful owner." Ignoring Daniel's outstretched hand, John approached Clara and affixed the wilting flower to a button. "I hope, Clara, that you will do us the honor of letting us use some of your beautiful roses for our wedding."

I turned to him with a look of anger, but he ignored me. He seemed intent on watching Dr. Lewiston.

Both of the Lewistons appeared startled, but good breeding quickly changed their expressions to polite interest. Clara's pale eyes seemed to shrink despite her smile. "Then let me be the first to congratulate you. I will be happy to have you as our neighbor." She laid her hands on my shoulders and brushed her lips against my cheek.

Dr. Lewiston stepped forward. "Yes, of course. Congratulations are certainly called for. It is just a bit of a shock, especially after . . ." His words fell away, but each of us knew the implication.

John inclined his head. "I thank you for the congratulations. The wedding will be small, under the circumstances, but you will be receiving an invitation soon."

Without further comment, John placed his hand at my elbow and led me out of the grotto. I asked the Lewistons again if they would stay, but again they declined. I did not know why it was so imperative not to be left alone with John, especially since I had agreed to be his wife. But the feeling persisted.

After the Lewistons left, John turned to me, a knowing look in his eyes. "I am hoping your eagerness for guests has nothing to do with there being something lacking in my company."

Heat enflamed my cheeks at having been read so accurately. "Not at all. I merely enjoy their company."

He raised an eyebrow but made no further comment. Instead, he bowed slightly and said, "Please excuse me. I have business matters to attend to. I look forward to seeing you at supper." With an amused glint in his eyes, he raised my fingers to his lips. Instead of kissing the top of my hand, he turned it over and let his lips brush the inside of my wrist. The sensations that swirled through my veins at his touch nearly undid me. With a knowing glance, he turned and left. I tried to force myself not to stare after him, but found I could not.

I retired to my room and tried to read, but my thoughts were too easily diverted. I tried to gauge the Lewistons' reaction to John's announcement, and wondered if it was because it was simply too soon after Elizabeth's death. But then there was Daniel's veiled warning to me, and even Judge Patterson's, and it was clear that both men believed there to be something at Whispering Oaks over which I should be alarmed. It was not clear to me, however, if both warnings had been referring to the same thing.

Absently, I picked Rose's lodestone off of the dressing table and felt its cold smoothness against my palm. I recalled the older woman's words about the two men in my life and of a great betrayal, and wondered anew at her meaning. Had she been referring to Robert? His suicide had been the greatest betrayal I had ever faced, the bullet that had killed him having shattered my own life, leaving me with mere fragments to try to piece together again. But who was the other man? I was contemplating sharing my life with John, but could she have been speaking of him? Or was she referring to someone else—someone whom I would love and want to share my life with?

But I was afraid my battered heart had no room for such a fickle affection—an emotion that rode the waves of one's life, lifting a person up to the highest frothy crest and then plummeting her below, creating a frantic struggle for air beneath the surface. I set the lodestone back on my dresser, determined not to let such silliness affect my reasoning.

The window in my room had been opened to let in the late-summer air, bringing with it the heavy odor of the river. I watched as the sky picked up its darkening hues, an unseen hand painting strokes of magenta and burnt sienna across the horizon. It reminded me of the sunsets at home, and I surrendered myself to the glory of it. It was time to dress for supper, but the lovely image of the sunset transfixed me, and I sat in peace for the first time since my arrival. The irony that my first moments of serenity had come only with a memory of home did not evade me.

I sat up suddenly, my ears straining to hear the faint notes of music that crept in through the window. The fine hair at the nape of my neck bristled as I recognized the odd tune and Rebecca's voice. I stood and left my room to find my niece, even though the humming had stopped abruptly.

I stopped in front of Delphine, who was waxing the foyer floor. "Have you seen Rebecca?"

"Yes, ma'am. She be in her room, resting afore supper."

I shook my head. "But I just heard her singing and it was most definitely not coming from her room."

"That be where I puts her, Miss Catherine, and she cain' get by me without me seeing her, so she must still be there."

Confused, I stepped past her until I reached the rear door. I found Rebecca on the back steps with Samantha on her lap. She did not look up as I approached but stared out at the gathering gloom. I sat down next to her and began smoothing her hair with my hand.

"How did you manage to sneak past Delphine?"

I saw her cheek crinkle in a smile but she still did not look up at me. Night had completely descended, leaving only the moon and the stars in the sky, like a queen with her court. "It is a secret."

"A secret? Does that mean I cannot know?"

She looked at me finally, her bright eyes shining like two more stars in the moonlight. "Not yet, Aunt Cat."

I nodded, not wanting to press her. "It is too dark for you to be outside and I do not want you to catch a chill. Why do you not come inside now and get dressed for supper?"

She shook her head vehemently, her coiled curls shaking in agreement. "No—not yet. It is too dark in there."

I put my arm around her small shoulders and drew her closer. "But it is darker out here. Inside we have the lamps lit."

I felt her shiver under my hands. "No, Aunt Cat. Inside there are dark places I am afraid of. There are shadows that live in the corners and I do not want them to get me." Her wide eyes shone as she raised them to mine. "Like they got my mama."

I wanted to refute her words, but I could not. I knew the dark shadows she spoke of, had felt them even as a child, and could not deny them now as an adult. As much as I wanted to dismiss her fears as a child's fancy, I could not. They were all too real to me. Instead, I held her close and patted her head.

She pointed a chubby finger up to the moon, full and round like a ripened peach. "Marguerite says that on nights with a full moon, the Indian lady walks with her baby." She tilted her head, as if trying to hear a far-off sound. "If you listen real good, you can hear the baby crying. Marguerite says the baby cries because she and her mama were buried under the house and they want to get out."

I raised my ear to the slight breeze, listening intently, and I heard it. A high-pitched cry, shifting in and out at the whim of the wind. I stood and moved down the steps to hear it better. I heard it again and I started, a mother's first reaction at the sound of a crying child. My own child's cries were forever stilled, yet the plaintive cry reached out to me with silent fingers of need.

"Do you hear it, Aunt Cat?"

I nodded and stepped slowly off the bottom stair. Then I remembered the glass bottles and realized where the sound was coming from. I turned to Rebecca. "It is the wind blowing through those old bottles that are hung on the trees. It sounds just like a baby crying."

Her wide-eyed look was one of certain disbelief, but she did not say anything. Taking her hand, I said, "Come on. Let us go get dressed."

She placed her hand inside mine and followed. As I guided Rebecca up to her room, I thought of the Indian woman and her child buried under this house, their spirits crying to be free. And I thought of Elizabeth, her spirit just as wistful and strong, and wondered if her time here made her feel as if she had been buried within the four walls of this dark house and had ached to the point of desperation to be set free.

The evening meal passed slowly. I felt John's constant gaze upon me and was grateful for Rebecca's presence. The child charmed me, and I found myself seeing more of her than just the things that reminded me

476 · Karen White

of Jamie. Her blue eyes would still suddenly catch me off guard at times, causing a cascade of grief that I struggled to keep hidden. But her indomitable spirit and sweet hugs had begun to take the chill out of my cold heart.

When Delphine arrived to take Rebecca to her room, I rose, too, eager to excuse myself. But John stayed me with his hand. "Please wait. I have something I wish to give to you."

I nodded and allowed myself to be led into his library. He strode over to his desk and, after unlocking the top drawer, took out a black velvet rectangular box. He returned to stand in front of me again, but made no move to either present the box to me or to open it himself.

"I first met your father in New Orleans. It was at my club there, and he had been invited by an associate of mine to discuss business. I found him a very charming man, and was especially enthralled with his stories of his beautiful Saint Simons. I think that he loved it almost as much as you do."

He smiled at me gently, as if he knew that speaking to me of my father and of my home needed to be handled with great care. "But I soon realized that what he loved most of all were his two daughters. He spoke of you both, but the one he spoke most about was the daughter who loved openly and freely, whose beauty was inside and out, and whose nature was as wild as the waves she liked to race into with bare feet. She was an artist who painted the natural beauty of her island with a lover's touch." He lowered his eyes, staring at the box. "I think I fell in love with her then. She seemed so foreign and exotic compared to the prim Bostonian misses my mother had been tossing in my direction since I had grown out of boyhood." His gaze met mine again and I caught sight of an emotion I thought I recognized before he hid it again from me.

Holding up the box, he opened the lid. "I had these made for that girl, before I had even met her, knowing I wanted her for my wife."

I looked inside and held my breath. The double-strand necklace was composed of the most perfectly formed pearls I had ever seen, faultless in their round, creamy beauty. They circled the strand, each in graduating size before coming to an end in a large, tear-shaped ruby. I didn't move, but continued to stare at the necklace.

He continued. "I pictured these on her flawless skin and against her long black hair." He reached behind me and began to loosen the pins in my hair. I heard them fall one by one to the floor behind me, each one a discarded drop of my resistance.

"Did Elizabeth ever wear it?" I held my breath, awaiting his answer. His eyes darkened. "No. I never gave them to her."

I waited for him to continue, my lungs filling with unspent air and a distant hope.

"Your father never told me how young you were. It was not until my visit when I saw you that I realized. But it was too late then. I had come for a wife, and I was not a man used to disappointment. And Elizabeth . . ." Slowly he raised the pearls from their black box. "Elizabeth used all her charms on me, making me believe that she and you shared more than just appearance."

I did not move as he placed the pearls around my throat, leaning over me to clasp it in back. He lifted my unbound hair and placed it about my shoulders, then studied me closely, his warm breath brushing my neck. "Yes," he whispered. "This is how I pictured you."

I stepped back, my defenses rallying at the first taste of hope. "I am no silly virgin so easily seduced."

He moved toward me and bent his head near my ear. "Neither was Elizabeth."

I looked up at him in shock. "You lie!"

"I am no liar, madam." He took a deep breath, his gaze locked with mine. "And that is the last I shall speak of it." He moved his lips down to my throat, almost making me forget the implications.

"Why did you not press for an annulment?" I had to force the words out, my lungs gasping for air.

"Because I fancied myself in love with her." He lifted his face to look into mine, his emotions completely hidden from me. "But for you and me, Catherine, our motives to marry are much more tangible, are they not?"

My hope crumbled with the hairpins at my feet. I tried to push away, but he would not allow me.

"My dear Catherine. We have made our decision. Now let us make the best of it."

He lowered his mouth to mine and I discovered I had no more will to fight him. I eagerly opened my lips to his, letting him devour me with a passion that seemed to fill us both. His hands swept down the bodice of my dress, pulling me closer in an intimate embrace. His hands teased my hips, sliding upward to my waist. I felt as if I should stop him, but my traitorous arms wrapped themselves around his neck instead, pulling him even closer.

Suddenly, he stopped, and he lifted his face to give me a mocking look. "Madam. It would seem that you are as impatient for our wedding as I."

Ashamed to have to admit the feelings that he stirred in me, I said nothing.

Abruptly, he stepped back, only a sheen of perspiration on his forehead belying his true emotions. "I will not be bothering you any more this evening. You are free to retire."

He bowed, then left the room, but not before I caught sight of a satisfied smile on his face. I was not sure what his game was, but I was quite certain I did not like being a part of it. Perhaps he was testing me—to see how much alike I was to Elizabeth. I wondered at his abrupt dismissal of me, and if my physical response to him had been an affirmation or a warning.

My hands reached up to the chilled beads on my neck, their touch like cool fingers of warning. Slowly, I undid the clasp, then dropped the pearls into their coffinlike box, leaving them on his desk to find in the morning. Turning down the lamp, I climbed the stairs to my room, ignoring the deepening shadows that seemed to reach out to me from the darkened corners of the house.

———◆———

CHAPTER FOURTEEN

I awoke the following morning feeling as if I had not slept at all. I could tell from the brilliant white-yellow glow of the sun peering in between the wooden slats that it was late morning. Slowly, I sat up. It was then that I noticed the black box on my night table.

Reaching over, I picked it up and flicked open the lid. Inside lay the pearl necklace, and I did not doubt for one moment how it had come to be in my bedroom. I wondered how long he had stayed, watching me sleep, if he had stayed at all. But I knew why he had felt compelled to leave the box instead of waiting until morning. He was not a man accustomed to having his wants and desires curtailed in any way. If he wanted me to have the necklace, then have it I would.

I rang for Marguerite to help me dress. While outwardly she continued with the appearance of the dutiful servant, I watched her closely. According to Clara Lewiston, Marguerite had been Elizabeth's confidante, and I wondered how much Marguerite knew of Elizabeth's secret life and of her death. I felt like a mouse, and Marguerite seemed like a cat—toying with me while I tried to pry loose a morsel of truth.

"Marguerite, how well did you know my sister?" I sat at the dresser, waiting for her to fix my hair, and watched her in the mirror.

She smiled faintly. "I was her maid. I suppose I knew her no more or no less than other maids know their mistresses."

"Did she ever tell you anything personal—something only you were privy to?"

She lifted my hair off my shoulders, smoothing it down my back with her hand. "She told me lots of personal things."

I waited for her to continue, but when it was apparent that she would not, I said, "Did she ever tell you anything that might have been some clue as to why she would want her life to end?"

Her eyes glittered in the mirror with an indecipherable emotion, and I imagined that her loyalties toward her former mistress still held firm. Gently, I said, "She is gone now, Marguerite. I only try to understand a sister I loved dearly, to make some sense from her passing. To manage to find peace with the knowledge that I will never see her again."

She took a deep breath. "Miss Elizabeth was not a happy woman, no matter what she had. There was nothing that could make her happy. She was like a child crying for the moon, and even if Mr. John had roped it and brought it down for her, Miss Elizabeth would have quickly tired of it." She pulled the brush through my hair in a long, slow stroke. "And she did not care whose life she made miserable while she was searching for her happiness."

"Do you mean John? Was their life together really that unbearable?"

She shrugged. "There are some who bear it better than others and some who just look until they find a way out."

She fixed my hair in silence, allowing me to mull over our conversation and John's words of the previous evening. If it were true that Elizabeth had not been a virgin on her wedding night, then Elizabeth had been set in her ways long before she married John. I felt no little relief at the thought. I did not want to think that my soon-to-be husband had anything to do with Elizabeth's restlessness. Then again, since she and I had been raised in the same home, would I, too, be susceptible? Or were Elizabeth's demons hers and hers alone?

Due to the lateness of the hour, I ate breakfast alone. The quiet darkness of the house smothered me, and I made a mental note to do something to brighten the interior soon. I listened for Rebecca's voice, but only the brooding silence of the house answered.

After eating, I found Rebecca and took her for a jaunt along the levee in her mother's small buggy. I enjoyed listening to her laugh and hearing her stories of her life on the plantation. It did not escape my notice that she never mentioned her mother at all.

When we were through, I placed her in Delphine's care while I retired to John's study to attend to some personal correspondence. Since my arrival at Whispering Oaks, I had not yet written to my friends and neighbors on Saint Simons. I had been putting off telling them that I would not be returning, but the time had come. John had given me a wedding date two weeks hence, and I needed to adjust myself to my new situation. Writing our names together with a wedding date in a letter seemed to be a prudent way to go about it.

I had been writing for more than an hour when I heard the front door open. Heavy footsteps approached the library, and I chastised myself for the excitement I felt when I recognized who it was.

John seemed surprised to see me at his desk, but his surprise was quickly replaced by a smile. He clutched a medium-sized traveling trunk he held in his arms.

"I am afraid I have been caught."

"Caught?" I raised an eyebrow.

He stepped forward and placed the trunk on the floor by the desk. "Yes. I drove into town to pick up your wedding present. I asked for these from an artist friend in New Orleans shortly after your arrival here. And now I have a reason to give them to you."

I stared at the trunk, unsure of my response. "I thought the necklace was my wedding gift."

He sent me a knowing look, as if realizing we were both thinking of the box sitting on my night table. "No, seeing you wear it is your gift to me. This is my gift to you."

I stood and walked around to his side of the desk, trying to give all my attention to the trunk. But it was hopeless. Whenever he was near me, I could scarce remember to breathe, much less take note of anything else.

"Here—you might find use for this." He reached down and flicked one of the latches with his fingers.

"Oh yes. Of course." My fingers fumbled as I tried to unlatch the two metal loops on the front of the trunk. I managed the first, but I couldn't seem to get my fingers to do the second.

John seemed amused, as if he knew the source of my discomfiture. He stooped to help me. "How about I do this for you?"

With ease, he flicked open the latch and lifted the lid. Stepping back, he indicated the open trunk. "I remembered shortly after you arrived here you mentioned that the Union soldiers had destroyed all your canvases and paints. And that there was nothing left for you to paint. I hope that my gift will soften your heart for at least one Yankee."

Cautiously, I peered inside. When I recognized what it was, my first instinct was to cry. It had been so long since I had received a gift, much less a gift so personal and so full of meaning. Cradled inside wadded mounds of newspaper lay an artist's palette and an array of small glass jars filled with different colored paints. Rolled and fitted neatly in the corners of the trunk were canvases of various sizes.

John stood close to me, studying my face as if to gauge my reaction. When I did not speak, he said, "I had some of the paint pigments already mixed for you—and I hope I chose the colors you would have. I tried to re-create the colors of your home—of the ocean and sand and the marsh."

I waited for a moment, trying to find my voice. "This . . . this is extraordinary." I found it hard to find the appropriate words.

"I want you to be happy here."

I looked into his eyes and wondered if he were thinking of his first wife and her desperate unhappiness. I felt hurt that he would again confuse me with my sister. I gently closed the lid of the box, not wanting him to see the longing in my eyes as I contemplated painting again. "I am not Elizabeth, John. You do not need to bribe me to keep me here."

He stiffened, and the hope I had seen in his eyes was quickly hidden by his usual sardonic smile. He took a step away, as if to distance himself from me. "My dear, I thought the offer of my bed was enough of a bribe to get you to stay. This gift is merely gravy."

I stepped back, the gift nearly ruined for me. He had cut me deeply and I did not want him to see it. I moved to walk past him, but he grabbed my arm.

"I am sorry, Catherine. I should not have said that."

I faced him, trying to keep my fury under the surface. "I am not my sister, and I do not expect you to treat me as if I were. Whatever was between you two, it is past. And if you expect a real marriage between us, then you had best remember it."

He pulled me closer to him, and my wanting of him nearly consumed me. He angered me, yet I still could not resist him. "Forgive me," he said, and before I could contemplate what he was asking forgiveness from, he covered my lips with his, obliterating all thought.

The world seemed to spiral out of control for a moment as my hands grabbed his hair and pulled him closer. He pressed me backward against the desk, our bodies touching intimately. With visible control, he pulled himself back, disentangling my arms from around his neck. His eyes burned as he watched me try to find my breath. "I could never mistake you for Elizabeth. Only a fool could do that."

Embarrassed again by my easy acquiescence to his touch, I backed away from him and then fled up to my room. I paced for a few moments before my gaze caught sight of a piece of Elizabeth's riding habit stuck in the doors of the armoire. Yanking off my clothes, I pulled on the habit, struggling in my haste with the row of tiny buttons up the back. I desperately needed to burn off the energy that John's presence created in me. Perhaps then I could be calm and impartial when next he approached me.

As I pinned the riding hat to my hair, I recalled the glimmer of hope in John's eyes when he had given me the paints. John McMahon was a difficult man to fathom, but the very gesture of the gift told me that perhaps within the dark depths of his soul lay a kind and tender heart. A side to him, if it existed, he was not at all comfortable in letting others see.

Not sure why I did it, I slipped the lodestone into my pocket before walking quickly to the stables. I spotted Mr. O'Rourke and greeted him warmly. He still treated me with aloofness, due to the accident on the flooded road, no doubt, which was why I always gave him my biggest smile. I had the strong feeling that I would need as many friends as I could find if I were to make a home for myself at Whispering Oaks.

He saddled Jezebel for me and allowed me to go by myself only after I solemnly promised to stay on the levee road and not venture anywhere else. I gave Mr. O'Rourke a bright smile; then Jezebel and I took off at a brisk walk.

I kept a sedate pace as we passed through the lane of weeping oaks, then gave Jezebel the lead as we raced toward the levee. I loved the feel of the wind kissing my face and tugging at my hair. I was a little girl again, with no concerns or worries, my future laid out ahead of me as sparkling as the sun-dappled river.

Slowing my mount, I allowed her to trot along the levee road as I stared into the murky depths of the Mississippi. How tranquil the water seemed, yet I knew of the strong undercurrents that could sweep one under without warning. Unlike my ocean, who showed his wrath with froth-tipped waves, the river was an insidious thing; so unassuming on the surface yet turbulent and deadly underneath.

As I turned my horse to head back, I caught sight of another rider approaching me. The rakish angle of his hat and foppish dress gave away his identity before I even recognized the face of Philip Herndon.

His face seemed unusually pale as he drew alongside me, and for a moment he did not speak. Finally, as if remembering his manners, he doffed his hat and bowed low. "My dear Cat, forgive me my manners. I was so struck by your beauty that I was paralyzed for a few moments."

The stunned expression on his face made me almost believe his words until I recalled that I wore Elizabeth's riding habit. From a distance, I must have resembled her greatly.

"Hello, Philip. This is an unexpected pleasure."

He nodded, his smile wary. "Are you alone?"

"Yes, I am. But only because I promised not to get into trouble." I smiled, but it was not returned.

He leaned close to me. "Forgive the impudence, but I am glad to find you alone. I need to speak with you, and I would not be able to speak candidly if you had company." It was clear from his implication as to whom "company" referred.

Jezebel stepped forward to nuzzle Philip's mount as if they were old friends. He continued. "I heard from the Lewistons that there is to be a wedding soon at Whispering Oaks."

I lifted my chin. "Yes, there is. John and I are to be married."

His face darkened. "How could you, Cat? Especially after what he did to Elizabeth!"

"Whatever happened to Elizabeth, Philip, was of her own doing. I do not hold him responsible."

He scoffed, looking up to the sky momentarily. "Not responsible? But she is dead! Can you honestly tell me that you do not believe he had anything to do with it?"

"Yes, I can." I realized with a start that I was telling the truth. Despite all the unknowns, I had believed John when he claimed innocence in Elizabeth's death.

Philip grabbed Jezebel's bridle and leaned close to me. "Do not believe him. He is a dangerous man, Cat. And a Yankee. He's not to be trusted."

Growing impatient, I pulled away. "It is none of your concern, Philip, and I would appreciate it if you would not be intent on spreading unfounded rumors. I have Rebecca to think of."

His eyes softened. "Yes, Elizabeth's child. Thank God you are here to see to her upbringing." Somber again, he said, "If you are intent on marrying him, just remember that I am only a short ride from you. Do not hesitate to call on me if you should need anything. Anything."

I wondered at his words as he bowed again and replaced his hat. "It is best that I leave now. Good day, Cat." To my surprise, he reached for my hand and held it to his mouth, his lips lingering longer than necessary. Jezebel stepped back, and I pulled away. His eyes darkened as he regarded me, but there was something in them that told me he was not seeing me but some distant vision from his memory. I wondered if it had anything to do with Elizabeth. He looked past my shoulder and then, without another word, he bowed again and took off at a canter.

In a contemplative mood, I stared after him until he was out of sight, oblivious to the pounding of hooves approaching me from the rear. At the last moment, I turned to see John approaching, his face a mask of fury. He drew up his horse quickly, making it rear.

"So, we are not yet married and you are already having assignations. If you are to meet with men other than your husband, at least have the decency to choose a more worthy adversary. That fop is not even worth the energy of pulling out my pistol."

I was dumbfounded for a minute as I contemplated his implication. In an unaccustomed rage, borne of weariness and anxiety over the recent and dramatic turns in my life, I raised my hand to strike out at him. He leaned back, avoiding the blow, and I lost my balance, tumbling over the neck of my horse and down the embankment toward the swirling river below.

The abject terror of touching the water consumed me, and I acted as a wild woman, scraping and clawing at the grassy mud, trying to find something of which to grab hold. My struggles were rewarded when I managed to grasp a withered root, its frizzled ends reaching out from the dark mud like a groping hand. With desperation I hung on with all my strength.

"Catherine!"

It was then that I remembered I was not alone, and I clung to John's voice with hope. The relief nearly weakened me, but I dared not let go.

"Hold on—I think I can reach you and pull you up. Just do not let go." I saw his gaze travel to the slurp and splash of the river below me. He disappeared for a moment and then returned.

"I have tied myself to my horse so there is no danger of me falling in and taking you with me." He lay on his stomach and inched himself slightly over the precipice, his hands reaching toward me, his fingertips nearly touching mine.

"Give me your hand."

I hesitated, thinking back on Philip's words. Could I trust this man?

"Cat, give me your hand."

His dark eyes bored into mine. With a deep breath, I let go with my right hand and placed it into John's strong palm. His fingers closed about mine in a firm grip, and I had no more doubt. Without waiting for him to ask, I let go with my other hand and placed it into his other palm.

His face contorted in strain and concentration as he began to pull me up. I used my feet to find footholds, using them for leverage as John slid back toward his horse. Slowly but surely, I inched my way up to the top, and when we were both safe, we lay on our backs, panting.

John sat up and reached for me, pulling me into his lap. I did not resist and allowed him to cradle me in his arms, much the same way I had seen him holding Rebecca, and I felt him tremble. I was warm and safe in his care, and my doubts of marrying him began to fade. "You called me Cat," I said foolishly. Only my family and those who had known me since childhood called me by that name, and I found his use of it oddly comforting and familiar.

"Yes. I did."

I felt his lips on my hair as we huddled together, his arms tight around me.

We rode back together on his horse, leading Jezebel, as John would not be separated from me. When we arrived, Mr. O'Rourke took the horses and John insisted on carrying me up to my bedroom.

Despite my assertions that I was quite all right, I was still surprised that John did not suggest we call for Dr. Lewiston. As he settled me on the bed, he said, "There is no need to send for Daniel. I am quite capable of taking care of you, and he would only look upon your accident as another reason for you to stay at Belle Meade." He tried to force a grin but failed. "It would not do to have the neighbors thinking that you might be in some sort of danger from me."

I found his words odd, especially after having spoken with Philip and Judge Patterson. But John had saved my life, and I now knew their concerns to be unfounded.

Marguerite helped me undress and settled me into bed with an herbal tea to help me sleep. I felt like a child but acquiesced, realizing that the afternoon had taken a toll on my nerves. The soothing brew settled in my brain like a warm blanket, and I was soon fast asleep.

It was near dark when I awoke, and I knew that I was not alone. John sat on the edge of my bed, watching me. His expression was grim, his face pale.

"I came close to losing you today, and know I am partially to blame." He took a deep breath, and it almost sounded like a sigh. "I wanted to offer you an apology."

I sat up, pulling the blankets along with me to cover my nightgown. I was all too aware that I was barely dressed and alone in my bedroom with this disturbing man. "I met with Philip today simply by accident. It was not planned." I took a deep breath. "John, I am learning to trust you, and you should be doing the same with me. I do not know if I can marry you if you are going to interpret every innocent action or remark as something circumspect. A marriage without trust is like a prison for the soul."

My heart clenched as I recalled the painful weeks following Robert's return from the war when he had learned that our Jamie had drowned. Robert had gone to his grave believing that the woman to whom he had entrusted the care of his only son had betrayed him. And his harsh words had me almost believing him. I met John's troubled gaze. "I would rather have my destitution on Saint Simons than live in such a prison again."

He took my hand and held it to his lips. My pulse leapt through my veins at his gesture, my breath quickening. "There are reasons for my behavior, some of which you understand and some of which I hope you never try to fathom. But I swear to you that I will do my best to be more trusting." His dark eyes bored into mine. "And you must do the same. I am not the evil man that some are eager to make me appear." His thumb stroked the top of my hand, and I wondered if he could hear the scattered beating of my heart. "I can be quite gentle, if given the chance."

Reluctantly, I pulled my hand away. "Do not try to seduce me with your words. I will pack my bags and return to Saint Simons tomorrow if you have no intention of building trust into our marriage."

"Then I give you my word."

I bowed my head so he could not see the hope I knew must be shimmering in my eyes. "Then I will marry you as we planned."

He took my hand again and squeezed it. Bending close to me, he kissed me chastely on the cheek. My skin burned where his lips had been, and I looked up as he stood. "I will have a tray sent up for you. I think you should remain in bed until morning."

I nodded. "Thank you."

He raised an eyebrow.

"For saving my life."

"Then I must thank you for the same reason. Sometimes I think that you may have saved my own as well."

With a brief bow, he left. My hand went to my night table, where I had placed the lodestone when getting undressed. I rubbed its cool, smooth hardness as I contemplated his words, until Marguerite arrived with my tray.

Halfway through my meal, I looked up to see the door of my room slowly being pushed open.

"Hello?" I called.

I saw Samantha's head first, shortly followed by Rebecca's blond head, her face covered by her doll. Without answering or waiting to be invited in, Rebecca climbed up on the footstool by the side of my bed and plopped herself down at the foot, Samantha in her lap.

I stopped chewing, noticing the doll's face. It was completely covered in dirt, and the yellow yarn of her hair had fared no better. Rebecca's hand rested in Samantha's lap and her nails were caked with dark earth. When the child peeked around her doll's head, it was hard to tell the two apart, so filthy were the usually rosy cheeks.

"Rebecca, what has happened to you?"

She giggled, that high, appealing child sound that I had come to love. I tried to look stern and admonishing, but it was so difficult when faced with so much guileless charm. I pressed my napkin to my mouth to hide my smile.

She pretended to pout. "Samantha is all dirty. She made me get dirty, too."

I nodded solemnly. "I see. And how did she make you get dirty?"

Rebecca pursed her lips into a perfect rosebud shape and placed her little finger against them. "Sshh. It is a secret."

I tilted my head. "I promise not to tell."

She shrugged, her gaze wandering around the room, apparently losing interest in the direction of our conversation.

I continued. "Well, whether or not you tell me your secret, you should not be getting yourself and Samantha so dirty. Where was Delphine?"

She shook her head, her blond curls bouncing, a mischievous smile on her lips. "I ran away from her when she was not looking."

I put down my fork, feeling anxious. I remembered the cottonmouth snake and knew that dangers lurked everywhere for small children. Even under the serene waters of the ocean—or a pond. "Promise me, Rebecca, that you will never do that again. I do not care that you are all dirty, but I do care if you get hurt. That is why you must never run off by yourself. Do you understand?"

She looked at me as if she were about to cry, and I realized that my tone had taken on a sense of urgency. I reached out and took her hand. "I care about you, Rebecca, and I do not want anything to happen to you. Can you understand that? And can you promise me that you won't run off again?"

With a small sniff, she nodded. I patted her hand, noticing again the dirt-encrusted nails. Gently, I asked, "Are you sure you won't tell me where you and Samantha have been?"

She looked up at me with those clear blue eyes, and my heart skipped a beat. I fleetingly wondered if I would ever be able to look at this child and not see the one I had lost. "Somebody is buried under the orange trees, and me and Samantha were trying to dig it up."

Something hit the floor, and it took me a moment to realize that it was the lodestone that had slipped from my hand onto the wood floor and now lay cold and still. I thought I saw a movement by the door and imagined the sound of stealthy footsteps walking down the passageway outside. I hastily moved aside the tray and slid from the bed. When I stepped outside my bedroom door, all was still and quiet in the darkening house.

I walked down the passageway, not caring who might see me in my nightdress. I continued down the corridor toward John's room but saw no one. I returned and peered down the hallway toward the attic door, but nothing stirred.

I returned to my room to find Rebecca gone. I had not heard her leave, nor had she passed me on the way to her room. When I bent to look for the child under my bed, I noticed that the lodestone was missing from my floor. Looking up, I spotted it on my night table, a diminutive statue full of secrets and hidden meaning, surrounded with a sprinkling kiss of dirt.

CHAPTER FIFTEEN

———◆———

I had no time to pursue the absurdities of Rebecca's claims, as the preparations for the wedding consumed my time and energy. She was apparently a child with a rich imagination, and I did not want to discourage it. To assuage my curiosity, I would soon have to take her with me to investigate her mysterious place in the orange grove. Then, perhaps, I could put it out of my mind. But for now, the child's secretive smile and earnest words made sure it was never far from my thoughts.

John's work on the plantation and at the sugar mill kept him out of the house from sunrise to sunset. But I always knew when he was near, as if something about him had heightened all my senses, creating an awareness of his presence.

Despite his long absences during the day, he would join us for supper in the evenings. I enjoyed his company, his intelligent conversation, and even his smoldering looks. But I was also glad of Rebecca's presence. The days in which I could make the excuse to retire to the privacy of my own room alone were dwindling, and I mourned the passing of each one. I had been my own person for a long time, and the thought of answering to a man again was not appealing. Especially this man, whose mere touch could make me forget all reason and agree to anything he wished. I hated myself for this one weakness, while at the same time I enjoyed the tiny flashes of heat I felt every time our eyes met.

Our relationship seemed to have progressed since my accident at the levee. We no longer spoke of Elizabeth, and he seemed to have stopped making comparisons. It was as if Elizabeth were truly gone and buried, leaving us alone to start a new life together. I had no illusions as to our marriage. It was not a love match, but perhaps in time the bond between us could grow into something even longer lasting than that elusive emotion. If not, I would at least have the comfort of food and shelter and old memories. My bargain with John still made me feel at times like a compromised woman, but I had done what I did for mere survival. I had not made it this far past the war and loss to die of starvation.

My one consolation was that I would have Rebecca—and any other children I might bear through our union. The thought always made me flush like a virginal bride. But I was hardly that, and chastised myself for my foolish notions and weak knees that appeared every time he entered the room.

We were married on the last Friday in September. In addition to the new clothes that John had ordered for me shortly after my arrival at Whispering Oaks, I had had several new dresses made, including a wedding gown of dove gray silk, as I could not imagine wearing either one of my own or one of Elizabeth's. The dresses John had ordered for me were brightly colored reds, blues, and yellows, making a travesty of my mourning. I had thanked him, then had them put away in an armoire in one of the guest rooms.

At the dressmaker's, I had felt like a child in a candy store, choosing between the multihued bolts of cloth. Still clinging to my mourning, I picked out only muted colors of gray and brown, but when I looked at my reflection I felt almost beautiful.

The clouds dripped halfheartedly on the small wedding party, anointing our hair with tiny kisses of rain. I stood on the church steps and smiled at my groom, intent on casting off any dark thoughts brought about by the weather. Marguerite, pausing earlier while helping me dress, had clucked her tongue as she looked out the window of my bedroom. "It is a bad sign for it to rain on your wedding day."

I had shrugged, determined not to let her words sour my wedding, but a little shiver of apprehension crept down my spine, settling in my stomach. I had stared at the reflection of the pearl necklace about my neck and could not help but remember Elizabeth's wedding day, when the clouds had blackened, unleashing a torrent of rain that had saturated the earth and turned the roads into muddy creeks.

Whenever I smell the odor of wet leaves and moist earth, I remember that day as I stood at the altar of Grace Episcopal Church in Saint

Francisville next to John and exchanged vows to last until death did us part. His kiss burned my lips, as if branding me his.

We were to honeymoon in New Orleans, and after extracting promises from Delphine and Mary not to let Rebecca out of their sight, we set off in a closed carriage driven by Mr. O'Rourke.

John sat next to me and took my hand. Slowly, he drew off my glove and moved my fingers to his lips. "So. It is done."

I looked into those dark, unfathomable eyes and wondered what he meant. "I would not say it is done, but, rather, that this is the beginning."

He gripped my hand tightly. "But all endings are the beginnings of something new."

I nodded, then leaned against the back of the seat, suddenly tired. He moved my head to his shoulder, and I must have slept, for when I awoke, we were on the outskirts of the city.

I had always loved New Orleans, with its brash mixture of French and American customs and the grand mansions of the Garden District and Vieux Carré. The intricate iron balconies and balustrades delighted me with their foreign appeal, and I had thought as a child that they always made the buildings appear gift-wrapped.

We checked into a small hotel on Royal Street, the accommodations intimate yet exquisitely furnished. Our suite consisted of two main rooms, a sitting room and bedroom, and I paused with trepidation in the threshold of the room with the large rice poster bed with heavy silk drapes.

After the porter had delivered our bags, John came to stand behind me and kissed me on the neck. "All in good time, my dear," he said. "But, alas, I have reservations at Antoine's for a late supper. Shall I help you dress?" He removed my traveling cloak while I tried to breathe calmly.

All of my senses seemed sharpened somehow; every color, every sound, every touch seemed brighter, louder, and more sensitive. "No." My voice shook. "I would like a maid sent up, please. I need help unpacking and selecting a gown."

He nodded, his eyes once again hiding his thoughts from me. I turned away, thankful for his compliance. I needed time to fortify my mind before he touched me and all rational thought deserted me.

We sat in the glow of the candlelight at Antoine's, eating and drinking and talking intimately. I do not recall what was said or what we ate, but I do remember how I felt. The way he looked at me and the way he held my hand made me feel more whole than I had since I had lost my son. The grieving mother and destitute widow was not the woman in the dark amber silk gown with her hair piled high on her head and pearls glowing at her throat. This woman was new to me; she was a woman desired by the man across the snowy white table linens from her, and a woman equally capable of the same desires.

The ride back to the hotel was quiet, but the darkness inside the coach was filled with a heady anticipation that was thick enough to fill my lungs. John lifted me out of the carriage in front of our hotel, his touch solicitous and chaste, but my response was the same as if he had touched my naked flesh.

He opened the door to our room and allowed me to enter first. Before I could turn around, his hands were on me, the pins from my hair pulled out and scattered on the plush rug at our feet. With quick hands he expertly undid the myriad buttons of my gown, leaving it in a pool of silk at my feet.

His lips ravaged mine as his hands efficiently disrobed me, his fingers adept at every nuance of a woman's clothing. I stood trembling, wearing only my chemise, as he knelt in front of me to remove my stockings. Strong fingers slid up my nearly bare legs, coming to rest on my exposed thighs. We said nothing, but each of us knew the steps to this primal dance; no words were needed. Slowly, he slid the stockings down one leg, then the other, his eyes never leaving my face.

He stood, bringing the hem of my chemise with him, carefully lifting it over my head. He reached his hand out to my neck and I realized that I still wore the pearls. "Yes," he whispered. "This is how I saw you."

He bent his head toward me, his lips brushing my neck. I had never felt this wanting before, this need. It frightened me yet it exhilarated me, too, awakening the woman in me that had lain dormant for so long. I shed the skin of the grieving widow and became John McMahon's wife: cherished and desired, a woman of passion.

John lifted me and carried me to the bed, laying me down on the turned-back covers. He began to undress and I sat up to watch him, a craving rising within me like I had never known. The lamps burned low, casting deep shadows on the walls. But instead of being foreboding, they warmed the room, creating the impression of being in a cocoon. My bare feet sank deeply into the sheets on the bed and I arched my spine in a luxurious stretch, feeling his eyes upon me.

I lay back, my arms reaching for him, and he came to me, pressing his warm flesh against mine. There was no tenderness between us in our hunger. It was as if we knew we would have a lifetime for discovery, but this first time would be to claim each other.

Afterward he rolled to my side but held me close. His eyes shone from the streetlamp outside the window, and the look in them made me catch my breath. He had claimed my body, and now he seemed intent on claiming my very soul. *Had he ever looked at Elizabeth in the same way? And is that what drove her away?*

He must have felt my slight withdrawal, for he reached for me, pulling me on top of him. "I knew it would be this way between us."

I turned my face away, my cheek against his bare chest, embarrassment at my wantonness flooding over me.

Lifting my chin, he raised my face to his. "Do not be ashamed, Cat. This is the way it is supposed to be between man and wife. What has gone before no longer matters. It is just you and me now."

His hands slid down my bare body, coming to rest on the dip of my waist. Raising his head, he ran his tongue along the sensitive skin of my neck, making me shudder. I fought to keep my voice steady. "I do not want this to be all there is between you and me." My skin shivered as his hands caressed my bare back while his eyes continued to glitter in the darkness.

His hands moved behind my neck, brushing the pearls and lifting my hair, bringing my face closer to his. "My dear, there was never any question of that." He pressed his lips against mine, and I soon forgot all of my questions and concerns, lost as I was in the riptide of his lovemaking. I was not sure whether I was drowning or swimming, and as the hours of that first night together ticked on, I simply did not care.

Ours was an idyllic honeymoon. We ate in wonderful restaurants, strolled along the river, and spent hours in the shops, purchasing things for the house and gifts for Rebecca. I still had the suspicion that there were things John preferred to keep hidden from me, but in our time together, I learned that he was capable of great thought and feeling. He made me laugh again, a sound that had become foreign to my ears. For that, I was grateful.

He expressed concern over my thinness and questioned me closely over the condition of my home in Saint Simons. He seemed to be storing away the information for future use, but when questioned about it, he only smiled and diverted my attention to a street vendor selling pralines.

I no longer feared the night, but instead looked forward to the sunset with breathless anticipation. John had awakened a passion in me I had not known existed but which he insisted he had known had always dwelled within. We would make love through the long hours of the night, then sleep in each other's arms until late morning. The hotel maids instinctively knew not to disturb us and let us sleep. It was terribly decadent, but John's touch consumed me, erasing all other concerns.

Throughout my days and nights with John on our honeymoon, I would think back to that girl I had once been: Robert's wife and Jamie's mother. When I looked at myself in the mirror, it seemed she was no longer there. I still bore my grief for my son, but I could now regard Robert's absence in my life as a gift of freedom, and felt very little remorse at the thought.

On our last night in New Orleans we dined at the St. Charles, and we were both surprised when we looked up during the main course and saw Philip Herndon approaching.

John did not stand to greet his neighbor, but placed his fork deliberately on the white tablecloth with a snap.

Philip bowed to me, then turned to John. "Allow me to congratulate you both on your recent nuptials. I have been in town for a while and I missed the big celebration."

I thanked him, while John merely stared at him with barely concealed dislike.

Philip continued. "I can only hope that this marriage has a much happier ending. I have a great fondness for Cat, and I would hate to have her dead, too."

John stood suddenly, his chair wobbling but, blessedly, not falling over. Heads had already begun to turn. "I demand an apology for that remark, Herndon."

Philip stared at him insolently. "So you can call me out and kill me, too? Everyone knows you are a crack shot, John. But what is one more murder on your hands?"

I knew I had to intervene before matters disintegrated further. Standing, I put myself between them. "Please," I whispered urgently to both men. "Do not cause a scene. Surely this matter can be settled when you have both had a chance to cool off, and in a more appropriate place."

John looked at me and must have read the pleading in my eyes, for he stepped back. "My wife has uncommon good sense. But I do not wish to speak with you later—or ever. I have no use for irrational men."

I clasped John's arm, hoping to create the impression of a united front. We were husband and wife, and I wanted Philip to understand that attacking John would be akin to attacking me.

Philip leaned close so that only John and I could hear. "I will not forget what you have done. You have taken away the most precious thing in my life, and I will see that you, too, shall lose that which you hold in the highest regard."

With a brief glance at me, he turned and left, oblivious to the heads turning to follow him out.

Shaking, John sat down. The meal was ruined for both of us and we soon left the restaurant, not even waiting to finish the last course.

His lovemaking that night was fierce, his touch tender yet his passions boiling under the surface of his skin. When I touched him, he was as if a man with fever, and I found myself arching toward him, trying to match his heated ardor. Afterward, he cradled me in his arms, making me feel more cherished than I had since I was a small child. I laid my head on his shoulder and slept.

Our honeymoon ended after only a week. John promised me an extended European honeymoon the following year, but for now he was needed at the plantation and mill and he did not want to leave Rebecca so soon after her mother's death.

I did not argue, as I was also anxious to return to Rebecca. I wished only that we would be returning to Saint Simons instead of Whispering Oaks. When I thought of my new home, it was always with apprehension. The dark shadows, unseen footsteps, and haunted past seemed to follow me like a ghost—a ghost who refused to be exorcised.

We were both subdued on our return journey, John's brow furrowed with dark thoughts that he did not share with me, and me with my own. I thought back on Philip's words and wondered at his threats. He obviously still believed that John had something to do with Elizabeth's death. I did trust in John's innocence. He had given me his word. Then why the small shadow of doubt that threatened to obscure my new happiness?

I looked up suddenly to find John watching me closely. I colored, imagining that he could read my mind, and looked away. Whether he guessed my thoughts, he did not say. We had promised not to speak of Elizabeth's death again, for it was a topic we both preferred to avoid. My reasons were obvious: I simply did not wish to be reminded of the person my sister had become. But for John, his reasons went unexplained to me.

Rebecca ran out to greet us, enthusiastically hugging us each in turn. She greedily unwrapped the porcelain doll with yellow hair and blue eyes, easily putting it aside with the fickle nature of small children, when she saw the sweets we had brought. I had deliberately avoided buying her licorice, knowing how she disliked it, and enjoyed her cries of pleasure when she spotted the peppermint sticks.

After greeting his daughter, John went immediately to the sugar mill, leaving me alone with Rebecca. While my bags were brought up and Marguerite unpacked for me, the child and I went for a walk. She sucked on a peppermint stick as we walked, her words garbled. I smiled at her attempts to speak and suggested she remove the candy for me to understand her better, but she stubbornly refused.

I held her hand, now sticky from the candy, as we walked along the perimeter of the pond, me with a constant wariness over how close we came to the edge. She paused on the far side and pointed toward the orange grove. "Do you want to see my secret now?"

Her fingernails were filthy, and it was clear that she had been digging near the orange trees again. Feeling I should humor her, I agreed.

It was late afternoon, and the early-autumn sky was beginning to darken. The trees in the grove had been severely damaged in a storm several years before and had long since given up their fruit. Now the naked limbs reached up to the sky in silent supplication like the arms of barren mothers.

I realized for the first time how quiet it was in the grove. Even the screech of insects seemed to bypass this place, as if they, too, respected its peaceful solitude. Elizabeth had once told me that the orange grove had been the site of another burial mound, smaller than the one on which the house had been built. I thought again of Rebecca's claims of finding a dead body and wondered with trepidation if indeed she had.

She ran to the farthest corner of the grove, an area completely out of sight from the main house, and knelt down beside a tree trunk. "Over here, Aunt Cat." Even from where I was, I could tell where new dirt had been replaced by old, the topsoil removed and then scraped back. A deep indentation in the middle of the small rectangle of dark soil showed where small fingers had been diligently digging.

I stood looking down at the disturbed earth and was about to suggest we go find help to finish the digging when a glimmer of something shiny caught my attention.

Kneeling down, I placed my hands on the cool earth and peered into the hole. I stared hard, not really believing what I saw until I reached out and touched it. The letterbox.

With my heart thumping, I stuck my hands in the dirt and began frantically scraping away. I sent Rebecca to go find a couple of sharp sticks and she returned, excitedly holding up our new digging instruments.

Knowing the size of the box, I easily outlined the shape with one of the sticks, which made the process easier. It hadn't been buried deep, and it took less than half an hour to release it from its grave. The sky had almost completely darkened by now, leaving only thin traces of glowing orange to guide us back to the house.

I sent Rebecca to the kitchen to wash up while I went to the front of the house, knowing that the servants at this time would be mostly by the kitchen. I had no idea who had buried the box, but whoever it was had obviously wished for it to remain hidden.

Cautiously, I opened the front door and entered. As I reached the bottom step, I heard movement in the dining room. Peering over my shoulder, I spied Marguerite setting the table. Our gazes met but I kept my back to her, only nodding as I proceeded up the stairs. As I pushed open my bedroom door I noticed behind me the trail of dirt, and I made a note to sweep the steps before anybody saw.

I quickly hid the letterbox under the bed, then stood, taking note of my surroundings with dismay. All of my things were gone. The armoire doors stood open, exposing empty shelves and hooks, and my dressing table had been completely stripped. I realized with a mix of excitement and apprehension that my things had been taken to the master bedroom.

But where was the key? When I had left for my honeymoon, I had hidden it in the back of my dresser drawer, tucking it among stockings and chemises. I walked quickly over to the dresser and yanked open the drawer. My heart slammed in my chest when I saw the gaping cavity.

Calming myself, I left the room and walked to the end of the corridor to John's room. The door stood partially ajar, and I waited for a moment before pushing it open. To my relief, I found the room empty, but I still felt uncomfortable advancing further. This was John's room. My gaze strayed to the empty spot on the wall where Elizabeth's portrait had been, and then to the great mahogany bed. I flushed, imagining what we would be doing beneath its sheets later in the evening.

Elizabeth had had her own room, but her ghost seemed to be everywhere in this one. Even as I looked at the bed, I wondered if she had ever passed the night there, wrapped in John's arms and enjoying his caresses. I turned away, trying to avert my thoughts, and saw the trunk of paints and supplies John had given me. It sat in the corner, untouched, and I smiled again, remembering his thoughtfulness. One of the first things I would do to become settled would be to set up a place in the house for my painting.

I closed the door quietly behind me and leaned against it, contemplating where my things would have been placed. I was reluctant to go around blatantly opening drawers, still feeling like an intruder in somebody else's room. A large chest-on-chest occupied the space between the windows, and I was fairly certain it contained John's personal items. My gaze strayed to a lowboy against the far wall, and I thought that it would be the ideal place for my things.

With my breath held, I slid open the first drawer and, to my delight, found my underpinnings. Wiping my hands on my underskirt, I began digging into the drawer, hoping to feel the hard brass key easily under the light fabrics of my clothing. I almost cried out when my fingers found it, wrapped in a pair of stockings, as I had left it, and pulled it from the drawer.

I had started sliding the drawer closed when I spotted something unfamiliar in the back. It appeared to be a large linen handkerchief, certainly not one of my own, and when I pulled on it, it seemed stuck. I realized it was caught on the back of the drawer and would have been easily overlooked had I not had the drawer pulled all the way out.

I held it out to the light and saw the embroidered initials JEM and knew it belonged to my new husband, as I had seen him in possession of several identical to this one. It was filthy, covered in dirt, with long streaks of mud bisecting the cloth. It was as if somebody had wiped very dirty fingers on it and then stuffed it in the back of the drawer to be hidden and forgotten.

My gaze strayed to my own dirty hands, and they began to tremble as the realization of why it was there struck me. I remembered the ride to the questioning at the town hall, and how I had smelled freshly turned earth on John's jacket. I raised my eyes to the mirror over the chest and saw John standing in the doorway, watching me closely.

I turned quickly to face him, my hands behind my back and pressed against the lowboy. He approached with long strides, his eyes holding a dangerous spark. He stood so close to me that I couldn't move away without pushing against him.

His voice was like dark velvet when he spoke. "What are you hiding, Cat?"

"Nothing," I stammered. "I was simply cleaning and my hands are filthy. I was embarrassed to let you see them."

He placed his hands on my shoulders and slowly let them slide down to my elbows. "There is nothing about you that I do not think is beautiful." His eyes bored into mine. "Let me see."

I felt like an animal in a trap, with nowhere to run and hide. Without preamble, I moved my hands out from behind my back and raised them in front of me. One finger at a time, I opened my hands, revealing the key in one and the handkerchief in the other.

His eyes darkened, and the first flash of fear I had experienced in over a year coursed through me. The key hit the floor with a small *thud* as the handkerchief drifted out of my fingers. John lowered his face to mine, those obsidian eyes glittering, and I clenched my own eyes tightly, waiting for what was to come.

Chapter Sixteen

——◆——

"Why were you hiding these from me?" His voice was low and thick, like a dam holding back the words of accusation I knew he wanted to say.

I opened my eyes and faced him, forcing myself to raise my chin. "I should ask you the same thing. Why was your dirty handkerchief hidden in the back of your drawer? Did you use it to wipe your fingers after burying the letterbox from the attic?"

I waited for him to answer, my fingers clutching the lowboy behind me. To my surprise, he gave a low chuckle, but there was no mirth in it.

"Do you mean to say you are standing here acting like a hunted fox because you found a dirty handkerchief belonging to me?" He threw back his head and laughed. "I am a planter, my dear wife. I get my fingers dirty quite often, which is why I always carry a handkerchief. Feel free to interview the laundress, and she will inform you that, yes, I always have dirty and muddy handkerchiefs that need her attention."

He narrowed his eyes at me, all traces of laughter gone. "Now you might answer a question of my own. Why is that key on a chain, and why would you hide it from me?"

I felt suddenly foolish and found myself staring at him dumbly, unable to find any words that would defend myself.

He leaned closer to me and I felt his heat. "I thought we had an agreement between us. An agreement to trust. It was even you who said you could not have a marriage without it."

I nodded, my eyes stinging at his chastisement. He moved his head lower, his lips close to my ear. "I want you, Cat. But I want your trust even more. Can you understand that?"

"Yes," I said, my voice barely audible. He was pressing me against the chest while his hands slowly raised my skirts. I wanted to protest, but I wanted him as much as I wanted his forgiveness for doubting him.

His moist lips moved to my neck as his fingers deftly raised my chemise. "I want you . . . now," he whispered against my throat.

I was too aroused to tell him to stop, too enflamed by his passion to even want him to, but something in the back of my head told me that propriety should make me ashamed and disdainful of what we were about to do.

Instead, I allowed him to lift me on top of the low chest. "Cat," he whispered into my ear, and he moved his hands to my hips and slid me closer. I moaned into his mouth, and as he whispered my name again, time seemed to stop. He pressed me backward until I felt the wall behind me, my hair tumbling about my shoulders. I should have been ashamed, but all I could think of was my wanting of this man and his desire for me, and I pulled him closer.

I felt him shudder at the same time as my passion consumed me, leaving me trembling as I fell back down to earth. We held each other for a long moment, he with his lips on my hair and my fingers clutching his shirt. Finally, he lifted me off the chest and my legs slid down to the ground. He didn't let go of me, and I was grateful for his support because I was sure my legs would have otherwise buckled.

He looked honestly chagrined as he studied my face. "I am sorry," he whispered, his voice hoarse. Gently, he pulled me toward him, kissing me softly on my forehead. "I am sorry," he said again. "I did not mean for that to happen. But this wanting I have for you . . ."

I felt the sting of tears in my eyes—but they were not tears of shame. The fire we had shared was new to me, new and liberating, and he had made me feel wanted again. I knew, once I was alone again, I would be shocked at our behavior, but now I was simply grateful. He had made me a woman to be desired, not pitied, scorned, or accused. Robert's suicide had done all those things to me, had, indeed, deadened all emotions in me. John made me feel alive again, allowed me to feel passion and heat, to see colors where I had once only seen black and white.

He saw my tears and looked stricken. With the pads of his thumbs he gently wiped them away. "Forgive me, Cat."

I grabbed his wrists, stilling his hands. "There is nothing to forgive." I kissed his palm, then cradled my face in his hand.

He placed his lips on the hair at my temple, now damp from the sweat of our lovemaking. "I will send Marguerite to help you dress."

Drawing back, he adjusted his clothing, then left the room. As I watched the door close, I realized with a start that he had never actually denied burying the box. He had certainly implied it by giving an explanation as to how a dirty handkerchief would come to be shoved in the back of his drawer, but that was not a claim to innocence. I wanted to trust him, but I knew asking him would never allay my suspicions. I would need to discover the truth on my own before I could lay to rest all of my doubts.

I stooped to pick up the key, intent now on finding the contents of the box and why somebody was so determined that I not discover it.

As I moved toward the door, it opened and Marguerite came in, her strange eyes regarding me dispassionately. "I've ordered bathwater to be sent up."

"Thank you, Marguerite."

As she moved to the armoire to lay out my dinner gown, I slid the key into a drawer, then turned around and asked for her assistance with unbuttoning the back of my traveling costume. When she didn't approach, I faced her. "Is there something the matter?"

Her face remained impassive, but her eyes were alive with a hidden light. "I brought you a message from Dr. Lewiston. He asked me to tell you to keep it private and away from Mr. McMahon."

I looked at her, startled. "For me? Are you quite sure?"

Her eyes narrowed slightly. "Yes, ma'am. I am used to delivering messages for Dr. Lewiston."

"Thank you, Marguerite," I said, wondering at her implication, but knowing I wouldn't ask her. She was playing a game with me, I knew, except I refused to take a turn. I took the sealed note and left it unopened on my dressing table, waiting to open it in private. I was baffled by Daniel's actions, but from what I knew of the doctor, I felt confident that he would have a sound explanation.

I bathed and dressed for dinner, waiting until Marguerite left until I opened the note. It had tested the limits of my patience to wait so long, and I ripped it with a savage tear and took the note from the envelope. It read, *I am concerned for your welfare and would like to speak to you in private. I will be in the grotto tomorrow at two thirty.* It was signed simply *DL.*

Thoughtfully, I folded the note, then placed it under a tray in my jewelry box. Sliding open my drawer, I spotted the key I had hidden earlier and took it out. Ascertaining that I still had a few minutes before supper, I walked down the hallway to my old room and pushed open the door.

The blinds had been left down and no candle had been lit. Still, I was familiar enough with my surroundings to be able to feel my way to the bed and kneel beside it. As my fingers brushed the hard wood of the box, I heard John calling my name from downstairs. I froze, then stood quickly, hiding the key under the mattress. Confident that no one would be entering the room, I left as quietly as I had come in, walking slowly down the stairs, my calm demeanor belying the fluttering of my heart.

Supper was a peaceful affair, with Rebecca chatting excitedly the entire time about her new presents and about everything she had done while we were gone. I watched her animated face, and for a moment I saw my Jamie, telling me about the size of a fish he had caught or how fast he had gone on his pony. But the image faded quickly, leaving me with only the vision of this beautiful little girl, happily sharing with her parents the precious things of her life.

She still called me Aunt Cat, and I did not ask her to change it. It had not been so long since she had called Elizabeth *Mama*, and I had no intention of erasing that. If she chose, in future, to call me by another name, I would welcome it, but it would have to be in her own time.

After we ate, Delphine came to take Rebecca to bed, and John and I retired to the parlor. I played the piano for him, and he stood behind me, not touching but near enough that I could feel his heat. I smelled brandy mixed with his male scent, and I found the combination to be near intoxicating. I missed a note but continued playing. I had chosen a Chopin nocturne, its melody haunting, each key pressed a sensual ode to the evocative music.

He touched the pearls about my throat, then bent to kiss my exposed shoulder. My fingers collapsed on the keyboard, unable to continue. I turned on the bench and looked up at my husband, and I knew the desire in his eyes mirrored my own.

Without speaking, I rose from the piano and allowed him to escort me up the stairs. His hand never left my arm, and I burned from his touch. When the door closed to our bedroom, it was as if the afternoon's events had inspired us both to a new height of passion. My need for him was as fierce as his need for me, and we were still partially dressed when he pressed me on the bed. It was not until after we were both completely sated that he began to make love to me slowly, taking off my remaining clothes bit by bit and loving my body with his hands and mouth until I shouted out with the pleasure of it.

We lay in each other's arms long after the lamps had been turned down and we could no longer hear the stirrings of the servants. The room was in near darkness, and I rested with my back pressed up to John, staring out at my new surroundings. Moonlight lent an eerie cast to the various pieces of furniture, and, like a glaring reproof, illuminated the large empty space on the wall where Elizabeth's portrait had once hung.

I waited until his breathing slowed to a deep and heavy pace before I stealthily slipped from the bed and put on my nightdress. I paused for a moment to stare down at my sleeping husband, feeling an unfamiliar tenderness. At that moment, I thought of my actions as a betrayal, but I quickly dismissed them. This was simply to ease my mind and to help me pack away my doubts forever.

Tiptoeing across the room, I let myself out and scurried down the quiet corridor and entered my old bedroom. Finding my way to the window, I opened the blinds, letting in the soft glow from the moon. In a yellow shaft of light I slid the box out from under the bed and sat on the floor next to it to avoid getting dirt on my nightgown. Fumbling my way through the bedspread, I found the key and, with no little effort in the murky light, fit it into the keyhole.

With my breath held, I felt the key slide into place and the latch click as I turned it. I waited for a brief moment for the pounding of my heart to settle before slowly opening the lid.

I blinked twice, wondering if the moonlight was playing tricks on my eyesight, but was rewarded with the same vision each time: an empty box, just the dusty brown wood staring blankly up at me.

I leaned back against the bed, disappointment flooding me. I did not know what I had hoped to find—evidence of Elizabeth's descent into depression and desperation and of the thing she feared enough to write to me? Or perhaps evidence of John's innocence? I no longer knew which was more important to me; all I knew was that I had nothing now but John's words and my own suspicions of Elizabeth's true nature.

I placed the key inside the box, the chain making a hollow clatter, before closing the lid and replacing it under the bed. With a heavy heart, I stood and went back to my own room, moving quietly so as not to awaken John.

I slid back into bed, trying not to touch him, then turned to watch his face. His breathing remained slow and steady as I studied his dark shape. He was still an enigma to me, his strange allure all-consuming. I told myself I trusted him, and ignored the small doubts I harbored deep in the recesses of my mind. *Who buried the letterbox and why? And where are the letters?*

I ignored the questions pressing into my brain and continued to watch my husband. His heavy breathing continued, a sign of deep sleep. Slowly, I lifted my hand and touched his cheek, the heavy stubble from his beard rough on my fingers. I traced the line of his jaw lightly with my finger, coming to rest on the sensual curve of his lips. John was usually so aloof and stoic in public that those lips seemed almost incongruous on his stern face. I doubted I was the only woman who had known the passion behind the man, and his mouth was certainly a hint of his true nature. I moved forward to press my lips against his and felt his hand grasp my wrist.

"Where have you been?"

I tried to pull my hand away, embarrassed not only that I had opened the letterbox in secret, but that he had caught me touching him when I thought he was asleep.

"I wanted to check on Rebecca. She kicks the covers off frequently and I did not want her to catch a chill." The lie came easily, although I was not quite sure why I had not told him the truth. I again smelled the odor of fresh dirt in my memory, and a small doubt that had been hidden deep inside me wriggled free.

He let go of my wrist, his fingers sliding under the sleeves of my nightdress. Goose bumps rippled up my arms. He propped himself up on an elbow. "You seem to have caught a chill yourself. Let me warm you." He kissed me, his hard body moving over mine, and I soon forgot all about doubts and trust and the stale smell of loose dirt.

I spent most of the following morning making a few steps forward in organizing the household. I interviewed the servants to discern what their assigned duties were, reassigning them where responsibilities overlapped. I devised a cleaning schedule, including a long-overdue spring cleaning that would involve taking down all the drapes and beating them outside. I wondered how the old house would react to having the drapes down and all the sunlight creeping inside, trickling into its dark corners.

The hall clock chimed twice, alerting me to the time. Daniel's note had said two thirty, and I did not want to be late. His secrecy seemed odd to me, but I was sure he would explain it once we met. I knew that his objective was to speak to me without John being present, so I took pains to avoid being seen as I left the house and skirted the pond before heading out across the back lawn to the grotto.

I had arrived first and sat upon the bench to wait for him. As I waited, I thought I heard rustling in the bushes behind me and jumped up, remembering the cottonmouth. But I saw nothing, and settled back down to wait.

I did not wait long before Daniel appeared on the grotto path, his friendly smile warming me. I hoped that I would soon be able to claim Clara as a close friend. Because of my fondness for her husband, I wanted to be equally comfortable with both.

He kissed my hand as he had done on the last occasion when we had met at the grotto. "You are a picture of loveliness, Catherine. Marriage suites you." He tilted his head, an odd look on his face. "I remember many times seeing Elizabeth sitting here just like that. The resemblance is uncanny, you know."

A shadow passed over his face, drawing away the warmth of his smile. He sat down next to me and I turned to him. "You miss her a great deal."

Nodding, he looked away toward the thick greenery blocking our view of the house. "Yes. We were good friends. . . ." His voice trailed away and he did not say anything else.

I touched his shoulder, feeling his sadness. "Is that why you brought me here today—to talk about Elizabeth?"

He faced me, his clear gray eyes dimming. "Not exactly. I wanted to talk about you." His lips turned up in a slight smile. "And please forgive my secrecy. I love John like a brother, but he is rather possessive when it comes to you. I wanted to speak to you in private and I could think of no other way." He pressed my hand, then let it go. "Thank you."

Daniel stood, as if preparing for a speech. "I have known John for a long time, and I know him to be a good man." Bracing himself with one hand against a tree, he leveled me with his gaze. "There might be . . . aspects of his personality that you are not aware of, but perhaps should be." He took a deep breath. "John has a fierce temper—I have certainly witnessed it myself growing up with him in Boston. But here, well, you must know how servants talk, and there were stories brought to us about the arguments he and Elizabeth would have."

I felt my blood cool in my veins. "Did he ever . . . harm her?"

Daniel shook his head. "No—not that I ever heard. And Elizabeth never mentioned it, either." His eyes clouded. "But she was afraid of him—she told me that much." He began to pace, his boots crunching the dead leaves and pine straw underfoot. "Elizabeth was not as strong as you, Catherine. She was emotionally . . . vulnerable. She craved love and attention, and when she did not get it from John, she sought it elsewhere."

Again, I imagined I heard a soft crunching of ground cover from behind me, but when Daniel showed no sign of noticing, I dismissed it. Lots of small animals lived in the pine forests that dotted West Feliciana Parish, and even though I would have avoided the dark and shadowed ones surrounded Whispering Oaks, the deer and raccoons would not.

I shifted uncomfortably on the bench, feeling myself flush at the mention of Elizabeth's infidelities. Daniel came and sat down next to me again and took my hand, holding it in his warm palms. "I am sorry to be indelicate, but I thought you should know. Even if it is only to understand why John would be so possessive of you." He smiled again, his eyes brightening. "It is so amazing how much you resemble her. But one only has to be in your presence for a few minutes to know that the similarities end with your beautiful face."

I pulled my hand from his and pretended to rearrange my skirts as I slid to the edge of the bench. He seemed to notice and his demeanor sobered considerably.

"Catherine, I am sorry. I did not mean to make you uncomfortable. I just wanted to warn you."

"Warn me? About my own husband?"

"Yes, and to offer you refuge. I know I have said this before, but if there is ever a time that you need to seek sanctuary, please know that you have a place at Belle Meade. I will welcome you there without questions."

I noted his omission of Clara's name. "I thank you for your concern, Daniel, but I can assure you that I am not my sister and I have no intention of raising my husband's ire. And, as you mentioned, I am stronger than she was. I can handle his temper without fleeing to the nearest neighbor."

He studied me carefully for a moment before speaking. "You defend him so readily."

"He is my husband."

Daniel dropped his head and stared at his hands. His fingers were long and slender, almost delicate. They were the hands of a doctor, unused to physical labor. So unlike John's, which were strong and powerful, hiding their remarkable tenderness. "And he was Elizabeth's husband, too, and now she is dead."

I stood, anger flooding me. "What are you implying, Daniel?"

He stood, too. "I am not making any accusations, but in Boston I witnessed John kill a man when thoroughly provoked. I could not say he would not do it again."

"It was in self-defense!"

He raked his fingers through his hair. "Yes, it was. But if John had left the man alone instead of inciting his anger, the man would still be alive."

I shook my head. "But that is in the past and has nothing to do with Elizabeth or me."

I thought of the baby Elizabeth carried and John's knowledge that it was not his, and could only imagine his anger. With a steady gaze, I said, "You were her doctor and knew of the baby she carried. Did she tell you the identity of the child's father?"

His face blanched and he stared at me for a moment without speaking.

"I am sorry," I said. "That was rather rash of me. Then I assume you did not know?"

"Yes, of course I did. I was her doctor, and everything she told me was held in confidence. I just did not expect you to know."

"John told me—before we were married. I suppose it was his way of letting me know that the Elizabeth I had known was not the same Elizabeth she had become."

"I am sorry. It must have been a great shock for you."

"Yes, it was. But I would rather know the truth."

He turned away for a moment, studying the small trickle of water under the dilapidated bridge. "So, does John know the identity of the child's father?"

"He said she had many lovers and that it would be difficult to name just one." I took a deep breath. "We have put Elizabeth to rest. There is no need to continue delving into a past that no longer matters."

He smiled again. "Yes. I am sure you are right. I just want you—and John—to be happy." He came toward me and placed both hands on my shoulders. "And you certainly are a picture of happiness. I am glad. You both deserve contentment in your lives."

I warmed to him. "Thank you, Daniel. We are lucky to have such a friend as you. And please do not worry about me. I appreciate your concern, but I am not afraid of my husband, and there is no cause for you to worry. Remember, I am not my sister."

He dropped his hands from my shoulders, his face sobering. "No, Catherine, you certainly are not." He studied me for a long moment, his eyes narrowed. "I do not even know if I should tell you this, but I think it would be important to you. As much as Elizabeth's behavior is reprehensible to us both, there was a reason for it." He continued to study me, making me shift uncomfortably. "Never having met you, I did not understand it at the time, but now I do. She was extremely envious of you."

I stepped back. "Of me? You must be mistaken."

Daniel shook his head. "Oh no. She all but admitted it to me. She envied your happiness—or should I say your ability to be happy. You did not need material things to be content. She said a blue sky or a smile from your father would set you adrift on a sea of contentment, as she put it." His face darkened. "But it was never that easy for her. She needed things—not just material things, but the undiluted attention of everyone she met. I do not think it was easy for her growing up in your household and having to divide your father's affections."

I shook my head. "I still cannot believe it. Elizabeth had everything. . . ."

"Everything but happiness. It hurt her deeply that that which she sought so vainly came so easily to you."

"I never knew. . . ."

His voice was gentle. "But now you do. It certainly does not excuse her behavior, but perhaps it will help you to understand it."

I nodded and thanked him, then allowed him to escort me to the edge of the grotto. Taking my hand from his elbow, he faced me. "I think it best that we not be seen together. I have hidden my horse over by the levee and I can walk through the forest to get to her."

As he was saying goodbye, I happened to look toward the lane of oaks and spotted a man sitting on a horse. The man's mount stomped the ground, then stilled. Squinting my eyes, I realized the man was looking in our direction. There was something familiar about him, and I pointed him out to Daniel.

Daniel stepped back into the shadow of the grotto while staring hard at the man on horseback. After a moment, he said with distaste, "It is Philip Herndon. If he knows what is good for him, he will get off of John's property before he is spotted."

"I will go see what he wants."

Daniel stilled me with a hand on my arm. "No, Catherine. That could only fuel John's anger. I will go get my horse and approach the lane as if I am just getting here for a visit. I will see what he wants and get him to leave."

I nodded, seeing reason in his suggestion. "All right. Just tell me later what he is up to."

He bent to kiss my hand. "I will be sure to do that. Goodbye, Catherine. Take care of yourself, and I will see you soon."

Feeling fortunate to have found such a good friend so quickly, I turned and began walking back toward the house, my skirts brushing the brittle summer grass. My good spirits dimmed as I approached the looming white structure, the windows like foreboding eyes warning me away. But I had no intention of fleeing. Instead my determination to change the house deepened, and I marched toward the front porch with confident steps.

John met me in the foyer, a look of concern on his face. "Where have you been? I have been waiting for you. I have something to show you."

"I went for a walk," I said, hating my half lie. I pushed aside my guilt, justifying it by assuring myself that when our marriage was not so new it would be strong enough to handle unpleasantness. But for now, I was reveling in our honeymoon period, and I did not want to cast any shadows on it.

I went to him and reached for his hands. He immediately pulled me into an embrace, and I was lost in his touch completely.

"You are overheated. Perhaps you should go upstairs and change first."

I looked into his face and saw his mocking smile. "John," I said, pretending to be shocked. "It is the middle of the afternoon."

"Mrs. McMahon, I am insulted that you could think I would be such a cad as to be suggesting anything other than changing your clothes." He bent to kiss my ear. "Of course, what I want to show you is upstairs in the bedroom. . . ." His voice was smothered as he rained kisses down my neck, my bones melting in his hands.

Footsteps in the back passage made him straighten in time to see Marguerite approaching with two freshly polished candelabra in her hands for the dining-room table. She sent me a knowing look, and I flushed. I was not sure if the look was intended to remind me that she knew of the note from Daniel, or if she knew what John and I had been discussing.

I headed up the stairs, John following close behind. When we reached the bedroom, he closed the door behind him, then locked it.

"John—"

He held his finger to his lips. "Sshh. Let me show you your surprise now."

He went to a door on the far wall that had led to a small sitting room in my grandmother's day. I had not yet been inside, assuming it to be unused. He opened the door and indicated that I should enter.

I held my breath as I walked in, my face flushing with pleasure. The windows had been stripped of their heavy drapes, leaving them bare for the sunshine to pour in through slatted blinds. A large chest stood open on the opposing wall, its shelves displaying my paints and brushes. In the middle of the room were two easels, each holding a blank canvas.

John came to stand behind me, his hands on my arms. "I had Mr. O'Rourke and Marguerite fix this room for you while we were in New Orleans. I put the paints and brushes in myself today, seeing as how they were still in a box on the floor of the bedroom."

I could not speak, afraid that I would burst out crying if I did. Instead I walked toward the window and raised the blind. The view was of the long stand of pines that hid the grotto from sight. I knew if I turned to look out of the right corner of the window, I would see the pond, its dark, placid waters still a place I did not willingly visit.

I turned to John, wrapping my arms around his neck, happiness flooding my spirit. "This is the most precious gift anyone has ever given me. How can I ever thank you?"

He reached for me, his powerful hands caressing my back. "Let me show you."

I felt his fingers beginning to undo the buttons on the back of my dress and I pressed myself against him. Unbidden came Daniel's words to me about John's temper and his penchant for violence.

As John's hands found my bare skin, Daniel's words faded into nothingness, lost as I was in my husband's gentle touch, thoughts of his anger easily forgotten.

Chapter Seventeen

---◆---

My days passed serenely as I settled in as the new mistress of Whispering Oaks. I felt proud of my ability to organize the household and to understand the ebb and flow of the workload on a sugar plantation. John took great pride in taking me for long rides and showing me the lay of the land. He showed respect for my intelligence and took pains to explain the problems of the encroaching Mississippi River and the never-ending battle to shore up the levee.

John spent a great portion of his day out of the house, and I came to know in time that it had nothing to do with me but, rather, the house. As much as he loved the rich, fertile earth and the things he was able to coax from it, the house held no appeal for him at all. I had brought a measure of brightness to it with new draperies and furnishings, but for all the sunshine that now lapped at the creamy white walls, a pervasive darkness lingered over the old rooms, like a nightmare that followed one into the waking hours.

I had begun to paint again, and it was not until I first put my brush to canvas that I realized how much I had changed in the last years. Whereas before all I had painted had been flora and fauna and the blue ocean of Saint Simons, now I wanted to paint people. I wanted to study these new inhabitants of my life, examine each feature separately, as if they were puzzle pieces that might add up to the sum of this new existence of mine.

My first subject had been, remarkably, Rebecca. Perhaps it was the desire to capture Jamie's eyes on canvas, but her pixielike face called to me, insisting that I paint it. I hoped that one day I might find the strength to paint Jamie from memory, but for now I reveled in capturing his endearing little cousin on canvas. I looked forward to our painting sessions on those early-fall mornings, which I can remember with a vividness of thought and color that are foreign to most of my memories. Perhaps it is with the knowledge of hindsight now that I recall those happy times with such clarity. I cling to the memory so as to block out the events that would soon change our lives forever.

On a bright October morning, I sat painting Rebecca. It was still warm, as fall in the Delta rarely brought cold weather, but the heavy humidity had lifted. Rebecca sat on a blanket with Samantha by the pond, the sunlight spinning her hair into gold. I was not comfortable being this close to the water, but the child had insisted, and I knew she was right. The sun reflecting off the water and the big house in the background were perfect for a portrait.

Still, I felt unease, as if the restless spirits of the Indian woman and her child were watching us. The breeze teased at my neck, making my skin prick like little breaths of warning, and I found it hard to focus on my task.

As I mixed my paints for her hair, I realized with a start what I was doing. It was the same combination of gold and yellows I had once used when painting a miniature portrait of Robert. It seemed as if he were mocking me now, calling to mind his beautiful hair and the thick red river of blood running through it. As if that one gunshot had not ended his life but merely perpetuated his existence to haunt me forever.

I realized my hand was shaking, and I went to sit next to Rebecca until I could calm myself. I sat with my back to the water, and the little girl laid her head in my lap, her small arms clutching her doll. I ran my hands through her glorious hair, reveling in the thick texture of it. It was not baby-fine, as most children's hair, but more like that of an adult. My hand stilled, an unbidden memory assaulting me. A memory of Robert and me on the beach for a picnic, with his head in my lap and me stroking his hair, so full and rich and gold.

I let my hand fall to my side, clutching at the grass and dirt as if to ground my thoughts. I had come to a place in my mind where I could almost bear the memories of Jamie. Even though they were still tinged with great sadness, his conjured image could sometimes make me smile with remembered joy.

But memories of Robert were not allowed. John had helped me

banish Robert from the marriage bed, but at other times thoughts of him caught me unaware. And each time it brought back the terrifying memory of a gunshot and red blood on white sheets. I closed my eyes, trying my best to focus on the smell of the earth and grass and the feel of the beautiful child in my lap.

Rebecca began to hum the strange, haunting melody, her eyes transfixed on the still waters of the pond.

I listened for a while, still trying to identify where I had heard the music before. It was so familiar, yet so elusive. Despite receiving no answer to my question before, I thought I would try again. "Rebecca, where did you learn that song? I feel I should know it, but I cannot seem to recall where I have heard it before."

She turned her head in my lap to face me, her eyes squinting in the bright sunlight. "It is a secret and I am not supposed to tell."

I leaned forward to block the sun from her face. "Who told you that you were not supposed to tell?"

She faced the pond again and didn't answer.

"Was it Marguerite?"

She shook her head vigorously.

I prodded again. "Was it your mama?"

"You are my mama now."

My heart lurched at this declaration, but I restrained myself from lifting this child high in the air and swinging her about. The thought was obviously as new to her as it was to me, and I wanted us both to get used to the idea.

Gently, I continued. "It is such a beautiful song and I would like to learn it, too. I promise I will not tell anybody you told me."

She furrowed her pale brows for a moment, as if in deep thought. Then she turned back to me, her face stricken. "But then I would not get any more candy."

I looked down at the cherubic face of my niece and wondered momentarily if her mother's neglect had had any negative effect on her developing person. Leaning over, I kissed her forehead, determined not to press the matter further for the time being.

We sat in silence for a long time, enjoying the soft breeze and the crisp smell of the approaching autumn. Our fickle climate would allow for the heat and humidity to return for brief periods of time, but for now the clear air was a welcome respite.

Rebecca continued to gaze out at the pond, her brows puckered. Finally, she said, "I think they are down there."

I sat up with alarm. "Who is down there?"

"The Indian mama and her baby. They buried them under the house, but when their bones were found, the people threw them into the pond."

I kept my voice calm. "Who told you this, Rebecca?"

She did not speak for a moment but eventually turned her face to stare up at me. "They did. And they want me to get them out."

A frigid finger of dread slipped down my spine as I stared at the wide-eyed innocence of this child. I continued stroking her hair. "Who do you mean by 'they,' Rebecca?"

"They come to talk to me at night—after my lamps are turned down and it is all dark. Sometimes they scare me, but not a lot." She turned away from me and sighed, her fingers restlessly plucking at her dress. "It is the Indian lady and her baby. The mama does all of the talking. She tells me how lonely they are and how much they want me to come with them."

My hand stilled on her hair. "Where do they want you to go?"

I watched her profile as her long golden lashes closed over her eyes. "To the bottom of the pond. Then they will be free."

Dread gripped at my heart. I reached down and lifted her, sitting her on my lap to face me. "Rebecca, you must listen to me. These voices are not your friends—do you hear me? They are in your imagination and you must not listen to them. The pond is a dangerous place for you to go alone and you must never, ever go there without me or another grown person. Do you understand me? Do you understand?"

The child's bottom lip began to quiver, and I realized how harsh my voice must have sounded to her. I felt ashamed at having scared her, but the heaviness in my heart would not dissipate. I clutched her closely to my chest, not hearing her cries of protest. It was only when her hands began to push me away that I let go.

She sat on my lap, gazing at me, her blue eyes questioning. I touched her soft cheek, brushing away fat tears. "I am so sorry. I did not mean to make you cry, but you scared me so. Can you understand that I do not want anything to happen to you? You mean so much to me and to your papa, and I just want to keep you safe from harm. I did not mean to frighten you."

Rebecca touched my face. "You are crying."

I reached up and pressed my fingers to my own cheek and realized she was right.

As quickly as this child had lodged herself in my heart, she leapt at me, throwing her small arms around me and burying her face into my neck. "I do not want to make you cry. My old mama would cry and say it was my fault and that she was going to leave. And then she went away. Does this mean you are going away, too?"

I cradled her head on my shoulder, my heart breaking for this motherless child. "Oh no. I will never leave you. If you make me cry, they will be tears of happiness, for there is nothing that you can ever do that would make me go away. You bring so much joy to my life, Rebecca, and I will always want you in it." I realized with a start that I had meant every word.

She pulled back to contemplate me, her puckered brows telling me she had not understood everything I'd said, but perhaps enough. "You are not leaving?"

I shook my head vigorously. "Not ever."

She threw her arms around me again and squeezed tightly. Then she laid her head on my shoulder, putting her thumb in her mouth, and I felt her pat my back, just as I had done to comfort her. We sat like that for a long while, watching the sun slide lazily across the pond. Then, very softly, her voice heavy with drowsiness, she said, "I love you, Mama."

Tears pricked at my eyes. It seemed like an eternity and more since I had last heard those words. I began to cry in earnest now, recalling how I had emotionally pushed this child away, thinking of her only as a reminder of the child I had lost. Instead she had become a large piece of my salvation, warming a corner of my heart that I had considered forever dead. I placed my cheek against hers and whispered, "I love you too, Rebecca."

She fell asleep in my arms and I held her closely, reveling in the joy of being a mother again and vowing to myself that the bond would never be broken.

After I put the sleeping Rebecca into her bed for a nap, I passed Marguerite in the hallway outside my room. I was still unsure of her position in the household and unsettled about her seemingly permanent place in it. I knew John would balk at my suggestion to dismiss her, so I tried my best to assert my authority.

"Marguerite, I need to speak to you for a moment."

She inclined her head slightly in acknowledgment of my request, but her expression lacked any semblance of servitude.

"I am enjoying my art room very much and I wanted to thank you for helping Mr. McMahon surprise me with it."

She regarded me evenly. "I always do what I am asked."

I was taken aback by her response but tried not to show it. Instead I said, "Yes, well, thank you anyway. The room has proven to be a real pleasure to me."

Bobbing her head, she moved to pass me, but I called out to her. "I also wanted to speak to you about Rebecca."

She turned slowly, her eyes narrowing. "She is not my responsibility anymore."

"That is true, but I thought you might know who has been putting ideas into her head. She has told me that she hears the voices of an Indian lady at night after she goes to bed. I know it is all in her imagination, but somebody has to be planting the seeds for her to be thinking such things."

Her odd green eyes widened. "And what makes you think that it is not real?"

I was at a loss for words. Finally, I said, "Well, of course they are not real. The story of the Indian woman and her child is only a legend. And I do not want Rebecca to hear any more of those stories—they will only frighten her."

"There are things you do not understand, but that does not mean they do not exist."

I tried to remain calm. "They are irrational and frightening, and I do not want Rebecca hearing any more about it. I will speak to the other servants and make sure my wishes are clear, and I expect you to help me enforce my orders."

Her eyes regarded me calmly. "If that is what you want."

"That is what I want, and I expect my orders obeyed. If you find that you cannot, then you will be dismissed."

She lifted her chin. "You will have to talk to Mr. McMahon about that."

I squared my shoulders. "Do not be too sure of that, Marguerite. I am in charge of the household staff."

"Maybe with the others. But Mr. McMahon hired me, and only he can fire me."

Bristling, I walked past her. "We will see about that. If you cannot accept my authority, then I do not feel you should be working here."

"I would think twice about that, Mrs. McMahon. I know what a temper Mr. McMahon has, and I do not like to think how he would like knowing that the doctor has sent you a note and you met in private."

I froze, my back to her. "That is not your concern."

"Maybe it is, and maybe it is not, but it is certainly your husband's concern to know that his wife's been meeting with another man."

I turned quickly, my skirts whirling about my ankles, to face her. "You would not dare."

She simply raised an eyebrow and silently walked past me.

My heart hammered in my chest as I ran to my room, taking the time to shut the door calmly. With my breath held, I opened my jewelry box and lifted the tray where I had thrown Daniel's note. It was gone. I threw everything out of the box, leaving it in a tangled mess on the dresser, but there was no note.

I shoved everything back in the box, too agitated to take the time to put it away neatly. I tried to force my breathing to slow down, rationalizing to myself that all I needed to do was speak to John and everything would be sorted out.

But I thought with longing of the weeks since our marriage, of the bonds of trust that we had forged, and I thought also of his anger when I had discovered the dirty handkerchief in his drawer. I closed my eyes, clutching the edge of the dresser. Marguerite had to be dealt with—but

I was loath to create any ripples in the river of my new marriage just yet. It could wait.

Slowly, I took everything out of the jewelry box again and replaced it inside neatly and orderly.

A brief tapping on the door made me look up. Marguerite appeared, a knowing smile on her lips when she saw what I was doing. I did not acknowledge it, but simply asked her what she needed.

"Mrs. Lewiston is here to see you. I showed her into the parlor and will ask Rose to bring tea."

"Thank you, Marguerite." I stared after her long after she had gone, then smoothed my hair and went downstairs.

When I entered the parlor, Clara stood by one of the windows, her pale hands clutching the draperies, staring out toward the front drive. She did not appear to have heard me come in, so I moved to stand next to her.

"She is a beautiful child."

Clara's voice startled me. I followed her gaze to where Rebecca played on the front lawn with Delphine. They each had a large wooden hoop with a stick and were racing each other down the drive, seeing who could roll theirs the fastest without making it fall over.

"She is supposed to be napping. But she is beautiful, is she not? I am afraid I cannot take any credit for that. We must thank her parents."

Clara gave me an odd look, then returned to gaze out the window. "How are you finding the child? Does she seem normal and healthy?"

I stared at Clara's profile, the pale skin and nearly lashless eyes. "She is a wonderful child—unique among most children I have known, but very typical of a girl her age. She is intelligent and loving and very charming—especially when she wants to get her way." I smiled but it was not returned. "Why do you ask?"

Rose appeared with a tea tray, and we seated ourselves on the sofa. As I poured tea, Clara said, "I am just concerned. There have always been . . . rumors concerning Rebecca, and I was just wondering if you had noticed anything out of the ordinary."

I thought momentarily of mentioning the voices Rebecca said she had been hearing, but I kept it to myself. I did not want my daughter's name dragged through the rumor mill. Despite any assurances, I doubted

Clara would be able to keep a tidbit like that a secret. Instead I shook my head. "No, I have noticed nothing unusual. What sorts of rumors have you been hearing?"

She concentrated on putting sugar into her tea and stirring it slowly, her eyebrows tightly knit. "Just that she has imaginary friends—that she sees people who are not there and speaks to them. Daniel even mentioned to me that Rebecca has spoken to him of her mother as if she were still seeing her. As if she still lived."

Tepid brown eyes focused on me, and I returned her stare without blinking. "Clara, having imaginary friends is quite common for children Rebecca's age. My own son had an imaginary friend, too—an old fisherman." I laughed, trying to add levity to our conversation. "Perhaps it is in our blood, for I know not every child has such an active imagination as Jamie and Rebecca."

There. I had done it. Used Jamie's name in a sentence and not completely fallen apart. In fact, it was good to hear his name spoken. It was as if I had buried his existence at his memorial service, never to be brought into the light again. How wrong I had been.

Clara smiled warmly. "I am sure you are right—and you would know more of these things than I. After all, you have been a mother and I have not been so blessed. Yet." She smiled again. "I simply wanted to broach the subject with you so that you would know I am more than happy to discuss it. I can only imagine how hard it must be for you here, far from your true home. It must be so lonely."

I took a sip of my tea. "We have had so many visitors since we returned from our honeymoon. I feel as if I know the whole parish by now. And Daniel's become a dear friend, too. It is my hope that we can all spend time together."

She looked down into her cup, hiding her expression. "Yes, I would like that, too. When Elizabeth was alive . . ." She paused, glancing up at me. "John and Elizabeth were our closest friends, and I sorely miss the companionship."

I placed my hand on hers and squeezed. "As soon as our mourning is over, we can be more social, and I hope to see you and Daniel as frequently as possible."

"Yes. That would be nice." She took her hand away and reached for a tea cookie. "So, how are you adjusting to being the new Mrs. Mc-Mahon?"

I chewed on a cookie, trying to will away the flush I felt creeping up my cheeks. "Very well, thank you. John has been nothing but kind in answering all my questions and helping me learn everything there is to know about the plantation. He has been very patient with me."

Clara put her teacup down in its saucer. "I do not think I have ever heard John McMahon's name and the word 'patient' used in the same sentence."

"Really?"

Her lips pulled over her teeth for a moment as she contemplated her next words. "I just recall certain aspects of Elizabeth's behavior that John was not so patient with."

I held my teacup loosely, afraid that I might snap the fragile handle. "Like what?"

Clara stood and walked back over to the window and stared out. "Elizabeth had . . . friends that she liked to visit. She would just take off without a word, returning when the whim took her. John would go into a fury when she returned—something of which I had never seen the likes of before. He was so insanely jealous. . . ." Her voice trailed off as she turned to face me.

She continued. "He did not even like her visiting Daniel. I knew there was nothing more to their friendship, but John could not be reasoned with when it came to Elizabeth. She infuriated him and he was powerless to do anything about it. I understand she was the same way when she lived in Boston during the war." Almost as an afterthought, she added, "I always wondered why she stayed with him."

I sat up straight, feeling the heat pervade my cheeks. "Perhaps, like me, she had nowhere else to go." I heard the acrimony in my voice, but her frivolous gossip regarding my dead sister had raised my ire.

Clara held her hand to her mouth and looked truly chagrined. "Please forgive me, Catherine. I did not mean . . ." She looked down to her lap for a moment, studiously straightening her skirt. "And please do not think that you have no place to go. There is always Belle Meade, and if you need to get farther away, I would see that you returned to Saint Simons."

My voice was cool. "That will not be necessary. And I must resent the implication that I would have need of leaving my husband."

Clara's pale eyes blinked rapidly. "I have wounded you, and I am deeply sorry. It is just that Elizabeth and I used to be so frank with each other, and I suppose I forgot you were not her."

A booming voice sounded from the threshold. "Catherine is most definitely not Elizabeth." John entered the room and strode toward me, then placed a lingering kiss on my cheek. I was sure it was for Clara's benefit, but his touch thrilled me nonetheless.

John greeted Clara with a deep grin that made her squirm. I supposed he was using a little revenge to repay her for her gossiping.

"My, my. Where does the time go to?" She stood hastily, knocking her teaspoon on the floor in a fluster. "I really need to be going, but I wanted to extend to you both a supper invitation at Belle Meade. I realize you are still in mourning, so it will be a very small affair, but I feel it necessary to introduce you into our society. Of course, many remember you from your grandmother's days, but they need to meet you as the new mistress of Whispering Oaks." She glanced from me to John, like a child seeking approval. "How about Wednesday evening in two weeks? We will dine at eight."

My anger toward her lessened somewhat. I knew from John that Belle Meade had suffered greatly during the war and that it would be a struggle to entertain graciously, as Clara would have been used to. Still, she was making the effort to bring me into her social circle, and for that I was grateful.

"Thank you, Clara. We would be delighted to accept. Thank you so much for your kindness." I took her hand and held it, hoping she would realize it was an apology and an offer of a truce.

She smiled warmly at me. "No, Catherine—thank you. Thank you for putting up with my gossiping, and thank you for accepting my invitation. It will be a real pleasure." She moved to leave, then turned back to add, "For me and for Daniel, I am sure."

John and I saw her out. After she had gone, I turned to my husband. During my conversation with Clara, my thoughts had been in turmoil. It had become very clear that my concern for Rebecca far outweighed any anxiety I might suffer at my husband's anger.

I took a deep breath before I spoke. "We must talk about Marguerite. I do not feel as if she should stay here—she is insolent and rude and does not take well to my direction. And somebody has been feeding Rebecca nonsense about the ghosts of the Indian woman and her baby—that they are under the pond and she needs to save them."

He looked at me intently. "And you think Rebecca believes it?"

I nodded. "She is young and impressionable. But I think I convinced her that it's not true and that she should never go to the pond without an adult. But still . . ."

He spoke gently. "Catherine, I understand how this is all very upsetting to you but, as you said, it is nonsense. We will speak to the servants and make it clear that no one is to mention the legend to Rebecca again, and that she must not be allowed by the pond by herself."

"But, John, I feel Marguerite is behind it—that she wishes Rebecca ill for some reason. I cannot forget the time when she left Rebecca out in the thunderstorm as punishment. It chills me to the bone."

I saw him grit his teeth, his jawbone working furiously. "I will speak to her, but I am sure you are mistaken. I have known Marguerite for years. Yes, her ways are strange, but I have never known her to wish evil on anyone."

I touched his sleeve, fighting to keep the desperation out of my voice. "I do not want her in this house. Please send her away. Give her a large severance and a good reference, if it will make you feel better, but please, John. Dismiss her."

He looked away, avoiding my eyes. "I said I would speak to her. But I will not dismiss her for ungrounded reasons. I know your concerns are real, but perhaps they are born of being uncertain and in a new situation rather than any solid reasons." He turned and kissed me on the cheek. "I have to return to the mill."

I watched his retreating form, bristling at how easily he had dismissed my fears. But maybe he was right and I was being foolish. Maybe I had imagined harmful intentions on Marguerite's part. Perhaps I should trust John and try harder to accept Marguerite's presence in my house, for the sake of harmony.

And then I recalled the note and Marguerite's veiled threat. I shrugged—it did not matter. I could only tell the truth, and the truth had nothing to hide.

I stared after John as he walked toward the mill, finally admitting to myself that the heady rush I felt whenever I saw him was perhaps more than fascination. The soft smiles that he reserved for Rebecca and me belied his stern demeanor, and made them all the more special for their rarity. Our tender bond had taken root in deep hurt and grief, and now I could only wonder if such fragile beginnings could blossom into something more.

I returned to the house, closing the door quietly behind me. The bright afternoon sun had begun its descent into the twilight sky, and I stood in the foyer for a long moment, watching the play of light on the walls.

A shadow caught my attention and I turned, thinking something moved in the mirror. I stared into the murky glass, watching with unblinking eyes. I spun around to see if what I had seen had been a reflection, but found myself staring at the empty wall on the opposite side of the foyer.

I approached the old mirror slowly, marveling at the fear I felt lodged in my throat. Could it be that my new sense of contentment, now that I had something to lose, had resurrected my sense of fear?

Reaching out, I allowed my fingertips to graze the cold glass of the mirror. I dropped my hands, watching them as I slowly lowered them to my sides. I gasped as the top of the hall table came into view, then blinked to clear my eyes in the dim light.

Scattered over the table's surface lay a handful of oleander leaves, their tender corners lifted as if waving goodbye. I stared at them for a long moment before gathering them in my fists, squeezing tightly as if to choke the life out of them. I shoved them into my pockets, obliterating them from my sight, as if they, and the threat they represented to my newfound happiness, had never existed at all.

Chapter Eighteen

———◆———

I awoke with a scream trapped in my mouth, the room of my dream still surrounding me, the pool of bloodred oleander leaves drowning me. I reached for John, but his side of the bed was empty, the pillow cool.

I sat on the edge of the bed, my teeth chattering, waiting for my eyes to adjust to the dark shadows of the furniture. Softly, I called out his name, but there was no reply. Sliding to the floor, I felt the cool wood touch my feet, sending more shivers up my spine. Carefully, I walked to the door and opened it, the hinges singing a faint protest.

A thin triangle of light fanned the far wall of the corridor, and I followed it like a lost ship guided by a lighthouse beacon. I hesitated at the bend in the hallway when I realized the light came from Elizabeth's room. Slowly, I approached the door, my feet padding softly on the carpet runner. I had not brought my wrapper, and I trembled in the cool night air.

My fingers, seemingly disembodied in the dark, bisected the illumination, making them glow before I pushed gently on the door.

John sat at Elizabeth's dressing table, a glass of Scotch not far from his hand. He was fully dressed, and I recalled how I had retired before he did. His jacket was missing, his hair mussed, as if he had spent many wretched moments ruggedly sweeping his hands through it.

With a start, I noticed that her hairbrush, comb, and mirror sat on her dresser top. Had I imagined they were missing when I had first come into this room? Or perhaps they were merely someplace in the room and had been put back.

I turned my attention back to John. He did not see me right away, and I stayed where I was, watching as he picked up her hairbrush and held it idly in his hands, then lifted it to his nose to smell deeply. He turned his head away quickly, as if the scent from the brush was not what he wished for.

He lifted his eyes and spied me in the mirror, but did not act surprised to see me.

"What are you doing, John?"

Taking a sip from his glass, he remained silent. I entered the room and closed the door behind me. I had already grown used to the knowledge that these walls had ears, and I had no intention of fueling the gossip mill any more than I had already. "What are you doing?" I asked again.

He dropped the brush, the clatter glaring in the quiet room, and stood to face me. "I am not sure," he said slowly. "Perhaps I am simply trying to ascertain that you and Elizabeth are not one and the same."

I smiled, thinking he was jesting, until I caught sight of the crumpled note on the dresser. I knew without asking that it was Daniel's note, and I realized Marguerite had made good on her threat. Still, I was not sorry I had spoken to John about dismissing her. As Rebecca's mother, I knew the child's welfare had to come first.

I sobered quickly, the blood draining from my head. Nausea rose to my throat, and I had to sit down on the corner of the bed for fear of fainting. "I can explain that," I said weakly.

Silence pervaded the room for a long moment as we watched each other warily. "I am sure you can. Elizabeth always had good explanations, too. Until she felt that she no longer need bother with such trivialities."

I tasted bile and grimaced as I swallowed it down. I stared up at him, my anger rising. "So, that is the way it is? I am guilty regardless of the truth, and you are judge and jury. How dare you?" I struggled to stand, clutching one of the bedposts for support.

His face was ragged, his torment plain to see. "What else am I supposed to think, Catherine?"

"That your wife is innocent." I glared at him, struggling to ignore the nausea that threatened to engulf me. "This wife—not Elizabeth. What about trust, John? Can one simple misunderstanding erase everything we have built so far?"

He stared at me for a long moment, his face hidden in shadow.

Slowly, he put his glass down on the dressing table, the small clinking sound an intrusion in the heavy silence.

I leaned against the tall bed, pressing my forehead against the bedpost, seeking something cool. I heard the resignation in my voice. "I told you before we were married: I would rather have my freedom and starve on Saint Simons than live this way."

He took a step toward me out of the shadows, and I raised my face to his. "Daniel was simply concerned for my welfare, and he did not want to raise your ire by questioning my well-being in your presence. Your mistrust and jealousies are building a prison for me. Is this how it started with Elizabeth? Did your jealousies imprison her, too?"

The words I hurled at him hit their mark and I closed my eyes, unable to look at the hurt in his. I took long, deep breaths and felt the cool wood of the bedpost against my face. I opened them again to look into his inscrutable eyes and spoke the words that I had never intended to utter. "If only you knew what is in my heart."

Dark eyes stared at me, unblinking, a flash of hope flickering within. "How can you expect me to know what is in your heart when you are meeting with other men without my knowledge, when my best friend is sending you private notes? Elizabeth—"

"I am not Elizabeth, John. If you have any question as to my behavior, ask me and I will tell you the truth. I have nothing to hide. And what lies in my heart is worthless if you cannot trust me with your secrets. You say that it is to protect me, but I am telling you that it is killing me—little by little. It is leaching the strength and energy from my blood. It is starvation of the soul, which is far worse than starvation of the body. And I have experienced both."

I shook as I spoke and felt my knees weaken beneath me. He crossed the room in two long strides and lifted me in his arms. Gently, he sat on the bed with me in his lap, cradling me like a child. "I am sorry," he whispered. "I am sorry."

Soft lips brushed my forehead, and it must have been a healing kiss, for my wave of nausea vanished. I still felt cold and clammy, and I snuggled deeply into John's arms, closing my eyes and relishing his scent.

His words fell softly on my ear. "What is really in your heart, Cat?"

I did not open my eyes. I had no desire to banish my hope by not seeing what I wanted reflected in his. Instead I tilted my head to face him, but kept my eyes tightly shut. "I feel weak whenever you walk in a room. And my blood seems to move faster and my heart beats louder when you look at me or when you make Rebecca laugh." I took a deep breath, still not daring to look at him. "And when you touch me, I feel as if I have found a part of paradise here on earth. I would die for just your touch, for I find myself living just to have you pull me toward you each night."

Small kisses touched my eyelids, and I opened them in surprise.

His eyes darkened as he gazed down at me. "And I feel as if I have always known you, as if there has never been a time in my life in which you were not a part of it."

I kept my eyes open as he kissed me, his lips caressing me, his mere touch arousing all of my senses.

I struggled to sit up, clutching his sleeves for support, intent on speaking before I lost my will and allowed my being to dissolve under his fingertips. "Then let us start anew. Let us pretend that all that has gone before us never happened. That there was no pain, loss, and betrayal. That there was simply us, waiting to find each other."

His face stilled, his voice heavy and dark when he spoke. "If only I could share in your optimism—that it is possible to forgive and forget old betrayals. That it is possible to pretend they never happened, despite the fact that the evidence of their existence is within eyesight." He pressed his lips to my forehead, holding me close. "I swear that I will do all that I can to help you remain so innocent and forgiving. I would preserve it in you even if I am incapable of forgetting or forgiving."

I struggled to read his eyes, but he had once again masked his true emotions, hiding his thoughts and tucking whatever secrets he kept from me far back into the recesses of his mind.

I felt emboldened by his words and I turned to him with confidence. "There is already something you can do."

He raised an eyebrow. "What is it?" Those impenetrable dark eyes flickered.

I kept my voice low, the sound of it rasping into the dark night. "Dismiss Marguerite. There is something . . . unholy about her. She is working against my authority here, and I am afraid of her influence on

Rebecca." I made no mention of the oleander leaves or the obvious way John had received the note from Daniel. The one true way to steer an issue to his core would be to invoke Rebecca's name.

His arms stiffened around me. "It sounds as if you are suggesting blackmail. You will stay if I dismiss Marguerite."

I shook my head vehemently, a sick feeling churning in the pit of my stomach. "No, I am asking for your trust. You are keeping Marguerite here for a reason that you will not divulge to me. Trust me, John, with your secret. Whatever my reaction to it, it cannot possibly be worse than the damage should Marguerite stay."

To my astonishment, John moved me from his lap, settling me onto the bed, and then stood, turning his back to me. I watched as he brushed his hands over his head, sweeping the hair off his forehead in uncharacteristic agitation. "I cannot. With all your talk of trust, why can you not trust me in this matter?" He shook his head, then turned to look at me with haunted eyes. "And the matter is not to be discussed further."

I slid off the bed and approached him, my hands on his sleeves. "What do you mean that you cannot? If it is due to a promise you made to the Lewistons, I am sure they would understand if you would just explain—"

His words cut me off. "I said I cannot, and nothing will change that. The matter is closed."

He resembled a madman, his hair looking storm-tossed and his face ravaged. Very quietly, I said, "Then everything you have said to me tonight in this room has been a lie."

I waited for him to refute my words, to apologize or make some move of reconciliation, but he did not. Slowly, I turned from him and left, waiting until I was safely behind the closed door of my old room to let the tears fall.

The next few days were difficult, as relations between John and me remained strained. I had slept in my old room the first night, and had continued to do so in the ensuing days. I made a show of retiring to the room I shared with John to ready myself for bed, but would return to the room down the hall as soon as the servants had gone to bed. I was too angry and hurt to sleep with him, and I knew all he would have to do would be to touch me and I would forget all his empty promises and the damage they had caused in our blossoming relationship.

We ate our meals together and I would sense his gaze resting heavily on me. I spoke civilly to him, for Rebecca's sake, but refused any intimate conversation or contact. He accepted my withdrawal coolly, never acknowledging it outright, but aware nonetheless. He would watch me as a cat might watch a mouse, waiting for the first show of weakness to catch me.

On the third night, I excused myself with Rebecca, and helped her get ready for bed. Since her revelation of her conversations with the dead woman and her baby, I had been seeing to Rebecca. I dressed her in the morning and put her to bed each night, sitting in a chair by her bed until I was satisfied that she was sound asleep. I would sit in the darkness and strain my ears for voices or a baby's cry, but would hear only the silence.

I fought fatigue as I slid her nightgown over her head and tucked her in bed, and when she was asleep, I gratefully walked down the corridor to the master bedroom to change for bed. I rang for Marguerite and began pulling the pins from my hair, the dark strands falling past my shoulders and almost to my waist. It was the one feature Elizabeth and I had in common that I had not resented. We would spend long hours braiding each other's hair into elaborate twists and styles, each one more beautiful than the next.

I paused for a moment at the memory, relieved that it had been a good one. I leaned into the mirror at my dressing table, the candlelight making my hair and skin glow, and saw the smile on my lips.

The door swung open behind me, making the candle flame shiver and swirl. I swiveled in my seat and stood to watch John enter the room.

I cleared my throat. "I rang for Marguerite."

"And I told her not to come. I will see to your needs tonight."

"No, John. I would rather not."

I could see his visible efforts to control his impatience. "You cannot keep me from your bed forever, you know."

I stepped back. "It is just that . . . I need time away from you. To think."

He took a step forward, tension outlined in his face. "To think about what?"

I realized I was wringing my hands and stopped. "The way things are between us."

His face relaxed, as if he had been expecting another answer. "We are married. I already told you that I did not want a cold marriage bed. And my bed has been very cold these past few nights." He held out his hand. "Come back to me."

As he spoke he approached, and I retreated until my heels hit the wall behind me. "No, John, not until this is settled between us."

He reached me, and I had nowhere else to go. "Avoiding me and my bed will not settle anything." With a light touch of his finger, he stroked my cheek, the gentle touch nearly undoing my resolve.

I turned my head, making him drop his hand. "You treat my concerns lightly."

"And I tell you that you have no reason for concerns. I have promised you that I will learn to trust more freely. You know it is not easy for me, and I am only learning. Be patient with me."

"What of Marguerite?"

His face darkened. "That is still a subject not open to discussion." He placed his palms on the wall behind me and leaned in closer. "I have sworn to protect you with my life, Cat. You need never fear anything as long as I am here. And I will do all that I can to give you the gentle life you so deserve." His warm breath fell softly on my skin, making me sigh. "Surely there is nothing more you could ask of me."

He kissed my cheek, his lips and deep voice the final caress needed to banish my resolve. I turned my head to face him, feeling the change in the air between us. I almost felt that if I lifted my finger to touch him, a great ball of fire would erupt, burning us to ashes.

"Let me love you, Cat. Let me show you that all is right between us."

I hated myself at that moment. I hated myself for putting my arms around his neck and pulling him closer. And for allowing his fingers to undress me and for his lips to arouse me. I willingly succumbed to self-loathing and denial just to be in his arms again.

When we were undressed, he lifted me in his arms and carried me to the bed. His lovemaking was sweet and tender, reminding me of our

honeymoon, before the realities of our married life together had in-
truded. I clung to him, forgetting all that had gone between us, and
cried out my passion for this man as he loved me into oblivion.

He turned to me several times that night, and each time I welcomed
him. It was as if we had been starved of food and now could not be
sated. As dawn approached, I lay in his arms, our bodies cooling under
the thin cotton sheet, the other bedclothes thrown in rumpled heaps
on the floor.

Stroking my bare shoulder, he kissed my temple and moved me
closer to his side. "Tell me about Robert."

I stiffened, startled at his request. "Why would you want to know
about my first husband?"

"It is only natural curiosity. You know about Elizabeth, and I feel
the desire to know about Robert. I want to know everything about
you, Cat."

I pressed my cheek against his chest and sighed. "There is not much
to tell, really. We were only married a short time before the war. But we
had known each other from childhood. Our mothers were great friends,
so we saw them quite a bit, even though their cotton plantation was on
the mainland."

I shut my eyes tightly against the memories that were assailing my
heart—the memories of happy childhood days on warm sunny beaches
and of sand beneath bare toes and the stirrings of what I had thought
to be love.

"Elizabeth was always our leader—she was quite bossy. Even though
Robert was Elizabeth's age, he always agreed to follow. I was the younger
sister and had always been the little soldier for Elizabeth, and I suppose
both Robert and I were in awe of her. She would get us into scrapes and
we would let her. I rarely remember her getting punished for them, either. She would feign illness or true remorse, leaving Robert and me,
who were far less clever, to face our fathers' switches. Not that we ever
learned our lessons, of course. We would be up to the same old tricks as
soon as our bottoms had healed."

I felt John's cheek smile against the top of my head.

"I always thought that she would marry him, and I think our parents
did, too, even though she never treated Robert any differently than she

would have a brother." I slid my hand underneath the sheet as I talked, smoothing John's taut chest, my fingers curled in the thick black hairs.

"I do not believe she paid any attention to him at all until he started courting me." I recalled then the look of rage on Elizabeth's face when she had caught Robert trying to steal a kiss from me. At the time I had thought that she had been angered that he would take such liberties with her sister, who was barely fourteen. But now, for the first time, I looked back on that memory anew.

"It was during your visit—when you and Elizabeth became engaged. I suppose Robert had realized that Elizabeth was forever lost to him, so he turned his interest to me." I rolled over, placing both arms on top of John's chest, my chin cradled on my hands. "She became the most outrageous flirt. Even though she was engaged, she sought Robert out at every opportunity. I heard other mothers and their daughters calling her fast, but it did not stop her. It was only after she married you and moved away did she stop."

He pushed the hair away from my forehead with gentle fingers. "Did you love him?"

I laid my head down on my clasped hands and closed my eyes for a moment, opening them quickly at the remembered sight of blood-stained sheets. "I think I did—at least in the beginning. I thought what I felt for him was love. But what does a young girl really know of love? We were good friends, and I thought that would be a fine start to a marriage. And he was going off to war and looked so handsome in his uniform. We were just all caught up in the excitement of it. We were young and happy with no idea of the harsh realities of life or of the devastation of war. And it never occurred to us that perhaps whatever we had based our marriage on was not strong enough to help us survive the bad times."

I looked up at him again, and he used a roughened thumb to wipe away the wetness on my cheeks. "No, I do not think I really loved him. He gave me my beautiful son and I was grateful to him for that, but I can't say that I loved him."

His large hands closed about my waist and lifted me on top of him. My hands spread on the pillow behind his head to support me, my long hair brushing his face and chest.

538 · *Karen White*

"I am glad," he said. "I have no intention of sharing your heart with another man."

Our passion was frenzied this time, as if the heat and rising tide of our emotions was needed to negate the past and forge new, stronger bonds. The image of sandy beaches and bloodstained sheets evaporated in a sea of feeling and need for this man, and for the refuge he offered my bruised and battered heart.

It was only later, when his breathing had slowed to the deep and heavy rhythm of sleep and I watched the dawn light the sky, that my doubts returned. His reluctance to dismiss Marguerite alerted me to a secret that had been kept hidden from me. But I was powerless against his will. My last thought before I lapsed into a deep sleep was that perhaps I was being unreasonable by not accepting his word that he would protect me. And that, indeed, there were some secrets best kept hidden.

CHAPTER NINETEEN

———◆———

I kept Rebecca close to my side, her dreams of ghosts and voices calling to her from the pond haunting me. I had spoken to all of the servants and threatened them with dismissal if I ever heard that one of them had mentioned the Indian woman and her baby to Rebecca. Still, I wanted the child with me, trusting my protection more than any promises.

With the heavy heat of summer gone, we spent a great deal of time outside. I would speak soon to John about buying a pony for Rebecca and teaching her to ride, but for now, we would go for long drives in the small buggy that had been Elizabeth's favorite. We would race along the lane of oaks in front of the house and beyond, but I would slow the horse as soon as we reached the levee road.

I was still uncomfortable on the levee after my fall, and would have avoided it altogether if the child had not clamored for it. She loved the view of the water and could never be convinced to try a different route.

On an overcast morning, just as Rebecca and I approached the levee, we were hailed by a lone rider. With dismay, I thought at first it was Philip Herndon but soon realized that it was Dr. Lewiston. I smiled warmly and waved back.

He bowed grandly to both Rebecca and me, wiggling his golden eyebrows as he did so and making her giggle. "What a lovely surprise to find two such beautiful ladies out for their morning ride. I would be so flattered to accompany you, if only so I can bask in your beauty."

Rebecca laughed harder and I had to smile, too, despite my trepidation. I could only imagine John's anger were he to find out I had seen Daniel again without John's presence.

Daniel pretended to be hurt, and pressed his hat to his heart. "You wound me, ladies. I am merely trying to brighten this terribly cloudy day, yet you laugh at me."

He winked at Rebecca, then reached into his jacket pocket and pulled out a string of licorice. "And this, my dear, is for you. I always carry it around in case I am lucky enough to see you."

Rebecca reached up to take it, her smile never fading. Then she placed it in her lap, one of her gloved hands on top lest it should fall off. I assumed she was protecting it to make sure it made it to her collection in the bottom of her bureau drawer.

Despite my wariness, I could not help but show my genuine gladness to see him. "It is good to see you again."

I smiled up at him and he grinned back, but his eyes were serious. "You are looking as lovely as ever, Catherine."

I looked down at my gloved hands, attempting to hide my discomfiture. I knew Daniel was simply being gallant, but I doubted John would have considered it so innocently. The thought of John sobered me considerably, casting another cloud onto my day. I considered Daniel my friend and felt I should not be made to feel guilty for spending time with him.

"Thank you, Daniel. Your flattery goes too far, but it is always nice to hear. But I am afraid we need to be returning home."

Daniel looked disappointed. "But surely you could spare a little bit of time for me to show you Rebecca's secret place."

Intrigued, I looked at the little girl beside me. She jumped up and down on the seat, her eyes pleading. "Please? There is my own little waterfall, and sometimes I find bird eggs and rocks for my collection. I have not been there since my other mama went up to heaven." Her blue eyes shimmered.

Reluctantly, I nodded, hoping that our extended excursion would not be noticed. "All right, Rebecca. But just for a little while."

Daniel leaned over and reached for Rebecca. "Then come on, little peanut—let us go for a ride and show your aunt our special place."

"She is not my aunt anymore, Dr. Lewiston. She is my new mama."

Daniel's eyes met mine over Rebecca's blond head and he nodded approvingly.

"Let us go, then," I said, and flicked the reins on my horse. I followed Daniel and Rebecca along the levee for a short distance before turning off onto a narrow dirt road hardly wider than a trail. It bisected a dense pine forest, a thin line of brown against lush green. We dismounted and tied the horses, then followed Daniel into the woods.

It was hard to imagine that we were so close to the river in this secluded place. The only sounds were those of the birds and other small forest creatures who inhabited the tall, scrubby pines. A thick layer of pine needles lay across the path, bristling and cracking underneath our feet. Rebecca held the doctor's hand, and I followed quietly, not wanting my voice to ruin the magic of this place.

We soon came to a clearing, a brilliant white gazebo marking the end of the path. It was large—large enough for a couple to dance the waltz—and the roof had been painted a dark green. A weathered brass hawk perched on the cupola, its eyes bright and penetrating, frightening away any small birds who might come to perch there. In the far distance, a great house rose into view, its unprotected back glaring at us. Half of the roof was missing, the charred walls like blackened bruises on the white house. A flock of sparrows lifted off what had once been the attic, darkening the sky and leaving us in the quiet solitude of the ruined mansion.

"Where are we?" I asked, completely lost.

Daniel smiled. "We are at Pine Grove—the King family's cotton plantation. Not that it can be called that anymore, since no crop has been planted in almost five years. It burned in the first year of the war, and they left. Nobody has heard from them since."

A frown crossed his face for a moment and I looked away, studying the gazebo. It, too, appeared to be in disrepair, with floorboards missing and paint peeling, and a great sadness fell on me. It seemed that whatever the Yankees had not outright destroyed during the war had been left to face a slow and lingering death. Watching my own house burn to the ground had wounded my spirit more than a bullet to my heart ever could, yet at least I didn't have to watch it slowly fall to the ground as a mother would watch a sick child slowly founder out of this life.

I turned to face Daniel. "It is so quiet here."

He walked onto the octagonal floor of the gazebo, carefully stepping over a protruding board. Rebecca followed closely behind him, easily avoiding the first board and then skipping, with the agility of a child who had done the same movement many times, over two more gaping holes before finding a seat on the far wall.

Daniel leaned against an archway and studied me carefully. "Yes, it is. It is reminiscent of so many lives after the war, is it not? Everything in ruins."

I walked around the gazebo, taking note of the late-fall scarlet camellias, their bright, leafy bushes hiding the base of the structure, which was nearly completely swallowed by brambles and vines. I turned back to Daniel, eager to turn the conversation. I had no wish to remember those desolate days following Robert's return. "I have not had the chance to ask you what Philip was doing at Whispering Oaks the last time we met."

Before he spoke, Daniel turned to Rebecca. "Go see if you can find any eggs—but stay away from the water until we come, all right?"

Eagerly, the child nodded and skipped off in the direction of a dirt path close to the one we had just been on.

"Is it safe?" I asked, remembering the dangers of our grotto.

Daniel nodded. "She has been there many a time and always stays away from the water—even though it is merely a trickle and cannot cause her more harm than wetting her pinafore." He smiled. "She knows to not venture far from the path, and it only meanders into the woods for a short distance. She is perfectly safe and will wait for us until we are ready to come and get her."

I wrinkled my brow. "It sounds like she has been here often."

"Yes, she loves it here. Her mother and I would bring her here quite a bit."

I nodded, remembering Mr. O'Rourke explaining to me the jaunts Elizabeth would take with Rebecca. How desperately Elizabeth must have wanted to get away from that house. She had hated the outdoors with a passion and had always gone to great lengths to avoid it.

I watched Rebecca disappear and waited for Daniel to answer my question about Philip. The doctor leaned down and picked up a long sliver of wood that had been dislodged from a floorboard and rubbed it between his fingers. Without looking at me, he said, "He was there to see you, regardless of what John might think about it. Luckily, I was able to persuade him otherwise."

"He wanted to see me? Whatever for? I am quite sure he understands that his behavior toward my husband the last time we met is completely unacceptable to me. I will not see him."

Daniel's gaze traveled to the neglected camellias, their gentle beauty now hidden under tall grass and weeds. "I told him that, but he seems quite obsessed with you."

"But that is absurd. We have known each other since we were children. It was always Elizabeth that Philip was interested in." I took a deep breath, the memory of the baby that had died with Elizabeth never far from me. "I also gather that their relationship may have continued after Elizabeth's marriage."

A shade of sadness passed across Daniel's face. "Perhaps. I do not listen to gossip, nor will I speak ill of the dead. But as for Philip, I think it would be wise to avoid him. His antagonism toward John could be due in part to the fact that John's a Yankee and may have nothing to do with Elizabeth at all. I avoid him simply because he is a member of that rabble-rousing White League." He dropped the scrap of wood, hitting the gazebo floor with an oddly hollow and lonely sound.

"He has threatened John. Philip said that John had taken his most cherished thing from him and now Philip would repay him. He is not the same boy I knew."

Daniel swept his hand along a balustrade, peeling paint flaking off and drifting down onto the camellias. "No, Philip has changed. He ran away from the war and now is stirring up trouble in the hopes that people will forget his cowardice. But I would avoid him—especially now that he has all but admitted to being obsessed with you."

I waved my hand in the air, dismissing his words. "He was obsessed with Elizabeth, and she and I bear strong resemblance—that is all. He certainly never gave me a second glance all through those summers of coming here to our grandmother's." I said it without bitterness, glad to have been left to my own devices to paint and read instead of worry about what my hair and dress looked like at all times.

Daniel smiled. "Perhaps Elizabeth's shadow was simply too large for you to emerge from. But now that it is no longer here, we all see how you shine."

I turned away to study the camellias, embarrassed at his words.

He stepped down the gazebo's steps and stood near me. Reluctantly, I looked up.

"Are you happy, Catherine?"

He stood so close, and I suddenly felt uncomfortable. I shot a glance toward the path where Rebecca had gone, feeling somewhat safer with her nearby. I stepped backward, still smiling, but trying to maintain a distance between us.

With a self-deprecating look, he stepped back, too. "I am sorry, Catherine. I forget sometimes that we have known each other for such a short time. Perhaps it is your resemblance to Elizabeth that makes me believe that I have known you for much longer."

I looked sharply at him, curious as to how well he really did know my sister.

As if reading my thoughts, he quickly added, "Elizabeth and I were good friends. She needed someone to confide in, and she chose me. I know she confided in Clara, too, but I think that perhaps Elizabeth might have been more reticent in sharing certain things with her than with me. I was her doctor, after all."

I nodded, my doubts satisfied. I glanced down at the scarlet camellias, their showy blooms staring out from among the glossy green leaves and the climbing weeds. Taking pity on the vain flowers, I knelt down and began plucking as many as I could fit in my hand. The weeds would soon choke out their beauty, withering their buds on the vines. I brought the cluster close to my face and closed my eyes, feeling the velvet softness of the flowers against my chin. These blossoms were so much like my dead sister: brash and vibrant, yet so vulnerable to the weeds of vanity and the fruitless search for happiness that had finally choked out her life. For a moment, I felt only pity for her instead of the anger that had resided in my heart since her death—my anger at her desperate and ultimately selfish act of leaving me completely and utterly alone.

A gentle touch on my arm made me open my eyes, and I saw Daniel's compassionate ones staring into mine.

"Are you well?"

I nodded, then buried my face in the blooms again until I felt Elizabeth's memory drift back into the dark recesses of my mind, where they belonged. "Let us go find Rebecca. We need to get back."

We found her crouched in front of a thin rivulet, the water valiantly struggling over mud and rocks, creating a small, dripping waterfall that had entranced the little girl. It lay in the middle of an unexpectedly large clearing. I noticed with delight that the old camellias had found their way into this place and were pushing their heads toward the daylight sky.

Rebecca squealed in delight as Daniel swung her up on his back. I noticed the pockets of her pinafore bulged and I laughed. "Did you find many treasures, sweetheart?"

She nodded exuberantly. "Oh yes. No eggs today, but lots of pretty things."

I smiled at her childish enthusiasm. "That is wonderful. You will have to show me everything when we get home."

Daniel added, "We need to leave now, before people begin to worry."

I looked at him with alarm, knowing to whom he was referring. "Yes, let us leave. I want to paint Rebecca in this light, and I probably have less than an hour before it changes."

Following them down the dirt trail, I glanced at the camellias clutched in my hands, their stems sticking to my sweaty palms. They no longer seemed beautiful to me but, rather, were sad reminders of Elizabeth's life and untimely death. They were also one more thing to explain to John, and I had no desire to travel that path.

Slowly, I opened my palm and let the flowers fall from my hand, scattering the bright red petals on the dirt path like spilled blood.

Daniel escorted us as far as the lane of trees leading up to Whispering Oaks. As we waved goodbye and watched him ride off for home, I again heard the keening cry of a baby. My skin chilled as if a breath had been brushed against the back of my neck.

Rebecca touched my arm, her eyes wide, and then I remembered the glass bottles. Turning in my seat, I spied Marguerite, half-hidden behind a tree trunk, a roll of twine and empty bottles at her feet. A movement from a low branch caught my attention, and I looked up to see Delphine clinging to a branch, a newly tied bottle dangling below her.

Marguerite looked at me for a moment, then turned her head in the direction in which the doctor had ridden. When our eyes met again, hers were all-knowing. Quickly, she bowed her head. "Good afternoon, ma'am."

"Good afternoon, Marguerite." I looked past her toward the bottles hanging in the tree and swaying in the wind, their ghostly cry spiraling among the gnarled oaks. "Does Mr. McMahon approve of having these here?"

"I do not know. I have never asked him."

"Nor did you ask me, and I do not approve. The sound frightens Rebecca." I looked up at Delphine so she would understand I was speaking to her, too. "I want all of these removed right now, and I do not want to see them again."

Marguerite stared at me in silence for a long moment before nodding and saying, "Yes, ma'am."

Not wanting further discussion, I picked up the reins and headed toward the house. In the short time since we had left the gazebo, heavier clouds had moved in, obscuring the light and changing my plans for painting Rebecca. I was not completely disappointed. I had been battling fatigue for more than a week, and I was happy for the excuse to lie down when Rebecca napped.

After a quick midday meal, eaten without John, who had remained at the mill office, I slowly climbed the stairs and put Rebecca to bed, barely able to keep my eyes open. When I reached my room, I collapsed on the bed, not taking the time to remove my clothes, and quickly fell into oblivious sleep.

When I awoke, John sat on the foot of the bed, staring at me with a contemplative look. My smile was not returned, and he morosely moved off the bed and went to the window, staring out at the pond.

Unease bled through my body, and I wondered if Marguerite had told him of my being with Daniel. I sat up, willing to do battle and defend my freedom and innocence. "What is wrong?"

He didn't look at me when he spoke. "While you were out with Rebecca, Philip Herndon came to call."

My unease scattered into relief. "What did he want?"

He turned to face me. "I do not know. It was you he wanted to see."

"After our confrontation in New Orleans, I truly have no desire to ever speak to the man again."

Without comment, John faced the window again. "He gave me the same threats he has given me before, and I told him I would shoot him if I ever found him on my property again. Not that I think I would. The man is not mentally stable, I am afraid, and I need to speak with his parents about seeking treatment for him."

I slid off the bed to stand near him. "Surely not, John. I know you do not want to hear this, but he . . . cared for Elizabeth very much. He is grieving." I touched his sleeve, willing him to look in my eyes. "Let someone grieve for her as she deserved."

He touched my face with a gentle caress. "You are too kind and loving to people who are not deserving of it."

"She was my sister, John. That will never change."

He flinched slightly, and I was about to ask him why when the door was flung open. Rebecca stood in the doorway, her underclothing wrinkled from her nap and her unbound hair flying in all directions. She wore a wide smile, given only to those she loved the most, and in her chubby hands clutched two bright red clusters of camellias.

My heart skidded when I spied them. I remembered her bulging pockets and, knowing her love for flowers, it would have been inevitable that she would have wanted some to bring home with her.

John walked to her and knelt by her side. "These are lovely, Rebecca. Who are they for?"

"For both of you," she said with glee, thrusting out her hand to John.

I stayed where I was, paralyzed, a sick feeling of nausea burning my stomach.

He took them from her and gave her a hug and kiss. "And where did you find such beautiful flowers?"

"Dr. Lewiston took me and Mama to our secret place, where these pretty flowers grow. I knew you would like them, so I picked a lot."

An abrupt stillness seemed to fall on John, and Rebecca sensed it, too.

"What is wrong, Papa? Do you not like them?"

He had to clear his throat before getting the words out. "Yes, of course. Now, you go find Delphine to help you dress. I need to speak to your mama."

She gave him a loud kiss on the cheek before skipping out of the room, taking all the warmth with her.

Slowly, John stood and faced me. "Well?"

I tried to push back the wave of nausea and squared my shoulders. "Well, what? I took Rebecca for a ride, and we ran into Daniel quite by accident. He showed us to the most lovely spot, and we chatted for a while before returning."

His eyes flickered but he remained silent.

"For God's sake, John! Daniel is your best friend, and I am your wife. Do you really think for one second that either one of us would ever betray you? I pity you if you cannot find it in your heart to trust those of us who love you best. And Rebecca was with us. Do you doubt my love for your child so much that you think I could be so despicable as to place her in that sort of situation? Maybe Philip Herndon is not the only one who is mentally unhinged. Perhaps you both should seek treatment."

He placed his fingers under my jaw, his hand trembling from trying to control his emotions, and brought my face up to meet his. His words were harsh. "I can believe the worst of people for a reason. Remember that, my dear wife."

His eyes flashed as they bored into mine for a long moment before he dropped his hand. With great deliberation, he raised his other hand and closed it tightly, crushing the fragile blooms inside, then letting them drift to the floor.

I trembled from hurt and nausea and his coldness, and was glad when he left the room without another word. I barely made it to the washstand before I vomited, taking the last of my energy. Collapsing to the floor, I sat there for a long time, feeling anger, hurt, and grief wash over me in continual succession. When numbness finally seeped into my heart and brain, I stood and cleansed my face. As I slowly dried myself, I spotted the lodestone sitting on my dressing table amid my brushes and jars of perfume.

Picking it up, I rolled it in my palms, noticing how my touch did not warm it. Instead it remained a frigid lump in my hand, as if my blood had chilled to such a degree that there was no more warmth to give.

Still clutching the stone, I slipped a pair of earbobs into my pocket, then left the room, intent on finding Rose. I was too exhausted to contemplate my next course of action, but perhaps she could help me find my way.

I found her alone in the kitchen, and she looked up as if she were expecting me. The black pot over the stove simmered, creating that oddly pungent odor I remembered from before. She greeted me, then motioned for me to sit while she stirred the pot, whisking the steam toward her face and breathing in deeply. Reaching into a glass jar on a high shelf, she pinched a crimson-colored powder and threw it into the pot, making it hiss and bubble.

Dipping the ladle into the pot, she poured the contents into two tin cups, then handed one to me. I turned away from the bitter brew, the odor making my stomach twist. Looking up, I caught Rose watching me closely, her eyes wide and knowing.

She sat down at the stained wooden table in the same seat she had used before and closed her eyes, the smoke from her cup rising in front of her and distorting her face like a reflection in old glass.

When she spoke, her deeply accented voice had once again transformed itself, its grainy thickness calling to mind moist river silt, carrying fertile words heavy with meaning. "Does your husband know you secret?"

I raised an eyebrow, my breath held. Until this moment, I had not even ventured to hope, but now joy leapt inside me and I knew. "No. I was not sure. . . ."

She waved her hand, her eyes tightly shut in her dark, wrinkled face. "You be giving you husband a son." A corner of her mouth tilted up at a vision unseen by me. "That chile will be dark like his father, so Mr. McMahon don' need to wonder no more about your true feelings for him."

I flinched as her eyes flickered open and she stared at me, unseeing. "But there be many bridges to cross afore you can find that happiness you be searchin' for." She placed her elbows on the table and leaned over to me. "You and that girl chile be in terrible danger. She need you love and protection now, and you need it more than her. But you needs to know who you friends be and who not you friend."

Her hand crept across the table like a large, dark spider. She grabbed my hand, prying open the fingers. She touched the lodestone, and it seemed to burn in my hand. I let it roll off my palm, and she replaced it quickly. "You carry always. You need it for protection now. And you needs to find out who you friends be."

The cloudiness in her eyes passed and she gave me a clear gaze. "There be things you don' know, that people wants to keep hidden. But you needs to know these things so you can understand the true nature of those closest to you." She patted my hand. "You be hurt, but you soul mate—he be the one to get you through 'dis dark time."

I cleared my throat. "You mentioned before two men I share my life with, and one who betrays me. Is there any more you can tell me?"

She sat up and wrapped her fingers around her mug. "No. I only see what I suppose to see. It be up to you to figure out what I means."

Nodding, I stood, clutching the edge of the table for support. Leaning heavily on it, I thanked her and handed her the pair of earbobs Robert had given me to show my appreciation. Turning to leave, I felt a touch on my sleeve.

Rose's eyes seemed to flicker in the dimness of the kitchen. "You watch Marguerite. Her power be much stronger than mine. And don' you forgets to carry that lodestone." Her fingers tightened over my hand with the lodestone and squeezed tightly. "You be needin' it now more than ever."

I thanked her again and left, the joy of my impending motherhood mixed inexorably with Rose's dour warnings. Needing fresh air, I walked around the house, avoiding the pond, toward the front. As I passed the side, I looked up, a movement in a window capturing my attention. I realized the window belonged to Elizabeth's old room, and there was no reason for anybody to be in there. Watching closely, I saw an almost imperceptible swing of the blinds, as if somebody were gently replacing them against the window.

I raced around to the front of the house and took the steps two at a time until I reached Elizabeth's room. The door was shut and I flung it open, waiting for the bang as it hit the wall.

The room lay still and empty, just as Elizabeth had left it, her hairbrush and bottles now gathering dust on her dressing table. I blinked my eyes, noticing something dark and round hovering behind a wooden jewel box. Walking closer, my breath caught. I stared at the object for a long time before finding the nerve to pick it up. Lifting it toward the light creeping in from the blinds, I examined it closely. It appeared to be a short, thick, and twisted root of some kind, and it emitted an acrid odor, as if it had been soaked in some sort of oil. The object was dark and slick, the roots intertwined on one another and oddly resembling an old and withered face.

Staring at it, I nearly dropped it. Carefully laced in between the sinews of the root was a thin gold chain—my chain that I had left in the letterbox under my old bed, the key to the empty box hanging from the middle.

My hand shook as I held the gris-gris away from me. I had no doubt who had left it, and it was time to face my husband and his demons and hopefully put to rest some of my own.

Squaring my shoulders, I left the room, closing the door firmly on the emptiness inside.

CHAPTER TWENTY

———◆———

I had heard John come in and I knew he was somewhere in the house. After searching the library and his study, I paused in the foyer, listening to distant voices. Many of the windows had been raised to let the cool air cleanse the house, and I realized that the voices were being carried in from outside.

Walking to the back door, I quietly opened it, then stopped. Sitting on the top step was John, his daughter cradled in his lap while he read to her from a book. Her fingers curled on his shirt collar and her head nestled comfortably in the crook of his arm. She laughed at something he read, and when he looked at her, my knees weakened. It was a look so open, so warm, and so full of love that I knew then why I had to be strong and fight whatever forces were pulling me away from him and this place of secrets. His ability to love this child so completely, thus showing his true heart, had stolen my own heart. I loved him, I realized, so fully and utterly it took my breath away. At the same time it instilled a fear so terrorizing, I was afraid to even acknowledge it. For I had learned that to love so fiercely could bring loss and grief just as fierce.

Placing my hand over my still-smooth abdomen, I took a deep breath. For the sake of not only Rebecca, but also for the child I knew grew inside, I could not give up. The hope of a future with John and our growing family consumed me, giving me something to fight for—something I had not had since Jamie's death.

I tucked the gris-gris in among the folds of my dress, unsure as to how to proceed. If John were still willing to keep Marguerite at Whispering Oaks even with her threat to Rebecca, the power she held over him had to be something so awful that I could not even consider it.

John turned his head and saw me, and my heart lurched. Had I imagined that he looked at me with the same glow in his eyes with which he had regarded Rebecca? If only I could erase all the blackness and doubt that lingered between us—thin and wispy like smoke, but as impenetrable as a brick wall.

I joined them on the step, sitting close to John. Rebecca reached with her free hand to hold mine, and we listened to John's deep voice as he finished the story. By the time he had finished, Rebecca had fallen sound asleep.

Slowly, John rose, his daughter gathered in his arms, and I followed him up the stairs to Rebecca's room. He laid her on her bed, and I gently covered her with a blanket. We stood there for a long moment, watching her sleep, before leaving.

I waited for him to close the door behind him before speaking. "John."

He looked at me with shadowed eyes, the emotion I had seen on the porch hidden away from my view. Had I imagined what I had seen? Could I truly expect to fight for us and our family if he were not willing to stand by my side and fight with me? I almost blurted out my news then, but something made me hesitate. Perhaps it was the knowledge that if he knew of the baby, I would be tied to him forever, living in this prison of distrust and jealousy.

Silently, I held up the root, the gold chain winking in the light from the window.

He sucked in his breath. "Where did you find that?"

"In Elizabeth's room. I know it came from Marguerite, and you and I both know what it is. It is bad gris-gris. And whether or not we believe in it, it is proof that she means us harm in some way. What have I done to her to make her hate me so?"

I heard his slow, deliberate breaths in the silent corridor. "I do not know. Maybe she resents your replacement of Elizabeth. Or perhaps it is simply your resemblance to your sister."

I shook my head in exasperation. "None of that matters now, John. What matters is our peace of mind. Whatever her reasons, she cannot stay here. Let her go. I can accept whatever hold she has on you." I swallowed thickly, searching for the courage to utter my next words. "Whatever she has to say will never change the way I feel about you."

He looked down at me, and for a moment I thought I saw pity in his eyes. He gave an almost imperceptible shake of his head and I dropped my hand, deeply wounded.

I tried to keep the desperation out of my voice. "I cannot live this way—with doubt and suspicion clouding my every move. I told you that before we were married. I cannot stay here if things remain the way they are." My voice caught, and I choked on my words, thinking of the child that grew inside. The one thing to bind me here, to this place and to John—if he should find out. "I cannot stay if you continue to make it clear that you distrust me so much that you feel you cannot confide in me. I have already survived so much. Surely whatever you are hiding cannot be as devastating to the spirit as that which I have already suffered. I am your wife, John. Treat me as such."

He gripped my arm and his voice shook. "I am trying to protect you from things you are better off not knowing. Why can you not accept that?"

I pulled away, tears flowing freely down my cheeks. "Because I am not a silly girl who prefers to be coddled. I have faced the worst things life can give—there is nothing that can wound me more deeply than I already have been. Except your distrust. Please, John, tell me. Tell me what secret Marguerite hides."

His dark eyes bored into mine as a fleeting emotion flickered behind them. "I cannot," he whispered. Then, his words urgent and low, he said, "Do not leave me."

I looked at him sharply. Were his words pleading or a threat? I thought of Elizabeth, supposedly killed by her own hand, and wondered if her real misdeed had been to threaten to leave her husband.

We stood almost touching in the darkened hallway, the air thick with unspoken words. He sighed, the sound of pain mixed with desire, then bent to kiss me. With all my will, I turned away, and his lips brushed my cheek. He stayed there for a long moment, his heated breath teasing my neck, and it took all my determination not to turn back and reach for him. But he had hurt me more than a physical blow would have, and I remained as I was.

Eventually, he straightened. Saying my name quietly, he brushed his finger against my jaw, but I remained impassive, despite the warring between my heart and my mind. I did not turn my head until I heard his boots descending the stairs. I watched him in silence, the joyful words of my impending motherhood stilled on my lips.

He did not come to my bed that night or the next, and I did not search for him. My heart and body screamed for him, but my mind clung to reason and I resolved to hold on to that as long as I could, for my sake as much as for the sake of my unborn child.

It had been a long while since I had last cried, but I would wake up in the middle of those desolate nights with a pillow sodden with tears and I would reach for John's warmth, only to feel the cold emptiness of the bed beside me.

On the third evening, he came into the bedroom as I was preparing to dress for supper at the Lewistons'. I was seated at the dressing table, rummaging through my jewelry box, when he came to stand behind me.

He placed a hand on my shoulder, his finger tracing the line of my collarbone. "You look tired."

I looked in the mirror at the dark circles under my eyes and wondered if he were mocking me. But when our gazes met in the glass, his expression showed genuine concern.

"Perhaps I can send Mr. O'Rourke with our excuses and we can stay home tonight."

I shook my head, perhaps too vigorously, knowing how weak my defenses were. I could not give in to my physical desires and hope to cling on to any self-respect. "No. Daniel and Clara would be so disappointed. I will be fine."

A dark shadow clouded his features. Leaning over me, he reached for the pearls nestled in the top tray of the jewelry box. "Then wear these. I miss seeing you in them."

"The clasp is a little loose—I would like to have the jeweler look at it before I wear them again."

He picked the necklace up and held it to the light, his long fingers stroking the creamy smoothness of the pearls. "The clasp is fine. And it looks lovely with your amber silk gown." With slow, deliberate movements, he wrapped the necklace around my neck and fastened it. His touch and the coolness of the pearls caressed my skin, making me burn.

Our eyes met again in the mirror. Before I could move away, he bent and kissed my neck, sending dangerous sparks throughout my body.

Quietly, he said in my ear, "I will be waiting for you downstairs."

I finished dressing, then left the room to go down to the foyer. I moved slowly, my fatigue weighing heavily on me, and dreading the evening ahead. My mood was not conducive to small talk nor Clara's incessant chatter. Nor were my defenses strong enough to fight the inevitable longing for John's touch whenever I was in his presence.

As I approached him, he turned to face me, my wrap in his hands. I swallowed deeply, trying not to show how his mere appearance affected me. His starched white shirt accentuated his skin, darkened by the sun. The black dinner jacket hung on his broad shoulders, outlining their powerful breadth.

His gaze swept over me in an appreciative glance, then moved behind me to set the wrap on my shoulders. I reached for it and our fingers touched. I jerked my hands away, as if I'd been burned, and stepped toward the door.

Rebecca rushed into the room, Delphine following close behind her.

"Mama, Mama!" the little girl shouted before launching herself into my arms.

I hugged her close and kissed her soft cheek before letting her go. As she ran to her father, I turned to Delphine.

"Remember, you are in charge tonight. Do not let her out of your sight, and I want you to stay in the room with her after you put her to bed, until she falls asleep. Do you understand?"

Delphine nodded. "Yes'm."

Confident I could trust the young girl, I thanked her, then allowed John to escort me out the door and into the carriage. I moved over to my usual spot on the far side of the carriage, pressing against the door so as not to touch my husband inadvertently.

Mr. O'Rourke drove, and John sat next to me. I fell against him when the coach lurched, and it took all my will to move away. We did not speak for a long while, and I watched the changing landscape out the window. It was a windless night, with a full moon and clear air, the stars brilliant diamonds in the black sky.

I felt compelled to face John and found him watching me closely.

His eyes held the same haunting look as they had when we had spoken in the hallway outside Rebecca's room several days before. His words tossed about my mind, pleading and threatening at the same time. *Do not leave me.* As if reading my thoughts, he said, "It is an appropriate night for All Hallows' Eve, is it not? Nothing seems quite real."

The carriage pulled up on the levee road, bumping and swaying over the uneven surface. The water seemed so close, too near, and I clutched at my reticule, feeling silly that I had put the lodestone in it but glad that I had done so.

I turned back to look at the water, so calm and peaceful under the light of the moon, its undercurrents hidden under placid ripples. I looked at John and wondered what perilous undercurrents ran through his blood. My hand rested on my abdomen, and I wondered if we might find a peace between us and I could share the news that would only be good for both of us.

I was still unwilling to inexorably tie myself to John with so many unanswered questions between us, as if my growing feelings for John and Rebecca had not already done so. But I could not help harboring the hope that this child could be the one thing that would erase all doubts and misunderstandings between us and bring us back to that place of wild contentment that had been upon us the first weeks of our marriage.

I looked out again at the moonlit water, the nonsalty smell of it still so foreign to me. A bat launched itself from a tree on the bank, swooping low and fluttering fast, until it disappeared behind the carriage. A metallic *click* sounded from the outside of the carriage, unrelated to the usual bumps and jars, and I found myself holding my breath.

A feeling of danger suddenly consumed me, making me sick with it, and I pressed myself against the side of the carriage. John reached toward me, taking my arm with one hand as he reached for the door near me with his other.

I looked at his face for a moment, but it was hidden in shadow. His grip on me tightened as I remembered his words in the hall. *Do not leave me.*

I gave a strangled cry as the carriage door swung open behind me at the same time John lifted me out of the seat. The skirts of my gown whipped furiously in the wind outside the gaping coach door, and I clung to John's arms.

Mr. O'Rourke shouted from above, and then I found myself smothered against John's solid chest, the smell of wool and freshly pressed linen heavy in my nose. I did not open my eyes again until the carriage came to a complete stop.

"Are you all right?" John's voice was thick in my ear.

I nodded, not yet able to speak.

"Thank God. I saw the door opening and knew that one bump in the road would send you out of the carriage. I got to you just in time."

Mr. O'Rourke climbed down from his perch and stood in the empty doorway. Holding a lantern aloft, he said, "The paint is marred—it is like someone tampered with the latch."

John continued to hold me tightly to him. Softly, he said, "You are shaking. We should go home."

I shook my head. I felt the need to be with other people besides John. I could not help but remember John gripping my arm before we heard Mr. O'Rourke's shout, and my wild thoughts wondered what his true intent had been had the driver not noticed the open door. His words reverberated again and again in my head, my mind trying to decipher them as plea or threat. *Do not leave me.*

John gave Mr. O'Rourke instructions to continue on and, after he had fiddled with the latch to get it to stay, the carriage started again. I stayed close to John and away from the door, wondering for the remainder of the journey if I were truly safer in his arms. I wanted to believe it with all my heart, but I could not stop myself from thinking of Elizabeth. *Had she ever threatened to leave and was that why she now lay buried in the old family mausoleum?*

I turned to look at my husband in the dark interior of the carriage and saw no malice. He brushed the hair from my forehead and kissed me gently, then gazed out his window, his thoughts hidden from me.

Daniel met us at the door of Belle Meade, an imposing Greek Revival mansion. I noticed the absence of a servant to greet us and take our cloaks, as well as the faded and peeling wallpaper in the grand foyer—both examples of the demise of a way of life that I acknowledged we would never see again.

As Daniel led us into the front parlor, conversation halted as all eyes turned to us, more specifically to me. I felt a flush steal over my shoulders as the uncomfortable silence continued, until Daniel took my arm and led me to a chair. As he seated me, he leaned toward my ear and whispered, "You look so much like Elizabeth tonight—it is the way you have done your hair, I think. It is quite stunning."

Self-consciously, I reached up to touch the coil of hair at the nape of my neck, remembering how Elizabeth, after teasing me about my propensity for wearing my long hair unbound, had taught me how to roll and tuck my hair in a fair imitation of the style she preferred. After securing it, she had quickly pulled it out again, saying it did not suit me. But now, no longer willing to accept Marguerite's help in getting me dressed or fixing my hair, it was the only formal style I knew how to do myself.

Clara greeted me with a kiss on each cheek, her smile cheerful and warm as she played the consummate hostess with a skill that had been bred in her since the cradle. Despite the dingy furniture and dusty drapes, she exuded the same hospitality that she would have when her home shone and sparkled and the paint didn't peel from the massive columns across the front.

She wore a dinner gown in a dated style, but the celery-colored silk lifted the usual pallor of her skin, making her eyes shine. When she smiled, as she invariably did when looking at her husband, she was almost pretty. She seemed to flit among her guests like a moth around an open flame, but always seemed to come to rest by her husband's side. She reminded me of a small child with a favorite toy, afraid to leave it alone too long, lest somebody come along and take it from her.

As Clara had assured me, it was a small gathering. Besides the Lewistons, Clara's elderly father, Mr. Brier, John and me, Judge Patterson, and the elder Herndons completed the party. I was surprised to see the latter until Daniel quietly explained that they were no longer on speaking terms with their son and that he had moved out of their house several weeks prior and they had not seen him since. When Daniel straightened after whispering in my ear, I looked up to see Clara and John watching us closely. Before I could respond, Clara was at Daniel's side, whisking him away to a conversation with Mr. and Mrs. Herndon.

At dinner, as one of the guests of honor, I was seated at Daniel's right side, with Judge Patterson on my right and Clara's father across from me. I remembered Mr. Brier's assertion that he had seen Elizabeth in Baton Rouge before we had found her body, and John's claim that the old man was not in his right mind. I assumed him to be in his late seventies or early eighties, and time would have taken a toll on his mind and body. Stooped and wrinkled, he walked with the assistance of a cane, and one of the servants had to cut his meal into tiny bites. He did not speak, so I assumed he could not, and when he ate, drool fell from the corner of his mouth. But when he looked up, his eyes were bright and clear, and it was obvious that he was following the conversation around him intently.

John sat to Clara's right, putting him diagonally across from me, and every time I looked in his direction, I would see his dark, brooding eyes on me before I quickly looked away.

Conversation at the table seemed strained, as if we were all trying too hard to avoid the obvious topics that would be deemed unsuitable. We talked of the weather and politics and the recent disappearance and murder of a sheriff in a neighboring parish. But the recent war, the dilapidated house, the missing son, and my dead sister seemed to float behind the dining-room chairs like ghosts, unseen but as present in the room as the scarred furniture.

As a young female servant cleared away the dinner dishes and brought out dessert and coffee, Clara addressed me from the other end of the table, ensuring everyone could hear.

"Catherine, is the food to your liking? You look pale."

It was true that the aromas of food were making my stomach churn, no doubt on account of the baby. I had thought that I had stirred the food up enough on my plate to warrant a pretense of an appetite.

"The food is delicious, thank you. I am just feeling a little tired— that is all."

"Well, it has been almost two months since your honeymoon. Since we are all close friends, I was wondering if perhaps you had some news for us."

I tried to give her a warning look as I answered. "I am not quite sure what you mean. If you are speaking of my first completed portrait, yes—Rebecca's has been finished, and I am quite proud of it. When you visit us next, you can see it hanging in the library."

Her eyes never wavered from my face. "No, dear. I was hoping you and John might have some more exciting news for us." She lowered her lashes, her composure returned to the reserved Clara I knew. Quietly smoothing her linen napkin in her lap, she said, "I am sorry if I have embarrassed you by speaking out of turn. It is just that I thought— well, I hoped—that we might have something to celebrate this evening. There is precious little good news as it is."

My gaze slid to John. His eyes had darkened, his face stilled, his hand tightly clutching his wineglass. I turned away and saw Clara, who, remarkably, had her eyes fixed on Daniel, as if to study his reaction.

Clara must have already known the truth—probably from Marguerite. I looked down at my plate, knowing that to lie now would be futile. "Yes, we do have good news. John and I are expecting a child."

There was a call for a toast, and Daniel immediately stood to refill the wineglasses. I noticed how his hand shook as he poured my wine. The sound of broken glass brought our attention to John. The glass in his hand had shattered, leaving spilled wine, shards of crystal, and blood from his cut hand on the crisp white tablecloth.

Daniel placed the wine bottle on the table and hesitated a moment before approaching John. "Let me take you to my office, where I can make sure there is no glass left in your hand and wrap it properly."

John glanced up at his old friend with darkened eyes and, after a long pause, accepted Daniel's offer. With a bow and an apology, he excused himself, his gaze carefully avoiding mine.

I felt sick to my stomach and was grateful for Judge Patterson's assistance in helping me out of my chair and escorting me back to the parlor. Because of the small group and the absence of John and Daniel, the ladies and gentlemen convened in the same room. I assumed the three remaining men were waiting for the return of the other two before retiring to the library for port and cigars.

Mr. Brier sat next to me on a horsehair sofa. To my surprise, he reached for my hand and patted it solicitously. His skin was surprisingly soft and warm, and I found comfort in his gesture. Still, I felt hot and clammy, almost as if I were suffocating, the need to see John all-consuming. His anger at the table had been palpable and certainly understandable, and I needed to be with him to explain.

The old man leaned toward me, then surprised me by speaking. "Do not pay any mind to my Clara." He pointed to his wrinkled and age-spotted forehead. "Her own lack of children has become an obsession with her. Almost as much as her obsession with Daniel."

After speaking, he immediately sat back on the sofa, closed his eyes, and began to snore softly.

I was soon joined by Judge Patterson. I struggled to stand, but he urged me back. "You are pale and need to rest." He fixed a knowing gaze on me. "You let the men work on their own problems—it has nothing to do with you, you understand?"

Numbly, I nodded, not sure I did understand.

He moved closer, so that his words would be heard only by me. "So, it would seem that you and John are finding marriage to each other quite suitable."

I flushed and looked down at my hands.

"No need to be embarrassed, child. A good and fruitful marriage is something to be rejoiced over. I know his first marriage was difficult, and it was my greatest hope that you both would find happiness." He sat down next to me, peering at me with a gentle smile. "But I also understand that a new marriage in an unfamiliar place may have bumps in the road. If you ever have need of a friend, please remember that my old ears are still good for listening. You know where to find me."

I looked into his kind eyes and knew I was not alone.

"Thank you," was all I said.

He leaned toward me, speaking quietly. "The old man isn't as senile as some would like you to believe."

"What do you mean?"

Before he could answer, there was a loud pounding on the front door. The judge held out his hand, holding Clara back. "You stay here. I will go see who it is."

As soon as he had opened the door, the sound of a high-pitched, excited voice reached us. With panic tearing at my heart, I raced toward the foyer, recognizing the voice.

"Delphine! What is wrong?"

Her dark skin was streaked with sweat, her clothes damp and disheveled. Rufus hovered in the background, Jezebel flicking her tail behind him, sweat glistening on her flank. It appeared that they had run all the way from Whispering Oaks.

Delphine took several deep breaths before filling her lungs enough to be able to answer. "She be gone, Miz McMahon. Miss Rebecca—she be gone!"

CHAPTER TWENTY-ONE

Spots swam before my eyes, but I held on, convincing myself that I could not help Rebecca if I did not remain strong. I felt a familiar touch on my shoulder, and I melded into John's side, drawing strength from him.

John spoke, his words clipped, his anger and fear held in tight control. "What do you mean she is gone? Your instructions were to stay with her after she went to bed."

Delphine began sobbing, her words unintelligible. I went to her and brought her inside, asking for a drink of water. A glass was soon pressed into her shaking hands. As soon as she took a sip, I asked her, "What happened, Delphine? Tell us everything so that we might find her as quickly as possible."

She took another sip and nodded. "I did as I was told, Miz McMahon. She be in my sight the whole time. And I sat in that chair by her bed until she falls asleep."

I pressed on, the urge to bolt out the door and run to Whispering Oaks nearly overpowering my calm. "Then what happened?"

"I thought she was asleep, but as I stood to go, she asks for drink of water." She sniffed and brought the back of her hand across her nose. "So I went down the stairs and I passed Marguerite. She asks what I doin' and I tells her. Marguerite say I works hard enough and that she bring the water to Miss Rebecca."

She started sobbing harder, and I felt the claw of fear take hold of my heart with sharp talons.

Through sniffs, Delphine managed to continue. "Later, I starts to worry, since I's suppose to be in charge. So I went back to her room, and her bed be empty." Tears leaked out of her dark eyes as she stared up at me with fear and remorse. "I shouted for her, and I looks all over, but she not in the house."

"What about Marguerite? Where is she?" The panic clawed through my words.

Delphine sobbed louder. "Nowhere. She and Miss Rebecca just be gone!"

John's grip on my shoulder tightened. "Catherine, I want you and Delphine to stay here with Clara and the other women. Daniel and I will ride back to see what has happened and find Rebecca. I will send Mr. O'Rourke back with news."

I turned to my husband, my hands wildly clutching at him. "No, John. I must come with you. I cannot stay here and worry." Hearing the sob at the back of my throat, I lowered my voice. "Please let me help."

His eyes softened as he regarded me, then gave a sharp nod. Daniel brought our cloaks, and we raced out the door, not bothering with the formalities of saying goodbye.

We tore down the levee road, me clutching John's arm and staying away from the broken door, while Daniel and Rufus followed closely behind on their own mounts. John's hand reached for mine and I took it, looking into his eyes and feeling the unity of our spirits. *Yes,* I thought, *this is how it should be. Together, as one, through all the good and bad.* It went far deeper than trust, and I pulled our entwined hands to my heart so we could both feel its beating and know that it beat for us, for Rebecca, and for the tiny child growing within me.

When we pulled up in front of Whispering Oaks, I jumped out quickly without waiting for John's assistance. I noted the lack of servants to meet us and I wondered why until I smelled the smoke. The pungent smell of burning wood carried its way to us in the thin air, like thick fists grabbing us and pulling us around the side of the house.

Daniel saw it first and pointed. "Fire at the sugar mill!"

"Rebecca!" I shouted, ready to run as fast as my legs and full skirts would allow me.

Instead, John held tight to my arms. "Daniel and I will go see what we can do. I need you to sound the alarm so the field hands can come and help us with water. Then go search the house for Rebecca and send word when you find her."

His dark gaze bored into me and I nodded, understanding his meaning. He needed to be reassured that Rebecca was not in the burning building. Without warning, he grasped my head in his large hands and pulled me toward him, kissing me brutally.

He let go of me and began running toward the burning mill. I nearly stumbled as I turned and ran blindly back toward the house and to the edge of the field, where a large bell hung in its wooden casing. The evening wind whipped inside of it, causing it to moan into the clear night. I pulled on the suspended rope, making the bell chime in a low, monotonous clang, and waited until several men appeared from their quarters to investigate.

I sent one to ride to the neighboring plantations to ask for help, and the remainder to rouse as many people as they could and to go directly to the well with as many buckets as they could gather. Then I ran for the house, frantically searching for Rebecca. I almost sprawled over a large stump of an oak tree, the ax protruding from its middle, where Mr. O'Rourke had left it. Finding my footing again, I continued to run toward the front entrance to the house.

I flung open the door to complete stillness. With the exception of Marguerite and Delphine, I had seen all the house servants outside by the bell. I ran up the stairs two at a time, shouting out Rebecca's name. My lungs pressed against my stays, searching for air that they could not get. Forcing myself to slow down, I took slow, deep breaths as I walked purposefully toward Rebecca's room.

The sheets had been turned down and the pillow had the indentation of a small head, but Rebecca was conspicuously absent. My heart lurched when I spotted Samantha on the floor, facedown. I ran out of the room, my voice near hysteria as I shouted Rebecca's name again and again. She would never willingly go anywhere without her doll, and wherever she was would not be a place she wanted to be.

I ran through the house, opening every door and closet, looking under every bed and calling her name. I even climbed up to the attic, candle held aloft, searching, but found no trace of the child.

A sick dread settled in my stomach as I caught sight of the growing flames from the mill. What if Rebecca was in the mill? Feeling almost faint from my exertion, I sped out of the house toward the burning mill, now the scene of a growing number of men and women who had formed lines from the well, transporting buckets of water to overcome the flames. My eyes stung from the smoke as they searched the crowd for John's towering form, but he was nowhere to be found. I asked several of the men hauling buckets, but they hadn't seen him. People swarmed everywhere, the air heavy with smoke, making it difficult to see. My mind screamed. *Where are you, John? Where are you?*

Thinking that maybe he had found Rebecca and brought her back to the house, I turned back. As my feet fled over the dry grass, I felt a prickling sensation on the back of my neck that made me turn around toward the house. I thought I imagined a solid thumping on window glass and I stopped in my tracks, small spots of light gathering before my eyes as I struggled to maintain consciousness. A candle had been lit in my art room, and there, silhouetted against the window, was the sweet face of the child I had come to love as my own flesh and blood.

With a strangled shout, I ran back into the house and up the stairs to the little art room off my bedroom. I smelled candle smoke, as if a candle had just been extinguished, and no light shone under the crack in the door. I approached the room cautiously, wondering if I had just imagined Rebecca's face in the window.

I pushed at the door, watching it soundlessly glide open. "Rebecca?"

The room was completely black, the mixed odors of smoke and paints turning my stomach and making me feel faint. Pressing one hand against the doorframe to steady myself, I held my other hand to my nose and called Rebecca's name again.

A small sound came from the far corner of the room, and I approached slowly. "Rebecca, it is your mama. Everything is all right and I am here to take care of you. Can you come out now?"

A slight rasping came from the corner again, quickly followed by the sound of the door shutting behind me and the key turning in the lock.

I spun quickly, my skirts knocking over an easel and dumping the canvas to the floor with a crash. Feeling my way to the door, I grasped at the handle and tugged hard. It did not move.

"Rebecca? Is that you? Please let me out. Somebody please let me out."

In the inky silence, I heard the rasping sound again, a creeping noise in the far dark corner, and cold perspiration crawled up my skin. *Snake.* I could almost see the black, scaly skin of a cottonmouth as it slithered toward me in the darkness. I knew it would not attack me unless provoked, but I could not see it nor avoid stepping on it if it came nearer.

I turned back to the door, banging on it in earnest. "Help me. Please, somebody help me. Please let me out!" I thumped louder, feeling the reverberations up to my shoulders.

Again, the white spots appeared before my eyes, but I clung on to consciousness with every fiber of my being. I had not survived so much of life already to die now, now that so much mattered to me. I banged on the door again with renewed strength, knowing my life and the life of my unborn child depended on it.

I stopped for a moment to listen, but heard nothing except the muted shouts from the mill. Gingerly hugging the wall, I crept toward the window, hoping to find somebody in the yard below. I nearly sagged with relief as I spied Mr. O'Rourke, the ax from the stump in his hand, walking quickly back toward the fire. I fumbled with the window latch, scraping my fingers until they bled, but was unable to open it. Instead, I banged loudly on the glass, praying against all hope that I could break it or that he would hear me banging and look up. I imagined I felt something brush against the skirt of my dress, and I pounded even harder.

Mr. O'Rourke glanced up and I waved my hands, hoping he would spot the movement. I hit my fists against the glass again so he would realize where I was and watched, with thin hope nearly smothered with desperation, as he turned back toward the house, ax in hand.

Pressing myself against the wall, I strained my ears, imagining I heard movement from all four corners of the blackened room. The darkness fell all around me, encroaching upon my very mind, but I fought it with my last resources of energy. I placed my cheek against the cool plaster of the wall, concentrating on the reality of it and forcing myself to stay upright.

A pounding sounded from the other side of the door. "Mrs. Mc-Mahon, are you in there? Do you need me?"

"Mr. O'Rourke—yes! Somebody has locked me in here and I need to get out. There is a snake in here. Please hurry!"

"There's no key in the lock. Stand back, and I will use my ax."

I crouched by the window and listened as the ax shattered the door, splinters of wood flying into the room and hitting my bowed head.

When enough of the door had been destroyed, Mr. O'Rourke kicked the door in, the jamb fracturing in half. I stood, and a movement outside the window caused me to turn my head. Rebecca's back was toward me and she was walking in the direction of the pond, her long white nightgown glowing in the light of the full moon.

"Rebecca!" I screamed at the closed window. I stepped back and felt something smooth and rigid under my foot. A solid force hit the skirt of my gown and I looked down to see the shimmering scales of the cotton-mouth in the light of the open door, its fangs buried in the folds of my skirt. Mr. O'Rourke raised his ax and brought it down with a sickening *thud*, severing the serpent in half. In a daze, I watched as he grabbed the head of the snake and yanked it from my dress, ripping the silk.

I turned to Mr. O'Rourke. "Go get Mr. McMahon and bring him to the pond—now!" Without another word, I dashed out of the room, my fingers frantically ripping at my dress, then my stays, to loosen them so I could breathe. Or swim. All I knew was that I had to get to Rebecca before she reached the pond. I could not lose another child. The light that had begun to shine in my soul would surely be darkened forever.

I saw Rebecca hesitating by the edge of the pond and heard her sobs. As I neared her, I heard her voice cry out to me, and it sounded so much like Jamie that my steps faltered and I fell.

"Mama, Mama. Where are you, Mama?"

I scraped my fingernails in the dirt, trying to stand, my mind reeling. Was that Jamie's voice or was it Rebecca's?

I found my footing again and raced toward her, watching in horror as she stepped into the black water.

"Rebecca, stop! Mama's here. Stay there and I will come get you."

Slowly, she turned around and stared at me, her blond hair shimmering in the moonlight like a halo. "Mama?" Her eyes were dreamlike, as if she were walking in her sleep.

I pulled my gown over my head, throwing it on the grass, and stepped out of my underskirts. Reaching out my arms, I walked slowly to her, barely aware of the shouts and running feet approaching from behind.

As if in slow motion, I watched as she seemed to lose her balance, her arms swinging in wide arcs at her side before she fell backward, slowly sinking out of sight within the embrace of the dark, treacherous arms of the pond.

My skin seemed stuck to my bones, making me ponderous, lethargic, unable to move. I smelled salt water and heard a seagull's cry. The grass under my feet became warm sand, and waves rolled toward me, lapping at my now-bare toes. Jamie was just beyond my reach, his fingers stretching toward me before his head fell beneath the waves one last time. I cried out, his name sweet on my lips, my heart heavy with grief.

Then the fear that had remained so elusive in the last year struck me with the force of a human hand, taking the breath from my lungs and jolting my muscles into action. It was no longer the fear of water but the fear of loss. Without conscious thought, I dove into the pond where I had last seen Rebecca, the chill of the water sending pinpricks of misery to every pore of my skin.

I dove deep into the darkness, my hands reaching out to grab anything. But my fingertips brushed only the cold water, sending it in ripples down the length of my body. I swam to the bottom, feeling the thick, heavy mud, then kicked myself up toward the surface. I followed the light of the moon, its edges soft and uneven through the water but still a beacon for me.

I burst through the water, my lungs hurting. I glanced quickly around, ignoring Mr. O'Rourke and those he had gathered now approaching the bank, and looked for any sign of Rebecca. Only the small ripples caused by my movement marred the still surface of the dark water. With a deep breath, I plunged into the dark depths again.

I used the broadest stroke I could, stretching as far as possible, my fingers lonely hunters in the murky coldness. I reached the empty bottom again, pushing aside my despair that I had not yet found Rebecca. Turning on my back, I stared up to the surface, my loosened hair swimming snakelike around my face. I pushed it away and watched as a dark shadow passed above me.

With my toes finding purchase in the siltlike bottom, I crouched and pushed upward, my fingers reaching for the small flailing hands that seemed to move slower and slower. I skimmed through the water and touched her, then grabbed her around the waist with my other arm before I broke the surface.

Gasping for air, I struggled with Rebecca's limp form until I felt two strong arms grab hold of us and bring us the rest of the way to the bank, where my feet could touch the bottom. Daniel took the child from my arms, and I was at first reluctant to let her go.

John's strained voice shook. "Give her to Daniel, Cat. He needs to get the water out of her lungs."

With shaking hands I let go, then allowed myself to be lifted in my husband's arms.

We waited until we heard Rebecca's cry, and then she and I were both carried inside the house. I insisted that Rebecca be put in my bed with me. The threat of pneumonia was real, and I trusted no one to watch her as I could. We were dried and dressed in our nightclothes, then bundled into bed with a roaring fire heating the room.

I cringed when I looked at the shattered door to my art room, trying not to remember the cold sweat of fear. Looking up at John, I grabbed hold of his sleeve. "You have not asked about the door."

He leaned over to tuck Rebecca in, his sleeve brushing across my chest. "Mr. O'Rourke told me. I will have it replaced tomorrow."

I fell back, trying to read his inscrutable face. I pulled on his arm as he straightened. "It was no accident. I was led there on purpose and locked inside. Now do you believe me about Marguerite? Do you have any doubts about her intentions now? I know I cannot prove anything, but there is no doubt in my mind that she means us harm. Including Rebecca."

"Did you see her so that you know for sure? I know that Philip Herndon was here—my burning mill is proof of that. He is the one who swore to take what was most precious to me. If anybody had a motive to harm you, it would be him."

I pushed myself up, forcing my voice to remain calm. "But what about Rebecca? We know that Marguerite was with her last." I swallowed thickly. "Rebecca could have died tonight."

He flinched, then resumed his stolid expression. "Hush, now—you are overwrought. You both need your rest. I have asked Rose to make you a tea to help you sleep. She will bring it up when it is ready."

He stood, and I held on to his hand. To my surprise, I realized it was shaking. "John, please!"

Gently, he pulled his hand away. "Go to sleep. We will talk when you are feeling better."

He bent and kissed Rebecca's forehead and then mine before leaving. I turned to face my art room, as if to make sure nothing would slither out. An unbidden thought crossed my mind: the memory of how I searched in vain for John at the burning mill before returning to the house, lured by Rebecca's image in the window and where I had been locked in a room with certain death. *Where were you, John?*

I pushed the recollection aside, dismissing it as nerves brought on by the events of the evening. He could have been lost in the crush of people attempting to put out the fire, and it would have been easy to miss him.

I watched Rebecca fall asleep while I waited for Rose's tea. It was steaming hot and bitter, but I drank it down, wondering if I would ever feel warm again, and quickly joined Rebecca in oblivious sleep.

The sound of hushed, arguing voices awakened me. The fire had sputtered to a faint glow and a chill enveloped the room. The heated embers were the only source of light, giving me the impression that it was the middle of the night. Something heavy weighed upon my neck and I realized that my pearl necklace had not been removed when I had been dried and dressed in my nightclothes. My fingers patted it lightly, and I remembered the loose clasp, thankful it had not fallen into the water.

After checking Rebecca's slow, even breathing to make sure she was asleep, I slipped from bed and padded toward the door. Opening it a crack, I listened for voices, but heard nothing but the quiet ticking of the grandfather clock in the foyer. I was about to close the door again when I heard someone speaking. I recognized the deep voice as John's and I waited for a long moment to hear to whom he was talking.

It was a woman's voice, deep and resonant and highly distinguishable. *Marguerite.* I heard her laugh, a sound from deep in her throat, and it made my blood chill. I stepped into the hallway and closed the door, locking it with a soft *click* behind me. Slowly, I descended the stairs, gripping the banister to guide my way, following the voices.

A light shone from under the library door, thin like the light of a single candle, and I walked toward it and placed my hand on the knob. The sound of Marguerite's voice gave me pause.

"You know that if she finds out the truth, she will leave. She will go back to where she belongs. Or maybe that is what you have been wanting all along—for her to be gone. Yet you are afraid that she will take the child with her once she knows."

With my heart hammering wildly in my chest, my hand flew from the brass doorknob as if scorched.

I heard the control in John's voice. "You will not blackmail me with this any longer. I will not have it."

Marguerite laughed a bitter laugh. "You stand to lose a lot more than I ever could. When she finds out how you have been deceiving her, she and that child will be gone. Then you will be left with no child and no one to warm your bed at night." She chuckled again, low and evil, the sound fighting the rigid pulse in my neck. "Maybe that is what you deserve."

A glass crashed to the floor, and I jumped back.

"How dare you! Rebecca and Catherine could have been killed tonight because of your negligence, and no amount of threats from you will ever make me ignore that fact."

Marguerite's tone darkened. "I put Rebecca to bed. If the voices of the dead spoke to her, then that is the way of it. Those are powers that are stronger than mine, and I cannot stand in their way." She gave a low chuckle. "And somebody locked Catherine in that room tonight. Who is to say it was not you?"

"Stop it! I should have listened to Catherine and dismissed you long ago. You are a danger to my daughter, and I will no longer tolerate your presence here. You are dismissed, and I never want to see you in this house again." Two quick and heavy footfalls sounded in the library and I pictured him walking closer to Marguerite, his height towering over her, and she staring defiantly up at him. "Get out. Tonight. And if you ever breathe a word to Catherine, I will kill you. It will be so swift and so sudden that your last living thought will be to wonder how it happened." He lowered his voice further, making me strain to hear him. "I have killed before and I will do it again. I am not a man to be thwarted."

Steps approached the door, and I drew back into the alcove under the stairs, my eyes mesmerized by the mirror opposite. It seemed to create its own light, casting an ethereal glow that shimmered in the darkness. I clenched my eyes, not wanting to see whatever should materialize in its corrupted glass.

The door flew open and John hissed, "Get out."

Opening my eyes, I peered out of my hiding place.

Marguerite turned to John with equal fervor. "I will do that, but you can be sure that once your precious wife finds out that Rebecca is not your child, she will know why you married her. And she will try to leave, just like your Elizabeth. Maybe this wife will be more successful in escaping than her sister." She barked a mirthless laugh. "Maybe you should show her Elizabeth's letters before she leaves. If you do not think they will kill her. Or maybe that is what you want."

I heard John draw in a sudden breath. "You are lucky I am not throwing you in jail or worse. Now leave before I change my mind!"

Her voice was insolent as she turned to him in the threshold of the room. "You have far more to hide than I do."

She turned to leave, but he grabbed her elbow and pulled her back. "What do you mean?"

Facing him slowly, she turned to smile at him. "I saw Elizabeth before you got to her and took your glove and the gris-gris. Her traveling bag was with her, too, like she was planning on leaving you. The authorities would be interested in hearing all about it."

"There was nothing to incriminate me—only evidence that would have destroyed Rebecca's standing in the community."

"It was your glove, remember? And the gris-gris was one for an unfaithful lover. But you know that, do you not?"

"Get out," he said again through gritted teeth, letting go of her arm in a rough gesture.

Her skirts swung in a graceful arc as she turned back to the darkened foyer. I flattened myself against the wall, grasping at the necklace around my neck, their words reverberating in my head. *I need you, dear sister. I am so afraid.* Had I finally discovered what she had been so afraid of? Her husband, the man with a known temper and penchant for violence?

I hugged the wall, blending into the darkened alcove to avoid being seen by Marguerite as she walked by. I heard her words again, and fear curled up in my blood. *Rebecca is not your child.*

Why had John not told me? I already knew about the unborn child Elizabeth carried when she died, so the fact that Rebecca was not his, either, would have come as no surprise. I almost gasped aloud as the next thought occurred to me. *He had no claim to Rebecca, a child he loved as if she were his own flesh and blood. The only sure way to keep her with him would have been to marry the child's aunt.*

The hope that I had carried inside me, the hope that John had married me for other reasons, turned to ash as quickly as a thin leaf in a flame. John was a willful man. He would stop at nothing to get what he wanted. If I were threatening to leave and knew he had no claims to Rebecca, what would he do to stop me? The same thing that had been done to Elizabeth?

I clenched my eyes, pressing my forehead against the wall. Marguerite had gone, but I had not heard John move from the doorway of the library. After a few breathless moments, I heard his slow footsteps walk back into the room and the squeak of his desk chair as he sat.

Taking a step out of the alcove, a loud clattering sound came from the wood floor, as if something had dropped. Not wanting to waste any time to see if John had heard it, too, I fled up the stairs, then hid in the dark corridor above and waited.

John walked out into the middle of the foyer and stopped. "Marguerite? Is that you?" In the stillness of the night, I heard the precise snap of a pistol's hammer and held my breath.

After several long moments, he retreated back into his library and shut the door, the sound of the lock sliding into place loud and deliberate.

Slowly, I stood on shaking legs and made my way back to my room. After turning the key in the lock, I stirred the fire, the heat unable to penetrate the bone-chilling numbness that seemed to have seeped into my soul.

I had no hope of sleep, but the warmth of the bed beckoned me, so I slipped into the cold sheets and snuggled next to Rebecca. *What kind of a man is your father?* I wanted to ask. *He possesses unknown depths of love and kindness in the same soul that harbors so much darkness. And I am afraid. So afraid.*

Too numb to weep, I lay beside Rebecca, absorbing her warmth and keeping my eyes transfixed on the ceiling as I waited for dawn.

CHAPTER TWENTY-TWO

———◆———

As soon as the light of day touched the windows, I crept from the bed, making sure I did not awaken Rebecca, and unlocked the door. I paused by her side and felt her forehead. It was warm but not overly so, and her breathing was slow and even. Assured, I stepped back and began to dress. I had been busy making plans all through the long, wakeful night, and I had much to do.

While I sat at the dressing table, twisting my hair on top of my head, the door opened and John entered. He was still in the evening clothes he had worn the night before, his hair rumpled. Dark stubble covered his jaw, making him look as dangerous as a knife blade. My traitorous heart leapt at the sight of him, and the familiar burn inside of me ached. I turned away, focusing on my reflection in the mirror.

He went to the bed and sat down next to Rebecca, watching her as she slept. Then, as I had done, he pressed the back of his hand to her forehead and left it for a long moment. "She is very warm."

I nodded, searching for my voice. "Yes, I noticed that, too. But I think it is just from sleep. We will see how she is when she wakes."

His dark eyes rested on me for a moment before he went to the fireplace and restarted the fire with more logs. Then he came to me and stood next to my chair, not saying anything.

Unnerved by his proximity, I glanced at him. Without a word, he fell to his knees in front of me, placing his large hand on my abdomen where our child grew inside.

"The child—he is well?"

A large lump lodged itself in my throat. I remembered his anger of the night before when he had learned of the child's existence and noticed the absence of the words "our child." Still, his gentleness disarmed me, and I was left floundering for a foothold. "Yes. Our child is fine. He is well protected."

He leaned forward and kissed me where his hand had been a moment before, his hot breath moving through the fabric of my gown to my bare flesh. I suppressed a moan and the need to run my hands through his black hair, and instead pushed myself back into my chair.

He lifted his head and his eyes searched mine. "You risked so much last night." His fingers lightly traced my jawbone, his touch heating my blood, until they came to rest on my collarbone. "I remember what you told me of Jamie's death, and I believe I can understand what strength it took from you to save Rebecca."

Tears pricked at my eyes as I realized the enormity of the previous night's occurrences. There was so much unsaid between us, but my uncertainty hovered near. "I love her." There was nothing more I could say.

"So do I," he said, his voice full of meaning. His hand dropped and the light shining in his eyes dimmed. Softly, he said, "How lucky Rebecca is to be loved so completely and selflessly that you would risk everything for her."

I longed to fall into his arms and tell him that the love I felt for him was the same, but I could not. The words I had overheard between him and Marguerite had built a strong wall around my heart, a wall not easily breached.

I turned back to my dressing table and lifted the brush. One by one I picked out the long, dark strands from the bristles, letting them fall soundlessly to the floor. "She is but a child and has been denied the true love of a mother for too long. I am glad that we have found each other."

He rose swiftly, his movements stiff, and I knew that my words of omission had hurt him. He, too, seemed to have expected me to say something else. "You have told me many times that you wish for a loving marriage built on truth and trust. Yet I feel there is something heavy hanging between us—something unsaid. Is there something you wish to say to me?"

I thought of my questions and accusations, certain he would have answers for me. But not the truth. The lingering suspicion that I could not bear the truth clouded my mind, and I wanted to answer him from my heart. *I want to leave you now—now before I learn that which I cannot bear.* I shook my head. "I am content," I lied, wishing that he would leave so I would not have to see my own betrayal in his eyes.

His expression hardened before he looked away. With another glance at Rebecca, he turned to leave. "Let me know when she wakes."

I nodded and watched him as he left the room. I turned back to the mirror and stared at my reflection, realizing something was not right. My hand flew to my throat and I realized the pearl necklace was missing.

I jumped up and ran to the bed, pulling back the bedclothes to see if it had fallen off while I slept. Then a sickening realization flooded my veins. I remembered the clattering sound of something hitting the wood floor as I stood hidden in the alcove under the stairs. Uselessly, my fingers swept across the soft skin of my neck, searching for the pearls that now lay abandoned on the wood floor of the foyer.

Quickly finishing my toilette, I sped down the stairs, thankful nobody was there to witness my desperate search. I followed the curve of the banister to the alcove, my heart firmly lodged in my throat. The honey-gold color of the wood shone brilliantly under a new layer of wax. I swished my foot across the expanse of wood, hoping to kick something that I could not see, but all I felt under the soles of my shoes was the smooth surface of the floor.

I lifted my head rapidly at the sound of approaching footsteps, making spots dance before my eyes. John stood before me with a questioning look in his eyes.

"Are you looking for something?"

Too ashamed to admit my guilt, I shook my head. "No, I am just light-headed. I think I need to eat breakfast."

"I will call for Mary to sit with Rebecca while you eat." He solicitously offered me his arm and I reluctantly took it, understanding the power of his touch and its effect on me. "You need to keep up your strength."

I allowed myself to be escorted into the dining room. John sent for Mary to go upstairs and then poured himself a cup of coffee. He filled a plate with food and put it in front of me before sitting down across the table. I felt my skin flame at the intensity of his gaze.

Forcing myself to remain calm, I returned his appraisal and searched for conversation. The events of the previous night meant I didn't have to search far. "How is the mill?"

"Severely damaged. It is a good thing the harvesting is done, or a lot of farmers would be losing their land over this. It will take a good six months to put it in working order again." I knew that John leased out the use of his mill to local farmers, saving them the trouble and expense of transporting their sugarcane to mills far away. He had acknowledged that he did it cheaply, but that it was necessary to maintain the local economy.

"Do you know how it started?"

He put his coffee cup into the saucer a little too forcefully, making some of the coffee splash up over the sides. "It was undoubtedly arson, since it bears the marks of the White League. I have no doubt that Philip Herndon is behind this."

I put my fork down and faced him. "How can you be sure?"

A dark brow rose over an eye. "We have an eyewitness. Rufus said he spied Philip several days ago lurking around the mill, and warned him off. Unfortunately, Rufus did not think enough of the incident to tell me about it." He took a deep breath. "I assume Philip had also been by the coach house to tamper with the latch. I do not think it mattered to him whom he harmed, as long as I or somebody close to me got hurt."

I remembered Philip's threats and felt certain that John's suspicions were not unfounded. "Have they found Philip yet for questioning?"

John shook his head. "No. The sheriff stopped by while you were upstairs. He has sent some men to look for him, but so far they have not found a trace of him." He picked up his cup and seemed to take a deliberately long sip from it. "The sheriff seems to think Philip had help in escaping. He has disappeared so completely that it would have been impossible to do so on his own, especially with his lack of funds."

I placed my hands flat on the surface of the hard mahogany table. "What are you suggesting?"

He stood and kissed me lightly on the temple. "Not a thing, dear wife. Unless there is something you think might shed light on the situation."

Having lost my appetite completely, I slid back from the table. "I have nothing to hide—especially not the truth. I have not spoken with

Philip since that horrible scene in New Orleans. Believe what you will, but that is the truth."

A dark flush stained his handsome features. "Nothing to hide, Cat? I have noticed that you have not asked about Marguerite, nor made note of her absence."

Doubt and fear flashed through my mind. I stood, facing him with my chin lifted. "Where is she?"

Leaning close to me, he reached for my hand, sending unbidden shivers of anticipation up my arm. Lifting it, he held it between us and opened up my palm. Wordlessly, he reached into his pocket and dumped the pearl necklace in my hand.

My fingers closed over the cool beads and I noticed my hand shook. Slowly, I raised my eyes to his. "Is that why you married me, then? To keep Rebecca with you? Surely you know that the law would be on your side. Simply being married to her mother would have made you the child's legal father."

He opened his mouth to say something, then seemed to change his mind. He turned away, his back to me, before speaking. "I am a foreigner here—a damned Yankee, regardless of my years here or my commitment to the parish. With your friends' and neighbors' help, I am sure they would have spirited you and Rebecca away to her rightful family without regard to my legal status. Despite their destitute state, they would have found the means to keep both of you hidden from me indefinitely."

The small glimmer of hope that I had sheltered inside of me fragmented like a broken mirror, and I was afraid all the pieces could never be put back where the scars would not be seen or felt. With a drowning sensation in my chest, I realized it was for the best. In the long hours of the night, I had made the decision to leave him and his dark secrets. He did not trust me, much less love me, and I loved him far more than good reason dictated.

"And now I am your wife . . ." I did not have the courage to finish the sentence.

"And we both love Rebecca. She could find worse parents to raise her."

With a mocking bow, he moved toward the doorway.

My words called him back. "If you are not Rebecca's father, then who is?"

He paused and I heard a deep intake of breath. Looking at me over his shoulder, he said, "I do not know. But rest assured, regardless of what man gave her mother his seed, I will never cease to be her father. And I pity whoever would try to separate us."

I listened as his footsteps crossed the foyer to the library, my hollow heart aching. My hand fell to my abdomen. He must have believed for a time that Rebecca was his. But of Elizabeth's second child, he had had no such assumption. Would her second proof of infidelity have angered him enough to be rid of her forever? And what of his doubts of me and my child?

I tried to shut out the insidious thoughts, but they spread through my mind like poison from an oleander petal. It took only a small dose to claim its victim, and I was afraid that I had already succumbed.

A door opened upstairs, quickly followed by the sound of running feet on the steps. I rushed out into the foyer and nearly ran into Mary.

"Missus MacMahon, Miss Rebecca's awake. She is asking for her papa."

I looked at the young girl, worry gnawing at me. Her skin was flushed, her freckles standing out in stark relief. "What is wrong, Mary?"

She wrung her hands. "Rebecca is burning up, she is. Burning with the fever."

I took the stairs two at a time, with John, who had emerged from his study, close behind me. When I approached Rebecca's bed, she twitched and moaned, her face pale and wan. Her bright blue eyes stared at me but did not seem to see me. I touched her cheek and her skin nearly burned my hand.

John turned to Mary, who had followed us up the stairs. "Go get Mr. O'Rourke and send him to find Dr. Lewiston and bring him here. Now."

Mary bobbed her head several times, still wringing her hands, then ran from the room, her feet clattering down the steps.

Rebecca clutched at my dress. "Mama, Mama. So hot." Her voice rasped, her lips cracked and dry.

I sat at the edge of the bed and brushed her hair off her forehead. "I know, baby. I am going to try to cool you off."

Quietly, John said, "I will go to Rose and have her bring fresh water and bathing cloths."

I looked at him for the first time and saw the tight restraint and despair in his eyes. I wanted to take his hand and offer comfort, but I could not. I simply nodded and turned back to Rebecca while I listened as his footsteps faded away down the hall.

Rebecca lingered in a feverish delirium for almost four days. We moved her back to her own room, and I began a vigil by her bedside. She could not hold down food, and I spent hours simply squeezing drops of water between her dry and cracked lips from a clean washcloth.

Daniel came frequently, as much to comfort John and me as to tend to Rebecca. He listened to her chest and gave us the promising news that it was not pneumonia. He ruled out many childhood diseases, but could not determine what was afflicting Rebecca. Her fever remained unabated, regardless of our treatment, and I lived through those nights and days with fear as my constant shadow. I sat transfixed at her bedside, afraid to leave her if only for a moment. Jamie had drowned when I had looked away, and the guilt and grief still weighed heavily on my heart. Perhaps I could earn forgiveness if I protected Rebecca in a way that had been denied my beloved son.

On the second night of her illness, while I was bathing Rebecca's forehead yet again with a cool cloth, John silently opened the door. I sensed him before I saw him, my emotions an odd mixture of joy and wariness.

I looked up and saw dark circles under his eyes and a beard growing on his strong jaw. If there had been any doubts before at all that he loved this child as his own flesh and blood, they would have fled completely now.

He took the cloth from my hand and led me away from the bed. He grasped my hands in his and I felt how chilled they were—as if his life's blood were flowing out to the child who needed it more than he.

"I want you to go your room and seek rest. And then I want you to pray. That is the only thing I will allow you to do."

I wrenched my hands away. "No, John. Do not deny me this!"

His hands spanned my waist, his palms pressing against my abdomen. "And what of the baby? You are compromising not only your own health but that of the unborn child." His dark eyes bored into mine. "I will take your place and not leave her side. I promise you that. Can you trust me enough to tend her with all the love and care that you would?"

I looked back at the frail and flushed face of the child I had grown to love so much and then looked back at my husband. I knew he was right, yet I agonized over the decision. How could anyone care for Rebecca as well as I could? I stared into John's eyes and knew the truth.

Slowly, I nodded. "You will send for me if you need anything? Or if she calls for me?"

Relief flooded his handsome features. "Yes. Of course. Now go get your rest. You will need all of your strength."

Reluctantly, I stepped back, the warmth of his hands deserting me, and knew that Rebecca would be well tended. I wanted to reach for him, to hold him and read in his eyes that he felt the same, yet we both stood facing each other, each one holding back our own truth and secrets.

I turned away and bent to kiss Rebecca on the forehead, then left the room without a word.

John stayed in her room, nursing his daughter day and night as he had promised. I was allowed in to hold her hand and give her water and to help change her bedclothes, but John always sent me back to my room to rest. I knew he was right, but I longed to be at his side, watching over our daughter.

On the second day of his vigil I brought his shaving materials and a clean change of clothes. He opened the door at my knock, and I barely recognized the disheveled man as my husband.

"How is she?" I asked.

"The same." He opened the door wider to let me in, eyeing the bundle in my hands. "Thank you."

I forced a smile on my face that I did not feel. "You will be needing these right now, I think. What if she awakens and sees you as you are? She will think you a monster and start screaming." His stomach grumbled, and I added, "A food tray will be brought up shortly."

White teeth showed as he grinned, disarming my resolve completely, and I realized it had been too long since I had seen him smile.

He reached for the stack in my hands and his fingers touched mine.

I let go quickly, almost dropping everything, and he caught it with a quick grab. His eyes sobered. "She will be fine, Cat. I will it to be so."

My voice was harsher than I intended, my exhaustion and worry no doubt sharpening my tongue. "And no one would dare thwart your wants and desires—not even God."

He said nothing. I reached into my pocket, feeling the cool smoothness of the lodestone. I held it up to him and he took it. "Put this by Rebecca. It is to chase away evil and bring her goodness. She needs it more than I."

Without waiting for a response, I kissed Rebecca's hot cheek and left. I would return to prayer, for that was the only thing I could do for her. Rose was in her kitchen, casting spells and offering up sacrifices. I no longer thought of it as pagan, for it seemed to take its root in this dark, humid place, seeming more at home than Christianity. As long as Rebecca recovered, it did not matter to me what means guided her there.

And when she was well, I would take her away. I would bring her home to the bright light that dispersed the darkness away from weary hearts and where the rhythm of the ocean waves lulled one to sleep and kept the nightmares at bay. And where a child could grow in a place without shadows lurking in every corner and where dark secrets did not obscure the purity of love.

I did not know when I had come to the decision to take Rebecca with me, but even with a heavy heart I knew that I had made the right choice. The walls of this place emanated deceit and danger, and I knew she would be in peril if she should remain. Leaving would save both our lives; of that I had no doubt. John would grieve her loss, for his love for her was greater than I had ever seen from a father toward his natural child. But that broken bond, I could not consider. The remembered pain of losing a child weighed heavily on my heart if I did, and I would not carry John's grief for him. For if I did, my scarred heart would surely break open, spilling out my resolve to leave along with the only chance of saving our lives and our very souls.

Rebecca's fever broke on the fifth day. I waited in the hall as Daniel examined her and then reappeared, a shadow of a smile on his face.

"I think she is well on the road to complete health. There seems to be no damage to her sight or hearing, and I expect her to have a full recovery."

Relief flooded my bones, making me shake. I wanted to throw my arms around him but restrained myself. "Thank you, Daniel, for caring for her."

He put a calming hand on my arm. "I need you to take care of yourself, too. If you show the first sign of fever, you are to call me immediately. I do not think you realize the danger to your unborn child."

Unbidden, my hands went to my bodice. "I will," I promised. I walked the doctor down the stairs, my heart lighter for the first time in more than a week.

Daniel paused for a moment at the door, a perplexed expression darkening his brow. "I thought you might want to know that Marguerite is at Belle Meade now. We cannot afford to pay her, yet Clara insists that she stay, and Marguerite seems satisfied with a room and food. I hope that does not dismay you too much. John has told me of some of the doubts you harbored regarding Marguerite."

I closed my eyes, shaking my head. "As long as she is out of my house, her whereabouts do not concern me, but thank you for telling me. I know she practically raised Clara, so I cannot fault either one of them for their closeness."

I opened the door and he stepped out onto the porch. The late-afternoon sun glinted off his hair and I paused in midsentence, staring at it. It was so much like Robert's—all the gentle shadings of gold and yellow. So much like Rebecca's. I grabbed his arm and he turned, his gaze focused on my tight grip.

"What is wrong, Catherine?"

"You, Daniel. You . . ."

I could not seem to form the words. I thought back on Rebecca's secret place behind the burned plantation house, and how she had disappeared to a secluded place so Daniel and I could be alone. As if she had done it many times before.

He turned to face me, his expression one of worry. "What is wrong? Do you need to sit down?"

I shook my head. "No. No, I do not." I could not tell him. I did not want to acknowledge it. Because then I would have to tell John. Regardless of what I believed John capable of, my heart could not stand the knowledge that he would lose not only his wife and child, but his best friend as well.

His eyes remained guarded. "Are you quite sure?"

"Yes. Really, I am fine. I am just tired, I think."

He kissed my hand, his gray eyes warm. "You are so strong, Catherine. John and Rebecca are very lucky to have you." A deep and abiding sadness seem to cross his face for a brief moment, quickly replaced by his smile. "Take care of yourself, remember. It will take a long time for Rebecca to completely recover and regain her strength. You will have need of your own strength to see her through."

I thanked him, grateful for Rebecca's recovery but concerned over the delay in my departure. "How long do you think it will be before she is well again?"

He brightened. "By Christmas, I expect. She loves the bonfires along the levee, and she should be well enough by then to join in the festivities."

By Christmas, then. I had plenty of time to finalize my plans. Daniel said his goodbyes, and I watched him get into his carriage, his hat not completely hiding his hair, the sun glinting off those beautiful yellow-gold strands.

CHAPTER TWENTY-THREE

With Rebecca out of danger, the darkness that had seemed to be hovering over me lifted, although my troubles did not go away. John had been sleeping on a small pallet in her room, but now she no longer needed him there. I could not allow John to return to my bed. His touch had a way of lowering my defenses, of creating breaches in my wall of reason. I wondered how long it would take John to demand my presence in his bed again.

On a chilly November evening, John and I sat facing each other at the dining-room table. I forced myself to eat for the sake of the baby, whose presence was now made known by a small mound under my loosened corset. John also seemed to have other thoughts on his mind. From the corner of my eye, I saw him eat little but refill his wineglass three times. When I forced myself to look at him directly, I found his black eyes scrutinizing me as a hunter watches his prey.

I excused myself before dessert, with plans to change for bed and be fast asleep before John came up. He had begun the habit of retiring to his study for a cigar and brandy, thus giving me ample time.

As I ascended the stairs, I felt a presence behind me and turned. John had followed me and was walking up the steps in my wake. I headed down the hall toward our bedroom, hoping he would go to Rebecca's room. Instead he followed me, even opening the door of the bedroom for me.

I moved to ring for Mary, but John stayed my hand. "I will help you with your dress."

Knowing I had no choice, I bent my head forward and allowed his hands to unfasten the buttons and slide the gown over my shoulders. Long fingers slid down my chemise, sliding forward to cup my breasts, now heavy and swollen from my impending motherhood. One hand slid down farther, touching the mound of my stomach as he moved me against him.

I wanted to turn in his arms, to forget all that had happened between us and all my doubts and suspicions, but I could not. I owed it to the child that grew inside me, as well as to Rebecca, to make sure they were safe forever.

I stepped away, pulling up my fallen bodice to cover myself. "Stop. Please."

He looked genuinely surprised. "Why, Cat? I know you miss me as much as I miss you."

"It is . . . the baby. I do not think we should."

Stepping forward, he lifted my chin and stared into my eyes for a long moment, his own eyes dark and secretive. "Is that really the reason?"

I closed my eyes and turned away from him. "Of course it is. I do not want anything to happen to this baby."

He was silent, and I moved to my dresser to remove a nightgown, keeping my hands busy so I would not have to listen to my heart.

He moved so silently that I was not aware of it until I felt his hot breath on the back of my neck. I closed my eyes, recalling the passion we had shared for such a short time, and a longing to recapture it pulled at my resolve. He held my heart, for I had seen the goodness that resided inside him. But there was darkness, too, one I fleetingly wished I could cut out like a surgeon's knife on a cancer. I had tried and failed, and now I knew I had to escape the darkness that threatened to suffocate me like a heavy cloak.

For the long years of the war and the time afterward, I had lived in such a shadow that I would rather die than return to it. Rebecca and the child growing inside me were my light, guiding me through the blackness that encroached, moving me toward the brightness that beckoned at the end of my journey home.

"You cannot deny me, Catherine. It is not the child—there is something else." His soft voice caressed my skin, the temptation pulling at me like fingers in honey. "Tell me."

I straightened, making him step away. "It is the child, John. It is not safe for me to share your bed until he is born."

His hands were rough as he forced me to turn and look at him. "I know that is not true." He lowered his face close to mine and I could feel his all-consuming heat. "Marguerite is gone. What is it that you fear?"

I need you, dear sister. I am so afraid. The images of Elizabeth's letter, John's glove, and the empty letterbox jumbled in my mind, and I nearly suffocated with the urge to shout out all my suspicions. But I held back, knowing if I did, I would jeopardize all. In the deepest part of my heart, I knew that he would not give me answers. And his reticence would be for reasons that my soul could not bear to contemplate.

I stared into his eyes as they flashed with anger. He dropped his arms but did not step back. "What about this trust between us that you hold so dear? Practice what you preach, Catherine, and tell me why you suddenly have no desire to share my bed." His lips narrowed as his eyes became guarded, blocking out all emotion. "Have you found someone else who stirs your passions more than I?" His gaze slid down to my stomach, coming to rest on the small mound.

I sucked in my breath, shocked to hear him so blatantly voice his suspicion. I drew back my hand to slap him, but he grabbed my wrist. I knew I was being a hypocrite; at least he had the courage to speak of his doubts. But I knew my own truth, whereas his truth was muddied and twisted like the grass in the fields after a hard rain.

He let go and turned away, and my arm fell to my side, useless. He glanced back at me from the doorway. "I do not want you to leave Whispering Oaks without me or Mr. O'Rourke. And if you should leave with Mr. O'Rourke, I want to know about it beforehand."

I took a step toward him. "You want to make a prisoner out of me! I am not a slave or your kept woman with no mind of her own. You cannot do this."

He opened the door. "As your husband, I can. It is for your own protection. Philip Herndon has not been found, and I know he has sworn to harm me and those I love." His gaze flickered to the swell of my abdomen once more. "And I will not suffer the embarrassment of having you seek him out."

The implication was clear. My anger, softened by his mention of love, rekindled itself. "Is this why Elizabeth was trying to get away from you? Because you accused her of vile things and then tried to keep her locked in this prison? I am not Elizabeth, though I do not think you will ever understand that. But maybe, finally, I think I can understand why my sister behaved the way she did."

His face paled. Inexplicably, I felt sick with the knowledge that I had hurt him badly. I wanted to go to him, to tell him I was sorry, but my pride, anger, and suspicion held me back.

Slowly, he opened the door. "From the first day of my marriage to Elizabeth, I thought that I had married the wrong sister. And now I see it really did not matter."

Words strangled my throat and my eyes blurred as I watched him walk through the doorway and close the door behind him. The last image of him was of his eyes—eyes of a wildcat who had been hunted into a corner, but whose intention was to fight to the death those who threatened him.

I did not see John for two weeks. I learned from Mr. O'Rourke that he had gone to Baton Rouge on business. I slept in our bed, safe in the knowledge that John was far away, and had the pallet removed from Rebecca's room. She was out of danger from the fever but still very weak. *But for this,* I told myself, *I would take advantage of the opportunity of John's absence and flee.*

As it was, I did not leave the plantation. The threat of Philip Herndon lingered, although to a lesser degree, since he seemed to have vanished. I knew John had hired guards to keep watch over the plantation night and day, and it offered a measure of security. Mr. O'Rourke found excuses to work close to the house, and I wondered if it were for my protection or to keep John informed of my whereabouts in his absence.

Even with John gone, I did not sleep easily. Several times I would lie in bed and imagine I heard footsteps in the hallway. When I rose to investigate, I would find nothing. Twice I thought that I detected the faint smell of lavender, reminding me of Elizabeth. I would stare out into the hallway, cloaked in night, for long moments, as if waiting for my dead sister to appear. Always disappointed, I would close my door and turn the key before returning to bed for another restless night.

Two weeks after John's departure, I awoke with a start out of a dark dream in the deepest part of night. The sound that had brought me awake had been the distinct noise of a door latch snapping into place. I blinked my eyes, trying to identify the dark shapes of the furniture.

Rain pelted at the glass like unseen fingers tapping to gain my attention. I left the bed and moved to a window, pulling aside the curtains and staring out into the rain-clogged fields. As a child I had always loved the heavy rain from the ocean-born tempests. My father had made a habit of pacing the front porch of our house during storms, as if to guard the house from lightning and wind, and at a very early age I had joined him.

Our waterlogged conversations had created a bond between us, a bond that even Elizabeth could not traverse and which was not broken until his death. I pressed my forehead against the cool glass, missing him as suddenly as if he had just died, and feeling more alone and adrift than I had in my entire life.

A movement by the pond caught my attention and I squinted, trying to see through the blur of raindrops. A light, as if from a bobbing lantern, glittered through the rain for a brief moment and then extinguished. I stared out the window for a long time, not knowing if it had been my imagination. I thought I saw a brief flicker moving toward the pond before that, too, disappeared. My eyes strained to see into the eternal darkness of the night, but saw only the blackness pressing in on me.

My nape prickled, and I realized that the blackness came from within the house as well, as if it were a dark soul whose menacing presence infested the very air I breathed. I slowly backed away from the window, convincing myself it had been my imagination and pressing away more morbid thoughts. *Will I, too, soon be hearing voices of the dead calling me to come to them?*

I took a lit lamp and walked quickly out of the room and down the hall to Rebecca's. I pushed open the door and held the lantern high, my heart tumbling with relief when I spied her small body tucked under the covers, Samantha pressed against her cheek.

I left the room and noticed for the first time the strong odor of something burning fill my nostrils. Moving toward the stairs, I sniffed deeply. Too strong to be the lingering odors from the burnt mill, and definitely not the scent of burning wood. I would remember that smell until the day I died, as I had good reason to never forget it.

Gingerly descending the stairs, I followed the scent to the library. John's pipe sat in an ashtray and I lifted it, feeling the warmth of the bowl. The fire in the grate still burned strong, as if recently tended, and I moved near, seeking warmth.

Putting down the lamp on the desk, I stood in front of the fireplace, my hands outstretched. My fingers straightened and clenched, then stilled as if of their own accord as my gaze rested on the pile of ash under the grate.

I knelt and reached in a hand, pulling out the corner of one of several burnt envelopes, its edge raw and sooty. A black slash of ink from a pen formed part of a word, the remainder obliterated forever by fire. The stroke of penmanship seemed oddly familiar to me, but there was not enough of it to identify. It gnawed at the back of my mind as I gazed at the heap of ashes, the heat from the fire burning my face.

Grabbing a poker, I scraped out what remnants of letters I could find, realizing with disappointment that no piece was large enough to be of any use.

I stood, the inevitable questions filling my mind. *Are these Elizabeth's letters?* I reached my hand in again, desperate for some word from my lost sister, but my hand got too close to the flame and I burned my finger and rapidly withdrew.

Stepping away and sucking on my singed finger, I stared into the fire, my mind in deep thought. Grabbing the lamp, I made my way cautiously up the stairs to Rebecca's room. Even without the light from the lamp, my body screamed in awareness of John's presence, betraying my resolve that I stay immune to him.

"Good evening, wife."

His voice held a note of flippancy, but I sensed a deeper, darker emotion—more akin to grief and loss.

"John," I stammered, his presence filling the room and shaking my senses. "I did not know when to expect you back." A brutal gust of wind knocked at the house, jarring me further.

He did not respond but leaned forward in the chair, his elbows

594 · *Karen White*

resting on his knees. Finally, he spoke, but his gaze rested on the sleeping child.

His voice sounded tired and very far away. "When I first saw Rebecca, she was well past the newborn stage and already had a look of you about her." He rubbed his hands over his face, the sound of skin against beard stubble rustling loudly enough to be heard over the tapping of rain.

"And as she grew, she became more and more as I remembered you—the girl you had been when I first saw you. Not so much in the way she looked, but her free spirit and her sweetness and joy for life. She reminded me so much of the girl dancing barefoot on the beach in Saint Simons, her hair loose in the wind. I wanted to spoil Rebecca by giving her all the love and attention that I would never be able to give you."

I fought the urge to go to him, to lay my head on his knee. To touch him. His words moved me, showing me the man I knew lived deep inside his forbidding form. But the darkness lurked within him, too, and I pulled away.

John continued, his voice just loud enough to be heard over the splattering rain. "And then as Elizabeth and I grew farther apart, Rebecca became even more important to me. She was mine to love unconditionally, and she freely shared her love with me. It was the first time I had ever experienced anything like it. Even my own mother had not seemed capable of it. All her love seemed to begin and end with my older brother, with not even scraps left for me. Which is why I left my home as soon as I could and have never been back. Not even for my mother's funeral." He lifted his eyes to mine, and they shimmered in the lamplight with potent meaning. "I do not take rejection easily."

My heart reverberated in my chest, crying out for this man at the same time my mind reeled with warning. I went to him and knelt before the chair. Tentatively, I reached for his hands and he grabbed them, pressing tightly.

His voice was gruff. "It is not good between us now, is it? And I do not know how to make it different. I thought that two weeks away from you would make my need for you lessen somehow, but it only made it stronger. I have been searching for some trace of Philip Herndon, hoping my mind would be occupied by something other than you." He paused for a moment, the tapping of the rain marking the passing time. "I almost hoped that you would be gone when I returned. Your rejection of me cuts deeper than a knife, wounding my soul. But now that I am back and I see you here, I know that I could never let you go. Never."

The pressure on my hands increased and I winced, but he seemed not to notice. I stared at him in the darkened room, listening to the rain beat against the house, almost smelling the salt air and the damp cotton of my beloved home and knowing that to return, I would lose part of my soul. Or worse.

I yearned to give him another chance, an opportunity to restore his soul—and mine. I leaned toward him, hearing the urgency in my own voice. "Tell me, then, John. The burned letters in the grate. Were they Elizabeth's?"

I felt more than heard his quick intake of air, but he made no move to answer.

"Tell me now, John. I am stronger that you think. There is nothing in her letters that can harm me now."

He let go of my hand and touched my cheek. "You do not know what you ask."

I leaned into his touch, feeling his heat. "Yes, I do. I ask that there be trust and truth between us. For without it, we have nothing."

Dropping his hand, he leaned back in the chair, his dark gaze resting on me. He said no more, and my heart and mind receded from him, resigned as to my course of action. His eyes widened as if he could read my thoughts, and I turned away. Slowly, I stood and walked toward the door.

"I am sleeping in the master bedroom and I keep it locked at night."

"I know."

The bluntness of his response startled me.

I looked at Rebecca, still peacefully asleep, then back at John. "Good night."

He did not respond, but I felt his brooding gaze on my back as I lifted the lamp and left the room.

As I took several steps, my foot slipped and I realized that the floor was scattered with small wet spots that resembled footsteps. Curious, I held the lantern high, following the spots for several feet until they dead-ended into a wall. Intrigued, I turned and followed them back in the other direction, realizing with a heavy heart that they led to my bedroom. *Were John's hair and clothes wet from the rain?* I could not recall, the emotions and words having obliterated all other senses. I stared at the small puddles traversing the hallway to my bedroom.

I turned the handle and pushed it wide. I held the lantern high, looking behind me to see if John followed. Reassured that he had not, I entered the bedroom. The wet footsteps stopped at the side of my bed and it did not take me long to realize why.

In the middle of the pulled-back coverlet lay a large black ball of wax. I knew without looking closer that it was a conjure ball. Some were said to contain human flesh, and my own skin rippled at the thought. Smooth pins stuck through the black wax made an even arc over the ball, and stripes of something wet and dark like blood or paint slashed across the side.

My knees trembled as I stared at the ball and I inadvertently cried out. I knew they were meant to bring death or misfortune to a household, and the fact that it lay in the middle of my bed gave me no doubt as to whom the harm was meant to befall.

I backed out of the room, mentally prepared to grab Rebecca and steal away into the night. But as I moved backward, I bumped into something hard and solid and looked up to find myself staring into the cold black eyes of my husband.

———◆———

CHAPTER TWENTY-FOUR

I faced John, noting for the first time his wet hair. Quickly, I glanced down at his feet and saw that he had taken off his boots. I noted, too, the absence of his jacket and coat. Had he seen them dripping in the hallway and taken them off?

I pushed at his chest, forcing him to step back through the doorway. He caught my wrist. "What is wrong? I heard you shout."

"Leave, John. And do not pretend you do not know the reason why." My voice shook with hurt, anger, and fear. *Please deny it. Please do not let me believe the worst of you.*

"Let me in." His voice held a note of warning.

My heart sank low in my chest. "No. I have already made that mistake more than once and I will not do it again."

He stood perfectly still, his gaze hard and unreadable. *Is he simply warning me with the conjure ball?* His voice held no malice. "Then I shall not trouble you again." Soundlessly, he turned away and strode down the corridor toward the stairs.

I closed the door, pressing my back against it, and stared at the insidious thing in the middle of my bed. *I do not take rejection easily.* I thought of Elizabeth and the price I suspected her of paying for the ultimate rejection of leaving him. My gaze strayed to the lower drawer of the dresser, where I had been gathering things to pack for my journey with Rebecca. His words crept unbidden into my mind. *And I pity whoever would try to separate us.*

I wrapped the evil conjure ball in one of John's linen handkerchiefs, ensuring that my fingers never brushed the object of my dread. Dragging a chair in front of the door, I crawled into it and stared at the brass door handle until the morning light touched the walls of my room.

* * *

The light of day did little to scatter the dark shadows in my mind. I quickly dressed before cautiously opening my door. With relief, I saw that the hallway was empty, then hurriedly crossed the corridor. Sliding into my old room, I placed the conjure ball under the bed, then left the room as silently as I had arrived and headed toward the stairs.

I paused at the top, hearing that ethereal humming sound again. It was certainly Rebecca's voice, so I approached the open door to her room. She was out of her sickbed, as evidenced by the wrinkled sheets and indentation on the pillow. Her nightgown lay on the floor, so she must have dressed. But she was nowhere in her room.

The humming came to me again and I turned to follow it out into the corridor. I spied the lodestone on her night table and picked it up as an afterthought. I would be needing it much more than she in the coming weeks.

I stepped out into the hall, and the humming abruptly ceased. I paused, listening, and caught sight of Samantha lying on the floor. She was crammed tightly against the wall, and as I stooped to pick her up, I realized that the doll lay in the exact spot where the wet footprints had disappeared into the wall the night before.

Stunned, I pressed my palms against the plaster. I knocked to see if there would be a hollow sound, and was surprised to hear someone knocking back, quickly followed by girlish giggles.

"Rebecca? Are you in there?"

I heard a slight *click* and then a small door opened in the wainscoting. The seams of the door had been perfectly hidden in the woodwork, rendering it virtually invisible. I wondered how many other such doors might be hidden in this house.

Rebecca stuck her face out of the opening, a bright smile crowning her lips. "You found my secret place, Mama!"

I had to kneel to see past the opening and was surprised to see a set of stairs. Sunlight poured into a high, round window. I had seen that window many times from the outside of the house but it never occurred to me that I had never seen it from the inside.

I took Rebecca's hands and helped her crawl out. "How did you ever find this place?"

She looked at me with wide blue eyes. "Do you promise you will not be mad at me?"

I nodded, my serious expression matching hers.

Very solemnly, she said, "I spied on my mama. I saw her use it one day and followed her. It goes outside, behind the bushy green plants by the back porch. She used it a lot but she never knew that it was my secret, too."

Smoothing the hair off her forehead, I asked, "Did you ever see anybody else use it?"

She looked down and did not answer.

"Rebecca, you can tell me. I promise not to be angry."

"I saw my papa. But only two times. Once, he followed my mama. I saw her leave and then he left, too. I thought they were playing a game."

I spoke gently. "You said you saw your papa use these stairs two times. When was the other time?"

She looked up at me with wide blue eyes. "On the same day Papa told me Mama had gone to heaven, I saw him coming back up these stairs with Mama's traveling bag. But how could she brush her hair if she did not have her brush? Maybe Papa didn't think she'd need it in heaven and that's why he brought her bag back."

Small pinpricks of fear dusted the back of my neck. I forced a smile. "Did he see you?"

Rebecca shook her head. "No, I am too fast to let anybody see me." She plucked at her skirt. "But I was not sad. I know Mama did not want to be here with me. She made me cry."

I watched as her lower lip quivered and touched her cheek to soothe her lonely heart, recalling how she would scream when I had first arrived and was easily confused for Elizabeth.

"Did you see anybody else?"

"Yes. Marguerite used them all the time. She says it is faster to get outside this way."

My fingers trembled as I stroked Rebecca's cheek. *Is this what Marguerite had meant when she told John that he had more to hide than she? And if Elizabeth had been running away, to whom had she been running?*

The sands of grief and loss sifted through my fingers again, yet I was afraid to catch them and look closely, unwilling to see the truth. So I let them fall to the ground, unheeded, and occupied my mind with plans to leave. My mistrust and doubts were enough for me. To know more would damage my heart beyond repair and perhaps move me closer to danger than I already was.

I found Philip Herndon two days later, his bloated body floating face-down in the pond behind the house. I had gone to rid myself of the conjure ball, having decided that whether I believed in it or not, it needed to be out of the house. I was walking, trying to organize my thoughts and to ignore the heavy weight of the ball in my hand, when I had spotted something undoubtedly human in the pond.

My heart had twisted at the sight and I had dropped the ball, not able to stop my thoughts of Jamie. With a small relief, I soon realized that the form in the water was that of an adult. For a moment, I thought that it was John and I had sunk to my knees, unable to fathom the loss or my reaction to it. Someone, possibly Mr. O'Rourke, spotted me and shouted the alarm. Nobody made mention of the conjure ball at my feet, or if they did, I did not hear.

I do not remember much past being led inside the house and the news whispered in my ear that it was Philip. I sat in the parlor with my feet propped on a footstool and recalled the night of John's return, when I thought I had seen a light by the pond and then John's wet hair. I felt the sickening realization that my love for John was wrong, that he had undoubtedly unleashed his fury on Elizabeth and her lover, and that I was in mortal danger. I should have realized that a woman as vain as Elizabeth would never have taken her own life. But my love for John had blinded me, and my unwillingness to see filled me with shame and remorse. I gathered my loss and grief around me yet again, finally forcing myself to stare the truth in the face.

John rode to the Herndons' plantation to tell them about Philip. As soon as he disappeared down the lane of oaks, I fetched Rebecca and went to find Mr. O'Rourke to ready our buggy.

He protested at first, but after I reminded him that the threat of Philip no longer existed, he let me go. I snapped the reins and set off at a brisk trot. When I neared the end of the lane, out of sight from the house, a dark figure stepped out and waved me down.

Instinctively, my hand flew to Rebecca, my main concern to protect her. I sighed with relief when I recognized Rose and slowed to a stop.

"What are you doing out here, Rose?"

"I be having dark dreams about you. You still carry that lodestone I gives you?"

I patted the pocket of my dress, feeling the smooth lump underneath, and felt foolish. "Yes, Rose. I carry it with me wherever I go."

She stepped closer to the buggy. "Good. You needs it bad." Placing a hand on the side of the buggy, she stared up at me. "You needs to tell the Herndons to put fresh eggs in Master Herndon's hands, then tie his wrists together before they put him facedown in the coffin. Then sprinkle eggshells on top of his grave, and he who done kilt him be revealed." She nodded, satisfied that she had told me.

"Thank you, Rose. I will certainly think about it, but I am not quite sure that Mr. and Mrs. Herndon will take my suggestions. They will be grieving very much for their son."

Rose patted the side of the buggy before stepping away. "You just do you best, Miz McMahon. If'n you want the killer caught." Her eyes were full of meaning as she glanced at me one last time before turning away back down the lane, toward the house.

I snapped the reins again and felt Rebecca tugging at my sleeve. I had almost forgotten she was with me. "Are you all right?" I asked.

She nodded, then reached over with her small hand and patted the lodestone in my pocket.

I had not been to Judge Patterson's home since my return, but I remembered where it was located. Off the main River Road, it was set back on a smaller parcel of land than Whispering Oaks. He had raised oranges and rare birds instead of investing in cash crops, his fortune having been inherited from his father, a shipping merchant. I remembered the exotic screens, vases, and artwork from my visits to his raised cottage as a child. I would always wonder if it was our visits to Gracehaven that had fueled Elizabeth's wanderlust. The Oriental paintings, with their odd black splashes that substituted for our alphabet, and the unique teas and curries we'd dine on always lent an otherworldly feel that would last for days after our visits with our grandmother.

A man came to help us and take the buggy as we approached the single-floor structure. The redbrick pillars supporting the white house reminded me of pelicans with their skinny legs standing on muddy banks, their fluffy white torsos perched precariously on top.

The judge greeted us warmly and then, as if reading my mind, sent Rebecca to the kitchen for something sweet. She lifted her face, still peaked after her illness, with a questioning look.

"You may go, but just eat a little. You are not used to eating very much right now. And if you get tired, come back to me." With a bright smile on her pale face, she left us, and the judge ushered me into his library.

He rang for tea and then offered me a seat by the fire. Joining me in an adjacent chair, he regarded me with a warm expression. "Forgive me for my bluntness, but you are not looking well, Catherine."

I shook my head, then lowered my gaze to my lap, trying to find my composure. His sympathy was all I needed to lose the control I had so tightly maintained in the last weeks. Finally, I raised my eyes to his. "You once offered your assistance in whatever way you could, and I have come to call you on your offer. I need to leave here—with Rebecca. And I cannot let John know that I am leaving."

He leaned forward, resting his elbows on his knees. "I have known you since you were a little girl, Catherine, and I know you are not prone to flights of fancy. But what you are asking of me is very serious, and I need to be sure that this is not a rash decision on your part. Because once you leave, it would be very difficult for you to return."

I nodded. "I thank you for your concern, but this is a decision that has tormented me for quite some time. I have made up my mind and there is no turning back."

"I see. Does this have anything to do with Elizabeth?"

I looked at him sharply. "Yes, in a way. I . . . I think John may have been responsible for her death. And now Philip Herndon has been found dead." I paused for a moment, weighing my words. "I think we both know that John would have had the best motive for wanting Philip killed."

My hand was shaking and he put his gnarled hand over mine, and I relished the warmth. The tea arrived and he poured for me, though I still could not trust my hands to hold a teacup.

"How did Philip die?"

"I found him in the pond behind our house. I overheard Dr. Lewiston telling John that Philip had a severe gash on the back of his head. And his . . . his tongue had been cut out." I shivered despite the roaring fire in the fireplace.

He took a sip. "Do you have proof of John's involvement in either death?"

"Two nights before, when John returned to Whispering Oaks, I thought I saw lights out by the pond. And then John appeared inside, and he was wet, as if he had been outside in the rain."

The judge spoke gently. "But if he had just returned from his trip, he would have been traveling in the elements. It would not be inconceivable that he would be wet from the rain."

I nodded. "But he also lied to me. He told me that when he found Elizabeth's body, his glove and an evil gris-gris were next to her. He removed them, telling me that Elizabeth had placed them there to implicate him. He never mentioned her traveling bag, but Rebecca saw him bringing it into the house after she disappeared, and I remember seeing her personal items reappear on her dressing table after her death."

I told the judge about John's pipe in the attic and the buried letterbox with the missing letters and the scent of earth on John's jacket. The old man nodded silently while I talked, his fingers steepled under his chin.

I pressed my cold hands against the cup, trying to draw the warmth. "I know that most of my suspicions can be construed as purely coincidental, which is why I cannot go to the authorities. I only have suspicions and doubts—and Rebecca's recollection. It would appear that Elizabeth was intent on leaving John when she was killed." I looked the judge squarely in the eye. "I do not know a great many people who are contemplating suicide who pack a traveling bag."

He nodded. "And the words of a four-year-old would never be accepted in a court of law."

"Nor would I subject Rebecca to the torment. I need to take her far away from here, away from him." I choked back a sob.

"You love him."

I stood, nearly knocking over the tea table. "I cannot help myself.

There is so much goodness in him, but to know that he is also capable of such violence . . ." I took a deep breath before facing the judge again. "Which is why I need to take Rebecca away. It will kill him to lose her, but I have to think of what is best for her."

Judge Patterson stood next to me, and I put a hand on his arm. "And I also wanted to tell another person of my suspicions. My sister is dead, and no matter how she might have provoked him, justice should be served. I will tell you everything I know so that in future, perhaps you might stand in a court of law and see John McMahon pay for his crimes."

My voice had descended into a whisper, my agony ripping the strength from me. He helped me sit again and handed me back my cup. After I had calmed down, I reached for my reticule. Slowly and deliberately, I pulled out the pearl necklace that John had given me as a wedding gift.

"I want you to sell this for me. I will need cash for my journey, and this should give me a bit left over, too. I will be going to my mother-in-law's home in Brunswick, Georgia, not far from Saint Simons. I eventually will want to return to my home, but John will look for us there first. Robert's mother has not spoken to me since his funeral, but I have nowhere else to go. Bringing her funds and an extra pair of hands to help should be welcome. Since Robert's death, she has been all alone."

I swallowed at the thick cloud of despair that threatened to settle over me. My mother-in-law had become a shriveled, unhappy woman over the course of the war in which she had lost not only her husband, but also her three sons. I was sure she blamed me for Robert's suicide, and the loss of the one child who had had the skill and luck to survive the war but not the strength of spirit to survive the anguish of coming home.

He clasped my hands in his. "When will you need the money?"

"I plan to leave at Christmas—in less than three weeks' time. Dr. Lewiston said Rebecca would be well enough to travel by then."

The judge looked at me in surprise. "Does he know, then?"

"No. He is John's friend and I will not jeopardize that." I thought back on the day when the terrible knowledge came to me concerning Rebecca's father.

"Will you need to stay at Gracehaven until you leave?"

I shook my head. "That would only alert John's suspicions. Besides, he will be gone for two of those weeks on business in New Orleans. For the remaining week I will be very watchful. And I do not intend to be alone for a single moment."

"Surely the child you carry will keep you safe."

I looked down at the ground, my face heating. "John does not think it is his."

The judge had the good grace not to appear shocked. "He has never truly recovered from Elizabeth's infidelities. Perhaps it has driven him mad." He patted my hand. "I will call frequently to check in on you. How is that?"

Impulsively, I kissed his cheek. "I would welcome that under any circumstances. Thank you."

"I do not want you to worry about anything. I will see that everything is arranged for you."

I found Rebecca in the kitchen, eating a helping of corn bread heaped with butter, and my heart softened at the sight. She was too thin from her illness, and to see her with an appetite again filled me with joy.

The judge tucked a blanket around us in the buggy, warding off the chill December air, and stood waving goodbye until we rounded a bend and he disappeared from sight.

CHAPTER TWENTY-FIVE

The first week after my visit to Judge Patterson left my nerves on edge and my mind fractured like a war-worn battlefield. John had been aloof yet watchful. He asked me to accompany him to New Orleans, suggesting that while he was conducting business I could use the opportunity to select fabrics and furnishings for the nursery we would soon be needing.

I had looked away, afraid that my lack of preparations in this area had alerted John to my plans. I had declined, stating my unwillingness to leave Rebecca before her complete recovery. John seemed to accept my answer, but at times I would find him watching me closely, his eyes narrowed and his expression blank, making me feel like a corpse under the measuring gaze of the undertaker.

I continued the pretense of calm serenity, outwardly going about my duties as mistress of Whispering Oaks, while in my head I marked the days until my departure. I had not yet told Rebecca. Not only was I afraid that she would be unable to keep the confidence, but I was also afraid that she would not leave her father.

I grieved for her, knowing the depth of her loss and knowing that I could never tell her the real reason of why we had to go. I would bear the weight for her and free her innocent soul from the torment of knowing the truth.

Rebecca bristled with excitement over the coming holidays, and I pretended to join in her enthusiasm. The traditional bonfires were to be lit on Christmas Eve, and I would use the noise and confusion of the festivities to disappear under cover of darkness.

Two days before Christmas, while John was still in New Orleans, Daniel called at the house to check on Rebecca. I had just put her down for a nap, so I brought him up the stairs to her room.

By the time we arrived, she had already settled into a heavy slumber. I watched Daniel carefully as he studied the child. He stood by the side of her bed for a long moment, watching her sleep. Reaching out a hand, he tenderly pushed her gold hair from her face.

"She is so much like her mother," he said.

I stepped closer to the foot of the bed. "But not anything like her father." I watched his face carefully.

To my surprise, he showed no reaction to my words. Instead he turned to me. "I used to think that Elizabeth was the most intoxicating woman ever born." He stared at me intently. "Until I met you. But your beauty is deeper than your arresting face. Something Elizabeth could never claim."

Embarrassed, I felt heat color my cheeks. "Really, Daniel. I do not think you should be speaking to me in this way."

He set down his black bag and approached me. "But surely you have guessed my feelings for you."

I looked away from the intensity of his gaze. "We are friends, Daniel. Nothing more. Nor are we free to pursue a deeper relationship, even if that were something I desired."

He reached for my hand but I pulled away. "Catherine, my feelings for you have grown far beyond friendship. I know it is wrong, but I cannot seem to help myself. I want to be with you. Always. And I know you are not happy with John. I have sensed a restlessness in you this last month. He made Elizabeth's life miserable and now I see he has done the same to you."

I stepped back. "Daniel, I want you to stop this now. Please do not destroy the high regard I have for you. I am not my sister, easily seduced."

He shook his head and approached me again. "No, you are not Elizabeth. You are much too good and too beautiful. I suppose it was too much to hope for that you might feel the same affection for me."

"Daniel, you have been a good friend. I am sorry if any of my actions or anything I have said might have led you to believe that my feelings went further than friendship. I am flattered, certainly, that a man such as you would hold me in such high regard. But you are married, as am I, and I am only in need of your friendship now."

He took a deep breath and regarded me with soft gray eyes. "I apologize if I have offended you. I am afraid that I have spoken out of turn. It was wrong of me to confess my feelings, knowing that your honor would never allow you to feel the same way about me."

I saw the way his golden hair shimmered in the bright light of the afternoon sun streaming in from the windows. "I am not my sister," I said again.

"No, you are not, and I have been wrong to think otherwise." He started to turn away but stopped, his expression that of a man intent on finding the absolution of confession. "Remember when I told you that I married Clara because it was love at first sight? I lied. I had seen Elizabeth on my visit with John and I could not leave. So I married Clara to be near your sister. I am so ashamed. My only hope is that you can find it in your generous heart to forgive me."

"Why are you telling me all this now?"

"Because I have been carrying the burden of my secret around for so long. And your forgiveness would be a balm to my soul."

I looked at him wearily. "It is not from me you need to beg forgiveness, but your wife. She loves you so. And from John."

A flash of anger momentarily crossed his fine features. "I owe nothing to John."

I looked down at the sleeping child, her spun-gold hair shimmering against the whiteness of her pillow. "I beg to differ."

His gaze followed mine, but his expression remained blank. "I did not steal his wife's affections, if that is to what you are referring. She kept those all to herself."

I swallowed, as if digesting his words. "So you are telling me that she never returned your feelings?"

A slow breath escaped him, like the last sigh of a dying man. "No."

I felt relief for a moment in the knowledge that Daniel's infatuation with Elizabeth had remained chaste. Rebecca stirred, and we watched her in silence for a moment. *Then who is your father, sweet child? Was it somebody your mother truly loved?* In my heart of hearts, I wished for it to be true. The thought of a cold and indifferent Elizabeth finding death without it was too hard to bear.

I lifted my eyes to find Daniel watching me intently. I did not look away. "But you did betray your friendship with John, if only with your feelings for his wife."

His lips curled into a grimace. "It was his own fault. He could not make Elizabeth happy, and he gave up trying. He drove her to take her own life. And I see how John has already dimmed your spirit and I fear for you, too."

I turned away, not wanting him to read the secret in my eyes.

"If you are unhappy, let me take you away from here. As your friend, let me help you."

I looked back at him to refuse, but he must have seen something in my face, for he stopped suddenly. "You have already made plans to leave, have you not?"

I started to shake my head, to deny it, but the weight of my secret longed to be lightened. "It is not what you think, Daniel. I am not going with another man. I simply need . . . to get away."

His face colored. "Has he hurt you in any way?"

I turned away to face the window. "No. But I have reason to believe that he is a dangerous man."

"Because of Philip?"

I nodded. "And Elizabeth. Did you know she was leaving John when she died? I think she might have been going with Philip, and now he is dead, too."

He looked ashen but kept his gaze steadily on me. "Why do you think it was Philip?"

I closed my eyes tightly for a moment, trying to erase the picture of Philip floating facedown in the pond. "I do not think either one of them tried to keep their affair secret. John certainly knew."

His voice was almost a whisper. "And then she was found dead." He shook his head. "I had no doubts when John said it was suicide. Her mental health had always been frail at best, although she kept it hidden from most. I thought I could save her from her inner torment, but my love was never enough for her. Nothing ever was." Defeat and desolation crowded his words, but I could feel little sympathy for him. "And now you are telling me that John . . ."

I rested my hand on his arm. "I have nothing but suspicion. But I do not feel safe here."

Solemn gray eyes bored into mine. "Let me do the right thing for a change. Let me help you. I will fight to bring John to justice, but first I need to see you safe."

"How can I trust you, Daniel? You have deceived your wife and your closest friend. How could I be sure that you would not betray me?"

His shoulders slumped in an attitude of defeat. "I need to redeem my soul and this is my last chance. I could never hope for forgiveness from Clara, and it is already too late for Elizabeth. You are my last chance to save me from this dark hell that chases me night and day."

My resolve weakened as I stared at this man whom my sister had destroyed. I did believe I could trust him, but I still had other doubts. "Judge Patterson has already offered his help."

He took a step forward. "But the judge is old and feeble. What if John finds out and pursues you? Do you really think the judge is strong enough to protect you and Rebecca from John's fury?"

I looked at Rebecca again, sleeping peacefully with her doll securely tucked under her arm. Daniel was right. The judge would be no match against John, and I would not put an innocent man in the path of John's wrath. Daniel was eager and willing to do so and, perhaps, find his own forgiveness. Pressing back golden hair from Rebecca's face, I rationalized that she might not be as frightened on our journey if she had the doctor with her in the beginning.

Slowly, I nodded. "You must swear you will not tell anyone."

He agreed and I knew I could trust him.

"In two days' time, when they light the bonfires out on the levee, I will need a carriage to take me to New Orleans. I was planning to take one of John's but if he finds it missing, it will be easier for him to search for us."

"Us?"

"Yes. I am taking Rebecca with me."

His features tightened for a brief moment but he said nothing.

"She is not safe here." I reached for his hand and squeezed it. "I was hoping you could tell me that she would be well enough to travel now."

"Yes. She is almost completely recovered."

"Good. If you can get us to New Orleans, I have enough funds to hire a coach to take me to Brunswick. Could you do that without arousing suspicion?"

A dreaded calm seemed to settle on him. "Yes. I will find a way."

"And if John finds out that you helped me?"

With a determined shift of his head, he said, "He has more to fear from me. From what you have told me, I now have information that implicates him in Elizabeth's death."

He stopped to pick up his bag, and I grabbed his arm. "Please tell me that John was not always like that. I still see so much good in him." I choked on a sob.

"Elizabeth changed him—she changed us both. It was for her I betrayed both my best friend and my wife, and I doubt I will ever find forgiveness from either, regardless of who John has become." His eyes were looking inside himself, into the deepest reaches of his heart, and what he saw there saddened me. "But being with Elizabeth, nothing else seemed to matter."

With shoulders stooped with defeat, he faced me. "I will send a message to you as to when and where to meet me. Have everything ready before the bonfire so we will not be delayed."

"Thank you, Daniel. I will be ready."

He nodded and placed his hat on his head, then left the room.

I sat on the side of Rebecca's bed and watched her sleep. Besides the hair, I saw little else to remind me of Daniel, and I was relieved that at least John had not suspected as much.

The back of my neck prickled and I sat up. A slight scratching sounded from what I thought was the wall, as if a fingernail were being slid along the plaster. I bounded off the bed and ran to the deserted corridor.

"Mary? Delphine? Is anybody there?"

There was no answer.

I sped down the stairs to the empty foyer and called out again.

As I stood listening to the deserted house around me, I looked into the old mirror, noting again the irregularities in the glass. I moved to stand in front of it, noticing how distorted my reflection appeared. With a sad grimace, I turned away, thinking how accurate the mirror's portrayal of me was.

612 · *Karen White*

* * *

John returned from New Orleans on Christmas Eve, in time for the festivities. I was in the library, reading, when I heard the carriage, but I did not go into the foyer to greet him.

I heard Delphine tell him where I was, and he soon joined me, his presence filling the room and drawing me to him before I even looked up from the pages of my book. Having him so near still affected me in ways I could not control, regardless of what I knew of him.

Several parcels tottered in his outstretched arms and he knelt on the floor beside me, letting the packages slide to the ground. A boyish grin lit his face, making my mouth go dry, and I had to look away.

"I have been shopping," he said unnecessarily.

"I can see that."

He lifted the lid from a small hatbox and pulled out a miniature rabbit-fur hat and muff. "I thought Rebecca might like this."

I nodded, finding it not too difficult to put a smile on my face. His enthusiasm was contagious.

"And this," he said, pulling a slim box from his pocket, "is for you. You can have it now or wait until tomorrow."

I almost said to wait, but instead I closed my book and held out my hand. Something mercenary in me realized that if it were valuable jewelry, I could sell it and use the funds for survival once we reached Brunswick. Slowly, I opened the box and gasped. Two beautiful teardrop earbobs rested on black velvet, each large round-cut diamond as big as a thumbnail.

"A diamond for each of our children. I hope to someday give you a necklace full of diamonds."

I felt hot and clammy, the taste of bile thick in my mouth. *What game are you playing?* I wanted to ask him. *These are not the words of a man who doubts his wife's fidelity.* The mixed emotions of betrayal, regret, wanting, and loss coursed through me, leaving me empty and shaking.

"Are you ill?" The note of concern in his voice was unmistakable.

"I am fine. It must have been something I ate." I managed a smile. "These are beautiful. Thank you."

He moved to kiss me but I turned away. He kept his head lowered, his breath brushing my neck but not speaking. Then, unable to stop myself, I leaned into him and placed my lips against his cheek like the kiss of Judas. I held my face close to his for several heartbeats, smelling his intoxicating scent and my mind reeling at his nearness, then pulled back.

His dark eyes searched mine. "You are welcome," he said, before pulling away and standing. "The bonfires will be lit at dusk. I suggest you and Rebecca get ready so we can leave."

"Yes. Of course." I managed to stand on unsteady legs before leaving the room, feeling his brooding eyes on my back as I walked away.

The blazing lights of bonfires along the levee stretched as far down the river as I could see. The pyramid-shaped wooden log structures towered in the night sky, flames licking upward toward the stars perched on top, an almost-pagan ritual to welcome the birth of the Christ child.

Stalks of sugarcane had been piled on top of the wood, creating a rapid succession of shotlike sounds as the steam expanded inside the stalks, causing them to explode. Smoke rose from the tops of the pyramids like the wispy spirits of those no longer with us, their cloudlike arms stretching heavenward.

I kept Rebecca close to me, afraid to get separated in the crowd. John stayed at our side, his presence worrying me. I would have to find a good enough excuse to leave with Rebecca when the time came.

The smells of roasting pork and burning sugarcane thickened the chilly air, but I could not find my appetite. I made sure Rebecca ate, not knowing when we would have the chance to stop and eat again. For appearances, I accepted a tin plate heaped with food, although I barely managed to force down more than crumbled corn bread.

John stopped to speak with a cluster of men from neighboring plantations, and I turned quickly to disappear with Rebecca into the crowd. A hand grabbed at my arm and I twisted around in fear, keeping Rebecca behind my skirts. I let out my breath in relief when I saw it was Rose.

She leaned close to me to be heard over the noise of the people and the bonfire. "I sprinkled them eggshells over Master Philip's grave. The man who done kilt him be revealed. My signs say it be tonight."

Rebecca pulled at my skirts, diverting my attention. "Mama, can I have some saltwater taffy? I promise I will not be messy."

I answered her question, and when I turned back to Rose, she had gone.

Clutching Rebecca's hand tightly, I began to weave in and out of the crowd, hoping to make it difficult for John to spot us. Because of his height, I had no problems locating him and made sure I stayed far away from him.

I patted the bulge in my skirt pocket, taking comfort in the coins in the leather pouch. Judge Patterson had sold my necklace in New Orleans for a very large sum and had visited Whispering Oaks as promised the previous week to give me the proceeds.

I spotted Rose again and approached her, my question about her words ready on my tongue. As I stood in front of her, her gaze fell behind me, her eyes wide with fear. Pushing Rebecca behind me again, I turned to stand face-to-face with Marguerite.

Straightening my back, I said, "You are not welcome here. Surely Belle Meade has their own bonfire."

Her green eyes smoldered in the light from the fire, making them seem to flicker with their own internal flame. "Dr. Lewiston sent me with a message for you. He is waiting for you at Belle Meade in his office behind the house. He says you will know what it is about."

I stared at her for a long moment, wondering why Daniel would have thought to trust her to deliver the message.

As if reading my mind, she said, "He trusts me not to speak of this to anyone else." She narrowed her eyes. "He says your husband is too suspicious, which is why the doctor did not come tonight. He did not want to draw attention to you or to him. He says it is best if you leave tonight from Belle Meade. Take your horse, and he will make arrangements to return her before anyone notices she is gone."

I looked at her closely, to see if I could determine how much she really knew about our plans. But her face was inscrutable, the only movement that of her flickering green eyes. "But why would he send you? He could have given anybody a note."

She grinned in the firelight, her eyes receding into shadows. "Because he knew that if John saw us talking, he would never suspect that I was here to help you."

I thought for a long moment. Everything she had said made sense, although I still had misgivings. But if she knew of our plans, Daniel must have trusted her enough to tell her. I closed my eyes for a moment, trying to think, and when I opened them I knew. This could be my one chance to escape, and I owed it to Rebecca and my unborn child to do whatever was necessary.

"All right," I said, keeping Rebecca behind me. "I will go to him." I took a few steps back to separate us, then turned toward the house.

We walked quickly through the grass, one hand clutching Rebecca's and my other holding up my skirts so I could go faster. "I have a surprise for you," I said to the child running at my side.

"A surprise?" Her eyes widened with excitement.

"Yes. We are going on a journey. Just you and me."

Her face fell. "But what about Papa? Will he not be lonely?"

I swallowed the lump rising in my throat. "He will miss you, but he will be keeping busy with business matters. He will want you to have fun, though. And Dr. Lewiston will be with us for a little while."

She nodded but did not say anything else, her young mind seemingly immersed in thought.

We ran into the house and grabbed the satchel I had packed for the journey, then raced out the back door toward the stables. Jezebel greeted me with a soft whinny as I set about saddling her in the semidarkness. Finally, I reached for Rebecca and hoisted her onto the horse, then climbed up behind her. With a gentle kick on Jezebel's flank, we left the stables, circled around the house, and headed toward Belle Meade.

CHAPTER TWENTY-SIX

The breeze off the Mississippi picked up, lifting my cape and rustling the leaves beneath us like old voices. I stayed far away from the levee until I was certain we would not be seen by any of the people from Whispering Oaks, then climbed the levee road. The bonfires lit my way, and I kept the hood over my face and my cloak wrapped around Rebecca to keep us hidden. I did not once look back—whether to test my resolve or because I had no desire to see it again, I could not say. Perhaps it was a mixture of both.

I slowed as we approached the lane leading to Belle Meade. No lamps were lit within the house, nor were torches blazing on the outside of the house and grounds. The windows were dark indentations on the faded white of the house, and the front doorway gaped darkly like an open mouth, lending it the appearance of an empty skull. I shivered, gooseflesh rippling up my arms, and hugged Rebecca close to me.

Long arms of clouds reached around the full moon in a celestial embrace, lighting our way while casting sporadic shadows. Jezebel picked her way across the side of the house with its barren garden, and to the large brick-and-frame cottage in the rear that housed Daniel's medical practice.

I spied a light in the window of the office with a surge of relief. I slid off the horse, then took Rebecca and Samantha from the horse and tied Jezebel's reins to a tree. Taking Rebecca's hand, I went to the door of the cottage.

I knocked loudly and waited for an answer. After several minutes, I knocked again, but heard only silence. Then, to my surprise, Rebecca turned the latch and opened the door.

A small lamp burned on a table in what appeared to be a waiting room. This was the oldest portion of the cottage and consisted of three brick walls. The fourth wall, part of the newer addition and consisting of frame and plaster, had a wooden door built in the middle, apparently leading to an examining room. A group of chairs clustered together on a braided rug, and a fireplace, devoid of fire, covered an entire side of the room. "Daniel?" I called, my voice loud in the empty room.

Rebecca stepped past me to a large music box on a pedestal table. I gave a start as I recognized it as my wedding gift to John and Elizabeth. Curious, I walked toward it and opened the lid, startled to recognize the bright, tinny song that floated up to me.

Rebecca stood next to me and began to hum the odd, off-key melody, and it hit a strange chord in me. I thought back on all of Elizabeth's doctor's visits and the drawer full of licorice sticks and Rebecca's familiarity with this song, and I knew. *Elizabeth was not running away with Philip, was she, Daniel? And the child she carried was yours.* I recalled Clara's lamentations of her own barren state, and wondered if she knew about Elizabeth and Daniel, and I prayed she did not. The knowledge would be too hard to bear. I glanced down at Rebecca and tried to see Daniel in her face, but could not.

I noticed a door on the far side of the room and knocked on it, calling Daniel's name. Unease settled in my belly when I again heard no response. I pushed open the door farther and it opened slightly, then hit something solid that was blocking it. Peering inside, I saw Daniel Lewiston lying on the floor, a thin trickle of blood seeping from his forehead. His body was wedged behind the door, making it nearly impossible to open.

"Where is Dr. Lewiston, Mama?"

Forcing my voice to remain calm, I said, "I am going to find out. But I need you and Samantha to sit down in that chair while I look for him, all right? And promise me that you will not go anywhere."

Solemnly, she nodded, then settled herself and her large rag doll into a chair.

With all of my might, I pushed on the door and managed to open it a little more, giving me enough room to squeeze through the doorway. The only illumination came from a flickering candle on the desk, casting thick shadows in the across the room. I knelt by Daniel on the floor and lifted his head.

I called his name and pressed my fingers to his neck. His pulse was faint and erratic, but at least he was still alive. I needed to get help, for I could not tend to his injuries alone.

Leaning over him, I whispered, "Daniel, I have to leave you to get help. I promise to be back as quickly as I can." Gently I lowered his head, then took off my cloak and put it on him, using a portion of it to pillow his head.

As I stood, I spotted a movement in the shadows and I held up my arm in defense. "John!" I cried. To my shock and horror, I saw that it was not my husband who emerged from the dark corner of the room.

Clara's eyes were wild in the flickering light. "Your husband will not be able to save you now, Catherine."

I ignored her, not quite understanding yet. "Clara, Daniel is hurt. I must go get help." My voice faded as I spied the mallet in her hand and it became all too clear as to how Daniel had been hurt.

I barely recognized the voice coming from the mousy Clara that I knew. "Men are so weak. I knew it was only a matter of time before Daniel would transfer his affection for Elizabeth to you. You are more alike than you think, you know. You attract men like bees to honey. Just like her."

"Clara, you are confused. There is nothing between Daniel and me. He was only helping me escape. . . ." A sick feeling spilled itself in my belly. I was escaping John because I thought he had harmed Elizabeth and Philip, and meant to harm me. But Clara had just struck Daniel, perhaps with the intent to kill him. "Did you . . ." I swallowed. "Did you hurt Elizabeth?"

She threw back her head and laughed an evil laugh I would have never thought her capable of. "Of course I did. She was carrying the baby that was meant for me and taking what was mine, as you are trying to do now. I will never let that happen."

Daniel moaned and I looked down at him. "If you care anything for your husband, you will let me seek help."

She also glanced at Daniel and her lower lip quivered. "He does not love me. He never has. I had once hoped that my love would be enough."

She looked back to me, and the wild cast was in her eyes again. "I wanted you to go away before Daniel noticed you. I tried to warn you away. Marguerite helped—locked you in the attic and put the snake in your room. But *I* put the doll in the pond. I knew how you let your little boy die. You all thought I was not smart, but I am. Everyone knows to stay away from oleander leaves, but you never seemed to understand. If only you had not looked so much like her . . ."

Tumbling images crowded my mind as I tried to make sense of her words. Acid churned in my stomach as I realized my own folly. In my haste to get away from the one person who could protect me, I had run straight into the arms of the one set to destroy me.

I forced my voice to stay strong. "And what of Philip? Did he have a part in any of your plans?"

"That fool. I told him that we would help him get rid of John if he would get rid of you. You are the reason my Daniel will not love me and you need to be gone. Like Elizabeth."

I tried to speak rationally with her, make her talk of her plans to get her to calm down. "But why would Philip agree to such a thing?"

"Greed. It is as deadly a sin as lust. His parents had disowned him and he needed money to leave the country. Seems he knew too much about some lynchings." She slid the mallet so that her hands were on the pole near its head.

Her eyes brightened and she appeared completely normal, her tone of voice no different from when we were sitting in my parlor and drinking tea. But her words chilled me to the bone.

"You were supposed to take a tumble from the carriage, and when that failed, he set the fire in the mill to distract everyone, and then he waited in the house for you. But the man was weak, like all men, and he could not harm you. He was supposed to lock you in the room after Marguerite put the snake in there and then stop anybody from helping you. He had brought a gun, hoping John would come to your rescue so he could kill him."

She shook with fury, the knuckles of the hand gripping the mallet turning white. "But he could not bear the thought of being responsible for your death. So he left, the coward. I had no choice but to kill him. He was of no use to me if he would not get rid of you. But he knew enough of my plans to ensure he would not live long to tell." She grinned a feral smile, her white teeth flashing in the dimness. "I killed him right where you are standing now and where Daniel stood not more than an hour ago. And then Marguerite helped me dump him in your pond, where we hoped you would find him. That was the night Marguerite laid the conjure ball on your bed, too. And now we will see that its prophecy will come true."

She looked down at the worn mallet in her hand as if contemplating how heavy a blow it would take to fell me. Then her eyes sought mine again. "I know you found the secret stairs in the house, but you never found the hidden rooms. Marguerite and I would hide in them and listen to every word you said. Or pretend to be a ghost for Rebecca. That is how I knew things. But you never suspected, did you? You were too busy trying to get Daniel to fall in love with you. That is how I know that you and Daniel are planning to run away tonight together. But I cannot let that happen."

She took a step toward me, but froze at the tapping on the door.

"Mama? I am scared out here by myself. Who are you talking to?"

I threw myself at the blocked door, desperate to keep her away. "Run, Rebecca, run! Go find your papa—anybody. Get help. Now!"

"Mama?" Her voice was full of questions and uncertainty.

Clara moved quickly toward me but tripped on Daniel, falling on her knees.

Frantically, I turned back to the partially open door, blocking it with my body. "Rebecca, do it now. Please. Just run—run as far as you can and hide."

"Mama?"

"Do it!"

I heard her run across the room and then fling the front door open before I turned to face Clara. She had regained her balance and was now advancing on me.

"She cannot hide from me. Marguerite will find her eventually. But it is you and your lover I need to deal with now."

I backed up against the door. "Why would you want to hurt an innocent child?"

Clara's mouth erupted in a bitter laugh. "There is no such thing as an innocent child, is there? Especially not that one. Daniel might not be her father"—she shrugged, looking incongruous with the mallet clutched in her hand—"but it is quite certain that John is not, either."

Fear and despair began winning out over courage and I had to choke back sobs. "Please—please do not hurt her. She is just a child."

"You are not really in a position to tell me what I can and cannot do, now, are you? At first she was merely a means to an end. I thought if something happened to her, surely you would leave. But now she has been here and seen things. She knows my voice."

I said a silent prayer that Rebecca had listened to me and had hidden herself far away from the cottage.

"You are making a terrible mistake. Daniel is only helping me escape—he is not coming with me. There is nothing between us."

With a hiss, she threw a crumpled letter at me. It hit my shoulder before falling on the rug. "That is a farewell note he wrote to me. He was not planning on coming back."

Rage seemed to flood her features as she raised the mallet over her head with both arms. With a grunt, she swung at me, narrowly missing my head as I ducked. It slammed the door closed while leaving a splintery scar in the wood panel.

I ran to the desk while glancing frantically around the room for a weapon with which to defend myself, but to no avail. Too late, I looked up to see Clara hoisting the mallet over her head again, its thick end aimed at my skull. Seeing no other recourse, I threw myself at her, my head hitting her forcibly in the chest, pushing her backward and making her grunt. The mallet struck my back with a glancing blow, knocking the wind out of me momentarily.

She fell backward and I on top of her, the mallet hitting the floor behind us with a solid *thud*. We both grappled to stand and find the weapon first. My hands settled around the smooth wood of the stick before I felt Clara's nails claw into the tender skin at the back of my neck as she tried to pull me away.

Her hands slid down to the neckline of my dress and I heard a loud rending of fabric as my dress tore away, taking Clara with it. I struggled to a stand, surprised at the heaviness of the mallet. Breathing deeply, I said, "I do not want to hurt you. If you cooperate with me and go with me to find help for Daniel, I will see that you get the help you need. You have endured a lot, Clara. There are many people who will understand and will come to your aid."

Her thin brown hair had come loose from our struggle and now hung raggedly over her face and shoulders. I forced myself to count my heartbeats as I waited for her answer.

As before, I witnessed her rage and jealousy feed her muscles as she came at me again. "I have lost everything, and somebody has to pay!" Her fingers flew to my throat and she began to squeeze the breath from me. Still, I clung to the mallet, not yet willing to use it. The light began to dim from my eyes, and for a moment I was tempted to let the battle I had been fighting for so long be over. My battle for survival had been a futile, uphill struggle, and I was ready to put the load down and be done with it.

From far away I thought I heard my name being called and the pounding of hoofbeats. *John.* I forced my eyes open but could barely see the shadow of the woman choking the life from me.

"Catherine!"

It was him, and his voice was like a fire in my blood. With my last ounce of energy I shoved at Clara, knocking her away. As I gasped for breath, I blindly swung the mallet, hitting something soft yet solid.

Clara flew sideways, falling into the desk before sliding to the ground. The candle wobbled at the impact, and I watched it move from side to side, as if undecided as to what it should do, before finally collapsing and rolling off the desk, the flame catching the long draperies on fire. I watched, mesmerized, as long fingers of flame spread along the length of the curtains, creating a wall of heat that nearly singed my skin.

Dropping the mallet, I grabbed Daniel by the shoulders and tugged with a strength I did not know I possessed. Maneuvering him out of the way, I swung open the door and pulled him through it. Billows of smoke covered us, making me cough and my eyes sting as I dragged Daniel through the waiting area and to the front door.

My lungs felt as if they would explode and spots danced in front of my eyes as I searched for air in the suffocating room. I dropped to my knees, no longer having the strength to stand, and found the air clearer near the floor.

As if by my will alone, the door opened and John stood in the threshold. Strong hands grabbed me, then lifted me. I heard him issue orders for someone else to get Daniel, and then I was breathing the sweet outside air once again.

He laid me on the grass while I struggled for breath and words. I clutched at his coat. "Clara . . . she is still . . . inside."

He uttered a low curse. "I will find her." With a quick touch to my cheek, he disappeared in the direction of the burning building. I could find no breath to carry my words of caution to him or to call him back.

Daniel was laid next to me, and I blinked up and recognized the judge and two men from Whispering Oaks. Daniel had regained consciousness and now struggled to rise, managing to lift up on his elbows. Relieved to see him alive, I let my head fall back upon the grass, grateful to feel the prickly sweetness of it.

Judge Patterson knelt by my head and brushed the hair from my face. Lifting me slightly, he gave me water to drink from a cup. I drank it thankfully, feeling the cool, soothing liquid slide down my parched throat. "Have . . . you found . . . Rebecca? She is . . . hiding."

As if in answer to my prayer, she came running from behind a large magnolia, the white bow in her hair glowing like a star in the night. She bounded to me and I hugged her to my side, burying my face in her hair. It smelled of smoke and sweat and fear, and I cursed Clara silently for inflicting such harm on this child.

As the judge moved to stand, I grabbed his wrist. "John?"

He shifted his eyes away for a moment toward the building, which now had flames dancing on its roof and crying out from every window. There was nothing anybody could do but watch it burn.

He turned back to me. "He went around to the back of the house to see if he could get in that way. He has not come out yet."

I closed my eyes, remembering how I had felt when I heard John call my name, and tried to summon that strength again. When I felt my blood surge, I willed my strength and hope and love to him and waited. My hand crept to the pocket of my skirt and I found the lodestone, wrapped my fingers around it, and squeezed tightly.

The judge spoke, his voice solemn. "I want you to know that I did not go back on my word to keep your secret. I was approached earlier this evening by Philip's father, with a letter Philip had left in his desk drawer before he died. It explained the fire at the sugar mill and Clara's involvement and reasons for it, as well as some other interesting things I do not want to go into now. And when I saw you leave after speaking with Marguerite, I knew there was trouble. So I told John, knowing him to be innocent of trying to harm you. I hope you will forgive me."

I grabbed his hand and squeezed.

"Marguerite has disappeared into the swamp. We will find her and bring her in to see that justice is served, but I have a feeling that the swamp will serve its own particular brand of justice." I shuddered, recalling the night my carriage overturned and the sounds of the prowling night predators.

Patting my shoulder, the judge stood and turned toward the house. I held Rebecca's hand in mine, drawing strength from her sturdy little spirit and taking comfort in her presence. She rested her head on my shoulder and sucked her thumb as the burning house popped and crackled behind us, sending smoke into the sky like an offering. Daniel looked at me for a moment, but the horror and grief in his eyes said more than I could find words for. He turned away, and I stared up into the black sky and began counting stars, keeping the dark thoughts at bay.

I became aware of movement all around me. More men had arrived, perhaps noticing the fire from the levee. Several stopped to check on Daniel and me, and at our request sat us up against a tree. My lungs burned and I still found it hard to breathe deeply. We sat in silence, coughing sporadically, our eyes turned toward the burning building.

A gasp went up among the crowd, all eyes riveted on the south end of the small cottage. With a creaking groan, the wall collapsed, sending sparks and splintered wood toward the onlookers. I stared at the flaming house, then dropped my head onto my drawn-up knees and wept.

Rebecca tugged at my hand and then let go. I felt her warmth leave my side and I jerked my head up. Moving slowly, a dark shadow appeared against the flaming backdrop of the cottage. My heart seemed to stick in my throat as I watched the shadow loom larger as it approached.

"Papa!" Rebecca ran to him and propelled herself into John's arms. He staggered slightly and did not lift her. Instead he put his hand on her head and walked toward me. A loud cheer spread out from the gathering men. His face was blackened with ash, a bleeding cut bisecting his left cheek. He stopped in front of us but did not say anything.

To my surprise, Daniel struggled to a stand, supporting himself against the tree. "I will watch Rebecca. You two have much to talk about."

The two men faced each other, one man's expression wary and the other impassive. John's voice was deep and hollow, singed from the smoke. "I could not save Clara. She regained consciousness while I was carrying her through the door. She struggled with me and ran back inside. That is when the wall collapsed and I could not go back in."

Daniel stared at John for a brief moment, his face ashen. "She told me she killed Elizabeth and Philip. I had no idea. . . ."

He turned away then and took Rebecca's hand. With slow, halting steps, he walked to the huge magnolia that Rebecca had hidden behind and he sat, resting his head against it as if still in great pain, and nestled her under his arm.

John collapsed next to me and I listened to his ragged breath. He coughed, then turned to look at me. "Judge Patterson told me everything. It is beyond my comprehension how you could have believed the worst of me." Anger and pain emanated from his eyes, but he reached for my hand and clutched it tightly as if making a peace offering. His touch told me that despite the anger, his relief at finding me alive was all that mattered.

The emotions of anger and relief chased each other in a circle in my own mind, along with questions yet to be answered. "It is not as if you have always told me the truth. Rebecca saw you on the secret stairs, bringing up Elizabeth's traveling bag. Yet you did not think it important enough to tell me, and I was left with no choice but to believe the worst."

He let go of my hand and ground the heels of his palms into his eyes. "I only did that to protect myself. I truly believed that she had killed herself and had tried to implicate me. Hence the traveling bag to make people believe she was leaving and to give me motive to kill her. And, to seal my fate, the placement of my glove and the gris-gris. I shudder to think what would have happened if I had not been the first to discover her body. I knew you would never accept my story if you learned of the traveling bag, so I kept it secret. If I had not heard Elizabeth's threats to kill herself, even I would have had difficulty accepting it."

"But there was also the letterbox and the missing letters. Even though I found your pipe in the attic and the burning letters in the fireplace, you still denied any knowledge of the letterbox. I knew you were lying to me, but you wouldn't tell me the truth."

He sat so close to me our shoulders touched, our heat nearly matching that of the flickering flames. "I took the letterbox from the attic and buried it. But after I heard you and Rebecca talking about it, I dug it up again to remove the letters. I did not have the key, so I had to unscrew the hinges and removed the letters before reburying it. I did not want to risk you ever finding them and reading them."

Tears stung my eyes and I was not sure whether they were from the burning building. "You should have trusted me with the truth. That is all I have ever asked of you."

"And you should have trusted me to take care of you. All I wanted was to protect you." He took my hands and brought them to his lips. "I want us to start over—far away from this place. We will go back to Saint Simons, if that is what you want, and rebuild your home. I love you, Cat. I have since the first moment I saw you dancing barefoot on the beach." He closed his eyes and I could feel his blood pulsing in his hands. "Please give me another chance to make you happy."

I took his face in my hands, using my thumbs to wipe off the dark smudges on his cheeks. "Even when I thought the worst of you, you still managed to claim my heart. I do want to start over—but I want to start with no secrets between us. They are like dark shadows in the corners of our lives, and I cannot live with them." I touched my lips to his, sealing my fate. "I need to know what was in Elizabeth's letters."

His hands reached up to cover mine and I felt them tremble. "Do not, Cat. You do not know what you are asking."

I didn't release him. "Yes, I do. I am stronger than you think."

He dark eyes searched mine, our faces close enough to kiss. "When I tell you, I want you to know that you are not alone. And that you are loved and cherished by me and that nothing else matters."

Fear blossomed in me then—not fear of my own mortality, for I had already faced that, but fear of losing my final innocence. But his touch gave me strength. "Tell me," I whispered.

His hands tightened on mine, and his eyes did not leave my face. "The letters in the letterbox were from your husband, Robert, to Elizabeth. They were love letters, dating from before her marriage to me up until the time of his return to Saint Simons after the war."

I started shaking then, as bright bubbles of light seemed to surface and explode in my brain. He continued. "They talked of their intimacy and of a child they conceived when Robert was in Maryland in the army and she visited him there."

Rose's voice came back to me. *There be two men in your life—two men you share your life with. But one of them is not who you thinks he be. He betray you in a terrible way.*

"Oh, God," I whispered, shaking uncontrollably now. Still, he did not let me go.

"Rebecca is their child."

I wanted to scream in denial, but my voice, hoarse from the smoke, deadened my grief. John gathered me in his arms and held me close, his kisses on my hair soft and gentle. I felt as if I were drowning in a sea of betrayal that threatened to pull me under and steal the life from me. He let me cry until I had no more tears left.

When I was finished, John brought my tear-streaked face up to his and kissed me. Grabbing his hands, I allowed him to pull me out of the darkness. I reached for him, feeling the beginning of my salvation in the beating of his heart. The darkness still tugged at me, as I knew it might always do, but John would bear me up to face it.

Together, we walked over to Daniel to claim Rebecca, and then took her home.

Epilogue

———◆———

Sometimes I come down to the beach and take off my shoes, delighting in the feel of the shifting sand beneath my feet. I can listen to the waves now without hearing the cries of my lost child, and I am more at peace than I have ever been.

I have begun to swim in the ocean again, and John has asked me to teach Rebecca and our son, Samuel, when he is old enough. We will do so together, John and I, as we have done everything in our lives since the night of the fire.

Robert and Elizabeth's betrayal will always be with me, like a scar from an old wound. The pain is gone, but at times the fingers of my memory touch the ridges of the scar, a medal of survival and a reminder of John's love for me. Forgiveness is an elusive ghost to me still, but I try. Every day I try.

My home and family have become a great tide pool of my own creation, and my love the dam that protects them from the encroaching waves. I can face the vastness of the ocean now, with the salt wind whipping at my hair and banishing the gnawing hunger from my soul, and feel only possibility and an overflowing well of contentment.

When I think back on those first tumultuous months of our marriage, I see it as a macabre dance: John and I waltzing around a circle, with the dark shadow of betrayal lurking in the middle, waiting to consume us. But now the light of my beloved island shines on us, illuminating the corners of our lives and our hearts. We take delight in the building of our house and the joyful cries of our children. His touch strengthens me, and mine him. We have waited all of our lives for this, and know that we are blessed.

Photo by Claudio Marinesco

Karen White is the *New York Times* bestselling author of twenty novels, including *Flight Patterns*, *The Sound of Glass*, *A Long Time Gone*, and *The Time Between*, and the coauthor of *The Forgotten Room* with *New York Times* bestselling authors Beatriz Williams and Lauren Willig. She grew up in London but now lives with her husband and two children near Atlanta, Georgia.